Agatha Christie is known througho
Her books have sold over a billion c
in foreign languages. She is the mos author of all time and in any language, outsold only by the Bible and Shakespeare. She is the author of 80 crime novels and short story collections, 20 plays, and six novels written under the name of Mary Westmacott.

Agatha Christie's first novel, *The Mysterious Affair at Styles*, was written towards the end of the First World War, in which she served as a VAD. In it she created Hercule Poirot, the little Belgian detective who was destined to become the most popular detective in crime fiction since Sherlock Holmes. It was eventually published by The Bodley Head in 1920.

In 1926, after averaging a book a year, Agatha Christie wrote her masterpiece. *The Murder of Roger Ackroyd* was the first of her books to be published by Collins and marked the beginning of an author–publisher relationship which lasted for 50 years and well over 70 books. *The Murder of Roger Ackroyd* was also the first of Agatha Christie's books to be dramatized – under the name *Alibi* – and to have a successful run in London's West End. *The Mousetrap*, her most famous play of all, opened in 1952 and is the longest-running play in history.

Agatha Christie was made a Dame in 1971. She died in 1976, since when a number of books have been published posthumously: the bestselling novel *Sleeping Murder* appeared later that year, followed by her autobiography and the short story collections *Miss Marple's Final Cases*, *Problem at Pollensa Bay* and *While the Light Lasts*. In 1998 *Black Coffee* was the first of her plays to be novelized by another author, Charles Osborne.

THE AGATHA CHRISTIE COLLECTION

The Man in the Brown Suit
The Secret of Chimneys
The Seven Dials Mystery
The Mysterious Mr Quin
The Sittaford Mystery
The Hound of Death
The Listerdale Mystery
Why Didn't They Ask Evans?
Parker Pyne Investigates
Murder is Easy
And Then There Were None
Towards Zero
Death Comes as the End
Sparkling Cyanide
Crooked House
They Came to Baghdad
Destination Unknown
Ordeal by Innocence
The Pale Horse
Endless Night
Passenger to Frankfurt
Problem at Pollensa Bay
While the Light Lasts

Poirot
The Mysterious Affair at Styles
The Murder on the Links
Poirot Investigates
The Murder of Roger Ackroyd
The Big Four
The Mystery of the Blue Train
Peril at End House
Lord Edgware Dies
Murder on the Orient Express
Three-Act Tragedy
Death in the Clouds
The ABC Murders
Murder in Mesopotamia
Cards on the Table
Murder in the Mews
Dumb Witness
Death on the Nile
Appointment With Death
Hercule Poirot's Christmas
Sad Cypress
One, Two, Buckle My Shoe
Evil Under the Sun
Five Little Pigs
The Hollow
The Labours of Hercules
Taken at the Flood
Mrs McGinty's Dead
After the Funeral
Hickory Dickory Dock
Dead Man's Folly
Cat Among the Pigeons
The Adventure of the Christmas Pudding
The Clocks
Third Girl
Hallowe'en Party
Elephants Can Remember
Poirot's Early Cases
Curtain: Poirot's Last Case

Marple
The Murder at the Vicarage
The Thirteen Problems
The Body in the Library
The Moving Finger
A Murder is Announced
They Do It With Mirrors
A Pocket Full of Rye
4.50 from Paddington
The Mirror Crack'd from Side to Side
A Caribbean Mystery
At Bertram's Hotel
Nemesis
Sleeping Murder
Miss Marple's Final Cases

Tommy & Tuppence
The Secret Adversary
Partners in Crime
N or M?
By the Pricking of My Thumbs
Postern of Fate

Published as Mary Westmacott
Giant's Bread
Unfinished Portrait
Absent in the Spring
The Rose and the Yew Tree
A Daughter's a Daughter
The Burden

Memoirs
An Autobiography
Come, Tell Me How You Live

Play Collections
The Mousetrap and Selected Plays
Witness for the Prosecution
and Selected Plays

Play Adaptations by Charles Osborne
Black Coffee (Poirot)
Spider's Web
The Unexpected Guest

Agatha Christie

POIROT

THE COMPLETE ARIADNE OLIVER

VOLUME 2

•

THIRD GIRL

•

HALLOWE'EN PARTY

•

ELEPHANTS CAN REMEMBER

•

THE PALE HORSE

•

HarperCollins*Publishers*

HarperCollins*Publishers*
77–85 Fulham Palace Road,
Hammersmith, London W6 8JB
www.harpercollins.co.uk

This edition first published 2005
2

ISBN-13 978-0-00-719068-3
ISBN-10 0-00-719068-9

Typeset in Plantin Light and Gill Sans by
Palimpsest Book Production Limited,
Polmont, Stirlingshire

Printed and bound in Great Britain by
Clays Ltd, St Ives plc

CONTENTS

THIRD GIRL 1

•

HALLOWE'EN PARTY 201

•

ELEPHANTS CAN REMEMBER 385

•

THE PALE HORSE 545

•

THIRD GIRL

To Norah Blackmore

CHAPTER I

Hercule Poirot was sitting at the breakfast table. At his right hand was a steaming cup of chocolate. He had always had a sweet tooth. To accompany the chocolate was a *brioche.* It went agreeably with chocolate. He nodded his approval. This was from the fourth shop he had tried. It was a Danish *pâtisserie* but infinitely superior to the so-called French one nearby. That had been nothing less than a fraud.

He was satisfied gastronomically. His stomach was at peace. His mind also was at peace, perhaps somewhat too much so. He had finished his *Magnum Opus*, an analysis of great writers of detective fiction. He had dared to speak scathingly of Edgar Allen Poe, he had complained of the lack of method or order in the romantic outpourings of Wilkie Collins, had lauded to the skies two American authors who were practically unknown, and had in various other ways given honour where honour was due and sternly withheld it where he considered it was not. He had seen the volume through the press, had looked upon the results and, apart from a really incredible number of printer's errors, pronounced that it was good. He had enjoyed this literary achievement and enjoyed the vast amount of reading he had had to do, had enjoyed snorting with disgust as he flung a book across the floor (though always remembering to rise, pick it up and dispose of it tidily in the waste-paper basket) and had enjoyed appreciatively nodding his head on the rare occasions when such approval was justified.

And now? He had had a pleasant interlude of relaxation, very necessary after his intellectual labour. But one could not relax for ever, one had to go on to the next thing. Unfortunately he had no idea what the next thing might be. Some further literary accomplishment? He thought not. Do a thing well then leave it alone. That was his maxim. The truth of the matter was, he was bored. All this strenuous mental activity in which he had been indulging – there had been too much of it. It had got him into bad habits, it had made him restless . . .

Vexatious! He shook his head and took another sip of chocolate.

The door opened and his well-trained servant, George, entered. His manner was deferential and slightly apologetic. He coughed and murmured, 'A –' he paused, '– a – young lady has called.'

Poirot looked at him with surprise and mild distaste.

'I do not see people at this hour,' he said reprovingly.

'No, sir,' agreed George.

Master and servant looked at each other. Communication was sometimes fraught with difficulties for them. By inflexion or innuendo or a certain choice of words George would signify that there was something that might be elicited if the right question was asked. Poirot considered what the right question in this case might be.

'She is good-looking, this young lady?' he inquired carefully.

'In my view – no, sir, but there is no accounting for tastes.'

Poirot considered his reply. He remembered the slight pause that George had made before the phrase – young lady. George was a delicate social recorder. He had been uncertain of the visitor's status but had given her the benefit of the doubt.

'You are of the opinion that she is a young lady rather than, let us say, a young person?'

'I think so, sir, though it is not always easy to tell nowadays.' George spoke with genuine regret.

'Did she give a reason for wishing to see me?'

'She said –' George pronounced the words with some reluctance, apologising for them in advance as it were, 'that she wanted to consult you about a murder she might have committed.'

Hercule Poirot stared. His eyebrows rose. '*Might* have committed? Does she not *know*?'

'That is what she said, sir.'

'Unsatisfactory, but possibly interesting,' said Poirot.

'It might – have been a joke, sir,' said George, dubiously.

'Anything is possible, I suppose,' conceded Poirot, 'but one would hardly think –' He lifted his cup. 'Show her in after five minutes.'

'Yes, sir.' George withdrew.

Poirot finished the last sip of chocolate. He pushed aside his cup and rose to his feet. He walked to the fireplace and adjusted his moustaches carefully in the mirror over the chimney piece. Satisfied, he returned to his chair and awaited the arrival of his visitor. He did not know exactly what to expect . . .

He had hoped perhaps for something nearer to his own estimate of female attraction. The outworn phrase 'beauty in distress' had occurred to him. He was disappointed when George returned ushering in the visitor; inwardly he shook his head and sighed. Here was no beauty – and no noticeable distress either. Mild perplexity would seem nearer the mark.

'Pha!' thought Poirot disgustedly. 'These girls! Do they not even try to make something of themselves? Well made up, attractively dressed, hair that has been arranged by a good hairdresser, then perhaps she might pass. But now!'

His visitor was a girl of perhaps twenty-odd. Long straggly hair of indeterminate colour strayed over her shoulders. Her eyes, which were large, bore a vacant expression and were of a greenish blue. She wore what were presumably the chosen clothes of her generation. Black high leather boots, white open-work woollen stockings of doubtful cleanliness, a skimpy skirt, and a long and sloppy pullover of heavy wool. Anyone of Poirot's age and generation would have had only one desire. To drop the girl into a bath as soon as possible. He had often felt this same reaction walking along the streets. There were hundreds of girls looking exactly the same. They all looked dirty. And yet – a contradiction in terms – this one had the look of having been recently drowned and pulled out of a river. Such girls, he reflected, were not perhaps really dirty. They merely took enormous care and pains to look so.

He rose with his usual politeness, shook hands, drew out a chair.

'You demanded to see me, mademoiselle? Sit down, I pray of you.'

'Oh,' said the girl, in a slightly breathless voice. She stared at him.

'*Eh bien?*' said Poirot.

She hesitated. 'I think I'd – rather stand.' The large eyes continued to stare doubtfully.

'As you please.' Poirot resumed his seat and looked at her. He waited. The girl shuffled her feet. She looked down on them then up again at Poirot.

'You – you *are* Hercule Poirot?'

'Assuredly. In what way can I be of use to you?'

'Oh, well, it's rather difficult. I mean –'

Poirot felt that she might need perhaps a little assistance. He said helpfully, 'My manservant told me that you wanted to consult me because you thought you "might have committed a murder". Is that correct?'

The girl nodded. 'That's right.'

'Surely that is not a matter that admits of any doubt. You must know yourself whether you have committed a murder or not.'

'Well, I don't know quite how to put it. I mean –'

'Come now,' said Poirot kindly. 'Sit down. Relax the muscles. Tell me all about it.'

'I don't think – oh dear, I don't know how to – You see, it's all so difficult. I've – I've changed my mind. I don't want to be rude but – well, I think I'd better go.'

'Come now. Courage.'

'No, I can't. I thought I could come and – and ask you, ask you what I ought to do – but I can't, you see. It's all so different from –'

'From what?'

'I'm awfully sorry and I really don't want to be rude, but –'

She breathed an enormous sigh, looked at Poirot, looked away, and suddenly blurted out, '*You're too old.* Nobody told me you were so old. I really don't want to be rude but – there it is. *You're too old.* I'm really very sorry.'

She turned abruptly and blundered out of the room, rather like a desperate moth in lamplight.

Poirot, his mouth open, heard the bang of the front door.

He ejaculated: '*Nom d'un nom d'un nom* . . .'

CHAPTER 2

I

The telephone rang.

Hercule Poirot did not even seem aware of the fact.

It rang with shrill and insistent persistence.

George entered the room and stepped towards it, turning a questioning glance towards Poirot.

Poirot gestured with his hand.

'Leave it,' he said.

George obeyed, leaving the room again. The telephone continued to ring. The shrill irritating noise continued. Suddenly it stopped. After a minute or two, however, it commenced to ring again.

'Ah *Sapristi*! That must be a woman – undoubtedly a woman.'

He sighed, rose to his feet and came to the instrument.

He picked up the receiver. ''Allo,' he said.

'Are you – is that M. Poirot?'

'I, myself.'

'It's Mrs Oliver – your voice sounds different. I didn't recognise it at first.'

'*Bonjour*, Madame – you are well, I hope?'

'Oh, I'm all right.' Ariadne Oliver's voice came through in its usual cheerful accents. The well-known detective story writer and Hercule Poirot were on friendly terms.

'It's rather early to ring you up, but I want to ask you a favour.'

'Yes?'

'It is the annual dinner of our Detective Authors' Club; I wondered if you would come and be our Guest Speaker this year. It would be very very sweet of you if you would.'

'When is this?'

'Next month – the twenty-third.'

A deep sigh came over the telephone.

'Alas! I am too old.'

'Too old? What on earth do you mean? You're not old at all.'

'You think not?'

'Of course not. You'll be wonderful. You can tell us lots of lovely stories about real crimes.'

'And who will want to listen?'

'Everyone. They – M. Poirot, is there anything the matter? Has something happened? You sound upset.'

'Yes, I am upset. My feelings – ah, well, no matter.'

'But tell me about it.'

'Why should I make a fuss?'

'Why shouldn't you? You'd better come and tell me all about it. When will you come? This afternoon. Come and have tea with me.'

'Afternoon tea, I do not drink it.'

'Then you can have coffee.'

'It is not the time of day I usually drink coffee.'

'Chocolate? With whipped cream on top? Or a tisane. You love sipping tisanes. Or lemonade. Or orangeade. Or would you like decaffeinated coffee if I can get it –'

'*Ah ça, non, par example!* It is an abomination.'

'One of those sirops you like so much. I know, I've got half a bottle of Ribena in the cupboard.'

'What is Ribena?'

'Blackcurrant flavour.'

'Indeed, one has to hand it to you! You really do try, Madame. I am touched by your solicitude. I will accept with pleasure to drink a cup of chocolate this afternoon.'

'Good. And then you'll tell me all about what's upset you.'

She rang off.

II

Poirot considered for a moment. Then he dialled a number. Presently he said: 'Mr Goby? Hercule Poirot here. Are you very fully occupied at this moment?'

'Middling,' said the voice of Mr Goby. 'Middling to fair. But to oblige you, Monsieur Poirot, if you're in a hurry, as you usually are – well, I wouldn't say that my young men couldn't manage mostly what's on hand at present. Of course good boys aren't as easy to get as they used to be. Think too much of themselves nowadays. Think they know it all before they've started to learn. But there! Can't expect old heads on young shoulders. I'll be pleased to put myself at your disposal, M. Poirot. Maybe I can put one or two of the better lads on the job. I suppose it's the usual – collecting information?'

He nodded his head and listened whilst Poirot went into details of exactly what he wanted done. When he had finished with Mr Goby, Poirot rang up Scotland Yard where in due course he got through to a friend of his. When he in turn had listened to Poirot's requirements, he replied,

'Don't want much, do you? Any murder, *anywhere*. Time, place and victim unknown. Sounds a bit of a wild goose chase, if you ask me, old boy.' He added disapprovingly, 'You don't seem really to know *anything*!'

III

At 4.15 that afternoon Poirot sat in Mrs Oliver's drawing-room sipping appreciatively at a large cup of chocolate topped with foaming whipped cream which his hostess had just placed on a small table beside him. She added a small plate full of *langue de chats* biscuits.

'*Chère* Madame, what kindness.' He looked over his cup with faint surprise at Mrs Oliver's coiffure and also at her new wallpaper. Both were new to him. The last time he had seen Mrs Oliver, her hair style had been plain and severe. It now displayed a richness of coils and twists arranged in intricate patterns all over her head. Its prolific luxury was, he suspected, largely artificial. He debated in his mind how many switches of hair might unexpectedly fall off if Mrs Oliver was to get suddenly excited, as was her wont. As for the wallpaper . . .

'These cherries – they are new?' he waved a teaspoon. It was, he felt, rather like being in a cherry orchard.

'Are there too many of them, do you think?' said Mrs Oliver. 'So hard to tell beforehand with wallpaper. Do you think my old one was better?'

Poirot cast his mind back dimly to what he seemed to remember as large quantities of bright coloured tropical birds in a forest. He felt inclined to remark '*Plus ça change, plus c'est la même chose*,' but restrained himself.

'And now,' said Mrs Oliver, as her guest finally replaced his cup on its saucer and sat back with a sigh of satisfaction, wiping remnants of foaming cream from his moustache, 'what *is* all this about?'

'That I can tell you very simply. This morning a girl came to see me. I suggested she might make an appointment. One has one's routine, you comprehend. She sent back word that she wanted to see me at once because she thought she might have committed a murder.'

'What an odd thing to say. Didn't she *know*?'

'Precisely! *C'est inouï!* so I instructed George to show her in. She stood there! She refused to sit down. She just stood there staring at me. She seemed quite half-witted. I tried to encourage her. Then suddenly she said that she'd changed her mind. She said she didn't want to be rude but that – (what do you think?) – but that I was *too old* . . .'

Mrs Oliver hastened to utter soothing words. 'Oh well, girls are like that. Anyone over thirty-five they think is half dead. They've no *sense*, girls, you must realise that.'

'It wounded me,' said Hercule Poirot.

'Well, I shouldn't worry about it, if I were you. Of course it was a very rude thing to say.'

'That does not matter. And it is not only *my* feelings. I am worried. Yes, I am worried.'

'Well, I should forget all about it if I were you,' advised Mrs Oliver comfortably.

'You do not understand. I am worried about this girl. She came to me for *help*. Then she decided that I was too old. Too old to be of any use to her. She was wrong of course, that goes without saying, and then she just ran away. But I tell you that girl *needs* help.'

'I don't suppose she does really,' said Mrs Oliver soothingly. 'Girls make a fuss about things.'

'No. You are wrong. *She needs help.*'

'You don't think she really has committed a murder?'

'Why not? She said she had.'

'Yes, but –' Mrs Oliver stopped. 'She said she *might* have,' she said slowly. 'But what can she possibly mean by that?'

'Exactly. It does not make sense.'

'Who did she murder or did she think she murdered?'

Poirot shrugged his shoulders.

'And why did she murder someone?'

Again Poirot shrugged his shoulders.

'Of course it could be all sorts of things.' Mrs Oliver began to brighten as she set her ever prolific imagination to work. 'She could have run over someone in her car and not stopped. She could have been assaulted by a man on a cliff and struggled with him and managed to push him over. She could have given someone the wrong medicine by mistake. She could have gone to one of those purple pill parties and had a fight with someone. She could have come to and found she had stabbed someone. She –'

'*Assez*, madame, *assez!*'

But Mrs Oliver was well away.

'She might have been a nurse in the operating theatre and administered the wrong anaesthetic or –' she broke off, suddenly anxious for clearer details. 'What did she look like?'

Poirot considered for a moment.

'An Ophelia devoid of physical attraction.'

'Oh dear,' said Mrs Oliver. 'I can almost *see* her when you say that. How queer.'

'She is not competent,' said Poirot. 'That is how I see her. She is not one who can cope with difficulties. She is not one of those who can see beforehand the dangers that must come. She is one of whom others will look round and say "we want a victim. That one will do".'

But Mrs Oliver was no longer listening. She was clutching her rich coils of hair with both hands in a gesture with which Poirot was familiar.

'Wait,' she cried in a kind of agony. 'Wait!'

Poirot waited, his eyebrows raised.

'You didn't tell me her name,' said Mrs Oliver.

'She did not give it. Unfortunate, I agree with you.'

'Wait!' implored Mrs Oliver, again with the same agony. She relaxed her grip on her head and uttered a deep sigh. Hair detached itself from its bonds and tumbled over her shoulders, a super imperial coil of hair detached itself completely and fell on the floor. Poirot picked it up and put it discreetly on the table.

'Now then,' said Mrs Oliver, suddenly restored to calm. She

pushed in a hairpin or two, and nodded her head while she thought. 'Who told this girl about you, M. Poirot?'

'No one, so far as I know. Naturally, she had heard about me, no doubt.'

Mrs Oliver thought that 'naturally' was not the word at all. What was natural was that Poirot himself was sure that everyone had always heard of him. Actually large numbers of people would only look at you blankly if the name of Hercule Poirot was mentioned, especially the younger generation. 'But how am I going to put that to him,' thought Mrs Oliver, 'in such a way that it won't hurt his feelings?'

'I think you're wrong,' she said. 'Girls – well, girls and young men – they don't know very much about detectives and things like that. They don't hear about them.'

'Everyone must have heard about Hercule Poirot,' said Poirot, superbly.

It was an article of belief for Hercule Poirot.

'But they are all so badly educated nowadays,' said Mrs Oliver. 'Really, the only people whose names they know are pop singers, or groups, or disc jockeys – that sort of thing. If you need someone special, I mean a doctor or a detective or a dentist – well, then, I mean you would *ask* someone – ask who's the right person to go to? And then the other person says – "My dear, you must go to that absolutely wonderful man in Queen Anne's Street, twists your legs three times round your head and you're cured," or "All my diamonds were stolen, and Henry would have been furious, so I couldn't go to the police, but there's a simply uncanny detective, *most* discreet, and he got them back for me and Henry never knew a thing." – That's the way it happens all the time. *Someone* sent that girl to you.'

'I doubt it very much.'

'You wouldn't know until you were told. *And you're going to be told now.* It's only just come to me. *I* sent that girl to you.'

Poirot stared. 'You? But why did you not say so at once?'

'Because it's only just come to me – when you spoke about Ophelia – long wet-looking hair, and rather plain. It seemed a description of someone I'd actually *seen*. Quite lately. And then it came to me who it was.'

'Who is she?'

'I don't actually know her name, but I can easily find out. We were talking – about private detectives and private eyes – and I spoke about you and some of the amazing things you had done.'

'And you gave her my address?'

'No, of course I didn't. I'd no idea she wanted a detective or anything like that. I thought we were just talking. But I'd mentioned the name several times, and of course it would be easy to look you up in the telephone book and just come along.'

'Were you talking about murder?'

'Not that I can remember. I don't even know how we came to be talking about detectives – unless, yes, perhaps it was *she* who started the subject . . .'

'Tell me then, tell me all you can – even if you do not know her name, tell me all you know about her.'

'Well, it was last weekend. I was staying with the Lorrimers. They don't come into it except that they took me over to some friends of theirs for drinks. There were several people there – and I didn't enjoy myself much because, as you know, I don't really like drink, and so people have to find a soft drink for me which is rather a bore for them. And then people *say* things to me – you know – how much they like my books, and how they've been longing to meet me – and it all makes me feel hot and bothered and rather silly. But I manage to cope more or less. And they say how much they love my awful detective Sven Hjerson. If they knew how *I* hated him! But my publisher always says I'm not to say so. Anyway, I suppose the talk about detectives in real life grew out of all that, and I talked a bit about you, and this girl was standing around listening. When you said an unattractive Ophelia it clicked somehow. I thought: "Now who does that remind me of?" And then it came to me: "Of course. The girl at the party that day." I rather think she belonged there unless I'm confusing her with some other girl.'

Poirot sighed. With Mrs Oliver one always needed a lot of patience.

'Who were these people with whom you went to have drinks?'

'Trefusis, I think, unless it was Treherne. That sort of name – he's a tycoon. Rich. Something in the City, but he's spent most of his life in South Africa –'

'He has a wife?'

'Yes. Very good-looking woman. Much younger than he is. Lots of golden hair. Second wife. The daughter was the first wife's daughter. Then there was an uncle of incredible antiquity. Rather deaf. He's frightfully distinguished – strings of letters after his name. An admiral or an air-marshal or something. He's an astronomer too, I think. Anyway, he's got a kind of big telescope sticking out of the roof. Though I suppose that might be just a hobby. There was a foreign girl there, too, who sort of trots about after the old boy. Goes up to London with him, I believe, and sees he doesn't get run over. Rather pretty, she was.'

Poirot sorted out the information Mrs Oliver had supplied him with, feeling rather like a human computer.

'There lives then in the house Mr and Mrs Trefusis –'

'It's not Trefusis – I remember now – It's Restarick.'

'That is not at all the same type of name.'

'Yes it is. It's a Cornish name, isn't it?'

'There lives there then, Mr and Mrs Restarick, the distinguished elderly uncle. Is his name Restarick too?'

'It's Sir Roderick something.'

'And there is the *au pair* girl, or whatever she is, and a daughter – any more children?'

'I don't think so – but I don't really know. The daughter doesn't live at home, by the way. She was only down for the weekend. Doesn't get on with the stepmother, I expect. She's got a job in London, and she's picked up with a boy friend they don't much like, so I understand.'

'You seem to know quite a lot about the family.'

'Oh well, one picks things up. The Lorrimers are great talkers. Always chattering about someone or other. One hears a lot of gossip about the people all around. Sometimes, though, one gets them mixed up. I probably have. I wish I could remember that girl's Christian name. Something connected with a song . . . Thora? *Speak to me, Thora.* Thora, Thora. Something like that, or Myra? Myra, *oh Myra my love is all for thee.* Something like that. I *dreamt I dwelt in marble halls.* Norma? Or do I mean Maritana? Norma – Norma Restarick. That's right, I'm sure.' She added inconsequently, 'She's a third girl.'

'I thought you said you thought she was an only child.'

'So she is – or I think so.'

'Then what do you mean by saying she is the third girl?'

'Good gracious, don't you know what a third girl is? Don't you read *The Times*?'

'I read the births, deaths, and marriages. And such articles as I find of interest.'

'No, I mean the front advertisement page. Only it isn't in the front now. So I'm thinking of taking some other paper. But I'll show you.'

She went to a side table and snatched up *The Times*, turned the pages over and brought it to him. 'Here you are – look. "THIRD GIRL *for comfortable second floor flat, own room, central heating, Earl's Court.*" "*Third girl wanted to share flat. 5gns. week own room.*" "*4th girl wanted. Regent's park. Own room.*" It's the way girls like living now. Better than PGs or a hostel. The main girl takes a furnished flat, and then shares out the rent. Second girl is usually a friend. Then they find a third girl by advertising if they don't know one. And, as you see, very often they manage to squeeze in a fourth girl. First girl takes the best room, second girl pays rather less, third girl less still and is stuck in a cat-hole. They fix it among themselves which one has the flat to herself which night a week – or something like that. It works reasonably well.'

'And where does this girl whose name might just possibly be Norma live in London?'

'As I've told you I don't really know anything about her.'

'But you could find out?'

'Oh yes, I expect that would be quite easy.'

'You are sure there was no talk, no mention of an unexpected death?'

'Do you mean a death in London – or at the Restaricks' home?'

'Either.'

'I don't think so. Shall I see what I can rake up?'

Mrs Oliver's eyes sparkled with excitement. She was by now entering into the spirit of the thing.

'That would be very kind.'

'I'll ring up the Lorrimers. Actually now would be quite a good time.' She went towards the telephone. 'I shall have to think of reasons and things – perhaps invent things?'

She looked towards Poirot rather doubtfully.

'But naturally. That is understood. You are a woman of imagination – you will have no difficulty. But – not too fantastic, you understand. Moderation.'

Mrs Oliver flashed him an understanding glance.

She dialled and asked for the number she wanted. Turning her head, she hissed: 'Have you got a pencil and paper – or a notebook – something to write down names or addresses or places?'

Poirot had already his notebook arranged by his elbow and nodded his head reassuringly.

Mrs Oliver turned back to the receiver she held and launched herself into speech. Poirot listened attentively to one side of a telephone conversation.

'Hallo. Can I speak to – Oh, it's you, Naomi. Ariadne Oliver here. Oh, yes – well, it was rather a crowd . . . Oh, you mean the old boy? . . . No, you know I don't . . . Practically blind? . . . I thought he was going up to London with the little foreign girl . . . Yes, it must be rather worrying for them sometimes – but she seems to manage him quite well . . . One of the things I rang up for was to ask you what the girl's address was – No, the Restarick girl, I mean – somewhere in South Ken, isn't it? Or was it Knightsbridge? Well, I promised her a book and I wrote down the address, but of course I've lost it as usual. I can't even remember her name. Is it Thora or Norma? . . . Yes, I *thought* it was Norma: . . . Wait a minute, I'll get a pencil . . . Yes, I'm ready . . . 67 Borodene Mansions . . . I know – that great block that looks rather like Wormwood Scrubs prison . . . Yes, I believe the flats are very comfortable with central heating and everything . . . Who are the other two girls she lives with? . . . Friends of hers? . . . or advertisements? . . . Claudia Reece-Holland . . . her father's the MP, is he? Who's the other one? . . . No, I suppose you wouldn't know – she's quite nice, too, I suppose . . . What do they all do? They always seem to be secretaries, don't they? . . . Oh, the other girl's an interior decorator – you think – or to do with an art gallery – No, Naomi, of course I don't *really* want to know – one just wonders – what *do* all the girls do nowadays? – well, it's useful for me to know because of my books – one wants to keep up to date . . . What was it you told me about some boy friend . . . Yes, but one's so helpless, isn't one? I mean girls do just exactly as they like . . . does he look very awful? Is he the unshaven dirty kind? Oh, *that* kind – Brocade waistcoats, and long curling chestnut hair – lying on his shoulders – yes, so hard to tell whether they're girls or boys, isn't it? – Yes, they do look like Vandykes sometimes if they're good looking . . . What did you say? That Andrew Restarick simply hates him? . . . Yes, men usually do . . . Mary Restarick? . . . Well, I suppose you do usually have rows with a stepmother. I expect she was quite thankful when the girl got a job in London. What do you mean about people saying things . . . Why, couldn't they find out what was the matter with her? . . . *Who* said? . . . Yes, but *what* did they hush up? . . . Oh – a nurse? – talked to the Jenners' governess? Do you mean her *husband*? Oh, I see – The doctors couldn't find out . . . No, but people are so ill-natured. I do agree with you. These things are usually *quite* untrue . . . Oh, gastric, was it? . . . But how ridiculous. Do you mean people said what's his name – Andrew – You mean it would be easy with all those weed killers about – Yes, but why? . . . I mean, it's not a case of some wife he's hated for years – she's the second wife – and much younger than he is and good looking . . . Yes, I suppose *that* could be – but why should the foreign girl want to either? . . . You mean she might have resented things that Mrs Restarick said to her . . . She's quite an attractive little thing – I suppose Andrew might have taken a fancy to her – nothing serious of course – but it might have annoyed Mary, and then she might have pitched into the girl and –'

Out of the corner of her eye, Mrs Oliver perceived Poirot signalling wildly to her.

'Just a moment, darling,' said Mrs Oliver into the telephone. 'It's the baker.' Poirot looked affronted. 'Hang on.'

She laid down the receiver, hurried across the room, and backed Poirot into a breakfast nook.

'Yes,' she demanded breathlessly.

'A baker,' said Poirot with scorn. 'Me!'

'Well, I had to think of something quickly. What were you signalling about? Did you understand what she –'

Poirot cut her short.

'You shall tell me presently. I know enough. What I want you to do is, with your rapid powers of improvisation, to arrange some plausible pretext for me to visit the Restaricks – an old friend of yours, shortly to be in the neighbourhood. Perhaps you could say –'

'Leave it to me. I'll think of something. Shall you give a false name?'

'Certainly not. Let us at least try to keep it simple.'

Mrs Oliver nodded, and hurried back to the abandoned telephone.

'Naomi? I can't remember what we were saying. Why does something always come to interrupt just when one has settled down to a nice gossip? I can't even remember now what I rang you up for to begin with – Oh yes – that child Thora's address – Norma, I mean – and you gave it to me. But there was something else I wanted to – oh, I remember. An old friend of mine. A most fascinating little man. Actually I was talking about him the other day down there. Hercule Poirot his name is. He's going to be staying quite close to the Restaricks and he is most tremendously anxious to meet old Sir Roderick. He knows a lot about him and has a terrific admiration for him, and for some wonderful discovery of his in the war – or some scientific thing he did – anyway, he is very anxious to "call upon him and present his respects", that's how he put it. Will that be all right, do you think? Will you warn them? Yes, he'll probably just turn up out of the blue. Tell them to make him tell them some wonderful espionage stories . . . He – what? Oh! your mowers? Yes, of course you must go. Goodbye.'

She put back the receiver and sank down in an armchair. 'Goodness, how exhausting. Was that all right?'

'Not bad,' said Poirot.

'I thought I'd better pin it all to the old boy. Then you'll get to see the lot which I suppose is what you want. And one can always be vague about scientific subjects if one is a woman, and you can think up something more definite that sounds probable by the time you arrive. Now, do you want to hear what she was telling me?'

'There has been gossip, I gather. About the health of Mrs Restarick?'

'That's it. It seems she had some kind of mysterious illness – gastric in nature – and the doctors were puzzled. They sent her into hospital and she got quite all right, but there didn't seem any real cause to account for it. And she went home, and it all began to start again – and again the doctors were puzzled. And then people began to *talk.* A rather irresponsible nurse started it and her sister told a neighbour, and the neighbour went out on daily work and told someone else, and how queer it all was. And then people began saying that her husband must be trying to poison her. The sort of thing people always say – but in this case it really didn't seem to make sense. And then Naomi and I wondered about the *au pair* girl, she's a kind of secretary companion to the old boy – so really there isn't any kind of reason why she should administer weed killer to Mrs Restarick.'

'I heard you suggesting a few.'

'Well, there is usually something *possible* . . .'

'*Murder desired* . . .' said Poirot thoughtfully . . . 'But not yet committed.'

CHAPTER 3

Mrs Oliver drove into the inner court of Borodene Mansions. There were six cars filling the parking space. As Mrs Oliver hesitated, one of the cars reversed out and drove away. Mrs Oliver hurried neatly into the vacant space.

She descended, banged the door and stood looking up to the sky. It was a recent block, occupying a space left by the havoc of a land mine in the last war. It might, Mrs Oliver thought, have been lifted *en bloc* from the Great West Road and, first deprived of some such legend as SKYLARK'S FEATHER RAZOR BLADES, have been deposited as a block of flats *in situ.* It looked extremely functional and whoever had built it had obviously scorned any ornamental additions.

It was a busy time. Cars and people were going in and out of the courtyard as the day's work came to a close.

Mrs Oliver glanced down at her wrist. Ten minutes to seven. About the right time, as far as she could judge. The kind of time when girls in jobs might be presumed to have returned, either to renew their make up, change their clothes to tight exotic pants or whatever their particular addiction was, and go out again, or else to settle down to home life and wash their smalls and their stockings. Anyway, quite a sensible time to try. The block was exactly the same on the east and the west, with big swing doors set in the centre. Mrs Oliver chose the left hand side but immediately found that she was wrong. All this side was numbers from 100 to 200. She crossed over to the other side.

No. 67 was on the sixth floor. Mrs Oliver pressed the button of the lift. The doors opened like a yawning mouth with a menacing clash. Mrs Oliver hurried into the yawning cavern. She was always afraid of modern lifts.

Crash. The doors came to again. The lift went up. It stopped almost immediately (that was frightening too!). Mrs Oliver scuttled out like a frightened rabbit.

She looked up at the wall and went along the right hand passage. She came to a door marked 67 in metal numbers affixed to the centre of the door. The numeral 7 detached itself and fell on her feet as she arrived.

'This place doesn't like me,' said Mrs Oliver to herself as she winced with pain and picked the number up gingerly and affixed it by its spike to the door again.

She pressed the bell. Perhaps everyone was out.

However, the door opened almost at once. A tall handsome girl stood in the doorway. She was wearing a dark well-cut suit with a very short skirt, a white silk shirt, and was very well shod. She had swept-up dark hair, good but discreet make up, and for some reason was slightly alarming to Mrs Oliver.

'Oh,' said Mrs Oliver, galvanising herself to say the right thing. 'Is Miss Restarick in, by any chance?'

'No, I'm sorry, she's out. Can I give her a message?'

Mrs Oliver said, 'Oh' again – before proceeding. She made a play of action by producing a parcel rather untidily done up in brown paper. 'I promised her a book,' she explained. 'One of mine that she hadn't read. I hope I've remembered actually which it was. She won't be in soon, I suppose?'

'I really couldn't say. I don't know what she is doing tonight.'

'Oh. Are you Miss Reece-Holland?'

The girl looked slightly surprised.

'Yes, I am.'

'I've met your father,' said Mrs Oliver. She went on, 'I'm Mrs

Oliver. I write books,' she added in the usual guilty style in which she invariably made such an announcement.

'Won't you come in?'

Mrs Oliver accepted the invitation, and Claudia Reece-Holland led her into a sitting-room. All the rooms of the flats were papered the same with an artificial raw wood pattern. Tenants could then display their modern pictures or apply any forms of decoration they fancied. There was a foundation of modern built-in furniture, cupboard, bookshelves and so on, a large settee and a pull-out type of table. Personal bits and pieces could be added by the tenants. There were also signs of individuality displayed here by a gigantic Harlequin pasted on one wall, and a stencil of a monkey swinging from branches of palm fronds on another wall.

'I'm sure Norma will be thrilled to get your book, Mrs Oliver. Won't you have a drink? Sherry? Gin?'

This girl had the brisk manner of a really good secretary. Mrs Oliver refused.

'You've got a splendid view up here,' she said, looking out of the window and blinking a little as she got the setting sun straight in her eyes.

'Yes. Not so funny when the lift goes out of order.'

'I shouldn't have thought *that* lift would dare to go out of order. It's so – so – robot-like.'

'Recently installed, but none the better for that,' said Claudia. 'It needs frequent adjusting and all that.'

Another girl came in, talking as she entered.

'Claudia, have you any idea where I put –'

She stopped, looking at Mrs Oliver.

Claudia made a quick introduction.

'Frances Cary – Mrs Oliver. Mrs *Ariadne* Oliver.'

'Oh, how exciting,' said Frances.

She was a tall willowy girl, with long black hair, a heavily made up dead white face, and eyebrows and eyelashes slightly slanted upwards – the effect heightened by mascara. She wore tight velvet pants and a heavy sweater. She was a complete contrast to the brisk and efficient Claudia.

'I brought a book I'd promised Norma Restarick,' said Mrs Oliver.

'Oh! – what a pity she's still in the country.'

'Hasn't she come back?'

There was quite definitely a pause. Mrs Oliver thought the two girls exchanged a glance.

'I thought she had a job in London,' said Mrs Oliver, endeavouring to convey innocent surprise.

'Oh yes,' said Claudia. 'She's in an interior decorating place. She's sent down with patterns occasionally to places in the country.' She smiled. 'We live rather separate lives here,' she explained. 'Come and go as we like – and don't usually bother to leave messages. But I won't forget to give her your book when she does get back.'

Nothing could have been easier than the casual explanation.

Mrs Oliver rose. 'Well, thank you very much.'

Claudia accompanied her to the door. 'I shall tell my father I've met you,' she said. 'He's a great reader of detective stories.'

Closing the door she went back into the sitting-room.

The girl Frances was leaning against the window.

'Sorry,' she said. 'Did I boob?'

'I'd just said that Norma was out.'

Frances shrugged her shoulders.

'I couldn't tell. Claudia, where *is* that girl? Why didn't she come back on Monday? Where has she gone?'

'I can't imagine.'

'She didn't stay on down with her people? That's where she went for the weekend.'

'No. I rang up, actually, to find out.'

'I suppose it doesn't really matter . . . All the same, she is – well, there's something queer about her.'

'She's not really queerer than anyone else.' But the opinion sounded uncertain.

'Oh yes, she is,' said Frances. 'Sometimes she gives me the shivers. She's not normal, you know.'

She laughed suddenly.

'Norma isn't normal! You know she isn't, Claudia, although you won't admit it. Loyalty to your employer, I suppose.'

CHAPTER 4

Hercule Poirot walked along the main street of Long Basing. That is, if you can describe as a main street a street that is to all intents and purposes the only street, which was the case in Long Basing. It was one of those villages that exhibit a tendency to length without breadth. It had an impressive church with a tall tower and a yew tree of elderly dignity in its churchyard. It had its full quota of village shops disclosing much variety. It had two antique shops, one mostly consisting of stripped pine chimney pieces, the other disclosing a full house of piled up ancient maps, a good deal of porcelain, most of it chipped, some worm-eaten old oak chests, shelves of glass, some Victorian silver, all somewhat hampered in display by lack of space. There were two cafés, both rather nasty, there was a basket shop, quite delightful, with a large variety of home-made wares, there was a post office-cum-greengrocer, there was a draper's which dealt largely in millinery and also a shoe department for children and a large miscellaneous selection of haberdashery of all kinds. There was a stationery and newspaper shop which also dealt in tobacco and sweets. There was a wool shop which was clearly the aristocrat of the place. Two white-haired severe women were in charge of shelves and shelves of knitting materials of every description. Also large quantities of dress-making patterns and knitting patterns and which branched off into a counter for art needlework. What had lately been the local grocer's had now blossomed into calling itself 'a supermarket' complete with stacks of wire baskets and packaged materials of every cereal and cleaning material, all in dazzling paper boxes. And there was a small establishment with one small window with Lillah written across it in fancy letters, a fashion display of one French blouse, labelled 'Latest chic', and a navy skirt and a purple striped jumper labelled 'separates'. These were displayed by being flung down as by a careless hand in the window.

All of this Poirot observed with a detached interest. Also contained within the limits of the village and facing on the street were several small houses, old-fashioned in style, sometimes retaining Georgian purity, more often showing some signs of

Victorian improvement, as a veranda, bow window, or a small conservatory. One or two houses had had a complete face lift and showed signs of claiming to be new and proud of it. There were also some delightful and decrepit old-world cottages, some pretending to be a hundred or so years older than they were, others completely genuine, any added comforts of plumbing or such being carefully hidden from any casual glance.

Poirot walked gently along digesting all that he saw. If his impatient friend, Mrs Oliver, had been with him, she would have immediately demanded why he was wasting time, as the house to which he was bound was a quarter of a mile beyond the village limits. Poirot would have told her that he was absorbing the local atmosphere; that these things were sometimes important. At the end of the village there came an abrupt transition. On one side, set back from the road, was a row of newly built council houses, a strip of green in front of them and a gay note set by each house having been given a different coloured front door. Beyond the council houses the sway of fields and hedges resumed its course interspersed now and then by the occasional 'desirable residences' of a house agent's list, with their own trees and gardens and a general air of reserve and of keeping themselves to themselves. Ahead of him farther down the road Poirot descried a house, the top storey of which displayed an unusual note of bulbous construction. Something had evidently been tacked on up there not so many years ago. This no doubt was the Mecca towards which his feet were bent. He arrived at a gate to which the nameplate Crosshedges was attached. He surveyed the house. It was a conventional house dating perhaps to the beginning of the century. It was neither beautiful nor ugly. Commonplace was perhaps the word to describe it. The garden was more attractive than the house and had obviously been the subject of a great deal of care and attention in its time, though it had been allowed to fall into disarray. It still had smooth green lawns, plenty of flower beds, carefully planted areas of shrubs to display a certain landscape effect. It was all in good order. A gardener was certainly employed in this garden, Poirot reflected. A personal interest was perhaps also taken, since he noted in a corner near the house a woman bending over one of the flower beds, tying up dahlias, he thought. Her head showed as a bright circle of pure gold colour.

She was tall, slim but square-shouldered. He unlatched the gate, passed through and walked up towards the house. The woman turned her head and then straightened herself, turning towards him inquiringly.

She remained standing, waiting for him to speak, some garden twine hanging from her left hand. She looked, he noted, puzzled.

'Yes?' she said.

Poirot, very foreign, took off his hat with a flourish and bowed. Her eyes rested on his moustaches with a kind of fascination.

'Mrs Restarick?'

'Yes. I –'

'I hope I do not derange you, Madame.'

A faint smile touched her lips. 'Not at all. Are you –'

'I have permitted myself to pay a visit on you. A friend of mine, Mrs Ariadne Oliver –'

'Oh, of course. I know who you must be. Monsieur Poiret.'

'Monsieur Poirot,' he corrected her with an emphasis on the last syllable. 'Hercule Poirot, at your service. I was passing through this neighbourhood and I ventured to call upon you here in the hope that I might be allowed to pay my respects to Sir Roderick Horsefield.'

'Yes. Naomi Lorrimer told us you might turn up.'

'I hope it is not inconvenient?'

'Oh, it is not inconvenient at all. Ariadne Oliver was here last weekend. She came over with the Lorrimers. Her books are most amusing, aren't they? But perhaps you don't find detective stories amusing. You are a detective yourself, aren't you – a real one?'

'I am all that there is of the most real,' said Hercule Poirot.

He noticed that she repressed a smile. He studied her more closely. She was handsome in a rather artificial fashion. Her golden hair was stiffly arranged. He wondered whether she might not at heart be secretly unsure of herself, whether she were not carefully playing the part of the English lady absorbed in her garden. He wondered a little what her social background might have been.

'You have a very fine garden here,' he said.

'You like gardens?'

'Not as the English like gardens. You have for a garden a

special talent in England. It means something to you that it does not to us.'

'To French people, you mean? Oh yes. I believe that Mrs Oliver mentioned that you were once with the Belgian Police Force?'

'That is so. Me, I am an old Belgian police dog.' He gave a polite little laugh and said, waving his hands, 'But your gardens, you English, I admire. I sit at your feet! The Latin races, they like the formal garden, the gardens of the château, the Château of Versailles in miniature, and also of course they invented the *potager*. Very important, the *potager*. Here in England you have the *potager*, but you got it from France and you do not love your *potager* as much as you love your flowers. *Hein*? That is so?'

'Yes, I think you are right,' said Mary Restarick. 'Do come into the house. You came to see my uncle.'

'I came, as you say, to pay homage to Sir Roderick, but I pay homage to you also, Madame. Always I pay homage to beauty when I meet it.' He bowed.

She laughed with slight embarrassment. 'You mustn't pay me so many compliments.'

She led the way through an open french window and he followed her.

'I knew your uncle slightly in 1944.'

'Poor dear, he's getting quite an old man now. He's very deaf, I'm afraid.'

'It was long ago that I encountered him. He will probably have forgotten. It was a matter of espionage and of scientific developments of a certain invention. We owed that invention to the ingenuity of Sir Roderick. He will be willing, I hope, to receive me.'

'Oh, I'm sure he'll love it,' said Mrs Restarick. 'He has rather a dull life in some ways nowadays. I have to be so much in London – we are looking for a suitable house there.' She sighed and said, 'Elderly people can be very difficult sometimes.'

'I know,' said Poirot. 'Frequently I, too, am difficult.'

She laughed. 'Ah no, M. Poirot, come now, you mustn't pretend you're old.'

'Sometimes I am told so,' said Poirot. He sighed. 'By young girls,' he added mournfully.

'That's very unkind of them. It's probably the sort of thing that our daughter would do,' she added.

'Ah, you have a daughter?'

'Yes. At least, she is my stepdaughter.'

'I shall have much pleasure in meeting her,' said Poirot politely.

'Oh well, I'm afraid she is not here. She's in London. She works there.'

'The young girls, they all do jobs nowadays.'

'Everybody's supposed to do a job,' said Mrs Restarick vaguely. 'Even when they get married they're always being persuaded back into industry or back into teaching.'

'Have they persuaded you, Madame, to come back into anything?'

'No. I was brought up in South Africa. I only came here with my husband a short time ago – It's all – rather strange to me still.'

She looked round her with what Poirot judged to be an absence of enthusiasm. It was a handsomely furnished room of a conventional type – without personality. Two large portraits hung on the walls – the only personal touch. The first was that of a thin lipped woman in a grey velvet evening dress. Facing her on the opposite wall was a man of about thirty-odd with an air of repressed energy about him.

'Your daughter, I suppose, finds it dull in the country?'

'Yes, it is much better for her to be in London. She doesn't like it here.' She paused abruptly, and then as though the last words were almost dragged out of her, she said, '– and she doesn't like me.'

'Impossible,' said Hercule Poirot, with Gallic politeness.

'Not at all impossible! Oh well, I suppose it often happens. I suppose it's hard for girls to accept a stepmother.'

'Was your daughter very fond of her own mother?'

'I suppose she must have been. She's a difficult girl. I suppose most girls are.'

Poirot sighed and said, 'Mothers and fathers have much less control over daughters nowadays. It is not as it used to be in the old good-fashioned days.'

'No indeed.'

'One dare not say so, Madame, but I must confess I regret that they show so very little discrimination in choosing their – how do you say it? – their boy friends?'

'Norma has been a great worry to her father in that way. However, I suppose it is no good complaining. People must make their own experiments. But I must take you up to Uncle Roddy – he has his own rooms upstairs.'

She led the way out of the room. Poirot looked back over his shoulder. A dull room, a room without character – except perhaps for the two portraits. By the style of the woman's dress, Poirot judged that they dated from some years back. If that was the first Mrs Restarick, Poirot did not think that he would have liked her.

He said, 'Those are fine portraits, Madame.'

'Yes. Lansberger did them.'

It was the name of a famous and exceedingly expensive fashionable portrait painter of twenty years ago. His meticulous naturalism had now gone out of fashion, and since his death, he was little spoken of. His sitters were sometimes sneeringly spoken of as 'clothes props', but Poirot thought they were a good deal more than that. He suspected that there was a carefully concealed mockery behind the smooth exteriors that Lansberger executed so effortlessly.

Mary Restarick said as she went up the stairs ahead of him:

'They have just come out of storage – and been cleaned up and –'

She stopped abruptly – coming to a dead halt, one hand on the stair-rail.

Above her, a figure had just turned the corner of the staircase on its way down. It was a figure that seemed strangely incongruous. It might have been someone in fancy dress, someone who certainly did not match with this house.

He was a figure familiar enough to Poirot in different conditions, a figure often met in the streets of London or even at parties. A representative of the youth of today. He wore a black coat, an elaborate velvet waistcoat, skin tight pants, and rich curls of chestnut hair hung down on his neck. He looked exotic and rather beautiful, and it needed a few moments to be certain of his sex.

'David!' Mary Restarick spoke sharply. 'What on earth are you doing here?'

The young man was by no means taken aback. 'Startled you?' he asked. 'So sorry.'

'What are you doing here – in this house? You – have you come down here with Norma?'

'Norma? No, I hoped to find her here.'

'Find her here – what do you mean? She's in London.'

'Oh, but my dear, she isn't. At any rate, she's not at 67 Borodene Mansions.'

'What do you mean, she isn't there?'

'Well, since she didn't come back this weekend, I thought she was probably here with you. I came down to see what she was up to.'

'She left here Sunday night as usual.' She added in an angry voice, 'Why didn't you ring the bell and let us know you were here? What are you doing roaming about the house?'

'Really, darling, you seem to be thinking I'm going to pinch the spoons or something. Surely it's natural to walk into a house in broad daylight. Why ever not?'

'Well, we're old-fashioned and we don't like it.'

'Oh dear, dear.' David sighed. 'The fuss everyone makes. Well, my dear, if I'm not going to have a welcome and you don't seem to know where your stepdaughter is, I suppose I'd better be moving along. Shall I turn out my pockets before I go?'

'Don't be absurd, David.'

'Ta-ta, then.' The young man passed them, waved an airy hand and went on down and out through the open front door.

'Horrible creature,' said Mary Restarick, with a sharpness of rancour that startled Poirot. 'I can't bear him. I simply can't stand him. Why is England absolutely full of these people nowadays?'

'Ah, Madame, do not disquiet yourself. It is all a question of fashion. There have always been fashions. You see less in the country, but in London you meet plenty of them.'

'Dreadful,' said Mary. 'Absolutely dreadful. Effeminate, exotic.'

'And yet not unlike a Vandyke portrait, do you not think so, Madame? In a gold frame, wearing a lace collar, you would not then say he was effeminate or exotic.'

'Daring to come down here like that. Andrew would have been furious. It worries him dreadfully. Daughters can be very worrying. It's not even as though Andrew knew Norma well.

He's been abroad since she was a child. He left her entirely to her mother to bring up, and now he finds her a complete puzzle. So do I for that matter. I can't help feeling that she is a very odd type of girl. One has no kind of authority over them these days. They seem to like the worst type of young men. She's absolutely infatuated with this David Baker. One can't do anything. Andrew forbade him the house, and look, he turns up here, walks in as cool as a cucumber. I think – I almost think I'd better not tell Andrew. I don't want him to be unduly worried. I believe she goes about with this creature in London, and not only with him. There are some much worse ones even. The kind that don't wash, completely unshaven faces and funny sprouting beards and greasy clothes.'

Poirot said cheerfully, 'Alas, Madame, you must not distress yourself. The indiscretions of youth pass.'

'I hope so, I'm sure. Norma is a *very* difficult girl. Sometimes I think she's not right in the head. She's so peculiar. She really looks sometimes as though she isn't all there. These extraordinary dislikes she takes –'

'Dislikes?'

'She hates me. Really hates me. I don't see why it's necessary. I suppose she was very devoted to her mother, but after all it's only reasonable that her father should marry again, isn't it?'

'Do you think she really hates you?'

'Oh, I know she does. I've had ample proof of it. I can't say how relieved I was when she went off to London. I didn't want to make trouble –' She stopped suddenly. It was as though for the first time she realised that she was talking to a stranger.

Poirot had the capacity to attract confidences. It was as though when people were talking to him they hardly realised who it was they were talking to. She gave a short laugh now.

'Dear me,' she said, 'I don't really know why I'm saying all this to you. I expect every family has these problems. Poor stepmothers, we have a hard time of it. Ah, here we are.'

She tapped on a door.

'Come in, come in.'

It was a stentorian roar.

'Here is a visitor to see you, Uncle,' said Mary Restarick, as she walked into the room, Poirot behind her.

A broad-shouldered, square-faced, red-cheeked, irascible looking elderly man had been pacing the floor. He stumped forward towards them. At the table behind him a girl was sitting sorting letters and papers. Her head was bent over them, a sleek, dark head.

'This is Monsieur Hercule Poirot, Uncle Roddy,' said Mary Restarick.

Poirot stepped forward gracefully into action and speech. 'Ah, Sir Roderick, it is many years – many years since I have had the pleasure of meeting you. We have to go back, so far as the last war. It was, I think, in Normandy the last time. How well I remember, there was there also Colonel Race and there was General Abercromby and there was Air-Marshal Sir Edmund Collingsby. What decisions we had to take! And what difficulties we had with security. Ah, nowadays, there is no longer the need for secrecy. I recall the unmasking of that secret agent who succeeded for so long – you remember Captain Henderson.'

'Ah. Captain Henderson indeed. Lord, that damned swine! Unmasked!'

'You may not remember me, Hercule Poirot.'

'Yes, yes, of course I remember you. Ah, it was a close shave that, a close shave. You were the French representative, weren't you? There were one or two of them, one I couldn't get on with – can't remember his name. Ah well, sit down, sit down. Nothing like having a chat over old days.'

'I feared so much that you might not remember me or my colleague, Monsieur Giraud.'

'Yes, yes, of course I remember both of you. Ah, those were the days, those were the days indeed.'

The girl at the table got up. She moved a chair politely towards Poirot.

'That's right, Sonia, that's right,' said Sir Roderick. 'Let me introduce you,' he said, 'to my charming little secretary here. Makes a great difference to me. Helps me, you know, files all my work. Don't know how I ever got on without her.'

Poirot bowed politely. '*Enchanté*, mademoiselle,' he murmured.

The girl murmured something in rejoinder. She was a small creature with black bobbed hair. She looked shy. Her dark blue eyes were usually modestly cast down, but she smiled up sweetly and shyly at her employer. He patted her on the shoulder.

'Don't know what I should do without her,' he said. 'I don't really.'

'Oh, no,' the girl protested. 'I am not much good really. I cannot type very fast.'

'You type quite fast enough, my dear. You're my memory, too. My eyes and my ears and a great many other things.'

She smiled again at him.

'One remembers,' murmured Poirot, 'some of the excellent stories that used to go the round. I don't know if they were exaggerated or not. Now, for instance, the day that someone stole your car and –' he proceeded to follow up the tale.

Sir Roderick was delighted. 'Ha, ha, of course now. Yes, indeed, well, bit of exaggeration, I expect. But on the whole, that's how it was. Yes, yes, well, fancy your remembering *that*, after all this long time. But I could tell you a better one than that now.' He launched forth into another tale. Poirot listened, applauded. Finally he glanced at his watch and rose to his feet.

'But I must detain you no longer,' he said. 'You are engaged, I can see, in important work. It was just that being in this neighbourhood I could not help paying my respects. Years pass, but you, I see, have lost none of your vigour, of your enjoyment of life.'

'Well, well, perhaps you may say so. Anyway, you mustn't pay me too many compliments – but surely you'll stay and have tea. I'm sure Mary will give you some tea.' He looked round. 'Oh, she's gone away. Nice girl.'

'Yes, indeed, and very handsome. I expect she has been a great comfort to you for many years.'

'Oh! They've only married recently. She's my nephew's second wife. I'll be frank with you. I've never cared very much for this nephew of mine, Andrew – not a steady chap. Always restless. His elder brother Simon was my favourite. Not that I knew him well, either. As for Andrew, he behaved very badly to his first wife. Went off, you know. Left her high and dry. Went off with a thoroughly bad lot. Everybody knew about her. But he was infatuated with her. The whole thing broke up in a year or two: silly fellow. The girl he's married seems all right. Nothing wrong with her as far as I know. Now Simon was a steady chap – damned dull, though. I can't say I liked it when my sister married into that family. Marrying into trade, you know. Rich, of course, but money isn't everything – we've usually married into the Services. I never saw much of the Restarick lot.'

'They have, I believe, a daughter. A friend of mine met her last week.'

'Oh, Norma. Silly girl. Goes about in dreadful clothes and has picked up with a dreadful young man. Ah well, they're all alike nowadays. Long-haired young fellows, beatniks, Beatles, all sorts of names they've got. I can't keep up with them. Practically talk a foreign language. Still, nobody cares to hear an old man's criticisms, so there we are. Even Mary – I always thought she was a good, sensible sort, but as far as I can see she can be thoroughly hysterical in some ways – mainly about her health. Some fuss about going to hospital for observation or something. What about a drink? Whisky? No? Sure you won't stop and have a drop of tea?'

'Thank you, but I am staying with friends.'

'Well, I must say I have enjoyed this chat with you very much. Nice to remember some of the things that happened in the old days. Sonia, dear, perhaps you'll take Monsieur – sorry, what's your name, it's gone again – ah, yes, Poirot. Take him down to Mary, will you?'

'No, no,' Hercule Poirot hastily waved aside the offer. 'I could not dream of troubling Madame any more. I am quite all right. Quite all right. I can find my way perfectly. It has been a great pleasure to meet you again.'

He left the room.

'Haven't the faintest idea who that chap was,' said Sir Roderick, after Poirot had gone.

'You do not know who he was?' Sonia asked, looking at him in a startled manner.

'Personally I don't remember who half the people are who come up and talk to me nowadays. Of course, I have to make a good shot at it. One learns to get away with that, you know. Same thing at parties. Up comes a chap and says, "Perhaps you don't remember me. I last saw you in 1939." I have to say "Of course I remember," but I don't. It's a handicap being nearly blind and deaf. We got pally with a lot of frogs like that towards the end of the war. Don't remember half of them. Oh, he'd been there all right. He knew me and I knew a good many of the chaps he talked about. That story about me and the stolen car, that was true enough. Exaggerated a bit, of course, they made a pretty good story of it at the time. Ah well, I don't think he knew I didn't remember him. Clever chap, I should say, but a thorough frog, isn't he? You know, mincing and dancing and bowing and scraping. Now then, where were we?'

Sonia picked up a letter and handed it to him. She tentatively proffered a pair of spectacles which he immediately rejected.

'Don't want those damned things – I can see all right.'

He screwed up his eyes and peered down at the letter he was holding. Then he capitulated and thrust it back into her hands.

'Well, perhaps you'd better read it to me.'

She started reading it in her clear soft voice.

CHAPTER 5

I

Hercule Poirot stood upon the landing for a moment. His head was a little on one side with a listening air. He could hear nothing from downstairs. He crossed to the landing window and looked out. Mary Restarick was below on the terrace, resuming her gardening work. Poirot nodded his head in satisfaction. He walked gently along the corridor. One by one in turn he opened the doors. A bathroom, a linen cupboard, a double bedded spare room, an occupied single bedroom, a woman's room with a double bed (Mary Restarick's?). The next door was that of an adjoining room and was, he guessed, the room belonging to Andrew Restarick. He turned to the other side of the landing. The door he opened first was a single bedroom. It was not, he judged, occupied at the time, but it was a room which possibly was occupied at weekends. There were toilet brushes on the dressing-table. He listened carefully, then tip-toed in. He opened the wardrobe. Yes, there were some clothes hanging up there. Country clothes.

There was a writing table but there was nothing on it. He opened the desk drawers very softly. There were a few odds and ends, a letter or two, but the letters were trivial and dated some time ago. He shut the desk drawers. He walked downstairs, and going out of the house, bade farewell to his hostess. He refused her offer of tea. He had promised to get back, he said, as he had to catch a train to town very shortly afterwards.

'Don't you want a taxi? We could order you one, or I could drive you in the car.'

'No, no, Madame, you are too kind.'

Poirot walked back to the village and turned down the lane by the church. He crossed a little bridge over a stream. Presently he came to where a large car with a chauffeur was waiting discreetly under a beech tree. The chauffeur opened the door of the car, Poirot got inside, sat down and removed his patent leather shoes, uttering a gasp of relief.

'Now we return to London,' he said.

The chauffeur closed the door, returned to his seat and the car purred quietly away. The sight of a young man standing by the roadside furiously thumbing a ride was not an unusual one. Poirot's eyes rested almost indifferently on this member of the fraternity, a brightly dressed young man with long and exotic hair. There were many such but in the moment of passing him Poirot suddenly sat upright and addressed the driver.

'If you please, stop. Yes, and if you can reverse a little . . . There is someone requesting a lift.'

The chauffeur turned an incredulous eye over his shoulder. It was the last remark he would have expected. However, Poirot was gently nodding his head, so he obeyed.

The young man called David advanced to the door. 'Thought you weren't going to stop for me,' he said cheerfully. 'Much obliged, I'm sure.'

He got in, removed a small pack from his shoulders and let it slide to the floor, smoothed down his copper brown locks. 'So you recognised me,' he said.

'You are perhaps somewhat conspicuously dressed.'

'Oh, do you think so? Not really. I'm just one of a band of brothers.'

'The school of Vandyke. Very dressy.'

'Oh. I've never thought of it like that. Yes, there may be something in what you say.'

'You should wear a cavalier's hat,' said Poirot, 'and a lace collar, if I might advise.'

'Oh, I don't think we go quite as far as that.' The young man laughed. 'How Mrs Restarick dislikes the mere sight of me. Actually I reciprocate her dislike. I don't care much for Restarick, either. There is something singularly unattractive about successful tycoons, don't you think?'

'It depends on the point of view. You have been paying attentions to the daughter, I understand.'

'That is such a nice phrase,' said David. 'Paying attentions to the daughter. I suppose it might be called that. But there's plenty of fifty-fifty about it, you know. She's paying attention to me, too.'

'Where is Mademoiselle now?'

David turned his head rather sharply. 'And why do you ask that?'

'I should like to meet her.' He shrugged his shoulders.

'I don't believe she'd be your type, you know, any more than I am. Norma's in London.'

'But you said to her stepmother –'

'Oh! We don't tell stepmothers everything.'

'And where is she in London?'

'She works in an interior decorator's down the King's Road somewhere in Chelsea. Can't remember the name of it for the moment. Susan Phelps, I think.'

'But that is not where she lives, I presume. You have her address?'

'Oh yes, a great block of flats. I don't really understand your interest.'

'One is interested in so many things.'

'What do you mean?'

'What brought you to that house – (what is its name? – Crosshedges) today. Brought you secretly into the house and up the stairs.'

'I came in the back door, I admit.'

'What were you looking for upstairs?'

'That's my business. I don't want to be rude – but aren't you being rather nosy?'

'Yes, I am displaying curiosity. I would like to know exactly where this young lady is.'

'I see. Dear Andrew and dear Mary – lord rot 'em – are employing you, is that it? They are trying to find her?'

'As yet,' said Poirot, 'I do not think they know that she is missing.'

'Someone must be employing you.'

'You are exceedingly perceptive,' said Poirot. He leant back.

'I wondered what you were up to,' said David. 'That's why I hailed you. I hoped you'd stop and give me a bit of dope. She's my girl. You know that, I suppose?'

'I understand that that is supposed to be the idea,' said Poirot cautiously. 'If so, you should know where she is. Is that not so, Mr – I am sorry, I do not think I know your name beyond, that is, that your Christian name is David.'

'Baker.'

'Perhaps, Mr Baker, you have had a quarrel.'

'No, we haven't had a quarrel. Why should you think we had?'

'Miss Norma Restarick left Crosshedges on Sunday evening, or was it Monday morning?'

'It depends. There is an early bus you can take. Gets you to London a little after ten. It would make her a bit late at work, but not too much. Usually she goes back on Sunday night.'

'She left there Sunday night but she has not arrived at Borodene Mansions.'

'Apparently not. So Claudia says.'

'This Miss Reece-Holland – that is her name, is it not? – was she surprised or worried?'

'Good lord, no, why should she be. They don't keep tabs on each other all the time, these girls.'

'But you thought she was going back there?'

'She didn't go back to work either. They're fed up at the shop, I can tell you.'

'Are *you* worried, Mr Baker?'

'No. Naturally – I mean, well, I'm damned if I know. I don't see any reason I should be worried, only time's getting on. What is it today – Thursday?'

'She has not quarrelled with you?'

'No. We don't quarrel.'

'But you are worried about her, Mr Baker?'

'What business is it of yours?'

'It is no business of mine but there has, I understand, been trouble at home. She does not like her stepmother.'

'Quite right too. She's a bitch, that woman. Hard as nails. She doesn't like Norma either.'

'She has been ill, has she not? She had to go to hospital.'

'Who are you talking about – Norma?'

'No, I am not talking about Miss Restarick. I am talking about Mrs Restarick.'

'I believe she did go into a nursing home. No reason she should. Strong as a horse, I'd say.'

'And Miss Restarick hates her stepmother.'

'She's a bit unbalanced sometimes, Norma. You know, goes off the deep end. I tell you, girls always hate their stepmothers.'

'Does that always make stepmothers ill? Ill enough to go to hospital?'

'What the hell are you getting at?'

'Gardening perhaps – or the use of weed killer.'

'What do you mean by talking about weed killer? Are you suggesting that Norma – that she'd dream of – that –'

'People talk,' said Poirot. 'Talk goes round the neighbourhood.'

'Do you mean that somebody has said that Norma has tried to poison her stepmother? That's ridiculous. It's absolutely absurd.'

'It is very unlikely, I agree,' said Poirot. 'Actually, people have *not* been saying that.'

'Oh. Sorry. I misunderstood. But – what *did* you mean?'

'My dear young man,' said Poirot, 'you must realise that there are rumours going about, and rumours are almost always about the same person – a husband.'

'What, poor old Andrew? Most unlikely I should say.'

'Yes. Yes, it does not seem to me very likely.'

'Well, what were you there for then? You *are* a detective, aren't you?'

'Yes.'

'Well, then?'

'We are talking at cross purposes,' said Poirot. 'I did not go down there to inquire into any doubtful or possible case of poisoning. You must forgive me if I cannot answer your question. It is all very hush-hush, you understand.'

'What on earth do you mean by that?'

'I went there,' said Poirot, 'to see Sir Roderick Horsefield.'

'What, that old boy? He's practically ga-ga, isn't he?'

'He is a man,' said Poirot, 'who is in possession of a great many secrets. I do not mean that he takes an active part in such things nowadays, but he knows a good deal. He was connected with a great many things in the past war. He *knew* several people.'

'That's all over years ago, though.'

'Yes, yes, *his* part in things is all over years ago. But do you not realise that there are certain things that it might be useful to know?'

'What sort of things?'

'Faces,' said Poirot. 'A well known face perhaps, which Sir Roderick might recognise. A face or a mannerism, a way of talking, a way of walking, a gesture. People do remember, you know. Old people. They remember, not things that have happened last week or last month or last year, but they remember something that happened, say, nearly twenty years ago. And they may remember someone who does not want to be remembered. And they can tell you certain things about a certain man or a certain woman or something they were mixed up in – I am speaking very vaguely, you understand. I went to him for information.'

'You went to him for information, did you? *That* old boy? Ga-ga. And he gave it to you?'

'Let us say that I am quite satisfied.'

David continued to stare at him. 'I wonder now,' he said. 'Did you go to see the old boy or did you go to see the little girl, eh? Did you want to know what *she* was doing in the house? I've wondered once or twice myself. Do you think she took that post there to get a bit of past information out of the old boy?'

'I do not think,' said Poirot, 'that it will serve any useful purpose to discuss these matters. She seems a very devoted and attentive – what shall I call her – secretary?'

'A mixture of a hospital nurse, a secretary, a companion, an *au pair* girl, an uncle's help? Yes, one could find a good many names for her, couldn't one? He's besotted about her. You noticed that?'

'It is not unnatural under the circumstances,' said Poirot primly.

'I can tell you someone who doesn't like her, and that's our Mary.'

'And she perhaps does not like Mary Restarick either.'

'So that's what you think, is it?' said David. 'That Sonia doesn't like Mary Restarick. Perhaps you go as far as thinking that she may have made a few inquiries as to where the weed killer was kept? Bah,' he added, 'the whole thing's ridiculous. All right. Thanks for the lift. I think I'll get out here.'

'Aha. This is where you want to be? We are still a good seven miles out of London.'

'I'll get out here. Goodbye, M. Poirot.'

'Goodbye.'

Poirot leant back in his seat as David slammed the door.

II

Mrs Oliver prowled round her sitting-room. She was very restless. An hour ago she had parcelled up a typescript that she had just finished correcting. She was about to send it off to her publisher who was anxiously awaiting it and constantly prodding her about it every three or four days.

'There you are,' said Mrs Oliver, addressing the empty air and conjuring up an imaginary publisher. 'There you are, and I hope you like it! *I* don't. I think it's *lousy*! I don't believe *you* know whether anything I write is good or bad. Anyway, I warned you. I *told* you it was frightful. You said "Oh! no, no, I don't believe that for a moment."

'You just wait and see,' said Mrs Oliver vengefully. 'You just wait and see.'

She opened the door, called to Edith, her maid, gave her the parcel and directed that it should be taken to the post at once.

'And now,' said Mrs Oliver, 'what am I going to do with myself?'

She began strolling about again. 'Yes,' thought Mrs Oliver, 'I wish I had those tropical birds and things back on the wall instead of these idiotic cherries. I used to feel like something in a tropical wood. A lion or a tiger or a leopard or a cheetah! What could I possibly feel like in a cherry orchard except a bird scarer?'

She looked round again. 'Cheeping like a bird, that's what I ought to be doing,' she said gloomily. 'Eating cherries . . . I wish it was the right time of year for cherries. I'd like some cherries. I wonder now –' She went to the telephone. 'I will ascertain, Madam,' said the voice of George in answer to her inquiry. Presently another voice spoke.

'Hercule Poirot, at your service, Madame,' he said.

'Where've you been?' said Mrs Oliver. 'You've been away all day. I suppose you went down to look up the Restaricks. Is that it? Did you see Sir Roderick? What did you find out?'

'Nothing,' said Hercule Poirot.

'How dreadfully dull,' said Mrs Oliver.

'No, I do not think it is really so dull. It is rather astonishing that I have *not* found out anything.'

'Why is it so astonishing? I don't understand.'

'Because,' said Poirot, 'it means either there was nothing to find out, and that, let me tell you, does not accord with the facts; or else something was being very cleverly concealed. That, you see, would be interesting. Mrs Restarick, by the way, did not know the girl was missing.'

'You mean – she has nothing to do with the girl having disappeared?'

'So it seems. I met there the young man.'

'You mean the unsatisfactory young man that nobody likes?'

'That is right. The unsatisfactory young man.'

'Did you think he *was* unsatisfactory?'

'From whose point of view?'

'Not from the girl's point of view, I suppose.'

'The girl who came to see me I am sure would have been highly delighted with him.'

'Did he look very awful?'

'He looked very beautiful,' said Hercule Poirot.

'Beautiful?' said Mrs Oliver. 'I don't know that I *like* beautiful young men.'

'Girls do,' said Poirot.

'Yes, you're quite right. They like beautiful young men. I don't mean good-looking young men or smart-looking young men or well-dressed or well-washed looking young men. I mean they either like young men looking as though they were just going on in a Restoration comedy, or else very dirty young men looking as though they were just going to take some awful tramp's job.'

'It seemed that he also did not know where the girl is now –'

'Or else he wasn't admitting it.'

'Perhaps. He had gone down there. Why? He was actually in the house. He had taken the trouble to walk in without anyone seeing him. Again why? For what reason? Was he looking for the girl? Or was he looking for something else?'

'You think he *was* looking for something?'

'He was looking for something in the girl's room,' said Poirot.

'How do you know? Did you see him there?'

'No, I only saw him coming down the stairs, but I found a very nice little piece of damp mud in Norma's room that could have come from his shoe. It is possible that she herself may have asked him to bring her something from that room – there are a lot of possibilities. There is another girl in that house – and a pretty one – He may have come down there to meet *her*. Yes – many possibilities.'

'What are you going to do next?' demanded Mrs Oliver.

'Nothing,' said Poirot.

'That's very dull,' said Mrs Oliver disapprovingly.

'I am going to receive, perhaps, a little information from those I have employed to find it; though it is quite possible that I shall receive nothing at all.'

'But aren't you going to *do* something?'

'Not till the right moment,' said Poirot.

'Well, I shall,' said Mrs Oliver.

'Pray, pray be very careful,' he implored her.

'What nonsense! What could happen to me?'

'Where there is murder, anything can happen. I tell that to you. I, Poirot.'

CHAPTER 6

I

Mr Goby sat in a chair. He was a small shrunken little man, so nondescript as to be practically nonexistent.

He looked attentively at the claw foot of an antique table and addressed his remarks to it. He never addressed anybody direct.

'Glad you got the names for me, Mr Poirot,' he said. 'Otherwise, you know, it might have taken a lot of time. As it is, I've got the main facts – and a bit of gossip on the side . . . Always useful, that. I'll begin at Borodene Mansions, shall I?'

Poirot inclined his head graciously.

'Plenty of porters,' Mr Goby informed the clock on the chimney piece. 'I started there, used one or two different young men. Expensive, but worth it. Didn't want it thought that there was anyone making any particular inquiries! Shall I use initials, or names?'

'Within these walls you can use the names,' said Poirot.

'Miss Claudia Reece-Holland spoken of as a very nice young lady. Father an MP. Ambitious man. Gets himself in the news a lot. She's his only daughter. She does secretarial work. Serious girl. No wild parties, no drink, no beatniks. Shares flat with two others. Number two works for the Wedderburn Gallery in Bond Street. Arty type. Whoops it up a bit with the Chelsea set. Goes around to places arranging exhibitions and art shows.

'The third one is *your* one. Not been there long. General opinion is that she's a bit "wanting". Not all there in the top storey. But it's all a bit vague. One of the porters is a gossipy type. Buy him a drink or two and you'll be surprised at the things he'll tell you! Who drinks, and who drugs, and who's having trouble with his income tax, and who keeps his cash behind the cistern. Of course you can't believe it all. Anyway, there was some story about a revolver being fired one night.'

'A revolver fired? Was anyone injured?'

'There seems a bit of doubt as to that. His story is he heard a shot fired one night, and he comes out and there was this girl, *your* girl, standing there with a revolver in her hand. She looked sort of dazed. And then one of the other young ladies – or both of them, in fact – they come running along. And Miss Cary (that's the arty one) says, "Norma, what on earth have you done?" and Miss Reece-Holland, she says sharp-like, "Shut up, can't you, Frances. Don't be a fool!" and she took the revolver away from your girl and says, "Give me that." She slams it into her handbag and then she notices this chap Micky, and goes over to him and says, laughing-like, "That must have startled you, didn't it?" and Micky he says it gave him quite a turn, and she says, "You needn't worry. Matter of fact, we'd no idea this thing was loaded. We were just fooling about." And then she says: "Anyway, if anybody asks you questions, tell them it is quite all right," and then she says: "Come on, Norma," and took her arm and led her along to the elevator, and they all went up again.

'But Micky said he was a bit doubtful still. He went and had a good look round the courtyard.'

Mr Goby lowered his eyes and quoted from his notebook:

'"I'll tell you, I found something, I did! I found some wet patches. Sure as anything I did. Drops of blood they were. I touched them with my finger. I tell you what *I* think. Somebody had been shot – some man as he was running away . . . I went upstairs and I asked if I could speak to Miss Holland. I says to her: 'I think there may have been someone shot, Miss,' I says. 'There are some drops of blood in the courtyard.' 'Good gracious,' she says, 'How ridiculous. I expect, you know,' she says, 'it must have been one of the pigeons.' And then she says: 'I'm sorry if it gave you a turn. Forget about it,' and she slipped me a five pound note. Five pound note, no less! Well, naturally, I didn't open my mouth after that."

'And then, after another whisky, he comes out with some more. "If you ask me, she took a pot shot at that low class young chap that comes to see her. I think she and he had a row and she did her best to shoot him. That's what I think. But least said soonest mended, so I'm not repeating it. If anyone asks me anything I'll say I don't know what they're talking about."' Mr Goby paused.

'Interesting,' said Poirot.

'Yes, but it's as likely as not that it's a pack of lies. Nobody else seems to know anything about it. There's a story about a gang of young thugs who came barging into the courtyard one night, and had a bit of a fight – flick-knives out and all that.'

'I see,' said Poirot. 'Another possible source of blood in the courtyard.'

'Maybe the girl did have a row with her young man, threatened to shoot him, perhaps. And Micky overheard it and mixed the whole thing up – especially if there was a car backfiring just then.'

'Yes,' said Hercule Poirot, and sighed, 'that would account for things quite well.'

Mr Goby turned over another leaf of his notebook and selected his confidant. He chose an electric radiator.

'Joshua Restarick Ltd. Family firm. Been going over a hundred years. Well thought of in the City. Always very sound. Nothing spectacular. Founded by Joshua Restarick in 1850. Launched out after the first war, with greatly increased investments abroad, mostly South Africa, West Africa and Australia. Simon and Andrew Restarick – the last of the Restaricks. Simon, the elder brother, died about a year ago, no children. His wife had died some years previously. Andrew Restarick seems to have been a restless chap. His heart was never really in the business though everyone says he had plenty of ability. Finally ran off with some woman, leaving his wife and a daughter of five years old. Went to South Africa, Kenya, and various other places. No divorce. His wife died two years ago. Had been an invalid for some time. He travelled about a lot, and wherever he went he seems to have made money. Concessions for minerals mostly. Everything he touched prospered.

'After his brother's death, he seems to have decided it was time to settle down. He'd married again and he thought the right thing to do was to come back and make a home for his daughter. They're living at the moment with his uncle Sir Roderick Horsefield – uncle by marriage that is. That's only temporary. His wife's looking at houses all over London. Expense no object. They're rolling in money.'

Poirot sighed. 'I know,' he said. 'What you outline to me is a success story! Everyone makes money! Everybody is of good family and highly respected. Their relations are distinguished. They are well thought of in business circles.

'There is only one cloud in the sky. A girl who is said to be "a bit wanting", a girl who is mixed up with a dubious boy friend who has been on probation more than once. A girl who may quite possibly have tried to poison her stepmother, and who either suffers from hallucinations, or else has committed a crime! I tell you, none of that accords well with the success story you have brought me.'

Mr Goby shook his head sadly and said rather obscurely:

'There's one in every family.'

'This Mrs Restarick is quite a young woman. I presume she is *not* the woman he originally ran away with?'

'Oh no, that bust up quite soon. She was a pretty bad lot by all accounts, and a tartar as well. He was a fool ever to be taken in by her.' Mr Goby shut his notebook and looked inquiringly at Poirot. 'Anything more you want me to do?'

'Yes. I want to know a little more about the late Mrs Andrew Restarick. She was an invalid, she was frequently in nursing homes. What *kind* of nursing homes? Mental homes?'

'I take your point, Mr Poirot.'

'And any history of insanity in the family – on either side?'

'I'll see to it, Mr Poirot.'

Mr Goby rose to his feet. 'Then I'll take leave of you, sir. Good night.'

Poirot remained thoughtful after Mr Goby had left. He raised and lowered his eyebrows. He wondered, he wondered very much.

Then he rang Mrs Oliver:

'I told you before,' he said, 'to be careful. I repeat that – Be very careful.'

'Careful of what?' said Mrs Oliver.

'Of yourself. I think there might be danger. Danger to anyone who goes poking about where they are not wanted. There is murder in the air – I do not want it to be yours.'

'Have you had the information you said you might have?'

'Yes,' said Poirot, 'I have had a little information. Mostly rumour and gossip, but it seems something happened at Borodene Mansions.'

'What sort of thing?'

'Blood in the courtyard,' said Poirot.

'Really!' said Mrs Oliver. 'That's just like the title of an old-fashioned detective story. *The Stain on the Staircase.* I mean nowadays you say something more like *She Asked for Death.*'

'Perhaps there may not have been blood in the courtyard. Perhaps it is only what an imaginative, Irish porter imagined.'

'Probably an upset milk bottle,' said Mrs Oliver. 'He couldn't see it at night. What happened?'

Poirot did not answer directly.

'The girl thought she "might have committed a murder". Was that the murder she meant?'

'You mean she *did* shoot someone?'

'One might presume that she did shoot *at* someone, but for all intents and purposes missed them. A few drops of blood . . . That was all. No body.'

'Oh dear,' said Mrs Oliver, 'it's all very confused. Surely if anyone could still run out of a courtyard, you wouldn't think you'd killed him, would you?'

'*C'est difficile,*' said Poirot, and rang off.

II

'I'm worried,' said Claudia Reece-Holland.

She refilled her cup from the coffee percolator. Frances Cary gave an enormous yawn. Both girls were breakfasting in the small kitchen of the flat. Claudia was dressed and ready to start for her day's work. Frances was still in dressing-gown and pyjamas. Her black hair fell over one eye.

'I'm worried about Norma,' continued Claudia.

Frances yawned.

'I shouldn't worry if I were you. She'll ring up or turn up sooner or later, I suppose.'

'Will she? You know, Fran, I can't help wondering –'

'I don't see why,' said Frances, pouring herself out more coffee. She sipped it doubtfully. 'I mean – Norma's not really our business, is she? I mean, we're not looking after her or spoon-feeding her or anything. She just shares the flat. Why all this motherly solicitude? I certainly wouldn't worry.'

'I daresay *you* wouldn't. You never worry over anything. But it's not the same for you as it is for me.'

'Why isn't it the same? You mean because you're the tenant of the flat or something?'

'Well, I'm in rather a special position, as you might say.'

Frances gave another enormous yawn.

'I was up too late last night,' she said. 'At Basil's party. I feel dreadful. Oh well, I suppose black coffee will be helpful. Have some more before I've drunk it all? Basil *would* make us try some new pills – Emerald Dreams. I don't think it's really worth trying all these silly things.'

'You'll be late at your gallery,' said Claudia.

'Oh well, I don't suppose it matters much. Nobody notices or cares.

'I saw David last night,' she added. 'He was all dressed up and really looked rather wonderful.'

'Now don't say *you're* falling for him, too, Fran. He really is too *awful*.'

'Oh, I know *you* think so. You're such a conventional type, Claudia.'

'Not at all. But I cannot say I care for all your arty set. Trying out all these drugs and passing out or getting fighting mad.'

Frances looked amused.

'I'm not a drug fiend, dear – I just like to see what these things are like. And some of the gang are all right. David can paint, you know, if he wants to.'

'David doesn't very often want to, though, does he?'

'You've always got your knife into him, Claudia . . . You hate him coming here to see Norma. And talking of knives . . .'

'Well? Talking of knives?'

'I've been worrying,' said Frances slowly, 'whether to tell you something or not.'

Claudia glanced at her wrist-watch.

'I haven't got time now,' she said. 'You can tell me this evening if you want to tell me something. Anyway, I'm not in the mood. Oh dear,' she sighed, 'I wish I knew what to do.'

'About Norma?'

'Yes. I'm wondering if her parents ought to know that *we* don't know where she is . . .'

'That would be *very* unsporting. Poor Norma, why shouldn't she slope off on her own if she wants to?'

'Well, Norma isn't exactly –' Claudia stopped.

'No, she isn't, is she? *Non compos mentis*. That's what you meant. Have you rung up that terrible place where she works? "Homebirds", or whatever it's called? Oh yes, of course you did. I remember.'

'So where *is* she?' demanded Claudia. 'Did David say anything last night?'

'David didn't seem to know. Really, Claudia, I *can't* see that it matters.'

'It matters for me,' said Claudia, 'because my boss happens to be her father. Sooner or later, if anything peculiar *has* happened to her, they'll ask me why I didn't mention the fact that she hadn't come home.'

'Yes, I suppose they might pitch on you. But there's no real reason, is there, why Norma should have to report to us every time she's going to be away from here for a day or two. Or even a few nights. I mean, she's not a paying guest or anything. You're not in charge of the girl.'

'No, but Mr Restarick did mention he felt glad to know that she had got a room here with us.'

'So that entitles *you* to go and tittle-tattle about her every time she's absent without leave? She's probably got a crush on some new man.'

'She's got a crush on David,' said Claudia. 'Are you sure she isn't holed up at his place?'

'Oh, I shouldn't think so. He doesn't really care for her, you know.'

'You'd like to think he doesn't,' said Claudia. 'You are rather sweet on David yourself.'

'Certainly not,' said Frances sharply. 'Nothing of the kind.'

'David's really keen on her,' said Claudia. 'If not, why did he come round looking for her here the other day?'

'*You* soon marched him out again,' said Frances. 'I think,' she added, getting up and looking at her face in a rather unflattering small kitchen mirror, 'I think it *might* have been me he really came to see.'

'You're too idiotic! He came here looking for Norma.'

'That girl's mental,' said Frances.

'Sometimes I really think she is!'

'Well, I *know* she is. Look here, Claudia, I'm going to tell you that something *now*. You ought to know. I broke the string of my bra the other day and I was in a hurry. I know you don't like anyone fiddling with *your* things –'

'I certainly don't,' said Claudia.

'– but Norma never minds, or doesn't notice. Anyway, I went into her room and I rootled in her drawer and I – well, I found something. A knife.'

'A knife!' said Claudia, surprised. 'What sort of a knife?'

'You know we had that sort of shindy thing in the courtyard? A group of beats, teenagers who'd come in here and were having a fight with flick-knives and all that? And Norma came in just after.'

'Yes, yes, I remember.'

'One of the boys got stabbed, so a reporter told me, and he ran away. Well, the knife in Norma's drawer was a flick-knife. It had got a stain on it – looked like dried blood.'

'Frances! You're being absurdly dramatic.'

'Perhaps. But I'm sure that's what it was. And what on earth was that doing hidden away in Norma's drawer, I should like to know?'

'I suppose – she might have picked it up.'

'What – a souvenir? And hidden it away and never told us?'

'What did you do with it?'

'I put it back,' said Frances slowly. 'I – I didn't know what else to do . . . I couldn't decide whether to tell you or not. Then yesterday I looked again and *it was gone, Claudia*. Not a trace of it.'

'You think she sent David here to get it?'

'Well, she might have done . . . I tell you, Claudia, in future I'm going to keep my door locked at night.'

CHAPTER 7

Mrs Oliver woke up dissatisfied. She saw stretching before her a day with nothing to do. Having packed off her completed manuscript with a highly virtuous feeling, work was over. She had now only, as many times before, to relax, to enjoy herself; to lie fallow until the creative urge became active once more. She walked about her flat in a rather aimless fashion, touching things, picking them up, putting them down, looking in the drawers of her desk, realising that there were plenty of letters there to be dealt with but feeling also that in her present state of virtuous accomplishment, she was certainly not going to deal with anything so tiresome as that now. She wanted something *interesting* to do. She wanted – what did she want?

She thought about the conversation she had had with Hercule Poirot, the warning he had given her. Ridiculous! After all, why shouldn't she participate in this problem which she was sharing with Poirot? Poirot might choose to sit in a chair, put the tips of his fingers together, and set his grey cells whirring to work while his body reclined comfortably within four walls. That was not the procedure that appealed to Ariadne Oliver. She had said, very forcibly, that she at least was going to do something. She was going to find out more about this mysterious girl. Where was Norma Restarick? What was she doing? What more could she, Ariadne Oliver, find out about her?

Mrs Oliver prowled about, more and more disconsolate. What *could* one do? It wasn't very easy to decide. Go somewhere and ask questions? Should she go down to Long Basing? But Poirot had already been there – and found out presumably what there was to be found out. And what excuse could she offer for barging into Sir Roderick Horsefield's house?

She considered another visit to Borodene Mansions. Something still to be found out there, perhaps? She would have to think of another excuse for going there. She wasn't quite sure *what* excuse she would use but anyway, that seemed the only possible place where more information could be obtained. What was the time? Ten a.m. There were certain possibilities . . .

On the way there she concocted an excuse. Not a very original excuse. In fact, Mrs Oliver would have liked to have found something more intriguing, but perhaps, she reflected prudently, it was just as well to keep to something completely everyday and plausible. She arrived at the stately if grim elevation of Borodene Mansions and walked slowly round the courtyard considering it.

A porter was conversing with a furniture van – A milkman, pushing his milk-float, came to join Mrs Oliver near the service lift.

He rattled bottles, cheerfully whistling, whilst Mrs Oliver continued to stare abstractedly at the furniture van.

'Number 76 moving out,' explained the milkman to Mrs Oliver, mistaking her interest. He transferred a clutch of bottles from his float to the lift.

'Not that she hasn't moved already in a manner of speaking,' he added, emerging again. He seemed a cheery kind of milkman.

He pointed a thumb upwards.

'Pitched herself out of a window – seventh floor – only a week ago, it was. Five o'clock in the morning. Funny time to choose.'

Mrs Oliver didn't think it so funny.

'Why?'

'Why did she do it? Nobody knows. Balance of mind disturbed, they said.'

'Was she – young?'

'Nah! Just an old trout. Fifty if she was a day.'

Two men struggled in the van with a chest of drawers. It resisted them and two mahogany drawers crashed to the ground – a loose piece of paper floated toward Mrs Oliver who caught it.

'Don't smash everything, Charlie,' said the cheerful milkman reprovingly, and went up in the lift with his cargo of bottles.

An altercation broke out between the furniture movers. Mrs Oliver offered them the piece of paper, but they waved it away.

Making up her mind, Mrs Oliver entered the building and went up to No. 67. A clank came from inside and presently the door was opened by a middle-aged woman with a mop who was clearly engaged in household labours.

'Oh,' said Mrs Oliver, using her favourite monosyllable. 'Good morning. Is – I wonder – is anyone in?'

'No, I'm afraid not, Madam. They're all out. They've gone to work.'

'Yes, of course . . . As a matter of fact when I was here last I left a little diary behind. *So* annoying. It must be in the sitting-room somewhere.'

'Well, I haven't picked up anything of the kind, Madam, as far as I know. Of course I mightn't have known it was yours. Would you like to come in?' She opened the door hospitably, set aside the mop with which she had been treating the kitchen floor, and accompanied Mrs Oliver into the sitting-room.

'Yes,' said Mrs Oliver, determined to establish friendly relations, 'yes, I see here – that's the book I left for Miss Restarick, Miss Norma. Is she back from the country yet?'

'I don't think she's living here at the moment. Her bed wasn't slept in. Perhaps she's still down with her people in the country. I know she was going there last weekend.'

'Yes, I expect that's it,' said Mrs Oliver. 'This was a book I brought her. One of *my* books.'

One of Mrs Oliver's books did not seem to strike any chord of interest in the cleaning woman.

'I was sitting here,' went on Mrs Oliver, patting an armchair, 'at least I *think* so. And then I moved to the window and perhaps to the sofa.'

She dug down vehemently behind the cushions of the chair. The cleaning woman obliged by doing the same thing to the sofa cushions.

'You've no idea how maddening it is when one loses something like that,' went on Mrs Oliver, chattily. 'One has all one's engagements written down there. I'm quite sure I'm lunching with someone very important today, and I can't remember who it was or where the luncheon was to be. Only, of course, it may be *tomorrow*. If so, I'm lunching with someone else *quite* different. Oh dear.'

'Very trying for you, ma'am, I'm sure,' said the cleaning woman with sympathy.

'They're such nice flats, these,' said Mrs Oliver, looking round.

'A long way up.'

'Well, that gives you a very good view, doesn't it?'

'Yes, but if they face east you get a lot of cold wind in winter. Comes right through these metal window frames. Some people have had double windows put in. Oh yes, I wouldn't care for a flat facing this way in winter. No, give me a nice ground floor flat every time. Much more convenient too if you've got children. For prams and all that, you know. Oh yes, I'm all for the ground floor, I am. Think if there was to be a fire.'

'Yes, of course, that would be terrible,' said Mrs Oliver. 'I suppose there are fire escapes?'

'You can't always get to a fire door. Terrified of fire, I am. Always have been. And they're ever so expensive, these flats. You wouldn't believe the rents they ask! That's why Miss Holland, she gets two other girls to go in with her.'

'Oh yes, I think I met them both. Miss Cary's an artist, isn't she?'

'Works for an art gallery, she does. Don't work at it very hard, though. She paints a bit – cows and trees that you'd never recognise as being what they're meant to be. An untidy young lady. The state her room is in – you wouldn't believe it! Now Miss Holland, everything is always as neat as a new pin. She was a secretary in the Coal Board at one time but she's a private secretary in the City now. She likes it better, she says. She's secretary to a very rich gentleman just come back from South America or somewhere like that. He's Miss Norma's father, and it was he who asked Miss Holland to take her as a boarder when the last young lady went off to get married – and she mentioned as she was looking for another girl. Well, she couldn't very well refuse, could she? Not since he was her employer.'

'Did she want to refuse?'

The woman sniffed.

'I think she would have – if she'd known.'

'Known what?' The question was too direct.

'It's not for me to say anything, I'm sure. It's not my business –'

Mrs Oliver continued to look mildly inquiring. Mrs Mop fell.

'It's not that she isn't a nice young lady. Scatty but then they're nearly all scatty. But I think as a doctor ought to see her. There are times when she doesn't seem to know rightly what she's doing, or where she is. It gives you quite a turn, sometimes – Looks just how my husband's nephew does after he's had a fit. (Terrible fits he has – you wouldn't believe!) Only I've never known her have fits. Maybe she takes things – a lot do.'

'I believe there is a young man her family doesn't approve of.'

'Yes, so I've heard. He's come here to call for her once or twice – though I've never seen him. One of these Mods by all accounts. Miss Holland doesn't like it – but what can you do nowadays? Girls go their own way.'

'Sometimes one feels very upset about girls nowadays,' said Mrs Oliver, and tried to look serious and responsible.

'Not brought up right, that's what *I* says.'

'I'm afraid not. No, I'm afraid not. One feels really a girl like Norma Restarick would be better at home than coming all alone to London and earning her living as an interior decorator.'

'She don't like it at home.'

'Really?'

'Got a stepmother. Girls don't like stepmothers. From what I've heard the stepmother's done her best, tried to pull her up, tried to keep flashy young men out of the house, that sort of thing. She knows girls pick up with the wrong young man and a lot of harm may come of it. Sometimes –' the cleaning woman spoke impressively, '– I'm thankful I've never had any daughters.'

'Have you got sons?'

'Two boys, we've got. One's doing very well at school, and the other one, he's in a printer's, doing well there too. Yes, very nice boys they are. Mind you, boys can cause you trouble, too. But girls is more worrying, I think. You feel you ought to be able to do something about them.'

'Yes,' said Mrs Oliver, thoughtfully, 'one does feel that.'

She saw signs of the cleaning woman wishing to return to her cleaning.

'It's too bad about my diary,' she said. 'Well, thank you very much and I hope I haven't wasted your time.'

'Well, I hope you'll find it, I'm sure,' said the other woman obligingly.

Mrs Oliver went out of the flat and considered what she should do next. She couldn't think of anything she could do further that day, but a plan for tomorrow began to form in her mind.

When she got home, Mrs Oliver, in an important way, got out a notebook and jotted down in it various things under the heading 'Facts I have learned.' On the whole the facts did not amount to very much but Mrs Oliver, true to her calling, managed to make the most of them that could be made. Possibly the fact that Claudia Reece-Holland was employed by Norma's father was the most salient fact of any. She had not known that before, she rather doubted if Hercule Poirot had known it either. She thought of ringing him up on the telephone and acquainting him with it but decided to keep it to herself for the moment because of her plan for the morrow. In fact, Mrs Oliver felt at this moment less like a detective novelist than like an ardent bloodhound. She was on the trail, nose down on the scent, and tomorrow morning – well, tomorrow morning we would see.

True to her plan, Mrs Oliver rose early, partook of two cups of tea and a boiled egg and started out on her quest. Once more she arrived in the vicinity of Borodene Mansions. She wondered whether she might be getting a bit well known there, so this time she did not enter the courtyard, but skulked around either one entrance to it or the other, scanning the various people who were turning out into the morning drizzle to trot off on their way to work. They were mostly girls, and looked deceptively alike. How extraordinary human beings were when you considered them like this, emerging purposefully from these large tall buildings – just like anthills, thought Mrs Oliver. One had never considered an anthill properly, she decided. It always looked so aimless, as one disturbed it with the toe of a shoe. All those little things rushing about with bits of grass in their mouths, streaming along industriously, worried, anxious, looking as though they were running to and fro and going nowhere, but presumably they were just as well organised as these human beings here. That man, for instance, who had just passed her. Scurrying along, muttering to himself. 'I wonder what's upsetting *you*,' thought Mrs Oliver. She walked up and down a little more, then she drew back suddenly.

Claudia Reece-Holland came out of the entranceway walking at a brisk businesslike pace. As before, she looked very well turned out. Mrs Oliver turned away so that she should not be recognised. Once she had allowed Claudia to get a sufficient distance ahead of her, she wheeled round again and followed in her tracks. Claudia Reece-Holland came to the end of the street and turned right into a main thoroughfare. She came to a bus stop and joined the queue. Mrs Oliver, still following her, felt a momentary uneasiness. Supposing Claudia should turn round, look at her, recognise her? All Mrs Oliver could think of was to do several protracted but noiseless blows of the nose. But Claudia Reece-Holland seemed totally absorbed in her own thoughts. She looked at none of her fellow waiters for buses. Mrs Oliver was about third in the queue behind her. Finally the right bus came and there was a surge forward. Claudia got on the bus and went straight up to the top. Mrs Oliver got inside and was able to get a seat close to the door as the uncomfortable third person. When the conductor came round for fares Mrs Oliver pressed a reckless one and sixpence into his hand. After all, she had no idea by what route the bus went or indeed how far the distance was to what the cleaning woman had described vaguely as 'one of those new buildings by St Paul's'. She was on the alert and ready when the venerable dome was at last sighted. Any time now, she thought to herself, and fixed a steady eye on those who descended from the platform above. Ah yes, there came Claudia, neat and chic in her smart suit. She got off the bus. Mrs Oliver followed her in due course and kept at a nicely calculated distance.

'Very interesting,' thought Mrs Oliver. 'Here I am actually *trailing* someone! Just like in my books. And, what's more, I must be doing it very well because she hasn't the least idea.'

Claudia Reece-Holland, indeed, looked very much absorbed in her own thoughts. 'That's a very capable looking girl,' thought Mrs Oliver, as indeed she had thought before. 'If I was thinking of having a go at guessing a murderer, a good capable murderer, I'd choose someone very like her.'

Unfortunately, nobody had been murdered yet, that is to say, unless the girl Norma had been entirely right in her assumption that she herself had committed a murder.

This part of London seemed to have suffered or profited from a large amount of building in the recent years. Enormous skyscrapers, most of which Mrs Oliver thought very hideous, mounted to the sky with a square matchbox-like air.

Claudia turned into a building. 'Now I shall find out exactly,' thought Mrs Oliver and turned into it after her. Four lifts appeared to be all going up and down with frantic haste. This, Mrs Oliver thought, was going to be more difficult. However, they were of a very large size and by getting into Claudia's one at the last minute Mrs Oliver was able to interpose large masses of tall men between herself and the figure she was following. Claudia's destination turned out to be the fourth floor. She went along a corridor and Mrs Oliver, lingering behind two of her tall men, noted the door where she went in. Three doors from the end of the corridor. Mrs Oliver arrived at the same door in due course and was able to read the legend on it. 'Joshua Restarick Ltd.' was the legend it bore.

Having got as far as that Mrs Oliver felt as though she did not quite know what to do next. She had found Norma's father's place of business and the place where Claudia worked, but now, slightly disabused, she felt that this was not as much of a discovery as it might have been. Frankly, did it help? Probably it didn't.

She waited around a few moments, walking from one end to the other of the corridor looking to see if anybody else interesting went in at the door of Restarick Enterprises. Two or three girls did but they did not look particularly interesting. Mrs Oliver went down again in the lift and walked rather disconsolately out of the building. She couldn't quite think what to do next. She took a walk round the adjacent streets, she meditated a visit to St Paul's.

'I might go up in the Whispering Gallery and whisper,' thought Mrs Oliver. 'I wonder now how the Whispering Gallery would do for the scene of a murder?

'No,' she decided, 'too profane, I'm afraid. No, I don't think that would be quite nice.' She walked thoughtfully towards the Mermaid Theatre. That, she thought, had far more possibilities.

She walked back in the direction of the various new buildings. Then, feeling the lack of a more substantial breakfast than she had had, she turned into a local café. It was moderately well filled with people having extra late breakfast or else early 'elevenses'. Mrs Oliver, looking round vaguely for a suitable table, gave a gasp. At a table near the wall the girl Norma was sitting, and opposite her was sitting a young man with lavish chestnut hair curled on his shoulders, wearing a red velvet waistcoat and a very fancy jacket.

'David,' said Mrs Oliver under her breath. 'It must be David.' He and the girl Norma were talking excitedly together.

Mrs Oliver considered a plan of campaign, made up her mind, and nodding her head in satisfaction, crossed the floor of the café to a discreet door marked 'Ladies'.

Mrs Oliver was not quite sure whether Norma was likely to recognise her or not. It was not always the vaguest looking people who proved the vaguest in fact. At the moment Norma did not look as though she was likely to look at anybody but David, but who knows?

'I expect I can *do* something to myself anyway,' thought Mrs Oliver. She looked at herself in a small fly-blown mirror provided by the café's management, studying particularly what she considered to be the focal point of a woman's appearance, her hair. No-one knew this better than Mrs Oliver, owing to the innumerable times that she had changed her mode of hairdressing, and had failed to be recognised by her friends in consequence. Giving her head an appraising eye she started work. Out came the pins, she took off several coils of hair, wrapped them up in her handkerchief and stuffed them into her handbag, parted her hair in the middle, combed it sternly back from her face and rolled it up into a modest bun at the back of her neck. She also took out a pair of spectacles and put them on her nose. There was a really earnest look about her now! 'Almost intellectual,' Mrs Oliver thought approvingly. She altered the shape of her mouth by an application of lipstick, and emerged once more into the café; moving carefully since the spectacles were only for reading and in consequence the landscape was blurred. She crossed the café, and made her way to an empty table next to that occupied by Norma and David. She sat down so that she was facing David. Norma, on the near side, sat with her back to her. Norma, therefore, would not see her unless she turned her head right round. The waitress drifted up. Mrs Oliver ordered a cup of coffee and a Bath bun and settled down to be inconspicuous.

Norma and David did not even notice her. They were deeply in the middle of a passionate discussion. It took Mrs Oliver just a minute or two to tune in to them.

'. . . But you only fancy these things,' David was saying. 'You *imagine* them. They're all utter, utter nonsense, my dear girl.'

'I don't know. I can't tell.' Norma's voice had a queer lack of resonance in it.

Mrs Oliver could not hear her as well as she heard David, since Norma's back was turned to her, but the dullness of the girl's tone struck her disagreeably. There was something wrong here, she thought. Very wrong. She remembered the story as Poirot had first told it to her. '*She thinks she may have committed a murder.*' What *was* the matter with the girl? Hallucinations? Was her mind really slightly affected, or was it no more and no less than truth, and in consequence the girl had suffered a bad shock?

'If you ask me, it's all fuss on Mary's part! She's a thoroughly stupid woman anyway, and she imagines she has illnesses and all that sort of thing.'

'She *was* ill.'

'All right then, she *was* ill. Any sensible woman would get the doctor to give her some antibiotic or other, and not get het up.'

'She thought *I* did it to her. My father thinks so too.'

'I tell you, Norma, you imagine all these things.'

'You just say that to me, David. You say it to me to cheer me up. Supposing I *did* give her the stuff?'

'What do you mean, suppose? You must *know* whether you did or you didn't. You can't be so idiotic, Norma.'

'I *don't* know.'

'You keep saying that. You keep coming back to that, and saying it again and again. "I don't know." "I don't know."'

'You don't understand. You don't understand in the least what hate is. I hated her from the first moment I saw her.'

'I know. You told me that.'

'That's the queer part of it. I told you that, and yet I don't even *remember* telling you that. D'you see? Every now and then I – I tell people things. I tell people things that I want to do, or that I have done, or that I'm going to do. But I don't even remember telling them the things. It's as though I was *thinking* all these things in my mind, and sometimes they come out in the open and I say them to people. I did say them to you, didn't I?'

'Well – I mean – look here, don't let's harp back to that.'

'But I did say it to you? Didn't I?'

'All right, all right! One says things like that. "I hate her and I'd like to kill her. I think I'll poison her!" But that's only kid stuff, if you know what I mean, as though you weren't quite grown up. It's a very natural thing. Children say it a lot. "I hate so and so. I'll cut off his head!" Kids say it at school. About some master they particularly dislike.'

'You think it was just that? But – that sounds as though *I* wasn't grown up.'

'Well, you're not in some ways. If you'd just pull yourself together, realise how silly it all is. What can it matter if you do hate her? You've got away from home and don't have to live with her.'

'Why shouldn't I live in my own home – with my own father?'

said Norma. 'It's not fair. It's not fair. First he went away and left my mother, and now, just when he's coming back to me, he goes and marries Mary. Of course I hate her and she hates me too. I used to think about killing her, used to think of ways of doing it. I used to enjoy thinking like that. But then – when she *really* got ill . . .'

David said uneasily:

'You don't think you're a witch or anything, do you? You don't make figures in wax and stick pins into them or do that sort of thing?'

'Oh no. That would be silly. What I did was real. Quite real.'

'Look here, Norma, what do you mean when you say it was real?'

'The bottle was there, in my drawer. Yes, I opened the drawer and found it.'

'What bottle?'

'*The Dragon Exterminator. Selective weed killer.* That's what it was labelled. Stuff in a dark green bottle and you were supposed to spray it on things. And it had labels with *Caution* and *Poison*, too.'

'Did you buy it? Or did you just find it?'

'I don't know where I got it, but it was there, in my drawer, and it was half empty.'

'And then you – you – remembered –'

'Yes,' said Norma. 'Yes . . .' Her voice was vague, almost dreamy. 'Yes . . . I think it was then it all came back to me. You think so too, don't you, David?'

'I don't know what to make of you, Norma. I really don't. I think in a way, you're making it all up, you're telling it to *yourself*.'

'But she went to hospital, for observation. They said they were puzzled. Then they said they couldn't find anything wrong so she came home – and then she got ill again, and I began to be frightened. My father began looking at me in a queer sort of way, and then the doctor came and they talked together, shut up in Father's study. I went round outside, and crept up to the window and I tried to listen. I wanted to hear what they were saying. They were planning together – to send me away to a place where I'd be shut up! A place where I'd have a "course of treatment" – or something. They thought, you see, that I was crazy, and I was frightened . . . Because – because I wasn't sure what I'd done or what I hadn't done.'

'Is that when you ran away?'

'No – that was later –'

'Tell me.'

'I don't want to talk about it any more.'

'You'll have to let them know sooner or later where you are –'

'I won't! I hate them. I hate my father as much as I hate Mary. I wish they were dead. I wish they were both dead. Then – then I think I'd be happy again.'

'Don't get all het up! Look here, Norma –' He paused in an embarrassed manner – 'I'm not very set on marriage and all that rubbish . . . I mean I didn't think I'd ever do anything of that kind . . . oh well, not for years. One doesn't want to tie oneself up – but I think it's the best thing we could do, you know. Get married. At a registry office or something. You'll have to say you're over twenty-one. Roll up your hair, put on some spectacles or something. Make you look a bit older. Once we're married, your father can't do a thing! He can't send you away to what you call a "place". He'll be powerless.'

'I hate him.'

'You seem to hate everybody.'

'Only my father and Mary.'

'Well, after all, it's quite natural for a man to marry again.'

'Look what he did to my mother.'

'All that must have been a long time ago.'

'Yes. I was only a child, but I remember. He went away and left us. He sent me presents at Christmas – but he never came himself. I wouldn't even have known him if I'd met him in the street by the time he did come back. He didn't mean anything to me by then. I think he got my mother shut up, too. She used to go away when she was ill. I don't know where. I don't know what was the matter with her. Sometimes I wonder . . . I wonder, David. I think, you know, there's something wrong in my head, and some day it will make me do something really bad. Like the knife.'

'What knife?'

'It doesn't matter. Just a knife.'

'Well, can't you tell me what you're talking about?'

'I think it had bloodstains on it – it was hidden there . . . under my stockings.'

'Do you remember hiding a knife there?'

'I think so. But I can't remember what I'd done with it *before* that. I can't remember where I'd *been* . . . There is a whole hour gone out of that evening. A whole hour I didn't know where I'd been. I'd been somewhere and done something.'

'Hush!' He hissed it quickly as the waitress approached their table. 'You'll be all right. I'll look after you. Let's have something more,' he said to the waitress in a loud voice, picking up the menu – 'Two baked beans on toast.'

CHAPTER 8

I

Hercule Poirot was dictating to his secretary, Miss Lemon.

'*And while I much appreciate the honour you have done me, I must regretfully inform you that . . .*'

The telephone rang. Miss Lemon stretched out a hand for it. 'Yes? Who did you say?' She put her hand over the receiver and said to Poirot, 'Mrs Oliver.'

'Ah . . . Mrs Oliver,' said Poirot. He did not particularly want to be interrupted at this moment, but he took the receiver from Miss Lemon. ''Allo,' he said, 'Hercule Poirot speaks.'

'Oh, M. Poirot, I'm so glad I got you! I've found her for you!'

'I beg your pardon?'

'*I've found her for you.* Your girl! You know, the one who's committed a murder or thinks she has. She's talking about it too, a great deal. I think she is off her head. But never mind that now. Do you want to come and get her?'

'Where are you, *chère* Madame?'

'Somewhere between St Paul's and the Mermaid Theatre and all that. Calthorpe Street,' said Mrs Oliver, suddenly looking out of the telephone box in which she was standing. 'Do you think you can get here quickly? They're in a restaurant.'

'They?'

'Oh, she and what I suppose is the unsuitable boy friend. He is rather nice really, and he seems very fond of her. I can't think why. People are odd. Well, I don't want to talk because I want to get back again. I followed them, you see. I came into the restaurant and saw them there.'

'Aha? You have been very clever, Madame.'

'No, I haven't really. It was a pure accident. I mean, I walked into a small café place and there the girl was, just sitting there.'

'Ah. You had the good fortune then. That is just as important.'

'And I've been sitting at the next table to them, only she's got her back to me. And anyway I don't suppose she'd recognise me. I've done things to my hair. Anway, they've been talking as though they were alone in the world, and when they ordered another course – baked beans – (I can't bear baked beans, it always seems to me so funny that people should) –'

'Never mind the baked beans. Go on. You left them and came out to telephone. Is that right?'

'Yes. Because the baked beans gave me time. And I shall go back now. Or I might hang about outside. Anway, try and get here quickly.'

'What is the name of this café?'

'The Merry Shamrock – but it doesn't look very merry. In fact, it looks rather sordid, but the coffee is quite good.'

'Say no more. Go back. In due course, I will arrive.'

'Splendid,' said Mrs Oliver, and rang off.

II

Miss Lemon, always efficient, had preceded him to the street, and was waiting by a taxi. She asked no questions and displayed no curiosity. She did not tell Poirot how she would occupy her time whilst he was away. She did not need to tell him. She always knew what she was going to do and she was always right in what she did.

Poirot duly arrived at the corner of Calthorpe Street. He descended, paid the taxi, and looked around him. He saw The Merry Shamrock but he saw no one in its vicinity who looked at all like Mrs Oliver, however well disguised. He walked to the end of the street and back. No Mrs Oliver. So either the couple in which they were interested had left the café and Mrs Oliver had gone on a shadowing expedition, or else – To answer 'or else' he went to the café door. One could not see the inside very well from the outside, on account of steam, so he pushed the door gently open and entered. His eyes swept round it.

He saw at once the girl who had come to visit him at the breakfast table. She was sitting by herself at a table against the wall. She was smoking a cigarette and staring in front of her. She seemed to be lost in thought. No, Poirot thought, hardly that. There did not seem to be any thought there. She was lost in a kind of oblivion. She was somewhere else.

He crossed the room quietly and sat down in the chair opposite her. She looked up then, and he was at least gratified to see that he was recognised.

'So we meet again, Mademoiselle,' he said pleasantly. 'I see you recognise me.'

'Yes. Yes, I do.'

'It is always gratifying to be recognised by a young lady one has only met once and for a very short time.'

She continued to look at him without speaking.

'And how did you know me, may I ask? What made you recognise me?'

'Your moustache,' said Norma immediately. 'It couldn't be anyone else.'

He was gratified by that observation and stroked it with the pride and vanity that he was apt to display on these occasions.

'Ah yes, very true. Yes, there are not many moustaches such as mine. It is a fine one, hein?'

'Yes – well, yes – I suppose it is.'

'Ah, you are perhaps not a connoisseur of moustaches, but I can tell you, Miss Restarick – Miss Norma Restarick, is it not? – that it is a very fine moustache.'

He had dwelt deliberately upon her name. She had at first looked so oblivious to everything around her, so far away, that he wondered if she would notice. She did. It startled her.

'How did you know my name?' she said.

'True, you did not give your name to my servant when you came to see me that morning.'

'How did you know it? How did you get to know it? Who told you?'

He saw the alarm, the fear.

'A friend told me,' he said. 'One's friends can be very useful.'

'Who was it?'

'Mademoiselle, you like keeping your little secrets from me. I, too, have a preference for keeping my little secrets from you.'

'I don't see *how* you could know who I was.'

'I am Hercule Poirot,' said Poirot, with his usual magnificence. Then he left the initiative to her, merely sitting there smiling gently at her.

'I –' she began, then stopped. '– Would –' Again she stopped.

'We did not get very far that morning, I know,' said Hercule Poirot. 'Only so far as your telling me that you had committed a murder.'

'Oh *that*!'

'Yes, Mademoiselle, *that*.'

'But – I didn't mean it of course. I didn't mean anything like that. I mean, it was just a joke.'

'*Vraiment*? You came to see me rather early in the morning, at breakfast time. You said it was urgent. The urgency was because you might have committed a murder. That is your idea of a joke, eh?'

A waitress who had been hovering, looking at Poirot with a fixed attention, suddenly came up to him and proffered him what appeared to be a paper boat such as is made for children to sail in a bath.

'This for you?' she said. 'Mr Porritt? A lady left it.'

'Ah yes,' said Poirot. 'And how did you know who I was?'

'The lady said I'd know by your moustache. Said I wouldn't have seen a moustache like that before. And it's true enough,' she added, gazing at it.

'Well, thank you very much.'

Poirot took the boat from her, untwisted it and smoothed it out; he read some hastily pencilled words: 'He's just going. She's staying behind, so I'm going to leave her for you, and follow him.' It was signed Ariadne.

'Ah yes,' said Hercule Poirot, folding it and slipping it into his pocket. 'What were we talking about? Your sense of humour, I think, Miss Restarick.'

'Do you know just my name or – or do you know everything about me?'

'I know a few things about you. You are Miss Norma Restarick, your address in London is 67 Borodene Mansions. Your home address is Crosshedges, Long Basing. You live there with a father, a stepmother, a great-uncle and – ah yes, an *au pair* girl. You see, I am quite well informed.'

'You've been having me followed.'

'No, no,' said Poirot. 'Not at all. As to that, I give you my word of honour.'

'But you are not police, are you? You didn't say you were.'

'I am not police, no.'

Her suspicion and defiance broke down.

'I don't know what to do,' she said.

'I am not urging you to employ me,' said Poirot. 'For that you have said already that I am too old. Possibly you are right. But since I know who you are and something about you, there is no reason we should not discuss together in a friendly fashion the troubles that afflict you. The old, you must remember, though considered incapable of action, have nevertheless a good fund of experience on which to draw.'

Norma continued to look at him doubtfully, that wide-eyed stare that had disquieted Poirot before. But she was in a sense trapped, and she had at this particular moment, or so Poirot judged, a wish to talk about things. For some reason, Poirot had always been a person it was easy to talk to.

'They think I'm crazy,' she said bluntly. 'And – and I rather think I'm crazy, too. Mad.'

'That is most interesting,' said Hercule Poirot, cheerfully. 'There are many different names for these things. Very grand names. Names rolled out happily by psychiatrists, psychologists and others. But when you say crazy, that describes very well what the general appearance may be to ordinary, everyday people. *Eh bien*, then, you are crazy, or you appear crazy or you think you are crazy, and possibly you *may* be crazy. But all the same that is not to say the condition is serious. It is a thing that people suffer from a good deal, and it is usually easily cured with the proper treatment. It comes about because people have had too much mental strain, too much worry, have studied too much for examinations, have dwelled too much perhaps on their emotions, have too much religion or have a lamentable lack of religion, or have good reasons for hating their fathers or their mothers! Or, of course, it can be as simple as having an unfortunate love affair.'

'I've got a stepmother. I hate her and I rather think I hate my father too. That seems rather a lot, doesn't it?'

'It is more usual to hate one or the other,' said Poirot. 'You were, I suppose, very fond of your own mother. Is she divorced or dead?'

'Dead. She died two or three years ago.'

'And you cared for her very much?'

'Yes. I suppose I did. I mean of course I did. She was an invalid, you know, and she had to go to nursing homes a good deal.'

'And your father?'

'Father had gone abroad a long time before that. He went to South Africa when I was about five or six. I think he wanted Mother to divorce him but she wouldn't. He went to South Africa and was mixed up with mines or something like that. Anyway, he used to write to me at Christmas, and send me a Christmas present or arrange for one to come to me. That was about all. So he didn't really seem very real to me. He came home about a year ago because he had to wind up my uncle's affairs and all that sort of financial thing. And when he came home he – he brought this new wife with him.'

'And you resented the fact?'

'Yes, I did.'

'But your mother was dead by then. It is not unusual, you know, for a man to marry again. Especially when he and his wife have been estranged for many years. This wife he brought, was she the same lady he had wished to marry previously, when he asked your mother for a divorce?'

'Oh, no, this one is quite young. And she's very good-looking and she acts as though she just owns my father!'

She went on after a pause – in a different, rather childish voice. 'I thought perhaps when he came home this time he would be fond of *me* and take notice of *me* and – but she won't let him. She's *against* me. She's crowded me out.'

'But that does not matter at all at the age you are. It is a good thing. You do not need anyone to look after you now. You can stand on your own feet, you can enjoy life, you can choose your own friends –'

'You wouldn't think so, the way they go on at home! Well, I mean to choose my own friends.'

'Most girls nowadays have to endure criticism about their friends,' said Poirot.

'It was all so different,' said Norma. 'My father isn't at all like I remember him when I was five years old. He used to play with me, all the time, and be so gay. He's not gay now. He's worried and rather fierce and – oh quite different.'

'That must be nearly fifteen years ago, I presume. People change.'

'But ought people to change so much?'

'Has he changed in appearance?'

'Oh no – no, not that. Oh no! If you look at his picture just over his chair, although it's of him when he was much younger, it's exactly like him now. But it isn't at all the way I remember him.'

'But you know, my dear,' said Poirot gently, 'people are never like what you remember them. You make them, as the years go by, more and more the way you *wish* them to be, and as you *think* you remember them. If you want to remember them as agreeable and gay and handsome, you make them far more so than they actually were.'

'Do you think so? Do you really think so?' She paused and then said abruptly, 'But why do you think I want to kill people?' The question came out quite naturally. It was there between them. They had, Poirot felt, got at last to a crucial moment.

'That may be quite an interesting question,' said Poirot, 'and there may be quite an interesting reason. The person who can probably tell you the answer to that will be a doctor. The kind of doctor who *knows*.'

She reacted quickly.

'I won't go to a doctor. I won't go *near* a doctor! They wanted to send me to a doctor, and then I'll be shut up in one of those loony places and they won't let me out again. I'm not going to do anything like that.' She was struggling now to rise to her feet.

'It is not I who can send you to one! You need not be alarmed. You could go to a doctor entirely on your own behalf if you liked. You can go and say to him the things you have been saying to me, and you may ask him *why*, and he will perhaps tell you the cause.'

'That's what David says. That's what David says I should do but I don't think – I don't think he *understands*. I'd have to tell a doctor that I – I might have tried to do things . . .'

'What makes you think you have?'

'Because I don't always remember what I've done – or where I've been. I lose an hour of time – two hours – and I can't *remember*. I was in a corridor once – a corridor outside a door, her door. I'd something in my hand – I don't know how I got it. She came walking along towards me – But when she got near me, her face changed. It wasn't her at all. She'd changed into somebody else.'

'You are remembering, perhaps, a nightmare. There people do change into somebody else.'

'It wasn't a nightmare. I picked up the revolver – It was lying there at my feet –'

'In a corridor?'

'No, in the courtyard. She came and took it away from me.'

'Who did?'

'Claudia. She took me upstairs and gave me some bitter stuff to drink.'

'Where was your stepmother then?'

'She was there, too – No, she wasn't. She was at Crosshedges. Or in hospital. That's where they found out she was being poisoned – and that it was me.'

'It need not have been you – It could have been someone else.'

'Who else could it have been?'

'Perhaps – her husband.'

'Father? Why on earth should Father want to poison *Mary*. He's devoted to her. He's silly about her!'

'There are others in the house, are there not?'

'Old Uncle Roderick? Nonsense!'

'One does not know,' said Poirot, 'he might be mentally afflicted. He might think it was his duty to poison a woman who might be a beautiful spy. Something like that.'

'That would be very interesting,' said Norma, momentarily

diverted, and speaking in a perfectly natural manner. 'Uncle Roderick *was* mixed up a good deal with spies and things in the last war. Who else is there? Sonia? I suppose *she* might be a beautiful spy, but she's not quite my idea of one.'

'No, and there does not seem very much reason why she should wish to poison your stepmother. I suppose there might be servants, gardeners?'

'No, they just come in for the days. I don't think – well, they wouldn't be the kind of people to have any *reason*.'

'She might have done it herself.'

'Committed *suicide*, do you mean? Like the other one?'

'It is a possibility.'

'I can't imagine *Mary* committing suicide. She's far too sensible. And why should she want to?'

'Yes, you feel that if she did, she would put her head in the gas oven, or she would lie on a bed nicely arranged and take an overdose of sleeping draughts. Is that right?'

'Well, it would have been more natural. So you see,' said Norma earnestly, '*it must have been me*.'

'Aha,' said Poirot, 'that interests me. You would almost, it would seem, *prefer* that it should be you. You are attracted to the idea that it was your hand who slipped the fatal dose of this, that or the other. Yes, you *like* the idea.'

'How dare you say such a thing! How can you?'

'*Because I think it is true*,' said Poirot. 'Why does the thought that you may have committed murder excite you, please you?'

'It's not true.'

'I wonder,' said Poirot.

She scooped up her bag and began feeling in it with shaking fingers.

'I'm not going to stop here and have you say these horrible things to me.' She signalled to the waitress who came, scribbled on a pad of paper, detached it and laid it down by Norma's plate.

'Permit me,' said Hercule Poirot.

He removed the slip of paper deftly, and prepared to draw his notecase from his pocket. The girl snatched it back again.

'No, I won't let you pay for me.'

'As you please,' said Poirot.

He had seen what he wanted to see. The bill was for two.

It would seem therefore that David of the fine feathers had no objection to having his bills paid by an infatuated girl.

'So it is you who entertain a friend to elevenses, I see.'

'How did you know that I was with anyone?'

'I tell you, I know a good deal.'

She placed coins on the table and rose. 'I'm going now,' she said, 'and I forbid you to follow me.'

'I doubt if I could,' said Poirot. 'You must remember my advanced age. If you were to run down the street I should certainly not be able to follow you.'

She got up and went towards the door.

'Do you hear? You are *not* to follow me.'

'You permit me at least to open the door for you.' He did so with something of a flourish. '*Au revoir*, Mademoiselle.'

She threw a suspicious glance at him and walked away down the street with a rapid step, turning her head back over her shoulder from time to time. Poirot remained by the door watching her, but made no attempt to gain the pavement or to catch her up. When she was out of sight, he turned back into the café.

'And what the devil does all that mean?' said Poirot to himself.

The waitress was advancing upon him, displeasure on her face. Poirot regained his seat at the table and placated her by ordering a cup of coffee. 'There is something here very curious,' he murmured to himself. 'Yes, something very curious indeed.'

A cup of pale beige fluid was placed in front of him. He took a sip of it and made a grimace.

He wondered where Mrs Oliver was at this moment.

CHAPTER 9

Mrs Oliver was seated in a bus. She was slightly out of breath though full of the zest of the chase. What she called in her own mind the Peacock, had led a somewhat brisk pace. Mrs Oliver was not a rapid walker. Going along the Embankment she followed him at a distance of some twenty yards or so. At Charing Cross he got into the underground. Mrs Oliver also got into the underground. At Sloane Square he got out, so did Mrs Oliver.

She waited in a bus queue some three or four people behind him. He got on a bus and so did she. He got out at World's End, so did Mrs Oliver. He plunged into a bewildering maze of streets between King's Road and the river. He turned into what seemed a builder's yard. Mrs Oliver stood in the shadow of a doorway and watched. He turned into an alleyway, Mrs Oliver gave him a moment or two and then followed – he was nowhere to be seen. Mrs Oliver reconnoitred her general surroundings. The whole place appeared somewhat decrepit. She wandered farther down the alleyway. Other alleyways led off from it – some of them cul-de-sacs. She had completely lost her sense of direction when she once more came to the builder's yard and a voice spoke behind her, startling her considerably. It said, politely, 'I hope I didn't walk too fast for you.'

She turned sharply. Suddenly what had recently been almost fun, a chase undertaken light-heartedly and in the best of spirits, now was that no longer. What she felt now was a sudden unexpected throb of fear. Yes, she was afraid. The atmosphere had suddenly become tinged with menace. Yet the voice was pleasant, polite; but behind it she knew there was anger. The sudden kind of anger that recalled to her in a confused fashion all the things one read in newspapers. Elderly women attacked by gangs of young men. Young men who were ruthless, cruel, who were driven by hate and the desire to do harm. This was the young man whom she had been following. He had known she was there, had given her the slip and had then followed her into this alleyway, and he stood there now barring her way out. As is the precarious fashion of London, one moment you are amongst people all round you and the next moment there is nobody in sight. There must be people in the next street, someone in the houses near, but nearer than that is a masterful figure, a figure with strong cruel hands. She felt that in this moment he was thinking of using those hands . . . The Peacock. A proud peacock. In his velvets, his tight, elegant black trousers, speaking in that quiet ironical amused voice that held behind it anger . . . Mrs Oliver took three big gasps. Then, in a lightning moment of decision she put up a quickly imagined defence. Firmly and immediately she sat down on a dustbin which was against the wall quite close to her.

'Goodness, how you startled me,' she said. 'I'd no idea you were there. I hope you're not annoyed.'

'So you *were* following me?'

'Yes, I'm afraid I was. I expect it must have been rather annoying to you. You see I thought it would be such an excellent opportunity. I'm sure you're frightfully angry but you needn't be, you know. Not really. You see –' Mrs Oliver settled herself more firmly on the dustbin, 'you see I write books. I write detective stories and I've really been very worried this morning. In fact I went into a café to have a cup of coffee just to try and think things out. I'd just got to the point in my book where I was following somebody. I mean my hero was following someone and I thought to myself, "Really I know very little about following people." I mean, I'm always using the phrase in a book and I've read a lot of books where people do follow other people, and I wondered if it was as easy as it seems to be in some people's books or if it was as almost entirely impossible as it seemed in other people's books. So I thought "Well, really, the only thing was to try it out *myself*" – because until you try things out yourself you can't really tell what it's like. I mean you don't know what you feel like, or whether you get worried at losing a person. As it happened, I just looked up and you were sitting at the next table to me in the café and I thought you'd be – I hope you won't be annoyed again – but I thought you'd be an especially good person to follow.'

He was still staring at her with those strange, cold blue eyes, yet she felt somehow that the tension had left them.

'Why was I an especially good person to follow?'

'Well, you were so decorative,' explained Mrs Oliver. 'They are really very attractive clothes – almost Regency, you know, and I thought, well, I might take advantage of your being fairly easy to distinguish from other people. So you see, when you went out of the café I went out too. And it's not really easy at all.' She looked up at him. 'Do you mind telling me if you knew I was there all the time?'

'Not at once, no.'

'I see,' said Mrs Oliver thoughtfully. 'But of course I'm not as distinctive as you are. I mean you wouldn't be able to tell me very easily from a lot of other elderly women. I don't stand out very much, do I?'

'Do you write books that are published? Have I ever come across them?'

'Well, I don't know. You may have. I've written forty-three by now. My name's Oliver.'

'Ariadne Oliver?'

'So you do know my name,' said Mrs Oliver. 'Well, that's rather gratifying, of course, though I daresay you wouldn't like my books very much. You probably would find them rather old-fashioned – not violent enough.'

'You didn't know me personally beforehand?'

Mrs Oliver shook her head. 'No, I'm sure I don't – didn't, I mean.'

'What about the girl I was with?'

'You mean the one you were having – baked beans, was it – with in the café? No, I don't think so. Of course I only saw the back of her head. She looked to me – well, I mean girls do look rather alike, don't they?'

'She knew you,' said the boy suddenly. His tone in a moment had a sudden acid sharpness. 'She mentioned once that she'd met you not long ago. About a week ago, I believe.'

'Where? Was it at a party? I suppose I might have met her. What's her name? Perhaps I'd know that.'

She thought he was in two moods whether to mention the name or not, but he decided to and he watched her face very keenly as he did so.

'Her name's Norma Restarick.'

'Norma Restarick. Oh, of course, yes, it was at a party in the country. A place called – wait a minute – Long Norton was it? – I don't remember the name of the house. I went there with some friends. I don't think I would have recognised her anyway, though I believe she did say something about my books. I even promised I'd give her one. It's very odd, isn't it, that I should make up my mind and actually choose to follow a person who was sitting with somebody I more or less knew. Very odd. I don't think I could put anything like that in my book. It would look rather too much of a coincidence, don't you think?'

Mrs Oliver rose from her seat.

'Good gracious, what have I been sitting on? A dustbin! Really!

Not a very nice dustbin either.' She sniffed. 'What *is* this place I've got to?'

David was looking at her. She felt suddenly that she was completely mistaken in everything she had previously thought. 'Absurd of me,' thought Mrs Oliver, 'absurd of me. Thinking that he was dangerous, that he might do something to me.' He was smiling at her with an extraordinary charm. He moved his head slightly and his chestnut ringlets moved on his shoulders. What fantastic creatures there were in the way of young men nowadays!

'The least I can do,' he said, 'is to show you, I think, where you've been brought to, just by following me. Come on, up these stairs.' He indicated a ramshackle outside staircase running up to what seemed to be a loft.

'Up those stairs?' Mrs Oliver was not so certain about this. Perhaps he was trying to lure her up there with his charm, and he would then knock her on the head. 'It's no good, Ariadne,' said Mrs Oliver to herself, 'you've got yourself into this spot, and now you've got to go on with it and find out what you can find out.'

'Do you think they'll stand my weight?' she said, 'they look frightfully rickety.'

'They're quite all right. I'll go up first,' he said, 'and show you the way.'

Mrs Oliver mounted the ladder-like stairs behind him. It was no good. She was, deep down, still frightened. Frightened, not so much of the Peacock, as frightened of where the Peacock might be taking her. Well, she'd know very soon. He pushed open the door at the top and went into a room. It was a large, bare room and it was an artist's studio, an improvised kind of one. A few mattresses lay here and there on the floor, there were canvasses stacked against the wall, a couple of easels. There was a pervading smell of paint. There were two people in the room. A bearded young man was standing at an easel, painting. He turned his head as they entered.

'Hallo, David,' he said, 'bringing us company?'

He was, Mrs Oliver thought, quite the dirtiest-looking young man she'd ever seen. Oily black hair hung in a kind of circular bob down the back of his neck and over his eyes in front. His face apart from the beard was unshaven, and his clothes seemed mainly composed of greasy black leather and high boots. Mrs Oliver's glance went beyond him to a girl who was acting as a model. She was on a wooden chair on a dais, half flung across it, her head back and her dark hair drooping down from it. Mrs Oliver recognised her at once. It was the second one of the three girls in Borodene Mansions. Mrs Oliver couldn't remember her last name, but she remembered her first one. It was the highly decorative and languid-looking girl called Frances.

'Meet Peter,' said David, indicating the somewhat revolting looking artist. 'One of our budding geniuses. And Frances who is posing as a desperate girl demanding abortion.'

'Shut up, you ape,' said Peter.

'I believe I know you, don't I?' said Mrs Oliver, cheerfully, without any air of conscious certainty. 'I'm sure I've met you somewhere! Somewhere quite lately, too.'

'You're Mrs Oliver, aren't you?' said Frances.

'That's what she said she was,' said David. 'True, too, is it?'

'Now, where *did* I meet you,' continued Mrs Oliver. 'Some party, was it? No. Let me think. I know. It was Borodene Mansions.'

Frances was sitting up now in her chair and speaking in weary but elegant tones. Peter uttered a loud and miserable groan.

'Now you've ruined the pose! Do you have to have all this wriggling about? Can't you keep still?'

'No, I couldn't any longer. It was an awful pose. I've got the most frightful crick in my shoulder.'

'I've been making experiments in following people,' said Mrs Oliver. 'It's much more difficult than I thought. Is this an artist's studio?' she added, looking round her brightly.

'That's what they're like nowadays, a kind of loft – and lucky if you don't fall through the floor,' said Peter.

'It's got all you need,' said David. 'It's got a north light and plenty of room and a pad to sleep on, and a fourth share in the loo downstairs – and what they call cooking facilities. And it's got a bottle or two,' he added. Turning to Mrs Oliver, but in an entirely different tone, one of utter politeness, he said, 'And can we offer you a drink?'

'I don't drink,' said Mrs Oliver.

'The lady doesn't drink,' said David. 'Who would have thought it!'

'That's rather rude but you're quite right,' said Mrs Oliver. 'Most people come up to me and say, "I always thought you drank like a fish".'

She opened her handbag – and immediately three coils of grey hair fell on the floor. David picked them up and handed them to her.

'Oh! thank you.' Mrs Oliver took them. 'I hadn't time this morning. I wonder if I've got any more hairpins.' She delved in her bag and started attaching the coils to her head.

Peter roared with laughter – 'Bully for you,' he said.

'How extraordinary,' Mrs Oliver thought to herself, 'that I should ever have had this silly idea that I was in danger. *Danger* – from *these* people? No matter what they look like, they're really very nice and friendly. It's quite true what people always say to me. I've far too much imagination.'

Presently she said she must be going, and David, with Regency gallantry, helped her down the rickety steps, and gave her definite directions as to how to rejoin the King's Road in the quickest way.

'And then,' he said, 'you can get a bus – or a taxi if you want it.'

'A taxi,' said Mrs Oliver. 'My feet are absolutely dead. The sooner I fall into a taxi the better. Thank you,' she added, 'for being so very nice about my following you in what must have seemed a very peculiar way. Though after all I don't suppose private detectives, or private eyes or whatever they call them, would look anything at all like me.'

'Perhaps not,' said David gravely. 'Left here – and then right, and then left again until you see the river and go towards it, and then sharp right and straight on.'

Curiously enough, as she walked across the shabby yard the same feeling of unease and suspense came over her. 'I mustn't let my imagination go again.' She looked back at the steps and the window of the studio. The figure of David still stood looking after her. 'Three perfectly nice young people,' said Mrs Oliver to herself. 'Perfectly nice and very kind. Left here, and then right. Just because they *look* rather peculiar, one goes and has silly ideas about their being dangerous. Was it right again? or left? Left, I think – Oh goodness, my feet. It's going to rain, too.' The walk seemed endless and the King's Road incredibly far away. She could hardly hear the traffic now – And where on earth was the river? She began to suspect that she had followed the directions wrongly.

'Oh! well,' thought Mrs Oliver, 'I'm bound to get *somewhere* soon – the river, or Putney or Wandsworth or somewhere.' She asked her way to the King's Road from a passing man who said he was a foreigner and didn't speak English.

Mrs Oliver turned another corner wearily and there ahead of her was the gleam of the water. She hurried towards it down a narrow passageway, heard a footstep behind her, half turned, when she was struck from behind and the world went up in sparks.

CHAPTER 10

I

A voice said:

'Drink this.'

Norma was shivering. Her eyes had a dazed look. She shrank back a little in the chair. The command was repeated. 'Drink this.' This time she drank obediently, then choked a little.

'It's – it's very strong,' she gasped.

'It'll put you right. You'll feel better in a minute. Just sit still and wait.'

The sickness and the giddiness which had been confusing her passed off. A little colour came into her cheeks, and the shivering diminished. For the first time she looked round her, noting her surroundings. She had been obsessed by a feeling of fear and horror but now things seemed to be returning to normal. It was a medium-sized room and it was furnished in a way that seemed faintly familiar. A desk, a couch, an armchair and an ordinary chair, a stethoscope on a side table and some machine that she thought had to do with eyes. Then her attention went from the general to the particular. The man who had told her to drink.

She saw a man of perhaps thirty-odd with red hair and a rather attractive ugly face, the kind of face that is craggy but interesting. He nodded at her in a reassuring fashion.

'Beginning to get your bearings?'

'I – I think so. I – did you – what happened?'

'Don't you remember?'

'The traffic. I – it came at me – it –' She looked at him. 'I was run over.'

'Oh no, you weren't run over.' He shook his head. 'I saw to that.'

'You?'

'Well, there you were in the middle of the road, a car bearing down on you and I just managed to snatch you out of its way. What were you thinking of to go running into the traffic like that?'

'I can't remember. I – yes, I suppose I must have been thinking of something else.'

'A Jaguar was coming pretty fast, and there was a bus bearing down on the other side of the road. The car wasn't trying to run you down or anything like that, was it?'

'I – no, no, I'm sure it wasn't. I mean I –'

'Well, I wondered – It just might have been something else, mightn't it?'

'What do you mean?'

'Well, it could have been deliberate, you know.'

'What do you mean by deliberate?'

'Actually I just wondered whether you were trying to get yourself killed?' He added casually, 'Were you?'

'I – no – well – no, of course not.'

'Damn' silly way to do it, if so.' His tone changed slightly. 'Come now, you must remember *something* about it.'

She began shivering again. 'I thought – I thought it would be all over. I thought –'

'So you were trying to kill yourself, weren't you? What's the matter? You can tell me. Boy friend? That can make one feel pretty bad. Besides, there's always the hopeful thought that if you kill yourself you make him sorry – but one should never trust to that. People don't like feeling sorry or feeling anything is their fault. All the boy friend will probably say is, "I always thought she was unbalanced. It's really all for the best." Just remember that next time you have an urge to charge Jaguars. Even Jaguars have feelings to be considered. *Was* that the trouble? Boy friend walk out on you?'

'No,' said Norma. 'Oh no. It was quite the opposite.' She added suddenly, 'He wanted to marry me.'

'That's no reason for throwing yourself down in front of a Jaguar.'

'Yes it is. I did it because –' She stopped.

'You'd better tell me about it, hadn't you?'

'How did I get here?' asked Norma.

'I brought you here in a taxi. You didn't seem injured – a few bruises, I expect. You merely looked shaken to death, and in a state of shock. I asked you your address, but you looked at me as though you didn't know what I was talking about. A crowd was about to collect. So I hailed a taxi and brought you here.'

'Is this a – a doctor's surgery?'

'This is a doctor's consulting room and I'm the doctor. Stillingfleet, my name is.'

'I don't want to see a doctor! I don't want to talk to a doctor! I don't –'

'Calm down, calm down. You've been talking to a doctor for the last ten minutes. What's the matter with doctors, anyway?'

'I'm afraid. I'm afraid a doctor would say –'

'Come now, my dear girl, you're not consulting me professionally. Regard me as a mere outsider who's been enough of a busybody to save you from being killed or, what is far more likely, having a broken arm or a fractured leg or a head injury or something extremely unpleasant which might incapacitate you for life. There are other disadvantages. Formerly, if you deliberately tried to commit suicide you could be had up in Court. You still can if it's a suicide pact. There now, you can't say I haven't been frank. You could oblige now by being frank with me, and telling me why on earth you're afraid of doctors. What's a doctor ever done to you?'

'Nothing. Nothing has been *done* to me. But I'm afraid that they might –'

'Might what?'

'Shut me up.'

Dr Stillingfleet raised his sandy eyebrows and looked at her.

'Well, well,' he said. 'You seem to have some very curious ideas about doctors. Why should I want to shut you up? Would you like a cup of tea,' he added, 'or would you prefer a purple heart or a tranquilliser? That's the kind of thing people of your age go in for. Done a bit yourself in that line, haven't you?'

She shook her head. 'Not – not *really*.'

'I don't believe you. Anyway, why the alarm and despondency? You're not really mental, are you? I shouldn't have said so. Doctors aren't at all anxious to have people shut up. Mental homes are far too full already. Difficult to squeeze in another body. In fact lately they've been letting a good many people out – in desperation – pushing them out, you might say – who jolly well ought to have been kept in. Everything's so over-crowded in this country.

'Well,' he went on, 'what are your tastes? Something out of my drug cupboard or a good solid old-fashioned English cup of tea?'

'I – I'd like some tea,' said Norma.

'Indian or China? That's the thing to ask, isn't it? Mind you, I'm not sure if I've got any China.'

'I like Indian better.'

'Good.'

He went to the door, opened it and shouted, 'Annie. Pot of tea for two.'

He came back and sat down and said, 'Now you get this quite clear, young lady. What's your name, by the way?'

'Norma Res—' she stopped.

'Yes?'

'Norma West.'

'Well, Miss West, let's get this clear. I'm not treating you, you're not consulting me. You are the victim of a street accident – that is the way we'll put it and that is the way I suppose you meant it to appear, which would have been pretty hard on the fellow in the Jaguar.'

'I thought of throwing myself off a bridge first.'

'Did you? You wouldn't have found that so easy. People who build bridges are rather careful nowadays. I mean you'd have had to climb up on to the parapet and it's not so easy. Somebody stops you. Well, to continue with my dissertation, I brought you home as you were in too much of a state of shock to tell me your address. What is it, by the way?'

'I haven't got an address. I – I don't live anywhere.'

'Interesting,' said Dr Stillingfleet. 'What the police call "of no fixed abode". What do you do – sit out on the Embankment all night?'

She looked at him suspiciously.

'I could have reported the accident to the police but there was no obligation upon me to do so. I preferred to take the view that in a state of maiden meditation you were crossing the street before looking left first.'

'You're not at all like my idea of a doctor,' said Norma.

'Really? Well, I've been getting gradually disillusioned in my profession in this country. In fact, I'm giving up my practice here and I'm going to Australia in about a fortnight. So you're quite safe from me, and you can if you like tell me how you see pink elephants walking out of the wall, how you think the trees are leaning out their branches to wrap round and strangle you, how you think you know just when the devil looks out of people's eyes, or any other cheerful fantasy, and I shan't do a thing about it! You *look* sane enough, if I may say so.'

'I don't think I am.'

'Well, you may be right,' said Dr Stillingfleet handsomely. 'Let's hear what your reasons are.'

'I do things and don't remember about them . . . I tell people things about what I've done but I don't *remember* telling them . . .'

'It sounds as though you have a bad memory.'

'You don't understand. They're all – wicked things.'

'Religious mania? Now that would be very interesting.'

'It's not religious. It's just – just *hate*.'

There was a tap at the door and an elderly woman came in with a tea tray. She put it down on the desk and went out again.

'Sugar?' said Dr Stillingfleet.

'Yes, please.'

'Sensible girl. Sugar is very good for you when you've had a shock.' He poured out two cups of tea, set hers at her side and placed the sugar basin beside it. 'Now then,' he sat down. 'What were we talking about? Oh yes, hate.'

'It is possible, isn't it, that you could hate someone so much that you really want to kill them?'

'Oh, yes,' said Stillingfleet, cheerfully still. 'Perfectly possible. In fact, most natural. But even if you really want to do it you can't always screw yourself up to the point, you know. The human being is equipped with a natural braking system and it applies the brakes for you just at the right moment.'

'You make it sound so ordinary,' said Norma. There was a distinct overtone of annoyance in her voice.

'Oh, well, it is quite natural. Children feel like it almost every day. Lose their tempers, say to their mothers or their fathers: "You're wicked, I hate you, I wish you were dead." Mothers, being sometimes sensible people, don't usually pay any attention. When you grow up, you still hate people, but you can't take quite so much trouble wanting to kill them by then. Or if you still do – well, then you go to prison. That is, if you actually brought yourself to do such a messy and difficult job. You aren't putting all this on, are you, by the way?' he asked casually.

'Of course not.' Norma sat up straight. Her eyes flashed with anger. 'Of course not. Do you think I would say such awful things if they weren't true?'

'Well, again,' said Dr Stillingfleet, 'people do. They say all sorts of awful things about themselves and enjoy saying them.' He took her empty cup from her. 'Now then,' he said, 'you'd better tell me all about everything. Who you hate, why you hate them, what you'd like to do to them.'

'Love can turn to hate.'

'Sounds like a melodramatic ballad. But remember hate can turn to love, too. It works both ways. And you say it's not a boy friend. *He was your man and he did you wrong*. None of that stuff, eh?'

'No, no. Nothing like that. It's – it's my stepmother.'

'The cruel stepmother *motif*. But that's nonsense. At your age you can get away from a stepmother. What has she done to you besides marrying your father? Do you hate him too, or are you so devoted to him that you don't want to share him?'

'It's not like that at all. Not at all. I used to love him once. I loved him dearly. He was – he was – I thought he was wonderful.'

'Now then,' said Dr Stillingfleet, 'listen to me. I'm going to suggest something. You see that door?'

Norma turned her head and looked in a puzzled fashion at the door.

'Perfectly ordinary door, isn't it? Not locked. Opens and shuts in the ordinary way. Go on, try it for yourself. You saw my housekeeper come in and go out through it, didn't you? No illusions. Come on. Get up. Do what I tell you.'

Norma rose from her chair and rather hesitatingly went to the door and opened it. She stood in the aperture, her head turned towards him inquiringly.

'Right. What do you see? A perfectly ordinary hallway, wants redecorating but it's not worth having it done when I'm just off to Australia. Now go to the front door, open it, also no tricks about it. Go outside and down to the pavement and that will show you that you are perfectly free with no attempts to shut you up in any way. After that, when you have satisfied yourself that you could walk out of this place at any minute you like, come back, sit in that comfortable chair over there and tell me all about yourself. After which I will give you my valuable advice. You needn't take it,' he added consolingly. 'People seldom do take advice, but you might as well have it. See? Agreed?'

Norma got up slowly, she went a little shakily out of the room, out into – as the doctor had described – the perfectly ordinary hallway, opened the front door with a simple catch, down four steps and stood on the pavement in a street of decorous but rather uninteresting houses. She stood there a moment, unaware that she was being watched through a lace blind by Dr Stillingfleet himself. She stood there for about two minutes, then with a slightly more resolute bearing she turned, went up the steps again, shut the front door and came back into the room.

'All right?' said Dr Stillingfleet. 'Satisfied you there's nothing up my sleeve? All clear and above board.'

The girl nodded.

'Right. Sit down there. Make yourself comfortable. Do you smoke?'

'Well, I –'

'Only reefers – something of that kind? Never mind, you needn't tell me.'

'Of course I don't take anything of that kind.'

'I shouldn't have said there was any "of course" about it, but one must believe what the patient tells one. All right. Now tell me about yourself.'

'I – I don't know. There's nothing to tell really. Don't you want me to lie down on a couch?'

'Oh, you mean your memory of dreams and all that stuff? No, not particularly. I just like to get a background. You know. You were born, you lived in the country or the town, you have brothers and sisters or you're an only child and so on. When your own mother died, were you very upset by her death?'

'Of course I was.' Norma sounded indignant.

'You're much too fond of saying of course, Miss West. By the way, West isn't really your name, is it? Oh, never mind, I don't want to know any other one. Call yourself West or East or North or anything you like. Anyway, what went on after your mother died?'

'She was an invalid for a long time before she died. In nursing homes a good deal. I stayed with an aunt, rather an old aunt, down in Devonshire. She wasn't really an aunt, she was Mother's first cousin. And then my father came home just about six months ago. It – it was wonderful.' Her face lighted up suddenly. She was unaware of the quick, shrewd glance the apparently casual young man shot at her. 'I could hardly remember him, you know. He must have gone away when I was about five. I didn't really think I'd ever see him again. Mother didn't very often talk about him. I think at first she hoped that he'd give up this other woman and come back.'

'Other woman?'

'Yes. He went away with someone. She was a very bad woman, Mother said. Mother talked about her very bitterly and very bitterly about Father too, but I used to think that perhaps – perhaps Father wasn't as bad as she thought, that it was all this woman's fault.'

'Did they marry?'

'No. Mother said she would never divorce Father. She was a – is it an Anglican? – very High Church, you know. Rather like a Roman Catholic. She didn't believe in divorce.'

'Did they go on living together? What was the woman's name or is that a secret too?'

'I don't remember her last name.' Norma shook her head. 'No, I don't think they lived together long, but I don't know much about it all, you see. They went to South Africa but I think they quarrelled and parted quite soon because that's when Mother said she hoped Father might come back again. But he didn't. He didn't write even. Not even to me. But he sent me things at Christmas. Presents always.'

'He was fond of you?'

'I don't know. How could I tell? Nobody ever spoke about him. Only Uncle Simon – his brother, you know. He was in business in the City and he was very angry that Father had chucked up everything. He said he had always been the same, could never settle to anything, but he said he wasn't a bad chap really. He said he was just weak. I didn't often see Uncle Simon. It was always Mother's friends. Most of them were dreadfully dull. My whole life has been very dull . . .

'Oh, it seemed so wonderful that Father was really coming home. I tried to remember him better. You know, things he had said, games he had played with me. He used to make me laugh a lot. I tried to see if I couldn't find some old snapshots or photographs of him. They seem all to have been thrown away. I think Mother must have torn them all up.'

'She had remained vindictive then.'

'I think it was really Louise she was vindictive against.'

'Louise?'

He saw a slight stiffening on the girl's part.

'I don't remember – I told you – I don't remember any names.'

'Never mind. You're talking about the woman your father ran away with. Is that it?'

'Yes. Mother said she drank too much and took drugs and would come to a bad end.'

'But you don't know whether she did?'

'I don't know anything.' . . . Her emotion was rising. 'I wish you wouldn't ask me questions! I don't know anything about her! I never heard of her again! I'd forgotten her until you spoke about her. I tell you I don't know *anything*.'

'Well, well,' said Dr Stillingfleet. 'Don't get so agitated. You don't need to bother about past history. Let's think about the future. What are you going to do next?'

Norma gave a deep sigh.

'I don't know. I've nowhere to go. I can't – it's much better – I'm sure it's much better to – to end it all – only –'

'Only you can't make the attempt a second time, is that it? It would be very foolish if you did, I can tell you that, my girl. All right, you've nowhere to go, no one to trust; got any money?'

'Yes, I've got a banking account, and Father pays so much into it every quarter but I'm not sure . . . I think perhaps, by now, they might be looking for me. *I don't want to be found.*'

'You needn't be. I'll fix that up for you all right. Place called Kenway Court. Not as fine as it sounds. It's a kind of convalescent nursing home where people go for a rest cure. It's got no doctors or couches, and you won't be shut up there, I can promise you. You can walk out any time you like. You can have breakfast in bed, stay in bed all day if you like. Have a good rest and I'll come down one day and talk to you and we'll solve a few problems together. Will that suit you? Are you willing?'

Norma looked at him. She sat, without expression, staring at him; slowly she nodded her head.

II

Later that evening Dr Stillingfleet made a telephone call.

'Quite a good operation kidnap,' he said. 'She's down at Kenway Court. Came like a lamb. Can't tell you much yet. The girl's full of drugs. I'd say she'd been taking purple hearts, and dream bombs, and probably LSD . . . She's been all hopped up for some time. She says no, but I wouldn't trust much to what she says.'

He listened for a moment. 'Don't ask me! One will have to go carefully there. She gets the wind up easy . . . Yes, she's scared of something, or she's pretending to be scared of something . . .

'I don't know yet, I can't tell. Remember people who take drugs are tricky. You can't believe what they say always. We haven't rushed things and I don't want to startle her . . .

'A father complex as a child. I'd say didn't care much for her mother who sounds a grim woman by all accounts – the self-righteous martyr type. I'd say Father was a gay one, and couldn't quite stand the grimness of married life – Know of anyone called Louise? . . . The name seemed to frighten her – She was the girl's first hate, I should say. She took Father away at the time the child was five. Children don't understand very much at that age, but they're very quick to feel resentment of the person they feel was responsible. She didn't see Father again until apparently a few months ago. I'd say she'd had sentimental dreams of being her father's companion and the apple of his eye. She got disillusioned apparently. Father came back with a wife, a new young attractive wife. *She's* not called Louise, is she? . . . Oh well, I only asked. I'm giving you roughly the picture, the general picture, that is.'

The voice at the other end of the wire said sharply, 'What is that you say? Say it again.'

'I said I'm giving you roughly the picture.'

There was a pause.

'By the way, here's one little fact might interest you. The girl made a rather ham-handed attempt to commit suicide. Does that startle you? . . .

'Oh, it doesn't . . . No, she didn't swallow the aspirin bottle, or put her head in the gas oven. She rushed into the traffic in the path of a Jaguar going faster than it should have done . . . I can tell you I only got to her just in time . . . Yes, I'd say it was a genuine impulse . . . She admitted it. Usual classic phrase – she "wanted to get out of it all".'

He listened to a rapid flow of words, then he said: 'I don't know. At this stage, I can't be sure – The picture presented is clear. A nervy girl, neurotic and in an overwrought state from taking drugs of too many kinds. No, I couldn't tell you definitely what kind. There are dozens of these things going about all producing slightly different effects. There can be confusion, loss of memory, aggression, bewilderment, or sheer fuzzleheadedness! The difficulty is to tell what the real reactions are as opposed to the reactions produced by drugs. There are two choices, you see. Either this is a girl who is playing herself up, depicting herself as neurotic and nervy and claiming suicidal tendencies. It could be actually so. Or it could be a whole pack of lies. I wouldn't put it past her to be putting up this story for some obscure reason of her own – wanting to give an entirely false impression of herself. If so, she's doing it very cleverly. Every now and then, there seems something not quite right in the picture she's giving. Is she a very clever little actress acting a part? Or is she a genuine semi-moronic suicidal victim? She could be either . . . What did you say? . . . Oh, the Jaguar! . . . Yes, it was being driven far too fast. You think it mightn't have been an attempt at suicide? That the Jaguar was deliberately meaning to run her down?'

He thought for a minute or two. 'I *can't* say,' he said slowly. 'It just *could* be so. Yes, it could be so, but I hadn't thought of it that way. The trouble is, everything's possible, isn't it? Anyway, I'm going to get more out of her shortly. I've got her in a position where she's semi-willing to trust me, so long as I don't go too far too quickly, and make her suspicious. She'll become more trusting soon, and tell me more, and if she's a genuine case, she'll pour out her whole story to me – force it on me in the end. At the moment she's frightened of something . . .

'If, of course, she's leading me up the garden path we'll have to find out the reason why. She's at Kenway Court and I *think* she'll stay there. I'd suggest that you keep someone with an eye on it for a day or so and if she does attempt to leave, someone she doesn't know by sight had better follow her.'

CHAPTER 11

I

Andrew Restarick was writing a cheque – he made a slight grimace as he did so.

His office was large and handsomely furnished in typical conventional tycoon fashion – the furnishing and fittings had been Simon Restarick's and Andrew Restarick had accepted them without interest and had made few changes except for removing a couple of pictures and replacing them by his own portrait which he had brought up from the country, and a water colour of Table Mountain.

Andrew Restarick was a man of middle age, beginning to put on flesh, yet strangely little changed from the man some fifteen years younger in the picture hanging above him. There was the same jutting out chin, the lips firmly pressed together, and the slightly raised quizzical eyebrows. Not a very noticeable man – an ordinary type and at the moment not a very happy man. His secretary entered the room – she advanced towards his desk, as he looked up.

'A Monsieur Hercule Poirot is here. He insists that he has an appointment with you – but I can find no trace of one.'

'A Monsieur Hercule Poirot?' The name seemed vaguely familiar, but he could not remember in what context. He shook his head – 'I can't remember anything about him – though I seem to have heard the name. What does he look like?'

'A very small man – foreign – French I should say – with an enormous moustache –'

'Of course! I remember Mary describing him. He came to see old Roddy. But what's all this about an appointment with me?'

'He says you wrote him a letter.'

'Can't remember it – even if I did. Perhaps Mary – Oh well, never mind – bring him in. I suppose I'd better see what this is all about.'

A moment or two later Claudia Reece-Holland returned ushering with her a small man with an egg-shaped head, large moustaches, pointed patent leather shoes and a general air of complacency which accorded very well with the description he had had from his wife.

'Monsieur Hercule Poirot,' said Claudia Reece-Holland.

She went out again as Hercule Poirot advanced towards the desk. Restarick rose.

'Monsieur Restarick? I am Hercule Poirot, at your service.'

'Oh yes. My wife mentioned that you'd called upon us or rather called upon my uncle. What can I do for you?'

'I have presented myself in answer to your letter.'

'What letter? I did not write to you, M. Poirot.'

Poirot stared at him. Then he drew from his pocket a letter, unfolded it, glanced at it and handed it across the desk with a bow.

'See for yourself, Monsieur.'

Restarick stared at it. It was typewritten on his own office stationery. His signature was written in ink at the bottom.

Dear Monsieur Poirot,
I should be very glad if you could call upon me at the above address at your earliest convenience. I understand from what my wife tells me and also from what I have learned by making various inquiries in London, that you are a man to be trusted when you agree to accept a mission that demands discretion.
Yours truly,
Andrew Restarick

He said sharply:
'When did you receive this?'
'This morning. I had no matters of moment on my hands so I came along here.'
'This is an extraordinary thing, M. Poirot. That letter was not written by me.'
'Not written by you?'
'No. My signature is quite different – look for yourself.' He cast out a hand as though looking for some example of his handwriting and without conscious thought turned the cheque book on which he had just written his signature, so that Poirot could see it. 'You see? The signature on the letter is not in the least like mine.'
'But that is extraordinary,' said Poirot. 'Absolutely extraordinary. Who could have written this letter?'
'That's just what I'm asking myself.'
'It could not – excuse me – have been your wife?'
'No, no. Mary would never do a thing like that. And anyway why should she sign it with my name? Oh no, she would have told me if she'd done such a thing, prepared me for your visit.'
'Then you have no idea why anyone might have sent this letter?'
'No, indeed.'
'Have you no knowledge, Mr Restarick, as to what the matter might be on which in this letter you apparently want to engage me?'
'How could I have an idea?'
'Excuse me,' said Poirot, 'you have not yet completely read this letter. You will notice at the bottom of the first page after the signature, there is a small p.t.o.'
Restarick turned the letter over. At the top of the next page the typewriting continued.

The matter on which I wish to consult you concerns my daughter, Norma.

Restarick's manner changed. His face darkened.

'So, that's it! But who could know – who could possibly meddle in this matter? Who knows about it?'

'Could it be a way of urging you to consult me? Some well-meaning friend? You have really *no* idea who the writer may have been?'

'I've no idea whatever.'

'And you are not in trouble over a daughter of yours – a daughter named Norma?'

Restarick said slowly:

'I have a daughter named Norma. My only daughter.' His voice changed slightly as he said the last words.

'And she is in trouble, difficulty of some kind?'

'Not that I know of.' But he hesitated slightly as he spoke the words.

Poirot leaned forward.

'I don't think that is exactly right, Mr Restarick. I think there *is* some trouble or difficulty concerning your daughter.'

'Why should you think that? Has someone spoken to you on the subject?'

'I was going entirely by your intonation, Monsieur. Many people,' added Hercule Poirot, 'are in trouble over daughters at the present date. They have a genius, young ladies, for getting into various kinds of trouble and difficulty. It is possible that the same obtains here.'

Restarick was silent for some few moments, drumming with his fingers on the desk.

'Yes, I am worried about Norma,' he said at last. 'She is a difficult girl. Neurotic, inclined to be hysterical. I – unfortunately I don't know her very well.'

'Trouble, no doubt, over a young man?'

'In a way, yes, but that is not entirely what is worrying me. I think –' he looked appraisingly at Poirot. 'Am I to take it that you are a man of discretion?'

'I should be very little good in my profession if I were not.'

'It is a case, you see, of wanting my daughter *found*.'

'Ah?'

'She came home last weekend as she usually does to our house in the country. She went back on Sunday night ostensibly to the flat which she occupies in common with two other girls, but I now find that she did *not* go there. She must have gone – somewhere else.'

'In fact, she has disappeared?'

'It sounds too much of a melodramatic statement, but it does amount to that. I expect there's a perfectly natural explanation, but – well, I suppose any father would be worried. She hasn't rung up, you see, or given any explanation to the girls with whom she shares her flat.'

'They too are worried?'

'No, I should not say so. I think – well, I think they take such things easily enough. Girls are very independent. More so than when I left England fifteen years ago.'

'What about the young man of whom you say you do not approve? Can she have gone away with him?'

'I devoutly hope not. It's possible, but I don't – my wife doesn't think so. You saw him, I believe, the day you came to our house to call on my uncle –'

'Ah yes, I think I know the young man of whom you speak. A very handsome young man but not, if I may say so, a man of whom a father would approve. I noticed that your wife was not pleased, either.'

'My wife is quite certain that he came to the house that day hoping to escape observation.'

'He knows, perhaps, that he is not welcome there?'

'He knows all right,' said Restarick grimly.

'Do you not then think that it is only too likely your daughter may have joined him?'

'I don't know what to think. I didn't – at first.'

'You have been to the police.'

'No.'

'In the case of anyone who is missing, it is usually much better to go to the police. They too are discreet and they have many means at their disposal which persons like myself have not.'

'I don't want to go to the police. It's my *daughter*, man, you understand? *My* daughter. If she's chosen to – to go away for a short time and not let us know, well, that's up to her. There's no reason to believe that she's in any danger or anything like that. I – I just want to know for my own satisfaction where she is.'

'Is it possible, Mr Restarick – I hope I am not unduly presuming, that that is not the only thing that is worrying you about your daughter?'

'Why should you think there was anything else?'

'Because the mere fact that a girl is absent for a few days without telling her parents, or the friends with whom she is living, where she is going, is not particularly unusual nowadays. It is that, taken in conjunction with *something else*, I think, which has caused you this alarm.'

'Well, perhaps you're right. It's –' he looked doubtfully at Poirot. 'It is very hard to speak of these things to strangers.'

'Not really,' said Poirot. 'It is infinitely easier to speak to strangers of such things than it would be to speak of them to friends or acquaintances. Surely you must agree to that?'

'Perhaps. Perhaps. I can see what you mean. Well, I will admit I am upset about my girl. You see she – she's not quite like other girls and there's been something already that has definitely worried me – worried us both.'

Poirot said: 'Your daughter, perhaps, is at that difficult age of young girlhood, an emotional adolescence when, quite frankly, they are capable of performing actions for which they are hardly to be held responsible. Do not take it amiss if I venture to make a surmise. Your daughter perhaps resents having a stepmother?'

'That is unfortunately true. And yet she has no reason to do so, M. Poirot. It is not as though my first wife and I had recently parted. The parting took place many years ago.' He paused and then said, 'I might as well speak frankly to you. After all, there has been no concealment about the matter. My first wife and I drifted apart. I need not mince matters. I had met someone else, someone with whom I was quite infatuated. I left England and went to South Africa with the other woman. My wife did not approve of divorce and I did not ask her for one. I made suitable financial provision for my wife and for the child – she was only five years old at the time –'

He paused and then went on:

'Looking back, I can see that I had been dissatisfied with life for some time. I'd been yearning to travel. At that period of my life I hated being tied down to an office desk. My brother reproached me several times with not taking more interest in the family business, now that I had come in with him. He said that I was not pulling my weight. But I didn't want that sort of life. I was restless. I wanted an adventurous life. I wanted to see the world and wild places . . .'

He broke off abruptly.

'Anyway – you don't want to hear the story of my life. I went to South Africa and Louise went with me. It wasn't a success. I'll admit that straight away. I was in love with her but we quarrelled incessantly. She hated life in South Africa. She wanted to get back to London and Paris – all the sophisticated places. We parted only about a year after we arrived there.'

He sighed.

'Perhaps I ought to have gone back then, back to the tame life that I disliked the idea of so much. But I didn't. I don't know whether my wife would have had me back or not. Probably she would have considered it her duty to do so. She was a great woman for doing her duty.'

Poirot noted the slight bitterness that ran through that sentence.

'But I ought to have thought more about Norma, I suppose. Well, there it was. The child was safely with her mother. Financial arrangements had been made. I wrote to her occasionally and sent her presents, but I never once thought of going back to England and seeing her. That was not entirely blameworthy on my part. I had adopted a different way of life and I thought it would be merely unsettling for the child to have a father who came and went, and perhaps disturbed her own peace of mind. Anyway, let's say I thought I was acting for the best.'

Restarick's words came fast now. It was as though he was feeling a definite solace in being able to pour out his story to a sympathetic listener. It was a reaction that Poirot had often noticed before and he encouraged it.

'You never wished to come home on your own account?'

Restarick shook his head very definitely. 'No. You see, I was living the kind of life I liked, the kind of life I was meant for. I went from South Africa to East Africa. I was doing very well financially, everything I touched seemed to prosper; projects with which I was associated, occasionally with other people, sometimes on my own, all went well. I used to go off into the bush and trek. That was the life I'd always wanted. I am by nature an out-of-door man. Perhaps that's why when I was married to my first wife I felt trapped, held down. No, I enjoyed my freedom and I'd no wish to go back to the conventional type of life that I'd led here.'

'But you did come back in the end?'

Restarick sighed. 'Yes. I did come back. Ah well, one grows old, I suppose. Also, another man and I had made a very good strike. We'd secured a concession which might have very important consequences. It would need negotiation in London. There I could have depended on my brother to act, but my brother died. I was still a partner in the firm. I could return if I chose and see to things myself. It was the first time I had thought of doing so. Of returning, I mean, to City life.'

'Perhaps your wife – your second wife –'

'Yes, you may have something there. I had been married to Mary just a month or two when my brother died. Mary was born in South Africa but she had been to England several times and she liked the life there. She liked particularly the idea of having an English garden!

'And I? Well, for the first time perhaps I felt I would like life in England, too. And I thought of Norma as well. Her mother had died two years earlier. I talked to Mary about it all, and she was quite willing to help me make a home for my daughter. The prospects all seemed good and so –' he smiled, '– and so I came home.'

Poirot looked at the portrait that hung behind Restarick's head. It was in a better light here than it had been at the house in the country. It showed very plainly the man who was sitting at the desk; there were the distinctive features, the obstinancy of the chin, the quizzical eyebrows, the poise of the head, but the portrait had one thing that the man sitting in the chair beneath it lacked. Youth!

Another thought occurred to Poirot. Why had Andrew Restarick moved the portrait from the country to his London office? The two portraits of him and his wife had been companion portraits done at the same time and by that particular fashionable artist of the day whose speciality was portrait painting. It would have been more natural, Poirot thought, to have left them together, as they had been meant to be originally. But Restarick had moved one portrait, his own, to his office. Was it a kind of vanity on his part – a wish to display himself as a City man, as someone important to the City? Yet he was a man who had spent his time in wild places, who professed to prefer wild places. Or did he perhaps do it in order to keep before his mind himself in his City personality? Did he feel the need of reinforcement?

'Or, of course,' thought Poirot, 'it could be simple vanity!

'Even I myself,' said Poirot to himself, in an unusual fit of modesty, 'even I myself am capable of vanity on occasions.'

The short silence, of which both men had seemed unaware, was broken. Restarick spoke apologetically.

'You must forgive me, M. Poirot. I seem to have been boring you with the story of my life.'

'There is nothing to excuse, Mr Restarick. You have been talking really only of your life as it may have affected that of your daughter. You are much disquieted about your daughter. But I do not think that you have yet told me the real reason. You want her found, you say?'

'Yes, I want her found.'

'You want her found, yes, but do you want her found by *me*? Ah, do not hesitate. *La politesse* – it is very necessary in life, but it is not necessary here. Listen. I tell you, if you want your daughter found I advise you, I – Hercule Poirot – to go to the police for they have the facilities. And from my own knowledge they can be discreet.'

'I won't go to the police unless – well, unless I get very desperate.'

'You would rather go to a private agent?'

'Yes. But you see, I don't know anything about private agents. I don't know who – who can be trusted. I don't know who –'

'And what do you know about me?'

'I do know something about you. I know, for instance, that you held a responsible position in Intelligence during the war, since, in fact, my own uncle vouches for you. That is an admitted fact.'

The faintly cynical expression on Poirot's face was not perceived by Restarick. The admitted fact was, as Poirot was well aware, a complete illusion – although Restarick must have known how undependable Sir Roderick was in the matter of memory and eyesight – he had swallowed Poirot's own account of himself, hook, line and sinker. Poirot did not disillusion him. It merely confirmed him in his long-held belief that you should never believe anything anyone said without first checking it. *Suspect everybody*, had been for many years, if not his whole life, one of his first axioms.

'Let me reassure you,' said Poirot. 'I have been throughout my career exceptionally successful. I have been indeed in many ways unequalled.'

Restarick looked less reassured by this than he might have been! Indeed, to an Englishman, a man who praised himself in such terms aroused some misgivings.

He said: 'What do you feel yourself, M. Poirot? Have you confidence that you can find my daughter?'

'Probably not as quickly as the police could do, but yes. I shall find her.'

'And – and if you do –'

'But if you wish me to find her, Mr Restarick, you must tell me all the circumstances.'

'But I have told them to you. The time, the place, where she ought to be. I can give you a list of her friends . . .'

Poirot was making some violent shakings of his head. 'No, no, I suggest you tell me the truth.'

'Do you suggest I haven't told you the truth?'

'You have not told me all of it. Of that I am assured. What are you afraid of? What are the unknown facts – the facts that I have to know if I am to have success? Your daughter dislikes her stepmother. That is plain. There is nothing strange about that. It is a very natural reaction. You must remember that she may have secretly idealised you for many many years. That is quite possible in the case of a broken marriage where a child has had a severe blow in her affections. Yes, yes, I know what I am talking about. You say a child forgets. That is true. Your daughter could have forgotten you in the sense that when she saw you again she might not remember your face or your voice. She would make her own image of you. You went away. She wanted you to come back. Her mother, no doubt, discouraged her from talking about you, and therefore she thought about you perhaps all the more. You *mattered* to her all the more. And because she could not talk about you to her own mother she had what is a very natural reaction with a child – the blaming of the parent who remains for the absence of the parent who has gone. She said to herself something in the nature of "Father was fond of me. It's Mother he didn't like," and from that was born a kind of idealisation, a kind of secret liaison between you and her. What had happened was not her father's fault. She will not believe it!

'Oh yes, that often happens, I assure you. I know something of the psychology. So when she learns that you are coming home, that you and she will be reunited, many memories that she has pushed aside and not thought of for years return. Her father is coming back! He and she will be happy together! She hardly realises the stepmother, perhaps, until she sees her. And then she is violently jealous. It is most natural, I assure you. She is violently jealous partly because your wife is a good-looking woman, sophisticated, and well poised, which is a thing girls often resent because they frequently lack confidence in themselves. She herself is possibly gauche with perhaps an inferiority complex. So when she sees her competent and good-looking stepmother, quite possibly she hates her; but hates her as an adolescent girl who is still half a child might do.'

'Well –' Restarick hesitated. 'That *is* more or less what the doctor said when we consulted him – I mean –'

'Aha,' said Poirot, 'so you consulted a doctor? You must have had some reason, is it not so, for calling in a doctor?'

'Nothing really.'

'Ah no, you cannot say that to Hercule Poirot. It was not *nothing*. It was something serious and you had better tell me, because if I know just what has been in this girl's mind, I shall make more progress. Things will go quicker.'

Restarick was silent for several moments, then he made up his mind.

'This is in absolute confidence, M. Poirot? I can rely on you – I have your assurance as to that?'

'By all means. What was the trouble?'

'I cannot be – be sure.'

'Your daughter entered into some action against your wife?

Something more than being merely childishly rude or saying unpleasant things. It was something worse than that – something more serious. Did she perhaps attack her *physically*?'

'No, it was not an attack – not a physical attack but – nothing was proved.'

'No, no. We will admit that.'

'My wife became far from well –' He hesitated.

'Ah,' said Poirot. 'Yes, I see . . . And what was the nature of her illness? Digestive, possibly? A form of enteritis?'

'You're quick, M. Poirot. You're very quick. Yes, it *was* digestive. This complaint of my wife's was puzzling, because she had always had excellent health. Finally they sent her to hospital for "observation", as they call it. A check-up.'

'And the result?'

'I don't think they were completely satisfied . . . She appeared to regain her health completely and was sent home in due course. But the trouble recurred. We went carefully over the meals she had, the cooking. She seemed to be suffering from a form of intestinal poisoning for which there appeared to be no cause. A further step was taken, tests were made of the dishes she ate. By taking samples of everything, it was definitely proved that a certain substance had been administered in various dishes. In each case it was a dish of which only my wife had partaken.'

'In plain language somebody was giving her arsenic. Is that right?'

'Quite right. In small doses which would in the end have a cumulative effect.'

'You suspected your daughter?'

'No.'

'I think you did. Who else could have done it? You suspected your daughter.'

Restarick gave a deep sigh.

'Frankly, yes.'

II

When Poirot arrived home, George was awaiting him:

'A woman named Edith rang up, sir –'

'Edith?' Poirot frowned.

'She is, I gather, in the service of Mrs Oliver. She asked me to inform you that Mrs Oliver is in St Giles's Hospital.'

'What has happened to her?'

'I understand she has been – er – coshed.' George did not add the latter part of the message, which had been – '– and you tell him it's been all his fault.'

Poirot clicked his tongue. 'I warned her – I was uneasy last night when I rang her up, and there was no answer. *Les Femmes*!'

CHAPTER 12

Let's buy a peacock,' said Mrs Oliver suddenly and unexpectedly. She did not open her eyes as she made this remark, and her voice was weak though full of indignation.

Three people brought startled eyes to bear upon her. She made a further statement.

'Hit on the head.'

She opened badly focused eyes and endeavoured to make out where she was.

The first thing she saw was a face entirely strange to her. A young man who was writing in a notebook. He held the pencil poised in his hand.

'Policeman,' said Mrs Oliver decisively.

'I beg your pardon, Madam?'

'I said you were a policeman,' said Mrs Oliver. 'Am I right?'

'Yes, Madam.'

'Criminal assault,' said Mrs Oliver and closed her eyes in a satisfied manner. When she opened them again, she took in her surroundings more fully. She was in a bed, one of those rather high hygienic-looking hospital beds, she decided. The kind that you shoot up and down and round and about. She was not in her own house. She looked round and decided on her environment.

'Hospital, or could be nursing home,' she said.

A sister was standing with an air of authority at the door, and a nurse was standing by her bed. She identified a fourth figure. 'Nobody,' said Mrs Oliver, 'could mistake those moustaches. What are you doing here, M. Poirot?'

Hercule Poirot advanced towards the bed. 'I told you to be careful, Madame,' he said.

'Anyone might lose their way,' said Mrs Oliver, somewhat obscurely, and added, 'My head aches.'

'With good cause. As you surmise, you were hit on the head.'

'Yes. By the Peacock.'

The policeman stirred uneasily then said, 'Excuse me, Madam, you say you were assaulted by a peacock?'

'Of course. I'd had an uneasy feeling for some time – you know, atmosphere.' Mrs Oliver tried to wave her hand in an appropriate gesture to describe atmosphere, and winced. 'Ouch,' she said, 'I'd better not try that again.'

'My patient must not get over-excited,' said the sister with disapproval.

'Can you tell me where this assault occurred?'

'I haven't the faintest idea. I'd lost my way. I was coming from a kind of studio. Very badly kept. Dirty. The other young man hadn't shaved for days. A greasy leather jacket.'

'Is this the man who assaulted you?'

'No, it's another one.'

'If you could just tell me –'

'I am telling you, aren't I? I'd followed him, you see, all the way from the café – only I'm not very good at following people. No practice. It's much more difficult than you'd think.'

Her eyes focused on the policeman. 'But I suppose you know all about that. You have courses – in following people, I mean? Oh, never mind, it doesn't matter. You see,' she said, speaking with sudden rapidity, 'it's quite simple. I had got off at The World's End, I think it was, and naturally I thought he had stayed with the others – or gone the other way. But instead, he came up behind me.'

'Who was this?'

'The Peacock,' said Mrs Oliver, 'and he startled me, you see. It does startle you when you find things are the wrong way round. I mean he following you instead of you following him – only it was earlier – and I had a sort of uneasy feeling. In fact, you know, I was *afraid*. I don't know why. He spoke quite politely but I was *afraid*. Anyway there it was and he said "Come up and see the studio" and so I came up rather a rickety staircase. A kind of ladder staircase and there was this other young man – the dirty young man – and he was painting a picture, and the girl was acting as model. She was quite clean. Rather pretty really. And so there we were and they were quite nice and polite, and then I said I must be getting home, and they told me the right way to get back to the King's Road. But they can't really have told me the right way. Of course I *might* have made a mistake. You know, when people tell you second left and third right, well, you sometimes do it the wrong way round. At least I do. Anyway, I got into a rather peculiar slummy part quite close to the river. The afraid feeling had gone away by then. I must have been quite off my guard when the Peacock hit me.'

'I think she's delirous,' said the nurse in an explanatory voice.

'No, I'm not,' said Mrs Oliver. 'I know what I'm talking about.'

The nurse opened her mouth, caught the sister's admonitory eye and shut it again quickly.

'Velvets and satins and long curly hair,' said Mrs Oliver.

'A peacock in satin? A real peacock, Madam. You thought you saw a peacock near the river in Chelsea?'

'A real peacock?' said Mrs Oliver. 'Of course not. How silly. What would a real peacock be doing down on Chelsea Embankment?'

Nobody appeared to have an answer to this question.

'He struts,' said Mrs Oliver, 'that's why I nicknamed him a peacock. Shows off, you know. Vain, I should think. Proud of his looks. Perhaps a lot of other things as well.' She looked at Poirot. 'David something. You know who I mean.'

'You say this young man of the name of David assaulted you by striking you on the head?'

'Yes I do.'

Hercule Poirot spoke. 'You *saw* him?'

'I didn't see him,' said Mrs Oliver, 'I didn't know anything about it. I just thought I heard something behind me, and before I could turn my head to look – it all happened! Just as if a ton of bricks or something fell on me. I think I'll go to sleep now,' she added.

She moved her head slightly, made a grimace of pain, and relapsed into what appeared to be a perfectly satisfactory unconsciousness.

CHAPTER 13

Poirot seldom used the key to his flat. Instead, in an old-fashioned manner, he pressed the bell and waited for that admirable factotum, George, to open the door. On this occasion, however, after his visit to the hospital, the door was opened to him by Miss Lemon.

'You've got two visitors,' said Miss Lemon, pitching her voice in an admirable tone, not as carrying as a whisper but a good many notes lower than her usual pitch. 'One's Mr Goby and the other is an old gentleman called Sir Roderick Horsefield. I don't know which you want to see first.'

'Sir Roderick Horsefield,' mused Poirot. He considered this with his head on one side, looking rather like a robin while he decided how this latest development was likely to affect the general picture. Mr Goby, however, materialised with his usual suddenness from the small room which was sacred to Miss Lemon's typewriting and where she had evidently kept him in storage.

Poirot removed his overcoat. Miss Lemon hung it up on the hall-stand, and Mr Goby, as was his fashion, addressed the back of Miss Lemon's head.

'I'll have a cup of tea in the kitchen with George,' said Mr Goby. 'My time is my own. I'll keep.'

He disappeared obligingly into the kitchen. Poirot went into his sitting-room where Sir Roderick was pacing up and down full of vitality.

'Run you down, my boy,' he said genially. 'Wonderful thing the telephone.'

'You remembered my name? I am gratified.'

'Well, I didn't exactly remember your name,' said Sir Roderick. 'Names, you know, have never been my strong point. Never forget a face,' he ended proudly. 'No. I rang up Scotland Yard.'

'Oh!' Poirot looked faintly startled, though reflecting that that was the sort of thing that Sir Roderick *would* do.

'Asked me who I wanted to speak to. I said, put me on to the top. That's the thing to do in life, my boy. Never accept second in charge. No good. Go to the top, that's what I say. I said who I was, mind you. Said I wanted to speak to the top brass and I got on to it in the end. Very civil fellow. Told him I wanted the address of a chap in Allied Intelligence who was out with me at a certain place in France at a certain date. The chap seemed a bit at sea, so I said: "You know who I mean." A Frenchman, I said, or a Belgian. Belgian, weren't you? I said: "He's got a Christian name something like Achilles. It's not Achilles," I said, "but it's *like* Achilles. Little chap," I said, "big moustaches." And then he seemed to catch on, and he said you'd be in the telephone book, he thought. I said that's all right, but I said: "He won't be listed under Achilles or Hercules (as he said it was), will he? and I can't remember his second name." So then he gave it me. Very civil sort of fellow. Very civil, I must say.'

'I am delighted to see you,' said Poirot, sparing a hurried thought for what might be said to him later by Sir Roderick's telephone acquaintance. Fortunately it was not likely to have been quite the top brass. It was presumably someone with whom he was already acquainted, and whose job it was to produce civility on tap for distinguished persons of a bygone day.

'Anyway,' said Sir Roderick, 'I got here.'

'I am delighted. Let me offer you some refreshment. Tea, a grenadine, a whisky and soda, some *sirop de cassis* –'

'Good lord, no,' said Sir Roderick, alarmed at the mention of *sirop de cassis*. 'I'll take whisky for choice. Not that I'm allowed it,' he added, 'but doctors are all fools, as we know. All they care for is stopping you having anything you've a fancy for.'

Poirot rang for George and gave him the proper instructions. The whisky and the siphon were placed at Sir Roderick's elbow and George withdrew.

'Now,' said Poirot, 'what can I do for you?'

'Got a job for you, old boy.'

After the lapse of time, he seemed even more convinced of the close liaison between him and Poirot in the past, which was as well, thought Poirot, since it would produce an even greater dependence on his, Poirot's, capabilities by Sir Roderick's nephew.

'Papers,' said Sir Roderick, dropping his voice. 'Lost some papers and I've got to find 'em, see? So I thought what with my eyes not being as good as they were, and the memory being a trifle off key sometimes, I'd better go to someone in the know. See? You came along in the nick of time the other day, just in time to be useful, because I've got to cough 'em up, you understand.'

'It sounds most interesting,' said Poirot. 'What are these papers, if I may ask?'

'Well, I suppose if you're going to find them, you'll have to ask, won't you? Mind you, they're very secret and confidential. Top secret – or they were once. And it seems as though they are going to be again. An inter-change of letters, it was. Not of any particular importance at the time – or it was thought they were of no importance; but then of course politics change. You know the way it is. They go round and face the other way. You know how it was when the war broke out. None of us knew whether we were on our head or on our heels. One war we're pals with the Italians, next war we're enemies. I don't know which of them all was the worst. First war the Japanese were our dear allies, and the next war there they are blowing up Pearl Harbor! Never knew where you were! Start one way with the Russians, and finish the opposite way. I tell you, Poirot, nothing's more difficult nowadays than the question of allies. They can change overnight.'

'And you have lost some papers,' said Poirot, recalling the old man to the subject of his visit.

'Yes. I've got a lot of papers, you know, and I've dug 'em out lately. I had 'em put away safely. In a bank, as a matter of fact, but I got 'em all out and I began sorting through them because I thought why not write my memoirs. All the chaps are doing it nowadays. We've had Montgomery and Alanbrooke and Auchinleck all shooting their mouths off in print, mostly saying what they thought of the other generals. We've even had old Moran, a respectable physician, blabbing about his important patient. Don't know what things will come to next! Anyway, there it is, and I thought I'd be quite interested myself in telling a few facts about some people I knew! Why shouldn't I have a go as well as everyone else? I was in it all.'

'I am sure it could be a matter of much interest to people,' said Poirot.

'Ah-ha, yes! One knew a lot of people in the news. Everyone looked at them with awe. They didn't know they were complete fools, but I knew. My goodness, the mistakes some of those brass-hats made – you'd be surprised. So I got out my papers, and I had the little girl help me sort 'em out. Nice little girl, that, and quite bright. Doesn't know English very well, but apart from that, she's very bright and helpful. I'd salted away a lot of stuff, but everything was in a bit of a muddle. The point of the whole thing is, *the papers I wanted weren't there*.'

'Weren't there?'

'No. We thought we'd given it a miss by mistake to begin with, but we went over it again and I can tell you, Poirot, a lot of stuff seemed to me to have been pinched. Some of it wasn't important. Actually, the stuff I was looking for wasn't particularly important – I mean, nobody had thought it was, otherwise I suppose I shouldn't have been allowed to keep it. But anyway, these particular letters weren't there.'

'I wish of course to be discreet,' said Poirot, 'but can you tell me at all the nature of these letters you refer to?'

'Don't know that I can, old boy. The nearest I can go is of somebody who's shooting off his mouth nowadays about what he did and what he said in the past. But he's not speaking the truth, and these letters just show exactly how much of a liar he is! Mind you, I don't suppose they'd be published now. We'll just send him nice copies of them, and tell him this is exactly what he did say at the time, and that we've got it in writing. I shouldn't be surprised if – well, things went a bit differently after that. See? I hardly need ask that, need I? You're familiar with all that kind of talky-talky.'

'You're quite right, Sir Roderick. I know exactly the kind of thing you mean, but you see also that it is not easy to help you recover something if one does not know what that something is, and where it is likely to be now.'

'First things first: I want to know who pinched 'em, because you see that's the important point. There may be more top secret stuff in my little collection, and I want to know who's tampering with it.'

'Have you any ideas yourself?'

'You think I ought to have, heh?'

'Well, it would seem that the principal possibility –'

'I know. You want me to say it's the little girl. Well, I don't think it *is* the little girl. She says she didn't, and I believe her. Understand?'

'Yes,' said Poirot with a slight sigh, 'I understand.'

'For one thing she's too young. She wouldn't know these things were important. It's before her time.'

'Someone else might have instructed her as to that,' Poirot pointed out.

'Yes, yes, that's true enough. But it's too obvious as well.'

Poirot sighed. He doubted if it was any use insisting in view of Sir Roderick's obvious partiality. 'Who else had access?'

'Andrew and Mary, of course, but I doubt if Andrew would even be interested in such things. Anyway, he's always been a very decent boy. Always was. Not that I've ever known him very well. Used to come for the holidays once or twice with his brother and that's about all. Of course, he ditched his wife, and went off with an attractive bit of goods to South Africa, but that might happen to any man, especially with a wife like Grace. Not that I ever saw much of her, either. Kind of woman who looked down her nose and was full of good works. Anyway you can't imagine a chap like Andrew being a spy. As for Mary, she seems all right. Never looks at anything but a rose bush as far as I can make out. There's a gardener but he's eighty-three and has lived in the village all his life, and there are a couple of women always dodging about the house making a noise with Hoovers, but I can't see them in the role of spies either. So you see it's got to be an outsider. Of course Mary wears a wig,' went on Sir Roderick rather inconsequently. 'I mean it might make you think she was a spy because she wore a wig, but that's not the case. She lost her hair in a fever when she was eighteen. Pretty bad luck for a young woman. I'd no idea she wore a wig to begin with but a rose bush caught in her hair one day and whisked it sideways. Yes, very bad luck.'

'I thought there was something a little odd about the way she had arranged her hair,' said Poirot.

'Anyway, the best secret agents never wear wigs,' Sir Roderick informed him. 'Poor devils have to go to plastic surgeons and get their faces altered. But someone's been mucking about with my private papers.'

'You don't think that you may perhaps have placed them in some different container – in a drawer or a different file. When did you see them last?'

'I handled these things about a year ago. I remember I thought then, they'd make rather good copy, and I noted those particular letters. Now they're gone. Somebody's taken them.'

'You do not suspect your nephew Andrew, his wife or the domestic staff. What about the daughter?'

'Norma? Well Norma's a bit off her onion, I'd say. I mean she *might* be one of those kleptomaniacs who take people's things without knowing they're taking them but I don't see her fumbling about among my papers.'

'Then what *do* you think?'

'Well, you've been in the house. You saw what the house is like. Anyone can walk in and out any time they like. We don't lock our doors. We never have.'

'Do you lock the door of your own room – if you go up to London, for instance?'

'I never thought of it as necessary. I do now of course, but what's the use of that? Too late. Anyway, I've only an ordinary key, fits any of the doors. Someone must have come in from outside. Why nowadays that's how all the burglaries take place. People walk in in the middle of the day, stump up the stairs, go into any room they like, rifle the jewel box, go out again, and nobody sees them or cares who they are. They probably look like mods or rockers or beatniks or whatever they call these chaps nowadays with the long hair and the dirty nails. I've seen more than one of them prowling about. One doesn't like to say "Who the devil are you?" You never know which sex they are, which is embarrassing. The place crawls with them. I suppose they're Norma's friends. Wouldn't have been allowed in the old days. But you turn them out of the house, and then you find out it's Viscount Endersleigh or Lady Charlotte Marjoribanks. Don't know where you are nowadays.' He paused. 'If anyone can get to the bottom of it, you can, Poirot.' He swallowed the last mouthful of whisky and got up.

'Well, that's that. It's up to you. You'll take it on, won't you?'

'I will do my best,' said Poirot.

The front-door bell rang.

'That's the little girl,' said Sir Roderick. 'Punctual to the minute. Wonderful, isn't it? Couldn't go about London without her, you know. Blind as a bat. Can't see to cross the road.'

'Can you not have glasses?'

'I've got some somewhere, but they're always falling off my nose or else I lose them. Besides, I don't like glasses. I've never had glasses. When I was sixty-five I could see to read without glasses and that's pretty good.'

'Nothing,' said Hercule Poirot, 'lasts for ever.'

George ushered in Sonia. She was looking extremely pretty. Her slightly shy manner became her very well, Poirot thought. He moved forward with Gallic *empressement*.

'*Enchanté*, Mademoiselle,' he said, bowing over her hand.

'I'm not late, am I, Sir Roderick,' she said, looking past him. 'I have not kept you waiting. Please I hope not.'

'Exactly to the minute, little girl,' said Sir Roderick. 'All ship-shape and Bristol fashion,' he added.

Sonia looked slightly perplexed.

'Made a good tea, I hope,' Sir Roderick went on. 'I told you, you know, to have a good tea, buy yourself some buns or éclairs or whatever it is young ladies like nowadays, eh? You obeyed orders, I hope.'

'No, not exactly. I took the time to buy a pair of shoes. Look, they are pretty, are they not?' She stuck out a foot.

It was certainly a very pretty foot. Sir Roderick beamed at it.

'Well, we must go and catch our train,' he said. 'I may be old-fashioned but I'm all for trains. Start to time and get there on time, or they should do. But these cars, they get in a queue in the rush hour and you may idle the time away for about an hour and a half more than you need. Cars! Pah!'

'Shall I ask Georges to get you a taxi?' asked Hercule Poirot. 'It will be no trouble, I assure you.'

'I have a taxi already waiting,' said Sonia.

'There you are,' said Sir Roderick, 'you see, she thinks of everything.' He patted her on the shoulder. She looked at him in a way that Hercule Poirot fully appreciated.

Poirot accompanied them to the hall door and took a polite

leave of them. Mr Goby had come out of the kitchen and was standing in the hall giving, it could be said, an excellent performance of a man who had come to see about the gas.

George shut the hall door as soon as they had disappeared into the lift, and turned to meet Poirot's gaze.

'And what is your opinion of that young lady, Georges, may I ask?' said Poirot. On certain points he always said George was infallible.

'Well, sir,' said George, 'if I might put it that way, if you'll allow me, I would say he'd got it badly, sir. All over her as you might say.'

'I think you are right,' said Hercule Poirot.

'It's not unusual of course with gentlemen of that age. I remember Lord Mountbryan. He'd had a lot of experience in his life and you'd say he was as fly as anyone. But you'd be surprised. A young woman as came to give him massage. You'd be surprised at what he gave her. An evening frock, and a pretty bracelet. Forget-me-nots, it was. Turquoise and diamonds. Not *too* expensive but costing quite a pretty penny all the same. Then a fur wrap – not mink, Russian ermine, and a petty point evening bag. After that her brother got into trouble, debt or something, though whether she ever *had* a brother I sometimes wondered. Lord Mountbryan gave her the money to square it – she was so upset about it! All platonic, mind you, too. Gentlemen seem to lose their sense that way when they get to that age. It's the clinging ones they go for, not the bold type.'

'I have no doubt that you are quite right, Georges,' said Poirot. 'It is all the same not a complete answer to my question. I asked what you thought of the *young lady*.'

'Oh, the young lady . . . Well, sir, I wouldn't like to say definitely, but she's quite a definite type. There's never anything that you could put your finger on. But they know what they're doing, I'd say.'

Poirot entered his sitting-room and Mr Goby followed him, obeying Poirot's gesture. Mr Goby sat down on an upright chair in his usual attitude. Knees together, toes turned in. He took a rather dog-eared little notebook from his pocket, opened it carefully and then proceeded to survey the soda water siphon severely.

'Re the backgrounds you asked me to look up.

'Restarick family, perfectly respectable and of good standing. No scandal. The father, James Patrick Restarick, said to be a sharp man over a bargain. Business has been in the family three generations. Grandfather founded it, father enlarged it, Simon Restarick kept it going. Simon Restarick had coronary trouble two years ago, health declined. Died of coronary thrombosis, about a year ago.

'Young brother Andrew Restarick came into the business soon after he came down from Oxford, married Miss Grace Baldwin. One daughter, Norma. Left his wife and went out to South Africa. A Miss Birell went with him. No divorce proceedings. Mrs Andrew Restarick died two and a half years ago. Had been an invalid for some time. Miss Norma Restarick was a boarder at Meadowfield Girls' School. Nothing against her.'

Allowing his eyes to sweep across Hercule Poirot's face, Mr Goby observed, 'In fact everything about the family seems quite OK and according to Cocker.'

'No black sheep, no mental instability?'

'It doesn't appear so.'

'Disappointing,' said Poirot.

Mr Goby let this pass. He cleared his throat, licked his finger, and turned over a leaf of his little book.

'David Baker. Unsatisfactory record. Been on probation twice. Police are inclined to be interested in him. He's been on the fringe of several rather dubious affairs, thought to have been concerned in an important art robbery but no proof. He's one of the arty lot. No particular means of subsistence but he does quite well. Prefers girls with money. Not above living on some of the girls who are keen on him. Not above being paid off by their fathers either. Thorough bad lot if you ask me but enough brains to keep himself out of trouble.'

Mr Goby shot a sudden glance at Poirot.

'You met him?'

'Yes,' said Poirot.

'What conclusions did you form, if I may ask?'

'The same as you,' said Poirot. 'A gaudy creature,' he added thoughtfully.

'Appeals to women,' said Mr Goby. 'Trouble is nowadays they

won't look twice at a nice hard-working lad. They prefer the bad lots – the scroungers. They usually say "he hasn't had a *chance*, poor boy".'

'Strutting about like peacocks,' said Poirot.

'Well, you might put it like that,' said Mr Goby, rather doubtfully.

'Do you think he'd use a cosh on anyone?'

Mr Goby thought, then very slowly shook his head at the electric fire.

'Nobody's accused him of anything like that. I don't say he'd be past it, but I wouldn't say it was his line. He is a smooth-spoken type, not one for the rough stuff.'

'No,' said Poirot, 'no, I should not have thought so. He could be bought off? That was your opinion?'

'He'd drop any girl like a hot coal if it was made worth his while.'

Poirot nodded. He was remembering something. Andrew Restarick turning a cheque towards him so that he could read the signature on it. It was not only the signature that Poirot had read, it was the person to whom the cheque was made out. It had been made out to David Baker and it was for a large sum. Would David Baker demur at taking such a cheque, Poirot wondered. He thought not on the whole. Mr Goby clearly was of that opinion. Undesirable young men had been bought off in any time or age, so had undesirable young women. Sons had sworn and daughters had wept but money was money. To Norma, David had been urging marriage. Was he sincere? Could it be that he really cared for Norma? If so, he would not be so easily paid off. He had sounded genuine enough. Norma no doubt believed him genuine. Andrew Restarick and Mr Goby and Hercule Poirot thought differently. They were very much more likely to be right.

Mr Goby cleared his throat and went on.

'Miss Claudia Reece-Holland? She's all right. Nothing against her. Nothing dubious, that is. Father a Member of Parliament, well off. No scandals. Not like some MPs we've heard about. Educated Roedean, Lady Margaret Hall, came down and did a secretarial course. First secretary to a doctor in Harley Street, then went to the Coal Board. First-class secretary. Has been secretary to Mr Restarick for the last two months. No special attachments, just what you'd call minor boy friends. Eligible and useful if she wants a date. Nothing to show there's anything between her and Restarick. I shouldn't say there is, myself. Has had a flat in Borodene Mansions for the last three years. Quite a high rent there. She usually has two other girls sharing it, no special friends. They come and go. Young lady, Frances Cary, the second girl, has been there some time. Was at RADA for a time, then went to the Slade. Works for the Wedderburn Gallery – well-known place in Bond Street. Specialises in arranging art shows in Manchester, Birmingham, sometimes abroad. Goes to Switzerland and Portugal. Arty type and has a lot of friends amongst artists and actors.'

He paused, cleared his throat and gave a brief look at the little notebook.

'Haven't been able to get much from South Africa yet. Don't suppose I shall. Restarick moved about a lot. Kenya, Uganda, Gold Coast, South America for a while. He just moved about. Restless chap. Nobody seems to have known him particularly well. He'd got plenty of money of his own to go where he liked. He made money, too, quite a lot of it. Liked going to out of the way places. Everyone who came across him seems to have liked him. Just seems as though he was a born wanderer. He never kept in touch with anyone. Three times I believe he was reported dead – gone off into the bush and not turned up again – but he always did in the end. Five or six months and he'd pop up in some entirely different place or country.

'Then last year his brother in London died suddenly. They had a bit of trouble in tracing him. His brother's death seemed to give him a shock. Perhaps he'd had enough, and perhaps he'd met the right woman at last. Good bit younger than him, she was, and a teacher, they say. The steady kind. Anyway he seems to have made up his mind then and there to chuck wandering about, and come home to England. Besides being a very rich man himself, he's his brother's heir.'

'A success story and an unhappy girl,' said Poirot. 'I wish I knew more about her. You have ascertained for me all that you could, the facts I needed. The people who surrounded that girl, who might have influenced her, who perhaps *did* influence her. I wanted to know something about her father, her stepmother, the boy she is in love with, the people she lived with, and worked for in London. You are sure that in connection with this girl there have been no deaths? That is important –'

'Not a smell of one,' said Mr Goby. 'She worked for a firm called Homebirds – on the verge of bankruptcy, and they didn't pay her much. Stepmother was in hospital for observation recently – in the country, that was. A lot of rumours flying about, but they didn't seem to come to anything.'

'She did not die,' said Poirot. 'What I need,' he added in a bloodthirsty manner, 'is a *death*.'

Mr Goby said he was sorry about that and rose to his feet. 'Will there be anything more you are wanting at present?'

'Not in the nature of information.'

'Very good, sir.' As he replaced his notebook in his pocket, Mr Goby said: 'You'll excuse me, sir, if I'm speaking out of turn, but that young lady you had here just now –'

'Yes, what about her?'

'Well, of course it's – I don't suppose it's anything to do with this, but I thought I might just mention it to you, sir –'

'Please do. You have seen her before, I gather?'

'Yes. Couple of months ago.'

'Where did you see her?'

'Kew Gardens.'

'Kew Gardens?' Poirot looked slightly surprised.

'I wasn't following *her*. I was following someone else, the person who met her.'

'And who was that?'

'I don't suppose as it matters mentioning it to you, sir. It was one of the junior attachés of the Hertzogovinian Embassy.'

Poirot raised his eyebrows. 'That is interesting. Yes, very interesting. Kew Gardens,' he mused. 'A pleasant place for a rendezvous. Very pleasant.'

'I thought so at the time.'

'They talked together?'

'No, sir, you wouldn't have said they knew each other. The young lady had a book with her. She sat down on a seat. She read the book for a little then she laid it down beside her. Then my bloke came and sat there on the seat also. They didn't speak – only the young lady got up and wandered away. He just sat there and presently he gets up and walks off. He takes with him the book that the young lady has left behind. That's all, sir.'

'Yes,' said Poirot. 'It is very interesting.'

Mr Goby looked at the bookcase and said good night to it. He went.

Poirot gave an exasperated sigh.

'*Enfin,*' he said, 'it is too much! There is far too much. Now we have espionage and counter espionage. All I am seeking is one perfectly simple murder. I begin to suspect that that murder only occurred in a drug addict's brain!'

CHAPTER 14

'*Chère* Madame,' Poirot bowed and presented Mrs Oliver with a bouquet, very stylised, a posy in the Victorian manner.

'M. Poirot! Well, really, that is very nice of you, and it's very like you somehow. All my flowers are always so untidy.' She looked towards a vase of rather temperamental-looking chrysanthemums, then back to the prim circle of rosebuds. 'And how nice of you to come and see me.'

'I come, Madame, to offer you my felicitations on your recovery.'

'Yes,' said Mrs Oliver, 'I suppose I am all right again.' She shook her head to and fro rather gingerly. 'I get headaches, though,' she said. 'Quite bad headaches.'

'You remember, Madame, that I warned you not to do anything dangerous.'

'Not to stick my neck out, in fact. That I suppose is just what I did do.' She added, 'I felt something evil was about. I was frightened, too, and I told myself I was a fool to be frightened, because what was I frightened of? I mean, it was London. Right in the middle of London. People all about. I mean – how *could* I be frightened? It wasn't like a lonely wood or anything.'

Poirot looked at her thoughtfully. He wondered, had Mrs Oliver really felt this nervous fear, had she really suspected the presence of evil, the sinister feeling that something or someone wished her ill, or had she read it into the whole thing afterwards? He knew only too well how easily that could be done. Countless clients had spoken in much the same words that Mrs Oliver had just used. 'I knew something was wrong. I could feel evil. I knew something was going to happen,' and actually they had not felt anything of the kind. What kind of a person was Mrs Oliver?

He looked at her consideringly. Mrs Oliver in her own opinion was famous for her intuition. One intuition succeeded another with remarkable rapidity and Mrs Oliver always claimed the right to justify the particular intuition which turned out to be right!

And yet one shared very often with animals the uneasiness of a dog or a cat before a thunderstorm, the knowledge that there is *something* wrong, although one does not know what it is that is wrong.

'When did it come upon you, this fear?'

'When I left the main road,' said Mrs Oliver. 'Up till then it was all ordinary and quite exciting and – yes, I was enjoying myself, though vexed at finding how difficult it was to trail anybody.'

She paused, considering. 'Just like a *game*. Then suddenly it didn't seem so much like a game, because there were queer little streets and rather sort of broken-down places, and sheds and open spaces being cleared for building – oh, I don't know, I can't explain it. But it was all *different*. Like a dream really. You know how dreams are. They start with one thing, a party or something, and then suddenly you find you're in a jungle or somewhere quite different – and it's all sinister.'

'A jungle?' said Poirot. 'Yet, it is interesting you should put it like that. So it felt to you as though you were in a jungle and you were afraid of a peacock?'

'I don't know that I was especially afraid of him. After all, a peacock isn't a dangerous sort of animal. It's – well I mean I thought of him as a peacock because I thought of him as a *decorative* creature. A peacock is very decorative, isn't it? And this awful boy is decorative too.'

'You didn't have any idea anyone was following you before you were hit?'

'No. No, I'd no idea – but I think he directed me wrong all the same.'

Poirot nodded thoughtfully.

'But of course it must have been the Peacock who hit me,' said Mrs Oliver. 'Who else? The dirty boy in the greasy clothes? He smelt nasty but he wasn't sinister. And it could hardly be that limp Frances something – she was draped over a packing case with long black hair streaming all over the place. She reminded me of some actress or other.'

'You say she was acting as a model?'

'Yes. Not for the Peacock. For the dirty boy. I can't remember if you've seen her or not.'

'I have not yet had that pleasure – if it is a pleasure.'

'Well, she's quite nice looking in an untidy, arty sort of way. Very much made up. Dead white and lots of mascara and the usual kind of limp hair hanging over her face. Works in an art gallery so I suppose it's quite natural that she should be all among the beatniks, acting as a model. How these girls *can*! I suppose she *might* have fallen for the Peacock. But it's probably the dirty one. All the same I don't see her coshing me on the head somehow.'

'I had another possibility in mind, Madame. Someone may have noticed you following David – and in turn followed you.'

'Someone saw *me* trailing David, and then they trailed *me*?'

'Or someone may have been already in the mews or the yard, keeping perhaps an eye on the same people that you were observing.'

'That's an idea, of course,' said Mrs Oliver. 'I wonder who they could be?'

Poirot gave an exasperated sigh. 'Ah, it is there. It is difficult – too difficult. Too many people, too many things. I cannot see anything clearly. I see only a girl who said that she may have committed a murder! That is all that I have to go on and you see even there there are difficulties.'

'What do you mean by difficulties?'

'Reflect,' said Poirot.

Reflection had never been Mrs Oliver's strong point.

'You always mix me up,' she complained.

'I am talking about a murder, but what murder?'

'The murder of the stepmother, I suppose.'

'But the stepmother is not murdered. She is alive.'

'You really are the most maddening man,' said Mrs Oliver.

Poirot sat up in his chair. He brought the tips of his fingers together and prepared – or so Mrs Oliver suspected – to enjoy himself.

'You refuse to reflect,' he said. 'But to get anywhere we *must* reflect.'

'I don't want to reflect. What I want to know is what you've been doing about everything while I've been in hospital. You must have done *something*. What *have* you done?'

Poirot ignored this question.

'We must begin at the beginning. One day you ring me up. I was in distress. Yes, I admit it, I was in distress. Something extremely painful had been said to me. You, Madame, were kindness itself. You cheered me, you encouraged me. You gave me a delicious *tasse de chocolat*. And what is more you not only offered to help me, but you *did* help me. You helped me to find a girl who had come to me and said that she thought she might have committed a murder! Let us ask ourselves, Madame, what about this murder? Who has been murdered? Where have they been murdered? Why have they been murdered?'

'Oh do stop,' said Mrs Oliver. 'You're making my head ache again, and that's bad for me.'

Poirot paid no attention to this plea. 'Have we got a murder at all? You say – the stepmother – but I reply that the stepmother is not dead – so as yet we *have* no murder. But there *ought* to have been a murder. So me, I inquire first of all, *who* is dead? Somebody comes to me and mentions a murder. A murder that has been committed somewhere and somehow. But I cannot *find* that murder, and what you are about to say once again, that the attempted murder of Mary Restarick will do very well, does not satisfy Hercule Poirot.'

'I really can't think what more you want,' said Mrs Oliver.

'*I want a murder*,' said Hercule Poirot.

'It sounds very bloodthirsty when you say it like that!'

'I look for a murder and I cannot find a murder. It is exasperating – so I ask you to reflect with me.'

'I've got a splendid idea,' said Mrs Oliver. 'Suppose Andrew Restarick murdered his first wife before he went off in a hurry to South Africa. Had you thought of that possibility?'

'I certainly did not think of any such thing,' said Poirot indignantly.

'Well, *I've* thought of it,' said Mrs Oliver. 'It's very interesting. He was in love with this other woman, and he wanted like Crippen to go off with her, and so he murdered the first one and nobody ever suspected.'

Poirot drew a long, exasperated sigh. '*But his wife did not die until eleven or twelve years after he'd left this country for South Africa*, and his child could not have been concerned in the murder of her own mother at the age of five years old.'

'She could have given her mother the wrong medicine or perhaps Restarick just said that she died. After all, we don't *know* that she's dead.'

'I do,' said Hercule Poirot. 'I have made inquiries. The first Mrs Restarick died on the 14th April, 1963.'

'How can you know these things?'

'Because I have employed someone to check the facts. I beg of you, Madame, do not jump to impossible conclusions in this rash way.'

'I thought I was being rather clever,' said Mrs Oliver obstinately. 'If I was making it happen in a book that's how *I* would arrange it. And I'd make the child have done it. Not meaning to, but just by her father telling her to give her mother a drink made of pounded up box hedge.'

'*Non d'un nom d'un nom!*' said Poirot.

'All right,' said Mrs Oliver. 'You tell it your way.'

'Alas, I have nothing to tell. I look for a murder and I do not find one.'

'Not after Mary Restarick is ill and goes to hospital and gets better and comes back and is ill again, and if they looked they'd probably find arsenic or something hidden away by Norma somewhere.'

'That is exactly what they did find.'

'Well, really, M. Poirot, what *more* do you want?'

'I want you to pay some attention to the meaning of language. That girl said to me the same thing as she had said to my manservant, Georges. She did not say on either occasion "I have tried to kill someone" or "I have tried to kill my stepmother." She spoke each time of a deed that *had* been *done*, something that had already *happened*. Definitely *happened*. In the *past* tense.'

'I give up,' said Mrs Oliver. 'You just won't believe that Norma tried to kill her stepmother.'

'Yes, I believe it is perfectly possible that Norma may have tried to kill her stepmother. I think it is probably what happened – it is in accord psychologically. With her distraught frame of mind. But it is not *proved.* Anyone, remember, could have hidden a preparation of arsenic amongst Norma's things. It could even have been put there by the husband.'

'You always seem to think that husbands are the ones who kill their wives,' said Mrs Oliver.

'A husband is usually the most likely person,' said Hercule Poirot, 'so one considers him first. It could have been the girl, Norma, or it could have been one of the servants, or it could have been the *au pair* girl, or it could have been old Sir Roderick. Or it could have been *Mrs Restarick herself.*'

'Nonsense. Why?'

'There *could* be reasons. Rather far-fetched reasons, but not beyond the bounds of belief.'

'Really, Monsieur Poirot, you can't suspect *everybody.*'

'*Mais oui,* that is just what I can do. I suspect everybody. First I suspect, then I look for reasons.'

'And what reason would that poor foreign child have?'

'It might depend on what she is doing in that house, and what her reasons are for coming to England and a good deal more beside.'

'You're really crazy.'

'Or it could have been the boy David. Your Peacock.'

'Much too far-fetched. David wasn't there. He's never been near the house.'

'Oh yes he has. He was wandering about its corridors the day I went there.'

'But not putting poison in Norma's room.'

'How do you know?'

'But she and that awful boy are in love with each other.'

'They appear to be so, I admit.'

'You always want to make everything difficult,' complained Mrs Oliver.

'Not at all. Things have been made difficult for *me.* I need information and there is only one person who can give me information. And she has disappeared.'

'You mean Norma.'

'Yes, I mean Norma.'

'But she hasn't disappeared. We found her, you and I.'

'She walked out of that café and once more she has disappeared.'

'And you let her go?' Mrs Oliver's voice quivered with reproach.

'Alas!'

'*You let her go?* You didn't even try to find her again?'

'I did not say I had not tried to find her.'

'But so far you have not succeeded. M. Poirot, I really am disappointed with you.'

'There is a pattern,' said Hercule Poirot almost dreamily. 'Yes, there is a pattern. But because there is one factor missing, the pattern does not make sense. You see that, don't you?'

'No,' said Mrs Oliver, whose head was aching.

Poirot continued to talk more to himself than his listener. If Mrs Oliver could be said to be listening. She was highly indignant with Poirot and she thought to herself that the Restarick girl had been quite right and that Poirot *was* too old! There, she herself had found the girl for him, had telephoned him so that he might arrive in time, had gone off herself to shadow the other half of the couple. She had left the girl to Poirot, and what had Poirot done – lost her! In fact she could not really see that Poirot had done anything at all of any use at any time whatever. She was disappointed in him. When he stopped talking she would tell him so again.

Poirot was quietly and methodically outlining what he called 'the pattern'.

'It interlocks. Yes, it interlocks and that is why it is difficult. One thing relates to another and then you find that it relates to something else that seems outside the pattern. But it is not outside the pattern. And so it brings more people again into a ring of suspicion. Suspicion of what? There again one does not know. We have first the girl and through all the maze of conflicting patterns I have to search the answer to the most poignant of questions. Is the girl a victim, is she in danger? Or is the girl very astute? Is the girl creating the impression she wants to create for her own purposes? It can be taken either way. I need something still. Some one sure pointer, and it is *there* somewhere. I am sure it is there somewhere.'

Mrs Oliver was rummaging in her handbag.

'I can't think why I can never find my aspirin when I want it,' she said in a vexed voice.

'We have one set of relationships that hook up. The father, the daughter, the stepmother. Their lives are interrelated. We have the elderly uncle, somewhat gaga, with whom they live. We have the girl Sonia. She is linked with the uncle. She works for him. She has pretty manners, pretty ways. He is delighted with her. He is, shall we say, a little soft about her. But what is her role in the household?'

'Wants to learn English, I suppose,' said Mrs Oliver.

'She meets one of the members of the Herzogovinian Embassy – in Kew Gardens. She meets him there, but she does not speak to him. She leaves behind her a book and he takes it away –'

'What is all this?' said Mrs Oliver.

'Has this anything to do with the other pattern? We do not as yet know. It seems unlikely but it may not be unlikely. Had Mary Restarick unwittingly stumbled upon something which might be dangerous to the girl?'

'Don't tell me all this has something to do with *espionage* or something.'

'I am not telling you. I am wondering.'

'You said yourself that old Sir Roderick was gaga.'

'It is not a question of whether he is gaga or not. He was a person of some importance during the war. Important papers passed through his hands. Important letters can have been written to him. Letters which he was at perfect liberty to have kept once they had lost their importance.'

'You're talking of the war and that was ages ago.'

'Quite so. But the past is not always done with, because it is ages ago. New alliances are made. Public speeches are made repudiating this, denying that, telling various lies about something else. And suppose there exist still certain letters or documents that will change the picture of a certain personality. I am not telling you anything, you understand. I am only making assumptions. Assumptions such as I have known to be true in the past. It might be of the utmost importance that some letters or papers should be destroyed, or else passed to some foreign government. Who better to undertake that task than a charming young lady who assists and aids an elderly notability to collect material for his memoirs. Everyone is writing their memoirs nowadays. One cannot stop them from doing so! Suppose that the stepmother gets a little something in her food on the day that the helpful secretary plus *au pair* girl is doing the cooking? And suppose it is she who arranges that suspicion should fall on Norma?'

'What a mind you have,' said Mrs Oliver. 'Tortuous, that's what I call it. I mean, *all* these things can't have happened.'

'That is just it. There are too many patterns. Which is the right one? The girl Norma leaves home, goes to London. She is, as you have instructed me, a third girl sharing a flat with two other girls. There again you may have a pattern. The two girls are strangers to her. But then what do I learn? Claudia Reece-Holland is private secretary to Norma Restarick's father. Here again we have a *link*. Is that mere chance? Or could there be a pattern of some kind behind it? The other girl, you tell me, acts as a model, and is acquainted with the boy you call "the Peacock" with whom Norma is in love. Again a link. More links. And what is David – the Peacock – doing in all this? Is he in love with Norma? It would seem so. Her parents dislike it as is only probable and natural.'

'It's odd about Claudia Reece-Holland being Restarick's secretary,' said Mrs Oliver thoughtfully. 'I should judge she was unusually efficient at anything she undertook. Perhaps it was she who pushed the woman out of the window on the seventh floor.'

Poirot turned slowly towards her.

'What are you saying?' he demanded. 'What are you saying?'

'Just someone in the flats – I don't even know her name, but she fell out of a window or threw herself out of a window on the seventh floor and killed herself.'

Poirot's voice rose high and stern.

'And you never told me?' he said accusingly.

Mrs Oliver stared at him in surprise.

'I don't know what you mean.'

'What I mean? I ask you to tell me of a death. That is what I mean. *A death*. And you say there are no deaths. You can think only of an attempted poisoning. *And yet here is a death*. A death at – what is the name of those mansions?'

'Borodene Mansions.'

'Yes, yes. And when did it happen?'

'This suicide? Or whatever it was? I think – yes – I think it was about a week before I went there.'

'Perfect! How did you hear about it?'

'A milkman told me.'

'A milkman, *bon Dieu*!'

'He was just being chatty,' said Mrs Oliver. 'It sounded rather sad. It was in the daytime – very early in the morning, I think.'

'What was her name?'

'I've no idea. I don't think he mentioned it.'

'Young, middle-aged, old?'

Mrs Oliver considered. 'Well, he didn't say her exact age. Fifty-ish, I think, was what he said.'

'I wonder now. Anyone the three girls knew?'

'How can I tell? Nobody has said anything about it.'

'And you never thought of telling me.'

'Well, really, M. Poirot, I cannot say that it has anything to do with all this. Well, I suppose it may have – but nobody seems to have said so, or thought of it.'

'But yes, there is the link. There is this girl, Norma, and she lives in those flats, and one day somebody commits suicide (for that, I gather, was the general impression). That is, somebody throws herself or falls out of a seventh-floor high window *and is killed*. And then? Some days later this girl Norma, after having heard you talk about me at a party, comes to call upon me and she says to me that she is afraid that she may have committed a murder. Do you not see? A death – and not many days later someone who thinks she may have committed a murder. Yes, *this must be the murder*.'

Mrs Oliver wanted to say 'Nonsense' but she did not quite dare to do so. Nevertheless, she thought it.

'This then must be the one piece of knowledge that had not yet come to me. This ought to tie up the whole thing! Yes, yes, I do not see yet *how*, but *it must be so*. I must think. That is what I must do. I must go home and think until slowly the pieces fit together – because this will be the key piece that ties them all together . . . Yes. At last. At last I shall see my way.'

He rose to his feet and said, '*Adieu, chère* Madame,' and hurried from the room. Mrs Oliver at last relieved her feelings.

'Nonsense,' she said to the empty room. 'Absolute nonsense. I wonder if four would be too many aspirins to take?'

CHAPTER 15

At Hercule Poirot's elbow was a tisane prepared for him by George. He sipped at it and thought. He thought in a certain way peculiar to himself. It was the technique of a man who selected thoughts as one might select pieces of a jigsaw puzzle. In due course they would be reassembled together so as to make a clear and coherent picture. At the moment the important thing was the selection, the separation. He sipped his tisane, put down the cup, rested his hands on the arms of his chair and let various pieces of his puzzle come one by one into his mind. Once he recognised them all, he would select. Pieces of sky, pieces of green bank, perhaps striped pieces like those of a tiger . . .

The painfulness of his own feet in patent-leather shoes. He started there. Walking along a road set on this path by his good friend, Mrs Oliver. A stepmother. He saw himself with his hand on a gate. A woman who turned, a woman bending her head cutting out the weak growth of a rose, turning and looking at him? What was there for him there? Nothing. A golden head, a golden head bright as a cornfield, with twists and loops of hair slightly reminiscent of Mrs Oliver's own in shape. He smiled a little. But Mary Restarick's hair was more tidily arranged than Mrs Oliver's ever was. A golden frame for her face that seemed just a little too large for her. He remembered that old Sir Roderick had said that she had to wear a wig, because of an illness. Sad for so young a woman. There was, when he came to think of it, something unusually heavy about her head. Far too static, too perfectly arranged. He considered Mary Restarick's wig – if it *was* a wig – for he was by no means sure that he could depend on Sir Roderick. He examined the possibilities of the wig in case they should be of significance. He reviewed the conversation they had had. Had they said anything important? He thought not. He remembered the room into which they had gone. A characterless room recently inhabited in someone else's house. Two pictures on the wall, the picture of a woman in a dove-grey dress. Thin mouth, lips set closely together. Hair that was greyish brown. The first Mrs Restarick. She looked as though she might have been older than her husband. His picture was on the opposite wall, facing her. Good portraits, both of them. Lansberger had been a good portrait painter. His mind dwelt on the portrait of the husband. He had not seen it so well that first day, as he had later in Restarick's office . . .

Andrew Restarick and Claudia Reece-Holland. Was there anything there? Was their association more than a merely secretarial one? It need not be. Here was a man who had come back to this country after years of absence, who had no near friends or relatives, who was perplexed and troubled over his daughter's character and conduct. It was probably natural enough that he should turn to his recently acquired eminently competent secretary and ask her to suggest somewhere for his daughter to live in London. It would be a favour on her part to provide that accommodation since she was looking for a Third Girl. Third girl . . . The phrase that he had acquired from Mrs Oliver always seemed to be coming to his mind. As though it had a second significance which for some reason he could not see.

His manservant, George, entered the room, closing the door discreetly behind him.

'A young lady is here, sir. The young lady who came the other day.'

The words came too aptly with what Poirot was thinking. He sat up in a startled fashion.

'The young lady who came at breakfast time?'

'Oh no, sir. I mean the young lady who came with Sir Roderick Horsefield.'

'Ah, indeed.'

Poirot raised his eyebrows. 'Bring her in. Where is she?'

'I showed her into Miss Lemon's room, sir.'

'Ah. Yes, bring her in.'

Sonia did not wait for George to announce her. She came into the room ahead of him with a quick and rather aggressive step.

'It has been difficult for me to get away, but I have come to tell you that I did not take those papers. I did not steal anything. You understand?'

'Has anybody said that you had?' Poirot asked. 'Sit down, Mademoiselle.'

'I do not want to sit down. I have very little time. I just came to tell you that it is absolutely untrue. I am very honest and I do what I am told.'

'I take your point. I have already taken it. Your statement is that you have not removed any papers, information, letters, documents of any kind from Sir Roderick Horsefield's house? That is so, is it not?'

'Yes, and I've come to tell you it is so. *He* believes me. *He* knows that I would not do such a thing.'

'Very well then. That is a statement and I note it.'

'Do you think you are going to find those papers?'

'I have other inquiries in hand,' said Poirot. 'Sir Roderick's papers will have to take their turn.'

'He is worried. He is very worried. There is something that I cannot say to him. I will say it to you. *He loses things*. Things are not put away where he thinks they are. He puts them in – how do you say it – in funny places. Oh I know. You suspect me. Everyone suspects me because I am foreign. Because I come from a foreign country and so they think – they think I steal secret papers like in one of your silly English spy stories. I am not like that. I am an intellectual.'

'Aha,' said Poirot. 'It is always nice to know.' He added: 'Is there anything else you wish to tell me?'

'Why should I?'

'One never knows.'

'What are these other cases you speak of?'

'Ah, I do not want to detain you. It is your day out, perhaps.'

'Yes. I have one day a week when I can do what I like. I can come to London. I can go to the British Museum.'

'Ah yes and to the Victoria and Albert also, no doubt.'

'That is so.'

'And to the National Gallery and see the pictures. And on a fine day you can go to Kensington Gardens, or perhaps as far as Kew Gardens.'

She stiffened . . . She shot him an angry questioning glance.

'Why do you say Kew Gardens?'

'Because there are some very fine plants and shrubs and trees there. Ah! you should not miss Kew Gardens. The admission fee is very small. A penny I think, or twopence. And for that you can go and see tropical trees, or you can sit on a seat and read a book.' He smiled at her disarmingly and was interested to notice that her uneasiness was increased. 'But I must not detain you, Mademoiselle. You have perhaps friends to visit at one of the Embassies, maybe.'

'Why do you say that?'

'No particular reason. You are, as you say, a foreigner and it is quite possible you may have friends connected with your own Embassy here.'

'Someone has told you things. Someone has made accusations against me! I tell you he is a silly old man who mislays things. That is all! And he knows nothing of importance. He has no secret papers or documents. He never has had.'

'Ah, but you are not quite thinking of what you are saying. Time passes, you know. He was once an important man who did know important secrets.'

'You are trying to frighten me.'

'No, no. I am not being so melodramatic as that.'

'Mrs Restarick. It is Mrs Restarick who has been telling you things. She does not like me.'

'She has not said so to me.'

'Well, I do not like *her*. She is the kind of woman I mistrust. I think *she* has secrets.'

'Indeed?'

'Yes, I think she has secrets from her husband. I think she goes up to London or to other places to meet other men. To meet at any rate one other man.'

'Indeed,' said Poirot, 'that is very interesting. You think she goes to meet another man?'

'Yes, I do. She goes up to London very often and I do not think she always tells her husband, or she says it is shopping or things she has to buy. All those sort of things. He is busy in the office and he does not think of why his wife comes up. She is more in London than she is in the country. And yet she pretends to like gardening so much.'

'You have no idea who this man is whom she meets?'

'How should I know? I do not follow her. Mr Restarick is not a suspicious man. He believes what his wife tells him. He thinks perhaps about business all the time. And, too, I think he is worried about his daughter.'

'Yes,' said Poirot, 'he is certainly worried about his daughter. How much do you know about the daughter? How well do you know her?'

'I do not know her very well. If you ask what I *think* – well, I tell you! I think she is mad.'

'You think she is mad? Why?'

'She says odd things sometimes. She sees things that are not there.'

'Sees things that are not there?'

'People that are not there. Sometimes she is very excited and other times she seems as though she is in a dream. You speak to her and she does not hear what you say to her. She does not answer. I think there are people who she would like to have dead.'

'You mean Mrs Restarick?'

'*And* her father. She looks at him as though she hates him.'

'Because they are both trying to prevent her marrying a young man of her choice?'

'Yes. They do not want that to happen. They are quite right, of course, but it makes her angry. Some day,' added Sonia, nodding her head cheerfully, 'I think she will kill herself. I hope she will do nothing so foolish, but that is the thing one does when one is much in love.' She shrugged her shoulders. 'Well – I go now.'

'Just tell me one thing. Does Mrs Restarick wear a wig?'

'A wig? How should I know?' She considered for a moment. 'She might, yes,' she admitted. 'It is useful for travelling. Also it is fashionable. I wear a wig myself sometimes. A *green* one! Or I did.' She added again, 'I go now,' and went.

CHAPTER 16

'Today I have much to do,' Hercule Poirot announced as he rose from the breakfast table next morning and joined Miss Lemon. 'Inquiries to make. You have made the necessary researches for me, the appointments, the necessary contacts?'

'Certainly,' said Miss Lemon. 'It is all here.' She handed him a small briefcase. Poirot took a quick glance at its contents and nodded his head.

'I can always rely on you, Miss Lemon,' he said. '*C'est fantastique*.'

'Really, Monsieur Poirot, I cannot see anything fantastic about it. You gave me instructions and I carried them out. Naturally.'

'Pah, it is not so natural as that,' said Poirot. 'Do I not give instructions often to the gas men, the electricians, the man who comes to repair things, and do they always carry out my instructions? Very, very seldom.'

He went into the hall.

'My slightly heavier overcoat, Georges. I think the autumn chill is setting in.'

He popped his head back in his secretary's room. 'By the way, what did you think of that young woman who came yesterday?'

Miss Lemon, arrested as she was about to plunge her fingers on the typewriter, said briefly, 'Foreign.'

'Yes, yes.'

'Obviously foreign.'

'You do not think anything more about her than that?'

Miss Lemon considered. 'I had no means of judging her capability in any way.' She added rather doubtfully, 'She seemed upset about something.'

'Yes. She is suspected, you see, of stealing! Not money, but papers, from her employer.'

'Dear, dear,' said Miss Lemon. 'Important papers?'

'It seems highly probable. It is equally probable though, that he has not lost anything at all.'

'Oh well,' said Miss Lemon, giving her employer a special look that she always gave and which announced that she wished to get rid of him so that she could get on with proper fervour with her work. 'Well, I always say that it's better to know where you are when you are employing someone, and buy British.'

Hercule Poirot went out. His first visit was to Borodene Mansions. He took a taxi. Alighting at the courtyard he cast his eyes around. A uniformed porter was standing in one of the doorways, whistling a somewhat doleful melody. As Poirot advanced upon him, he said:

'Yes, sir?'

'I wondered,' said Poirot, 'if you can tell me anything about a very sad occurrence that took place here recently.'

'Sad occurrence?' said the porter. 'Nothing that I know of.'

'A lady who threw herself, or shall we say fell from one of the upper storeys, and was killed.'

'Oh, *that*. I don't know anything about that because I've only been here a week, you see. Hi, Joe.'

A porter emerging from the opposite side of the block came over.

'You'd know about the lady as fell from the seventh. About a month ago, was it?'

'Not quite as much as that,' said Joe. He was an elderly, slow-speaking man. 'Nasty business it was.'

'She was killed instantly?'

'Yes.'

'What was her name? It may, you understand, have been a relative of mine,' Poirot explained. He was not a man who had any scruples about departing from the truth.

'Indeed, sir. Very sorry to hear it. She was a Mrs Charpentier.'

'She had been in the flat some time?'

'Well, let me see now. About a year – a year and a half perhaps. No, I think it must have been about two years. No. 76, seventh floor.'

'That is the top floor?'

'Yes, sir. A Mrs Charpentier.'

Poirot did not press for any other descriptive information since he might be presumed to know such things about his own relative. Instead he asked:

'Did it cause much excitement, much questioning? What time of day was it?'

'Five or six o'clock in the morning, I think. No warning or anything. Just down she came. In spite of being so early we got a crowd almost at once, pushing through the railing over there. You know what people are.'

'And the police, of course.'

'Oh yes, the police came quite quickly. And a doctor and an

ambulance. All the usual,' said the porter rather in the weary tone of one who had had people throwing themselves out of a seventh-storey window once or twice every month.

'And I suppose people came down from the flats when they heard what had happened.'

'Oh, there wasn't so many coming from the flats because for one thing with the noise of traffic and everything around here most of them didn't know about it. Someone or other said she gave a bit of a scream as she came down, but not so that it caused any real commotion. It was only people in the street, passing by, who saw it happen. And then, of course, they craned their necks over the railings, and other people saw them craning, and joined them. You know what an accident is!'

Poirot assured him he knew what an accident was.

'She lived alone?' he said, making it only half a question.

'That's right.'

'But she had friends, I suppose, among the other flat dwellers?'

Joe shrugged and shook his head. 'May have done. I couldn't say. Never saw her in the restaurant much with any of our lot. She had outside friends to dinner here sometimes. No, I wouldn't say she was specially pally with anybody here. You'd do best,' said Joe, getting slightly restive, 'to go and have a chat with Mr McFarlane who's in charge here if you want to know about her.'

'Ah, I thank you. Yes, that is what I mean to do.'

'His office is in that block over there, sir. On the ground floor. You'll see it marked up on the door.'

Poirot went as directed. He detached from his briefcase the top letter with which Miss Lemon had supplied him, and which was marked 'Mr McFarlane'. Mr McFarlane turned out to be a good-looking, shrewd-looking man of about forty-five. Poirot handed him the letter. He opened and read it.

'Ah yes,' he said, 'I see.'

He laid it down on the desk and looked at Poirot.

'The owners have instructed me to give you all the help I can about the sad death of Mrs Louise Charpentier. Now what do you want to know exactly, Monsieur' – he glanced at the letter again – 'Monsieur Poirot?'

'This is, of course, all quite confidential,' said Poirot. 'Her relatives have been communicated with by the police and by a solicitor, but they were anxious, as I was coming to England, that I should get a few more *personal* facts, if you understand me. It is distressing when one can get only official reports.'

'Yes, quite so. Yes, I quite understand that it must be. Well, I'll tell you anything I can.'

'How long had she been here and how did she come to take the flat?'

'She'd been here – I can look it up exactly – about two years. There was a vacant tenancy and I imagine that the lady who was leaving, being an acquaintance of hers, told her in advance that she was giving it up. That was a Mrs Wilder. Worked for the BBC. Had been in London for some time, but was going to Canada. Very nice lady – I don't think she knew the deceased well at all. Just happened to mention she was giving up the flat. Mrs Charpentier liked the flat.'

'You found her a suitable tenant?' There was a very faint hesitation before Mr McFarlane answered:

'She was a satisfactory tenant, yes.'

'You need not mind telling me,' said Hercule Poirot. 'There were wild parties, eh? A little too – shall we say – gay in her entertaining?'

Mr McFarlane stopped being so discreet.

'There *were* a few complaints from time to time, but mostly from elderly people.'

Hercule Poirot made a significant gesture.

'A bit too fond of the bottle, yes, sir – and in with quite a gay lot. It made for a bit of trouble now and again.'

'And she was fond of the gentlemen?'

'Well, I wouldn't like to go as far as *that.*'

'No, no, but one understands.'

'Of course she wasn't so young.'

'Appearances are very often deceptive. How old would you have said she was?'

'It's difficult to say. Forty – forty-five.' He added, 'Her health wasn't good, you know.'

'So I understand.'

'She drank too much – no doubt about it. And then she'd get

very depressed. Nervous about herself. Always going to doctors, I believe, and not believing what they told her. Ladies do get it into their heads – especially about that time of life – she thought that she had cancer. Was quite sure of it. The doctor reassured her but she didn't believe him. He said at the inquest that there was nothing really wrong with her. Oh well, one hears of things like that every day. She got all worked up and one fine day –' he nodded.

'It is very sad,' said Poirot. 'Did she have any special friends among the residents of the flats?'

'Not that I know of. This place, you see, isn't what I call the matey kind. They're mostly people in business, in jobs.'

'I was thinking possibly of Miss Claudia Reece-Holland. I wondered if they had known each other.'

'Miss Reece-Holland? No, I don't think so. Oh I mean they were probably acquaintances, talked when they went up in the lift together, that sort of thing. But I don't think there was much social contact of any kind. You see, they would be in a different generation. I mean –' Mr McFarlane seemed a little flustered. Poirot wondered why.

He said, 'One of the other girls who share Miss Holland's flat knew Mrs Charpentier, I believe – Miss Norma Restarick.'

'Did she? I wouldn't know – she's only come here quite recently, I hardly know her by sight. Rather a frightened-looking young lady. Not long out of school, I'd say.' He added, 'Is there anything more I can do for you, sir?'

'No, thank you. You've been most kind. I wonder if possibly I could see the flat. Just in order to be able to say –' Poirot paused, not particularising what he wanted to be able to say.

'Well, now, let me see. A Mr Travers has got it now. He's in the City all day. Yes, come up with me if you like, sir.'

They went up to the seventh floor. As Mr McFarlane introduced his key one of the numbers fell from the door and narrowly avoided Poirot's patent-leather shoe. He hopped nimbly and then bent to pick it up. He replaced the spike which fixed it on the door very carefully.

'These numbers are loose,' he said.

'I'm very sorry, sir. I'll make a note of it. Yes, they wear loose from time to time. Well, here we are.'

Poirot went into the living-room. At the moment it had little personality. The walls were papered with a paper resembling grained wood. It had conventional comfortable furniture, the only personal touch was a television set and a certain number of books.

'All the flats are partly furnished, you see,' said Mr McFarlane. 'The tenants don't need to bring anything of their own, unless they want to. We cater very largely for people who come and go.'

'And the decorations are all the same?'

'Not entirely. People seem to like this raw wood effect. Good background for pictures. The only things that are different are on the one wall facing the door. We have a whole set of frescoes which people can choose from.

'We have a set of ten,' said Mr McFarlane with some pride. 'There is the Japanese one – very artistic, don't you think? – and there is an English garden one; a very striking one of birds; one of trees, a Harlequin one, a rather interesting abstract effect – lines and cubes, in vividly contrasting colours, that sort of thing. They're all designs by good artists. Our furniture is all the same. Two choices of colours, or of course people can add what they like of their own. But they don't usually bother.'

'Most of them are not, as you might say, home-makers,' Poirot suggested.

'No, rather the bird of passage type, or busy people who want solid comfort, good plumbing and all that but aren't particularly interested in decoration, though we've had one or two of the do-it-yourself type, which isn't really satisfactory from our point of view. We've had to put a clause in the lease saying they've got to put things back as they found them – or pay for that being done.'

They seemed to be getting rather far away from the subject of Mrs Charpentier's death. Poirot approached the window.

'It was from here?' he murmured delicately.

'Yes. That's the window. The left-hand one. It has a balcony.'

Poirot looked out down below.

'Seven floors,' he said. 'A long way.'

'Yes, death was instantaneous, I am glad to say. Of course, it might have been an accident.'

Poirot shook his head.

'You cannot seriously suggest that, Mr McFarlane. It *must* have been deliberate.'

'Well, one always likes to suggest an easier possibility. She wasn't a happy woman, I'm afraid.'

'Thank you,' said Poirot, 'for your great courtesy. I shall be able to give her relations in France a very clear picture.'

His own picture of what had occurred was not as clear as he would have liked. So far there had been nothing to support his theory that the death of Louise Charpentier had been important. He repeated the Christian name thoughtfully. Louise . . . Why had the name Louise some haunting memory about it? He shook his head. He thanked Mr McFarlane and left.

CHAPTER 17

Chief Inspector Neele was sitting behind his desk looking very official and formal. He greeted Poirot politely and motioned him to a chair. As soon as the young man who had introduced Poirot to the presence had left, Chief Inspector Neele's manner changed.

'And what are you after now, you secretive old devil?' he said.

'As to that,' said Poirot, 'you already know.'

'Oh yes, I've rustled up some stuff but I don't think there's much for you from that particular hole.'

'Why call it a hole?'

'Because you're so exactly like a good mouser. A cat sitting over a hole waiting for the mouse to come out. Well, if you ask me, there isn't any mouse in this particular hole. Mind you, I don't say that you couldn't unearth *some* dubious transactions. You know these financiers. I dare say there's a lot of hoky-poky business, and all that, about minerals and concessions and oil and all those things. But Joshua Restarick Ltd. has got a good reputation. Family business – or used to be – but you can't call it that now. Simon Restarick hadn't any children, and his brother Andrew Restarick only has this daughter. There was an old aunt on the mother's side. Andrew Restarick's daughter lived with her after she left school and her own mother died. The aunt died of a stroke about six months ago. Mildly potty, I believe – belonged to a few rather peculiar religious societies. No harm in them. Simon Restarick was a perfectly plain type of shrewd business man, and had a social wife. They were married rather late in life.'

'And Andrew?'

'Andrew seems to have suffered from wanderlust. Nothing known against him. Never stayed anywhere long, wandered about South Africa, South America, Kenya and a good many other places. His brother pressed him to come back more than once, but he wasn't having any. He didn't like London or business, but he seems to have had the Restarick family flair for making money. He went after mineral deposits, things like that. He wasn't an elephant hunter or an archaeologist or a plant man or any of those things. All his deals were business deals and they always turned out well.'

'So he also in his way is conventional?'

'Yes, that about covers it. I don't know what made him come back to England after his brother died. Possibly a new wife – he's married again. Good-looking woman a good deal younger than he is. At the moment they're living with old Sir Roderick Horsefield whose sister had married Andrew Restarick's uncle. But I imagine that's only temporary. Is any of this news to you? Or do you know it all already?'

'I've heard most of it,' said Poirot. 'Is there any insanity in the family on either side?'

'Shouldn't think so, apart from old Auntie and her fancy religions. And that's not unusual in a woman who lives alone.'

'So all you can tell me really is that there is a lot of money,' said Poirot.

'Lots of money,' said Chief Inspector Neele. 'And all quite respectable. Some of it, mark you, Andrew Restarick brought into the firm. South African concessions, mines, mineral deposits. I'd say that by the time these were developed, or placed on the market, there'd be a very large sum of money indeed.'

'And who will inherit it?' said Poirot.

'That depends on how Andrew Restarick leaves it. It's up to him, but I'd say that there's no one obvious, except his wife and his daughter.'

'So they both stand to inherit a very large amount of money one day?'

'I should say so. I expect there are a good many family trusts and things like that. All the usual City gambits.'

'There is, for instance, no other woman in whom he might be interested?'

'Nothing known of such a thing. I shouldn't think it likely. He's got a good-looking new wife.'

'A young man,' said Poirot thoughtfully, 'could easily learn all this?'

'You mean and marry the daughter? There's nothing to stop him, even if she was made a ward of Court or something like that. Of course her father could then disinherit her if he wanted to.'

Poirot looked down at a neatly written list in his hand.

'What about the Wedderburn Gallery?'

'I wondered how you'd got on to that. Were you consulted by a client about a forgery?'

'Do they deal in forgeries?'

'People don't deal in forgeries,' said Chief Inspector Neele reprovingly. 'There *was* a rather unpleasant business. A millionaire from Texas over here buying pictures, and paying incredible sums for them. They sold him a Renoir and a Van Gogh. The Renoir was a small head of a girl and there was some query about it. There seemed no reason to believe that the Wedderburn Gallery had not bought it in the first place in all good faith. There was a case about it. A great many art experts came and gave their verdicts. In fact, as usual, in the end they all seemed to contradict each other. The gallery offered to take it back in any case. However, the millionaire didn't change his mind, since the latest fashionable expert swore that it was perfectly genuine. So he stuck to it. All the same there's been a bit of suspicion hanging round the gallery ever since.'

Poirot looked again at his list.

'And what about Mr David Baker? Have you looked him up for me?'

'Oh, he's one of the usual mob. Riff-raff – go about in gangs and break up night clubs. Live on purple hearts – heroin – Coke – Girls go mad about them. He's the kind they moan over saying his life has been so hard and he's such a wonderful genius. His painting is not *appreciated.* Nothing but good old sex, if you ask me.'

Poirot consulted his list again.

'Do you know anything about Mr Reece-Holland, MP?'

'Doing quite well, politically. Got the gift of the gab all right. One or two slightly peculiar transactions in the City, but he's wriggled out of them quite neatly. I'd say he was a slippery one. He's made quite a good deal of money off and on by rather doubtful means.'

Poirot came to his last point.

'What about Sir Roderick Horsefield?'

'Nice old boy but gaga. What a nose you have, Poirot, get it into everything, don't you? Yes, there's been a lot of trouble in the Special Branch. It's this craze for memoirs. Nobody knows what indiscreet revelations are going to be made next. All the old boys, service and otherwise, are racing hard to bring out their own particular brand of what they remember of the indiscretions of others! Usually it doesn't much matter, but sometimes – well, you know, Cabinets change their policies and you don't want to afront someone's susceptibilities or give the wrong publicity, so we have to try and muffle the old boys. Some of them are not too easy. But you'll have to go to the Special Branch if you want to nose into any of that. I shouldn't think there was much wrong. The trouble is they don't destroy the papers they should. They keep the lot. However, I don't think there is much in that, but we have evidence that a certain Power is nosing around.'

Poirot gave a deep sigh.

'Haven't I helped?' asked the Chief Inspector.

'I am very glad to get the real low-down from official quarters. But no, I don't think there is much help in what you have told me.' He sighed and then said, 'What would be your opinion if someone said to you casually that a woman – a young attractive woman – wore a wig?'

'Nothing in that,' said Chief Inspector Neele, and added, with a slight asperity, 'my wife wears a wig when we're travelling any time. It saves a lot of trouble.'

'I beg your pardon,' said Hercule Poirot.

As the two men bade each other good-bye, the Chief Inspector asked:

'You got all the dope, I suppose, on that suicide case you were asking about in the flats? I had it sent round to you.'

'Yes, thank you. The official facts, at least. A bare record.'

'There was something you were talking about just now that brought it back to my mind. I'll think of it in a moment. It was the usual, rather sad story. Gay woman, fond of men, enough money to live upon, no particular worries, drank too much and went down the hill. And then she gets what I call the health bug. You know, they're convinced they have cancer or something in that line. They consult a doctor and he tells them they're all right, and they go home and don't believe him. If you ask me it's usually because they find they're no longer as attractive as they used to be to men. That's what's really depressing them. Yes, it happens all the time. They're lonely, I suppose, poor devils. Mrs Charpentier was just one of them. I don't suppose that any –' he stopped. 'Oh yes, of course, I remember. You were asking about one of our MPs, Reece-Holland. He's a fairly gay one himself in a discreet way. Anyway, Louise Charpentier was his mistress at one time. That's all.'

'Was it a serious liaison?'

'Oh I shouldn't say so particularly. They went to some rather questionable clubs together and things like that. You know, we keep a discreet eye on things of that kind. But there was never anything in the Press about them. Nothing of that kind.'

'I see.'

'But it lasted for a certain time. They were seen together, off and on, for about six months, but I don't think she was the only one and I don't think he was the only one either. So you can't make anything of that, can you?'

'I do not think so,' said Poirot.

'But all the same,' he said to himself as he went down the stairs, 'all the same, it is a link. It explains the embarrassment of Mr McFarlane. It is a link, a tiny link, a link between Emlyn Reece-Holland, MP, and Louise Charpentier.' It didn't mean anything probably. Why should it? But yet – 'I know too much,' said Poirot angrily to himself. 'I know too much. I know a little about everything and everyone but I cannot get my pattern. Half these facts are irrelevant. I want a pattern. A pattern. My kingdom for a pattern,' he said aloud.

'I beg your pardon, sir,' said the lift boy, turning a startled head.

'It is nothing,' said Poirot.

CHAPTER 18

Poirot paused at the doorway of the Wedderburn Gallery to inspect a picture which depicted three aggressive-looking cows with vastly elongated bodies overshadowed by a colossal and complicated design of windmills. The two seemed to have nothing to do with each other or the very curious purple colouring.

'Interesting, isn't it?' said a soft purring voice.

A middle-aged man, who at first sight seemed to have shown a smile which exhibited an almost excessive number of beautiful white teeth, was at his elbow.

'Such *freshness*.'

He had large white plump hands which he waved as though he was using them in an arabesque.

'Clever exhibition. Closed last week. Claude Raphael show opened the day before yesterday. It's going to do well. Very well indeed.'

'Ah,' said Poirot and was led through grey velvet curtains into a long room.

Poirot made a few cautious if doubtful remarks. The plump man took him in hand in a practised manner. Here was someone, he obviously felt, who must not be frightened away. He was a very experienced man in the art of salesmanship. You felt at once that you were welcome to be in his gallery all day if you liked without making a purchase. Sheerly, solely looking at these delightful pictures – though when you entered the gallery you might not have thought that they *were* delightful. But by the time you went out you were convinced that delightful was exactly the word to describe them. After receiving some useful artistic instruction, and making a few of the amateur's stock remarks such as 'I rather like that one,' Mr Boscombe responded encouragingly by some such phrase as:

'Now that's very interesting that you should say that. It shows, if I may say so, great perspicacity. Of course you know it isn't the ordinary reaction. Most people prefer something – well, shall I say slightly *obvious* like that' – he pointed to a blue and green striped effect arranged in one corner of the canvas – 'but this, yes, you've spotted the quality of the thing. I'd say myself – of course it's only my personal opinion – that that's one of Raphael's masterpieces.'

Poirot and he looked together with both their heads on one side at an orange lop-sided diamond with two human eyes depending from it by what looked like a spidery thread. Pleasant relations established and time obviously being infinite, Poirot remarked:

'I think a Miss Frances Cary works for you, does she not?'

'Ah yes. Frances. Clever girl that. Very artistic and very competent too. Just come back from Portugal where she's been arranging an art show for us. Very successful. Quite a good artist herself, but not I should say really creative, if you understand me. She is better on the business side. I think she recognises that herself.'

'I understand that she is a good patron of the arts?'

'Oh yes. She's interested in *Les Jeunes*. Encourages talent, persuaded me to give a show for a little group of young artists last spring. It was quite successful – the Press noticed it – all in a small way, you understand. Yes, she has her protégés.'

'I am, you understand, somewhat old-fashioned. Some of these young men – *vraiment*!' Poirot's hands went up.

'Ah,' said Mr Boscombe indulgently, 'you mustn't go by their appearances. It's just a fashion, you know. Beards and jeans or brocades and hair. Just a passing phase.'

'David someone,' said Poirot. 'I forget his last name. Miss Cary seemed to think highly of him.'

'Sure you don't mean Peter Cardiff? He's her present protégé. Mind you, I'm not *quite* so sure about him as she is. He's really not so much *avant garde* as he is – well, positively reactionary. Quite – quite – Burne-Jones sometimes! Still, one never knows. You do get these reactions. She acts as his model occasionally.'

'David Baker – that was the name I was trying to remember,' said Poirot.

'He is not bad,' said Mr Boscombe, without enthusiasm. 'Not much *originality*, in my opinion. He was one of the group of artists I mentioned, but he didn't make any particular impression. A *good* painter, mind, but not striking. Derivative!'

Poirot went home. Miss Lemon presented him with letters to sign, and departed with them duly signed. George served him with an *omellette fines herbes* garnished, as you might say, with a discreetly sympathetic manner. After lunch, as Poirot was setting himself in his square-backed armchair with his coffee at his elbow, the telephone rang.

'Mrs Oliver, sir,' said George, lifting the telephone and placing it at his elbow.

Poirot picked up the receiver reluctantly. He did not want to talk to Mrs Oliver. He felt that she would urge upon him something which he did not want to do.

'M. Poirot?'

'*C'est moi.*'

'Well, what are you doing? What have you done?'

'I am sitting in this chair,' said Poirot. 'Thinking,' he added.

'Is that all?' said Mrs Oliver.

'It is the important thing,' said Poirot. 'Whether I shall have success in it or not I do not know.'

'But you must find that girl. She's probably been kidnapped.'

'It would certainly seem so,' said Poirot. 'And I have a letter here which came by the midday post from her father, urging me to come and see him and tell him what progress I have made.'

'Well, what progress *have* you made?'

'At the moment,' said Poirot reluctantly, 'none.'

'Really, M. Poirot, you really must take a grip on yourself.'

'You, too!'

'What do you mean, me too?'

'Urging me on.'

'Why don't you go down to that place in Chelsea, where I was hit on the head?'

'And get myself hit on the head also?'

'I simply don't understand you,' said Mrs Oliver. '*I* gave you a clue by finding the girl in the café. You said so.'

'I know, I know.'

'What about that woman who threw herself out of a window? Haven't you got anything out of that?'

'I have made inquiries, yes.'

'Well?'

'Nothing. The woman is one of many. They are attractive when young, they have affairs, they are passionate, they have still more affairs, they get less attractive, they are unhappy and drink too much, they think they have cancer or some fatal disease and so at last in despair and loneliness they throw themselves out of a window!'

'You said her death was important – that it *meant* something.'

'It ought to have done.'

'Really!' At a loss for further comment, Mrs Oliver rang off.

Poirot leant back in his armchair, as far as he could lean back since it was of an upright nature, waved to George to remove the coffee pot and also the telephone and proceeded to reflect upon what he did or did not know. To clarify his thoughts he spoke out loud. He recalled three philosophic questions.

'What do I know? What can I hope? What ought I to do?'

He was not sure that he got them in the right order or indeed if they were quite the right questions, but he reflected upon them.

'Perhaps I *am* too old,' said Hercule Poirot, at the bottom depths of despair. 'What *do* I know?'

Upon reflection he thought that he knew too much! He laid that question aside for the moment.

'What can I hope?' Well, one could always hope. He could hope that those excellent brains of his, so much better than anybody else's, would come up sooner or later with an answer to a problem which he felt uneasily that he did not really understand.

'What ought I to do?' Well, that was very definite. What he ought to do was to go and call upon Mr Andrew Restarick who was obviously distraught about his daughter, and who would no doubt blame Poirot for not having by now delivered the daughter in person. Poirot could understand that, and sympathised with his point of view, but disliked having to present himself in such a very unfavourable light. The only other thing he could do was to telephone to a certain number and ask what developments there had been.

But before he did that, he would go back to the question he had laid aside.

'What do I know?'

He knew that the Wedderburn Gallery was under suspicion – so far it had kept on the right side of the law, but it would not hesitate at swindling ignorant millionaires by selling them dubious pictures.

He recalled Mr Boscombe with his plump white hands and his plentiful teeth, and decided that he did not like him. He was the kind of man who was almost certainly up to dirty work, though he would no doubt protect *himself* remarkably well. That was a fact that might come into use because it might connect up with David Baker. Then there was David Baker himself, the Peacock. What did he know about him? He had met him, he had conversed with him, and he had formed certain opinions about him. He would do a crooked deal of any kind for money, he would marry a rich heiress for her money and not for love, he might perhaps be bought off. Yes, he probably could be bought off. Andrew Restarick certainly believed so and he was probably right. Unless –

He considered Andrew Restarick, thinking more of the picture on the wall hanging above him than of the man himself. He remembered the strong features, the jutting out chin, the air of resolution, of decision. Then he thought of Mrs Andrew Restarick, deceased. The bitter lines of her mouth . . . Perhaps he would go down to Crosshedges again and look at that portrait, so as to see it more clearly because there might be a clue to Norma in that. Norma – no, he must not think of Norma yet. What else was there?

There was Mary Restarick whom the girl Sonia said must have a lover because she went up to London so often. He considered that point but he did not think that Sonia was right. He thought Mrs Restarick was much more likely to go to London in order to look at possible properties to buy, luxury flats, houses in Mayfair, decorators, all the things that money in the metropolis could buy.

Money . . . It seemed to him that all the points that had been passing through his mind came to this in the end. Money. The importance of money. There was a great deal of money in this case. Somehow, in some way that was not obvious, money counted. Money played its part. So far there had been nothing to justify his belief that the tragic death of Mrs Charpentier had been the work of Norma. No sign of evidence, no motive; yet it seemed to him that there *was* an undeniable link. The girl had said that she 'might have committed a murder'. A death had taken place only a day or two previously. A death that had occurred in the building where she lived. Surely it would be too much of a coincidence that that death should not be connected in any way? He thought again of the mysterious illness which had affected Mary Restarick. An occurrence so simple as to be classic in its outline. A poison case where the poisoner was – must be – one of the household. Had Mary Restarick poisoned herself, had her husband tried to poison her, had the girl Sonia administered poison? Or had Norma been the culprit? Everything pointed, Hercule Poirot had to confess, to Norma as being the logical person.

'*Tout de même*,' said Poirot, 'since I cannot find anything, *et bien* then the logic falls out of the window.'

He sighed, rose to his feet and told George to fetch him a taxi. He must keep his appointment with Andrew Restarick.

CHAPTER 19

Claudia Reece-Holland was not in the office today. Instead, a middle-aged woman received Poirot. She said that Mr Restarick was waiting for him and ushered him into Restarick's room.

'Well?' Restarick hardly waited until he had come through the door. 'Well, what about my daughter?'

Poirot spread out his hands.

'As yet – nothing.'

'But look here, man, there must be something – some clue. A girl can't just disappear into thin air.'

'Girls have done it before now and will do it again.'

'Did you understand that no expense was to be spared, none whatever? I – I can't go on like this.'

He seemed completely on edge by this time. He looked thinner and his red-rimmed eyes spoke of sleepless nights.

'I know what your anxiety must be, but I assure you that I have done everything possible to trace her. These things, alas, cannot be hurried.'

'She may have lost her memory or – or she may – I mean, she might be sick. Ill.'

Poirot thought he knew what the broken form of the sentence meant. Restarick had been about to say 'she may perhaps be dead'.

He sat down on the other side of the desk and said:

'Believe me, I appreciate your anxiety and I have to say to you once again that the results would be a lot quicker if you consulted the police.'

'*No!*' The word broke out explosively.

'They have greater facilities, more lines of inquiry. I assure you it is not only a question of money. Money cannot give you the same result as a highly efficient organisation can do.'

'Man, it's no use your talking in that soothing way. Norma is my daughter. My only daughter, the only flesh and blood I've got.'

'Are you sure that you have told me everything – everything possible – about your daughter?'

'What more *can* I tell you?'

'That is for you to say, not me. Have there been, for instance, any incidents in the past?'

'Such as? What do you mean, man?'

'Any definite history of mental instability.'

'You think that – that –'

'How do I know? How can I know?'

'And how do I know?' said Restarick, suddenly bitter. 'What do I know of her? All these years. Grace was a bitter woman. A woman who did not easily forgive or forget. Sometimes I feel – I feel that she was the wrong person to have brought Norma up.'

He got up, walked up and down the room and then sat down again.

'Of course I shouldn't have left my wife. I know that. I left her to bring up the child. But then at the time I suppose I made excuses for myself. Grace was a woman of excellent character devoted to Norma. A thoroughly good guardian for her. But was she? Was she really? Some of the letters Grace wrote to me were as though they breathed anger and revenge. Well, I suppose that's natural enough. But I was away all those years. I should have come back, come back more often and found out how the child was getting on. I suppose I had a bad conscience. Oh, it's no good making excuses now.'

He turned his head sharply.

'Yes. I did think when I saw her again that Norma's whole attitude was neurotic, indisciplined. I hoped she and Mary would – would get on better after a little while but I have to admit that

I don't feel the girl was entirely normal. I felt it would be better for her to have a job in London and come home for weekends, but not to be forced into Mary's company the whole time. Oh, I suppose I've made a mess of everything. But where is she, M. Poirot? Where is she? Do you think she may have lost her memory? One hears of such things.'

'Yes,' said Poirot, 'that is a possibility. In her state, she may be wandering about quite unaware of who she is. Or she may have had an accident. That is less likely. I can assure you that I have made all inquiries in hospitals and other places.'

'You don't think she is – you don't think she's *dead*?'

'She would be easier to find dead than alive, I can assure you. Please calm yourself, Mr Restarick. Remember she may have friends of whom you know nothing. Friends in any part of England, friends whom she has known while living with her mother, or with her aunt, or friends who were friends of school friends of hers. All these things take time to sort out. It may be – you must prepare yourself – that she is with a boy friend of some kind.'

'David Baker? If I thought that –'

'She is not with David Baker. That,' said Poirot dryly, 'I ascertained first of all.'

'How do I know what friends she has?' He sighed. 'If I find her, *when* I find her – I'd rather put it that way – I'm going to take her out of all this.'

'Out of all what?'

'Out of this country. I have been miserable, M. Poirot, miserable ever since I returned here. I always hated City life. The boring round of office routine, continual consultations with lawyers and financiers. The life I liked was always the same. Travelling, moving about from place to place, going to wild and inaccessible places. That's the life for me. I should never have left it. I should have sent for Norma to come out to me and, as I say, when I find her that's what I'm going to do. Already I'm being approached with various take-over bids. Well, they can have the whole caboodle on very advantageous terms. I'll take the cash and go back to a country that *means* something, that's *real*.'

'Aha! And what will your wife say to that?'

'Mary? She's used to that life. That's where she comes from.'

'To *les femmes* with plenty of money,' said Poirot, 'London can be very attractive.'

'She'll see it my way.'

The telephone rang on his desk. He picked it up.

'Yes? Oh. From Manchester? Yes. If it's Claudia Reece-Holland, put her through.'

He waited a minute.

'Hallo, Claudia. Yes. Speak up – it's a very bad line, I can't hear you. They agreed? . . . Ah, pity . . . No, I think you did very well . . . Right . . . All right then. Take the evening train back. We'll discuss it further tomorrow morning.'

He replaced the telephone on its rest.

'That's a competent girl,' he said.

'Miss Reece-Holland?'

'Yes. Unusually competent. Takes a lot of bother off my shoulders. I gave her pretty well *carte blanche* to put through this deal in Manchester on her own terms. I really felt I couldn't concentrate. And she's done exceedingly well. She's as good as a man in some ways.'

He looked at Poirot, suddenly bringing himself back to the present.

'Ah yes, M. Poirot. Well, I'm afraid I've rather lost my grip. Do you need more money for expenses?'

'No, Monsieur. I assure you that I will do my utmost to restore your daughter sound and well. I have taken all possible precautions for her safety.'

He went out through the outer office. When he reached the street he looked up at the sky.

'A definite answer to one question,' he said, 'that is what I need.'

CHAPTER 20

Hercule Poirot looked up at the façade of the dignified Georgian house in what had been until recently a quiet street in an old-fashioned market town. Progress was rapidly overtaking it, but the new supermarket, the Gifte Shoppe, Margery's Boutique,

Peg's Café, and a palatial new bank, had all chosen sites in Croft Road and not encroached on the narrow High Street.

The brass knocker on the door was brightly polished, Poirot noted with approval. He pressed the bell at the side.

It was opened almost at once by a tall distinguished-looking woman with upswept grey hair and an energetic manner.

'M. Poirot? You are very punctual. Come in.'

'Miss Battersby?'

'Certainly.' She held back the door. Poirot entered. She deposited his hat on the hall stand and led the way to a pleasant room overlooking a narrow walled garden.

She waved towards a chair and sat down herself in an attitude of expectation. It was clear that Miss Battersby was not one to lose time in conventional utterances.

'You are, I think, the former Principal of Meadowfield School?'

'Yes. I retired a year ago. I understand you wished to see me on the subject of Norma Restarick, a former pupil.'

'That is right.'

'In your letters,' said Miss Battersby, 'you gave me no further details.' She added, 'I may say that I know who you are, M. Poirot. I should therefore like a little more information before I proceed further. Are you, for instance, thinking of employing Norma Restarick?'

'That is not my intention, no.'

'Knowing what your profession is you understand why I should want further details. Have you, for instance, an introduction to me from any of Norma's relations?'

'Again, no,' said Hercule Poirot. 'I will explain myself further.'

'Thank you.'

'In actual fact, I am employed by Miss Restarick's father, Andrew Restarick.'

'Ah. He has recently returned to England, I believe, after many years' absence.'

'That is so.'

'But you do not bring me a letter of introduction from him?'

'I did not ask him for one.'

Miss Battersby looked at him inquiringly.

'He might have insisted on coming with me,' said Hercule

Poirot. 'That would have hampered me in asking you the questions that I wish to ask, because it is likely that the answers to them might cause him pain and distress. There is no reason why he should be caused further distress than he is already suffering at this moment.'

'Has anything happened to Norma?'

'I hope not . . . There is, however, a possibility of that. You remember the girl, Miss Battersby?'

'I remember all my pupils. I have an excellent memory. Meadowfield, in any case, is not a very large school. Two hundred girls, no more.'

'Why have you resigned from it, Miss Battersby?'

'Really, M. Poirot, I cannot see that that is any of your business.'

'No, I am merely expressing my quite natural curiosity.'

'I am seventy. Is that not a reason?'

'Not in your case, I should say. You appear to me to be in full vigour and energy, fully capable of continuing your headmistress-ship for a good many years to come.'

'Times change, M. Poirot. One does not always like the way they are changing. I will satisfy your curiosity. I found I was having less and less patience with *parents*. Their aims for their daughters are short-sighted and quite frankly stupid.'

Miss Battersby was, as Poirot knew from looking up her qualifications, a very well-known mathematician.

'Do not think that I lead an idle life,' said Miss Battersby. 'I lead a life where the work is far more congenial to me. I coach senior students. And now, please, may I know the reason for your interest in the girl, Norma Restarick?'

'There is some occasion for anxiety. She has, to put it baldly, disappeared.'

Miss Battersby continued to look quite unconcerned.

'Indeed? When you say "disappeared", I presume you mean that she has left home without telling her parents where she was going. Oh, I believe her mother is dead, so without telling her father where she was going. That is really not at all uncommon nowadays, M. Poirot. Mr Restarick has not consulted the police?'

'He is adamant on that subject. He refuses definitely.'

'I can assure you that I have no knowledge as to where the girl is. I have heard nothing from her. Indeed, I have had no news from her since she left Meadowfield. So I fear I cannot help you in any way.'

'It is not precisely that kind of information that I want. I want to know *what kind of a girl she is* – how you would describe her. Not her personal appearance. I do not mean that. I mean as to her personality and characteristics.'

'Norma, at school, was a perfectly ordinary girl. Not scholastically brilliant, but her work was adequate.'

'Not a neurotic type?'

Miss Battersby considered. Then she said slowly: 'No, I would not say so. Not more, that is, than might be expected considering her home circumstances.'

'You mean her invalid mother?'

'Yes. She came from a broken home. The father, to whom I think she was very devoted, left home suddenly with another woman – a fact which her mother quite naturally resented. She probably upset her daughter more than she need have done by voicing her resentment without restraint.'

'Perhaps it may be more to the point if I ask you your opinion of the late Mrs Restarick?'

'What you are asking me for is my private opinion?'

'If you do not object?'

'No, I have no hesitation at all in answering your question. Home conditions are very important in a girl's life and I have always studied them as much as I can through the meagre information that comes to me. Mrs Restarick was a worthy and upright woman, I should say. Self-righteous, censorious and handicapped in life by being an extremely stupid one!'

'Ah,' said Poirot appreciatively.

'She was also, I would say, a *malade imaginaire*. A type that would exaggerate her ailments. The type of woman who is always in and out of nursing homes. An unfortunate home background for a girl – especially a girl who has no very definite personality of her own. Norma had no marked intellectual ambitions, she had no confidence in herself, she was not a girl to whom I would recommend a career. A nice ordinary job followed by marriage and children was what I would have hoped for her.'

'You saw – forgive me for asking – no signs at any time of mental instability?'

'Mental instability?' said Miss Battersby. 'Rubbish!'

'So that is what you say. Rubbish! And *not* neurotic?'

'Any girl, or almost any girl, can be neurotic, especially in adolescence, and in her first encounters with the world. She is still immature, and needs guidance in her first encounters with sex. Girls are frequently attracted to completely unsuitable, sometimes even dangerous young men. There are, it seems, no parents nowadays, or hardly any, with the strength of character to save them from this, so they often go through a time of hysterical misery, and perhaps make an unsuitable marriage which ends not long after in divorce.'

'But Norma showed no signs of mental instability?' Poirot persisted with the question.

'She is an emotional but normal girl,' said Miss Battersby. '*Mental instability!* As I said before – rubbish! She's probably run away with some young man to get married, and there's nothing more normal than that!'

CHAPTER 21

Poirot sat in his big square armchair. His hands rested on the arms, his eyes looked at the chimney-piece in front of him without seeing it. By his elbow was a small table and on it, neatly clipped together, were various documents. Reports from Mr Goby, information obtained from his friend, Chief Inspector Neele, a series of separate pages under the heading of 'Hearsay, gossip, rumour' and the sources from which it had been obtained.

At the moment he had no need to consult these documents. He had, in fact, read them through carefully and laid them there in case there was any particular point he wished to refer to once more. He wanted now to assemble together in his mind all that he knew and had learned because he was convinced that these things must form a pattern. There *must* be a pattern there. He was considering now, from what exact angle to approach it. He was not one to trust in enthusiasm for some particular intuition.

He was not an intuitive person – but he did have *feelings*. The important thing was not the feelings themselves – but what might have caused them. It was the cause that was interesting, the cause was so often not what you thought it was. You had very often to work it out by logic, by sense and by knowledge.

What did he *feel* about this case – what *kind* of a case was it? Let him start from the general, then proceed to the particular. What were the salient facts of this case?

Money was one of them, he thought, though he did not know *how*. Somehow or other, *money* . . . He also thought, increasingly so, that there was *evil* somewhere. He knew evil. He had met it before. He knew the tang of it, the taste of it, the way it went. The trouble was that here he did not yet know exactly where it *was*. He had taken certain steps to combat evil. He hoped they would be sufficient. Something was happening, something was in progress, *that was not yet accomplished*. Someone, somewhere, was in *danger*.

The trouble was that the facts pointed both ways. If the person he *thought* was in danger was really in danger, there seemed so far as he could see no reason *why*. Why should that particular person be in danger? There was no motive. If the person he thought was in danger was *not* in danger, then the whole approach might have to be completely reversed . . . Everything that pointed one way he must turn round and look at from the complete opposite point of view.

He left that for the moment in the balance, and he came from there to the personalities – to the *people*. What pattern did *they* make? What part were they playing?

First – Andrew Restarick. He had accumulated by now a fair amount of information about Andrew Restarick. A general picture of his life before and after going abroad. A restless man, never sticking to one place or purpose long, but generally liked. Nothing of the wastrel about him, nothing shoddy or tricky. Not, perhaps, a strong personality? Weak in many ways?

Poirot frowned, dissatisfied. That picture did not somehow fit the Andrew Restarick that he himself had met. Not *weak* surely, with that thrust-out chin, the steady eyes, the air of resolution. He had been a successful business man, too, apparently. Good at his job in the earlier years, and he had put through good deals in South Africa and in South America. He had increased his holdings. It was a success story that he had brought home with him, not one of failure. How then could he be a *weak* personality? Weak, perhaps, only where *women* were concerned. He had made a mistake in his marriage – married the wrong woman . . . Pushed into it perhaps by his family? And then he had met the other woman. Just that one woman? Or had there been several women? It was hard to find a record of that kind after so many years. Certainly he had not been a notoriously unfaithful husband. He had had a normal home, he had been fond, by all accounts, of his small daughter. But then he had come across a woman whom he had cared for enough to leave his home and to leave his country. It had been a real love affair.

But had it, perhaps, matched up with any additional motive? Dislike of office work, the City, the daily routine of London? He thought it might. It matched the pattern. He seemed, too, to have been a solitary type. Everyone had liked him both here and abroad, but there seemed no intimate friends. Indeed, it would have been difficult for him to have intimate friends abroad because he had never stopped in any one spot long enough. He had plunged into some gamble, attempted a coup, had made good, then tired of the thing and gone on somewhere else. Nomadic! A wanderer.

It still did not quite accord with his own picture of the man . . . A *picture*? The word stirred in his mind the memory of the picture that hung in Restarick's office, on the wall behind his desk. It had been a portrait of the same man fifteen years ago. How much difference had those fifteen years made in the man sitting there? Surprisingly little, on the whole! More grey in the hair, a heavier set to the shoulders, but the lines of character on the face were much the same. A determined face. A man who knew what he wanted, who meant to get it. A man who would take risks. A man with a certain ruthlessness.

Why, he wondered, had Restarick brought that picture up to London? They had been companion portraits of a husband and wife. Strictly speaking artistically, they should have remained together. Would a psychologist have said that subconsciously Restarick wanted to dissociate himself from his former wife once more, to separate himself from her? Was he then mentally still retreating from her personality although she was dead? An interesting point . . .

The pictures had presumably come out of storage with various other family articles of furnishing. Mary Restarick had no doubt selected certain personal objects to supplement the furniture of Crosshedges for which Sir Roderick had made room. He wondered whether Mary Restarick, the new wife, had liked hanging up that particular pair of portraits. More natural, perhaps, if she had put the first wife's portrait in an attic! But then he reflected that she would probably not have had an attic to stow away unwanted objects at Crosshedges. Presumably Sir Roderick had made room for a few family things whilst the returned couple were looking about for a suitable house in London. So it had not mattered much, and it would have been easier to hang both portraits. Besides, Mary Restarick seemed a sensible type of woman – not a jealous or emotional type.

'*Tout de même*,' thought Hercule Poirot to himself, '*les femmes*, they are all capable of jealousy, and sometimes the one you would consider the least likely!'

His thoughts passed to Mary Restarick, and he considered her in turn. It struck him that what was really odd was that he had so few thoughts about her! He had seen her only the once, and she had, somehow or other, not made much impression on him. A certain efficiency, he thought, and also a certain – how could he put it? – artificiality? ('But there, my friend,' said Hercule Poirot, again in parenthesis, 'there you are considering her wig!')

It was absurd really that one should know so little about a woman. A woman who was efficient and who wore a wig, and who was good-looking, and who was sensible, and who could feel anger. Yes, she had been angry when she had found the Peacock Boy wandering uninvited in her house. She had displayed it sharply and unmistakably. And the boy – he had seemed what? Amused, no more. But she had been angry, very angry at finding him there. Well, that was natural enough. He would not be any mother's choice for her daughter –

Poirot stopped short in his thoughts, shaking his head vexedly. Mary Restarick was *not* Norma's mother. Not for her the agony, the apprehension about a daughter making an unsuitable unhappy marriage, or announcing an illegitimate baby with an unsuitable father! What *did* Mary feel about Norma? Presumably, to begin with, that she was a thoroughly tiresome girl – who had picked up with a young man who was going to be obviously a source of worry and annoyance to Andrew Restarick. But after that? What had she thought and felt about a step-daughter who was apparently deliberately trying to poison her?

Her attitude seemed to have been the sensible one. She had wanted to get Norma out of the house, herself out of danger; and to co-operate with her husband in suppressing any scandal about what had happened. Norma came down for an occasional weekend to keep up appearances, but her life hence-forward was bound to centre in London. Even when the Restaricks moved into the house they were looking for, they would not suggest Norma living with them. Most girls, nowadays, lived away from their families. So that problem had been settled.

Except that, for Poirot, the question of who had administered poison to Mary Restarick was very far from settled. Restarick himself believed it was his daughter –

But Poirot wondered . . .

His mind played with the possibilities of the girl Sonia. What was she doing in that house? Why had she come there? She had Sir Roderick eating out of her hand all right – perhaps she had no wish to go back to her own country? Possibly her designs were purely matrimonial – old men of Sir Roderick's age married pretty young girls every day of the week. In the worldly sense, Sonia could do very well for herself. A secure social position, and widowhood to look forward to with a settled and sufficient income – or were her aims quite different? Had she gone to Kew Gardens with Sir Roderick's missing papers tucked between the pages of a book?

Had Mary Restarick become suspicious of her – of her activities, of her loyalties, of where she went on her days off, and of whom she met? And had Sonia, then, administered the substances which, in cumulative small doses, would arouse no suspicion of anything but ordinary gastroenteritis?

For the time being, he put the household at Crosshedges out of his mind.

He came, as Norma had come, to London, and proceeded to the consideration of three girls who shared a flat.

Claudia Reece-Holland, Frances Cary, Norma Restarick. Claudia

Reece-Holland, daughter of a well-known Member of Parliament, well off, capable, well trained, good-looking, a first-class secretary. Frances Cary, a country solicitor's daughter, artistic, had been to drama school for a short time, then to the Slade, chucked that also, occasionally worked for the Arts Council, now employed by an art gallery. Earned a good salary, was artistic and had bohemian associations. She knew the young man, David Baker, though not apparently more than casually. Perhaps she was in love with him? He was the kind of young man, Poirot thought, disliked generally by parents, members of the Establishment and also the police. Where the attraction lay for well-born girls Poirot failed to see. But one had to acknowledge it as a fact. What did he himself think of David?

A good-looking boy with the impudent and slightly amused air whom he had first seen in the upper storeys of Crosshedges, doing an errand for Norma (or reconnoitring on his own, who should say?). He had seen him again when he gave him a lift in his car. A young man of personality, giving indeed an impression of ability in what he chose to do. And yet there was clearly an unsatisfactory side to him. Poirot picked up one of the papers on the table by his side and studied it. A bad record though not positively criminal. Small frauds on garages, hooliganism, smashing up things, on probation twice. All those things were the fashion of the day. They did not come under Poirot's category of evil. He had been a promising painter, but had chucked it. He was the kind that did no steady work. He was vain, proud, a peacock in love with his own appearance. Was he anything more than that? Poirot wondered.

He stretched out an arm and picked up a sheet of paper on which was scribbled down the rough heads of the conversation held between Norma and David in the café – that is, as well as Mrs Oliver could remember them. And how well was that, Poirot thought? He shook his head doubtfully. One never knew quite at what point Mrs Oliver's imagination would take over! Did the boy care for Norma, really want to marry her? There was no doubt about her feelings for him. He had suggested marrying her. Had Norma got money of her own? She was the daughter of a rich man, but that was not the same thing. Poirot made an exclamation of vexation. He had forgotten to inquire the terms of the late Mrs Restarick's will. He flipped through the sheets of notes. No, Mr Goby had not neglected this obvious need. Mrs Restarick apparently had been well provided for by her husband during her lifetime. She had had, apparently, a small income of her own amounting perhaps to a thousand a year. She had left everything she possessed to her daughter. It would hardly amount, Poirot thought, to a motive for marriage. Probably, as his only child, she would inherit a lot of money at her father's death but that was not at all the same thing. Her father might leave her very little indeed if he disliked the man she had married.

He would say then, that David *did* care for her, since he was willing to marry her. And yet – Poirot shook his head. It was about the fifth time he had shaken it. All these things did not tie up, they did not make a satisfactory pattern. He remembered Restarick's desk, and the cheque he had been writing – apparently to buy off the young man – and the young man, apparently, was quite willing to be bought off! So that again did not tally. The cheque had certainly been made out to David Baker and it was for a very large – really a preposterous – sum. It was a sum that might have tempted any impecunious young man of bad character. And yet he had suggested marriage to her only a day before. That, of course, might have been just a move in the game – a move to raise the price he was asking. Poirot remembered Restarick sitting there, his lips hard. He must care a great deal for his daughter to be willing to pay so high a sum; and he must have been afraid too that the girl herself was quite determined to marry him.

From thoughts of Restarick, he went on to Claudia. Claudia and Andrew Restarick. Was it chance, sheer chance, that she had come to be his secretary? There might be a link between them. Claudia. He considered her. Three girls in a flat, Claudia Reece-Holland's flat. She had been the one who had taken the flat originally, and shared it first with a friend, a girl she already knew, and then with another girl, the third girl. *The third girl*, thought Poirot. Yes, it always came back to that. The third girl. And that is where *he* had come in the end. Where he had *had* to come. Where all this thinking out of patterns had led. To Norma Restarick.

A girl who had come to consult him as he sat at breakfast. A girl whom he had joined at a table in a café where she had recently been eating baked beans with the young man she loved.

(He always seemed to see her at meal times, he noted!) And what did he think about her? First, what did other people think about her? Restarick cared for her and was desperately anxious about her, desperately frightened for her. He not only suspected – he was quite sure, apparently, that she had tried to poison his recently married wife. He had consulted a doctor about her. Poirot felt he would like dearly to talk to that doctor himself, but he doubted if he would get anywhere. Doctors were very chary of parting with medical information to anyone but a duly accredited person such as the parents. But Poirot could imagine fairly well what the doctor had said. He had been cautious, Poirot thought, as doctors are apt to be. He'd hemmed and hawed and spoken perhaps of medical treatment. He had not stressed too positively a mental angle, but had certainly suggested it or hinted at it. In fact, the doctor probably was privately sure that that was what *had* happened. But he also knew a good deal about hysterical girls, and that they sometimes did things that were not really the result of mental causes, but merely of temper, jealousy, emotion, and hysteria. He would not be a psychiatrist himself nor a neurologist. He would be a GP who took no risks of making accusations about which he could not be sure, but suggested certain things out of caution. A job somewhere or other – a job in London, later perhaps treatment from a specialist?

What did anyone else think of Norma Restarick? Claudia Reece-Holland? He didn't know. Certainly not from the little that he knew about her. She was capable of hiding any secret, she would certainly let nothing escape her which she did not mean to let escape. She had shown no signs of wanting to turn the girl out – which she might have done if she had been afraid of her mental condition. There could not have been much discussion between her and Frances on the subject since the other girl had so innocently let escape the fact that Norma had not returned to them after her weekend at home. Claudia had been annoyed about that. It was possible that Claudia was more in the pattern than she appeared. She had brains, Poirot thought, and efficiency . . . He came back to Norma, came back once again to the third girl. What was *her* place in the pattern? The place that would pull the whole thing together. Ophelia, he thought? But there were two opinions to that, just as there were two opinions about Norma.

Was Ophelia mad or was she pretending madness? Actresses had been variously divided as to how the part should be played – or perhaps, he should say, producers. They were the ones who had the ideas. Was Hamlet mad or sane? Take your choice. Was Ophelia mad or sane?

Restarick would not have used the word 'mad' even in his thoughts about his daughter. *Mentally disturbed* was the term that everyone preferred to use. The other word that had been used of Norma had been 'batty'. 'She's a bit batty.' 'Not quite all there.' 'A bit wanting, if you know what I mean.' Were 'daily women' good judges? Poirot thought they might be. There *was* something odd about Norma, certainly, but she might be odd in a different way to what she seemed. He remembered the picture she had made slouching into his room, a girl of today, the modern type looking just as so many other girls looked. Limp hair hanging on her shoulders, the characterless dress, a skimpy look about the knees – all to his old-fashioned eyes looking like an adult girl pretending to be a child.

'*I'm sorry, you are too old.*'

Perhaps it was true. He'd looked at her through the eyes of someone old, without admiration, to him just a girl without apparently will to please, without coquetry. A girl without any sense of her own femininity – no charm or mystery or enticement, who had nothing to offer, perhaps, but plain biological sex. So it may be that she was right in her condemnation of him. He could not help her because he did not understand her, because it was not even possible for him to appreciate her. He had done his best for her, but what had that meant up to date? What had he done for her since that one moment of appeal? And in his thoughts the answer came quickly. *He had kept her safe.* That at least. If, indeed, she needed keeping safe. That was where the whole point lay. *Did* she need keeping safe? That preposterous confession! Really, not so much a confession as an announcement: '*I think I may have committed a murder*.'

Hold on to that, because that was the crux of the whole thing. That was his métier. To deal with murder, to clear up murder, to *prevent* murder! To be the good dog who hunts down murder. Murder announced. Murder *somewhere*. He had looked for it and had not found it. The pattern of arsenic in the soup? A pattern of young hooligans stabbing each other with knifes? The ridiculous and sinister phrase, *bloodstains in the courtyard.* A shot fired from a revolver. At whom, and why?

It was not as it ought to be, a form of crime that would fit with the words she had said: 'I may have committed a murder.' He had stumbled on in the dark, trying to see a pattern of crime, trying to see where the third girl fitted into that pattern, and coming back always to the same urgent need to know what this girl was really like.

And then with a casual phrase, Ariadne Oliver had, as he thought, shown him the light. The supposed suicide of a woman at Borodene Mansions. *That* would fit. It was where the third girl had her living quarters. It *must* be the murder that she had meant. Another murder committed about the same time would have been too much of a coincidence! Besides there was no sign or trace of any other murder that had been committed about then. No other death that could have sent her hot-foot to consult him, after listening at a party to the lavish admiration of his own achievements which his friend, Mrs Oliver, had given to the world. And so, when Mrs Oliver had informed him in a casual manner of the woman who had thrown herself out of the window, it had seemed to him that at last he had got what he had been looking for.

Here was the clue. The answer to his perplexity. Here he would find what he needed. The why, the when, the where.

'*Quelle déception,*' said Hercule Poirot, out loud.

He stretched out his hand, and sorted out the neatly typed résumé of a woman's life. The bald facts of Mrs Charpentier's existence. A woman of forty-three of good social position, reported to have been a wild girl – two marriages – two divorces – a woman who liked men. A woman who of late years had drunk more than was good for her. A woman who liked parties. A woman who was now reported to go about with men a good many years younger than herself. Living in a flat alone in Borodene Mansions, Poirot could understand and feel the sort of woman she was, and had been, and he could see why such a woman might wish to throw herself out of a high window one early morning when she awoke to despair.

Because she had cancer or thought she had cancer? *But at*

the inquest, the medical evidence had said very definitely that that was not so.

What he wanted was some kind of a link with Norma Restarick. He could not find it. He read through the dry facts again.

Identification had been supplied at the inquest by a solicitor. Louise Carpenter, though she had used a Frenchified form of her surname – Charpentier. Because it went better with her Christian name? Louise? Why was the name Louise familiar? Some casual mention? – a phrase? – his fingers riffled neatly through typewritten pages. Ah! there it was! Just that one reference. The girl for whom Andrew Restarick had left his wife had been a girl named Louise Birell. Someone who had proved to be of little significance in Restarick's later life. They had quarrelled and parted after about a year. The same pattern, Poirot thought. The same thing obtaining that had probably obtained all through this particular woman's life. To love a man violently, to break up his home, perhaps, to live with him, and then quarrel with him and leave him. He felt sure, absolutely sure, that this Louise Charpentier was the same Louise.

Even so, how did it tie up with the girl Norma? Had Restarick and Louise Charpentier come together again when he returned to England? Poirot doubted it. Their lives had parted years ago. That they had by any chance come together again seemed unlikely to the point of impossibility! It had been a brief and in reality unimportant infatuation. His present wife would hardly be jealous enough of her husband's past to wish to push his former mistress out of a window. Ridiculous! The only person so far as he could see who might have been the type to harbour a grudge over many long years, and wish to execute revenge upon the woman who had broken up her home, might have been the first Mrs Restarick. And that sounded wildly impossible also, and anyway, the first Mrs Restarick was dead!

The telephone rang. Poirot did not move. At this particular moment he did not want to be disturbed. He had a feeling of being on a trail of some kind . . . He wanted to pursue it . . . The telephone stopped. Good. Miss Lemon would be coping with it.

The door opened and Miss Lemon entered.

'Mrs Oliver wants to speak to you,' she said.

Poirot waved a hand. 'Not now, not now, *I pray you*! I cannot speak to her now.'

'She says there is something that she has just thought of – something she forgot to tell you. About a piece of paper – an unfinished letter, which seems to have fallen out of a blotter in a desk in a furniture van. A rather incoherent story,' added Miss Lemon, allowing a note of disapproval to enter her voice.

Poirot waved more frantically.

'Not *now*,' he urged. 'I beg of you, not *now*.'

'I will tell her you are busy.'

Miss Lemon retreated.

Peace descended once more upon the room. Poirot felt waves of fatigue creeping over him. Too much thinking. One *must* relax. Yes, one must relax. One must let tension go – in relaxation the pattern would come. He closed his eyes. There were all the components there. He was sure of that now, there was nothing more he could learn from *outside*. It must come from *inside*.

And quite suddenly – just as his eyelids were relaxing in sleep – *it came* . . .

It was all there – waiting for him! He would have to work it all out. But he *knew* now. All the bits were there, disconnected bits and pieces, all fitting in. A wig, a picture, 5 am, women and their hair-dos, the Peacock Boy – all leading to the phrase with which it had begun:

Third Girl . . .

'*I may have committed a murder* . . .' Of course!

A ridiculous nursery rhyme came into his mind. He repeated it aloud.

Rub a dub dub, three men in a tub
And who do you think they be?
A butcher, a baker, a candlestick maker . . .

Too bad, he couldn't remember the last line.

A baker, yes, and in a far-fetched way, a butcher –

He tried out a feminine parody:

Pat a cake, pat, three girls in a flat
And who do you think they be?
A Personal Aide and a girl from the Slade
And the Third is a –

Miss Lemon came in.

'Ah – I remember now – "*And they all came out of a weenie* POTATO."'

Miss Lemon looked at him in anxiety.

'Dr Stillingfleet insists on speaking to you at once. He says it is *urgent*.'

'Tell Dr Stillingfleet he can – *Dr Stillingfleet*, did you say?'

He pushed past her, caught up the receiver. 'I am here. Poirot speaking! Something has happened?'

'She's walked out on me.'

'What?'

'You heard me. She's walked out. Walked out through the front gate.'

'You let her go?'

'What else could I do?'

'You could have stopped her.'

'No.'

'To let her go was madness.'

'No.'

'You don't understand.'

'That was the arrangement. Free to go at any time.'

'You don't understand what may be involved.'

'All right then, I don't. But I know what *I*'m doing. And if I don't let her go, all the work I've done on her would go for nothing. And I *have* worked on her. Your job and my job aren't the same. We're not out for the same thing. I tell you I was getting somewhere. Getting somewhere, so that I was quite sure she *wouldn't* walk out on me.'

'Ah yes. And then, *mon ami*, she did.'

'Frankly, I can't understand it. I can't see why the setback came.'

'Something happened.'

'Yes, but what?'

'Somebody she saw, somebody who spoke to her, somebody who found out where she was.'

'I don't see how that could have happened . . . But what you don't seem to see is that she's a free agent. She had to be a free agent.'

'Somebody got at her. Somebody found out where she was. Did she get a letter, a telegram, a telephone call?'

'No, nothing of that kind. That I am quite sure of.'

'Then how – of course! Newspapers. You have newspapers, I suppose, in that establishment of yours?'

'Certainly. Normal everyday life, that's what I stand for in my place of business.'

'Then that is how they got at her. Normal, everyday life. What papers do you take?'

'Five.' He named the five.

'When did she go?'

'This morning. Half past ten.'

'Exactly. After she read the papers. That is good enough to start on. Which paper did she usually read?'

'I don't think she had any special choice. Sometimes one, sometimes another, sometimes the whole lot of them – sometimes only glanced at them.'

'Well, I must not waste time talking.'

'You think she saw an advertisement. Something of that kind?'

'What other explanation can there be? Goodbye, I can say no more now. I have to search. Search for the possible advertisement and then get on quickly.'

He replaced the receiver.

'Miss Lemon, bring me our two papers. The *Morning News* and the *Daily Comet*. Send Georges out for all the others.'

As he opened out the papers to the Personal advertisements and went carefully down them, he followed his line of thought.

He would be in time. He *must* be in time . . . There had been one murder already. There would be another one to come. But he, Hercule Poirot, would prevent that . . . If he was in time . . . He was Hercule Poirot – the avenger of the innocent. Did he not say (and people laughed when he said it), 'I do not approve of murder.' They had thought it an understatement. But it was not an understatement. It was a simple statement of *fact* without melodrama. He did not approve of murder.

George came in with a sheaf of newspapers.

'There are all this morning's, sir.'

Poirot looked at Miss Lemon, who was standing by waiting to be efficient.

'Look through the ones that I have searched in case I have missed anything.'

'The Personal column, you mean?'

'Yes. I thought there would be the name David perhaps. A girl's name. Some pet name or nickname. They would not use Norma. An appeal for help, perhaps, or to a meeting.'

Miss Lemon took the papers obediently with some distaste. This was not her kind of efficiency, but for the moment he had no other job to give her. He himself spread out the *Morning Chronicle*. That was the biggest field to search. Three columns of it. He bent over the open sheet.

A lady who wanted to dispose of her fur coat . . . Passengers wanted for a car trip abroad . . . Lovely period house for sale . . . Paying guests . . . Backward children . . . Home-made chocolates . . . '*Julia. Shall never forget. Always yours.*' That was more the kind of thing. He considered it, but passed on. Louis XVth furniture . . . Middle-aged lady to help run a hotel . . . '*In desperate trouble. Must see you. Come to flat 4.30 without fail. Our code Goliath.*'

He heard the doorbell ring just as he called out: 'Georges, a taxi,' slipped on his overcoat, and went into the hall just as George was opening the front door and colliding with Mrs Oliver. All three of them struggled to disentangle themselves in the narrow hall.

CHAPTER 22

I

Frances Cary, carrying her overnight bag, walked down Mandeville Road, chattering with the friend she had just met on the corner, towards the bulk of Borodene Mansions.

'Really, Frances, it's like living in a prison block, that building. Wormwood Scrubs or something.'

'Nonsense, Eileen. I tell you, they're frightfully comfortable, these flats. I'm very lucky and Claudia is a splendid person to share with – never bothers you. And she's got a wonderful daily. The flat's really very nicely run.'

'Are there just the two of you? I forget. I thought you had a third girl?'

'Oh, well, she seems to have walked out on us.'

'You mean she doesn't pay her rent?'

'Oh, I think the rent's all right. I think she's probably having some affair with a boy friend.'

Eileen lost interest. Boy friends were too much a matter of course.

'Where are you coming back from now?'

'Manchester. Private view was on. Great success.'

'Are you really going to Vienna next month?'

'Yes, I think so. It's pretty well fixed up by now. Rather fun.'

'Wouldn't it be awful if some of the pictures got stolen?'

'Oh, they're all insured,' said Frances. 'All the really valuable ones, anyway.'

'How did your friend Peter's show go?'

'Not terribly well, I'm afraid. But there was quite a good review by the critic of *The Artist*, and that counts a lot.'

Frances turned into Borodene Mansions, and her friend went on her way to her own small mews house farther down the road. Frances said 'Good evening' to the porter, and went up in the lift to the sixth floor. She walked along the passage, humming a little tune to herself.

She inserted her key in the door of the flat. The light in the hall was not on yet. Claudia was not due back from the office for another hour and a half. But in the sitting-room, the door of which was ajar, the light *was* on.

Frances said aloud: 'Light's on. That's funny.'

She slipped out of her coat, dropped her overnight bag, pushed the sitting-room door farther open and went in . . .

Then she stopped dead. Her mouth opened and then shut. She stiffened all over – her eyes staring at the prone figure on the floor; then they rose slowly to the mirror on the wall that reflected back at her her own horror-stricken face . . .

Then she drew a deep breath. The momentary paralysis over, she flung back her head and screamed. Stumbling over her bag on the hall floor and kicking it aside, she ran out of the flat and along the passage and beat frenziedly at the door of the next flat.

An elderly woman opened it.

'What on earth –'

'There's someone dead – someone *dead.* And I think it's someone I know . . . David Baker. He's lying there on the floor . . . I think he's stabbed . . . he must have been stabbed. There's blood – blood everywhere.'

She began to sob hysterically. Miss Jacobs shoved a glass into her hand. 'Stay there and drink it.'

Frances sipped obediently. Miss Jacobs went rapidly out of the door along the passage and through the open door from which the light was pouring out. The living-room door was wide open and Miss Jacobs went straight through it.

She was not the kind of woman who screams. She stood just within the doorway, her lips pursed hard together.

What she was looking at had a nightmarish quality. On the floor lay a handsome young man, his arms flung wide, his chestnut hair falling on his shoulders. He wore a crimson velvet coat, and his white shirt was dappled with blood . . .

She was aware with a start that there was a second figure with her in the room. A girl was standing pressed back against the wall, the great Harlequin above seeming to be leaping across the painted sky.

The girl had a white woollen shift dress on, and her pale brown hair hung limp on either side of her face. In her hand she was holding a kitchen knife.

Miss Jacobs stared at her and she stared back at Miss Jacobs.

Then she said in a quiet reflective voice, as though she was answering what someone had said to her:

'Yes, I've killed him . . . The blood got on my hands from the knife . . . I went into the bathroom to wash it off – but you can't really wash things like that off, can you? And then I came back in here to see if it was really *true* . . . But it *is* . . . Poor David . . . But I suppose I *had* to do it.'

Shock forced unlikely words from Miss Jacobs. As she said them, she thought how ridiculous they sounded!

'Indeed? Why did you have to do anything of the kind?'

'I don't know . . . At least – I suppose I do – really. He was in great trouble. He sent for me – and I came . . . But I wanted to be free of him. I wanted to get away from him. I didn't really love him.'

She laid the knife carefully on the table and sat down on a chair.

'It isn't safe, is it?' she said. 'To hate anyone . . . It isn't safe because you never know what you might do . . . Like Louise . . .'

Then she said quietly, 'Hadn't you better ring up the police?'

Obediently, Miss Jacobs dialled 999.

II

There were six people now in the room with the Harlequin on the wall. A long time had passed. The police had come and gone.

Andrew Restarick sat like a man stunned. Once or twice he said the same words. 'I can't believe it . . .' Telephoned for, he had come from his office, and Claudia Reece-Holland had come with him. In her quiet way, she had been ceaselessly efficient. She had put through telephone calls to lawyers, had rung Crosshedges and two firms of estate agents to try and get in touch with Mary Restarick. She had given Frances Cary a sedative and sent her to lie down.

Hercule Poirot and Mrs Oliver sat side by side on a sofa. They had arrived together at the same time as the police.

Last of all to arrive, when nearly everyone else had gone, had been a quiet man with grey hair and a gentle manner, Chief Inspector Neele of Scotland Yard, who had greeted Poirot with a slight nod, and been introduced to Andrew Restarick. A tall red-haired young man was standing by the window staring down into the courtyard.

What were they all waiting for? Mrs Oliver wondered. The body had been removed, the photographers and other police officers had done their work, they themselves, after being herded into Claudia's bedroom, had been re-admitted into the sitting-room, where they had been waiting, she supposed, for the Scotland Yard man to arrive.

'If you want me to go,' Mrs Oliver said to him uncertainly –

'Mrs Ariadne Oliver, aren't you? No, if you have no objection, I'd rather you remained. I know it hasn't been pleasant –'

'It didn't seem real.'

Mrs Oliver shut her eyes – seeing the whole thing again. The Peacock Boy, so picturesquely dead that he had seemed like a stage figure. And the girl – the girl had been different – not the uncertain Norma from Crosshedges – the unattractive Ophelia, as Poirot had called her – but some quiet figure of tragic dignity – accepting her doom.

Poirot had asked if he might make two telephone calls. One had been to Scotland Yard, and that had been agreed to, after the sergeant had made a preliminary suspicious inquiry on the phone. The sergeant had directed Poirot to the extension in Claudia's bedroom, and he had made his call from there, closing the door behind him.

The sergeant had continued to look doubtful, murmuring to his subordinate, 'They *say* it's all right. Wonder who he is? Odd-looking little bloke.'

'Foreign, isn't he? Might be Special Branch?'

'Don't think so. It was Chief Inspector Neele he wanted.'

His assistant raised his eyebrows and suppressed a whistle.

After making his calls, Poirot had re-opened the door and beckoned Mrs Oliver from where she was standing uncertainly inside the kitchen, to join him. They had sat down side by side on Claudia Reece-Holland's bed.

'I wish we could *do* something,' said Mrs Oliver – always one for action.

'Patience, *chère* Madame.'

'Surely *you* can do something?'

'I have. I have rung up the people it is necessary to ring up. We can do nothing here until the police have finished their preliminary investigations.'

'Who did you ring up after the inspector man? Her father? Couldn't he come and bail her out or something?'

'Bail is not likely to be granted where murder is concerned,' said Poirot dryly. 'The police have already notified her father. They got his number from Miss Cary.'

'Where is she?'

'Having hysterics in the flat of a Miss Jacobs next door, I understand. She was the one who discovered the body. It seems to have upset her. She rushed out of here screaming.'

'She's the arty one, isn't she? Claudia would have kept her head.'

'I agree with you. A very – poised young woman.'

'Who *did* you ring up, then?'

'First, as perhaps you heard, Chief Inspector Neele of Scotland Yard.'

'Will this lot like his coming and meddling?'

'He is not coming to meddle. He has of late been making certain inquiries for me, which may throw light on this matter.'

'Oh – I see . . . Who else did you ring up?'

'Dr John Stillingfleet.'

'Who's he? To say that poor Norma is potty and can't help killing people?'

'His qualifications would entitle him to give evidence to that effect in court if necessary.'

'Does he know anything about her?'

'A good deal, I should say. She has been in his care since the day you found her in the Shamrock café.'

'Who sent her there?'

Poirot smiled. 'I did. I made certain arrangements by telephone before I came to join you at the café.'

'What? All the time I was so disappointed in you and kept urging you to *do* something – you *had* done something? And you never *told* me! Really, Poirot! Not a *word*! How could you be so – so *mean*.'

'Do not enrage yourself, Madame, I beg. What I did, I did for the best.'

'People always say that when they have done something particularly maddening. What else did you do?'

'I arranged that my services should be retained by her father, so that I could make the necessary arrangements for her safety.'

'Meaning this Doctor Stillingwater?'

'Stilling*fleet*. Yes.'

'How on earth did you manage that? I shouldn't have thought for a moment that you would be the kind of person that her father would choose to make all these arrangements. He looks the kind of man who would be very suspicious of foreigners.'

'I forced myself upon him – as a conjurer forces a card. I called upon him, purporting to have received a letter from him asking me to do so.'

'And did he believe you?'

'Naturally. I showed the letter to him. It was typed on his office stationery and signed with his name – though as he pointed out to me, the handwriting was not his.'

'Do you mean you had actually written that letter yourself?'

'Yes. I judged correctly that it would awaken his curiosity, and that he would want to see me. Having got so far, I trusted to my own talents.'

'You told him what you were going to do about this Dr Stillingfleet?'

'No. I told no one. There was danger, you see.'

'Danger to Norma?'

'To Norma, or Norma was dangerous to someone else. From the very beginning there have always been the two possibilities. The facts could be interpreted in either way. The attempted poisoning of Mrs Restarick was not convincing – it was delayed too long, it was not a serious attempt to kill. Then there was an indeterminate story of a revolver shot fired here in Borodene Mansions – and another tale of flick-knives and bloodstains. Every time these things happen, Norma knows nothing about them, cannot remember, etcetera. She finds arsenic in a drawer – but does not remember putting it there. Claims to have had lapses of memory, to have lost long periods of time when she does not remember what she had been doing. So one has to ask oneself – is what she says *true*, or did she, for some reason of her own, *invent* it? Is she a potential victim of some monstrous and perhaps crazy plot – or is it she herself who is the moving spirit? Is she painting a picture of herself as a girl suffering from mental instability, or has she *murder* in mind, with a defence of diminished responsibility?'

'She was different today,' said Mrs Oliver slowly. 'Did you notice? *Quite* different. Not – not *scatty* any longer.'

Poirot nodded.

'Not Ophelia – Iphigeneia.'

A sound of added commotion outside in the flat diverted the attention of both of them.

'Do you think –' Mrs Oliver stopped. Poirot had gone to the

window and was looking down to the courtyard far below. An ambulance was drawn up there.

'Are they going to take It away?' asked Mrs Oliver in a shaky voice. And then added in a sudden rush of pity: 'Poor Peacock.'

'He was hardly a likeable character,' said Poirot coldly.

'He was very decorative . . . And so *young*,' said Mrs Oliver.

'That is sufficient for *les femmes*.' Poirot was opening the bedroom door a careful crack, as he peered out.

'Excuse me,' he said, 'if I leave you for a moment.'

'Where are you going?' demanded Mrs Oliver suspiciously.

'I understood that that was not a question considered delicate in this country,' said Poirot reproachfully.

'Oh, I beg your pardon.

'And that's not the way to the loo,' she breathed *sotto voce* after him, as she too applied an eye to the crack of the door.

She went back to the window to observe what was going on below.

'Mr Restarick has just driven up in a taxi,' she observed when Poirot slipped back quietly into the room a few minutes later, 'and Claudia has come with him. Did you manage to get into Norma's room, or wherever you really wanted to go?'

'Norma's room is in the occupation of the police.'

'How annoying for you. What are you carrying in that kind of black folder thing you've got in your hand?'

Poirot in his turn asked a question.

'What have you got in that canvas bag with Persian horses on it?'

'My shopping bag? Only a couple of Avocado pears, as it happens.'

'Then if I may, I will entrust this folder to you. Do not be rough with it, or squeeze it, I beg.'

'What is it?'

'Something that I hoped to find – and that I have found – Ah, things begin to pass themselves –' He referred to increased sounds of activities.

Poirot's words struck Mrs Oliver as being much more exactly descriptive than English words would have been. Restarick, his voice loud and angry. Claudia coming in to telephone. A glimpse of a police stenographer on an excursion to the flat next door to take statements from Frances Cary and a mythical person called Miss Jacobs. A coming and going of ordered business, and a final departure of two men with cameras.

Then unexpectedly the sudden incursion into Claudia's bedroom of a tall loosely-jointed young man with red hair.

Without taking any notice of Mrs Oliver, he spoke to Poirot.

'What's she done? Murder? Who is it? The boy friend?'

'Yes.'

'She admits it?'

'It would seem so.'

'Not good enough. Did she say so in definite words?'

'I have not heard her do so. I have had no chance of asking her anything myself.'

A policeman looked in.

'Dr Stillingfleet?' he asked. 'The police surgeon would like a word with you.'

Dr Stillingfleet nodded and followed him out of the room.

'So that's Dr Stillingfleet,' said Mrs Oliver. She considered for a moment or two. 'Quite something, isn't he?'

CHAPTER 23

Chief Inspector Neele drew a sheet of paper towards him, jotted one or two notes on it; and looked round at the other five people in the room. His voice was crisp and formal.

'Miss Jacobs?' he said. He looked towards the policeman who stood by the door. 'Sergeant Conolly, I know, has taken her statement. But I'd like to ask her a few questions myself.'

Miss Jacobs was ushered into the room a few minutes later. Neele rose courteously to greet her.

'I am Chief Inspector Neele,' he said, shaking hands with her. 'I am sorry to trouble you for a second time. But this time it is quite informal. I just want to get a clearer picture of exactly what you saw and heard. I'm afraid it may be painful –'

'Painful, no,' said Miss Jacobs, accepting the chair he offered her. 'It was a shock, of course. But no emotions were involved.' She added: 'You seem to have tidied up things.'

He presumed she was referring to the removal of the body.

Her eyes, both observant and critical, passed lightly over the assembled people, registering, for Poirot, frank astonishment (What on earth is *this*?), for Mrs Oliver, mild curiosity; appraisement for the back of Dr Stillingfleet's red head, neighbourly recognition for Claudia to whom she vouchsafed a slight nod, and finally dawning sympathy for Andrew Restarick.

'You must be the girl's father,' she said to him. 'There's not much point to condolences from a total stranger. They're better left unsaid. It's a sad world we live in nowadays – or so it seems to me. Girls study too hard in my opinion.'

Then she turned her face composedly towards Neele.

'Yes?'

'I would like you, Miss Jacobs, to tell me in your own words exactly what you saw and heard.'

'I expect it will vary from what I said before,' said Miss Jacobs unexpectedly. 'Things do, you know. One tries to make one's description as accurate as possible, and so one uses more words. I don't think one is any more accurate; I think, unconsciously, one adds things that you think you may have seen or ought to have seen – or heard. But I will do my best.

'It started with screams. I was startled. I thought someone must have been hurt. So I was already coming to the door when someone began beating on it, and still screaming. I opened it and saw it was one of my next-door neighbours – the three girls who live in 67. I'm afraid I don't know her name, though I know her by sight.'

'Frances Cary,' said Claudia.

'She was quite incoherent, and stammered out something about someone being dead – someone she knew – David Someone – I didn't catch his last name. She was sobbing and shaking all over. I brought her in, gave her some brandy, and went to see for myself.'

Everyone felt that throughout life that would be what Miss Jacobs would invariably do.

'You know what I found. Need I describe it?'

'Just briefly, perhaps.'

'A young man, one of these modern young men – gaudy clothes and long hair. He was lying on the floor and he was clearly dead. His shirt was stiff with blood.'

Stillingfleet stirred. He turned his head and looked keenly at Miss Jacobs.

'Then I became aware that there was a girl in the room. She was holding a kitchen knife. She seemed quite calm and self-possessed – really, most peculiar.'

Stillingfleet said: 'Did she say anything?'

'She said she had been into the bathroom to wash the blood off her hands – and then she said, "But you can't wash things like that off, can you?"'

'*Out, damnéd spot*, in fact?'

'I cannot say that she reminded me particularly of Lady Macbeth. She was – how shall I put it? – perfectly composed. She laid the knife down on the table and sat down on a chair.'

'What else did she say?' asked Chief Inspector Neele, his eyes dropping to a scrawled note in front of him.

'Something about *hate*. That it wasn't safe to *hate* anybody.'

'She said something about "poor David", didn't she? Or so you told Sergeant Conolly. And that she wanted to be free of him.'

'I'd forgotten that. Yes. She said something about his making her come here – and something about Louise, too.'

'What did she say about Louise?' It was Poirot who asked, leaning forward sharply. Miss Jacobs looked at him doubtfully.

'Nothing, really, just mentioned the name. "*Like Louise*," she said, and then stopped. It was after she had said about its not being safe to hate people . . .'

'And then?'

'Then she told me, quite calmly, I had better ring up the police. Which I did. We just – sat there until they came . . . I did not think I ought to leave her. We did not say anything. She seemed absorbed in her thoughts, and I – well, frankly, I couldn't think of anything to say.'

'You could see, couldn't you, that she was mentally unstable?' said Andrew Restarick. 'You could see that she didn't know what she had done or why, poor child?'

He spoke pleadingly – hopefully.

'If it is a sign of mental instability to appear perfectly cool and collected after committing a murder, then I will agree with you.'

Miss Jacobs spoke in the voice of one who quite decidedly did *not* agree.

Stillingfleet said:

'Miss Jacobs, did she at any time admit that she had killed him?'

'Oh yes. I should have mentioned that before – It was the very first thing she did say. As though she was answering some question I had asked her. She said, "*Yes. I've killed him.*" And then went on about having washed her hands.'

Restarick groaned and buried his face in his hands. Claudia put her hand on his arm.

Poirot said:

'Miss Jacobs, you say the girl put down the knife she was carrying on that table. It was quite near you? You saw it clearly? Did it appear to you that the knife also had been washed?'

Miss Jacobs looked hesitantly at Chief Inspector Neele. It was clear that she felt that Poirot struck an alien and unofficial note in this presumably official inquiry.

'Perhaps you would be kind enough to answer that?' said Neele.

'No – I don't think the knife had been washed or wiped in any way. It was stained and discoloured with some thick sticky substance.'

'Ah.' Poirot leaned back in his chair.

'I should have thought you would have known all about the knife yourself,' said Miss Jacobs to Neele accusingly. 'Didn't your police examine it? It seems to me very lax if they didn't.'

'Oh yes, the police examined it,' said Neele. 'But we – er – always like to get corroboration.'

She darted him a shrewd glance.

'What you really mean, I suppose, is that you like to find out how accurate the observation of your witnesses is. How much they make up, or how much they actually see, or think they have seen.'

He smiled slightly as he said:

'I don't think we need have doubts about you, Miss Jacobs. You will make an excellent witness.'

'I shan't enjoy it. But it's the kind of thing one has to go through with, I suppose.'

'I'm afraid so. Thank you, Miss Jacobs.' He looked round. 'No one has any additional questions?'

Poirot indicated that he had. Miss Jacobs paused near the doorway, displeased.

'Yes?' she said.

'About this mention of someone called Louise. Did you know who it was the girl meant?'

'How should I know?'

'Isn't it possible that she might have meant Mrs Louise Charpentier? You knew Mrs Charpentier, didn't you?'

'I did not.'

'You knew that she recently threw herself out of a window in this block of flats?'

'I knew that, of course. I didn't know her Christian name was Louise, and I was not personally acquainted with her.'

'Nor, perhaps, particularly wished to be?'

'I have not said so, since the woman is dead. But I will admit that that is quite true. She was a most undesirable tenant, and I and other residents have frequently complained to the management here.'

'Of what exactly?'

'To speak frankly, the woman drank. Her flat was actually on the top floor above mine and there were continual disorderly parties, with broken glass, furniture knocked over, singing and shouting, a lot of – er – coming and going.'

'She was, perhaps, a lonely woman,' suggested Poirot.

'That was hardly the impression she conveyed,' said Miss Jacobs acidly. 'It was put forward at the inquest that she was depressed over the state of her health. Entirely her own imagination. She seems to have had nothing the matter with her.'

And having disposed of the late Mrs Charpentier without sympathy, Miss Jacobs took her departure.

Poirot turned his attention to Andrew Restarick. He asked delicately:

'Am I correct in thinking, Mr Restarick, that you were at one time well acquainted with Mrs Charpentier?'

Restarick did not answer for a moment or two. Then he sighed deeply and transferred his gaze to Poirot.

'Yes. At one time, many years ago, I knew her very well indeed . . . Not, I may say, under the name of Charpentier. She was Louise Birell when I knew her.'

'You were – er – in love with her!'

'Yes, I was in love with her . . . Head over ears in love with her! I left my wife on her account. We went to South Africa. After barely a year the whole thing blew up. She returned to England. I never heard from her again. I never even knew what had become of her.'

'What about your daughter? Did she, also, know Louise Birell?'

'Not to remember her, surely. A child of five years old!'

'But did she know her?' Poirot persisted.

'Yes,' said Restarick slowly. 'She knew Louise. That is to say, Louise came to our house. She used to play with the child.'

'So it is possible that the girl *might* remember her, even after a lapse of years?'

'I don't know. I simply don't know. I don't know what she looked like; how much Louise might have changed. I never saw her again, as I told you.'

Poirot said gently, 'But you *heard* from her, didn't you, Mr Restarick? I mean, you have heard from her since your return to England?'

Again there came that pause, and the deep unhappy sigh:

'Yes – I heard from her . . .' said Restarick. And then, with sudden curiosity, he asked: 'How did you know that, M. Poirot?'

From his pocket, Poirot drew a neatly folded piece of paper. He unfolded it and handed it to Restarick.

The latter looked at it with a faintly puzzled frown.

Dear Andy

I see from the papers you're home again. We must meet and compare notes as to what we've both been doing all these years –

It broke off here – and started again.

Andy – Guess who this is from! Louise. Don't dare to say you've forgotten me! –

Dear Andy,

As you will see by this letterhead, I'm living in the same block of flats as your secretary. What a small world it is! We must meet. Could you come for a drink Monday or Tuesday next week?

Andy darling, I must see you again . . . Nobody has ever mattered to me but you – you haven't really forgotten me, either, have you?

'How did *you* get this?' asked Restarick of Poirot, tapping it curiously.

'From a friend of mine via a furniture van,' said Poirot, with a glance at Mrs Oliver.

Restarick looked at her without favour.

'I couldn't help it,' said Mrs Oliver, interpreting his look correctly. 'I suppose it was *her* furniture being moved out, and the men let go of a desk, and a drawer fell out and scattered a lot of things, and the wind blew this along the courtyard, so I picked it up and tried to give it back to them, but they were cross and didn't want it, so I just put it in my coat pocket without thinking. And I never even looked at it until this afternoon when I was taking things out of pockets before sending the coat to the cleaners. So it really wasn't my fault.'

She paused, slightly out of breath.

'Did she get her letter to you written in the end?' Poirot asked.

'Yes – she did – one of the more formal versions! I didn't answer it. I thought it would be wiser not to do so.'

'You didn't want to see her again?'

'She was the last person I wanted to see! She was a particularly difficult woman – always had been. And I'd heard things about her – for one that she had become a heavy drinker. And well – other things.'

'Did you keep her letter to you?'

'No, I tore it up!'

Dr Stillingfleet asked an abrupt question.

'Did your daughter ever speak about her to you?'

Restarick seemed unwilling to answer.

Dr Stillingfleet urged him:

'It might be significant if she did, you know.'

'You doctors! Yes, she did mention her once.'

'What did she say exactly?'

'She said quite suddenly: "I saw Louise the other day, Father." I was startled. I said: "Where did you see her?" And she said: "In the restaurant of our flats." I was a bit embarrassed. I said:

"I never dreamed you'd remembered her." And she said: "I've never forgotten. Mother wouldn't have let me forget, even if I wanted to."'

'Yes,' said Dr Stillingfleet. 'Yes, that could certainly be significant.'

'And you, Mademoiselle,' said Poirot, turning suddenly to Claudia. 'Did Norma ever speak to you about Louise Carpenter?'

'Yes – it was after the suicide. She said something about her being a wicked woman. She said it in rather a childish way, if you know what I mean.'

'You were here in the flats yourself on the night – or more correctly the early morning when Mrs Carpenter's suicide occurred?'

'I was not here that night, no! I was away from home. I remember arriving back here the next day and hearing about it.'

She half turned to Restarick . . . 'You remember? It was the twenty-third. I had gone to Liverpool.'

'Yes, of course. You were to represent me at the Hever Trust meeting.'

Poirot said:

'But Norma slept here that night?'

'Yes.' Claudia seemed uncomfortable.

'Claudia?' Restarick laid his hand on her arm. 'What *is* it you know about Norma? There's something. Something that you're holding back.'

'Nothing! What should I know about her?'

'You think she's off her head, don't you?' said Dr Stillingfleet in a conversational voice. 'And so does the girl with the black hair. And so do *you*,' he added, turning suddenly on Restarick. 'All of us behaving nicely and avoiding the subject and thinking the same thing! Except, that is, the chief inspector. He's not thinking anything. He's collecting the facts: mad or a murderess. What about *you*, Madam?'

'Me?' Mrs Oliver jumped. 'I – don't know.'

'You reserve judgment? I don't blame you. It's difficult. On the whole, most people agree on what they think. They use different terms for it – that's all. Bats in the Belfry. Wanting in the top storey. Off her onion. Mental. Delusions. Does *anyone* think that girl is sane?'

'Miss Battersby,' said Poirot.

'Who the devil is Miss Battersby?'

'A schoolmistress.'

'If I ever have a daughter I shall send her to that school . . . Of course I'm in a different category. *I know.* I know everything about that girl!'

Norma's father stared at him.

'Who is this man?' he demanded of Neele. 'What can he possibly *mean* by saying that he knows everything about my daughter?'

'I know about her,' said Stillingfleet, 'because she's been under my professional care for the last ten days.'

'Dr Stillingfleet,' said Chief Inspector Neele, 'is a highly qualified and reputable psychiatrist.'

'And how did she come into your clutches – without someone getting my consent first?'

'Ask Moustaches,' said Dr Stillingfleet, nodding towards Poirot.

'*You – you . . .*'

Restarick could hardly speak he was so angry.

Poirot spoke placidly.

'I had your instructions. You wanted care and protection for your daughter when she was found. I found her – and I was able to interest Dr Stillingfleet in her case. She was in danger, Mr Restarick, very grave danger.'

'She could hardly be in any more danger than she is now! Arrested on a charge of murder!'

'Technically she is not yet charged,' murmured Neele.

He went on:

'Dr Stillingfleet, do I understand that you are willing to give your professional opinion as to Miss Restarick's mental condition, and as to how well she knows the nature and meaning of her acts?'

'We can save the M'Naughten act for court,' said Stillingfleet. 'What you want to know now is, quite simply, if the girl is mad or sane? All right, I'll tell you. *That girl is sane* – as sane as any one of you sitting here in this room!'

CHAPTER 24

I

They stared at him.

'Didn't expect that, did you?'

Restarick said angrily: 'You're wrong. That girl *doesn't even know what she's done.* She's innocent – completely innocent. She can't be held responsible for what she doesn't know she's done.'

'You let *me* talk for a while. I know what I'm talking about. You don't. That girl is sane and responsible for her actions. In a moment or two we'll have her in and let her speak for herself. She's the only one who hasn't had the chance of speaking for herself! Oh yes, they've got her here still – locked up with a police matron in her bedroom. But before we ask her a question or two, I've got something to say that you'd better hear first.

'When that girl came to me *she was full of drugs*.'

'And *he* gave them to her!' shouted Restarick. 'That degenerate, miserable boy.'

'He started her on them, no doubt.'

'Thank God,' said Restarick. 'Thank God for it.'

'What are you thanking God for?'

'I misunderstood you. I thought you were going to throw her to the lions when you kept harping on her being sane. I misjudged you. It was the drugs that did it. Drugs that made her do things she would never have done of her own volition, and left her with no knowledge of having done them.'

Stillingfleet raised his voice:

'If you let *me* talk instead of talking so much yourself, and being so sure you know all about everything, we might get on a bit. First of all, *she's not an addict.* There are no marks of injections. She didn't sniff snow. Someone or other, perhaps the boy, perhaps someone else, was administering drugs to her without her knowledge. Not just a purple heart or two in the modern fashion. A rather interesting medley of drugs – LSD giving vivid dream sequences – nightmares or pleasurable. Hemp distorting the time factor, so that she might believe an experience has lasted an hour instead of a few minutes. And a good many other curious substances that I have no intention of letting any of you know about. Somebody who was clever with drugs played merry hell with that girl. Stimulants, sedatives, they all played their part in controlling her, and showing her *to herself* as a completely different person.'

Restarick interrupted: 'That's what I say. Norma wasn't responsible! Someone was hypnotising her to do these things.'

'You still haven't got the point! Nobody could make the girl do *what she didn't want to do*! What they *could* do, was make her *think* she had done it. Now we'll have her in and make her see what's been happening to her.'

He looked inquiringly at Chief Inspector Neele, who nodded.

Stillingfleet spoke over his shoulder to Claudia, as he went out of the sitting-room. 'Where'd you put that other girl, the one you took away from Jacobs, gave a sedative to? In her room on her bed? Better shake her up a bit, and drag her along, somehow. We'll need all the help we can get.'

Claudia also went out of the sitting-room.

Stillingfleet came back, propelling Norma, and uttering rough encouragement.

'There's a good girl . . . Nobody's going to bite you. Sit there.'

She sat obediently. Her docility was still rather frightening.

The policewoman hovered by the door looking scandalised.

'All I'm asking you to do is to speak the truth. It isn't nearly as difficult as you think.'

Claudia came in with Frances Cary. Frances was yawning heavily. Her black hair hung like a curtain hiding half her mouth as she yawned and yawned again.

'You need a pick-me-up,' said Stillingfleet to her.

'I wish you'd all let me go to sleep,' murmured Frances indistinctly.

'Nobody's going to have a chance of sleep until I've done with them! Now, Norma, you answer my questions – That woman along the passage says you admitted to her that you killed David Baker. Is that right?'

Her docile voice said:

'Yes. I killed David.'

'Stabbed him?'

'Yes.'

'How do you know you did?'

She looked faintly puzzled. 'I don't know what you mean. He was there on the floor – dead.'

'Where was the knife?'

'I picked it up.'

'It had blood on it?'

'Yes. And on his shirt.'

'What did it feel like – the blood on the knife? The blood that you got on your hand and had to wash off – Wet? Or more like strawberry jam?'

'It was like strawberry jam – sticky.' She shivered. 'I had to go and wash it off my hands.'

'Very sensible. Well, that ties up everything very nicely. Victim, murderer – you – all complete with the weapon. Do you remember actually *doing* it?'

'No . . . I don't remember *that* . . . But I must have done it, mustn't I?'

'Don't ask me! I wasn't there. It's you are the one who's saying it. But there was another killing before that, wasn't there? An earlier killing.'

'You mean – Louise?'

'Yes. I mean Louise . . . When did you first think of killing her?'

'Years ago. Oh, years ago.'

'When you were a child.'

'Yes.'

'Had to wait a long time, didn't you?'

'I'd forgotten all about it.'

'Until you saw her again and recognised her?'

'Yes.'

'When you were a child, you hated her. Why?'

'Because she took Father, my father, away.'

'And made your mother unhappy?'

'Mother hated Louise. She said Louise was a really wicked woman.'

'Talked to you about her a lot, I suppose?'

'Yes. I wish she hadn't . . . I didn't want to go on hearing about her.'

'Monotonous – I know. Hate isn't creative. When you saw her again did you *really* want to kill her?'

Norma seemed to consider. A faintly interested look came into her face.

'I didn't, really, you know . . . It seemed all so long ago. I couldn't imagine myself – that's why –'

'Why you weren't sure you *had*?'

'Yes. I had some quite wild idea that I *hadn't* killed her at all. That it had been all a dream. That perhaps she really *had* thrown herself out of the window.'

'Well – why not?'

'Because I knew I had done it – I *said* I had done it.'

'You said *you* had done it? Who did you say that to?'

Norma shook her head. 'I mustn't . . . It was someone who tried to be kind – to help me. She said she was going to pretend to have known nothing about it.' She went on, the words coming fast and excitedly: 'I was outside Louise's door, the door of 76, just coming out of it. I thought I'd been walking in my sleep. They – she – said there had been an accident. Down in the courtyard. She kept telling me it had been nothing to do with me. Nobody would ever know – And I couldn't remember what I had done – but there was stuff in my hand –'

'Stuff? What stuff? Do you mean *blood*?'

'No, not blood – torn curtain stuff. When I'd pushed her out.'

'You remember pushing her out, do you?'

'No, no. That's what was so awful. I didn't remember *anything*. That's why I *hoped*. That's why I went –' She turned her head towards Poirot – 'to *him* –'

She turned back again to Stillingfleet.

'I *never* remembered the things I'd done, none of them. But I got more and more frightened. Because there used to be quite long times that were blank – quite blank – hours I couldn't account for, or remember where I'd been and what I'd been doing. But I found things – things I must have hidden away myself. Mary was being poisoned by *me*, they found out she was being poisoned at the hospital. *And I found the weed killer I'd hidden away in the drawer.* In the flat here there was a flick-knife. And I had a revolver that I didn't even know I'd bought! I *did* kill people, but I didn't remember killing them, so I'm not really a murderer – I'm just – *mad*! I realised that at last. I'm mad, and I can't help it. People can't blame you if you do things when you are mad. If I could come here and even kill *David*, it *shows* I am mad, doesn't it?'

'You'd like to be mad, very much?'

'I – yes, I suppose so.'

'If so, why did you confess to someone that you had killed a woman by pushing her out of the window? Who was it you told?'

Norma turned her head, hesitated. Then raised her hand and pointed.

'I told Claudia.'

'That is absolutely untrue.' Claudia looked at her scornfully. 'You never said anything of the kind to me!'

'I did. I did.'

'When? Where?'

'I – don't know.'

'She told me that she had confessed it all to you,' said Frances indistinctly. 'Frankly, I thought she was hysterical and making the whole thing up.'

Stillingfleet looked across at Poirot.

'She could be making it all up,' he said judicially. 'There is quite a case for that solution. But if so, we would have to find the motive, a strong motive, for her desiring the death of those two people, Louise Carpenter and David Baker. A childish hate? Forgotten and done with years ago? Nonsense. David – just to be "free of him"? It is not for that that girls kill! We want better motives than that. A whacking great lot of money – say! – Greed!' He looked round him and his voice changed to a conventional tone.

'We want a little more help. There's still one person missing. Your wife is a long time joining us here, Mr Restarick?'

'I can't think where Mary can be. I've rung up. Claudia has left messages in every place we can think of. By now she ought to have rung up at least from somewhere.'

'Perhaps we have the wrong idea,' said Hercule Poirot. 'Perhaps Madame is at least partly here already – in a manner of speaking.'

'What on earth do you mean?' shouted Restarick angrily.

'Might I trouble you, *chère* Madame?'

Poirot leaned towards Mrs Oliver. Mrs Oliver stared.

'The parcel I entrusted to you –'

'Oh.' Mrs Oliver dived into her shopping bag. She handed the black folder to him.

He heard a sharply indrawn breath near him, but did not turn his head.

He shook off the wrappings delicately and held up – a wig of *bouffant* golden hair.

'Mrs Restarick is not here,' he said, 'but *her wig is*. Interesting.'

'Where the devil did you get that, Poirot?' asked Neele.

'From the overnight bag of Miss Frances Cary from which she had as yet no opportunity of removing it. *Shall we see how it becomes her?*'

With a single deft movement, he swept aside the black hair that masked Frances's face so effectively. Crowned with a golden aureole before she could defend herself, she glared at them.

Mrs Oliver exclaimed:

'Good gracious – it *is* Mary Restarick.'

Frances was twisting like an angry snake. Restarick jumped from his seat to come to her – but Neele's strong grip restrained him.

'No. We don't want any violence from you. The game's up, you know, Mr Restarick – or shall I call you Robert Orwell –'

A stream of profanity came from the man's lips. Frances's voice was raised sharply:

'Shut up, you damned fool!' she said.

II

Poirot had abandoned his trophy, the wig. He had gone to Norma, and taken her hand gently in his.

'Your ordeal is over, my child. The victim will not be sacrificed. You are neither mad, nor have you killed anyone. There are two cruel and heartless creatures who plotted against you, with cunningly administered drugs, with lies, doing their best to drive you either to suicide or to belief in your own guilt and madness.'

Norma was staring with horror at the other plotter.

'My *father*. My *father*? He could think of doing that to *me*. His daughter. My father who loved me –'

'Not your father, *mon enfant* – a man who came here after your father's death, to impersonate him and lay hands on an enormous fortune. Only one person was likely to recognise him – or rather to recognise that this man *was not Andrew Restarick* – the woman who had been Andrew Restarick's mistress fifteen years ago.'

CHAPTER 25

Four people sat in Poirot's room. Poirot in his square chair was drinking a glass of *sirop de cassis*. Norma and Mrs Oliver sat on the sofa. Mrs Oliver was looking particularly festive in unbecoming apple green brocade, surmounted by one of her more painstaking coiffures. Dr Stillingfleet was sprawled out in a chair with his long legs stretched out, so that they seemed to reach half across the room.

'Now then, there are lots of things I want to know,' said Mrs Oliver. Her voice was accusatory.

Poirot hastened to pour oil on troubled waters.

'But, *chère* Madame, consider. What I owe to you I can hardly express. All, but *all* my good ideas were suggested to me by you.'

Mrs Oliver looked at him doubtfully.

'Was it not you who introduced to me the phrase "Third Girl"? It is there that I started – and there, too, that I ended – at the third girl of three living in a flat. Norma was always technically, I suppose, the Third Girl – but when I looked at things *the right way round* it all fell into place. The missing answer, the lost piece of the puzzle, every time it was the same – the third girl.

'It was always, if you comprehend me, *the person who was not there*. She was a name to me, no more.'

'I wonder I never connected her with Mary Restarick,' said Mrs Oliver. 'I'd seen Mary Restarick at Crosshedges, talked to her. Of course the first time I saw Frances Cary, she had black hair hanging all over her face. That would have put anyone off!'

'Again it was you, Madame, who drew my attention to how easily a woman's appearance is altered by the way she arranges her hair. Frances Cary, remember, had had dramatic training. She knew all about the art of swift make-up. She could alter her voice at need. As Frances, she had long black hair, framing her face and half hiding it, heavy dead white *maquillage*, dark pencilled eyebrows and mascara, with a drawling husky voice. Mary Restarick, with her wig of formally arranged golden hair with crimped waves, her conventional clothes, her slight Colonial accent, her brisk way of talking, presented a complete contrast. Yet one felt, from the beginning, that she was not quite *real*. What kind of a woman *was* she? I did not know.

'I was not clever about her – No – I, Hercule Poirot, was not clever at all.'

'Hear, hear,' said Dr Stillingfleet. 'First time I've ever heard *you* say that, Poirot! Wonders will never cease!'

'I don't really see why she wanted two personalities,' said Mrs Oliver. 'It seems unnecessarily confusing.'

'No. It was very valuable to her. It gave her, you see, a perpetual alibi whenever she wanted it. To think that it was there, all the time, before my eyes, and I did not see it! There was the wig – I kept being subconsciously worried by it, but not seeing *why* I was worried. Two women – never, at any time, seen together. Their lives so arranged that no one noticed the large gaps in their time schedules when they were unaccounted for. Mary goes often to London, to shop, to visit house agents, to depart with a sheaf of orders to view, supposedly to spend her time that way. Frances goes to Birmingham, to Manchester, even flies abroad, frequents Chelsea with her special coterie of arty young men whom she employs in various capacities which would not be looked on with approval by the law. Special picture frames were designed for the Wedderburn Gallery. Rising young artists had "shows" there – their pictures sold quite well, and were shipped abroad or sent on exhibition with their frames stuffed with secret packets of heroin – Art rackets – skilful forgeries of the more obscure Old Masters – She arranged and organised all these things. David Baker was one of the artists she employed. He had the gift of being a marvellous copyist.'

Norma murmured: 'Poor David. When I first met him I thought he was wonderful.'

'That picture,' said Poirot dreamily. 'Always, always, I came back to that in my mind. Why had Restarick brought it up to his office? What special significance did it have for him? *Enfin*, I do not admire myself for being so dense.'

'I don't understand about the pictures.'

'It was a very clever idea. It served as a kind of certificate of identity. A pair of portraits, husband and wife, by a celebrated and fashionable portrait painter of his day. David Baker, when they come out of store, replaces Restarick's portrait with one of Orwell, making him about twenty years younger in appearance. Nobody would have dreamed that the portrait was a fake; the style, the brush strokes, the canvas, it was a splendidly convincing bit of work. Restarick hung it over his desk. Anyone who knew Restarick years ago, might say: "I'd hardly have known you!" Or "You've changed quite a lot," would look up at the portrait, but would only think he himself had really forgotten what the other man had looked like!'

'It was a great risk for Restarick – or rather Orwell – to take,' said Mrs Oliver thoughtfully.

'Less than you might think. He was never a *claimant*, you see, in the Tichborne sense. He was only a member of a well-known City firm, returning home after his brother's death to settle up his brother's affairs after having spent some years abroad. He brought with him a young wife recently acquired abroad, and took up residence with an elderly, half blind but extremely distinguished uncle by marriage who had never known him well after his schoolboy days, and who accepted him without question. He had no other near relations, except for the daughter whom he had last seen when she was a child of five. When he originally left for South Africa, the office staff had had two very elderly clerks, since deceased. Junior staff never remains anywhere long nowadays. The family lawyer is also dead. You may be sure that the whole position was studied very carefully on the spot by Frances after they had decided on their coup.

'She had met him, it seems, in Kenya about two years ago. They were both crooks, though with entirely different interests. He went in for various shoddy deals as a prospector – Restarick and Orwell went together to prospect for mineral deposits in somewhat wild country. There was a rumour of Restarick's death (probably true) which was later contradicted.'

'A lot of money in the gamble, I suspect?' said Stillingfleet.

'An enormous amount of money was involved. A terrific gamble – for a terrific stake. It came off. Andrew Restarick was a very rich man himself and he was his brother's heir. Nobody questioned his identity. And then – things went wrong. Out of the blue, he got a letter from a woman who, if she ever came face to face with him, would know at once that he wasn't Andrew Restarick. And a second piece of bad fortune occurred – David Baker started to blackmail him.'

'That might have been expected, I suppose,' said Stillingfleet thoughtfully.

'They didn't expect it,' said Poirot. 'David had never blackmailed before. It was the enormous wealth of this man that went to his head, I expect. The sum he had been paid for faking the portrait seemed to him grossly inadequate. He wanted more. So Restarick wrote him large cheques, and pretended that it was on account of his daughter – to prevent her from making an undesirable marriage. Whether he really wanted to marry her, I do not know – he may have done. But to blackmail two people like Orwell and Frances Cary was a dangerous thing to do.'

'You mean those two just cold-bloodedly planned to kill two people – quite calmly – just like that?' demanded Mrs Oliver.

She looked rather sick.

'They might have added you to their list, Madame,' said Poirot.

'Me? Do you mean that it was one of *them* who hit me on the head? Frances, I suppose? *Not* the poor Peacock?'

'I do not think it was the Peacock. But you had been already to Borodene Mansions. Now you perhaps follow Frances to Chelsea, or so she thinks, with a rather dubious story to account for yourself. So she slips out and gives you a nice little tap on the head to put paid to your curiosity for a while. You would not listen when I warned you there was danger about.'

'I can hardly believe it of her! Lying about in attitudes of a Burne-Jones heroine in that dirty studio that day. But why –' She looked at Norma – then back at Poirot. 'They used *her* – deliberately – worked upon her, drugged her, made her believe that she had murdered two people. Why?'

'They wanted a *victim* . . .' said Poirot.

He rose from his chair and went to Norma.

'*Mon enfant*, you have been through a terrible ordeal. It is a thing that need never happen to you again. Remember that now, you can have confidence in yourself always. To have known, at close quarters, what absolute evil means, is to be armoured against what life can do to you.'

'I suppose you are right,' said Norma. 'To think you are mad – really to *believe* it, is a frightening thing . . .' She shivered. 'I don't see, even now, *why* I escaped – why *anyone* managed to believe that I hadn't killed David – not when even *I* believed I had killed him?'

'Blood was wrong,' said Dr Stillingfleet in a matter-of-fact tone. 'Starting to coagulate. Shirt was "stiff with it", as Miss Jacobs said, not *wet*. You were supposed to have killed him not more than about five minutes before Frances's screaming act.'

'How did she –' Mrs Oliver began to work things out. 'She had been to Manchester –'

'She came home by an earlier train, changed into her Mary wig and make-up on the train. Walked into Borodene Mansions and went up in the lift as an unknown blonde. Went into the flat where David was waiting for her, as she had told him to do. He was quite unsuspecting, and she stabbed him. Then she went out again, and kept watch until she saw Norma coming. She slipped into a public cloakroom, changed her appearance, and joined a friend at the end of the road and walked with her, said goodbye to her at Borodene Mansions and went up herself and did her stuff – quite enjoying doing it, I expect. By the time the police had been called and got there, she didn't think anyone would suspect the time lag. I must say, Norma, you gave us all a hell of a time that day. Insisting on having killed everyone the way you did!'

'I wanted to confess and get it all over . . . Did you – did *you* think I might *really* have done it, then?'

'Me? What do you take me for? I know what my patients will do or won't do. But I thought you were going to make things damned difficult. I didn't know how far Neele was sticking his neck out. Didn't seem proper police procedure to me. Look at the way he gave Poirot here his head.'

Poirot smiled.

'Chief Inspector Neele and I have known each other for many years. Besides, he had been making inquiries about certain matters already. You were never really outside Louise's door. Frances changed the numbers. She reversed the 6 and the 7 on your own door. Those numbers were loose, stuck on with spikes. Claudia was away that night. Frances drugged you so that the whole thing was a nightmare dream to you.

'I saw the truth suddenly. The only other person who could have killed Louise was the real "third girl", Frances Cary.'

'You kept half recognising her, you know,' said Stillingfleet, 'when you described to me how one person seemed to turn into another.'

Norma looked at him thoughtfully.

'You were very rude to people,' she said to Stillingfleet. He looked slightly taken aback.

'Rude?'

'The things you said to everyone. The way you shouted at them.'

'Oh well, yes, perhaps I was . . . I've got in the way of it. People are so damned irritating.'

He grinned suddenly at Poirot.

'She's quite a girl, isn't she?'

Mrs Oliver rose to her feet with a sigh.

'I must go home.' She looked at the two men and then at Norma. 'What are we going to do with *her*?' she asked.

They both looked startled.

'I know she's staying with me at the moment,' she went on. 'And she says she's quite happy. But I mean there it is, quite a problem. Lots and lots of money because your father – the real one, I mean – left it all to you. And that will cause complications, and begging letters and all that. She *could* go and live with old Sir Roderick, but that wouldn't be fun for a girl – he's pretty deaf already as well as blind – and completely selfish. By the way, what about his missing papers, and the girl, and Kew Gardens?'

'They turned up where he thought he'd already looked – Sonia found them,' said Norma, and added, 'Uncle Roddy and Sonia are getting married – next week –'

'No fool like an old fool,' said Stillingfleet.

'Aha!' said Poirot. 'So the young lady prefers life in England to being embroiled in *la politique*. She is perhaps wise, that little one.'

'So that's that,' said Mrs Oliver with finality. 'But to go on about Norma, one has to be *practical.* One's got to make *plans*. The girl can't know what she wants to do all by *herself.* She's waiting for someone to *tell* her.'

She looked at them severely.

Poirot said nothing. He smiled.

'Oh, her?' said Dr Stillingfleet. 'Well, I'll tell you, Norma. I'm flying to Australia Tuesday week. I want to look around first – see if what's been fixed up for me is going to work, and all that. Then I'll cable you and you can join me. Then we get married. You'll have to take my word for it that it's not your money I want. I'm not one of those doctors who want to endow whacking great research establishments and all that. I'm just interested in *people.* I think, too, that you'd be able to manage *me* all right. All that about my being rude to people – I hadn't noticed it myself. It's odd, really, when you think of all the mess you've been in – helpless as a fly in treacle – yet it's not going to be *me* running *you*, it's going to be *you* running *me.*'

Norma stood quite still. She looked at John Stillingfleet very carefully, as though she was considering something that she knew from an entirely different point of view.

And then she smiled. It was a very nice smile – like a happy young nannie.

'All right,' she said.

She crossed the room to Hercule Poirot.

'*I* was rude, too,' she said. 'The day I came here when you were having breakfast. I said to you that you were too old to help me. That was a rude thing to say. *And it wasn't true . . .*'

She put her hands on his shoulders and kissed him.

'You'd better get us a taxi,' she said to Stillingfleet.

Dr Stillingfleet nodded and left the room. Mrs Oliver collected a handbag and a fur stole and Norma slipped on a coat and followed her to the door.

'*Madame, un petit moment –*'

Mrs Oliver turned. Poirot had collected from the recesses of the sofa a handsome coil of grey hair.

Mrs Oliver exclaimed vexedly: 'It's just like everything that they make nowadays, no good at all! Hairpins, I mean. They just slip out, and everything falls *off*!'

She went out frowning.

A moment or two later she poked her head round the door again. She spoke in a conspiratorial whisper:

'Just tell me – it's all right, I've sent her on down – did you send that girl to this particular doctor on purpose?'

'Of course I did. His qualifications are –'

'Never mind his qualifications. You know what I mean. He and she – Did you?'

'If you must know, yes.'

'I thought so,' said Mrs Oliver. 'You do think of things, don't you.'

HALLOWE'EN PARTY

To P.G. Wodehouse
whose books and stories have brightened my
life for many years. Also to show my pleasure
in his having been kind enough to tell me
that he enjoys *my* books

CHAPTER 1

Mrs Ariadne Oliver had gone with the friend with whom she was staying, Judith Butler, to help with the preparations for a children's party which was to take place that same evening.

At the moment it was a scene of chaotic activity. Energetic women came in and out of doors moving chairs, small tables, flower vases, and carrying large quantities of yellow pumpkins which they disposed strategically in selected spots.

It was to be a Hallowe'en party for invited guests of an age group between ten and seventeen years old.

Mrs Oliver, removing herself from the main group, leant against a vacant background of wall and held up a large yellow pumpkin, looking at it critically – 'The last time I saw one of these,' she said, sweeping back her grey hair from her prominent forehead, 'was in the United States last year – hundreds of them. All over the house. I've never seen so many pumpkins. As a matter of fact,' she added thoughtfully, 'I've never really known the difference between a pumpkin and a vegetable marrow. What's this one?'

'Sorry, dear,' said Mrs Butler, as she fell over her friend's feet.

Mrs Oliver pressed herself closer against the wall.

'My fault,' she said. 'I'm standing about and getting in the way. But it *was* rather remarkable, seeing so many pumpkins or vegetable marrows, whatever they are. They were everywhere, in the shops, and in people's houses, with candles or nightlights inside them or strung up. Very interesting really. But it wasn't for a Hallowe'en party, it was Thanksgiving. Now I've always associated pumpkins with Hallowe'en and that's the end of October. Thanksgiving comes much later, doesn't it? Isn't it November, about the third week in November? Anyway, here, Hallowe'en is definitely the 31st of October, isn't it? First Hallowe'en and then, what comes next? All Souls' Day? That's when in Paris you go to cemeteries and put flowers on graves. Not a sad sort of feast. I mean, all the children go too, and enjoy themselves. You go to flower markets first and buy lots and lots of lovely flowers. Flowers never look so lovely as they do in Paris in the market there.'

A lot of busy women were falling over Mrs Oliver occasionally, but they were not listening to her. They were all too busy with what they were doing.

They consisted for the most part of mothers, one or two competent spinsters; there were useful teenagers, boys of sixteen and seventeen climbing up ladders or standing on chairs to put decorations, pumpkins or vegetable marrows or brightly coloured witchballs at a suitable elevation; girls from eleven to fifteen hung about in groups and giggled.

'And after All Souls' Day and cemeteries,' went on Mrs Oliver, lowering her bulk on to the arm of a settee, 'you have All Saints' Day. I think I'm right?'

Nobody responded to this question. Mrs Drake, a handsome middle-aged woman who was giving the party, made a pronouncement.

'I'm not calling this a Hallowe'en party, although of course it is one really. I'm calling it the Eleven Plus party. It's that sort of age group. Mostly people who are leaving the Elms and going on to other schools.'

'But that's not very accurate, Rowena, is it?' said Miss Whittaker, resetting her pince-nez on her nose disapprovingly.

Miss Whittaker as a local school-teacher was always firm on accuracy.

'Because we've abolished the eleven-plus some time ago.'

Mrs Oliver rose from the settee apologetically. 'I haven't been making myself useful. I've just been sitting here saying silly things about pumpkins and vegetable marrows' – And resting my feet, she thought, with a slight pang of conscience, but without sufficient feeling of guilt to say it aloud.

'Now what can I do next?' she asked, and added, 'What lovely apples!'

Someone had just brought a large bowl of apples into the room. Mrs Oliver was partial to apples.

'Lovely red ones,' she added.

'They're not really very good,' said Rowena Drake. 'But they look nice and partified. That's for bobbing for apples. They're rather soft apples, so people will be able to get their teeth into them better. Take them into the library, will you, Beatrice? Bobbing for apples always makes a mess with the water slopping over, but that doesn't matter with the library carpet, it's so old. Oh! Thank you, Joyce.'

Joyce, a sturdy thirteen-year-old, seized the bowl of apples. Two rolled off it and stopped, as though arrested by a witch's wand, at Mrs Oliver's feet.

'You like apples, don't you,' said Joyce. 'I read you did, or perhaps I heard it on the telly. You're the one who writes murder stories, aren't you?'

'Yes,' said Mrs Oliver.

'We ought to have made you do something connected with murders. Have a murder at the party tonight and make people solve it.'

'No, thank you,' said Mrs Oliver. 'Never again.'

'What do you mean, never again?'

'Well, I did once, and it didn't turn out much of a success,' said Mrs Oliver.

'But you've written lots of books,' said Joyce, 'you make a lot of money out of them, don't you?'

'In a way,' said Mrs Oliver, her thoughts flying to the Inland Revenue.

'And you've got a detective who's a Finn.'

Mrs Oliver admitted the fact. A small stolid boy not yet, Mrs Oliver would have thought, arrived at the seniority of the eleven-plus, said sternly, 'Why a Finn?'

'I've often wondered,' said Mrs Oliver truthfully.

Mrs Hargreaves, the organist's wife, came into the room breathing heavily, and bearing a large green plastic pail.

'What about this,' she said, 'for the apple bobbing? Kind of gay, I thought.'

Miss Lee, the doctor's dispenser, said, 'Galvanized bucket's better. Won't tip over so easily. Where are you going to have it, Mrs Drake?'

'I thought the bobbing for apples had better be in the library.

The carpet's old there and a lot of water always gets spilt, anyway.'

'All right. We'll take them along. Rowena, here's another basket of apples.'

'Let me help,' said Mrs Oliver.

She picked up the two apples at her feet. Almost without noticing what she was doing, she sank her teeth into one of them and began to crunch it. Mrs Drake abstracted the second apple from her firmly and restored it to the basket. A buzz of conversation broke out.

'Yes, but where are we going to have the Snapdragon?'

'You ought to have the Snapdragon in the library, it's much the darkest room.'

'No, we're going to have that in the dining-room.'

'We'll have to put something on the table first.'

'There's a green baize to put on that and then the rubber sheet over it.'

'What about the looking-glasses? Shall we really see our husbands in them?'

Surreptitiously removing her shoes and still quietly champing at her apple, Mrs Oliver lowered herself once more on to the settee and surveyed the room full of people critically. She was thinking in her authoress's mind: 'Now, if I was going to make a book about all these people, how should I do it? They're nice people, I should think, on the whole, but who knows?'

In a way, she felt, it was rather fascinating *not* to know anything about them. They all lived in Woodleigh Common, some of them had faint tags attached to them in her memory because of what Judith had told her. Miss Johnson – something to do with the church, not the vicar's sister. Oh no, it was the organist's sister, of course. Rowena Drake, who seemed to run things in Woodleigh Common. The puffing woman who had brought in the pail, a particularly hideous plastic pail. But then Mrs Oliver had never been fond of plastic things. And then the children, the teenage girls and boys.

So far they were really only names to Mrs Oliver. There was a Nan and a Beatrice and a Cathie, a Diana and a Joyce, who was boastful and asked questions. I don't like Joyce much, thought Mrs Oliver. A girl called Ann, who looked tall and superior. There were two adolescent boys who appeared to have just got used to trying out different hair styles, with rather unfortunate results.

A smallish boy entered in some condition of shyness.

'Mummy sent these mirrors to see if they'd do,' he said in a slightly breathless voice.

Mrs Drake took them from him.

'Thank you so much, Eddy,' she said.

'They're just ordinary looking hand-mirrors,' said the girl called Ann. 'Shall we really see our future husbands' faces in them?'

'Some of you may and some may not,' said Judith Butler.

'Did you ever see your husband's face when you went to a party – I mean this kind of a party?'

'Of course she didn't,' said Joyce.

'She might have,' said the superior Beatrice. 'E.S.P. they call it. Extra sensory perception,' she added in the tone of one pleased with being thoroughly conversant with the terms of the times.

'I read one of your books,' said Ann to Mrs Oliver. '*The Dying Goldfish*. It was quite good,' she said kindly.

'I didn't like that one,' said Joyce. 'There wasn't enough blood in it. I like murders to have lots of blood.'

'A bit messy,' said Mrs Oliver, 'don't you think?'

'But exciting,' said Joyce.

'Not necessarily,' said Mrs Oliver.

'I *saw* a murder once,' said Joyce.

'Don't be silly, Joyce,' said Miss Whittaker, the school-teacher.

'I did,' said Joyce.

'Did you really?' asked Cathie, gazing at Joyce with wide eyes, 'really and truly see a murder?'

'Of course she didn't,' said Mrs Drake. 'Don't say silly things, Joyce.'

'I did see a murder,' said Joyce. 'I did. I did. I did.'

A seventeen-year-old boy poised on a ladder looked down interestedly.

'What kind of a murder?' he asked.

'I don't believe it,' said Beatrice.

'Of course not,' said Cathie's mother. 'She's just making it up.'

'I'm *not*. I *saw* it.'

'Why didn't you go to the police about it?' asked Cathie.

'Because I didn't know it *was* a murder when I saw it. It wasn't really till a long time afterwards, I mean, that I began to know that it was a murder. Something that somebody said only about a month or two ago suddenly made me think: Of course, that was a *murder* I saw.'

'You see,' said Ann, 'she's making it all up. It's nonsense.'

'When did it happen?' asked Beatrice.

'Years ago,' said Joyce. 'I was quite young at the time,' she added.

'Who murdered who?' said Beatrice.

'I shan't tell any of you,' said Joyce. 'You're all so horrid about it.'

Miss Lee came in with another kind of bucket. Conversation shifted to a comparison of buckets or plastic pails as most suitable for the sport of bobbing for apples. The majority of the helpers repaired to the library for an appraisal on the spot. Some of the younger members, it may be said, were anxious to demonstrate, by a rehearsal of the difficulties and their own accomplishment in the sport. Hair got wet, water got spilt, towels were sent for to mop it up. In the end it was decided that a galvanized bucket was preferable to the more meretricious charms of a plastic pail which overturned rather too easily.

Mrs Oliver, setting down a bowl of apples which she had carried in to replenish the store required for tomorrow, once more helped herself to one.

'I read in the paper that you were fond of eating apples,' the accusing voice of Ann or Susan – she was not quite sure which – spoke to her.

'It's my besetting sin,' said Mrs Oliver.

'It would be more fun if it was melons,' objected one of the boys. 'They're so juicy. Think of the mess it would make,' he said, surveying the carpet with pleasurable anticipation.

Mrs Oliver, feeling a little guilty at the public arraignment of greediness, left the room in search of a particular apartment, the geography of which is usually fairly easily identified. She went up the staircase and, turning the corner on the half landing, cannoned into a pair, a girl and a boy, clasped in each other's arms and leaning against the door which Mrs Oliver felt fairly certain was the door to the room to which she herself was anxious to gain access. The couple paid no attention to her. They sighed and they snuggled. Mrs Oliver wondered how old they were. The boy was fifteen, perhaps, the girl little more than twelve, although the development of her chest seemed certainly on the mature side.

Apple Trees was a house of fair size. It had, she thought, several agreeable nooks and corners. How selfish people are, thought Mrs Oliver. No consideration for others. That well-known tag from the past came into her mind. It had been said to her in succession by a nursemaid, a nanny, a governess, her grandmother, two great-aunts, her mother and a few others.

'Excuse me,' said Mrs Oliver in a loud, clear voice.

The boy and the girl clung closer than ever, their lips fastened on each other's.

'Excuse me,' said Mrs Oliver again, 'do you *mind* letting me pass? I want to get in at this door.'

Unwillingly the couple fell apart. They looked at her in an aggrieved fashion. Mrs Oliver went in, banged the door and shot the bolt.

It was not a very close fitting door. The faint sound of words came to her from outside.

'Isn't that like people?' one voice said in a somewhat uncertain tenor. 'They might *see* we didn't want to be disturbed.'

'People are so selfish,' piped a girl's voice. 'They never think of anyone but themselves.'

'No consideration for others,' said the boy's voice.

CHAPTER 2

Preparations for a children's party usually give far more trouble to the organizers than an entertainment devised for those of adult years. Food of good quality and suitable alcoholic refreshment – with lemonade on the side, that, to the right people, is quite enough to make a party go. It may cost more but the trouble is infinitely less. So Ariadne Oliver and her friend Judith Butler agreed together.

'What about teenage parties?' said Judith.

'I don't know much about them,' said Mrs Oliver.

'In one way,' said Judith, 'I think they're probably least trouble of all. I mean, they just throw all of us adults out. And say they'll do it all themselves.'

'And do they?'

'Well, not in our sense of the word,' said Judith. 'They forget to order some of the things, and order a lot of other things that nobody likes. Having turfed us out, then they say there were things we ought to have provided for them to find. They break a lot of glasses, and other things, and there's always somebody undesirable or who brings an undesirable friend. You know the sort of thing. Peculiar drugs and – what do they call it? – Flower Pot or Purple Hemp or L.S.D., which I always have thought just meant money; but apparently it doesn't.'

'I suppose it costs it,' suggested Ariadne Oliver.

'It's very unpleasant, and Hemp has a nasty smell.'

'It all sounds very depressing,' said Mrs Oliver.

'Anyway, this party will go all right. Trust Rowena Drake for that. She's a wonderful organizer. You'll see.'

'I don't feel I even want to go to a party,' sighed Mrs Oliver.

'You go up and lie down for an hour or so. You'll see. You'll enjoy it when you get there. I wish Miranda hadn't got a temperature – she's so disappointed at not being able to go, poor child.'

The party came into being at half past seven. Ariadne Oliver had to admit that her friend was right. Arrivals were punctual. Everything went splendidly. It was well imagined, well run and ran like clockwork. There were red and blue lights on the stairs and yellow pumpkins in profusion. The girls and boys arrived holding decorated broomsticks for a competition. After greetings, Rowena Drake announced the programme for the evening. 'First, judging of the broomstick competition,' she said, 'three prizes, first, second and third. Then comes cutting the flour cake. That'll be in the small conservatory. Then bobbing for apples – there's a list pinned upon the wall over there of the partners for that event – then there'll be dancing. Every time the lights go out you change partners. Then girls to the small study where they'll be given their mirrors. After that, supper, Snapdragon and then prize-giving.'

Like all parties, it went slightly stickily at first. The brooms were admired, they were very small miniature brooms, and on the whole the decorating of them had not reached a very high standard of merit, 'which makes it easier,' said Mrs Drake in an aside to one of her friends. 'And it's a very useful thing because I mean there are always one or two children one knows only too well won't win a prize at anything else, so one can cheat a little over this.'

'So unscrupulous, Rowena.'

'I'm not really. I just arrange so that things should be fair and evenly divided. The whole point is that everyone wants to win *something*.'

'What's the Flour Game?' asked Ariadne Oliver.

'Oh yes, of course, you weren't here when we were doing it. Well, you just fill a tumbler with flour, press it in well, then you turn it out in a tray and place a sixpence on top of it. Then everyone slices a slice off it very carefully so as not to tumble the sixpence off. As soon as someone tumbles the sixpence off, that person goes out. It's a sort of elimination. The last one left in gets the sixpence of course. Now then, away we go.'

And away they went. Squeals of excitement were heard coming from the library where bobbing for apples went on, and competitors returned from there with wet locks and having disposed a good deal of water about their persons.

One of the most popular contests, at any rate among the girls, was the arrival of the Hallowe'en witch played by Mrs Goodbody, a local cleaning woman who, not only having the necessary hooked nose and chin which almost met, was admirably proficient in producing a semi-cooing voice which had definitely sinister undertones and also produced magical doggerel rhymes.

'Now then, come along, Beatrice, is it? Ah, Beatrice. A very interesting name. Now you want to know what your husband is going to look like. Now, my dear, sit here. Yes, yes, under this light here. Sit here and hold this little mirror in your hand, and presently when the lights go out you'll see him appear. You'll see him looking over your shoulder. Now hold the mirror steady. *Abracadabra, who shall see? The face of the man who will marry me. Beatrice, Beatrice, you shall find, the face of the man who shall please your mind.*'

A sudden shaft of light shot across the room from a step-ladder, placed behind a screen. It hit the right spot in the room, which was reflected in the mirror grasped in Beatrice's excited hand.

'Oh!' cried Beatrice. 'I've seen him. I've seen him! I can see him in my mirror!'

The beam was shut off, the lights came on and a coloured photograph pasted on a card floated down from the ceiling. Beatrice danced about excitedly.

'That was him! That was him! I saw him,' she cried. 'Oh, he's got a *lovely* ginger beard.'

She rushed to Mrs Oliver, who was the nearest person.

'Do look, do look. Don't you think he's rather wonderful? He's like Eddie Presweight, the pop singer. Don't you think so?'

Mrs Oliver did think he looked like one of the faces she daily deplored having to see in her morning paper. The beard, she thought, had been an after-thought of genius.

'Where do all these things come from?' she asked.

'Oh, Rowena gets Nicky to make them. And his friend Desmond helps. He experiments a good deal with photography. He and a couple of pals of his made themselves up, with a great deal of hair or side-burns or beards and things. And then with the light on him and everything, of course it sends the girls wild with delight.'

'I can't help thinking,' said Ariadne Oliver, 'that girls are really very silly nowadays.'

'Don't you think they always were?' asked Rowena Drake.

Mrs Oliver considered.

'I suppose you're right,' she admitted.

'Now then,' cried Mrs Drake – 'supper.'

Supper went off well. Rich iced cakes, savouries, prawns, cheese and nut confections. The eleven-pluses stuffed themselves.

'And now,' said Rowena, 'the last one for the evening. Snapdragon. Across there, through the pantry. That's right. Now then. Prizes first.'

The prizes were presented, and then there was a wailing, banshee call. The children rushed across the hall back to the dining-room.

The food had been cleared away. A green baize cloth was laid across the table and here was borne a great dish of flaming raisins. Everybody shrieked, rushing forward, snatching the blazing raisins, with cries of 'Ow, I'm burned! Isn't it lovely?' Little by little the Snapdragon flickered and died down. The lights went up. The party was over.

'It's been a great success,' said Rowena.

'So it should be with all the trouble you've taken.'

'It was lovely,' said Judith quietly. 'Lovely.'

'And now,' she added ruefully, 'we'll have to clear up a bit. We can't leave everything for those poor women tomorrow morning.'

CHAPTER 3

In a flat in London the telephone bell rang. The owner of the flat, Hercule Poirot, stirred in his chair. Disappointment attacked him. He knew before he answered it what it meant. His friend Solly, with whom he had been going to spend the evening, reviving their never-ending controversy about the real culprit in the Canning Road Municipal Baths murder, was about to say that he could not come. Poirot, who had collected certain bits of evidence in favour of his own somewhat far-fetched theory, was deeply disappointed. He did not think his friend Solly would accept his suggestions, but he had no doubt that when Solly in his turn produced his own fantastic beliefs, he himself, Hercule Poirot, would just as easily be able to demolish them in the name of sanity, logic, order and method. It was annoying, to say the least of it, if Solly did not come this evening. But it is true that when they had met earlier in the day, Solly had been racked with a chesty cough and was in a state of highly infectious catarrh.

'He had a nasty cold,' said Hercule Poirot, 'and no doubt, in spite of the remedies that I have handy here, he would probably have given it to me. It is better that he should not come. *Tout de même*,' he added, with a sigh, 'it will mean that now I shall pass a dull evening.'

Many of the evenings were dull now, Hercule Poirot thought. His mind, magnificent as it was (for he had never doubted that fact) required stimulation from outside sources. He had never been of a philosophic cast of mind. There were times when he almost regretted that he had not taken to the study of theology instead of going into the police force in his early days. The number of angels who could dance on the point of a needle; it would be interesting to feel that that mattered and to argue passionately on the point with one's colleagues.

His manservant, George, entered the room.

'It was Mr Solomon Levy, sir.'

'Ah yes,' said Hercule Poirot.

'He very much regrets that he will not be able to join you this evening. He is in bed with a serious bout of 'flu.'

'He has not got 'flu,' said Hercule Poirot. 'He has only a nasty cold. Everyone always thinks they have 'flu. It sounds more important. One gets more sympathy. The trouble with a catarrhal cold is that it is hard to glean the proper amount of sympathetic consideration from one's friends.'

'Just as well he isn't coming here, sir, really,' said George. 'Those colds in the head are very infectious. Wouldn't be good for you to go down with one of those.'

'It would be extremely tedious,' Poirot agreed.

The telephone bell rang again.

'And now who has a cold?' he demanded. 'I have not asked anyone else.'

George crossed towards the telephone.

'I will take the call here,' said Poirot. 'I have no doubt that it is nothing of interest. But at any rate –' he shrugged his shoulders '– it will perhaps pass the time. Who knows?'

George said, 'Very good, sir,' and left the room.

Poirot stretched out a hand, raised the receiver, thus stilling the clamour of the bell.

'Hercule Poirot speaks,' he said, with a certain grandeur of manner designed to impress whoever was at the other end of the line.

'That's wonderful,' said an eager voice. A female voice, slightly impaired with breathlessness. 'I thought you'd be sure to be out, that you wouldn't be there.'

'Why should you think that?' inquired Poirot.

'Because I can't help feeling that nowadays things always happen to frustrate one. You want someone in a terrible hurry, you feel you can't wait, and you *have* to wait. I wanted to get hold of you urgently – absolutely urgently.'

'And who are you?' asked Hercule Poirot.

The voice, a female one, seemed surprised.

'Don't you *know*?' it said incredulously.

'Yes, I know,' said Hercule Poirot. 'You are my friend, Ariadne.'

'And I'm in a terrible state,' said Ariadne.

'Yes, yes, I can hear that. Have you also been running? You are very breathless, are you not?'

'I haven't exactly been running. It's emotion. Can I come and see you *at once*?'

Poirot let a few moments elapse before he answered. His friend, Mrs Oliver, sounded in a highly excitable condition. Whatever was the matter with her, she would no doubt spend a very long time pouring out her grievances, her woes, her frustrations or whatever was ailing her. Once having established herself within Poirot's sanctum, it might be hard to induce her to go home without a certain amount of impoliteness. The things that excited Mrs Oliver were so numerous and frequently so unexpected that one had to be careful how one embarked upon a discussion of them.

'Something has upset you?'

'Yes. Of course I'm upset. I don't know what to do. I don't know – oh, I don't know anything. What I feel is that I've got to come and tell you – tell you just what's happened, for you're the only person who might know what to do. Who might tell me what I ought to do. So can I come?'

'But certainly, but certainly. I shall be delighted to receive you.'

The receiver was thrown down heavily at the other end and Poirot summoned George, reflected a few minutes, then ordered lemon barley water, bitter lemon and a glass of brandy for himself.

'Mrs Oliver will be here in about ten minutes,' he said.

George withdrew. He returned with the brandy for Poirot, who accepted it with a nod of satisfaction, and George then proceeded to provide the teetotal refreshment that was the only thing likely to appeal to Mrs Oliver. Poirot took a sip of brandy delicately, fortifying himself for the ordeal which was about to descend upon him.

'It's a pity,' he murmured to himself, 'that she is so scatty. And yet, she has originality of mind. It could be that I am going to enjoy what she is coming to tell me. It could be –' he reflected a minute '– that it may take a great deal of the evening and that it will all be excessively foolish. *Eh bien*, one must take one's risks in life.'

A bell sounded. A bell on the outside door of the flat this time. It was not a single pressure of the button. It lasted for a long time with a kind of steady action that was very effective, the sheer making of noise.

'Assuredly, she has excited herself,' said Poirot.

He heard George go to the door, open it, and before any decorous announcement could be made the door of his sitting-room opened and Ariadne Oliver charged through it, with George in tow behind her, hanging on to something that looked like a fisherman's sou'wester and oilskins.

'What on earth are you wearing?' said Hercule Poirot. 'Let George take it from you. It's very wet.'

'Of course it's wet,' said Mrs Oliver. 'It's very wet out. I never thought about water before. It's a terrible thing to think of.'

Poirot looked at her with interest.

'Will you have some lemon barley water,' he said, 'or could I persuade you to a small glass of *eau de vie*?'

'I hate water,' said Mrs Oliver.

Poirot looked surprised.

'I hate it. I've never thought about it before. What it can do, and everything.'

'My dear friend,' said Hercule Poirot, as George extricated her from the flapping folds of watery oilskin. 'Come and sit down here. Let George finally relieve you of – what is it you are wearing?'

'I got it in Cornwall,' said Mrs Oliver. 'Oilskins. A real, proper fisherman's oilskin.'

'Very useful to him, no doubt,' said Poirot, 'but not, I think, so suitable for you. Heavy to wear. But come – sit down and tell me.'

'I don't know how,' said Mrs Oliver, sinking into a chair. 'Sometimes, you know, I can't feel it's really true. But it happened. It really happened.'

'Tell me,' said Poirot.

'That's what I've come for. But now I've got here, it's so difficult because I don't know where to begin.'

'At the beginning?' suggested Poirot, 'or is that too conventional a way of acting?'

'I don't know when the beginning was. Not really. It could have been a long time ago, you know.'

'Calm yourself,' said Poirot. 'Gather together the various threads of this matter in your mind and tell me. What is it that has so upset you?'

'It would have upset you, too,' said Mrs Oliver. 'At least, I suppose it would.' She looked rather doubtful. 'One doesn't know, really, what does upset you. You take so many things with a lot of calm.'

'It is often the best way,' said Poirot.

'All right,' said Mrs Oliver. 'It began with a party.'

'Ah yes,' said Poirot, relieved to have something as ordinary and sane as a party presented to him. 'A party. You went to a party and something happened.'

'Do you know what a Hallowe'en party is?' said Mrs Oliver.

'I know what Hallowe'en is,' said Poirot. 'The 31st of October.' He twinkled slightly as he said, 'When witches ride on broomsticks.'

'There *were* broomsticks,' said Mrs Oliver. 'They gave prizes for them.'

'Prizes?'

'Yes, for who brought the best decorated ones.'

Poirot looked at her rather doubtfully. Originally relieved at the mention of a party, he now again felt slightly doubtful. Since he knew that Mrs Oliver did not partake of spirituous liquor, he could not make one of the assumptions that he might have made in any other case.

'A children's party,' said Mrs Oliver. 'Or rather, an eleven-plus party.'

'Eleven-plus?'

'Well, that's what they used to call it, you know, in schools. I mean they see how bright you are, and if you're bright enough to pass your eleven-plus, you go on to a grammar school or something. But if you're not bright enough, you go to something called a Secondary Modern. A silly name. It doesn't seem to mean anything.'

'I do not, I confess, really understand what you are talking about,' said Poirot. They seemed to have got away from parties and entered into the realms of education.

Mrs Oliver took a deep breath and began again.

'It started really,' she said, 'with the apples.'

'Ah yes,' said Poirot, 'it would. It always might with you, mightn't it?'

He was thinking to himself of a small car on a hill and a large woman getting out of it, and a bag of apples breaking, and the apples running and cascading down the hill.

'Yes,' he said encouragingly, 'apples.'

'Bobbing for apples,' said Mrs Oliver. 'That's one of the things you do at a Hallowe'en party.'

'Ah yes, I think I have heard of that, yes.'

'You see, all sorts of things were being done. There was bobbing for apples, and cutting sixpence off a tumblerful of flour, and looking in a looking-glass –'

'To see your true love's face?' suggested Poirot knowledgeably.

'Ah,' said Mrs Oliver, 'you're beginning to understand at last.'

'A lot of old folklore, in fact,' said Poirot, 'and this all took place at your party.'

'Yes, it was all a great success. It finished up with Snapdragon. You know, burning raisins in a great dish. I suppose –' her voice faltered, '– I suppose that must be the actual time when it was done.'

'When what was done?'

'A murder. After the Snapdragon everyone went home,' said Mrs Oliver. 'That, you see, was when they couldn't find her.'

'Find whom?'

'A girl. A girl called Joyce. Everyone called her name and looked around and asked if she'd gone home with anyone else, and her mother got rather annoyed and said that Joyce must have felt tired or ill or something and gone off by herself, and that it was very thoughtless of her not to leave word. All the sort of things that mothers say when things like that happen. But anyway, we couldn't find Joyce.'

'And had she gone home by herself?'

'No,' said Mrs Oliver, 'she hadn't gone home . . .' Her voice faltered. 'We found her in the end – in the library. That's where – where someone did it, you know. Bobbing for apples. The bucket was there. A big, galvanized bucket. They wouldn't have the plastic one. Perhaps if they'd had the plastic one it wouldn't have happened. It wouldn't have been heavy enough. It might have tipped over –'

'What happened?' said Poirot. His voice was sharp.

'That's where she was found,' said Mrs Oliver. 'Someone, you know, someone had shoved her head down into the water with the apples. Shoved her down and held her there so that she was dead, of course. Drowned. *Drowned.* Just in a galvanized iron bucket nearly full of water. Kneeling there, sticking her head down to bob at an apple. I hate apples,' said Mrs Oliver. 'I never want to see an apple again.'

Poirot looked at her. He stretched out a hand and filled a small glass with cognac.

'Drink this,' he said. 'It will do you good.'

CHAPTER 4

Mrs Oliver put down the glass and wiped her lips.

'You were right,' she said. 'That – that helped. I was getting hysterical.'

'You have had a great shock, I see now. When did this happen?'

'Last night. Was it only last night? Yes, yes, of course.'

'And you came to me.'

It was not quite a question, but it displayed a desire for more information than Poirot had yet had.

'You came to me – why?'

'I thought you could help,' said Mrs Oliver. 'You see, it's – it's not simple.'

'It could be and it could not,' said Poirot. 'A lot depends. You must tell me more, you know. The police, I presume, are in charge. A doctor was, no doubt, called. What did he say?'

'There's to be an inquest,' said Mrs Oliver.

'Naturally.'

'Tomorrow or the next day.'

'This girl, Joyce, how old was she?'

'I don't know exactly. I should think perhaps twelve or thirteen.'

'Small for her age?'

'No, no, I should think rather mature, perhaps. Lumpy,' said Mrs Oliver.

'Well developed? You mean sexy-looking?'

'Yes, that is what I mean. But I don't think that was the kind of crime it was – I mean that would have been more simple, wouldn't it?'

'It is the kind of crime,' said Poirot, 'of which one reads every day in the paper. A girl who is attacked, a school child who is assaulted – yes, every day. This happened in a private house which makes it different, but perhaps not so different as all that. But all the same, I'm not sure yet that you've told me everything.'

'No, I don't suppose I have,' said Mrs Oliver. 'I haven't told you the reason, I mean, why I came to you.'

'You knew this Joyce, you knew her well?'

'I didn't know her at all. I'd better explain to you, I think, just how I came to be there.'

'There is *where*?'

'Oh, a place called Woodleigh Common.'

'Woodleigh Common,' said Poirot thoughtfully. 'Now where lately –' he broke off.

'It's not very far from London. About – oh, thirty to forty miles, I think. It's near Medchester. It's one of those places where there are a few nice houses, but where a certain amount of new building has been done. Residential. A good school nearby, and people can commute from there to London or into Medchester. It's quite an ordinary sort of place where people with what you might call everyday reasonable incomes live.'

'Woodleigh Common,' said Poirot again, thoughtfully.

'I was staying with a friend there. Judith Butler. She's a widow. I went on a Hellenic cruise this year and Judith was on the cruise and we became friends. She's got a daughter. A girl called Miranda who is twelve or thirteen. Anyway, she asked me to come and stay and she said friends of hers were giving this party for children, and it was to be a Hallowe'en party. She said perhaps I had some interesting ideas.'

'Ah,' said Poirot, 'she did not suggest this time that you should arrange a murder hunt or anything of that kind?'

'Good gracious, no,' said Mrs Oliver. 'Do you think I should ever consider such a thing again?'

'I should think it unlikely.'

'But it happened, that's what's so awful,' said Mrs Oliver. 'I mean, it couldn't have happened just because *I* was there, could it?'

'I do not think so. At least – Did any of the people at the party know who you were?'

'Yes,' said Mrs Oliver. 'One of the children said something about my writing books and that they liked murders. That's how it – well – that's what led to the thing – I mean to the thing that made me come to you.'

'Which you still haven't told me.'

'Well, you see, at first I didn't think of it. Not straight away. I mean, children do queer things sometimes. I mean there are queer children about, children who – well, once I suppose they would have been in mental homes and things, but they send them home now and tell them to lead ordinary lives or something, and then they go and do something like this.'

'There were some young adolescents there?'

'There were two boys, or youths as they always seem to call them in police reports. About sixteen to eighteen.'

'I suppose one of them might have done it. Is that what the police think?'

'They don't say what they think,' said Mrs Oliver, 'but they looked as though they might think so.'

'Was this Joyce an attractive girl?'

'I don't think so,' said Mrs Oliver. 'You mean attractive to boys, do you?'

'No,' said Poirot, 'I think I meant – well, just the plain simple meaning of the word.'

'I don't think she was a very nice girl,' said Mrs Oliver, 'not one you'd want to talk to much. She was the sort of girl who shows off and boasts. It's a rather tiresome age, I think. It sounds unkind what I'm saying, but –'

'It is not unkind in murder to say what the victim was like,' said Poirot. 'It is very, very necessary. The personality of the victim is the cause of many a murder. How many people were there in the house at the time?'

'You mean for the party and so on? Well, I suppose there were five or six women, some mothers, a school-teacher, a doctor's wife, or sister, I think, a couple of middle-aged married people, the two boys of sixteen to eighteen, a girl of fifteen, two or three of eleven or twelve – well that sort of thing. About twenty-five or thirty in all, perhaps.'

'Any strangers?'

'They all knew each other, I think. Some better than others. I think the girls were mostly in the same school. There were a couple of women who had come in to help with the food and the supper and things like that. When the party ended, most of the mothers went home with their children. I stayed behind with Judith and a couple of others to help Rowena Drake, the woman who gave the party, to clear up a bit, so the cleaning women who came in the morning wouldn't have so much mess to deal with. You know, there was a lot of flour about, and paper caps out of crackers and different things. So we swept up a bit, and we got to the library last of all. And that's when – when we found her. And then I remembered what she'd said.'

'What who had said?'

'Joyce.'

'What did she say? We are coming to it now, are we not? We are coming to the reason why you are here?'

'Yes. I thought it wouldn't mean anything to – oh, to a doctor or the police or anyone, but I thought it might mean something to you.'

'*Eh bien*,' said Poirot, 'tell me. Was this something Joyce said at the party?'

'No – earlier in the day. That afternoon when we were fixing things up. It was after they'd talked about my writing murder stories and Joyce said "I *saw* a murder once" and her mother or somebody said "Don't be silly, Joyce, saying things like that" and one of the older girls said "You're just making it up" and Joyce said "I did. I *saw* it I tell you. I did. I saw someone do a murder," but no one believed her. They just laughed and she got very angry.'

'Did *you* believe her?'

'No, of course not.'

'I see,' said Poirot, 'yes, I see.' He was silent for some moments, tapping a finger on the table. Then he said: 'I wonder – she gave no details – no names?'

'No. She went on boasting and shouting a bit and being angry because most of the other girls were laughing at her. The mothers, I think, and the older people, were rather cross with her. But the girls and the younger boys just laughed at her! They said things like "Go on, Joyce, when was this? Why did you never tell us about it?" And Joyce said, "I'd forgotten all about it, it was so long ago".'

'Aha! Did she say how long ago?'

'"Years ago",' she said. You know, in rather a would-be grown-up way.

'"Why didn't you go and tell the police then?" one of the girls said. Ann, I think, or Beatrice. Rather a smug, superior girl.'

'Aha, and what did she say to *that*?'

'She said: "Because I didn't know at the time it *was* a murder".'

'A very interesting remark,' said Poirot, sitting up rather straighter in his chair.

'She'd got a bit mixed up by then, I think,' said Mrs Oliver. 'You know, trying to explain herself and getting angry because they were all teasing her.

'They kept asking her why she hadn't gone to the police, and she kept on saying "Because I didn't know then that it was a murder. It wasn't until afterwards that it came to me quite suddenly that that was what I had seen".'

'But nobody showed any signs of believing her – and you yourself did not believe her – but when you came across her dead you suddenly felt that she might have been speaking the truth?'

'Yes, just that. I didn't know what I ought to do, or what I could do. But then, later, I thought of you.'

Poirot bowed his head gravely in acknowledgement. He was silent for a moment or two, then he said:

'I must pose to you a serious question, and reflect before you answer it. Do you think that this girl had *really* seen a murder? Or do you think that she merely *believed* that she had seen a murder?'

'The first, I think,' said Mrs Oliver. 'I didn't at the time. I just thought that she was vaguely remembering something she had once seen and was working it up to make it sound important and exciting. She became very vehement, saying, "I *did* see it, I tell you. I *did* see it happen".'

'And so.'

'And so I've come along to you,' said Mrs Oliver, 'because the only way her death makes sense is that there really *was* a murder and that she was a witness to it.'

'That would involve certain things. It would involve that one of the people who were at the party committed the murder, and that that same person must also have been there earlier that day and have heard what Joyce said.'

'You don't think I'm just imagining things, do you?' said Mrs Oliver. 'Do you think that it is all just my very farfetched imagination?'

'A girl was murdered,' said Poirot. 'Murdered by someone who had strength enough to hold her head down in a bucket of water. An ugly murder and a murder that was committed with what we might call, no time to lose. Somebody was threatened, and whoever it was struck as soon as it was humanly possible.'

'Joyce could not have known who it was who did the murder she saw,' said Mrs Oliver. 'I mean she wouldn't have said what she did if there was someone actually in the room who was concerned.'

'No,' said Poirot, 'I think you are right there. She saw a murder, but she did not see the murderer's face. We have to go beyond that.'

'I don't understand exactly what you mean.'

'It could be that someone who was there earlier in the day and heard Joyce's accusation knew about the murder, knew who committed the murder, perhaps was closely involved with that person. It may have been that someone thought he was the only person who knew what his wife had done, or his mother or his daughter or his son. Or it might have been a woman who knew what her husband or mother or daughter or son had done. Someone who thought that no one else knew. And then Joyce began talking . . .'

'And so –'

'Joyce had to die?'

'Yes. What are you going to do?'

'I have just remembered,' said Hercule Poirot, 'why the name of Woodleigh Common was familiar to me.'

CHAPTER 5

Hercule Poirot looked over the small gate which gave admission to Pine Crest. It was a modern, perky little house, nicely built. Hercule Poirot was slightly out of breath. The small, neat house in front of him was very suitably named. It was on a hill top, and the hill top was planted with a few sparse pines. It had a small neat garden and a large elderly man was trundling along a path a big tin galvanized waterer.

Superintendent Spence's hair was now grey all over instead of having a neat touch of grey hair at the temples. He had not shrunk much in girth. He stopped trundling his can and looked at the visitor at the gate. Hercule Poirot stood there without moving.

'God bless my soul,' said Superintendent Spence. 'It must be. It can't be but it is. Yes, it must be. Hercule Poirot, as I live.'

'Aha,' said Hercule Poirot, 'you know me. That is gratifying.'

'May your moustaches never grow less,' said Spence.

He abandoned the watering can and came down to the gate.

'Diabolical weeds,' he said. 'And what brings you down here?'

'What has brought me to many places in my time,' said Hercule Poirot, 'and what once a good many years ago brought *you* to see *me*. Murder.'

'I've done with murder,' said Spence, 'except in the case of weeds. That's what I'm doing now. Applying weed killer. Never so easy as you think, something's always wrong, usually the weather. Mustn't be too wet, mustn't be too dry and all the rest of it. How did you know where to find me?' he asked as he unlatched the gate and Poirot passed through.

'You sent me a Christmas card. It had your new address notified on it.'

'Ah yes, so I did. I'm old-fashioned, you know. I like to send round cards at Christmas time to a few old friends.'

'I appreciate that,' said Poirot.

Spence said, 'I'm an old man now.'

'We are both old men.'

'Not much grey in your hair,' said Spence.

'I attend to that with a bottle,' said Hercule Poirot. 'There is no need to appear in public with grey hair unless you wish to do so.'

'Well, I don't think jet black would suit me,' said Spence.

'I agree,' said Poirot. 'You look most distinguished with grey hair.'

'I should never think of myself as a distinguished man.'

'I think of you as such. Why have you come to live in Woodleigh Common?'

'As a matter of fact, I came here to join forces with a sister of mine. She lost her husband, her children are married and living abroad, one in Australia and the other in South Africa. So I moved in here. Pensions don't go far nowadays, but we do pretty comfortably living together. Come and sit down.'

He led the way on to the small glazed-in verandah where there were chairs and a table or two. The autumn sun fell pleasantly upon this retreat.

'What shall I get you?' said Spence. 'No fancy stuff here, I'm afraid. No blackcurrant or rose hip syrup or any of your patent things. Beer? Or shall I get Elspeth to make you a cup of tea? Or I can do you a shandy or Coca-Cola or some cocoa if you like it. My sister, Elspeth, is a cocoa drinker.'

'You are very kind. For me, I think a shandy. The ginger beer and the beer? That is right, is it not?'

'Absolutely so.'

He went into the house and returned shortly afterwards carrying two large glass mugs. 'I'm joining you,' he said.

He drew a chair up to the table and sat down, placing the two glasses in front of himself and Poirot.

'What was it you said just now?' he said, raising his glass. 'We won't say "Here's to crime." I've done with crime, and if you mean the crime I think you do, in fact which I think you have to do, because I don't recall any other crime just lately. I don't like the particular form of murder we've just had.'

'No. I do not think you would do so.'

'We *are* talking about the child who had her head shoved into a bucket?'

'Yes,' said Poirot, 'that is what I am talking about.'

'I don't know why you come to me,' said Spence. 'I'm nothing to do with the police nowadays. All that's over many years ago.'

'Once a policeman,' said Hercule Poirot, 'always a policeman. That is to say, there is always the point of view of the policeman behind the point of view of the ordinary man. I know, I who talk to you. I, too, started in the police force in my country.'

'Yes, so you did. I remember now your telling me. Well, I suppose one's outlook is a bit slanted, but it's a long time since I've had any active connection.'

'But you hear the gossip,' said Poirot. 'You have friends of your own trade. You will hear what they think or suspect or what they know.'

Spence sighed.

'One knows too much,' he said, 'that is one of the troubles nowadays. There is a crime, a crime of which the pattern is familiar, and you know, that is to say the active police officers know, pretty well who's probably done that crime. They don't tell the newspapers but they make their inquiries, and *they know*. But whether they're going to get any further than that – well, things have their difficulties.'

'You mean the wives and the girl friends and the rest of it?'

'Partly that, yes. In the end, perhaps, one gets one's man. Sometimes a year or two passes. I'd say, you know, roughly, Poirot, that more girls nowadays marry wrong 'uns than they ever used to in my time.'

Hercule Poirot considered, pulling his moustaches.

'Yes,' he said, 'I can see that that might be so. I suspect that girls have always been partial to the bad lots, as you say, but in the past there were safeguards.'

'That's right. People were looking after them. Their mothers looked after them. Their aunts and their older sisters looked after them. Their younger sisters and brothers knew what was going on. Their fathers were not averse to kicking the wrong young men out of the house. Sometimes, of course, the girls used to run away with one of the bad lots. Nowadays there's no need even to do that. Mother doesn't know who the girl's out with, father's not told who the girl is out with, brothers know who the girl is out with but they think "more fool her". If the parents refuse consent, the couple go before a magistrate and manage to get permission to marry, and then when the young man who everyone knows is a bad lot proceeds to prove to everybody, including his wife, that he *is* a bad lot, the fat's in the fire! But love's love; the girl doesn't want to think that her Henry has these revolting habits, these criminal tendencies, and all the rest of it. She'll lie for him, swear black's white for him and everything else. Yes, it's difficult. Difficult for us, I mean. Well, there's no good going on saying things were better in the old days. Perhaps we only thought so. Anyway, Poirot, how did you get yourself mixed up in all this? This isn't your part of the country, is it? Always thought you lived in London. You used to when I knew you.'

'I still live in London. I involved myself here at the request of a friend, Mrs Oliver. You remember Mrs Oliver?'

Spence raised his head, closed his eyes and appeared to reflect.

'Mrs Oliver? Can't say that I do.'

'She writes books. Detective stories. You met her, if you will throw your mind back, during the time that you persuaded me to investigate the murder of Mrs McGinty. You will not have forgotten Mrs McGinty?'

'Good lord, no. But it was a long time ago. You did me a good turn there, Poirot, a very good turn. I went to you for help and you didn't let me down.'

'I was honoured – flattered – that you should come to consult me,' said Poirot. 'I must say that I despaired once or twice. The man we had to save – to save his neck in those days I believe, it is long ago enough for that – was a man who was excessively difficult to do anything for. The kind of standard example of how not to do anything useful for himself.'

'Married that girl, didn't he? The wet one. Not the bright one with the peroxide hair. Wonder how they got on together. Have you ever heard about it?'

'No,' said Poirot. 'I presume all goes well with them.'

'Can't see what she saw in him.'

'It is difficult,' said Poirot, 'but it is one of the great consolations in nature that a man, however unattractive, will find that he is attractive – to some woman. One can only say or hope that they married and lived happily ever afterwards.'

'Shouldn't think they lived happily ever afterwards if they had to have Mother to live with them.'

'No, indeed,' said Poirot. 'Or Step-father,' he added.

'Well,' said Spence, 'here we are talking of old days again. All that's over. I always thought that man, can't remember his name now, ought to have run an undertaking parlour. Had just the face and manner for it. Perhaps he did. The girl had some money, didn't she? Yes, he'd have made a very good undertaker. I can see him, all in black, calling for orders for the funeral. Perhaps he can even have been enthusiastic over the right kind of elm or teak or whatever they use for coffins. But he'd never have made good selling insurance or real estate. Anyway, don't let's harp back.' Then he said suddenly, 'Mrs Oliver. Ariadne Oliver. *Apples*. Is that how she's got herself mixed up in this? That poor child got her head shoved under water in a bucket of floating apples, didn't she, at a party? Is that what interested Mrs Oliver?'

'I don't think she was particularly attracted because of the apples,' said Poirot, 'but she was at the party.'

'Do you say she lived here?'

'No, she does not live here. She was staying with a friend, a Mrs Butler.'

'Butler? Yes, I know her. Lives down not far from the church. Widow. Husband was an airline pilot. Has a daughter. Rather nice-looking girl. Pretty manners. Mrs Butler's rather an attractive woman, don't you think so?'

'I have as yet barely met her, but, yes, I thought she was very attractive.'

'And how does this concern you, Poirot? You weren't here when it happened?'

'No. Mrs Oliver came to me in London. She was upset, very upset. She wanted me to do something.'

A faint smile showed on Superintendent Spence's face.

'I see. Same old story. I came up to you, too, because I wanted you to do something.'

'And I have carried things one step further,' said Poirot. '*I* have come to *you*.'

'Because you want me to do something? I tell you, there's nothing I can do.'

'Oh yes there is. You can tell me all about the people. The

people who live here. The people who went to that party. The fathers and mothers of the children who were at the party. The school, the teachers, the lawyers, the doctors. Somebody, during a party, induced a child to kneel down, and perhaps, laughing, saying: "I'll show you the best way to get hold of an apple with your teeth. I know the trick of it." And then he or she – whoever it was – put a hand on that girl's head. There wouldn't have been much struggle or noise or anything of that kind.'

'A nasty business,' said Spence. 'I thought so when I heard about it. What do you want to know? I've been here a year. My sister's been here longer – two or three years. It's not a big community. It's not a particularly settled one either. People come and go. The husband has a job in either Medchester or Great Canning, or one of the other places round about. Their children go to school here. Then perhaps the husband changes his job and they go somewhere else. It's not a fixed community. Some of the people have been here a long time, Miss Emlyn, the school-mistress, has, Dr Ferguson has. But on the whole, it fluctuates a bit.'

'One supposes,' said Hercule Poirot, 'that having agreed with you that this was a nasty business, I might hope that you would know who are the nasty people here.'

'Yes,' said Spence. 'It's the first thing one looks for, isn't it? And the next thing one looks for is a nasty adolescent in a thing of this kind. Who wants to strangle or drown or get rid of a lump of a girl of thirteen? There doesn't seem to have been any evidence of a sexual assault or anything of that kind, which would be the first thing one looks for. Plenty of that sort of thing in every small town or village nowadays. There again, I think there's more of it than there used to be in my young day. We had our mentally disturbed, or whatever they call them, but not so many as we have now. I expect there are more of them let out of the place they ought to be kept safe in. All our mental homes are too full; over-crowded, so doctors say "Let him or her lead a normal life. Go back and live with his relatives," etc. And then the nasty bit of goods, or the poor afflicted fellow, whichever way you like to look at it, gets the urge again and another young woman goes out walking and is found in a gravel pit, or is silly enough to take lifts in a car. Children don't come home from school because they've accepted a lift from a stranger, although they've been warned not to. Yes, there's a lot of that nowadays.'

'Does that quite fit the pattern we have here?'

'Well, it's the first thing one thinks of,' said Spence. 'Somebody was at the party who had the urge, shall we say. Perhaps he'd done it before, perhaps he'd only wanted to do it. I'd say roughly that there might be some past history of assaulting a child somewhere. As far as I know, nobody's come up with anything of that kind. Not officially, I mean. There were two in the right age group at the party. Nicholas Ransom, nice-looking lad, seventeen or eighteen. He'd be the right age. Comes from the East Coast or somewhere like that, I think. Seems all right. Looks normal enough, but who knows? And there's Desmond, remanded once for a psychiatric report, but I wouldn't say there was much to it. It's got to be someone at the party, though of course I suppose anyone *could* have come in from outside. A house isn't usually locked up during a party. There's a side door open, or a side window. One of our half-baked people, I suppose could have come along to see what was on and sneaked in. A pretty big risk to take. Would a child agree, a child who'd gone to a party, to go playing apple games with anyone she *didn't* know? Anyway, you haven't explained yet, Poirot, what brings you into it. You said it was Mrs Oliver. Some wild idea of hers?'

'Not exactly a wild idea,' said Poirot. 'It is true that writers are prone to wild ideas. Ideas, perhaps, which are on the far side of probability. But this was simply something that she heard the girl say.'

'What, the child Joyce?'

'Yes.'

Spence leant forward and looked at Poirot inquiringly.

'I will tell you,' said Poirot.

Quietly and succinctly he recounted the story as Mrs Oliver had told it to him.

'I see,' said Spence. He rubbed his moustache. 'The girl said that, did she? Said she'd seen a murder committed. Did she say when or how?'

'No,' said Poirot.

'What led up to it?'

'Some remark, I think, about the murders in Mrs Oliver's

books. Somebody said something about it to Mrs Oliver. One of the children, I think, to the effect that there wasn't enough blood in her books or enough bodies. And then Joyce spoke up and said *she*'d seen a murder once.'

'Boasted of it? That's the impression you're giving me.'

'That's the impression Mrs Oliver got. Yes, she boasted of it.'

'It mightn't have been true.'

'No, it might not have been true at all,' said Poirot.

'Children often make these extravagant statements when they wish to call attention to themselves or to make an effect. On the other hand, it might have been true. Is that what you think?'

'I do not know,' said Poirot. 'A child boasts of having witnessed a murder. Only a few hours later, that child is dead. You must admit that there are grounds for believing that it might – it's a far-fetched idea perhaps – but it might have been cause and effect. If so, somebody lost no time.'

'Definitely,' said Spence. 'How many were present at the time the girl made her statement re murder, do you know exactly?'

'All that Mrs Oliver said was that she thought there were about fourteen or fifteen people, perhaps more. Five or six children, five or six grown-ups who were running the show. But for exact information I must rely on you.'

'Well, that will be easy enough,' said Spence. 'I don't say I know off-hand at the moment, but it's easily obtained from the locals. As to the party itself, I know pretty well already. A preponderance of women, on the whole. Fathers don't turn up much at children's parties. But they look in, sometimes, or come to take their children home. Dr Ferguson was there, the vicar was there. Otherwise, mothers, aunts, social workers, two teachers from the school. Oh, I can give you a list – and roughly about fourteen children. The youngest not more than ten – running on into teenagers.'

'And I suppose you would know the list of probables amongst them?' said Poirot.

'Well, it won't be so easy now if what you think is true.'

'You mean you are no longer looking for a sexually disturbed personality. You are looking instead for somebody who has committed a murder and got away with it, someone who never expected it to be found out and who suddenly got a nasty shock.'

'Blest if I can think who it could have been, all the same,' said Spence. 'I shouldn't have said we had any likely murderers round here. And certainly nothing spectacular in the way of murders.'

'One can have likely murderers anywhere,' said Poirot, 'or shall I say unlikely murderers, but nevertheless murderers. Because unlikely murderers are not so prone to be suspected. There is probably not very much evidence against them, and it would be a rude shock to such a murderer to find that there had actually been an eye-witness to his or her crime.'

'Why didn't Joyce say anything at the time? That's what I'd like to know. Was she bribed to silence by someone, do you think? Too risky surely.'

'No,' said Poirot. 'I gather from what Mrs Oliver mentioned that she didn't recognize that it *was* a murder she was looking at at the time.'

'Oh, surely that's most unlikely,' said Spence.

'Not necessarily,' said Poirot. 'A child of thirteen was speaking. She was remembering something she'd seen in the past. We don't know exactly when. It might have been three or even four years previously. She saw something but she didn't realize its true significance. That might apply to a lot of things you know, *mon cher*. Some rather peculiar car accident. A car where it appeared that the driver drove straight at the person who was injured or perhaps killed. A child might not realize it *was* deliberate *at the time*. But something someone said, or something she saw or heard a year or two later might awaken her memory and she'd think perhaps: "A or B or X did it *on purpose*." "Perhaps it was really a murder, not just an accident." And there are plenty of other possibilities. Some of them I will admit suggested by my friend, Mrs Oliver, who can easily come up with about twelve different solutions to everything, most of them not very probable but all of them faintly possible. Tablets added to a cup of tea administered to someone. Roughly that sort of thing. A push perhaps on a dangerous spot. You have no cliffs here, which is rather a pity from the point of view of likely theories. Yes, I think there could be plenty of possibilities. Perhaps it is some murder story that the girl reads which recalls to her an incident. It may have been an incident that puzzled her at the time, and she might, when she reads the story, say: "Well, *that* might have been so-and-so and so-and-so. I wonder if he or she did it on purpose?" Yes, there are a lot of possibilities.'

'And you have come here to inquire into them?'

'It would be in the public interest, I think, don't you?' said Poirot.

'Ah, we're to be public spirited, are we, you and I?'

'You can at least give me information,' said Poirot. 'You know the people here.'

'I'll do what I can,' said Spence. 'And I'll rope in Elspeth. There's not much about people she doesn't know.'

CHAPTER 6

Satisfied with what he had achieved, Poirot took leave of his friend.

The information he wanted would be forthcoming – he had no doubt as to that. He had got Spence interested. And Spence, once set upon a trail, was not one to relinquish it. His reputation as a retired high-ranking officer of the C.I.D. would have won him friends in the local police departments concerned.

And next – Poirot consulted his watch – he was to meet Mrs Oliver in exactly ten minutes' time outside a house called Apple Trees. Really, the name seemed uncannily appropriate.

Really, thought Poirot, one didn't seem able to get away from apples. Nothing could be more agreeable than a juicy English apple – And yet here were apples mixed up with broomsticks, and witches, and old-fashioned folklore, and a murdered child.

Following the route indicated to him, Poirot arrived to the minute outside a red brick Georgian style house with a neat beech hedge enclosing it, and a pleasant garden showing beyond.

He put his hand out, raised the latch and entered through the wrought iron gate which bore a painted board labelled 'Apple Trees'. A path led up to the front door. Looking rather like one of those Swiss clocks where figures come out automatically of a door above the clock face, the front door opened and Mrs Oliver emerged on the steps.

'You're absolutely punctual,' she said breathlessly. 'I was watching for you from the window.'

Poirot turned and closed the gate carefully behind him. Practically on every occasion that he had met Mrs Oliver, whether by appointment or by accident, a motif of apples seemed to be introduced almost immediately. She was either eating an apple or *had* been eating an apple – witness an apple core nestling on her broad chest – or was carrying a bag of apples. But today there was no apple in evidence at all. Very correct, Poirot thought approvingly. It would have been in very bad taste to be gnawing an apple here, on the scene of what had been not only a crime but a tragedy. For what else can it be but that? thought Poirot. The sudden death of a child of only thirteen years old. He did not like to think of it, and because he did not like to think of it he was all the more decided in his mind that that was exactly what he was going to think of until by some means or other, light should shine out of the darkness and he should see clearly what he had come here to see.

'I can't think why you wouldn't come and stay with Judith Butler,' said Mrs Oliver. 'Instead of going to a fifth-class guest house.'

'Because it is better that I should survey things with a certain degree of aloofness,' said Poirot. 'One must not get involved, you comprehend.'

'I don't see how you can avoid getting involved,' said Mrs Oliver. 'You've got to see everyone and talk to them, haven't you?'

'That most decidedly,' said Poirot.

'Who have you seen so far?'

'My friend, Superintendent Spence.'

'What's he like nowadays?' said Mrs Oliver.

'A good deal older than he was,' said Poirot.

'Naturally,' said Mrs Oliver, 'what else would you expect? Is he deafer or blinder or fatter or thinner?'

Poirot considered.

'He has lost a little weight. He wears spectacles for reading the paper. I do not think he is deaf, not to any noticeable extent.'

'And what does he think about it all?'

'You go too quickly,' said Poirot.

'And what exactly are you and he going to do?'

'I have planned my programme,' said Poirot. 'First I have seen and consulted with my old friend. I asked him to get me, perhaps, some information that would not be easy to get otherwise.'

'You mean the police here will be his buddies and he'll get a lot of inside stuff from them?'

'Well, I should not put it exactly like that, but yes, those are the lines along which I have been thinking.'

'And after that?'

'I come to meet you here, Madame. I have to see just where this thing happened.'

Mrs Oliver turned her head and looked up at the house.

'It doesn't look the sort of house there'd be a murder in, does it?' she said.

Poirot thought again: What an unerring instinct she has!

'No,' he said, 'it does not look at all that sort of a house. After I have seen *where*, then I go with you to see the mother of the dead child. I hear what she can tell me. This afternoon my friend Spence is making an appointment for me to talk with the local inspector at a suitable hour. I should also like a talk with the doctor here. And possibly the head-mistress at the school. At six o'clock I drink tea and eat sausages with my friend Spence and his sister again in their house and we discuss.'

'What more do you think he'll be able to tell you?'

'I want to meet his sister. She has lived here longer than he has. He came here to join her when her husband died. She will know, perhaps, the people here fairly well.'

'Do you know what you sound like?' said Mrs Oliver. 'A computer. You know. You're programming yourself. That's what they call it, isn't it? I mean you're feeding all these things into yourself all day and then you're going to see what comes out.'

'It is certainly an idea you have there,' said Poirot, with some interest. 'Yes, yes, I play the part of the computer. One feeds in the information –'

'And supposing you come up with all the wrong answers?' said Mrs Oliver.

'That would be impossible,' said Hercule Poirot. 'Computers do not do that sort of a thing.'

'They're not supposed to,' said Mrs Oliver, 'but you'd be surprised at the things that happen sometimes. My last electric light bill, for instance. I know there's a proverb which says "To err is human," but a human error is nothing to what a computer can do if it tries. Come on in and meet Mrs Drake.'

Mrs Drake was certainly something, Poirot thought. She was a tall, handsome woman of forty-odd, her golden hair was lightly tinged with grey, her eyes were brilliantly blue, she oozed competence from the fingertips downwards. Any party she had arranged would have been a successful one. In the drawing-room a tray of morning coffee with two sugared biscuits was awaiting them.

Apple Trees, he saw, was a most admirably kept house. It was well furnished, it had carpets of excellent quality, everything was scrupulously polished and cleaned, and the fact that it had hardly any outstanding object of interest in it was not readily noticeable. One would not have expected it. The colours of the curtains and the covers were pleasant but conventional. It could have been let furnished at any moment for a high rent to a desirable tenant, without having to put away any treasures or make any alterations to the arrangement of the furniture.

Mrs Drake greeted Mrs Oliver and Poirot and concealed almost entirely what Poirot could not help suspecting was a feeling of vigorously suppressed annoyance at the position in which she found herself as the hostess at a social occasion at which something as anti-social as murder had occurred. As a prominent member of the community of Woodleigh Common, he suspected that she felt an unhappy sense of having herself in some way proved inadequate. What had occurred should *not* have occurred. To someone else in someone else's house – yes. But at a party for children, arranged by her, given by her, organized by her, nothing like this ought to have happened. Somehow or other she ought to have seen to it that it did *not* happen. And Poirot also had a suspicion that she was seeking round irritably in the back of her mind for a reason. Not so much a reason for murder having taken place, but to find out and pin down some inadequacy on the part of someone who had been helping her and who had by some mismanagement or some lack of perception failed to realize that something like this *could* happen.

'Monsieur Poirot,' said Mrs Drake, in her fine speaking voice, which Poirot thought would come over excellently in a small lecture room or the village hall, 'I am so pleased you could come down here. Mrs Oliver has been telling me how invaluable your help will be to us in this terrible crisis.'

'Rest assured, Madame, I shall do what I can, but as you no doubt realize from your experience of life, it is going to be a difficult business.'

'Difficult?' said Mrs Drake. 'Of course it's going to be difficult. It seems incredible, absolutely *incredible*, that such an awful thing should have happened. I suppose,' she added, 'the police *may* know something? Inspector Raglan has a very good reputation locally, I believe. Whether or not they ought to call Scotland Yard in, I don't know. The idea seems to be that this poor child's death must have had a local significance. I needn't tell you, Monsieur Poirot – after all, you read the papers as much as I do – that there have been very many sad fatalities with children all over the countryside. They seem to be getting more and more frequent. Mental instability seems to be on the increase, though I must say that mothers and families generally are not looking after their children properly, as they used to do. Children are sent home from school alone, on dark evenings, go alone on dark early mornings. And children, however much you warn them, are unfortunately very foolish when it comes to being offered a lift in a smart-looking car. They believe what they're told. I suppose one cannot help that.'

'But what happened here, Madame, was of an entirely different nature.'

'Oh, I know – I know. That is why I used the term incredible. I still cannot quite believe it,' said Mrs Drake. 'Everything was entirely under control. All the arrangements were made. Everything was going perfectly, all according to plan. It just seems – seems incredible. Personally I consider myself that there *must* be what I call an *outside* significance to this. *Someone* walked into the house – not a difficult thing to do under the circumstances – someone of highly disturbed mentality, I suppose, the kind of people who are let out of mental homes simply because there is no room for them there, as far as I can see. Nowadays, room has to be made for fresh patients all the time. Anyone peeping in through a window could see a children's party was going on, and this poor wretch – if one can really feel pity for these people, which I really must say I find it very hard to do myself sometimes

– enticed this child away somehow and killed her. You can't think such a thing could happen, but it *did* happen.'

'Perhaps you would show me where –'

'Of course. No more coffee?'

'I thank you, no.'

Mrs Drake got up. 'The police seem to think it took place while the Snapdragon was going on. That was taking place in the dining-room.'

She walked across the hall, opened the door and, rather in the manner of someone doing the honours of a stately home to a party of charabanc goers, indicated the large dining-table and the heavy velvet curtains.

'It was dark here, of course, except for the blazing dish. And now –'

She led them across the hall and opened the door of a small room with arm-chairs, sporting prints and bookshelves.

'The library,' said Mrs Drake, and shivered a little. 'The bucket was *here*. On a plastic sheet, of course –'

Mrs Oliver had not accompanied them into the room. She was standing outside in the hall –

'I can't come in,' she said to Poirot. 'It makes me think of it too much.'

'There's nothing to see now,' said Mrs Drake. 'I mean, I'm just showing you *where*, as you asked.'

'I suppose,' said Poirot, 'there was water – a good deal of water.'

'There was water in the bucket, of course,' said Mrs Drake.

She looked at Poirot as though she thought that he was not quite all there.'

'And there was water on the sheet. I mean, if the child's head was pushed under water, there would be a lot of water splashed about.'

'Oh yes. Even while the bobbing was going on, the bucket had to be filled up once or twice.'

'So the person who did it? That person also would have got wet, one would think.'

'Yes, yes, I suppose so.'

'That was not specially noticed?'

'No, no, the Inspector asked me about that. You see, by the

end of the evening nearly everyone was a bit dishevelled or damp or floury. There doesn't seem to be any useful clues there at all. I mean, the police didn't think so.'

'No,' said Poirot. 'I suppose the only clue was the child herself. I hope you will tell me all you know about her.'

'About Joyce?'

Mrs Drake looked slightly taken aback. It was as though Joyce in her mind had by now retreated so far out of things that she was quite surprised to be reminded of her.

'The victim is always important,' said Poirot. 'The victim, you see, is so often the *cause* of the crime.'

'Well, I suppose, yes, I see what you mean,' said Mrs Drake, who quite plainly did not. 'Shall we come back to the drawing-room?'

'And then you will tell me about Joyce,' said Poirot.

They settled themselves once more in the drawing-room.

Mrs Drake was looking uncomfortable.

'I don't know really what you expect me to say, Monsieur Poirot,' she said. 'Surely all information can be obtained quite easily from the police or from Joyce's mother. Poor woman, it will be painful for her, no doubt, but –'

'But what I want,' said Poirot, 'is not a mother's estimate of a dead daughter. It is a clear, unbiased opinion from someone who has a good knowledge of human nature. I should say, Madame, that you yourself have been an active worker in many welfare and social fields here. Nobody, I am sure, could sum up more aptly the character and disposition of someone whom you know.'

'Well – it is a little difficult. I mean, children of that age – she was thirteen, I think, twelve or thirteen – are very much alike at a certain age.'

'Ah no, surely not,' said Poirot. 'There are very great differences in character, in disposition. Did you like her?'

Mrs Drake seemed to find the question embarrassing.

'Well, of course I – I liked her. I mean, well, I like all children. Most people do.'

'Ah, there I do not agree with you,' said Poirot. 'Some children I consider are *most* unattractive.'

'Well, I agree, they're not brought up very well nowadays. Everything seems left to the school, and of course they lead very permissive lives. Have their own choice of friends and – er – oh, really, Monsieur Poirot.'

'Was she a nice child or not a nice child?' said Poirot insistently.

Mrs Drake looked at him and registered censure.

'You must realize, Monsieur Poirot, that the poor child is *dead.*'

'Dead or alive, it matters. Perhaps if she was a nice child, nobody would have wanted to kill her, but if she was not a nice child, somebody might have wanted to kill her, and did so –'

'Well, I suppose – Surely it isn't a question of niceness, is it?'

'It could be. I also understand that she claimed to have seen a murder committed.'

'Oh *that,*' said Mrs Drake contemptuously.

'You did not take that statement seriously?'

'Well, of course I didn't. It was a very silly thing to say.'

'How did she come to say it?'

'Well, I think really they were all rather excited about Mrs Oliver being here. You are a very famous person, you must remember, dear,' said Mrs Drake, addressing Mrs Oliver.

The word 'dear' seemed included in her speech without any accompanying enthusiasm.

'I don't suppose the subject would ever have arisen otherwise, but the children were excited by meeting a famous authoress –'

'So Joyce said that she had seen a murder committed,' said Poirot thoughtfully.

'Yes, she said something of the kind. I wasn't really listening.'

'But you do remember that she said it?'

'Oh yes, she said it. But I didn't believe it,' said Mrs Drake. 'Her sister hushed her up at once, very properly.'

'And she was annoyed about that, was she?'

'Yes, she went on saying that it was true.'

'In fact, she boasted about it.'

'When you put it that way, yes.'

'It *might* have been true, I suppose,' said Poirot.

'Nonsense! I don't believe it for one minute,' said Mrs Drake. 'It's the sort of stupid thing Joyce would say.'

'She was a stupid girl?'

'Well, she was the kind, I think, who liked to show off,' said Mrs Drake. 'You know, she always wanted to have seen more or done more than other girls.'

'Not a very lovable character,' said Poirot.

'No indeed,' said Mrs Drake. 'Really the kind that you have to be shutting up all the time.'

'What did the other children who were here have to say about it? Were they impressed?'

'They laughed at her,' said Mrs Drake. 'So, of course, that made her worse.'

'Well,' said Poirot, as he rose, 'I am glad to have your positive assurance on that point.' He bowed politely over her hand. 'Good-bye, Madame, thank you so much for allowing me to view the scene of this very unpleasant occurrence. I hope it has not recalled unpleasant memories too definitely to you.'

'Of course,' said Mrs Drake, 'it *is* very painful to recall anything of this kind. I had so hoped our little party would go off well. Indeed, it *was* going off well and everyone seemed to be enjoying it so much till this terrible thing happened. However, the only thing one can do is to try and forget it all. Of course, it's very unfortunate that Joyce should have made this silly remark about seeing a murder.'

'Have you ever had a murder in Woodleigh Common?'

'Not that I can remember,' said Mrs Drake firmly.

'In this age of increased crime that we live in,' said Poirot, 'that really seems somewhat unusual, does it not?'

'Well, I think there was a lorry driver who killed a pal of his – something like that – and a little girl whom they found buried in a gravel pit about fifteen miles from here, but that was years ago. They were both rather sordid and uninteresting crimes. Mainly the result of drink, I think.'

'In fact, the kind of murder unlikely to have been witnessed by a girl of twelve or thirteen.'

'Most unlikely, I should say. And I can assure you, Monsieur Poirot, this statement that the girl made was solely in order to impress friends and perhaps interest a famous character.' She looked rather coldly across at Mrs Oliver.

'In fact,' said Mrs Oliver, 'it's all my fault for being at the party, I suppose.'

'Oh, of course not, my dear, of course I didn't mean it *that* way.'

Poirot sighed as he departed from the house with Mrs Oliver by his side.

'A very unsuitable place for a murder,' he said, as they walked down the path to the gate. 'No atmosphere, no haunting sense of tragedy, no character worth murdering, though I couldn't help thinking that just occasionally someone might feel like murdering Mrs Drake.'

'I know what you mean. She can be intensely irritating sometimes. So pleased with herself and so complacent.'

'What is her husband like?'

'Oh, she's a widow. Her husband died a year or two ago. He got polio and had been a cripple for years. He was a banker originally, I think. He was very keen on games and sport and hated having to give all that up and be an invalid.'

'Yes, indeed.' He reverted to the subject of the child Joyce. 'Just tell me this. Did anyone who was listening take this assertion of the child Joyce about murder seriously?'

'I don't know. I shouldn't have thought anyone did.'

'The other children, for instance?'

'Well, I was thinking really of them. No, I don't think they believed what Joyce was saying. They thought she was making up things.'

'Did you think that, too?'

'Well, I did really,' said Mrs Oliver. 'Of course,' she added, 'Mrs Drake would like to believe that the murder never really happened, but she can't very well go as far as that, can she?'

'I understand that this may be painful for her.'

'I suppose it is in a way,' said Mrs Oliver, 'but I think that by now, you know, she is actually getting quite pleased to talk about it. I don't think she likes to have to bottle it up all the time.'

'Do you like her?' asked Poirot. 'Do you think she's a nice woman?'

'You do ask the most difficult questions. Embarrassing ones,' said Mrs Oliver. 'It seems the only thing you are interested in is whether people are nice or not. Rowena Drake is the bossy type – likes running things and people. She runs this whole place more or less, I should think. But runs it very efficiently. It depends if you like bossy women. I don't much –'

'What about Joyce's mother whom we are on our way to see?'

'She's quite a nice woman. Rather stupid, I should think. I'm sorry for her. It's pretty awful to have your daughter murdered, isn't it? And everyone here thinks it was a sex crime which makes it worse.'

'But there was no evidence of sexual assault, or so I understand?'

'No, but people like to think these things happen. It makes it more exciting. You know what people are like.'

'One thinks one does – but sometimes – well – we do not really know at all.'

'Wouldn't it be better if my friend Judith Butler was to take you to see Mrs Reynolds? She knows her quite well, and I'm a stranger to her.'

'We will do as planned.'

'The Computer Programme will go on,' murmured Mrs Oliver rebelliously.

CHAPTER 7

Mrs Reynolds was a complete contrast to Mrs Drake. There was no air of poised competence about her, nor indeed was there ever likely to be.

She was wearing conventional black, had a moist handkerchief clasped in her hand and was clearly prepared to dissolve into tears at any moment.

'It's very kind of you, I'm sure,' she said to Mrs Oliver, 'to bring a friend of yours down here to help us.' She put a damp hand into Poirot's and looked at him doubtfully. 'And if he *can* help in any way I'm sure I'll be very grateful, though I don't see what anyone can do. Nothing will bring her back, poor child. It's awful to think of. How anyone could deliberately kill anyone of that age. If she had only cried out – though I suppose he rammed her head under water straight away and held it there. Oh, I can't bear to think of it. I really can't.'

'Indeed, Madame, I do not want to distress you. Please do not think of it. I only want to ask you a few questions that might help – help, that is, to find your daughter's murderer. You've no idea yourself, I suppose, who it can possibly be?'

'How could I have any idea? I shouldn't have thought there was anyone, anyone living here, I mean. This is such a nice place. And the people living here are such nice people. I suppose it was just someone – some awful man who came in through one of the windows. Perhaps he'd taken drugs or something. He saw the light and that it was a party, so he gate-crashed.'

'You are quite sure that the assailant was male?'

'Oh, it must have been.' Mrs Reynolds sounded shocked. 'I'm sure it was. It couldn't have been a *woman*, could it?'

'A woman might have been strong enough.'

'Well, I suppose in a way I know what you mean. You mean women are much more athletic nowadays and all that. But they wouldn't do a thing like this, I'm sure. Joyce was only a child – thirteen years old.'

'I don't want to distress you by staying here too long, Madame, or to ask you difficult questions. That already, I am sure, the police are doing elsewhere, and I don't want to upset you by dwelling on painful facts. It was just concerning a remark that your daughter made at the party. You were not there yourself, I think?'

'Well, no, I wasn't. I haven't been very well lately and children's parties can be very tiring. I drove them there, and then later I came back to fetch them. The three children went together, you know. Ann, that's the older one, she is sixteen, and Leopold who is nearly eleven. What was it Joyce said that you wanted to know about?'

'Mrs Oliver, who was there, will tell you what your daughter's words were exactly. She said, I believe, that she had once seen a murder committed.'

'Joyce? Oh, she couldn't have said a thing like that. What murder could she possibly have seen committed?'

'Well, everyone seems to think it was rather unlikely,' said Poirot. 'I just wondered if *you* thought it likely. Did she ever speak to you about such a thing?'

'Seeing a *murder*? Joyce?'

'You must remember,' said Poirot, 'that the term murder might have been used by someone of Joyce's age in a rather loose way. It might have been just a question of somebody being run over by a car, or of children fighting together perhaps and one pushing another into a stream or over a bridge. Something that was not meant seriously, but which had an unfortunate result.'

'Well, I can't think of anything like that happening here that Joyce could have seen, and she certainly never said anything about it to me. She must have been joking.'

'She was very positive,' said Mrs Oliver. 'She kept on saying that it was true and that she'd seen it.'

'Did anyone believe her?' asked Mrs Reynolds.

'I don't know,' said Poirot.

'I don't think they did,' said Mrs Oliver, 'or perhaps they didn't want to – er – well, encourage her by saying they believed it.'

'They were inclined to jeer at her and say she was making it all up,' said Poirot, less kind-hearted than Mrs Oliver.

'Well, that wasn't very nice of them,' said Mrs Reynolds. 'As though Joyce would tell a lot of lies about things like that.' She looked flushed and indignant.

'I know. It seems unlikely,' said Poirot. 'It was more possible, was it not, that she might have made a mistake, that she might have seen something she *did* think could have been described as a murder. Some accident, perhaps.'

'She'd have said something about it to me, if so, wouldn't she?' said Mrs Reynolds, still indignant.

'One would think so,' said Poirot. 'She did not say so at any time in the past? You might have forgotten. Especially if it wasn't really important.'

'When do you mean?'

'We don't know,' said Poirot. 'That is one of the difficulties. It might have been three weeks ago – or three years. She said she had been "quite young" at the time. What does a thirteen-year-old consider quite young? There was no sensational happening round here that you can recall?'

'Oh, I don't think so. I mean, you do hear of things. Or read about them in the papers. You know, I mean women being attacked, or a girl and her young man, or things like that. But nothing important that I can remember, nothing that Joyce took an interest in or anything of that kind.'

'But if Joyce said positively she saw a murder, would you think she really thought so?'

'She wouldn't say so unless she really did think so, would she?' said Mrs Reynolds. 'I think she must have got something mixed up really.'

'Yes, it seems possible. I wonder,' he asked, 'if I might speak to your two children who were also at the party?'

'Well, of course, though I don't know what you can expect them to tell you. Ann's doing her work for her "A" levels upstairs and Leopold's in the garden assembling a model aeroplane.'

Leopold was a solid, pudgy faced boy entirely absorbed, it seemed, in mechanical construction. It was some few moments before he could pay attention to the questions he was being asked.

'You were there, weren't you, Leopold? You heard what your sister said. What did she say?'

'Oh, you mean about the murder?' He sounded bored.

'Yes, that's what I mean,' said Poirot. 'She said she saw a murder once. Did she really see such a thing?'

'No, of course she didn't,' said Leopold. 'Who on earth would she see murdered? It was just like Joyce, that.'

'How do you mean, it was just like her?'

'Showing off,' said Leopold, winding round a piece of wire and breathing forcefully through his nose as he concentrated. 'She was an awfully stupid sort of girl,' he added. 'She'd say anything, you know, to make people sit up and take notice.'

'So you really think she invented the whole thing?'

Leopold shifted his gaze to Mrs Oliver.

'I expect she wanted to impress *you* a bit,' he said. 'You write detective stories, don't you? I think she was just putting it on so that you should take more notice of her than you did of the others.'

'That would also be rather like her, would it?' said Poirot.

'Oh, she'd say anything,' said Leopold. 'I bet nobody believed her though.'

'Were you listening? Do *you* think anyone believed it?'

'Well, I heard her say it, but I didn't really listen. Beatrice laughed at her and so did Cathie. They said "that's a tall story," or something.'

There seemed little more to be got out of Leopold. They went upstairs to where Ann, looking rather more than her sixteen years, was bending over a table with various study books spread round her.

'Yes, I was at the party,' she said.

'You heard your sister say something about having seen a murder?'

'Oh yes, I heard her. I didn't take any notice, though.'

'You didn't think it was true?'

'Of course it wasn't true. There haven't been any murders here for ages. I don't think there's been a proper murder for years.'

'Then why do you think she said so?'

'Oh, she likes showing off. I mean she used to like showing off. She had a wonderful story once about having travelled to India. My uncle had been on a voyage there and she pretended she went with him. Lots of girls at school actually *believed* her.'

'So you don't remember any what you call murders taking place here in the last three or four years?'

'No, only the usual kind,' said Ann. 'I mean, the ones you read every day in the newspaper. And they weren't actually *here* in Woodleigh Common. They were mostly in Medchester, I think.'

'Who do *you* think killed your sister, Ann? You must have known her friends, you would know any people who didn't like her.'

'I can't imagine who'd want to kill her. I suppose someone who was just batty. Nobody else would, would they?'

'There was no one who had – quarrelled with her or who did not get on with her?'

'You mean, did she have an enemy? I think that's silly. People don't have enemies really. There are just people you don't like.'

As they departed from the room, Ann said:

'I don't want to be nasty about Joyce, because she's dead, and it wouldn't be kind, but she really was the most awful liar, you know. I mean, I'm sorry to say things about my sister, but it's quite true.'

'Are we making any progress?' said Mrs Oliver as they left the house.

'None whatever,' said Hercule Poirot. 'That is interesting,' he said thoughtfully.

Mrs Oliver looked as though she didn't agree with him.

CHAPTER 8

It was six o'clock at Pine Crest. Hercule Poirot put a piece of sausage into his mouth and followed it up with a sip of tea. The tea was strong and to Poirot singularly unpalatable. The sausage, on the other hand, was delicious. Cooked to perfection. He looked with appreciation across the table to where Mrs McKay presided over the large brown teapot.

Elspeth McKay was as unlike her brother, Superintendent Spence, as she could be in every way. Where he was broad, she was angular. Her sharp, thin face looked out on the world with shrewd appraisal. She was thin as a thread, yet there was a certain likeness between them. Mainly the eyes and the strongly marked line of the jaw. Either of them, Poirot thought, could be relied upon for judgement and good sense. They would express themselves differently, but that was all. Superintendent Spence would express himself slowly and carefully as the result of due thought and deliberation. Mrs McKay would pounce, quick and sharp, like a cat upon a mouse.

'A lot depends,' said Poirot, 'upon the character of this child. Joyce Reynolds. This is what puzzles me most.'

He looked inquiringly at Spence.

'You can't go by me,' said Spence, 'I've not lived here long enough. Better ask Elspeth.'

Poirot looked across the table, his eyebrows raised inquiringly. Mrs McKay was sharp as usual in response.

'I'd say she was a proper little liar,' she said.

'Not a girl whom you'd trust and believe what she said?'

Elspeth shook her head decidedly.

'No, indeed. Tell a tall tale, she would, and tell it well, mind you. But I'd never believe her.'

'Tell it with the object of showing off?'

'That's right. They told you the Indian story, didn't they? There's many as believed that, you know. Been away for the holidays, the family had. Gone abroad somewhere. I don't know if it was her father and mother or her uncle and aunt, but they went to India and she came back from those holidays with tall tales of how she'd been taken there with them. Made a good story of it, she did. A Maharajah and a tiger shoot and elephants – ah, it was fine hearing and a lot of those around her here believed it. But I said straight along, she's telling more than ever happened. Could be, I thought at first, she was just exaggerating. But the story got added to every time. There were more tigers, if you know what I mean. Far more tigers than could possibly happen. And elephants, too, for that matter. I'd known her before, too, telling tall stories.'

'Always to get attention?'

'Aye, you're right there. She was a great one for getting attention.'

'Because a child told a tall story about a travel trip she never took,' said Superintendent Spence, 'you can't say that every tall tale she told was a lie.'

'It might not be,' said Elspeth, 'but I'd say the likelihood was that it usually would be.'

'So you think that if Joyce Reynolds came out with a tale that she'd seen a murder committed, you'd say she was probably lying and you wouldn't believe the story was true?'

'That's what I'd think,' said Mrs McKay.

'You might be wrong,' said her brother.

'Yes,' said Mrs McKay. 'Anyone may be wrong. It's like the old story of the boy who cried "Wolf, wolf," and he cried it once too often, when it was a real wolf, and nobody believed him, and so the wolf got him.'

'So you'd sum it up –'

'I'd still say the probabilities are that she wasn't speaking the truth. But I'm a fair woman. She may have been. She *may* have seen something. Not quite so much as she said she saw, but *something*.'

'And so she got herself killed,' said Superintendent Spence. 'You've got to mind that, Elspeth. She got herself killed.'

'That's true enough,' said Mrs McKay. 'And that's why I'm saying maybe I've misjudged her. And if so, I'm sorry. But ask anyone who knew her and they'll tell you that lies came natural to her. It was a party she was at, remember, and she was excited. She'd want to make an effect.'

'Indeed, they didn't believe her,' said Poirot.

Elspeth McKay shook her head doubtfully.

'Who could she have seen murdered?' asked Poirot.

He looked from brother to sister.

'Nobody,' said Mrs McKay with decision.

'There must have been deaths here, say, over the last three years.'

'Oh that, naturally,' said Spence. 'Just the usual – old folks or invalids or what you'd expect – or maybe a hit-and-run motorist –'

'No unusual or unexpected deaths?'

'Well –' Elspeth hesitated. 'I mean –'

Spence took over.

'I've jotted a few names down here.' He pushed the paper over to Poirot. 'Save you a bit of trouble, asking questions around.'

'Are these suggested victims?'

'Hardly as much as that. Say within the range of possibility.'

Poirot read aloud.

'Mrs Llewellyn-Smythe. Charlotte Benfield. Janet White. Lesley Ferrier –' He broke off, looked across the table and repeated the first name. Mrs Llewellyn-Smythe.

'Could be,' said Mrs McKay. 'Yes, you might have something there.' She added a word that sounded like 'opera.'

'Opera?' Poirot looked puzzled. He had heard of no opera.

'Went off one night, she did,' said Elspeth, 'was never heard of again.'

'Mrs Llewellyn-Smythe?'

'No, no. The opera girl. She could have put something in the medicine easily enough. And she came into all the money, didn't she – or so she thought at the time?'

Poirot looked at Spence for enlightenment.

'And never been heard of since,' said Mrs McKay. 'These foreign girls are all the same.'

The significance of the word 'opera' came to Poirot.

'An *au pair* girl,' he said.

'That's right. Lived with the old lady, and a week or two after the old lady died, the *au pair* girl just disappeared.'

'Went off with some man, I'd say,' said Spence.

'Well, nobody knew of him if so,' said Elspeth. 'And there's usually plenty to talk about here. Usually know just who's going with who.'

'Did anybody think there had been anything wrong about Mrs Llewellyn-Smythe's death?' asked Poirot.

'No. She'd got heart trouble. Doctor attended her regularly.'

'But you headed your list of possible victims with her, my friend?'

'Well, she was a rich woman, a very rich woman. Her death was not unexpected but it *was* sudden. I'd say off-hand that Dr Ferguson was surprised, even if only slightly surprised. I think he expected her to live longer. But doctors do have these surprises. She wasn't one to do as the doctor ordered. She'd been told not to overdo things, but she did exactly as she liked. For one thing, she was a passionate gardener, and that doesn't do heart cases any good.'

Elspeth McKay took up the tale.

'She came here when her health failed. She was living abroad before. She came here to be near her nephew and niece, Mr and Mrs Drake, and she bought the Quarry House. A big Victorian house which included a disused quarry which attracted her as having possibilities. She spent thousands of pounds on turning that quarry into a sunk garden or whatever they call the thing. Had a landscape gardener down from Wisley or one of these places to design it. Oh, I can tell you, it's something to look at.'

'I shall go and look at it,' said Poirot. 'Who knows – it might give me ideas.'

'Yes, I would go if I were you. It's worth seeing.'

'And she was rich, you say?' said Poirot.

'Widow of a big shipbuilder. She had packets of money.'

'Her death was not unexpected because she had a heart condition, but it *was* sudden,' said Spence. 'No doubts arose that it was due to anything but natural causes. Cardiac failure, or whatever the longer name is that doctors use. Coronary something.'

'No question of an inquest ever arose?'

Spence shook his head.

'It has happened before,' said Poirot. 'An elderly woman told to be careful, not to run up and down stairs, not to do any intensive gardening, and so on and so on. But if you get an energetic woman who's been an enthusiastic gardener all her life and done as she liked in most ways, then she doesn't always treat these recommendations with due respect.'

'That's true enough. Mrs Llewellyn-Smythe made a wonderful thing of the quarry – or rather, the landscape artist did. Three or four years they worked at it, he and his employer. She'd seen some garden, in Ireland I think it was, when she went on a National Trust tour visiting gardens. With that in mind, they fairly transformed the place. Oh yes, it has to be seen to be believed.'

'Here is a natural death, then,' said Poirot, 'certified as such by the local doctor. Is that the same doctor who is here now? And whom I am shortly going to see?'

'Dr Ferguson – yes. He's a man of about sixty, good at his job and well liked here.'

'But you suspect that her death *might* have been murder? For any other reason than those that you've already given me?'

'The opera girl, for one thing,' said Elspeth.

'Why?'

'Well, she must have forged the Will. Who forged the Will if she didn't?'

'You must have more to tell me,' said Poirot. 'What is all this about a forged Will?'

'Well, there was a bit of fuss when it came to probating, or whatever you call it, the old lady's Will.'

'Was it a new Will?'

'It was what they call – something that sounded like fish – a codi – a codicil.'

Elspeth looked at Poirot, who nodded.

'She'd made Wills before,' said Spence. 'All much the same. Bequests to charities, legacies to old servants, but the bulk of her fortune always went to her nephew and his wife, who were her near relatives.'

'And this particular codicil?'

'Left everything to the opera girl,' said Elspeth, '*because of her devoted care and kindness*. Something like that.'

'Tell me, then, more about the *au pair* girl.'

'She came from some country in the middle of Europe. Some long name.'

'How long had she been with the old lady?'

'Just over a year.'

'You call her the old lady always. How old was she?'

'Well in the sixties. Sixty-five or six, say.'

'That is not so very old,' said Poirot feelingly.

'Made several Wills, she had, by all accounts,' said Elspeth. 'As Bert has told you, all of them much the same. Leaving money to one or two charities and then perhaps she'd change the charities and some different souvenirs to old servants and all that. But the bulk of the money always went to her nephew and his wife, and I think some other old cousin who was dead, though, by the time she died. She left the bungalow she'd built to the landscape man, for him to live in as long as he liked, and some kind of income for which he was to keep up the quarry garden and let it be walked in by the public. Something like that.'

'I suppose the family claimed that the balance of her mind had been disturbed, that there had been undue influence?'

'I think probably it might have come to that,' said Spence. 'But the lawyers, as I say, got on to the forgery sharply. It was not a very convincing forgery, apparently. They spotted it almost at once.'

'Things came to light to show that the opera girl could have done it quite easily,' said Elspeth. 'You see, she wrote a great many of Mrs Llewellyn-Smythe's letters for her and it seems Mrs Llewellyn-Smythe had a great dislike of typed letters being sent to friends or anything like that. If it wasn't a business letter, she'd always say "write it in handwriting and make it as much like mine as you can and sign it with my name." Mrs Minden, the cleaning woman, heard her say that one day, and I suppose the girl got used to doing it and copying her employer's handwriting and then it came to her suddenly that she could do this and get away with it. And that's how it all came about. But as I say, the lawyers were too sharp and spotted it.'

'Mrs Llewellyn-Smythe's own lawyers?'

'Yes. Fullerton, Harrison and Leadbetter. Very respectable firm in Medchester. They'd always done all her legal business for her. Anyway, they got experts on to it and questions were asked and the girl was asked questions and got the wind up. Just walked out one day leaving half her things behind her. They were preparing to take proceedings against her, but she didn't wait for that. She just got out. It's not so difficult, really, to get out of this country, if you do it in time. Why, you can go on day trips on the Continent without a passport, and if you've got a little arrangement with someone on the other side, things can be arranged long before there is any real hue and cry. She's probably gone back to her own country or changed her name or gone to friends.'

'But everyone thought that Mrs Llewellyn-Smythe died a natural death?' asked Poirot.

'Yes, I don't think there was ever any question of that. I only say it's possible because, as I say, these things have happened before where the doctor has no suspicion. Supposing that girl Joyce had heard something, had heard the *au pair* girl giving medicines to Mrs Llewellyn-Smythe, and the old lady saying "this medicine tastes different to the usual one." Or "this has got a bitter taste" or "it's peculiar".'

'Anyone would think you'd been there listening to things yourself, Elspeth,' said Superintendent Spence. 'This is all your imagination.'

'When did she die?' said Poirot. 'Morning, evening, indoors, out of doors, at home or away from home?'

'Oh, at home. She'd come up from doing things in the garden one day, breathing rather heavily. She said she was very tired and she went to lie down on her bed. And to put it in one sentence, she never woke up. Which is all very natural, it seems, medically speaking.'

Poirot took out a little notebook. The page was already headed 'Victims.' Under, he wrote, 'No. 1. suggested, Mrs Llewellyn-Smythe.' On the next pages of his book he wrote down the other names that Spence had given him. He said, inquiringly:

'Charlotte Benfield?'

Spence replied promptly. 'Sixteen-year-old shop assistant. Multiple head injuries. Found on a footpath near the Quarry Wood. Two young men came under suspicion. Both had walked out with her from time to time. No evidence.'

'They assisted the police in their inquiries?' asked Poirot.

'As you say. It's the usual phrase. They didn't assist much. They were frightened. Told a few lies, contradicted themselves. They didn't carry conviction as likely murderers. But either of them *might* have been.'

'What were they like?'

'Peter Gordon, twenty-one. Unemployed. Had had one or two jobs but never kept them. Lazy. Quite good-looking. Had been on probation once or twice for minor pilferings, things of that kind. No record before of violence. Was in with a rather nasty lot of likely young criminals, but usually managed to keep out of serious trouble.'

'And the other one?'

'Thomas Hudd. Twenty. Stammered. Shy. Neurotic. Wanted to be a teacher, but couldn't make the grade. Mother a widow. The doting mother type. Didn't encourage girl friends. Kept him as close to her apron-strings as she could. He had a job in a stationer's. Nothing criminal known against him, but a possibility psychologically, so it seems. The girl played him up a good deal. Jealousy a possible motive, but no evidence that we could prosecute on. Both of them had alibis. Hudd's was his mother's. She would have sworn to kingdom come that he was indoors with her all that evening, and nobody can say he wasn't or had seen him elsewhere or in the neighbourhood of the murder. Young Gordon was given an alibi by some of his less reputable friends. Not worth much, but you couldn't disprove it.'

'This happened when?'

'Eighteen months ago.'

'And where?'

'In a footpath in a field not far from Woodleigh Common.'

'Three quarters of a mile,' said Elspeth.

'Near Joyce's house – the Reynolds' house?'

'No, it was on the other side of the village.'

'It seems unlikely to have been the murder Joyce was talking about,' said Poirot thoughtfully. 'If you see a girl being bashed on the head by a young man you'd be likely to think of murder straight away. Not to wait for a year before you began to think it was murder.'

Poirot read another name.

'Lesley Ferrier.'

Spence spoke again. 'Lawyer's clerk, twenty-eight, employed by Messrs Fullerton, Harrison and Leadbetter of Market Street, Medchester.'

'Those were Mrs Llewellyn-Smythe's solicitors, I think you said.'

'Yes. Same ones.'

'And what happened to Lesley Ferrier?'

'He was stabbed in the back. Not far from the Green Swan Pub. He was said to have been having an affair with the wife of the landlord, Harry Griffin. Handsome piece, she was, indeed still is. Getting perhaps a bit long in the tooth. Five or six years older than he was, but she liked them young.'

'The weapon?'

'The knife wasn't found. Les was said to have broken with her and taken up with some other girl, but what girl was never satisfactorily discovered.'

'Ah. And who was suspected in this case? The landlord or the wife?'

'Quite right,' said Spence. 'Might have been either. The wife seemed the more likely. She was half gypsy and a temperamental piece. But there were other possibilities. Our Lesley hadn't led a blameless life. Got into trouble in his early twenties, falsifying his accounts somewhere. With a spot of forgery. Was said to have come from a broken home and all the rest of it. Employers spoke up for him. He got a short sentence and was taken on by Fullerton, Harrison and Leadbetter when he came out of prison.'

'And after that he'd gone straight?'

'Well, nothing proved. He appeared to do so as far as his employers were concerned, but he *had* been mixed up in a few questionable transactions with his friends. He's what you might call a wrong 'un but a careful one.'

'So the alternative was?'

'That he might have been stabbed by one of his less reputable associates. When you're in with a nasty crowd you've got it coming to you with a knife if you let them down.'

'Anything else?'

'Well, he had a good lot of money in his bank account. Paid in in cash, it had been. Nothing to show where it came from. That was suspicious in itself.'

'Possibly pinched from Fullerton, Harrison and Leadbetter?' suggested Poirot.

'They say not. They had a chartered accountant to work on it and look into things.'

'And the police had no idea where else it might have come from?'

'No.'

'Again,' said Poirot, 'not Joyce's murder, I should think.'

He read the last name, 'Janet White.'

'Found strangled on a footpath which was a short cut from the schoolhouse to her home. She shared a flat there with another teacher, Nora Ambrose. According to Nora Ambrose, Janet White had occasionally spoken of being nervous about some man with whom she'd broken off relations a year ago, but who had frequently sent her threatening letters. Nothing was ever found out about this man. Nora Ambrose didn't know his name, didn't know exactly where he lived.'

'Aha,' said Poirot, 'I like this better.'

He made a good, thick black tick against Janet White's name.

'For what reason?' asked Spence.

'It is a more likely murder for a girl of Joyce's age to have witnessed. She could have recognized the victim, a school-teacher whom she knew and who perhaps taught her. Possibly she did not know the attacker. She might have seen a struggle, heard a quarrel between a girl whom she knew and a strange man. But thought no more of it than that at the time. When was Janet White killed?'

'Two and a half years ago.'

'That again,' said Poirot, 'is about the right time. Both for not realizing that the man she may have seen with his hands round Janet White's neck was not merely necking her, but might have been killing her. But then as she grew more mature, the proper explanation came to her.'

He looked at Elspeth. 'You agree with my reasoning?'

'I see what you mean,' said Elspeth. 'But aren't you going at all this the wrong way round? Looking for a victim of a past murder instead of looking for a man who killed a child here in Woodleigh Common not more than three days ago?'

'We go from the past to the future,' said Poirot. 'We arrive, shall we say, from two and a half years ago to three days ago. And, therefore, we have to consider – what you, no doubt, have already considered – who was there in Woodleigh Common amongst the people who were at the party who might have been connected with an older crime?'

'One can narrow it down a bit more than that now,' said Spence. 'That is if we are right in accepting your assumption that Joyce was killed because of what she claimed earlier in the day about seeing murder committed. She said those words during the time the preparations for the party were going on. Mind you, we may be wrong in believing that that was the motive for killing, but I don't think we are wrong. So let us say she claimed to have seen a murder, and someone who was present during the preparations for the party that afternoon could have heard her and acted as soon as possible.'

'Who *was* present?' said Poirot. 'You know, I presume.'

'Yes, I have the list for you here.'

'You have checked it carefully?'

'Yes, I've checked and re-checked, but it's been quite a job. Here are the eighteen names.'

List of people present during preparation
for Hallowe'en Party
Mrs Drake (owner of house)
Mrs Butler
Mrs Oliver
Miss Whittaker (school-teacher)
Rev. Charles Cotterell (Vicar)
Simon Lampton (Curate)
Miss Lee (Dr Ferguson's dispenser)
Ann Reynolds
Joyce Reynolds
Leopold Reynolds
Nicholas Ransom
Desmond Holland
Beatrice Ardley
Cathie Grant
Diana Brent
Mrs Garlton (household help)
Mrs Minden (cleaning woman)
Mrs Goodbody (helper)

'You are sure these are all?'

'No,' said Spence. 'I'm not sure. I can't really be sure. Nobody can. You see, odd people brought things. Somebody brought some coloured light bulbs. Somebody else supplied some mirrors. There were some extra plates. Someone lent a plastic pail. People brought things, exchanged a word or two and went away again. They didn't remain to help. Therefore such a person *could* have been overlooked and not remembered as being present. But that somebody, even if they had only just deposited a bucket in the hall, could have overheard what Joyce was saying in the sitting-room. She was shouting, you know. We can't really limit it to this list, but it's the best we can do. Here you are. Take a look at it. I've made a brief descriptive note against the names.'

'I thank you. Just one question. You must have interrogated some of these people, those for instance who were also at the party. Did anyone, *anyone* at all, mention what Joyce had said about seeing a murder?'

'I think not. There is no record of it officially. The first I heard of it is what you told me.'

'Interesting,' said Poirot. 'One might also say remarkable.'

'Obviously no one took it seriously,' said Spence.

Poirot nodded thoughtfully.

'I must go now to keep my appointment with Dr Ferguson, after his surgery,' he said.

He folded up Spence's list and put it in his pocket.

CHAPTER 9

Dr Ferguson was a man of sixty, of Scottish extraction with a brusque manner. He looked Poirot up and down with shrewd eyes under bristling eyebrows, and said:

'Well, what's all this about? Sit down. Mind that chair leg. The castor's loose.

'I should perhaps explain,' said Dr Ferguson. 'Everybody knows everything in a place like this. That authoress woman brought you down here as God's greatest detective to puzzle police officers. That's more or less right, isn't it?'

'In part,' said Poirot. 'I came here to visit an old friend ex-Superintendent Spence, who lives with his sister here.'

'Spence? Hm. Good type, Spence. Bull-dog breed. Good honest police officer of the old type. No graft. No violence. Not stupid either. Straight as a die.'

'You appraise him correctly.'

'Well,' said Ferguson, 'what did you tell him and what did he tell you?'

'Both he and Inspector Raglan have been exceedingly kind to me. I hope you will likewise.'

'I've nothing to be kind about,' said Ferguson. 'I don't know what happened. Child gets her head shoved in a bucket and is drowned in the middle of a party. Nasty business. Mind you, doing in a child isn't anything to be startled about nowadays. I've been called out to look at too many murdered children in the last seven to ten years – far too many. A lot of people who ought to be under mental restraint aren't under mental restraint. No room in the asylums. They go about, nicely spoken, nicely got up and looking like everybody else, looking for somebody they can do in. And enjoy themselves. Don't usually do it at a party, though. Too much chance of getting caught, I suppose, but novelty appeals even to a mentally disturbed killer.'

'Have you any idea who killed her?'

'Do you really suppose that's a question I can answer just like that? I'd have to have some evidence, wouldn't I? I'd have to be sure.'

'You could guess,' said Poirot.

'Anyone can guess. If I'm called in to a case I have to guess whether the chap's going to have measles or whether it's a case of an allergy to shell-fish or to feather pillows. I have to ask questions to find out what they've been eating, or drinking, or sleeping on, or what other children they've been meeting. Whether they've been in a crowded bus with Mrs Smith's or Mrs Robinson's children who've all got the measles, and a few other things. Then I advance a tentative opinion as to which it is of the various possibilities, and that, let me tell you, is what's called diagnosis. You don't do it in a hurry and you make sure.'

'Did you know this child?'

'Of course. She was one of my patients. There are two of us

here. Myself and Worrall. I happen to be the Reynolds' doctor. She was quite a healthy child, Joyce. Had the usual small childish ailments. Nothing peculiar or out of the way. Ate too much, talked too much. Talking too much hadn't done her any harm. Eating too much gave her what used to be called in the old days a bilious attack from time to time. She'd had mumps and chicken pox. Nothing else.'

'But she had perhaps talked too much on one occasion, as you suggest she might be able to do?'

'So that's the tack you're on? I heard some rumour of that. On the lines of "what the butler saw" – only tragedy instead of comedy. Is that it?'

'It could form a motive, a reason.'

'Oh yes. Grant you that. But there *are* other reasons. Mentally disturbed seems the usual answer nowadays. At any rate, it does always in the Magistrates' courts. Nobody gained by her death, nobody hated her. But it seems to me with children nowadays you don't need to look for the reason. The reason's in another place. The reason's in the killer's mind. His disturbed mind or his evil mind or his kinky mind. Any kind of mind you like to call it. I'm not a psychiatrist. There are times when I get tired of hearing those words: "Remanded for a psychiatrist's report," after a lad has broken in somewhere, smashed the looking-glasses, pinched the bottles of whisky, stolen the silver, knocked an old woman on the head. Doesn't matter much what it is now. Remand them for the psychiatrist's report.'

'And who would you favour, in this case, to remand for a psychiatrist's report?'

'You mean of those there at the "do" the other night?'

'Yes.'

'The murderer would have had to be there, wouldn't he? Otherwise there wouldn't have been a murder. Right? He was among the guests, he was among the helpers or he walked in through the window with malice aforethought. Probably he knew the fastenings of that house. Might have been in there before, looking round. Take your man or boy. He wants to kill someone. Not at all unusual. Over in Medchester we had a case of that. Came to light after about six or seven years. Boy of thirteen. Wanted to kill someone, so he killed a child of nine, pinched a car, drove it seven or eight miles into a copse, burned her there, went away, and as far as we know led a blameless life until he was twenty-one or two. Mind you, we have only his word for that, he may have gone on doing it. Probably did. Found he liked killing people. Don't suppose he's killed too many, or some police force would have been on to him before now. But every now and then he felt the urge. Psychiatrist's report. Committed murder while mentally disturbed. I'm trying to say myself that that's what happened here. That sort of thing, anyway. I'm not a psychiatrist myself, thank goodness. I have a few psychiatrist friends. Some of them are sensible chaps. Some of them – well, I'll go as far as saying they ought to be remanded for a psychiatrist's report themselves. This chap who killed Joyce probably had nice parents, ordinary manners, good appearance. Nobody'd dream anything was wrong with him. Ever had a bite at a nice red juicy apple and there, down by the core, something rather nasty rears itself up and wags its head at you? Plenty of human beings about like that. More than there used to be, I'd say nowadays.'

'And you've no suspicion of your own?'

'I can't stick my neck out and diagnose a murderer without some evidence.'

'Still, you admit it must have been someone at the party. You cannot have a murder without a murderer.'

'You can easily in some detective stories that are written. Probably your pet authoress writes them like that. But in this case I agree. The murderer must have been there. A guest, a domestic help, someone who walked in through the window. Easily done if he'd studied the catch of the window beforehand. It might have struck some crazy brain that it would be a novel idea and a bit of fun to have a murder at a Hallowe'en party. That's all you've got to start off with, isn't it? Just someone who was at the party.'

Under bushy brows a pair of eyes twinkled at Poirot.

'I was there myself,' he said. 'Came in late, just to see what was doing.'

He nodded his head vigorously.

'Yes, that's the problem, isn't it? Like a social announcement in the papers:

"Amongst those present was –
A Murderer".'

CHAPTER 10

Poirot looked up at The Elms and approved of it.

He was admitted and taken promptly by what he judged to be a secretary to the head-mistress's study. Miss Emlyn rose from her desk to greet him.

'I am delighted to meet you, Mr Poirot. I've heard about you.'

'You are too kind,' said Poirot.

'From a very old friend of mine, Miss Bulstrode. Former head-mistress of Meadowbank. You remember Miss Bulstrode, perhaps?'

'One would not be likely to forget her. A great personality.'

'Yes,' said Miss Emlyn. 'She made Meadowbank the school it is.' She sighed slightly and said, 'It has changed a little nowadays. Different aims, different methods, but it still holds its own as a school of distinction, of progress, and also of tradition. Ah well, we must not live too much in the past. You have come to see me, no doubt, about the death of Joyce Reynolds. I don't know if you have any particular interest in her case. It's out of your usual run of things, I imagine. You knew her personally, or her family perhaps?'

'No,' said Poirot. 'I came at the request of an old friend, Mrs Ariadne Oliver, who was staying down here and was present at the party.'

'She writes delightful books,' said Miss Emlyn. 'I have met her once or twice. Well, that makes the whole thing easier, I think, to discuss. So long as no personal feelings are involved, one can go straight ahead. It was a horrifying thing to happen. If I may say so, it was an unlikely thing to happen. The children involved seem neither old enough nor young enough for it to fall into any special class. A psychological crime is indicated. Do you agree?'

'No,' said Poirot. 'I think it was a murder, like most murders, committed for a motive, possibly a sordid one.'

'Indeed. And the reason?'

'The reason was a remark made by Joyce; not actually at the party, I understand, but earlier in the day when preparations were being made by some of the older children and other helpers. She announced that she had once seen a murder committed.'

'Was she believed?'

'On the whole, I think she was *not* believed.'

'That seems the most likely response. Joyce – I speak plainly to you, Monsieur Poirot, because we do not want unnecessary sentiment to cloud mental faculties – she was a rather mediocre child, neither stupid nor particularly intellectual. She was, quite frankly, a compulsive liar. And by that I do not mean that she was specially deceitful. She was not trying to avoid retribution or to avoid being found out in some peccadillo. She boasted. She boasted of things that had not happened, but that would impress her friends who were listening to her. As a result, of course, they inclined not to believe the tall stories she told.'

'You think that she boasted of having seen a murder committed in order to make herself important, to intrigue someone –?'

'Yes. And I would suggest that Ariadne Oliver was doubtless the person whom she wanted to impress . . .'

'So you don't think Joyce saw a murder committed at all?'

'I should doubt it very much.'

'You are of the opinion that she made the whole thing up?'

'I would not say that. She did witness, perhaps, a car accident, or someone perhaps who was hit with a ball on the golf links and injured – something that she could work up into an impressive happening that might, just conceivably, pass as an attempted murder.'

'So the only assumption we can make with any certainty is that there was a murderer present at the Hallowe'en party.'

'Certainly,' said Miss Emlyn, without turning a grey hair. 'Certainly. That follows on logically, does it not?'

'Would you have any idea who that murderer might be?'

'That is certainly a sensible question,' said Miss Emlyn. 'After all, the majority of the children at the party were aged between nine and fifteen, and I suppose nearly all of them had been or were pupils at my school. I ought to know something about them. Something, too, about their families and their backgrounds.'

'I believe that one of your own teachers, a year or two ago, was strangled by an unknown killer.'

'You are referring to Janet White? About twenty-four years of age. An emotional girl. As far as is known, she was out walking alone. She may, of course, have arranged to meet some young man. She was a girl who was quite attractive to men in a modest sort of way. Her killer has not been discovered. The police questioned various young men or asked them to assist them in their inquiries, as the technique goes, but they were not able to find sufficient evidence to bring a case against anyone. An unsatisfactory business from their point of view. And, I may say, from mine.'

'You and I have a principle in common. We do not approve of murder.'

Miss Emlyn looked at him for a moment or two. Her expression did not change, but Poirot had an idea that he was being sized up with a great deal of care.

'I like the way you put it,' she said. 'From what you read and hear nowadays, it seems that murder under certain aspects is slowly but surely being made acceptable to a large section of the community.'

She was silent for a few minutes, and Poirot also did not speak. She was, he thought, considering a plan of action.

She rose and touched a bell.

'I think,' she said, 'that you had better talk to Miss Whittaker.'

Some five minutes passed after Miss Emlyn had left the room and then the door opened and a woman of about forty entered. She had russet-coloured hair, cut short, and came in with a brisk step.

'Monsieur Poirot?' she said. 'Can I help you? Miss Emlyn seems to think that that might be so.'

'If Miss Emlyn thinks so, then it is almost a certainty that you can. I would take her word for it.'

'You know her?'

'I have only met her this afternoon.'

'But you have made up your mind quickly about her.'

'I hope you are going to tell me that I am right.'

Elizabeth Whittaker gave a short, quick sigh.

'Oh, yes, you're right. I presume that this is about the death of Joyce Reynolds. I don't know exactly how you come into it. Through the police?' She shook her head slightly in a dissatisfied manner.

'No, not through the police. Privately, through a friend.'

She took a chair, pushing it back a little so as to face him.

'Yes. What do you want to know?'

'I don't think there is any need to tell you. No need to waste time asking questions that may be of no importance. Something happened that evening at the party which perhaps it is well that I should know about. Is that it?'

'Yes.'

'You were at the party?'

'I was at the party.' She reflected a minute or two. 'It was a very good party. Well run. Well arranged. About thirty-odd people were there, that is, counting helpers of different kinds. Children – teenagers – grown-ups – and a few cleaning and domestic helpers in the background.'

'Did you take part in the arrangements which were made, I believe, earlier that afternoon or that morning?'

'There was nothing really to do. Mrs Drake was fully competent to deal with all the various preparations with a small number of people to help her. It was more domestic preparations that were needed.'

'I see. But you came to the party as one of the guests?'

'That is right.'

'And what happened?'

'The progress of the party, I have no doubt, you already know. You want to know if there is anything I can tell you that I specially noticed or that I thought might have a certain significance? I don't want to waste your time unduly, you understand.'

'I am sure you will not waste my time. Yes, Miss Whittaker, tell me quite simply.'

'The various events happened in the way already arranged for. The last event was what was really more a Christmas festivity or associated with Christmas, than it would be with Hallowe'en. The Snapdragon, a burning dish of raisins with brandy poured over them, and those round snatch at the raisins – there are squeals of laughter and excitement. It became very hot, though, in the room, with the burning dish, and I left it and came out in the hall. It was then, as I stood there, that I saw Mrs Drake coming out of the lavatory on the first floor landing. She was carrying a large vase of mixed autumn leaves and flowers. She stood at the angle of the staircase, pausing for a moment before coming downstairs. She was looking down over the well of the staircase. Not in my direction. She was looking towards the other end of the hall where there is a door leading into the library. It is set just across the hall from the door into the dining-room. As I say, she was looking that way and pausing for a moment before coming downstairs. She was shifting slightly the angle of the vase as it was a rather awkward thing to carry, and weighty if it was, as I presumed, full of water. She was shifting the position of it rather carefully so that she could hold it to her with one arm, and put out the other arm to the rail of the staircase as she came round the slightly shaped corner stairway. She stood there for a moment or two, still not looking at what she was carrying, but towards the hall below. And suddenly she made a sudden movement – a start I would describe it as – yes, definitely something had startled her. So much so that she relinquished her hold of the vase and it fell, reversing itself as it did so so that the water streamed over her and the vase itself crashed down to the hall below, where it broke in smithereens on the hall floor.'

'I see,' said Poirot. He paused a minute or two, watching her. Her eyes, he noticed, were shrewd and knowledgeable. They were asking now his opinion of what she was telling him. 'What did you think had happened to startle her?'

'On reflection, afterwards, I thought she had seen something.'

'You thought she had seen something,' repeated Poirot, thoughtfully. 'Such as?'

'The direction of her eyes, as I have told you, was towards the door of the library. It seems to me possible that she may have seen that door open or the handle turn, or indeed she might have seen something slightly more than that. She might have seen somebody who was opening that door and preparing to come out of it. She may have seen someone she did not expect to see.'

'Were you looking at the door yourself?'

'No. I was looking in the opposite direction up the stairs towards Mrs Drake.'

'And you think definitely that she saw something that startled her?'

'Yes. No more than that, perhaps. A door opening. A person, just possibly an unlikely person, emerging. Just sufficient to make her relinquish her grasp on the very heavy vase full of water and flowers, so that she dropped it.'

'Did you see anyone come out of that door?'

'No. I was not looking that way. I do not think anyone actually did come out into the hall. Presumably whoever it was drew back into the room.'

'What did Mrs Drake do next?'

'She made a sharp exclamation of vexation, came down the stairs and said to me, "Look what I've done now! What a mess!" She kicked some of the broken glass away. I helped her sweep it in a broken pile into a corner. It wasn't practicable to clear it all up at that moment. The children were beginning to come out of the Snapdragon room. I fetched a glass cloth and mopped her up a bit, and shortly after that the party came to an end.'

'Mrs Drake did not say anything about having been startled or make any reference as to what might have startled her?'

'No. Nothing of the kind.'

'But you think she *was* startled.'

'Possibly, Monsieur Poirot, you think that I am making a rather unnecessary fuss about something of no importance whatever?'

'No,' said Poirot, 'I do not think that at all. I have only met Mrs Drake once,' he added thoughtfully, 'when I went to her house with my friend, Mrs Oliver, to visit – as one might say, if one wishes to be melodramatic – the scene of the crime. It did not strike me during the brief period I had for observation that Mrs Drake could be a woman who is easily startled. Do you agree with my view?'

'Certainly. That is why I, myself, since have wondered.'

'You asked no special questions at the time?'

'I had no earthly reason to do so. If your hostess has been unfortunate to drop one of her best glass vases, and it has smashed to smithereens, it is hardly the part of a guest to say "What on earth made you do that?"; thereby accusing her of a clumsiness which I can assure you is not one of Mrs Drake's characteristics.'

'And after that, as you have said, the party came to an end. The children and their mothers or friends left, and Joyce could not be found. We know now that Joyce was behind the library door and that Joyce was dead. So who could it have been who was about to come out of the library door, a little while earlier, shall we say, and then hearing voices in the hall shut the door again and made an exit later when there were people milling about in the hall making their farewells, putting on their coats and all the rest of it? It was not until after the body had been found, I presume, Miss Whittaker, that you had time to reflect on what you had seen?'

'That is so.' Miss Whittaker rose to her feet. 'I'm afraid there's nothing else that I can tell you. Even this may be a very foolish little matter.'

'But noticeable. Everything noticeable is worth remembering. By the way, there is one question I should like to ask you. Two, as a matter of fact.'

Elizabeth Whittaker sat down again. 'Go on,' she said, 'ask anything you like.'

'Can you remember exactly the order in which the various events occurred at the party?'

'I think so.' Elizabeth Whittaker reflected for a moment or two. 'It started with a broomstick competition. Decorated broomsticks. There were three or four different small prizes for that. Then there was a kind of contest with balloons, punching them and batting them about. A sort of mild horse-play to get the children warmed up. There was a looking-glass business where the girls went into a small room and held a mirror where a boy's or young man's face reflected in it.'

'How was that managed?'

'Oh, very simply. The transom of the door had been removed, and so different faces looked through and were reflected in the mirror a girl was holding.'

'Did the girls know who it was they saw reflected in the glass?'

'I presume some of them did and some of them didn't. A little make-up was employed on the male half of the arrangement. You know, a mask or a wig, sideburns, a beard, some greasepaint effects. Most of the boys were probably known to the girls already and one or two strangers might have been included. Anyway, there was a lot of quite happy giggling,' said Miss Whittaker, showing for a moment or two a kind of academic contempt for this kind of fun. 'After that there was an obstacle race and then there was flour packed into a glass tumbler and reversed, sixpence laid on top and everyone took a slice off. When the flour collapsed that person was out of the competition and the others remained until the last one claimed the sixpence. After that there was dancing, and then there was supper. After that, as a final climax, came the Snapdragon.'

'When did you yourself see the girl Joyce last?'

'I've no idea,' said Elizabeth Whittaker. 'I don't know her very well. She's not in my class. She wasn't a very interesting girl so I wouldn't have been watching her. I do remember I saw her cutting the flour because she was so clumsy that she capsized it almost at once. So she was alive then – but that was quite early on.'

'You did not see her go into the library with anyone?'

'Certainly not. I should have mentioned it before if I had. *That* at least might have been significant and important.'

'And now,' said Poirot, 'for my second question or questions. How long have you been at the school here?'

'Six years this next autumn.'

'And you teach –?'

'Mathematics and Latin.'

'Do you remember a girl who was teaching here two years ago – Janet White by name?'

Elizabeth Whittaker stiffened. She half rose from her chair, then sat down again.

'But that – that has nothing to do with all this, surely?'

'It could have,' said Poirot.

'But how? In what way?'

Scholastic circles were less well informed than village gossip, Poirot thought.

'Joyce claimed before witnesses to have seen a murder done some years ago. Could that possibly have been the murder of Janet White, do you think? How did Janet White die?'

'She was strangled, walking home from school one night.'

'Alone?'

'Probably not alone.'

'But not with Nora Ambrose?'

'What do you know about Nora Ambrose?'

'Nothing as yet,' said Poirot, 'but I should like to. What were they like, Janet White and Nora Ambrose?'

'Over-sexed,' said Elizabeth Whittaker, 'but in different ways. How could Joyce have seen anything of the kind or know anything about it? It took place in a lane near Quarry Wood. She wouldn't have been more than ten or eleven years old.'

'Which one had the boy friend?' asked Poirot. 'Nora or Janet?'

'All this is past history.'

'*Old sins have long shadows*,' quoted Poirot. 'As we advance through life, we learn the truth of that saying. Where is Nora Ambrose now?'

'She left the school and took another post in the North of England – she was, naturally, very upset. They were – great friends.'

'The police never solved the case?'

Miss Whittaker shook her head. She got up and looked at her watch.

'I must go now.'

'Thank you for what you have told me.'

CHAPTER 11

Hercule Poirot looked up at the façade of Quarry House. A solid, well-built example of mid-Victorian architecture. He had a vision of its interior – a heavy mahogany sideboard, a central rectangular table also of heavy mahogany, a billiard room, perhaps, a large kitchen with adjacent scullery, stone flags on the floor, a massive coal range now no doubt replaced by electricity or gas.

He noted that most of the upper windows were still curtained. He rang the front-door bell. It was answered by a thin, grey-haired woman who told him that Colonel and Mrs Weston were away in London and would not be back until next week.

He asked about the Quarry Woods and was told that they were open to the public without charge. The entrance was about five minutes' walk along the road. He would see a notice-board on an iron gate.

He found his way there easily enough, and passing through the gate began to descend a path that led downwards through trees and shrubs.

Presently he came to a halt and stood there lost in thought. His mind was not only on what he saw, on what lay around him. Instead he was conning over one or two sentences, and reflecting over one or two facts that had given him at the time, as he expressed it to himself, furiously to think. A forged Will, a forged Will and a girl. A girl who had disappeared, the girl in whose favour the Will had been forged. A young artist who had come here professionally to make out of an abandoned quarry of rough stone a garden, a sunk garden. Here again, Poirot looked round him and nodded his head with approval of the phrase. A Quarry Garden was an ugly term. It suggested the noise of blasting rock, the carrying away by lorries of vast masses of stone for road making. It had behind it industrial demand. But a Sunk Garden – that was different. It brought with it vague remembrances in his own mind. So Mrs Llewellyn-Smythe had gone on a National Trust tour of gardens in Ireland. He himself, he remembered, had been in Ireland five or six years ago. He had gone there to investigate a robbery of old family silver. There had been some interesting points about the case which had aroused his curiosity, and having (as usual) – Poirot added this bracket to his thoughts – solved his mission with full success, he had put in a few days travelling around and seeing the sights.

He could not remember now the particular garden he had been to see. Somewhere, he thought, not very far from Cork. Killarney? No, not Killarney. Somewhere not far from Bantry Bay. And he remembered it because it had been a garden quite different from the gardens which he had so far acclaimed as the great successes of this age, the gardens of the Châteaux in France, the formal beauty of Versailles. Here, he remembered, he had started with a little group of people in a boat. A boat difficult to get into if two strong and able boatmen had not practically lifted him in. They had rowed towards a small island, not a very interesting island, Poirot had thought, and began to wish that he had not come. His feet were wet and cold and the wind was blowing through the crevices of his mackintosh. What beauty, he had thought, what formality, what symmetrical arrangement of great beauty could there be on this rocky island with its sparse trees? A mistake – definitely a mistake.

They had landed at the little wharf. The fishermen had landed him with the same adroitness they had shown before. The remaining members of the party had gone on ahead, talking and laughing. Poirot, readjusting his mackintosh in position and tying up his shoes again, had followed them up the rather dull path with shrubs and bushes and a few sparse trees either side. A most uninteresting park, he thought.

And then, rather suddenly, they had come out from among the scrub on to a terrace with steps leading down from it. Below it he had looked down into what struck him at once as something entirely magical. Something as it might have been if elemental beings such as he believed were common in Irish poetry, had come out of their hollow hills and had created there, not so much by toil and hard labour as by waving a magic wand, a garden. You looked down into the garden. Its beauty, the flowers and bushes, the artificial water below in the fountain, the path round it, enchanted, beautiful and entirely unexpected. He wondered how it had been originally. It seemed too symmetrical to have been a quarry. A deep hollow here in the raised ground of the island, but beyond it you could see the waters of the Bay and the hills rising the other side, their misty tops an enchanting scene. He thought perhaps that it might have been that particular garden which had stirred Mrs Llewellyn-Smythe to possess such a garden of her own, to have the pleasure of taking an unkempt quarry set in this smug, tidy, elementary and essentially conventional countryside of that part of England.

And so she had looked about for the proper kind of well-paid slave to do her bidding. And she had found the professionally qualified young man called Michael Garfield and had brought him here and had paid him no doubt a large fee, and had in due course built a house for him. Michael Garfield, thought Poirot, had not failed her.

He went and sat down on a bench, a bench which had been strategically placed. He pictured to himself what the sunken quarry would look like in the spring. There were young beech trees and birches with their white shivering barks. Bushes of thorn and white rose, little juniper trees. But now it was autumn, and autumn had been catered for also. The gold and red of acers, a parrotia or two, a path that led along a winding way to fresh delights. There were flowering bushes of gorse or Spanish broom – Poirot was not famous for knowing the names of either flowers or shrubs – only roses and tulips could he approve and recognize.

But everything that grew here had the appearance of having grown by its own will. It had not been arranged or forced into submission. And yet, thought Poirot, that is not really so. All has been arranged, all has been planned to this tiny little plant that grows here and to that large towering bush that rises up so fiercely with its golden and red leaves. Oh yes. All has been planned here and arranged. What is more, I would say that it had obeyed.

He wondered then whom it had obeyed. Mrs Llewellyn-Smythe or Michael Garfield? It makes a difference, said Poirot to himself, yes, it makes a difference. Mrs Llewellyn-Smythe was knowledgeable, he felt sure. She had gardened for many years, she was no doubt a Fellow of the Royal Horticultural Society, she went to shows, she consulted catalogues, she visited gardens. She took journeys abroad, no doubt, for botanical reasons. She would know what she wanted, she would say what she wanted. Was that enough? Poirot thought it was not quite enough. She could have given orders to gardeners and made sure her orders were carried out. But did she know – really know – see in her mind's eye exactly what her orders would look like when they had been carried out? Not in the first year of their planting, not even the second, but things that she would see two years later, three years later, perhaps, even six or seven years later. Michael Garfield, thought Poirot, Michael Garfield knows what she wants because she has told him what she wants, and he knows how to make this bare quarry of stone and rock blossom as a desert can blossom. He planned and he brought it about; he had no doubt the intense pleasure that comes to an artist who is commissioned by a client with plenty of money. Here was his conception of a fairy-land tucked away in a conventional and rather dull hillside, and here it would grow up. Expensive shrubs for which large cheques would have to be written, and rare plants that perhaps would only be obtainable through the goodwill of a friend, and here, too, the humble things that were needed and which cost next to nothing at all. In spring on the bank just to his left there would be primroses, their modest green leaves all bunched together up the side of it told him that.

'In England,' said Poirot, 'people show you their herbaceous borders and they take you to see their roses and they talk at inordinate length about their iris gardens, and to show they appreciate one of the great beauties of England, they take you on a day when the sun shines and the beech trees are in leaf, and underneath them are all the bluebells. Yes, it is a very beautiful sight, but I have been shown it, I think, once too often. I prefer –' the thought broke off in his mind as he thought back to what he had preferred. A drive through Devon lanes. A winding road with great banks up each side of it, and on those banks a great carpet and showing of primroses. So pale, so subtly and timidly yellow, and coming from them that sweet, faint, elusive smell that the primrose has in large quantities, which is the smell of spring almost more than any other smell. And so it would not be all rare shrubs here. There would be spring and autumn, there would be little wild cyclamen and there would be autumn crocus here too. It was a beautiful place.

He wondered about the people who lived in Quarry House now. He had their names, a retired elderly Colonel and his wife, but surely, he thought, Spence might have told him more about them. He had the feeling that whoever owned this now had not got the love of it that dead Mrs Llewellyn-Smythe had had. He got up and walked along the path a little way. It was an easy path, carefully levelled, designed, he thought, to be easy for an elderly person to walk where she would at will, without undue amount of steep steps, and at a convenient angle and convenient intervals a seat that looked rustic but was much less rustic than it looked. In fact, the angle for the back and for one's feet was remarkably comfortable. Poirot thought to himself, I'd like to see this Michael Garfield. He made a good thing of this. He knew his job, he was a good planner and he got experienced people to carry his plans out, and he managed, I think, to get his patron's plans so arranged that she would think that the whole planning had been hers. But I don't think it was only hers. It was mostly his. Yes, I'd like to see him. If he's still in the cottage – or the bungalow – that was built for him, I suppose – his thought broke off.

He stared. Stared across a hollow that lay at his feet where the path ran round the other side of it. Stared at one particular golden red branching shrub which framed something that Poirot did not know for a moment was really there or was a mere effect of shadow and sunshine and leaves.

What am I seeing? thought Poirot. Is this the result of enchantment? It could be. In this place here, it could be. Is it a human being I see, or is it – what could it be? His mind reverted to some adventures of his many years ago which he had christened 'The Labours of Hercules'. Somehow, he thought, this was not an English garden in which he was sitting. There was an atmosphere here. He tried to pin it down. It had qualities of magic, of enchantment, certainly of beauty, bashful beauty, yet wild. Here, if you were staging a scene in the theatre, you would have your nymphs, your fauns, you would have Greek beauty, you would have fear too. Yes, he thought, in this sunk garden there is fear. What did Spence's sister say? Something about a murder that took place in the original quarry years ago? Blood had stained the rock there, and afterwards, death had been forgotten, all had been covered over, Michael Garfield had come, had planned and had created a garden of great beauty, and an elderly woman who had not many more years to live had paid out money for it.

He saw now it was a young man who stood on the other side of the hollow, framed by golden red leaves, and a young man, so Poirot now recognized, of an unusual beauty. One didn't think of young men that way nowadays. You said of a young man that he was sexy or madly attractive, and these evidences of praise are often quite justly made. A man with a craggy face, a man with wild greasy hair and whose features were far from regular. You didn't say a young man was beautiful. If you did say it, you said it apologetically as though you were praising some quality that had been long dead. The sexy girls didn't want Orpheus with his lute, they wanted a pop singer with a raucous voice, expressive eyes and large masses of unruly hair.

Poirot got up and walked round the path. As he got to the other side of the steep descent, the young man came out from the trees to meet him. His youth seemed the most characteristic thing about him, yet, as Poirot saw, he was not really young. He was past thirty, perhaps nearer forty. The smile on his face was very, very faint. It was not quite a welcoming smile, it was just a smile of quiet recognition. He was tall, slender, with features of great perfection such as a classical sculptor might have produced. His eyes were dark, his hair was black and fitted him as a woven chain mail helmet or cap might have done. For a moment Poirot wondered whether he and this young man might not be meeting in the course of some pageant that was being rehearsed. If so, thought Poirot, looking down at his galoshes, I, alas, shall have to go to the wardrobe mistress to get myself better equipped. He said:

'I am perhaps trespassing here. If so, I must apologize. I am a stranger in this part of the world. I only arrived yesterday.'

'I don't think one could call it trespassing.' The voice was very quiet; it was polite yet in a curious way uninterested, as if this man's thoughts were really somewhere quite far away. 'It's not exactly open to the public, but people do walk round here. Old Colonel Weston and his wife don't mind. They would mind if there was any damage done, but that's not really very likely.'

'No vandalism,' said Poirot, looking round him. 'No litter that is noticeable. Not even a little basket. That is very unusual, is it not? And it seems deserted – strange. Here you would think,' he went on, 'there would be lovers walking.'

'Lovers don't come here,' said the young man. 'It's supposed to be unlucky for some reason.'

'Are you, I wonder, the architect? But perhaps I'm guessing wrong.'

'My name is Michael Garfield,' said the young man.

'I thought it might be,' said Poirot. He gesticulated with a hand around him. 'You made this?'

'Yes,' said Michael Garfield.

'It is beautiful,' said Poirot. 'Somehow one feels it is always rather unusual when something beautiful is made in – well, frankly, what is a dull part of the English landscape.

'I congratulate you,' he said. 'You must be satisfied with what you have done here.'

'Is one ever satisfied? I wonder.'

'You made it, I think, for a Mrs Llewellyn-Smythe. No longer alive, I believe. There is a Colonel and Mrs Weston, I believe? Do they own it now?'

'Yes. They got it cheap. It's a big, ungainly house – not easy to run – not what most people want. She left it in her Will to me.'

'And you sold it.'

'I sold the house.'

'And not the Quarry Garden?'

'Oh yes. The Quarry Garden went with it, practically thrown in, as one might say.'

'Now why?' said Poirot. 'It is interesting, that. You do not mind if I am perhaps a little curious?'

'Your questions are not quite the usual ones,' said Michael Garfield.

'I ask not so much for facts as for reasons. Why did A do so and so? Why did B do something else? Why was C's behaviour quite different from that of A and B?'

'You should be talking to a scientist,' said Michael. 'It is a matter – or so we are told nowadays – of genes or chromosomes. The arrangement, the pattern, and so on.'

'You said just now you were not entirely satisfied because no-one ever was. Was your employer, your patron, whatever you like to call her – was she satisfied? With this thing of beauty?'

'Up to a point,' said Michael. 'I saw to that. She was easy to satisfy.'

'That seems most unlikely,' said Hercule Poirot. 'She was, I have learned, over sixty. Sixty-five at least. Are people of that age often satisfied?'

'She was assured by me that what I had carried out was the exact carrying out of her instructions and imagination and ideas.'

'And was it?'

'Do you ask me that seriously?'

'No,' said Poirot. 'No. Frankly I do not.'

'For success in life,' said Michael Garfield, 'one has to pursue the career one wants, one has to satisfy such artistic leanings as one has got, but one has as well to be a tradesman. You have to sell your wares. Otherwise you are tied to carrying out other people's ideas in a way which will not accord with one's own. I carried out mainly my own ideas and I sold them, marketed them perhaps is a better word, to the client who employed me, as a direct carrying out of her plans and schemes. It is not a very difficult art to learn. There is no more to it than selling a child brown eggs rather than white ones. The customer has to be assured they are the best ones, the right ones. The essence of the countryside. Shall we say, the hen's own preference? Brown, farm, *country* eggs. One does not sell them if one says "they are just eggs. There is only one difference in eggs. They are new laid or they are not".'

'You are an unusual young man,' said Poirot. 'Arrogant,' he said thoughtfully.'

'Perhaps.'

'You have made here something very beautiful. You have added vision and planning to the rough material of stone hollowed out in the pursuit of industry, with no thought of beauty in that hacking out. You have added imagination, a result seen in the mind's eye, that you have managed to raise the money to fulfil. I congratulate you. I pay my tribute. The tribute of an old man who is approaching a time when the end of his own work is come.'

'But at the moment you are still carrying it on?'

'You know who I am, then?'

Poirot was pleased indubitably. He liked people to know who he was. Nowadays, he feared, most people did not.

'You follow the trail of blood . . . It is already known here. It is a small community, news travels. Another public success brought you here.'

'Ah, you mean Mrs Oliver.'

'Ariadne Oliver. A best seller. People wish to interview her, to know what she thinks about such subjects as student unrest, socialism, girls' clothing, should sex be permissive, and many other things that are no concern of hers.'

'Yes, yes,' said Poirot, 'deplorable, I think. They do not learn very much, I have noticed, from Mrs Oliver. They learn only that she is fond of apples. That has now been known for twenty years at least, I should think, but she still repeats it with a pleasant smile. Although now, I fear, she no longer likes apples.'

'It was apples that brought you here, was it not?'

'Apples at a Hallowe'en party,' said Poirot. 'You were at that party?'

'No.'

'You were fortunate.'

'Fortunate?' Michael Garfield repeated the word, something that sounded faintly like surprise in his voice.

'To have been one of the guests at a party where murder is committed is not a pleasant experience. Perhaps you have not experienced it, but I tell you, you are fortunate because –' Poirot became a little more foreign '– *il y a des ennuis, vous comprenez*? People ask you times, dates, impertinent questions.' He went on, 'You knew the child?'

'Oh yes. The Reynolds are well known here. I know most of the people living round here. We all know each other in Woodleigh Common, though in varying degrees. There is some intimacy, some friendships, some people remain the merest acquaintances, and so on.'

'What was she like, the child Joyce?'

'She was – how can I put it? – not important. She had rather an ugly voice. Shrill. Really, that's about all I remember about her. I'm not particularly fond of children. Mostly they bore me. Joyce bored me. When she talked, she talked about herself.'

'She was not interesting?'

Michael Garfield looked slightly surprised.

'I shouldn't think so,' he said. 'Does she have to be?'

'It is my view that people devoid of interest are unlikely to be murdered. People are murdered for gain, for fear or for love. One takes one's choice, but one has to have a starting point –'

He broke off and glanced at his watch.

'I must proceed. I have an engagement to fulfil. Once more, my felicitations.'

He went on down, following the path and picking his way carefully. He was glad that for once he was not wearing his tight patent leather shoes.

Michael Garfield was not the only person he was to meet in the sunk garden that day. As he reached the bottom he noted that three paths led from here in slightly different directions. At the entrance of the middle path, sitting on a fallen trunk of a tree, a child was awaiting him. She made this clear at once.

'I expect you are Mr Hercule Poirot, aren't you?' she said.

Her voice was clear, almost bell-like in tone. She was a fragile creature. Something about her matched the sunk garden. A dryad or some elf-like being.

'That is my name,' said Poirot.

'I came to meet you,' said the child. 'You are coming to tea with us, aren't you?'

'With Mrs Butler and Mrs Oliver? Yes.'

'That's right. That's Mummy and Aunt Ariadne.' She added with a note of censure: 'You're rather late.'

'I am sorry. I stopped to speak to someone.'

'Yes, I saw you. You were talking to Michael, weren't you?'

'You know him?'

'Of course. We've lived here quite a long time. I know everybody.'

Poirot wondered how old she was. He asked her. She said,

'I'm twelve years old. I'm going to boarding-school next year.'

'Will you be sorry or glad?'

'I don't really know till I get there. I don't think I like this place very much, not as much as I did.' She added, 'I think you'd better come with me now, please.'

'But certainly. But certainly. I apologize for being late.'

'Oh, it doesn't really matter.'

'What's your name?'

'Miranda.'

'I think it suits you,' said Poirot.

'Are you thinking of Shakespeare?'

'Yes. Do you have it in lessons?'

'Yes. Miss Emlyn read us some of it. I asked Mummy to read some more. I liked it. It has a wonderful sound. *A brave new world.* There isn't anything really like that, is there?'

'You don't believe in it?'

'Do you?'

'There is always a brave new world,' said Poirot, 'but only, you know, for very special people. The lucky ones. The ones who carry the making of that world within themselves.'

'Oh, I see,' said Miranda, with an air of apparently seeing with the utmost ease, though what she saw Poirot rather wondered.

She turned, started along the path and said,

'We go this way. It's not very far. You can go through the hedge of our garden.'

Then she looked back over her shoulder and pointed, saying:

'In the middle there, that's where the fountain was.'

'A fountain?'

'Oh, years ago. I suppose it's still there, underneath the shrubs and the azaleas and the other things. It was all broken up, you see. People took bits of it away but nobody has put a new one there.'

'It seems a pity.'

'I don't know. I'm not sure. Do you like fountains very much?'

'*Ca dépend*,' said Poirot.

'I know some French,' said Miranda. 'That's it depends, isn't it?'

'You are quite right. You seem very well educated.'

'Everyone says Miss Emlyn is a very fine teacher. She's our head-mistress. She's awfully strict and a bit stern, but she's terribly interesting sometimes in the things she tells us.'

'Then she is certainly a good teacher,' said Hercule Poirot. 'You know this place very well – you seem to know all the paths. Do you come here often?'

'Oh yes, it's one of my favourite walks. Nobody knows where I am, you see, when I come here. I sit in trees – on the branches, and watch things. I like that. Watching things happen.'

'What sort of things?'

'Mostly birds and squirrels. Birds are very quarrelsome, aren't they? Not like in the bit of poetry that says "birds in their little nests agree." They don't really, do they? And I watch squirrels.'

'And you watch people?'

'Sometimes. But there aren't many people who come here.'

'Why not, I wonder?'

'I suppose they are afraid.'

'Why should they be afraid?'

'Because someone was killed here long ago. Before it was a garden, I mean. It was a quarry once and then there was a gravel pile or a sand pile and that's where they found her. In that. Do you think the old saying is true – about you're born to be hanged or born to be drowned?'

'Nobody is born to be hanged nowadays. You do not hang people any longer in this country.'

'But they hang them in some other countries. They hang them in the streets. I've read it in the papers.'

'Ah. Do you think that is a good thing or a bad thing?'

Miranda's response was not strictly in answer to the question, but Poirot felt that it was perhaps meant to be.

'Joyce was drowned,' she said. 'Mummy didn't want to tell me, but that was rather silly, I think, don't you? I mean, I'm twelve years old.'

'Was Joyce a friend of yours?'

'Yes. She was a great friend in a way. She told me very interesting things sometimes. All about elephants and rajahs. She'd been to India once. I wish I'd been to India. Joyce and I used to tell each other all our secrets. I haven't so much to tell as Mummy. Mummy's been to Greece, you know. That's where she met Aunt Ariadne, but she didn't take me.'

'Who told you about Joyce?'

'Mrs Perring. That's our cook. She was talking to Mrs Minden who comes and cleans. Someone held her head down in a bucket of water.'

'Have you any idea who that someone was?'

'I shouldn't think so. They didn't seem to know, but then they're both rather stupid really.'

'Do *you* know, Miranda?'

'I wasn't there. I had a sore throat and a temperature so Mummy wouldn't take me to the party. But I think I could know. Because she was drowned. That's why I asked if you thought people were born to be drowned. We go through the hedge here. Be careful of your clothes.'

Poirot followed her lead. The entrance through the hedge from the Quarry Garden was more suited to the build of his childish guide with her elfin slimness – it was practically a highway to her. She was solicitous for Poirot, however, warning him of adjacent thorn bushes and holding back the more prickly components of the hedge. They emerged at a spot in the garden adjacent to a compost heap and turned a corner by a derelict cucumber frame to where two dustbins stood. From there on a small neat garden mostly planted with roses gave easy access to the small bungalow house. Miranda led the way through an open french window, announcing with the modest pride of a collector who has just secured a sample of a rare beetle:

'I've got him all right.'

'Miranda, you didn't bring him through the hedge, did you? You ought to have gone round by the path at the side gate.'

'This is a better way,' said Miranda. 'Quicker and shorter.'

'And much more painful, I suspect.'

'I forget,' said Mrs Oliver – 'I did introduce you, didn't I, to my friend Mrs Butler?'

'Of course. In the post office.'

The introduction in question had been a matter of a few moments while there had been a queue in front of the counter. Poirot was better able now to study Mrs Oliver's friend at close quarters. Before it had been a matter of a slim woman in a disguising head-scarf and a mackintosh. Judith Butler was a woman of about thirty-five, and whilst her daughter resembled a dryad or a wood-nymph, Judith had more the attributes of a water-spirit. She could have been a Rhine maiden. Her long blonde hair hung limply on her shoulders, she was delicately made with a rather long face and faintly hollow cheeks, whilst above them were big sea-green eyes fringed with long eyelashes.

'I'm very glad to thank you properly, Monsieur Poirot,' said Mrs Butler. 'It was very good of you to come down here when Ariadne asked you.'

'When my friend, Mrs Oliver, asks me to do anything I always have to do it,' said Poirot.

'What nonsense,' said Mrs Oliver.

'She was sure, quite sure, that you would be able to find out all about this beastly thing. Miranda, dear, will you go into the kitchen? You'll find the scones on the wire tray above the oven.'

Miranda disappeared. She gave, as she went, a knowledgeable smile directed at her mother that said as plainly as a smile could say, 'She's getting me out of the way for a short time.'

'I tried not to let her know,' said Miranda's mother, 'about this – this horrible thing that happened. But I suppose that was a forlorn chance from the start.'

'Yes indeed,' said Poirot. 'There's nothing that goes round any residential centre with the same rapidity as news of a disaster, and particularly an unpleasant disaster. And anyway,' he added, 'one cannot go long through life without knowing what goes on around one. And children seem particularly apt at that sort of thing.'

'I don't know if it was Burns or Sir Walter Scott who said "There's a chiel among you taking notes",' said Mrs Oliver, 'but he certainly knew what he was talking about.'

'Joyce Reynolds certainly seems to have noticed such a thing as a murder,' said Mrs Butler. 'One can hardly believe it.'

'Believe that Joyce noticed it?'

'I meant believe that if she saw such a thing she never spoke about it earlier. That seems very unlike Joyce.'

'The first thing that everybody seems to tell me here,' said Poirot, in a mild voice, 'is that this girl, Joyce Reynolds, was a liar.'

'I suppose it's possible,' said Judith Butler, 'that a child might make up a thing and then it might turn out to be true?'

'That is certainly the focal point from which we start,' said Poirot. 'Joyce Reynolds was unquestionably murdered.'

'And you *have* started. Probably you know already all about it,' said Mrs Oliver.

'Madame, do not ask impossibilities of me. You are always in such a hurry.'

'Why not?' said Mrs Oliver. 'Nobody would ever get anything done nowadays if they weren't in a hurry.'

Miranda returned at this moment with a plateful of scones.

'Shall I put them down here?' she asked. 'I expect you've finished talking by now, haven't you? Or is there anything else you would like me to get from the kitchen?'

There was a gentle malice in her voice. Mrs Butler lowered the Georgian silver teapot to the fender, switched on an electric kettle which had been turned off just before it came to the boil, duly filled the teapot and served the tea. Miranda handed hot scones and cucumber sandwiches with a serious elegance of manner.

'Ariadne and I met in Greece,' said Judith.

'I fell into the sea,' said Mrs Oliver, 'when we were coming back from one of the islands. It had got rather rough and the sailors always say "jump" and, of course, they always say jump just when the thing's at its furthest point which makes it come right for you, but you don't think that can possibly happen and so you dither and you lose your nerve and you jump when it looks close and, of course, that's the moment when it goes far away.'

She paused for breath. 'Judith helped fish me out and it made a kind of bond between us, didn't it?'

'Yes, indeed,' said Mrs Butler. 'Besides, I liked your Christian name,' she added. 'It seemed very appropriate, somehow.'

'Yes, I suppose it is a Greek name,' said Mrs Oliver. 'It's my own, you know. I didn't just make it up for literary purposes. But nothing Ariadne-like has ever happened to me. I've never been deserted on a Greek island by my own true love or anything like that.'

Poirot raised a hand to his moustache in order to hide the slight smile that he could not help coming to his lips as he envisaged Mrs Oliver in the rôle of a deserted Greek maiden.

'We can't all live up to our names,' said Mrs Butler.

'No, indeed. I can't see you in the rôle of cutting off your lover's head. That is the way it happened, isn't it, Judith and Holofernes, I mean?'

'It was her patriotic duty,' said Mrs Butler, 'for which, if I remember rightly, she was highly commended and rewarded.'

'I'm not really very well up in Judith and Holofernes. It's the Apocrypha, isn't it? Still, if one comes to think of it, people do give other people – their children, I mean – some very queer names, don't they? Who was the one who hammered some nails in someone's head? Jael or Sisera. I never remember which is the man or which is the woman there. Jael, I think. I don't think I remember any child having been christened Jael.'

'She laid butter before him in a lordly dish,' said Miranda unexpectedly, pausing as she was about to remove the tea-tray.

'Don't look at me,' said Judith Butler to her friend, 'it wasn't I who introduced Miranda to the Apocrypha. That's her school training.'

'Rather unusual for schools nowadays, isn't it?' said Mrs Oliver. 'They give them ethical ideas instead, don't they?'

'Not Miss Emlyn,' said Miranda. 'She says that if we go to church nowadays we only get the modern version of the Bible read to us in the lessons and things, and that it has no literary merit whatsoever. We should at least know the fine prose and blank verse sometimes of the Authorized Version. I enjoyed the story of Jael and Sisera very much,' she added. 'It's not a thing,' she said meditatively, 'that I should ever have thought of doing myself. Hammering nails, I mean, into someone's head when they were asleep.'

'I hope not indeed,' said her mother.

'And how *would* you dispose of your enemies, Miranda?' asked Poirot.

'I should be very kind,' said Miranda in a gently contemplative tone. 'It would be more difficult, but I'd rather have it that way because I don't like hurting things. I'd use a sort of drug that gives people euthanasia. They would go to sleep and have beautiful dreams and they just wouldn't wake up.' She lifted some tea cups and the bread and butter plate. 'I'll wash up, Mummy,' she said, 'if you like to take Monsieur Poirot to look at the garden. There are still some Queen Elizabeth roses at the back of the border.'

She went out of the room carefully carrying the tea-tray.

'She's an astonishing child, Miranda,' said Mrs Oliver.

'You have a very beautiful daughter, Madame,' said Poirot.

'Yes, I think she is beautiful *now*. One doesn't know what they will look like by the time they grow up. They acquire puppy fat and look like well-fattened pigs sometimes. But now – now she is like a wood-nymph.'

'One does not wonder that she is fond of the Quarry Garden which adjoins your house.'

'I wish she wasn't so fond of it sometimes. One gets nervous about people wandering about in isolated places, even if they are quite near people or a village. One's – oh, one's very frightened all the time nowadays. That's why – why you've got to find out why this awful thing happened to Joyce, Monsieur Poirot. Because until we know who that was, we shan't feel safe for a minute – about *our* children, I mean. Take Monsieur Poirot out in the garden, will you, Ariadne? I'll join you in a minute or two.'

She took the remaining two cups and a plate and went into the kitchen. Poirot and Mrs Oliver went out through the french window. The small garden was like most autumn gardens. It retained a few candles of golden rod and michaelmas daisies in a border, and some Queen Elizabeth roses held their pink statuesque heads up high. Mrs Oliver walked rapidly down to where there was a stone bench, sat down, and motioned Poirot to sit down beside her.

'You said you thought Miranda was like a wood-nymph,' she said. 'What do you think of Judith?'

'I think Judith's name ought to be Undine,' said Poirot.

'A water-spirit, yes. Yes, she does look as though she'd just come out of the Rhine or the sea or a forest pool or something. Her hair looks as though it had been dipped in water. Yet there's nothing untidy or scatty about her, is there?'

'She, too, is a very lovely woman,' said Poirot.

'What do you think about her?'

'I have not had time to think as yet. I just think that she is beautiful and attractive and that something is giving her great concern.'

'Well, of course, wouldn't it?'

'What I would like, Madame, is for you to tell me what *you* know or think about her.'

'Well, I got to know her very well on the cruise. You know, one does make quite intimate friends. Just one or two people. The rest of them, I mean, they like each other and all that, but you don't really go to any trouble to see them again. But one or two you do. Well, Judith was one of the ones I *did* want to see again.'

'You did not know her before the cruise?'

'No.'

'But you know something about her?'

'Well, just ordinary things. She's a widow,' said Mrs Oliver. 'Her husband died a good many years ago – he was an air pilot. He was killed in a car accident. One of those pile-up things, I think it was, coming off the M what-is-it that runs near here on to the ordinary road one evening, or something of that kind. He left her rather badly off, I imagine. She was very broken up about it, I think. She doesn't like talking about him.'

'Is Miranda her only child?'

'Yes. Judith does some part-time secretarial work in the neighbourhood, but she hasn't got a fixed job.'

'Did she know the people who lived at the Quarry House?'

'You mean old Colonel and Mrs Weston?'

'I mean the former owner, Mrs Llewellyn-Smythe, wasn't it?'

'I think so. I think I've heard that name mentioned. But she died two or three years ago, so of course one doesn't hear about her much. Aren't the people who are alive enough for you?' demanded Mrs Oliver with some irritation.

'Certainly not,' said Poirot. 'I have also to inquire into those who have died or disappeared from the scene.'

'Who's disappeared?'

'An *au pair* girl,' said Poirot.

'Oh well,' said Mrs Oliver, 'they're always disappearing, aren't they? I mean, they come over here and get their fare paid and then they go straight into hospital because they're pregnant and have a baby, and call it Auguste, or Hans or Boris, or some name like that. Or they've come over to marry someone, or to follow up some young man they're in love with. You wouldn't believe the things friends tell me! The thing about *au pair* girls seems to be either they're Heaven's gift to over-worked mothers and you never want to part with them, or they pinch your stockings – or get themselves murdered –' She stopped. 'Oh!' she said.

'Calm yourself, Madame,' said Poirot. 'There seems no reason to believe that an *au pair* girl has been murdered – quite the contrary.'

'What do you mean by quite the contrary? It doesn't make sense.'

'Probably not. All the same –'

He took out his notebook and made an entry in it.

'What are you writing down there?'

'Certain things that have occurred in the past.'

'You seem to be very perturbed by the past altogether.'

'The past is the father of the present,' said Poirot sententiously.

He offered her the notebook.

'Do you wish to see what I have written?'

'Of course I do. I daresay it won't mean anything to me. The things *you* think important to write down, I never do.'

He held out the small black notebook.

'Deaths: e.g. Mrs Llewellyn-Smythe (Wealthy). Janet White (School-teacher). Lawyer's clerk – Knifed, Former prosecution for forgery.'

Below it was written 'Opera girl disappears.'

'What opera girl?'

'It is the word my friend, Spence's sister, uses for what you and I call an *au pair* girl.'

'Why should she disappear?'

'Because she was possibly about to get into some form of legal trouble.'

Poirot's finger went down to the next entry. The word was simply 'Forgery', with two question marks after it.

'Forgery?' said Mrs Oliver. 'Why forgery?'

'That is what *I* asked. *Why* forgery?'

'What kind of forgery?'

'A Will was forged, or rather a codicil to a Will. A codicil in the *au pair* girl's favour.'

'Undue influence?' suggested Mrs Oliver.

'Forgery is something rather more serious than undue influence,' said Poirot.

'I don't see what that's got to do with the murder of poor Joyce.'

'Nor do I,' said Poirot. 'But, therefore, it is interesting.'

'What is the next word? I can't read it.'

'Elephants.'

'I don't see what that's got to do with anything.'

'It might have,' said Poirot, 'believe me, it might have.'

He rose.

'I must leave you now,' he said. 'Apologize, please, to my hostess for my not saying goodbye to her. I much enjoyed meeting her and her lovely and unusual daughter. Tell her to take care of that child.'

'"*My mother said I never should, play with the children in the wood*",' quoted Mrs Oliver. 'Well, goodbye. If you like to be mysterious, I suppose you will go on being mysterious. You don't even say what you're going to do next.'

'I have made an appointment for tomorrow morning with Messrs Fullerton, Harrison and Leadbetter in Medchester.'

'Why?'

'To talk about forgery and other matters.'

'And after that?'

'I want to talk to certain people who were also present.'

'At the party?'

'No – at the preparation for the party.'

CHAPTER 12

The premises of Fullerton, Harrison and Leadbetter were typical of an old-fashioned firm of the utmost respectability. The hand of time had made itself felt. There were no more Harrisons and no more Leadbetters. There was a Mr Atkinson and a young Mr Cole, and there was still Mr Jeremy Fullerton, senior partner.

A lean, elderly man, Mr Fullerton, with an impassive face, a dry, legal voice, and eyes that were unexpectedly shrewd. Beneath his hand rested a sheet of notepaper, the few words on which he had just read. He read them once again, assessing their meaning very exactly. Then he looked at the man whom the note introduced to him.

'Monsieur Hercule Poirot?' He made his own assessment of the visitor. An elderly man, a foreigner, very dapper in his dress, unsuitably attired as to the feet in patent leather shoes which were, so Mr Fullerton guessed shrewdly, too tight for him. Faint lines of pain were already etching themselves round the corners of his eyes. A dandy, a fop, a foreigner and recommended to him by, of all people, Inspector Henry Raglan, C.I.D., and also vouched for by Superintendent Spence (retired), formerly of Scotland Yard.

'Superintendent Spence, eh?' said Mr Fullerton.

Fullerton knew Spence. A man who had done good work in his time, had been highly thought of by his superiors. Faint memories flashed across his mind. Rather a celebrated case, more celebrated actually than it had showed any signs of being, a case that had seemed cut and dried. Of course! It came to him that his nephew Robert had been connected with it, had been Junior Counsel. A psychopathic killer, it had seemed, a man who had hardly bothered to try and defend himself, a man whom you might have thought really wanted to be hanged (because it had meant hanging at that time). No fifteen years, or indefinite number of years in prison. No. You paid the full penalty – and more's the pity they've given it up, so Mr Fullerton thought in his dry mind. The young thugs nowadays thought they didn't risk much by prolonging assault to the point where it became mortal. Once your man was dead, there'd be no witness to identify you.

Spence had been in charge of the case, a quiet, dogged man

who had insisted all along that they'd got the wrong man. And they *had* got the wrong man, and the person who found the evidence that they'd got the wrong man was some sort of an amateurish foreigner. Some retired detective chap from the Belgian police force. A good age then. And now – senile, probably, thought Mr Fullerton, but all the same he himself would take the prudent course. Information, that's what was wanted from him. Information which, after all, could not be a mistake to give, since he could not see that he was likely to have any information that could be useful in this particular matter. A case of child homicide.

Mr Fullerton might think he had a fairly shrewd idea of who had committed that homicide, but he was not so sure as he would like to be, because there were at least three claimants in the matter. Any one of three young ne'er-do-wells might have done it. Words floated through his head. Mentally retarded. Psychiatrist's report. That's how the whole matter would end, no doubt. All the same, to drown a child during a party – that was rather a different cup of tea from one of the innumerable school children who did not arrive home and who had accepted a lift in a car after having been repeatedly warned not to do so, and who had been found in a nearby copse or gravel pit. A gravel pit now. When was that? Many, many years ago now.

All this took about four minutes' time and Mr Fullerton then cleared his throat in a slightly asthmatic fashion, and spoke.

'Monsieur Hercule Poirot,' he said again. 'What can I do for you? I suppose it's the business of this young girl, Joyce Reynolds. Nasty business, very nasty business. I can't see actually where I can assist you. I know very little about it all.'

'But you are, I believe, the legal adviser to the Drake family?'

'Oh yes, yes. Hugo Drake, poor chap. Very nice fellow. I've known them for years, ever since they bought Apple Trees and came here to live. Sad thing, polio – he contracted it when they were holidaying abroad one year. Mentally, of course, his health was quite unimpaired. It's sad when it happens to a man who has been a good athlete all his life, a sportsman, good at games and all the rest of it. Yes. Sad business to know you're a cripple for life.'

'You were also, I believe, in charge of the legal affairs of Mrs Llewellyn-Smythe?'

'The aunt, yes. Remarkable woman really. She came here to live after her health broke down, so as to be near her nephew and his wife. Bought that white elephant of a place, Quarry House. Paid far more than it was worth – but money was no object to her. She was very well off. She could have found a more attractive house, but it was the quarry itself that fascinated her. Got a landscape gardener on to it, fellow quite high up in his profession, I believe. One of those handsome, long-haired chaps, but he had ability all right. He did well for himself in this quarry garden work. Got himself quite a reputation over it, illustrated in *Homes and Gardens* and all the rest of it. Yes, Mrs Llewellyn-Smythe knew how to pick people. It wasn't just a question of a handsome young man as a protégé. Some elderly women are foolish that way, but this chap had brains and was at the top of his profession. But I'm wandering on a bit. Mrs Llewellyn-Smythe died nearly two years ago.'

'Quite suddenly.'

Fullerton looked at Poirot sharply.

'Well, no, I wouldn't say that. She had a heart condition and doctors tried to keep her from doing too much, but she was the sort of woman that you couldn't dictate to. She wasn't a hypochondriac type.' He coughed and said, 'But I expect we are getting away from the subject about which you came to talk to me.'

'Not really,' said Poirot, 'although I would like, if I may, to ask you a few questions on a completely different matter. Some information about one of your employees, by name Lesley Ferrier.'

Mr Fullerton looked somewhat surprised. 'Lesley Ferrier?' he said. 'Lesley Ferrier. Let me see. Really you know, I'd nearly forgotten his name. Yes, yes, of course. Got himself knifed, didn't he?'

'That is the man I mean.'

'Well, I don't really know that I can tell you much about him. It took place some years ago. Knifed near the Green Swan one night. No arrest was ever made. I daresay the police had some idea who was responsible, but it was mainly, I think, a matter of getting evidence.'

'The motive was emotional?' inquired Poirot.

'Oh yes, I should think certainly so. Jealousy, you know. He'd been going steady with a married woman. Her husband had a pub. The Green Swan at Woodleigh Common. Unpretentious place. Then it seems young Lesley started playing around with another young woman – or more than one, it was said. Quite a one for the girls, he was. There was a bit of trouble once or twice.'

'You were satisfied with him as an employee?'

'I would rather describe it as not dissatisfied. He had his points. He handled clients well and was studying for his articles, and if only he'd paid more attention to his position and keeping up a good standard of behaviour, it would have been better instead of mixing himself up with one girl after another, most of whom I am apt in my old-fashioned way to consider as considerably beneath him in station. There was a row one night at the Green Swan, and Lesley Ferrier was knifed on his way home.'

'Was one of the girls responsible, or would it be Mrs Green Swan, do you think?'

'Really, it is not a case of knowing anything *definite*. I believe the police considered it was a case of jealousy – but –' He shrugged his shoulders.

'But you are not sure?'

'Oh, it happens,' said Mr Fullerton. '"*Hell hath no fury like a woman scorned.*" That is always being quoted in Court. Sometimes it's true.'

'But I think I discern that you yourself are not at all sure that that was the case here.'

'Well, I should have preferred rather more evidence, shall we say. The police would have preferred rather more evidence, too. Public prosecutor threw it out, I believe.'

'It *could* have been something quite different?'

'Oh yes. One could propound several theories. Not a very stable character, young Ferrier. Well brought up. Nice mother – a widow. Father not so satisfactory. Got himself out of several scrapes by the skin of his teeth. Hard luck on his wife. Our young man in some ways resembled his father. He was associated once or twice with rather a doubtful crowd. I gave him the benefit of the doubt. He was still young. But I warned him that he was getting himself mixed up with the wrong lot. Too closely connected with fiddling transactions outside the law. Frankly, but for his mother,

I wouldn't have kept him. He was young, and he had ability; I gave him a warning or two which I hoped might do the trick. But there's a lot of corruption about these days. It's been on the increase for the last ten years.'

'Someone might have had it in for him, you think?'

'Quite possible. These associations – gangs is a rather melodramatic word – but you run a certain danger when you get tangled up with them. Any idea that you may split on them, and a knife between your shoulder blades isn't an uncommon thing to happen.'

'Nobody saw it happen?'

'No. Nobody saw it happen. They wouldn't, of course. Whoever took the job on would have all the arrangements nicely made. Alibi at the proper place and time, and so on and so on.'

'Yet *somebody* might have seen it happen. Somebody quite unlikely. A child, for instance.'

'Late at night? In the neighbourhood of the Green Swan? Hardly a very credible idea, Monsieur Poirot.'

'A child,' persisted Poirot, 'who might remember. A child coming home from a friend's house. At some short distance, perhaps, from her own home. She might have been coming by a footpath or seen something from behind a hedge.'

'Really, Monsieur Poirot, what an imagination you have got. What you are saying seems to me *most* unlikely.'

'It does not seem so unlikely to me,' said Poirot. 'Children *do* see things. They are so often, you see, not expected to be where they are.'

'But surely when they go home and relate what they have seen?'

'They might not,' said Poirot. 'They might not, you see, be sure of what they *had* seen. Especially if what they had seen had been faintly frightening to them. Children do not always go home and report a street accident they have seen, or some unexpected violence. Children keep their secrets very well. Keep them and think about them. Sometimes they like to feel that they know a secret, a secret which they are keeping to themselves.'

'They'd tell their mothers,' said Mr Fullerton.

'I am not so sure of that,' said Poirot. 'In my experience the things that children do *not* tell their mothers are quite numerous.'

'What interests you so much, may I know, about this case of Lesley Ferrier? The regrettable death of a young man by a violence which is so lamentably often amongst us nowadays?'

'I know nothing about him. But I wanted to know something about him because his is a violent death that occurred not many years ago. That might be important to me.'

'You know, Mr Poirot,' said Mr Fullerton, with some slight acerbity. 'I really cannot quite make out why you have come to me, and in what you are really interested. You cannot surely suspect any tie-up between the death of Joyce Reynolds and the death of a young man of promise but slightly criminal activities who has been dead for some years?'

'One can suspect anything,' said Poirot. 'One has to find out more.'

'Excuse me, what one has to have in all matters dealing with crime, is evidence.'

'You have perhaps heard that the dead girl Joyce was heard by several witnesses to say that she had with her own eyes witnessed a murder.'

'In a place like this,' said Mr Fullerton, 'one usually hears any rumour that may be going round. One usually hears it, too, if I may add these words, in a singularly exaggerated form not usually worthy of credence.'

'That also,' said Poirot, 'is quite true. Joyce was, I gather, just thirteen years of age. A child of nine could remember something she had seen – a hit-and-run accident, a fight or a struggle with knives on a dark evening, or a school-teacher who was strangled, say – all these things might leave a very strong impression on a child's mind about which she would not speak, being uncertain, perhaps, of the actual facts she had seen, and mulling them over in her own mind. Forgetting about them even, possibly, until something happened to remind her. You agree that that is a possible happening?'

'Oh yes, yes, but I hardly – I think it is an extremely far-fetched supposition.'

'You had, also, I believe, a disappearance here of a foreign girl. Her name, I believe, was Olga or Sonia – I am not sure of the surname.'

'Olga Seminoff. Yes, indeed.'

'Not, I fear, a very reliable character?'

'No.'

'She was companion or nurse attendant to Mrs Llewellyn-Smythe, was she not, whom you described to me just now? Mrs Drake's aunt –'

'Yes. She had had several girls in that position – two other foreign girls, I think, one of them with whom she quarrelled almost immediately, and another one who was nice but painfully stupid. Mrs Llewellyn-Smythe was not one to suffer fools gladly. Olga, her last venture, seems to have suited her very well. She was not, if I remember rightly, a particularly attractive girl,' said Mr Fullerton. 'She was short, rather stocky, had rather a dour manner, and people in the neighbourhood did not like her very much.'

'But Mrs Llewellyn-Smythe *did* like her,' suggested Poirot.

'She became very much attached to her – unwisely so, it seemed at one moment.'

'Ah, indeed.'

'I have no doubt,' said Mr Fullerton, 'that I am not telling you anything that you have not heard already. These things, as I say, go round the place like wildfire.'

'I understand that Mrs Llewellyn-Smythe left a large sum of money to the girl.'

'A most surprising thing to happen,' said Mr Fullerton. 'Mrs Llewellyn-Smythe had not changed her fundamental testamentary disposition for many years, except for adding new charities or altering legacies left void by death. Perhaps I am telling you what you know already, if you are interested in this matter. Her money had always been left jointly to her nephew, Hugo Drake, and his wife, who was also his first cousin, and so also niece to Mrs Llewellyn-Smythe. If either of them predeceased her the money went to the survivor. A good many bequests were left to charities and to old servants. But what was alleged to be her final disposal of her property was made about three weeks before her death, and not, as heretofore, drawn up by our firm. It was a codicil written in her own handwriting. It included one or two charities – not so many as before – the old servants had no legacies at all, and the whole residue of her considerable fortune was left to Olga Seminoff in gratitude for the devoted service and affection she had shown her. A most astonishing disposition, one that seemed totally unlike anything Mrs Llewellyn-Smythe had ever done before.'

'And then?' said Poirot.

'You have presumably heard more or less the developments. From the evidence of handwriting experts, it became clear that the codicil was a complete forgery. It bore only a faint resemblance to Mrs Llewellyn-Smythe's handwriting, no more than that. Mrs Smythe had disliked the typewriter and had frequently got Olga to write letters of a personal nature, as far as possible copying her employer's handwriting – sometimes, even, signing the letter with her employer's signature. She had had plenty of practice in doing this. It seems that when Mrs Llewellyn-Smythe died the girl went one step further and thought that she was proficient enough to make the handwriting acceptable as that of her employer. But that sort of thing won't do with experts. No, indeed it won't.'

'Proceedings were about to be taken to contest the document?'

'Quite so. There was, of course, the usual legal delay before the proceedings actually came to court. During that period the young lady lost her nerve and well, as you said yourself just now, she – disappeared.'

CHAPTER 13

When Hercule Poirot had taken his leave and departed, Jeremy Fullerton sat before his desk drumming gently with his fingertips. His eyes, however, were far away – lost in thought.

He picked up a document in front of him and dropped his eyes down to it, but without focusing his glance. The discreet buzz of the house telephone caused him to pick up the receiver on his desk.

'Yes, Miss Miles?'

'Mr Holden is here, sir.'

'Yes. Yes, his appointment, I believe was for nearly three quarters of an hour ago. Did he give any reason for having been so late? . . . Yes, yes. I quite see. Rather the same excuse he gave last time. Will you tell him I've seen another client, and I am now too short of time. Make an appointment with him for next week, will you? We can't have this sort of thing going on.'

'Yes, Mr Fullerton.'

He replaced the receiver and sat looking thoughtfully down at the document in front of him. He was still not reading it. His mind was going over events of the past. Two years – close on two years ago – and that strange little man this morning with his patent leather shoes and his big moustaches, had brought it back to him, asking all those questions.

Now he was going over in his own mind a conversation of nearly two years ago.

He saw again, sitting in the chair opposite him, a girl, a short, stocky figure – the olive brown skin, the dark red generous mouth, the heavy cheekbones and the fierceness of the blue eyes that looked into his beneath the heavy, beetling brows. A passionate face, a face full of vitality, a face that had known suffering – would probably always know suffering – but would never learn to accept suffering. The kind of woman who would fight and protest until the end. Where was she now, he wondered? Somehow or other she had managed – what had she managed exactly? Who had helped her? Had anyone helped her? Somebody must have done so.

She was back again, he supposed, in some trouble-stricken spot in Central Europe where she had come from, where she belonged, where she had had to go back to because there was no other course for her to take unless she was content to lose her liberty.

Jeremy Fullerton was an upholder of the law. He believed in the law, he was contemptuous of many of the magistrates of today with their weak sentences, their acceptance of scholastic needs. The students who stole books, the young married women who denuded the supermarkets, the girls who filched money from their employers, the boys who wrecked telephone boxes, none of them in real need, none of them desperate, most of them had known nothing but over-indulgence in bringing-up and a fervent belief that anything they could not afford to buy was theirs to take. Yet along with his intrinsic belief in the administration of the law justly, Mr Fullerton was a man who had compassion. He could be sorry for people. He could be sorry, and was sorry, for Olga Seminoff though he was quite unaffected by the passionate arguments she advanced for herself.

'I came to you for help. I thought you would help me. You were kind last year. You helped me with forms so that I could remain another year in England. So they say to me: "You need not answer any questions you do not wish to. You can be represented by a lawyer." So I come to you.'

'The circumstances you have instanced –' and Mr Fullerton remembered how drily and coldly he had said that, all the more drily and coldly because of the pity that lay behind the dryness of the statement '– do not apply. In this case I am not at liberty to act for you legally. I am representing already the Drake family. As you know, I was Mrs Llewellyn-Smythe's solicitor.'

'But she is dead. She does not want a solicitor when she is dead.'

'She was fond of you,' said Mr Fullerton.

'Yes, she was fond of me. That is what I am telling you. That is why she wanted to give me the money.'

'All her money?'

'Why not? Why not? She did not like her relations.'

'You are wrong. She was very fond of her niece and nephew.'

'Well, then, she may have liked Mr Drake but she did not like Mrs Drake. She found her very tiresome. Mrs Drake interfered. She would not let Mrs Llewellyn-Smythe do always what she liked. She would not let her eat the food she liked.'

'She is a very conscientious woman, and she tried to get her aunt to obey the doctor's orders as to diet and not too much exercise and many other things.'

'People do not always want to obey a doctor's orders. They do not want to be interfered with by relations. They like living their own lives and doing what they want and having what they want. She had plenty of money. She could have what she wanted! She could have as much as she liked of everything. She was rich – rich – rich, and she could do what she liked with her money. They have already quite enough money, Mr and Mrs Drake. They have a fine house and clothes and two cars. They are very well-to-do. Why should they have any more?'

'They were her only living relations.'

'She wanted *me* to have the money. She was sorry for me.

She knew what I had been through. She knew about my father, arrested by the police and taken away. We never saw him again, my mother and I. And then my mother and how she died. All my family died. It is terrible, what I have endured. You do not know what it is like to live in a police state, as I have lived in it. No, no. You are on the side of the police. You are not on *my* side.'

'No,' Mr Fullerton said, 'I am not on your side. I am very sorry for what has happened to you, but you've brought this trouble about yourself.'

'That is not true! It is not true that I have done anything I should not do. What have I done? I was kind to her, I was nice to her. I brought her in lots of things that she was not supposed to eat. Chocolates and butter. All the time nothing but vegetable fats. She did not like vegetable fats. She wanted butter. She wanted lots of butter.'

'It's not just a question of butter,' said Mr Fullerton.

'I looked after her, I was nice to her! And so she was grateful. And then when she died and I find that in her kindness and her affection she has left a signed paper leaving all her money to me, then those Drakes come along and say I shall not have it. They say all sorts of things. They say I had a bad influence. And then they say worse things than that. Much worse. They say *I* wrote the Will myself. That is nonsense. *She* wrote it. *She* wrote it. And then she sent me out of the room. She got the cleaning woman and Jim the gardener. She said they had to sign the paper, not me. Because I was going to get the money. Why should not I have the money? Why should I not have some good luck in my life, some happiness? It seemed so wonderful. All the things I planned to do when I knew about it.'

'I have no doubt, yes, I have no doubt.'

'Why shouldn't I have plans? Why should not I rejoice? I am going to be happy and rich and have all the things I want. What did I do wrong? Nothing. *Nothing*, I tell you. *Nothing*.'

'I have tried to explain to you,' said Mr Fullerton.

'That is all lies. You say I tell lies. You say I wrote the paper myself. I did not write it myself. *She* wrote it. Nobody can say anything different.'

'Certain people say a good many things,' said Mr Fullerton. 'Now listen. Stop protesting and listen to me. It is true, is it not, that Mrs Llewellyn-Smythe in the letters you wrote for her, often asked you to copy her handwriting as nearly as you could? That was because she had an old-fashioned idea that to write typewritten letters to people who are friends or with whom you have a personal acquaintance, is an act of rudeness. That is a survival from Victorian days. Nowadays nobody cares whether they receive hand-written letters or typewritten ones. But to Mrs Llewellyn-Smythe that was discourtesy. You understand what I am saying?'

'Yes, I understand. And so she asks me. She says, "Now, Olga," she says. "These four letters you will answer as I have told you and that you have taken down in shorthand. But you will write them in handwriting and you will make the handwriting as close to mine as possible." And she told me to practise writing her handwriting, to notice how she made her a's, and her b's and her l's and all the different letters. "So long as it is reasonably like my handwriting," she said, "that will do, and then you can sign my name. But I do not want people to think that I am no longer able to write my own letters. Although, as you know, the rheumatism in my wrist is getting worse and I find it more difficult, but I don't want my personal letters typewritten".'

'You could have written them in your ordinary handwriting,' said Mr Fullerton, 'and put a note at the end saying "per secretary" or per initials if you liked.'

'She did not want me to do that. She wanted it to be thought that *she* wrote the letters herself.'

And that, Mr Fullerton thought, could be true enough. It was very like Louise Llewellyn-Smythe. She was always passionately resentful of the fact that she could no longer do the things she used to do, that she could no longer walk far or go up hills quickly or perform certain actions with her hands, her right hand especially. She wanted to be able to say 'I'm perfectly well, perfectly all right and there's nothing I can't do if I set my mind to it.' Yes, what Olga was telling him now was perfectly true, and because it was true it was one of the reasons why the codicil appended to the last Will properly drawn out and signed by Louise Llewellyn-Smythe had been accepted at first without suspicion. It was in his own office, Mr Fullerton reflected, that suspicions had arisen because both he and his younger partner knew Mrs Llewellyn-Smythe's handwriting very well. It was young Cole who had first said,

'You know, I really can't believe that Louise Llewellyn-Smythe wrote that codicil. I know she had arthritis lately but look at these specimens of her own writing that I've brought along from amongst her papers to show you. There's something wrong about that codicil.'

Mr Fullerton had agreed that there was something wrong about it. He had said they would take expert opinion on this handwriting question. The answer had been quite definite. Separate opinions had not varied. The handwriting of the codicil was definitely not that of Louise Llewellyn-Smythe. If Olga had been less greedy, Mr Fullerton thought, if she had been content to write a codicil beginning as this one had done – 'Because of her great care and attention to me and the affection and kindness she has shown me, I leave –' That was how it had begun, that was how it could have begun, and if it had gone on to specify a good round sum of money left to the devoted *au pair girl*, the relations might have considered it over-done, but they would have accepted it without questioning. But to cut out the relations altogether, the nephew who had been his aunt's residuary legatee in the last four wills she had made during a period of nearly twenty years, to leave everything to the stranger Olga Seminoff – that was not in Louise Llewellyn-Smythe's character. In fact, a plea of undue influence could upset such a document anyway. No. She had been greedy, this hot, passionate child. Possibly Mrs Llewellyn-Smythe had told her that some money would be left to her because of her kindness, because of her attention, because of a fondness the old lady was beginning to feel for this girl who fulfilled all her whims, who did whatever she asked her. And that had opened up a vista for Olga. She would have everything. The old lady should leave everything to her, and she would have *all* the money. All the money and the house and the clothes and the jewels. Everything. A greedy girl. And now retribution had caught up with her.

And Mr Fullerton, against his will, against his legal instincts and against a good deal more, felt sorry for her. Very sorry for her. She had known suffering since she was a child, had known the rigours of a police state, had lost her parents, lost a brother and a sister and known injustice and fear, and it had developed in her a trait that she had no doubt been born with but which she had never been able so far to indulge. It had developed a childish passionate greed.

'Everyone is against me,' said Olga. 'Everyone. You are all against me. You are not fair because I am a foreigner, because I do not belong to this country, because I do not know what to say, what to do. What *can* I do? Why do you not tell me what I can do?'

'Because I do not really think there is anything much you can do,' said Mr Fullerton. 'Your best chance is to make a clean breast of things.'

'If I say what you want me to say, it will be all lies and not true. She made that Will. She wrote it down there. She told me to go out of the room while the others signed it.'

'There is evidence against you, you know. There are people who will say that Mrs Llewellyn-Smythe often did not know what she was signing. She had several documents of different kinds, and she did not always re-read what was put before her.'

'Well, then she did not know what she was saying.'

'My dear child,' said Mr Fullerton, 'your best hope is the fact that you are a first offender, that you are a foreigner, that you understand the English language only in a rather rudimentary form. In that case you may get off with a minor sentence – or you may, indeed, get put on probation.'

'Oh, words. Nothing but words. I shall be put in prison and never let out again.'

'Now you are talking nonsense,' Mr Fullerton said.

'It would be better if I ran away, if I ran away and hid myself so that nobody could find me.'

'Once there is a warrant out for your arrest, you would be found.'

'Not if I did it quickly. Not if I went at once. Not if someone helped me. I could get away. Get away from England. In a boat or a plane. I could find someone who forges passports or visas, or whatever you have to have. Someone who will do something for me. I have friends. I have people who are fond of me. Somebody could help me to disappear. That is what I needed. I could put on a wig. I could walk about on crutches.'

'Listen,' Mr Fullerton had said, and he had spoken then with authority, 'I am sorry for you. I will recommend you to a lawyer who will do his best for you. You can't hope to disappear. You are talking like a child.'

'I have got enough money. I have saved money.' And then she had said, 'You have tried to be kind. Yes, I believe that. But you will not do anything because it is all the law – the law. But someone will help me. Someone will. And I shall get away where nobody will ever find me.'

Nobody, Mr Fullerton thought, had found her. He wondered – yes; he wondered very much – where she was or could be now.

CHAPTER 14

I

Admitted to Apple Trees, Hercule Poirot was shown into the drawing-room and told that Mrs Drake would not be long.

In passing through the hall he heard the hum of female voices behind what he took to be the dining-room door.

Poirot crossed to the drawing-room window and surveyed the neat and pleasant garden. Well laid out, kept studiously in control. Rampant autumn michaelmas daisies still survived, tied up severely to sticks; chrysanthemums had not yet relinquished life. There were still a persistent rose or two scorning the approach of winter.

Poirot could discern no sign as yet of the preliminary activities of a landscape gardener. All was care and convention. He wondered if Mrs Drake had been one too many for Michael Garfield. He had spread his lures in vain. It showed every sign of remaining a splendidly kept suburban garden.

The door opened.

'I am sorry to have kept you waiting, Monsieur Poirot,' said Mrs Drake.

Outside in the hall there was a diminishing hum of voices as various people took their leave and departed.

'It's our church Christmas fête,' explained Mrs Drake. 'A Committee Meeting for arrangements for it and all the rest of it. These things always go on much longer than they ought to, of course. Somebody always objects to something, or has a good idea – the good idea usually being a perfectly impossible one.'

There was a slight acerbity in her tone. Poirot could well imagine that Rowena Drake would put things down as quite absurd, firmly and definitely. He could understand well enough from remarks he had heard from Spence's sister, from hints of what other people had said and from various other sources, that Rowena Drake was that dominant type of personality whom everyone expects to run the show, and whom nobody has much affection for while she is doing it. He could imagine, too, that her conscientiousness had not been the kind to be appreciated by an elderly relative who was herself of the same type. Mrs Llewellyn-Smythe, he gathered, had come here to live so as to be near to her nephew and his wife, and that the wife had readily undertaken the supervision and care of her husband's aunt as far as she could do so without actually living in the house. Mrs Llewellyn-Smythe had probably acknowledged in her own mind that she owed a great deal to Rowena, and had at the same time resented what she had no doubt thought of as her bossy ways.

'Well, they've all gone now,' said Rowena Drake, hearing the final shutting of the hall door. 'Now what can I do for you? Something more about that dreadful party? I wish I'd never had it here. But no other house really seemed suitable. Is Mrs Oliver still staying with Judith Butler?'

'Yes. She is, I believe, returning to London in a day or two. You had not met her before?'

'No. I love her books.'

'She is, I believe, considered a very good writer,' said Poirot.

'Oh well, she *is* a good writer. No doubt of that. She's a very amusing person too. Has she any ideas herself – I mean about who might have done this dreadful thing?'

'I think not. And you, Madame?'

'I've told you already. I've no idea whatever.'

'You would perhaps say so, and yet – you might, might you not, have, perhaps, what amounts to a very good idea, but only an idea. A half-formed idea. A *possible* idea.'

'Why should you think that?'

She looked at him curiously.

'You might have seen something – something quite small and

unimportant but which on reflection might seem more significant to you, perhaps, than it had done at first.'

'You must have something in your mind, Monsieur Poirot, some definite incident.'

'Well, I admit it. It is because of what someone said to me.'

'Indeed! And who was that?'

'A Miss Whittaker. A school-teacher.'

'Oh yes, of course. Elizabeth Whittaker. She's the mathematics mistress, isn't she, at The Elms? She *was* at the party, I remember. Did she see something?'

'It was not so much that she saw something as she had the idea that *you* might have seen something.'

Mrs Drake looked surprised and shook her head.

'I can't think of anything I can possibly have seen,' said Rowena Drake, 'but one never knows.'

'It had to do with a vase,' said Poirot. 'A vase of flowers.'

'A vase of flowers?' Rowena Drake looked puzzled. Then her brow cleared. 'Oh, of course, I know. Yes, there was a big vase of autumn leaves and chrysanthemums on the table in the angle of the stairs. A very nice glass vase. One of my wedding presents. The leaves seemed to be drooping and so did one or two of the flowers. I remember noticing it as I passed through the hall – it was near the end of the party, I think, by then, but I'm not sure – I wondered why it looked like that, and I went up and dipped my fingers into it and found that some idiot must have forgotten to put any water into it after arranging it. It made me very angry. So I took it into the bathroom and filled it up. But what could I have seen in that bathroom? There was nobody in it. I am quite sure of that. I think one or two of the older girls and boys had done a little harmless, what the Americans call "necking", there during the course of the party, but there was certainly nobody when I went into it with the vase.'

'No, no, I do not mean that,' said Poirot. 'But I understood that there was an accident. That the vase slipped out of your hand and it fell to the hall below and was shattered to pieces.'

'Oh yes,' said Rowena. 'Broken to smithereens. I *was* rather upset about it because as I've said, it had been one of our wedding presents, and it was really a perfect flower vase, heavy enough to hold big autumn bouquets and things like that. It was very stupid of me. My fingers just slipped. It went out of my hand and crashed on the hall floor below. Elizabeth Whittaker was standing there. She helped me to pick up the pieces and sweep some of the broken glass out of the way in case someone stepped on it. We just swept it into a corner by the Grandfather clock to be cleared up later.'

She looked inquiringly at Poirot.

'Is that the incident you mean?' she asked.

'Yes,' said Poirot. 'Miss Whittaker wondered, I think, how you had come to drop the vase. She thought that something perhaps had startled you.'

'Startled me?' Rowena Drake looked at him, then frowned as she tried to think again. 'No, I don't think I was startled, anyway. It was just one of those ways things do slip out of your hands. Sometimes when you're washing up. I think, really, it's a result of being tired. I was pretty tired by that time, what with the preparations for the party and running the party and all the rest of it. It went very well, I must say. I think it was – oh, just one of those clumsy actions that you can't help when you're tired.'

'There was nothing – you are sure – that startled you? Something unexpected that you saw?'

'Saw? Where? In the hall below? I didn't see anything in the hall below. It was empty at the moment because everyone was in at the Snapdragon excepting, of course, for Miss Whittaker. And I don't think I even noticed her until she came forward to help when I ran down.'

'Did you see someone, perhaps, leaving the library door?'

'The library door . . . I see what you mean. Yes, I *could* have seen that.' She paused for quite a long time, then she looked at Poirot with a very straight, firm glance. 'I didn't see *anyone* leave the library,' she said. 'Nobody at all . . .'

He wondered. The way in which she said it was what aroused the belief in his mind that she was not speaking the truth, that instead she *had* seen someone or something, perhaps the door just opening a little, a mere glance perhaps of a figure inside. But she was quite firm in her denial. Why, he wondered, had she been so firm? Because the person she had seen was a person she did not want to believe for one moment had had anything to do with the crime committed on the other side of the door? Someone she cared about, or someone – which seemed more likely, he thought – someone whom she wished to protect. Someone, perhaps, who had not long passed beyond childhood, someone whom she might feel was not truly conscious of the awful thing they had just done.

He thought her a hard creature but a person of integrity. He thought that she was, like many women of the same type, women who were often magistrates, or who ran councils or charities, or interested themselves in what used to be called 'good works'. Women who had an inordinate belief in extenuating circumstances, who were ready, strangely enough, to make excuses for the young criminal. An adolescent boy, a mentally retarded girl. Someone perhaps who had already been – what is the phrase – 'in care'. If that had been the type of person she had seen coming out of the library, then he thought it possible that Rowena Drake's protective instinct might have come into play. It was not unknown in the present age for children to commit crimes, quite young children. Children of seven, of nine and so on, and it was often difficult to know how to dispose of these natural, it seemed, young criminals who came before the juvenile courts. Excuses had to be brought for them. Broken homes. Negligent and unsuitable parents. But the people who spoke the most vehemently for them, the people who sought to bring forth every excuse for them, were usually the type of Rowena Drake. A stern and censorious woman, except in such cases.

For himself, Poirot did not agree. He was a man who thought first always of justice. He was suspicious, had always been suspicious, of mercy – too much mercy, that is to say. Too much mercy, as he knew from former experience both in Belgium and this country, often resulted in further crimes which were fatal to innocent victims who need not have been victims if justice had been put first and mercy second.

'I see,' said Poirot. 'I see.'

'You don't think it's possible that Miss Whittaker might have seen someone go into the library?' suggested Mrs Drake.

Poirot was interested.

'Ah, you think that that might have been so?'

'It seemed to me merely a possibility. She might have caught sight of someone going in through the library, say, perhaps five minutes or so earlier, and then, when I dropped the vase it might have suggested to her that I could have caught a glimpse of the same person. That I might have seen who it was. Perhaps she doesn't like to say anything that might suggest, unfairly perhaps, some person whom she had perhaps only half glimpsed – not enough to be sure of. Some back view perhaps of a child, or a young boy.'

'You think, do you not, Madame, that it was – shall we say, a child – a boy or girl, a mere child, or a young adolescent? You think it was not any definite one of these but, shall we say, you think that that is the most likely type to have committed the crime we are discussing?'

She considered the point thoughtfully, turning it over in her mind.

'Yes,' she said at last, 'I suppose I do. I haven't thought it out. It seems to me that crimes are so often associated nowadays with the young. People who don't really know quite what they are doing, who want silly revenges, who have an instinct for destruction. Even the people who wreck telephone boxes, or who slash the tyres of cars, do all sorts of things just to hurt people, just because they hate – not anyone in particular, but the whole world. It's a sort of symptom of this age. So I suppose when one comes across something like a child drowned at a party for no reason really, one does assume that it's someone who is not yet fully responsible for their actions. Don't you agree with me that – that – well, that that is certainly the most likely possibility here?'

'The police, I think, share your point of view – or did share it.'

'Well, they should know. We have a very good class of policeman in this district. They've done well in several crimes. They are painstaking and they never give up. I think probably they will solve this murder, though I don't think it will happen very quickly. These things seem to take a long time. A long time of patient gathering of evidence.'

'The evidence in this case will not be very easy to gather, Madame.'

'No, I suppose it won't. When my husband was killed – He was a cripple, you know. He was crossing the road and a car ran over him and knocked him down. They never found the person who was responsible. As you know, my husband – or perhaps you don't know – my husband was a polio victim. He was partially paralyzed as a result of polio, six years ago. His condition had improved, but he was still crippled, and it would be difficult for him to get out of the way if a car bore down upon him quickly. I almost felt that I had been to blame, though he always insisted on going out without me or without anyone with him, because he would have resented very much being in the care of a nurse, or a wife who took the part of a nurse, and he was always careful before crossing a road. Still, one does blame oneself when accidents happen.'

'That came on top of the death of your aunt?'

'No. She died not long afterwards. Everything seems to come at once, doesn't it?'

'That is very true,' said Hercule Poirot. He went on: 'The police were not able to trace the car that ran down your husband?'

'It was a Grasshopper Mark 7, I believe. Every third car you notice on the road is a Grasshopper Mark 7 – or was then. It's the most popular car on the market, they tell me. They believe it was pinched from the Market Place in Medchester. A car park there. It belonged to a Mr Waterhouse, an elderly seed merchant in Medchester. Mr Waterhouse was a slow and careful driver. It was certainly not he who caused the accident. It was clearly one of those cases where irresponsible young men help themselves to cars. Such careless, or should I say such callous young men, should be treated, one sometimes feels, more severely than they are now.'

'A long gaol sentence, perhaps. Merely to be fined, and the fine paid by indulgent relatives, makes little impression.'

'One has to remember,' said Rowena Drake, 'that there are young people at an age when it is vital that they should continue with their studies if they are to have the chance of doing well in life.'

'The sacred cow of education,' said Hercule Poirot. 'That is a phrase I have heard uttered,' he added quickly, 'by people – well, should I say people who ought to know. People who themselves hold academic posts of some seniority.'

'They do not perhaps make enough allowances for youth, for a bad bringing up. Broken homes.'

'So you think they need something other than gaol sentences?'

'Proper remedial treatment,' said Rowena Drake firmly.

'And that will make – (another old-fashioned proverb) – a silk purse out of a sow's ear? You do not believe in the maxim "the fate of every man have we bound about his neck"?'

Mrs Drake looked extremely doubtful and slightly displeased.

'An Islamic saying, I believe,' said Poirot. Mrs Drake looked unimpressed.

'I hope,' she said, 'we do not take our ideas – or perhaps I should say our ideals – from the Middle East.'

'One must accept facts,' said Poirot, 'and a fact that is expressed by modern biologists – Western biologists –' he hastened to add, '– seems to suggest very strongly that the root of a person's actions lies in his genetic make-up. That a murderer of twenty-four was a murderer in potential at two or three or four years old. Or of course a mathematician or a musical genius.'

'We are not discussing murderers,' said Mrs Drake. 'My husband died as a result of an accident. An accident caused by a careless and badly adjusted personality. Whoever the boy or young man was, there is always the hope of eventual adjustment to a belief and acceptance that it is a duty to consider others, to be taught to feel an abhorrence if you have taken life unawares, simply out of what may be described as criminal carelessness that was not really criminal in intent?'

'You are quite sure, therefore, that it was not criminal in intent?'

'I should doubt it very much.' Mrs Drake looked slightly surprised. 'I do not think that the police ever seriously considered that possibility. I certainly did not. It was an accident. A very tragic accident which altered the pattern of many lives, including my own.'

'You say we are not discussing murderers,' said Poirot. 'But in the case of Joyce that is just what we are discussing. There was no accident about that. Deliberate hands pushed that child's head down into water, holding her there till death occurred. Deliberate intent.'

'I know. I know. It's terrible. I don't like to think of it, to be reminded of it.'

She got up, moving about restlessly. Poirot pushed on relentlessly.

'We are still presented with a choice there. We still have to find the motive involved.'

'It seems to me that such a crime must have been quite motiveless.'

'You mean committed by someone mentally disturbed to the extent of enjoying killing someone? Presumably killing someone young and immature.'

'One does hear of such cases. What is the original cause of them is difficult to find out. Even psychiatrists do not agree.'

'You refuse to accept a simpler explanation?'

She looked puzzled. 'Simpler?'

'Someone *not* mentally disturbed, *not* a possible case for psychiatrists to disagree over. Somebody perhaps who just wanted to be safe.'

'Safe? Oh, you mean –'

'The girl had boasted that same day, some hours previously, that she had seen someone commit a murder.'

'Joyce,' said Mrs Drake, with calm certainty, 'was really a very silly little girl. Not, I am afraid, always very truthful.'

'So everyone has told me,' said Hercule Poirot. 'I am beginning to believe, you know, that what everybody has told me must be right,' he added with a sigh. 'It usually is.'

He rose to his feet, adopting a different manner.

'I must apologize, Madame. I have talked of painful things to you, things that do not truly concern me here. But it seemed from what Miss Whittaker told me –'

'Why don't you find out more from her?'

'You mean –?'

'She is a teacher. She knows, much better than I can, what potentialities (as you have called them) exist amongst the children she teaches.'

She paused and then said:

'Miss Emlyn, too.'

'The head-mistress?' Poirot looked surprised.

'Yes. She knows things. I mean, she is a natural psychologist. You said I might have ideas – half-formed ones – as to who killed Joyce. I haven't – but I think Miss Emlyn might.'

'This is interesting . . .'

'I don't mean has *evidence.* I mean she just *knows. She* could tell you – but I don't think she will.'

'I begin to see,' said Poirot, 'that I have still a long way to go. People know things – but they will not tell them to me.' He looked thoughtfully at Rowena Drake.

'Your aunt, Mrs Llewellyn-Smythe, had an *au pair* girl who looked after her, a foreign girl.'

'You seem to have got hold of all the local gossip.' Rowena spoke dryly. 'Yes, that is so. She left here rather suddenly soon after my aunt's death.'

'For good reasons, it would seem.'

'I don't know whether it's libel or slander to say so – but there seems no doubt that she forged a codicil to my aunt's Will – or that someone helped her to do so.'

'Someone?'

'She was friendly with a young man who worked in a solicitor's office in Medchester. He had been mixed up in a forgery case before. The case never came to court because the girl disappeared. She realized the Will would not be admitted to probate, and that there was going to be a court case. She left the neighbourhood and has never been heard of since.'

'She too came, I have heard, from a broken home,' said Poirot.

Rowena Drake looked at him sharply but he was smiling amiably.

'Thank you for all you have told me, Madame,' he said.

II

When Poirot had left the house, he went for a short walk along a turning off the main road which was labelled 'Helpsly Cemetery Road.' The cemetery in question did not take him long to reach. It was at most ten minutes' walk. It was obviously a cemetery that had been made in the last ten years, presumably to cope with the rising importance of Woodleigh as a residential entity. The church, a church of reasonable size dating from some two or three centuries back, had had a very small enclosure round it already well filled. So the new cemetery had come into being with a foot-path connecting it across two fields. It was, Poirot thought, a business-like, modern cemetery with appropriate sentiments on marble or granite slabs; it had urns, chippings, small plantations of bushes or flowers. No interesting old epitaphs or inscriptions. Nothing much for an antiquarian. Cleaned, neat, tidy and with suitable sentiments expressed.

He came to a halt to read a tablet erected on a grave contemporary with several others near it, all dating within two or three years back. It bore a simple inscription, 'Sacred to the Memory of Hugo Edmund Drake, beloved husband of Rowena Arabella Drake, who departed this life March the 20th 19–'

He giveth his beloved sleep

It occurred to Poirot, fresh from the impact of the dynamic Rowena Drake, that perhaps sleep might have come in welcome guise to the late Mr Drake.

An alabaster urn had been fixed in position there and contained the remains of flowers. An elderly gardener, obviously employed to tend the graves of good citizens departed this life, approached Poirot in the pleasurable hopes of a few minutes' conversation while he laid his hoe and his broom aside.

'Stranger in these parts, I think,' he said, 'aren't you, sir?'

'It is very true,' said Poirot. 'I am a stranger with you as were my fathers before me.'

'Ah, aye. We've got that text somewhere or summat very like it. Over down the other corner, it is.' He went on, 'He was a nice gentleman, he were, Mr Drake. A cripple, you know. He had that infant paralysis, as they call it, though as often as not it isn't infants as suffer from it. It's grown-ups. Men and women too. My wife, she had an aunt, who caught it in Spain, she did. Went there with a tour, she did, and bathed somewhere in some river. And they said afterwards as it was the water infection, but I don't think they know much. Doctors don't, if you ask me. Still, it's made a lot of difference nowadays. All this inoculation they give the children, and that. Not nearly as many cases as there were. Yes, he were a nice gentleman and didn't complain, though he took it hard, being a cripple, I mean. He'd been a good sportsman, he had, in his time. Used to bat for us here in the village team. Many a six he's hit to the boundary. Yes, he were a nice gentleman.'

'He died of an accident, did he not?'

'That's right. Crossing the road, towards twilight this was. One of these cars come along, a couple of these young thugs in it with beards growing up to their ears. That's what they say. Didn't stop either. Went on. Never looked to see. Abandoned the car somewhere in a car park twenty miles away. Wasn't their own car either. Pinched from a car park somewhere. Ah, it's terrible, a lot of those accidents nowadays. And the police often can't do anything about them. Very devoted to him, his wife was. Took it very hard, she did. She comes here, nearly every week, brings flowers and puts them here. Yes, they were a very devoted couple. If you ask me, she won't stay here much longer.'

'Really? But she has a very nice house here.'

'Yes, oh yes. And she does a lot in the village, you know. All these things – women's institutes and teas and various societies and all the rest of it. Runs a lot of things, she does. Runs a bit too many for some people. Bossy, you know. Bossy and interfering, some people say. But the vicar relies on her. She starts things. Women's activities and all the rest of it. Gets up tours and outings. Ah yes. Often thought myself, though I wouldn't like to say it to my wife, that all these good works as ladies does, doesn't make you any fonder of the ladies themselves. Always know best, they do. Always telling you what you should do and what you shouldn't do. No freedom. Not much freedom anywhere nowadays.'

'Yet you think Mrs Drake may leave here?'

'I shouldn't wonder if she didn't go away and live somewhere abroad. They liked being abroad, used to go there for holidays.'

'Why do you think she wants to leave here?'

A sudden rather roguish smile appeared on the old man's face.

'Well, I'd say, you know, that she's done all she can do here. To put it scriptural, she needs another vineyard to work in. She needs more good works. Aren't no more good works to be done round here. She's done all there is, and even more than there need be, so some think. Yes.'

'She needs a new field in which to labour?' suggested Poirot.

'You've hit it. Better settle somewhere else where she can put a lot of things right and bully a lot of other people. She'd got us where she wants us here and there's not much more for her to do.'

'It may be,' said Poirot.

'Hasn't even got her husband to look after. She looked after him a good few years. That gave her a kind of object in life, as you might say. What with that and a lot of outside activities, she could be busy all the time. She's the type likes being busy all the time. And she's no children, more's the pity. So it's my view as she'll start all over again somewhere else.'

'You may have something there. Where would she go?'

'I couldn't say as to that. One of these Riviery places, maybe – or there's them as goes to Spain or Portugal. Or Greece – I've heard her speak of Greece – Islands. Mrs Butler, she's been to Greece on one of them tours. Hellenic, they call them, which sounds more like fire and brimstone to me.'

Poirot smiled.

'The isles of Greece,' he murmured. Then he asked: 'Do you like her?'

'Mrs Drake? I wouldn't say I exactly *like* her. She's a good woman. Does her duty to her neighbour and all that – but she'll always need a power of neighbours to do her duty to – and if you ask me, nobody really likes people who are always doing their duty. Tells me how to prune my roses which I know well enough myself. Always at me to grow some new-fangled kind of vegetable. Cabbage is good enough for me, and I'm sticking to cabbage.'

Poirot smiled. He said, 'I must be on my way. Can you tell me where Nicholas Ransom and Desmond Holland live?'

'Past the church, third house on the left. They board with Mrs Brand, go into Medchester Technical every day to study. They'll be home by now.'

He gave Poirot an interested glance.

'So that's the way your mind is working, is it? There's some already as thinks the same.'

'No, I think nothing as yet. But they were among those present – that is all.'

As he took leave and walked away, he mused, 'Among those present – I have come nearly to the end of my list.'

CHAPTER 15

Two pairs of eyes looked at Poirot uneasily.

'I don't see what else we can tell you. We've both been interviewed by the police, M. Poirot.'

Poirot looked from one boy to the other. They would not have described themselves as boys; their manner was carefully adult. So much so that if one shut one's eyes, their conversation could have passed as that of elderly clubmen. Nicholas was eighteen. Desmond was sixteen.

'To oblige a friend, I make my inquiries of those present on a certain occasion. Not the Hallowe'en party itself – the preparations for that party. You were both active in these.'

'Yes, we were.'

'So far,' Poirot said, 'I have interviewed cleaning women, I have had the benefit of police views, of talks to a doctor – the doctor who examined the body first – have talked to a school-teacher who was present, to the head-mistress of the school, to distraught relatives, have heard much of the village gossip – By the way, I understand you have a local witch here?'

The two young men confronting him both laughed.

'You mean Mother Goodbody. Yes, she came to the party and played the part of the witch.'

'I have come now,' said Poirot, 'to the younger generation, to those of acute eyesight and acute hearing and who have up-to-date scientific knowledge and shrewd philosophy. I am eager – very eager – to hear your views on this matter.'

Eighteen and sixteen, he thought to himself, looking at the two boys confronting him. Youths to the police, boys to him, adolescents to newspaper reporters. Call them what you will. Products of today. Neither of them, he judged, at all stupid, even if they were not quite of the high mentality that he had just suggested to them by way of a flattering sop to start the conversation. They had been at the party. They had also been there earlier in the day to do helpful offices for Mrs Drake.

They had climbed up step-ladders, they had placed yellow pumpkins in strategic positions, they had done a little electrical work on fairy lights, one or other of them had produced some clever effects in a nice batch of phoney photographs of possible husbands as imagined hopefully by teenage girls. They were also, incidentally, of the right age to be in the forefront of suspects in the mind of Inspector Raglan and, it seemed, in the view of an elderly gardener. The percentage of murders committed by this group had been increasing in the last few years. Not that Poirot inclined to that particular suspicion himself, but anything was possible. It was even possible that the killing which had occurred two or three years ago might have been committed by a boy, youth, or adolescent of fourteen or twelve years of age. Such cases had occurred in recent newspaper reports.

Keeping all these possibilities in mind he pushed them, as it were, behind a curtain for the moment, and concentrated instead on his own appraisement of these two, their looks, their clothes, their manner, their voices and so on and so forth, in the Hercule Poirot manner, masked behind a foreign shield of flattering words and much increased foreign mannerisms, so that they themselves should feel agreeably contemptuous of him, though hiding that under politeness and good manners. For both of them had excellent manners. Nicholas, the eighteen-year-old, was good-looking, wearing side-burns, hair that grew fairly far down his neck, and a rather funereal outfit of black. Not as a mourning for the recent tragedy, but what was obviously his personal taste in modern clothes. The younger one was wearing a rose-coloured velvet coat, mauve trousers and a kind of frilled shirting. They both obviously spent a good deal of money on their clothes which were certainly not purchased locally and were probably paid for by themselves and not by their parents or guardians.

Desmond's hair was ginger coloured and there was a good deal of fluffy profusion about it.

'You were there in the morning or afternoon of the party, I understand, helping with the preparations for it?'

'Early afternoon,' corrected Nicholas.

'What sort of preparations were you helping with? I have heard of preparation from several people, but I am not quite clear. They don't all agree.'

'A good deal of the lighting, for one thing.'

'Getting up on steps for things that had to be put high up.'

'I understand there were some very good photographic results too.'

Desmond immediately dipped into his pocket and took out a folder from which he proudly brought certain cards.

'We faked up these beforehand,' he said. 'Husbands for the girls,' he explained. 'They're all alike, birds are. They all want something up-to-date. Not a bad assortment, are they?'

He handed a few specimens to Poirot who looked with interest at a rather fuzzy reproduction of a ginger-bearded young man and another young man with an aureole of hair, a third one whose hair came to his knees almost, and there were a few assorted whiskers, and other facial adornments.

'Made 'em pretty well all different. It wasn't bad, was it?'

'You had models, I suppose?'

'Oh, they're all ourselves. Just make-up, you know. Nick and I got 'em done. Some Nick took of me and some I took of him. Just varied what you might call the hair *motif*.'

'Very clever,' said Poirot.

'We kept 'em a bit out of focus, you know, so that they'd look more like spirit pictures, as you might say.'

The other boy said,

'Mrs Drake was very pleased with them. She congratulated us. They made her laugh too. It was mostly electrical work we did at the house. You know, fitting up a light or two so that when the girls sat with the mirror one or other of us could take up a position, you'd only to bob up over a screen and the girl would see a face in the mirror with, mind you, the right kind of hair. Beard or whiskers or something or other.'

'Did they know it was you and your friend?'

'Oh, I don't think so for a moment. Not at the party, they didn't. They knew we had been helping at the house with some things, but I don't think they recognized us in the mirrors. Weren't smart enough, I should say. Besides, we'd got sort of an instant make-up to change the image. First me, then Nicholas. The girls squeaked and shrieked. Damned funny.'

'And the people who were there in the afternoon? I do not ask you to remember who was at the party.'

'At the party, there must have been about thirty, I suppose, knocking about. In the afternoon there was Mrs Drake, of course, and Mrs Butler. One of the school-teachers, Whittaker I think her name is. Mrs Flatterbut or some name like that. She's the organist's sister or wife. Dr Ferguson's dispenser, Miss Lee; it's her afternoon off and she came along and helped too and some of the kids came to make themselves useful if they could. Not that I think they were very useful. The girls just hung about and giggled.'

'Ah yes. Do you remember what girls there were there?'

'Well, the Reynolds were there. Poor old Joyce, of course. The one who got done in and her elder sister Ann. Frightful girl. Puts no end of side on. Thinks she's terribly clever. Quite sure she's going to pass all her "A" levels. And the small kid, Leopold, he's awful,' said Desmond. 'He's a sneak. He eavesdrops. Tells tales. Real nasty bit of goods. And there was Beatrice Ardley and Cathie Grant, who is dim as they make and a couple of useful women, of course. Cleaning women, I mean. And the authoress woman – the one who brought you down here.'

'Any men?'

'Oh, the vicar looked in if you count him. Nice old boy, rather dim. And the new curate. He stammers when he's nervous. Hasn't been here long. That's all I can think of now.'

'And then I understand you heard this girl – Joyce Reynolds – saying something about having seen a murder committed.'

'I never heard that,' said Desmond. 'Did she?'

'Oh, they're saying so,' said Nicholas. 'I didn't hear her, I suppose I wasn't in the room when she said it. Where was she – when she said that, I mean?'

'In the drawing-room.'

'Yes, well, most of the people were in there unless they were doing something special. Of course Nick and I,' said Desmond, 'were mostly in the room where the girls were going to look for their true loves in mirrors. Fixing up wires and various things like that. Or else we were out on the stairs fixing fairy lights. We were in the drawing-room once or twice putting the pumpkins up and hanging up one or two that had been hollowed out to hold lights in them. But I didn't hear anything of that kind when we were there. What about you, Nick?'

'I didn't,' said Nick. He added with some interest, 'Did Joyce really say that she'd seen a murder committed? Jolly interesting, you know, if she did, isn't it?'

'Why is it so interesting?' asked Desmond.

'Well, it's E.S.P., isn't it? I mean there you are. She saw a murder committed and within an hour or two she herself was murdered. I suppose she had a sort of vision of it. Makes you think a bit. You know these last experiments they've been having seems as though there is something you can do to help it by getting an electrode, or something of that kind, fixed up to your jugular vein. I've read about it somewhere.'

'They've never got very far with this E.S.P. stuff,' said Desmond, scornfully. 'People sit in different rooms looking at cards in a pack or words with squares and geometrical figures on them. But they never see the right things, or hardly ever.'

'Well, you've got to be pretty young to do it. Adolescents are much better than older people.'

Hercule Poirot, who had no wish to listen to this high-level scientific discussion, broke in.

'As far as you can remember, nothing occurred during your presence in the house which seemed to you sinister or significant in any way. Something which probably nobody else would have noticed, but which might have come to *your* attention.'

Nicholas and Desmond frowned hard, obviously racking their brains to produce some incident of importance.

'No, it was just a lot of clacking and arranging and doing things.'

'Have you any theories yourself?'

Poirot addressed himself to Nicholas.

'What, theories as to who did Joyce in?'

'Yes. I mean something that you might have noticed that could lead you to a suspicion on perhaps purely psychological grounds.'

'Yes, I can see what you mean. There might be something in that.'

'Whittaker for my money,' said Desmond, breaking into Nicholas's absorption in thought.

'The school-mistress?' asked Poirot.

'Yes. Real old spinster, you know. Sex starved. And all that teaching, bottled up among a lot of women. You remember, one of the teachers got strangled a year or two ago. She was a bit queer, they say.'

'Lesbian?' asked Nicholas, in a man of the world voice.

'I shouldn't wonder. D'you remember Nora Ambrose, the girl she lived with? She wasn't a bad looker. She had a boy friend or two, so they said, and the girl she lived with got mad with her about it. Someone said she was an unmarried mother. She was away for two terms with some illness and then came back. They'd say anything in this nest of gossip.'

'Well, anyway, Whittaker was in the drawing-room most of the morning. She probably heard what Joyce said. Might have put it into her head, mightn't it?'

'Look here,' said Nicholas, 'supposing Whittaker – what age is she, do you think? Forty odd? Getting on for fifty – Women do go a bit queer at that age.'

They both looked at Poirot with the air of contented dogs who have retrieved something useful which master has asked for.

'I bet Miss Emlyn knows if it is so. There's not much she doesn't know, about what goes on in her school.'

'Wouldn't she say?'

'Perhaps she feels she has to be loyal and shield her.'

'Oh, I don't think she'd do that. If she thought Elizabeth Whittaker was going off her head, well then, I mean, a lot of the pupils at the school might get done in.'

'What about the curate?' said Desmond hopefully. '*He* might be a bit off his nut. You know, original sin perhaps, and all that, and the water and the apples and the things and then – look here, I've got a good idea now. Suppose *he* is a bit barmy. Not been here very long. Nobody knows much about him. Supposing it's the Snapdragon put it into his head. Hell fire! All those flames going up! Then, you see, he took hold of Joyce and he said "come along with me and I'll show you something," and he took her to the apple room and he said "kneel down." He said "This is baptism," and pushed her head in. See? It would all fit. Adam and Eve and the apple and hell fire and the Snapdragon and being baptized again to cure you of sin.'

'Perhaps he exposed himself to her first,' said Nicholas hopefully. 'I mean, there's always got to be a sex background to all these things.'

They both looked with satisfied faces to Poirot.

'Well,' said Poirot, 'you've certainly given me something to think about.'

CHAPTER 16

Hercule Poirot looked with interest at Mrs Goodbody's face. It was indeed perfect as a model for a witch. The fact that it almost undoubtedly went with extreme amiability of character did not dispel the illusion. She talked with relish and pleasure.

'Yes, I was up there right enough, I was. I always does the witches round here. Vicar he complimented me last year and he said as I'd done such a good job in the pageant as he'd give me a new steeple hat. A witch's hat wears out just like anything else does. Yes, I was right up there that day. I does the rhymes, you know. I mean the rhymes for the girls, using their own Christian name. One for Beatrice, one for Ann and all the rest of it. And I gives them to whoever is doing the spirit voice and they recite it out to the girl in the mirror, and the boys, Master Nicholas and young Desmond, they send the phoney photographs floating down. Make me die of laughing, some of it does. See those boys sticking hair all over their faces and photographing each other. And what they dress up in! I saw Master Desmond the other day, and what he was wearing you'd hardly believe. Rose-coloured coat and fawn breeches. Beat the girls hollow, they do. All the girls can think of is to push their skirts higher and higher, and that's not much good to them because they've got to put on more underneath. I mean what with the things they call body stockings and tights, which used to be for chorus girls in my day and none other – they spend all their money on that. But the boys – my word, they look like kingfishers and peacocks or birds of paradise. Well, I like to see a bit of colour and I always think it must have been fun in those old historical days as you see on the pictures. You know, everybody with lace and curls and cavalier hats and all the rest of it. Gave the girls something to look at, they did. And doublet and hose. All the girls could think of in historical times, as far as I can see, was to put great balloon skirts on, crinolines they called them later, and great ruffles around their necks! My grandmother, she used to tell me that her young ladies – she was in service, you know, in a good Victorian family – and her young ladies (before the time of Victoria I think it was) – it was the time the King what had a head like a pear was on the throne – Silly Billy, wasn't it, William IVth – well then, her young ladies, I mean my grandmother's young ladies, they used to have muslin gowns very long down to their ankles, very prim but they used to damp their muslins with water so they stuck to them. You know, stuck to them so it showed everything there was to show. Went about looking ever so modest, but it tickled up the gentlemen, all right, it did.

'I lent Mrs Drake my witch ball for the party. Bought that witch ball at a jumble sale somewhere. There it is hanging up there now by the chimney, you see? Nice bright dark blue. I keep it over my door.'

'Do you tell fortunes?'

'Mustn't say I do, must I?' she chuckled. 'The police don't like that. Not that they mind the kind of fortunes *I* tell. Nothing to it, as you might say. Place like this you always know who's going with who, and so that makes it easy.'

'Can you look in your witch ball, look in there, see who killed that little girl, Joyce?'

'You got mixed up, you have,' said Mrs Goodbody. 'It's a crystal ball you look in to see things, not a witch ball. If I told you who I thought it was did it, you wouldn't like it. Say it was against nature, you would. But lots of things go on that are against nature.'

'You may have something there.'

'This is a good place to live, on the whole. I mean, people are decent, most of them, but wherever you go, the devil's always got some of his own. Born and bred to it.'

'You mean – black magic?'

'No, I don't mean that.' Mrs Goodbody was scornful. 'That's nonsense, that is. That's for people who like to dress up and do a lot of tomfoolery. Sex and all that. No, I mean those that the devil has touched with his hand. They're born that way. The sons of Lucifer. They're born so that killing don't mean nothing to them, not if they profit by it. When they want a thing, they want it. And they're ruthless to get it. Beautiful as angels, they can look like. Knew a little girl once. Seven years old. Killed her little brother and sister. Twins they were. Five or six months old, no more. Stifled them in their prams.'

'That took place here in Woodleigh Common?'

'No, no, it wasn't in Woodleigh Common. I came across that up in Yorkshire, far as I remember. Nasty case. Beautiful little creature she was, too. You could have fastened a pair of wings on her, let her go on a platform and sing Christmas hymns, and she'd have looked right for the part. But she wasn't. She was rotten inside. You'll know what I mean. You're not a young man. You know what wickedness there is about in the world.'

'Alas!' said Poirot. 'You are right. I do know only too well. If Joyce really saw a murder committed –'

'Who says she did?' said Mrs Goodbody.

'She said so herself.'

'That's no reason for believing. She's always been a little liar.' She gave him a sharp glance. 'You won't believe that, I suppose?'

'Yes,' said Poirot, 'I do believe it. Too many people have told me so, for me to continue disbelieving it.'

'Odd things crop up in families,' said Mrs Goodbody. 'You take the Reynolds, for example. There's Mr Reynolds. In the estate business he is. Never cut much ice at it and never will. Never got on much, as you'd say. And Mrs Reynolds, always getting worried and upset about things. None of their three children take after their parents. There's Ann, now, she's got brains. She's going to do well with her schooling, she is. She'll go to college, I shouldn't wonder, maybe get herself trained as a teacher. Mind you, she's pleased with herself. She's so pleased with herself that nobody can stick her. None of the boys look at her twice. And then there was Joyce. She wasn't clever like Ann, nor as clever as her little brother Leopold, either, but she wanted to be. She wanted always to know more than other people and to have done better than other people and she'd say anything to make people sit up and take notice. But don't you believe any single word she ever said was true. Because nine times out of ten it wasn't.'

'And the boy?'

'Leopold? Well, he's only nine or ten, I think, but he's clever all right. Clever with his fingers and other ways, too. He wants to study things like physics. He's good at mathematics, too. Quite surprised about it they were, in school. Yes, he's clever. He'll be one of these scientists, I expect. If you ask me, the things he does when he's a scientist and the things he'll think of – they'll be nasty, like atom bombs! He's one of the kind that studies and are ever so clever and think up something that'll destroy half the globe, and all us poor folk with it. You beware of Leopold. He plays tricks on people, you know, and eavesdrops. Finds out all their secrets. Where he gets all his pocket money from I'd like to know. It isn't from his mother or his father. They can't afford to give him much. He's got lots of money always. Keeps it in a drawer under his socks. He buys things. Quite a lot of expensive gadgets. Where does he get the money from? That's what I'd like to know. Finds people's secrets out, I'd say, and makes them pay him for holding his tongue.'

She paused for breath.

'Well, I can't help you, I'm afraid, in any way.'

'You have helped me a great deal,' said Poirot. 'What happened to the foreign girl who is said to have run away?'

'Didn't go far, in my opinion. "*Ding dong dell, pussy's in the well.*" That's what I've always thought, anyway.'

CHAPTER 17

'Excuse me, Ma'am, I wonder if I might speak to you a minute.'

Mrs Oliver, who was standing on the verandah of her friend's house looking out to see if there were any signs of Hercule Poirot approaching – he had notified her by telephone that he would be coming round to see her about now – looked round.

A neatly attired woman of middle age was standing, twisting her hands nervously in their neat cotton gloves.

'Yes?' said Mrs Oliver, adding an interrogation point by her intonation.

'I'm sorry to trouble you, I'm sure, Madam, but I thought – well, I thought . . .'

Mrs Oliver listened but did not attempt to prompt her. She wondered what was worrying the woman so much.

'I take it rightly as you're the lady who writes stories, don't I? Stories about crimes and murders and things of that kind.'

'Yes,' said Mrs Oliver, 'I'm the one.'

Her curiosity was now aroused. Was this a preface for a demand for an autograph or even a signed photograph? One never knew. The most unlikely things happened.

'I thought as you'd be the right one to tell me,' said the woman.

'You'd better sit down,' said Mrs Oliver.

She foresaw that Mrs Whoever-it-was – she was wearing a wedding ring so she was a Mrs – was the type who takes some time in getting to the point. The woman sat down and went on twisting her hands in their gloves.

'Something you're worried about?' said Mrs Oliver, doing her best to start the flow.

'Well, I'd like advice, and it's true. It's about something that happened a good while ago and I wasn't really worried at the time. But you know how it is. You think things over and you wish you knew someone you could go and ask about it.'

'I see,' said Mrs Oliver, hoping to inspire confidence by this entirely meretricious statement.

'Seeing the things what have happened lately, you never do know, do you?'

'You mean –?'

'I mean what happened at the Hallowe'en party, or whatever they called it. I mean it shows you there's people who aren't dependable here, doesn't it? And it shows you things before that weren't as you thought they were. I mean, they mightn't have been what you thought they were, if you understand what I mean.'

'Yes?' said Mrs Oliver, adding an even greater tinge of interrogation to the monosyllable. 'I don't think I know your name,' she added.

'Leaman. Mrs Leaman. I go out and do cleaning to oblige ladies here. Ever since my husband died, and that was five years ago. I used to work for Mrs Llewellyn-Smythe, the lady who lived up at the Quarry House, before Colonel and Mrs Weston came. I don't know if you ever knew her.'

'No,' said Mrs Oliver, 'I never knew her. This is the first time I have been down to Woodleigh Common.'

'I see. Well, you wouldn't know much about what was going on perhaps at that time, and what was said at that time.'

'I've heard a certain amount about it since I've been down here this time,' said Mrs Oliver.

'You see, I don't know anything about the law, and I'm worried always when it's a question of law. Lawyers, I mean. They might tangle it up and I wouldn't like to go to the police. It wouldn't be anything to do with the police, being a legal matter, would it?'

'Perhaps not,' said Mrs Oliver, cautiously.

'You know perhaps what they said at the time about the codi – I don't know, some word like codi. Like the fish I mean.'

'A codicil to the Will?' suggested Mrs Oliver.

'Yes, that's right. That's what I'm meaning. Mrs Llewellyn-Smythe, you see, made one of these cod – codicils and she left all her money to the foreign girl what looked after her. And it was a surprise, that, because she'd got relations living here, and she'd come here anyway to live near them. She was very devoted to them, Mr Drake, in particular. And it struck people as pretty queer, really. And then the lawyers, you see, they began saying things. They said as Mrs Llewellyn-Smythe hadn't written the codicil at all. That the foreign pair girl had done it, seeing as she got all the money left to her. And they said as they were going to law about it. That Mrs Drake was going to counterset the Will – if that is the right word.'

'The lawyers were going to contest the Will. Yes, I believe I did hear something about that,' said Mrs Oliver encouragingly. 'And you know something about it, perhaps?'

'I didn't mean no harm,' said Mrs Leaman. A slight whine came into her voice, a whine with which Mrs Oliver had been acquainted several times in the past.

Mrs Leaman, she thought, was presumably an unreliable woman in some ways, a snooper perhaps, a listener at doors.

'I didn't say nothing at the time,' said Mrs Leaman, 'because you see I didn't rightly know. But you see I thought it was queer and I'll admit to a lady like you, who knows what these things are, that I did want to know the truth about it. I'd worked for Mrs Llewellyn-Smythe for some time, I had, and one wants to know how things happened.'

'Quite,' said Mrs Oliver.

'If I thought I'd done what I oughtn't to have done, well, of course, I'd have owned up to it. But I didn't think as I'd done anything really wrong, you see. Not at the time, if you understand,' she added.

'Oh yes,' said Mrs Oliver, 'I'm sure I shall understand. Go on. It was about this codicil.'

'Yes, you see one day Mrs Llewellyn-Smythe – she hadn't felt too good that day and so she asked us to come in. Me that was, and young Jim who helps down in the garden and brings the sticks in and the coals, and things like that. So we went into her room, where she was, and she'd got papers before her there on the desk. And she turns to this foreign girl – Miss Olga we all called her – and said "You go out of the room now, dear, because you mustn't be mixed up in this part of it," or something like that. So Miss Olga, she goes out of the room and Mrs Llewellyn-Smythe, she tells us to come close and she says "This is my Will, this is." She got a bit of blotting paper over the top part of it but the bottom of it's quite clear. She said "I'm writing something here on this piece of paper and I want you to be a witness of what I've written and of my signature at the end of it." So she starts writing along the page. Scratchy pen she always used, she wouldn't use Biros or anything like that. And she writes two or three lines of writing and then she signed her name, and then she says to me, "Now, Mrs Leaman, you write your name there. Your name and your address" and then she says to Jim "And now you write your name underneath there, and your address too. There. That'll do. Now you've seen me write that and you've seen my signature and you've written your names, both of you, to say that's that." And then she says "That's all. Thank you very much." So we goes out of the room. Well, I didn't think nothing more of it at the time, but I wondered a bit. And it happened as I turns my head just as I was going out of the room. You see the door doesn't always latch properly. You have to give it a pull, to make it click. And so I was doing that – I wasn't really looking, if you know what I mean –'

'I know what you mean,' said Mrs Oliver, in a non-committal voice.

'And so I sees Mrs Llewellyn-Smythe pull herself up from the chair – she'd got arthritis and had pain moving about sometimes

– and go over to the bookcase and she pulled out a book and she puts that piece of paper she'd just signed – in an envelope it was – in one of the books. A big tall book it was in the bottom shelf. And she sticks it back in the bookcase. Well, I never thought of it again, as you might say. No, really I didn't. But when all this fuss came up, well, of course I felt – at least, I –' She came to a stop.

Mrs Oliver had one of her useful intuitions.

'But surely,' she said, 'you didn't wait as long as all that –'

'Well, I'll tell you the truth, I will. I'll admit I was curious. After all, I mean, you want to know when you've signed anything, *what* you've signed, don't you? I mean, it's only human nature.'

'Yes,' said Mrs Oliver, 'it's only human nature.'

Curiosity, she thought, was a highly component part in Mrs Leaman's human nature.

'So I will admit that next day, when Mrs Llewellyn-Smythe had driven into Medchester and I was doing her bedroom as usual – a bedsitting room she had because she had to rest a lot. And I thinks, "Well, one ought really to know when you've signed a thing, what it is you've signed." I mean they always say with these hire purchase things, you should read the small print.'

'Or in this case, the handwriting,' suggested Mrs Oliver.

'So I thought, well, there's no harm – it's not as though I was taking anything. I mean to say I'd had to sign my name there, and I thought I really ought to know what I'd signed. So I had a look along the bookshelves. They needed dusting anyway. And I found the one. It was on the bottom shelf. It was an old book, a sort of Queen Victoria's kind of book. And I found this envelope with a folded paper in it and the title of the book said *Enquire Within upon Everything*. And it seemed then as though it was, sort of meant, if you know what I mean?'

'Yes,' said Mrs Oliver. 'It was clearly meant. And so you took out the paper and looked at it.'

'That's right, Madam. And whether I did wrong or not I don't know. But anyway, there it was. It was a legal document all right. On the last page there was the writing what she'd made the morning before. New writing with a new scratchy pen she was using. It was clear enough to read, though, although she had a rather spiky handwriting.'

'And what did it say,' said Mrs Oliver, her curiosity now having joined itself to that previously felt by Mrs Leaman.

'Well, it said something like, as far as I remember – the exact words I'm not quite sure of – something about a codicil and that after the legacies mentioned in her Will, she bequeathed her entire fortune to Olga – I'm not sure of the surname, it began with an S. Seminoff, or something like that – in consideration of her great kindness and attention to her during her illness. And there it was written down and she'd signed it and I'd signed it, and Jim had signed it. So I put it back where it was because I shouldn't like Mrs Llewellyn-Smythe to know that I'd been poking about in her things.

'But well, I said to myself, well, this *is* a surprise. And I thought, fancy that foreign girl getting all that money because we all know as Mrs Llewellyn-Smythe was very rich. Her husband had been in shipbuilding and he'd left her a big fortune, and I thought, well, some people have all the luck. Mind you, I wasn't particularly fond of Miss Olga myself. She had a sharp way with her sometimes and she had quite a bad temper. But I will say as she was always very attentive and polite and all that, to the old lady. Looking out for herself, all right, she was, *and* she got away with it. And I thought, well, leaving all that money away from her own family. Then I thought, well, perhaps she's had a tiff with them and likely as not that will blow over, so maybe she'll tear this up and make another Will or codicil after all. But anyway, that was that, and I put it back and I forgot about it, I suppose.

'But when all the fuss came up about the Will, and there was talk of how it had been forged and Mrs Llewellyn-Smythe could never have written that codicil herself – for that's what they were saying, mind you, as it wasn't the old lady who had written that at all, it was somebody else –'

'I see,' said Mrs Oliver. 'And so, what did you do?'

'I didn't do anything. And that's what's worrying me . . . I didn't get the hang of things at once. And when I'd thought things over a bit I didn't know rightly *what* I ought to do and I thought, well, it was all talk because the lawyers were against the foreigner, like people always are. I'm not very fond of foreigners myself, I'll admit. At any rate, there it was, and the young lady herself was swanking about, giving herself airs, looking as pleased as Punch and I thought, well, maybe it's all a legal thing of some kind and they'll say she's no right to the money because she wasn't related to the old lady. So everything will be all right. And it was in a way because, you see, they gave up the idea of bringing the case. It didn't come to court at all and as far as anyone knew, Miss Olga ran away. Went off back to the Continent somewhere, where she came from. So it looks as though there must have been some hocus-pocus of some kind on her part. Maybe she threatened the old lady and made her do it. You never know, do you? One of my nephews who's going to be a doctor, says you can do wonderful things with hypnotism. I thought perhaps she hypnotized the old lady.'

'This was how long ago?'

'Mrs Llewellyn-Smythe's been dead for – let me see, nearly two years.'

'And it didn't worry you?'

'No, it didn't worry me. Not at the time. Because you see, I didn't rightly see that it mattered. Everything was all right, there wasn't any question of that Miss Olga getting away with the money, so I didn't see as it was any call for me –'

'But now you feel differently?'

'It's that nasty death – the child that was pushed into a bucket of apples. Saying things about a murder, saying she'd seen something or known something about a murder. And I thought maybe as Miss Olga had murdered the old lady because she knew all this money was coming to her and then she got the wind up when there was a fuss and lawyers and the police, maybe, and so she ran away. So then I thought well, perhaps I ought to – well, I ought to tell someone, and I thought you'd be a lady as has got friends in legal departments. Friends in the police perhaps, and you'd explain to them that I was only dusting a bookshelf, and this paper was there in a book and I put it back where it belonged. I didn't take it away or anything.'

'But that's what happened, was it, on that occasion? You saw Mrs Llewellyn-Smythe write a codicil to her Will. You saw her write her name and you yourself and this Jim someone were both there and you both wrote your own names yourselves. That's it, isn't it?'

'That's right.'

'So if you both saw Mrs Llewellyn-Smythe write her name, then that signature couldn't have been a forgery, could it? Not if you saw her write it herself.'

'I saw her write it herself and that's the absolute truth I'm speaking. And Jim'd say so too only he's gone to Australia, he has. Went over a year ago and I don't know his address or anything. He didn't come from these parts, anyway.'

'And what do you want me to do?'

'Well, I want you to tell me if there's anything I ought to say, or do – now. Nobody's asked me, mind you. Nobody ever asked me if I knew anything about a Will.'

'Your name is Leaman. What Christian name?'

'Harriet.'

'Harriet Leaman. And Jim, what was his last name?'

'Well, now, what was it? Jenkins. That's right. James Jenkins. I'd be much obliged if you could help me because it worries me, you see. All this trouble coming along and if that Miss Olga did it, murdered Mrs Llewellyn-Smythe, I mean, and young Joyce saw her do it . . . She was ever so cock-a-hoop about it all, Miss Olga was, I mean about hearing from the lawyers as she'd come into a lot of money. But it was different when the police came round asking questions, and she went off very sudden, she did. Nobody asked me anything, they didn't. But now I can't help wondering if I ought to have said something at the time.'

'I think,' said Mrs Oliver, 'that you will probably have to tell this story of yours to whoever represented Mrs Llewellyn-Smythe as a lawyer. I'm sure a good lawyer will quite understand your feelings and your motive.'

'Well, I'm sure if you'd say a word for me and tell them, being a lady as knows what's what, how it came about, and how I never meant to – well, not to do anything dishonest in any way. I mean, all I did –'

'All you did was to say nothing,' said Mrs Oliver. 'It seems quite a reasonable explanation.'

'And if it could come from you – saying a word for me first, you know, to explain, I'd be ever so grateful.'

'I'll do what I can,' said Mrs Oliver.

Her eyes strayed to the garden path where she saw a neat figure approaching.

'Well, thanks ever so much. They said as you were a very nice lady, and I'm sure I'm much obliged to you.'

She rose to her feet, replaced the cotton gloves which she had twisted entirely off in her anguish, made a kind of half nod or bob, and trotted off. Mrs Oliver waited until Poirot approached.

'Come here,' she said, 'and sit down. What's the matter with you? You look upset.'

'My feet are extremely painful,' said Hercule Poirot.

'It's those awful tight patent leather shoes of yours,' said Mrs Oliver. 'Sit down. Tell me what you came to tell me, and then *I'll* tell *you* something that you may be surprised to hear!'

CHAPTER 18

Poirot sat down, stretched out his legs and said: 'Ah! that is better.'

'Take your shoes off,' said Mrs Oliver, 'and rest your feet.'

'No, no, I could not do that.' Poirot sounded shocked at the possibility.

'Well, we're old friends together,' said Mrs Oliver, 'and Judith wouldn't mind if she came out of the house. You know, if you'll excuse me saying so, you oughtn't to wear patent leather shoes in the country. Why don't you get yourself a nice pair of suède shoes? Or the things all the hippy-looking boys wear nowadays? You know, the sort of shoes that slip on, and you never have to clean them – apparently they clean themselves by some extraordinary process or other. One of these labour-saving gimmicks.'

'I would not care for that at all,' said Poirot severely. 'No, indeed!'

'The trouble with you is,' said Mrs Oliver, beginning to unwrap a package on the table which she had obviously recently purchased, 'the trouble with you is that you insist on being *smart*. You mind more about your clothes and your moustaches and how you look and what you wear than *comfort*. Now comfort is really the great thing. Once you've passed, say, fifty, comfort is the only thing that matters.'

'Madame, chère Madame, I do not know that I agree with you.'

'Well, you'd better,' said Mrs Oliver. 'If not, you will suffer a great deal, and it will be worse year after year.'

Mrs Oliver fished a gaily covered box from its paper bag. Removing the lid of this, she picked up a small portion of its contents and transferred it to her mouth. She then licked her fingers, wiped them on a handkerchief, and murmured, rather indistinctly:

'Sticky.'

'Do you no longer eat apples? I have always seen you with a bag of apples in your hand, or eating them, or on occasions the bag breaks and they tumble out on the road.'

'I told you,' said Mrs Oliver, 'I told you that I never want to see an apple again. No. I hate apples. I suppose I shall get over it some day and eat them again, but – well, I don't like the associations of apples.'

'And what is it that you eat now?' Poirot picked up the gaily coloured lid decorated with a picture of a palm tree. 'Tunis dates,' he read. 'Ah, dates now.'

'That's right,' said Mrs Oliver. 'Dates.'

She took another date and put it in her mouth, removed a stone which she threw into a bush and continued to munch.

'Dates,' said Poirot. 'It is extraordinary.'

'What is extraordinary about eating dates? People do.'

'No, no, I did not mean that. Not eating them. It is extraordinary that you should say to me like that – *dates.*'

'Why?' asked Mrs Oliver.

'Because,' said Poirot, 'again and again you indicate to me the path, the how do you say, the *chemin* that I should take or that I should have already taken. You show me the way that I should go. Dates. Till this moment I did not realize how important dates were.'

'I can't see that dates have anything to do with what's happened here. I mean, there's no real *time* involved. The whole thing took place what – only five days ago.'

'The event took place four days ago. Yes, that is very true. But to everything that happens there has to be a past. A past which is by now incorporated in today, but which existed yesterday or last month or last year. The present is nearly always rooted in the past. A year, two years, perhaps even three years ago, a murder was committed. A child saw that murder. Because that child saw that murder on a certain date now long gone by, that child died four days ago. Is not that so?'

'Yes. That's so. At least, I suppose it is. It mightn't have been at all. It might be just some mentally disturbed nut who liked killing people and whose idea of playing with water is to push somebody's head under it and hold it there. It might have been described as a mental delinquent's bit of fun at a party.'

'It was not that belief that brought you to me, Madame.'

'No,' said Mrs Oliver, 'no, it wasn't. I didn't like the feel of things. I still don't like the feel of things.'

'And I agree with you. I think you are quite right. If one does not like the feel of things, one must learn why. I am trying very hard, though you may not think so, to learn why.'

'By going around and talking to people, finding out if they are nice or not and then asking them questions?'

'Exactly.'

'And what have you learnt?'

'Facts,' said Poirot. 'Facts which will have in due course to be anchored in their place by dates, shall we say.'

'Is that all? What else have you learnt?'

'That nobody believes in the veracity of Joyce Reynolds.'

'When she said she saw someone killed? But I heard her.'

'Yes, she *said* it. But nobody believes it is true. The probability is, therefore, that it was not true. That she saw no such thing.'

'It seems to me,' said Mrs Oliver, 'as though your facts were leading you backwards instead of remaining on the spot or going forward.'

'Things have to be made to accord. Take forgery, for instance. The fact of forgery. Everybody says that a foreign girl, the *au pair* girl, so endeared herself to an elderly and very rich widow that that rich widow left a Will, or a codicil to a Will, leaving all her money to this girl. Did the girl forge that Will or did somebody else forge it?'

'Who else could have forged it?'

'There was another forger in this village. Someone, that is, who had once been accused of forgery but had got off lightly as a first offender and with extenuating circumstances.'

'Is this a new character? One I know?'

'No, you do not know him. He is dead.'

'Oh? When did he die?'

'About two years ago. The exact date I do not as yet know. But I shall have to know. He is someone who had practised forgery and who lived in this place. And because of a little what you might call girl trouble arousing jealousy and various emotions, he was knifed one night and died. I have the idea, you see, that a lot of separated incidents might tie up more closely than anyone has thought. Not any of them. Probably not all of them, but several of them.'

'It sounds interesting,' said Mrs Oliver, 'but I can't see –'

'Nor can I as yet,' said Poirot. 'But I think dates might help. Dates of certain happenings, where people were, what happened to them, what they were doing. Everybody thinks that the foreign girl forged the Will and probably,' said Poirot, 'everybody was right. She was the one to gain by it, was she not? Wait – wait –'

'Wait for what?' said Mrs Oliver.

'An idea that passed through my head,' said Poirot.

Mrs Oliver sighed and took another date.

'You return to London, Madame? Or are you making a long stay here?'

'Day after tomorrow,' said Mrs Oliver. 'I can't stay any longer. I've got a good many things cropping up.'

'Tell me, now – in your flat, your house, I cannot remember which it is now, you have moved so many times lately, there is room there to have guests?'

'I never admit that there is,' said Mrs Oliver. 'If you ever admit that you've got a free guest room in London, you've asked for it. All your friends, and not only your friends, your acquaintances or indeed your acquaintances' third cousins sometimes, write you letters and say would you mind just putting them up for a night. Well, I do mind. What with sheets and laundry, pillow cases and wanting early morning tea and very often expecting meals served to them, people come. So I don't let on that I have got an available spare room. My *friends* come and stay with me. The people I *really* want to see, but the others – no, I'm not helpful. I don't like just being made use of.'

'Who does?' said Hercule Poirot. 'You are very wise.'

'And anyway, what's all this about?'

'You could put up one or two guests, if need arose?'

'I *could*,' said Mrs Oliver. 'Who do you want me to put up? Not you yourself. You've got a splendid flat of your own. Ultra modern, very abstract, all squares and cubes.'

'It is just that there might be a wise precaution to take.'

'For whom? Somebody else going to be killed?'

'I trust and pray not, but it might be within the bound of possibility.'

'But who? Who? I can't understand.'

'How well do you know your friend?'

'Know her? Not well. I mean, we liked each other on a cruise and got in the habit of pairing off together. There was something – what shall I say? – exciting about her. Different.'

'Did you think you might put her in a book some day?'

'I do hate that phrase being used. People are always saying it to me and it's not true. Not really. I don't put people in books. People I meet, people I know.'

'Is it perhaps not true to say, Madame, that you do put people in books sometimes? People that you meet, but *not*, I agree, people that you *know*. There would be no fun in that.'

'You're quite right,' said Mrs Oliver. 'You're really rather good at guessing things sometimes. It does happen that way. I mean, you see a fat woman sitting in a bus eating a currant bun and her lips are moving as well as eating, and you can see she's either saying something to someone or thinking up a telephone call that she's going to make, or perhaps a letter she's going to write. And you look at her and you study her shoes and the skirt she's got on and her hat and guess her age and whether she's got a wedding ring on and a few other things. And then you get out of the bus. You don't want ever to see her again, but you've got a story in your mind about somebody called Mrs Carnaby who is going home in a bus, having had a very strange interview somewhere where she saw someone in a pastry cook's and was reminded of someone she'd only met once and who she had heard was dead and apparently isn't dead. Dear me,' said Mrs Oliver, pausing for breath. 'You know, it's quite true. I did sit across from someone in a bus just before I left London, and here it is all working out beautifully inside my head. I shall have the whole story soon. The whole sequence, what she's going back to say, whether it'll run her into danger or somebody else into danger. I think I even know her name. Her name's Constance. Constance Carnaby. There's only one thing would ruin it.'

'And what is that?'

'Well, I mean, if I met her again in another bus, or spoke to her or she talked to me or I began to know something about her. That would ruin everything, of course.'

'Yes, yes. The story must be yours, the character is yours. She is your child. You have made her, you begin to understand her, you know how she feels, you know where she lives and you know what she does. But that all started with a real, live human being and if you found out what the real live human being was like – well then, there would be no story, would there?'

'Right again,' said Mrs Oliver. 'As to what you were saying about Judith, I think that is true. I mean, we were together a lot on the cruise, and we went to see the places but I didn't really get to know her particularly well. She's a widow, and her husband died and she was left badly off with one child, Miranda, whom you've seen. And it's true that I've got rather a funny feeling about them. A feeling as though they mattered, as though they're mixed up in some interesting drama. I don't want to know what the drama is. I don't want them to tell me. I want to think of the sort of drama I would like them to be in.'

'Yes. Yes, I can see that they are – well, candidates for inclusion for another best seller by Ariadne Oliver.'

'You really are a beast sometimes,' said Mrs Oliver. 'You make it all sound so vulgar.' She paused thoughtfully. 'Perhaps it is.'

'No, no, it is not vulgar. It is just human.'

'And you want me to invite Judith and Miranda to my flat or house in London?'

'Not yet,' said Poirot. 'Not yet until I am sure that one of my little ideas might be right.'

'You and your little ideas! Now I've got a piece of news for you.'

'Madame, you delight me.'

'Don't be too sure. It will probably upset your ideas. Supposing I tell you that the forgery you have been so busy talking about wasn't a forgery at all.'

'What is that you say?'

'Mrs Ap Jones Smythe, or whatever her name is, *did* make a

codicil to her Will leaving all her money to the *au pair* girl *and* two witnesses saw her sign it, and signed it also in the presence of each other. Put that in your moustache and smoke it.'

CHAPTER 19

'Mrs – Leaman –' said Poirot, writing down the name.

'That's right. Harriet Leaman. And the other witness seems to have been a James Jenkins. Last heard of going to Australia. And Miss Olga Seminoff seems to have been last heard of returning to Czechoslovakia, or wherever she came from. Everybody seems to have gone somewhere else.'

'How reliable do you think this Mrs Leaman is?'

'I don't think she made it all up, if that's what you mean. I think she signed something, that she was curious about it, and that she took the first opportunity she had of finding out what she'd signed.'

'She can read and write?'

'I suppose so. But I agree that people aren't very good sometimes, at reading old ladies' handwriting, which is very spiky and very hard to read. If there were any rumours flying about later, about this Will or codicil, she might have thought that that was what she'd read in this rather undecipherable handwriting.'

'A genuine document,' said Poirot. 'But there *was* also a forged codicil.'

'Who says so?'

'Lawyers.'

'Perhaps it wasn't forged at all.'

'Lawyers are very particular about these matters. They were prepared to come into court with expert witnesses.'

'Oh well,' said Mrs Oliver, 'then it's easy to see what must have happened, isn't it?'

'What is easy? What happened?'

'Well, of course, the next day or a few days later, or even as much as a week later, Mrs Llewellyn-Smythe either had a bit of a tiff with her devoted *au pair* attendant, or she had a delicious reconciliation with her nephew, Hugo, or her niece Rowena, and she tore up the Will or scratched out the codicil or something like that, or burnt the whole thing.'

'And after that?'

'Well, after that, I suppose, Mrs Llewellyn-Smythe dies, and the girl seizes her chance and writes a new codicil in roughly the same terms in as near to Mrs Llewellyn-Smythe's handwriting as she can, and the two witnessing signatures as near as she can. She probably knows Mrs Leaman's writing quite well. It would be on national health cards or something like that, and she produces it, thinking that someone will agree to having witnessed the Will and that all would be well. But her forgery isn't good enough and so trouble starts.'

'Will you permit me, chère Madame, to use your telephone?'

'I will permit you to use Judith Butler's telephone, yes.'

'Where is your friend?'

'Oh, she's gone to get her hair done. And Miranda has gone for a walk. Go on, it's in the room through the window there.'

Poirot went in and returned about ten minutes later.

'Well? What have you been doing?'

'I rang up Mr Fullerton, the solicitor. I will now tell you something. The codicil, the forged codicil that was produced for probate was not witnessed by Harriet Leaman. It was witnessed by a Mary Doherty, deceased, who had been in service with Mrs Llewellyn-Smythe but had recently died. The other witness was the James Jenkins, who, as your friend Mrs Leaman has told you, departed for Australia.'

'So there was a forged codicil,' said Mrs Oliver. 'And there seems to have been a real codicil as well. Look here, Poirot, isn't this all getting a little too complicated?'

'It is getting incredibly complicated,' said Hercule Poirot. 'There is, if I may mention it, too much forgery about.'

'Perhaps the real one is still in the library at Quarry House, within the pages of *Enquire Within upon Everything*.'

'I understand all the effects of the house were sold up at Mrs Llewellyn-Smythe's death, except for a few pieces of family furniture and some family pictures.'

'What we need,' said Mrs Oliver, 'is something like *Enquire Within* here now. It's a lovely title, isn't it? I remember my grandmother had one. You could, you know, inquire within about everything, too. Legal information and cooking recipes and how to take ink stains out of linen. How to make home-made face powder that would not damage the complexion. Oh – and lots more. Yes, wouldn't you like to have a book like that now?'

'Doubtless,' said Hercule Poirot, 'it would give the recipe for treatment of tired feet.'

'Plenty of them, I should think. But why don't you wear proper country shoes?'

'Madame, I like to look *soigné* in my appearance.'

'Well, then you'll have to go on wearing things that are painful, and grin and bear it,' said Mrs Oliver. 'All the same, I don't understand anything now. Was that Leaman woman telling me a pack of lies just now?'

'It is always possible.'

'Did someone *tell* her to tell a pack of lies?'

'That too is possible.'

'Did someone *pay* her to tell me a pack of lies?'

'Continue,' said Poirot, 'continue. You are doing very nicely.'

'I suppose,' said Mrs Oliver thoughtfully, 'that Mrs Llewellyn-Smythe, like many another rich woman, enjoyed making Wills. I expect she made a good many during her life. You know; benefiting one person and then another. Changing about. The Drakes were well off, anyway. I expect she always left them at least a handsome legacy, but I wonder if she ever left anyone else as much as she appears, according to Mrs Leaman and according to the forged Will as well, to that girl Olga. I'd like to know a bit more about that girl, I must say. She certainly seems a very successful disappearess.'

'I hope to know more about her shortly,' said Hercule Poirot.

'How?'

'Information that I shall receive shortly.'

'I know you've been asking for information down here.'

'Not here only. I have an agent in London who obtains information for me both abroad and in this country. I should have some news possibly soon from Herzogovinia.'

'Will you find out if she ever arrived back there?'

'That might be one thing I should learn, but it seems more likely that I may get information of a different kind – letters perhaps written during her sojourn in this country, mentioning friends she may have made here, and become intimate with.'

'What about the school-teacher?' said Mrs Oliver.

'Which one do you mean?'

'I mean the one who was strangled – the one Elizabeth Whittaker told you about?' She added, 'I don't like Elizabeth Whittaker much. Tiresome sort of woman, but clever, I should think.' She added dreamily, 'I wouldn't put it past her to have thought up a murder.'

'Strangle another teacher, do you mean?'

'One has to exhaust all the possibilities.'

'I shall rely, as so often, on your intuition, Madame.'

Mrs Oliver ate another date thoughtfully.

CHAPTER 20

When he left Mrs Butler's house, Poirot took the same way as had been shown him by Miranda. The aperture in the hedge, it seemed to him, had been slightly enlarged since last time. Somebody, perhaps, with slightly more bulk than Miranda, had used it also. He ascended the path in the quarry, noticing once more the beauty of the scene. A lovely spot, and yet in some way, Poirot felt as he had felt before, that it could be a haunted spot. There was a kind of pagan ruthlessness about it. It could be along these winding paths that the fairies hunted their victims down or a cold goddess decreed that sacrifices would have to be offered.

He could understand why it had not become a picnic spot. One would not want for some reason to bring your hard-boiled eggs and your lettuce and your oranges and sit down here and crack jokes and have a jollification. It was different, quite different. It would have been better, perhaps, he thought suddenly, if Mrs Llewellyn-Smythe had not wanted this fairy-like transformation. Quite a modest sunk garden could have been made out of a quarry without the atmosphere, but she had been an ambitious woman, ambitious and a very rich woman. He thought for a moment or two about Wills, the kind of Wills made by rich women, the kind of lies told about Wills made by rich women, the places in which the Wills of rich widows were sometimes hidden, and he tried to put himself back into the mind of a forger. Undoubtably the Will offered for probate had been a forgery. Mr Fullerton was a careful and competent lawyer. He was sure of that. The kind of lawyer, too, who would never advise a client to bring a case or to take legal proceedings unless there was very good evidence and justification for so doing.

He turned a corner of the pathway feeling for the moment that his feet were much more important than his speculations. Was he taking a short cut to Superintendent Spence's dwelling or was he not? As the crow flies, perhaps, but the main road might have been more good to his feet. This path was not a grassy or mossy one, it had the quarry hardness of stone. Then he paused.

In front of him were two figures. Sitting on an outcrop of rock was Michael Garfield. He had a sketching block on his knees and he was drawing, his attention fully on what he was doing. A little way away from him, standing close beside a minute but musical stream that flowed down from above, Miranda Butler was standing. Hercule Poirot forgot his feet, forgot the pains and ills of the human body, and concentrated again on the beauty that human beings could attain. There was no doubt that Michael Garfield was a very beautiful young man. He found it difficult to know whether he himself liked Michael Garfield or not. It is always difficult to know if you like anyone beautiful. You like beauty to look at, at the same time you dislike beauty almost on principle. Women could be beautiful, but Hercule Poirot was not at all sure that he liked beauty in men. He would not have liked to be a beautiful young man himself, not that there had ever been the least chance of that. There was only one thing about his own appearance which really pleased Hercule Poirot, and that was the profusion of his moustaches, and the way they responded to grooming and treatment and trimming. They were magnificent. He knew of nobody else who had any moustache half as good. He had never been handsome or good-looking. Certainly never beautiful.

And Miranda? He thought again, as he had thought before, that it was her gravity that was so attractive. He wondered what passed through her mind. It was the sort of thing one would never know. She would not say what she was thinking easily. He doubted if she would tell you what she was thinking, if you asked her. She had an original mind, he thought, a reflective mind. He thought too she was vulnerable. Very vulnerable. There were other things about her that he knew, or thought he knew. It was only thinking so far, but yet he was almost sure.

Michael Garfield looked up and said,

'Ha! Señor Moustachios. A very good afternoon to you, sir.'

'Can I look at what you are doing or would it incommode you? I do not want to be intrusive.'

'You can look,' said Michael Garfield, 'it makes no difference to me.' He added gently, 'I'm enjoying myself very much.'

Poirot came to stand behind his shoulder. He nodded. It was a very delicate pencil drawing, the lines almost invisible. The man could draw, Poirot thought. Not only design gardens. He said, almost under his breath:

'Exquisite!'

'I think so too,' said Michael Garfield.

He let it be left doubtful whether he referred to the drawing he was making, or to the sitter.

'Why?' asked Poirot.

'Why am I doing it? Do you think I have a reason?'

'You might have.'

'You're quite right. If I go away from here, there are one or two things I want to remember. Miranda is one of them.'

'Would you forget her easily?'

'Very easily. I am like that. But to have forgotten something or someone, to be unable to bring a face, a turn of a shoulder, a gesture, a tree, a flower, a contour of landscape, to know what it was like to see it but not to be able to bring that image in front of one's eyes, that sometimes causes – what shall I say – almost agony. You see, you record – and it all passes away.'

'Not the Quarry Garden or park. That has not passed away.'

'Don't you think so? It soon will. It soon will if no one is here. Nature takes over, you know. It needs love and attention and care and skill. If a Council takes it over – and that's what happens very often nowadays – then it will be what they call "kept up". The latest sort of shrubs may be put in, extra paths will be made, seats will be put at certain distances. Litter bins even may be erected. Oh, they are so careful, so kind at preserving. You can't preserve this. It's wild. To keep something wild is far more difficult than to preserve it.'

'Monsieur Poirot.' Miranda's voice came across the stream.

Poirot moved forward, so that he came within earshot of her.

'So I find you here. So you came to sit for your portrait, did you?'

She shook her head.

'I didn't come for that. That just happened.'

'Yes,' said Michael Garfield, 'yes, it just happened. A piece of luck sometimes comes one's way.'

'You were just walking in your favourite garden?'

'I was looking for the well, really,' said Miranda.

'A well?'

'There was a wishing well once in this wood.'

'In a former quarry? I didn't know they kept wells in quarries.'

'There was always a wood round the quarry. Well, there were always trees here. Michael knows where the well is but he won't tell me.'

'It will be much more fun for you,' said Michael Garfield, 'to go on looking for it. Especially when you're not at all sure it really exists.'

'Old Mrs Goodbody knows all about it.'

And added:

'She's a witch.'

'Quite right,' said Michael. 'She's the local witch, Monsieur Poirot. There's always a local witch, you know, in most places. They don't always call themselves witches, but everyone knows. They tell a fortune or put a spell on your begonias or shrivel up your peonies or stop a farmer's cow from giving milk and probably give love potions as well.'

'It was a wishing well,' said Miranda. 'People used to come here and wish. They had to go round it three times backwards and it was on the side of the hill, so it wasn't always very easy to do.' She looked past Poirot at Michael Garfield. 'I shall find it one day,' she said, 'even if you won't tell me. It's here somewhere, but it was sealed up, Mrs Goodbody said. Oh! years ago. Sealed up because it was said to be dangerous. A child fell into it years ago – Kitty Somebody. Someone else might have fallen into it.'

'Well, go on thinking so,' said Michael Garfield. 'It's a good local story, but there *is* a wishing well over at Little Belling.'

'Of course,' said Miranda. 'I know all about that one. It's a very common one,' she said. 'Everybody knows about it, and it's very silly. People throw pennies into it and there's not any water in it any more so there's not even a splash.'

'Well, I'm sorry.'

'I'll tell you when I find it,' said Miranda.

'You mustn't always believe everything a witch says. I don't believe any child ever fell into it. I expect a cat fell into it once and got drowned.'

'Ding dong dell, pussy's in the well,' said Miranda. She got up. 'I must go now,' she said. 'Mummy will be expecting me.'

She moved carefully from the knob of rock, smiled at both the men and went off down an even more intransigent path that ran the other side of the water.

'"Ding dong dell",' said Poirot, thoughtfully. 'One believes what one wants to believe, Michael Garfield. Was she right or was she not right?'

Michael Garfield looked at him thoughtfully, then he smiled.

'She is quite right,' he said. 'There is a well, and it is as she says sealed up. I suppose it may have been dangerous. I don't think it was ever a wishing well. I think that's Mrs Goodbody's own bit of fancy talk. There's a wishing tree, or there was once. A beech tree half-way up the hillside that I believe people did go round three times backwards and wished.'

'What's happened to that? Don't they go round it any more?'

'No. I believe it was struck by lightning about six years ago. Split in two. So that pretty story's gone west.'

'Have you told Miranda about that?'

'No. I thought I'd rather leave her with her well. A blasted beech wouldn't be much fun for her, would it?'

'I must go on my way,' said Poirot.

'Going back to your police friend?'

'Yes.'

'You look tired.'

'I am tired,' said Hercule Poirot. 'I am extremely tired.'

'You'd be more comfortable in canvas shoes or sandals.'

'Ah, *ça, non*.'

'I see. You are sartorially ambitious.' He looked at Poirot. 'The *tout ensemble*, it is very good and especially, if I may mention it, your superb moustache.'

'I am gratified,' said Poirot, 'that you have noticed it.'

'The point is rather, could anyone not notice it?'

Poirot put his head on one side. Then he said:

'You spoke of the drawing you are doing because you wish to remember the young Miranda. Does that mean you're going away from here?'

'I have thought of it, yes.'

'Yet you are, it seems to me, *bien placé ici*.'

'Oh yes, eminently so. I have a house to live in, a house small but designed by myself, and I have my work, but that is less satisfactory than it used to be. So restlessness is coming over me.'

'Why is your work less satisfactory?'

'Because people wish me to do the most atrocious things. People who want to improve their gardens, people who bought some land and they're building a house and want the garden designed.'

'Are you not doing her garden for Mrs Drake?'

'She wants me to, yes. I made suggestions for it and she seemed to agree with them. I don't think, though,' he added thoughtfully, 'that I really trust her.'

'You mean that she would not let you have what you wanted?'

'I mean that she would certainly have what *she* wanted herself and that though she is attracted by the ideas I have set out, she would suddenly demand something quite different. Something utilitarian, expensive and showy, perhaps. She would bully me, I think. She would insist on her ideas being carried out. I would not agree, and we should quarrel. So on the whole it is better I leave here before I quarrel. And not only with Mrs Drake but many other neighbours. I am quite well known. I don't need to stay in one spot. I could go and find some other corner of England, or it could be some corner of Normandy or Brittany.'

'Somewhere where you can improve, or help, nature? Somewhere where you can experiment or you can put strange things where they have never grown before, where neither sun will blister nor frost destroy? Some good stretch of barren land where you can have the fun of playing at being Adam all over again? Have you always been restless?'

'I never stayed anywhere very long.'

'You have been to Greece?'

'Yes. I should like to go to Greece again. Yes, you have something there. A garden on a Greek hillside. There may be cypresses there, not much else. A barren rock. But if you wished, what could there not be?'

'A garden for gods to walk –'

'Yes. You're quite a mind reader, aren't you, Mr Poirot?'

'I wish I were. There are so many things I would like to know and do not know.'

'You are talking now of something quite prosaic, are you not?'

'Unfortunately so.'

'Arson, murder and sudden death?'

'More or less. I do not know that I was considering arson. Tell me, Mr Garfield, you have been here some considerable time, did you know a young man called Lesley Ferrier?'

'Yes, I remember him. He was in a Medchester solicitor's office, wasn't he? Fullerton, Harrison and Leadbetter. Junior clerk, something of that kind. Good-looking chap.'

'He came to a sudden end, did he not?'

'Yes. Got himself knifed one evening. Woman trouble, I gather. Everyone seems to think that the police know quite well who did it, but they can't get the evidence they want. He was more or less tied up with a woman called Sandra – can't remember her name for the moment – Sandra Somebody, yes. Her husband kept the local pub. She and young Lesley were running an affair, and then Lesley took up with another girl. Or that was the story.'

'And Sandra did not like it?'

'No, she did not like it at all. Mind you, he was a great one for the girls. There were two or three that he went around with.'

'Were they all English girls?'

'Why do you ask that, I wonder? No, I don't think he confined himself to English girls, so long as they could speak enough English to understand more or less what he said to them, and he could understand what they said to him.'

'There are doubtless from time to time foreign girls in this neighbourhood?'

'Of course there are. Is there any neighbourhood where there aren't? *Au pair* girls – they're a part of daily life. Ugly ones, pretty ones, honest ones, dishonest ones, ones that do some good to distracted mothers and some who are no use at all and some who walk out of the house.'

'Like the girl Olga did?'

'As you say, like the girl Olga did.'

'Was Lesley a friend of Olga's?'

'Oh, that's the way your mind is running. Yes, he was. I don't think Mrs Llewellyn-Smythe knew much about it. Olga was rather careful, I think. She spoke gravely of someone she hoped to marry some day in her own country. I don't know whether that was true or whether she made it up. Young Lesley was an attractive young man, as I said. I don't know what he saw in Olga – she wasn't very beautiful. Still –' he considered a minute or two '– she had a kind of intensity about her. A young Englishman might have found that attractive, I think. Anyway, Lesley did all right, and his other girl friends weren't pleased.'

'That is very interesting,' said Poirot. 'I thought you might give me information that I wanted.'

Michael Garfield looked at him curiously.

'Why? What's it all about? Where does Lesley come in? Why this raking up of the past?'

'Well, there are things one wants to know. One wants to know how things come into being. I am even looking farther back still. Before the time that those two, Olga Seminoff and Lesley Ferrier, met secretly without Mrs Llewellyn-Smythe knowing about it.'

'Well, I'm not sure about that. That's only my – well, it's only my idea. I did come across them fairly frequently but Olga never confided in me. As for Lesley Ferrier, I hardly knew him.'

'I want to go back behind that. He had, I gather, certain disadvantages in his past.'

'I believe so. Yes, well, anyway it's been said here locally. Mr Fullerton took him on and hoped to make an honest man of him. He's a good chap, old Fullerton.'

'His offence had been, I believe, forgery?'

'Yes.'

'It was a first offence, and there were said to be extenuating circumstances. He had a sick mother or drunken father or something of that kind. Anyway, he got off lightly.'

'I never heard any of the details. It was something that he seemed to have got away with to begin with, then accountants came along and found him out. I'm very vague. It's only hearsay. Forgery. Yes, that was the charge. Forgery.'

'And when Mrs Llewellyn-Smythe died and her Will was to be admitted to probate, it was found the Will was forged.'

'Yes, I see the way your mind's working. You're fitting those two things as having a connection with each other.'

'A man who was up to a point successful in forging. A man who became friends with the girl, a girl who, if a Will had been accepted when submitted to probate, would have inherited the larger part of a vast fortune.'

'Yes, yes, that's the way it goes.'

'And this girl and the man who had committed forgery were great friends. He had given up his own girl and he'd tied up with the foreign girl instead.'

'What you're suggesting is that that forged Will was forged by Lesley Ferrier.'

'There seems a likelihood of it, does there not?'

'Olga was supposed to have been able to copy Mrs Llewellyn-Smythe's handwriting fairly well, but it seemed to me always that that was rather a doubtful point. She wrote handwritten letters for Mrs Llewellyn-Smythe but I don't suppose that they were really particularly similar. Not enough to pass muster. But if she and Lesley were in it together, that's different. I daresay he could pass off a good enough job and he was probably quite cocksure that it would go through. But then he must have been sure of that when he committed his original offence, and he was wrong there, and I suppose he was wrong this time. I suppose that when the balloon went up, when the lawyers began making trouble and difficulties, and experts were called in to examine things and started asking questions, it could be that she lost her nerve, and had a row with Lesley. And then she cleared out, hoping he'd carry the can.'

He gave his head a sharp shake. 'Why do you come and talk to me about things like that here, in my beautiful wood?'

'I wanted to know.'

'It's better not to know. It's better never to know. Better to leave things as they are. Not push and pry and poke.'

'You want beauty,' said Hercule Poirot. 'Beauty at any price. For me, it is truth I want. Always truth.'

Michael Garfield laughed. 'Go on home to your police friends and leave me here in my local paradise. Get thee beyond me, Satan.'

CHAPTER 21

Poirot went on up the hill. Suddenly he no longer felt the pain of his feet. Something had come to him. The fitting together of the things he had thought and felt, had known they were connected, but had not seen how they were connected. He was conscious now of danger – danger that might come to someone any minute now unless steps were taken to prevent it. Serious danger.

Elspeth McKay came out to the door to meet him. 'You look fagged out,' she said. 'Come and sit down.'

'Your brother is here?'

'No. He's gone down to the station. Something's happened, I believe.'

'Something has happened?' He was startled. 'So soon? Not possible.'

'Eh?' said Elspeth. 'What do you mean?'

'Nothing. Nothing. Something has happened to somebody, do you mean?'

'Yes, but I don't know who exactly. Anyway, Tim Raglan rang up and asked for him to go down there. I'll get you a cup of tea, shall I?'

'No,' said Poirot, 'thank you very much, but I think – I think I will go home.' He could not face the prospect of black bitter tea. He thought of a good excuse that would mask any signs of bad manners. 'My feet,' he explained. 'My feet. I am not very suitably attired as to footwear for the country. A change of shoes would be desirable.'

Elspeth McKay looked down at them. 'No,' she said. 'I can see they're not. Patent leather draws the feet. There's a letter for you, by the way. Foreign stamps on it. Come from abroad – c/o Superintendent Spence, Pine Crest. I'll bring it to you.'

She came back in a minute or two, and handed it to him.

'If you don't want the envelope, I'd like it for one of my nephews – he collects stamps.'

'Of course.' Poirot opened the letter and handed her the envelope. She thanked him and went back into the house.

Poirot unfolded the sheet and read.

Mr Goby's foreign service was run with the same competence that he showed in his English one. He spared no expense and got his results quickly.

True, the results did not amount to much – Poirot had not thought that they would.

Olga Seminoff had not returned to her home town. She had had no family still living. She had had a friend, an elderly woman, with whom she had corresponded intermittently, giving news of her life in England. She had been on good terms with her employer who had been occasionally exacting, but had also been generous.

The last letters received from Olga had been dated about a year and a half ago. In them there had been mention of a young man. There were hints that they were considering marriage, but the young man, whose name she did not mention, had, she said, his way to make, so nothing could be settled as yet. In her last letter she spoke happily of their prospects being good. When no more letters came, the elderly friend assumed that Olga had married her Englishman and changed her address. Such things happened frequently when girls went to England. If they were happily married they often never wrote again.

She had not worried.

It fitted, Poirot thought. Lesley had spoken of marriage, but might not have meant it. Mrs Llewellyn-Smythe had been spoken of as 'generous'. Lesley had been given money by someone, Olga perhaps (money originally given her by her employers), to induce him to do forgery on her behalf.

Elspeth McKay came out on the terrace again. Poirot consulted her as to his surmises about a partnership between Olga and Lesley.

She considered a moment. Then the oracle spoke.

'Kept very quiet about it, if so. Never any rumours about

those two. There usually is in a place like this if there's anything in it.'

'Young Ferrier was tied up to a married woman. He might have warned the girl not to say anything about him to her employer.'

'Likely enough. Mrs Smythe would probably know that Lesley Ferrier was a bad character, and would warn the girl to have nothing to do with him.'

Poirot folded up the letter and put it into his pocket.

'I wish you'd let me get you a pot of tea.'

'No, no – I must go back to my guest house and change my shoes. You do not know when your brother will be back?'

'I've no idea. They didn't say what they wanted him for.'

Poirot walked along the road to his guest house. It was only a few hundred yards. As he walked up to the front door it was opened and his landlady, a cheerful lady of thirty odd, came out to him.

'There's a lady here to see you,' she said. 'Been waiting some time. I told her I didn't know where you'd gone exactly or when you'd be back, but she said she'd wait.' She added, 'It's Mrs Drake. She's in a state, I'd say. She's usually so calm about everything, but really I think she's had a shock of some kind. She's in the sitting-room. Shall I bring you in some tea and something?'

'No,' said Poirot, 'I think it will be better not. I will hear first what she has to say.'

He opened the door and went into the sitting-room. Rowena Drake had been standing by the window. It was not the window overlooking the front path so she had not seen his approach. She turned abruptly as she heard the sound of the door.

'Monsieur Poirot. At last. It seemed so long.'

'I am sorry, Madame. I have been in the Quarry Wood and also talking to my friend, Mrs Oliver. And then I have been talking to two boys. To Nicholas and Desmond.'

'Nicholas and Desmond? Yes, I know. I wonder – oh! one thinks all sorts of things.'

'You are upset,' said Poirot gently.

It was not a thing he thought he would ever see. Rowena Drake upset, no longer mistress of events, no longer arranging everything, and enforcing her decisions on others.

'You've heard, haven't you?' she asked. 'Oh well, perhaps you haven't.'

'What should I have heard?'

'Something dreadful. He's – he's dead. Somebody killed him.'

'Who is dead, Madame?'

'Then you haven't really heard. And he's only a child, too, and I thought – oh, what a fool I've been. I should have told you. I should have told you when you asked me. It makes me feel terrible – terribly guilty for thinking I knew best and thinking – but I did mean it for the best, Monsieur Poirot, indeed I did.'

'Sit down, Madame, sit down. Calm yourself and tell me. There is a child dead – another child?'

'Her brother,' said Mrs Drake. 'Leopold.'

'Leopold Reynolds?'

'Yes. They found his body on one of the field paths. He must have been coming back from school and gone out of his way to play in the brook near here. Somebody held him down in the brook – held his head under water.'

'The same kind of thing as they did to the child Joyce?'

'Yes, yes. I can see it must be – it must be madness of some kind. And one doesn't know *who*, that's what's so awful. One hasn't the least idea. And I thought I knew. I really thought – I suppose, yes, it was a very wicked thing.'

'You must tell me, Madame.'

'Yes, I want to tell you. I came here to tell you. Because, you see, you came to me after you'd talked to Elizabeth Whittaker. After she'd told you that something had startled me. That I'd seen something. Something in the hall of the house, my house. I said that I hadn't seen anything and that nothing had startled me because, you see, I thought –' she stopped.

'What *did* you see?'

'I ought to have told you then. I saw the door of the library open, open rather carefully and – then he came out. At least, he didn't come right out. He just stood in the doorway and then pulled the door back quickly and went back inside.'

'Who was this?'

'Leopold. Leopold, the child that's been killed now. And you see, I thought I – oh, what a mistake, what an awful mistake.

If I'd told you, perhaps – perhaps you'd have got at what was behind it.'

'You thought?' Poirot said. 'You thought that Leopold had killed his sister. Is that what you thought?'

'Yes, that's what I thought. Not then, of course, because I didn't know she was dead. But he had a queer look on his face. He's always been a queer child. In a way you're a little afraid of him because you feel he's not – not quite right. Very clever and a high I.Q., but all the same not all there.

'And I thought "Why is Leopold coming out of there instead of being at the Snapdragon?" and I thought "What's he been doing – he looks so queer?" And then, well then I didn't think of it again after that, but I suppose, the way he looked upset me. And that's why I dropped the vase. Elizabeth helped me to pick up the glass pieces, and I went back to the Snapdragon and I didn't think of it again. Until we found Joyce. And that's when I thought –'

'You thought that Leopold had done it?'

'Yes. Yes, I did think that. I thought it explained the way he'd looked. I thought I knew. I always think – I've thought too much all my life that I know things, that I'm right about things. And I can be very wrong. Because, you see, his being killed must mean something quite different. He must have gone in there, and he must have found her there – dead – and it gave *him* a terrible shock and he was frightened. And so he wanted to come out of the room without anyone seeing him and I suppose he looked up and saw me and he got back into the room and shut the door and waited until the hall was empty before coming out. But *not* because he'd killed her. No. Just the shock of finding her dead.'

'And yet you said nothing? You didn't mention who it was you'd seen, even after the death was discovered?'

'No. I – oh, I couldn't. He's – you see, he's so young – *was* so young, I suppose I ought to say now. Ten. Ten – eleven at most and I mean – I felt he couldn't have known what he was doing, it couldn't have been his fault exactly. He must have been morally not responsible. He's always been rather queer, and I thought one could get treatment for him. Not leave it all to the police. Not send him to approved places. I thought one could get special psychological treatment for him, if necessary. I – I meant well. You must believe that, I meant well.'

Such sad words, Poirot thought, some of the saddest words in the world. Mrs Drake seemed to know what he was thinking.

'Yes,' she said, '"I did it for the best." "I meant well." One always thinks one knows what is best to do for other people, but one *doesn't*. Because, you see, the reason he looked so taken aback must have been that he either saw who the murderer was, or saw something that would give a clue to who the murderer might be. Something that made the murderer feel that he himself wasn't safe. And so – and so he's waited until he got the boy alone and then drowned him in the brook so that he shouldn't speak, so that he shouldn't tell. If I'd only spoken out, if I'd told you, or told the police, or told someone, but I thought I knew best.'

'Only today,' said Poirot, after he had sat silent for a moment or two, watching Mrs Drake where she sat controlling her sobs, 'I was told that Leopold had been very flush of money lately. Somebody must have been paying him to keep silent.'

'But who – who?'

'We shall find out,' said Poirot. 'It will not be long now.'

CHAPTER 22

It was not very characteristic of Hercule Poirot to ask the opinions of others. He was usually quite satisfied with his own opinions. Nevertheless, there were times when he made exceptions. This was one of them. He and Spence had had a brief conversation together and then Poirot had got in touch with a car hire service and after another short conversation with his friend and with Inspector Raglan, he drove off. He had arranged with the car to drive him back to London but he had made one halt on the way there. He drove to The Elms. He told the driver of the car that he would not be long – a quarter of an hour at most – and then he sought audience with Miss Emlyn.

'I am sorry to disturb you at this hour. It is no doubt the hour of your supper or dinner.'

'Well, I do you at least the compliment, Monsieur Poirot, to think you would not disturb me at either supper or dinner unless you have a valid reason for so doing.'

'You are very kind. To be frank, I want your advice.'

'Indeed?'

Miss Emlyn looked slightly surprised. She looked more than surprised, she looked sceptical.

'That does not seem very characteristic of you, Monsieur Poirot. Are you not usually satisfied with your own opinions?'

'Yes, I am satisfied with my own opinions, but it would give me solace and support if someone whose opinion I respected agreed with them.'

She did not speak, merely looked at him inquiringly.

'I know the killer of Joyce Reynolds,' he said. 'It is my belief that you know it also.'

'I have not said so,' said Miss Emlyn.

'No. You have not said so. And that might lead me to believe that it is on your part an opinion only.'

'A hunch?' inquired Miss Emlyn, and her tone was colder than ever.

'I would prefer not to use that word. I would prefer to say that you had a definite opinion.'

'Very well then. I will admit that I have a definite opinion. That does not mean that I shall repeat to you what my opinion is.'

'What I should like to do, Mademoiselle, is to write down four words on a piece of paper. I will ask you if you agree with the four words I have written.'

Miss Emlyn rose. She crossed the room to her desk, took a piece of writing paper and came across to Poirot with it.

'You interest me,' she said. 'Four words.'

Poirot had taken a pen from his pocket. He wrote on the paper, folded it and handed it to her. She took it, straightened out the paper and held it in her hand, looking at it.

'Well?' said Poirot.

'As to two of the words on that paper, I agree, yes. The other two, that is more difficult. I have no evidence and, indeed, the ideas had not entered my head.'

'But in the case of the first two words, you *have* definite evidence?'

'I consider so, yes.'

'Water,' said Poirot, thoughtfully. 'As soon as you heard that, you knew. As soon as I heard that I knew. You are sure, and I am sure. And now,' said Poirot, 'a boy has been drowned in a brook. You have heard that?'

'Yes. Someone rang me up on the telephone and told me. Joyce's brother. How was he concerned?'

'He wanted money,' said Poirot. 'He got it. And so, at a suitable opportunity, he was drowned in a brook.'

His voice did not change. It had, if anything, not a softened, but a harsher note,

'The person who told me,' he said, 'was riddled with compassion. Upset emotionally. But I am not like that. He was young, this second child who died, but his death was not an accident. It was, as so many things in life, a result of his actions. He wanted money and he took a risk. He was clever enough, astute enough to know he was taking a risk, but he wanted the money. He was ten years old but cause and effect is much the same at that age as it would be at thirty or fifty or ninety. Do you know what I think of first in such a case?'

'I should say,' said Miss Emlyn, 'that you are more concerned with justice than with compassion.'

'Compassion,' said Poirot, 'on my part would do nothing to help Leopold. He is beyond help. Justice, if we obtain justice, you and I, for I think you are of my way of thinking over this – justice, one could say, will also not help Leopold. But it might help some other Leopold, it might help to keep some other child alive, if we can reach justice soon enough. It is not a safe thing, a killer who has killed more than once, to whom killing has appealed as a way of security. I am now on my way to London where I am meeting with certain people to discuss a way of approach. To convert them, perhaps, to my own certainty in this case.'

'You may find that difficult,' said Miss Emlyn.

'No, I do not think so. The ways and means to it may be difficult but I think I can convert them to my knowledge of what has happened. Because they have minds that understand the criminal mind. There is one thing more I would ask you. I want your opinion. Your opinion only this time, not evidence. Your opinion of the character of Nicholas Ransom and Desmond Holland. Would you advise me to trust them?'

'I should say that both of them were thoroughly trustworthy. That is my opinion. They are in many ways extremely foolish, but that is only in the ephemeral things of life. Fundamentally, they are sound. Sound as an apple without maggots in it.'

'One always comes back to apples,' said Hercule Poirot sadly. 'I must go now. My car is waiting. I have one more call still to pay.'

CHAPTER 23

I

'Have you heard what's on at Quarry Wood?' said Mrs Cartwright, putting a packet of Fluffy Flakelets and Wonder White into her shopping bag.

'Quarry Wood?' said Elspeth McKay, to whom she was talking. 'No, I haven't heard anything particular.' She selected a packet of cereal. The two women were in the recently opened supermarket making their morning purchases.

'They're saying the trees are dangerous there. Couple of forestry men arrived this morning. It's there on the side of the hill where there's a steep slope and a tree leaning sideways. Could be I suppose, that a tree could come down there. One of them was struck by lightning last winter but that was farther over, I think. Anyway, they're digging round the roots of the trees a bit, and a bit farther down too. Pity. They'll make an awful mess of the place.'

'Oh well,' said Elspeth McKay, 'I suppose they know what they're doing. Somebody's called them in, I suppose.'

'They've got a couple of the police there, too, seeing that people don't come near. Making sure they keep away from things. They say something about finding out which the diseased trees are first.'

'I see,' said Elspeth McKay.

Possibly she did. Not that anyone had told her but then Elspeth never needed telling.

II

Ariadne Oliver smoothed out a telegram she had just taken as delivered to her at the door. She was so used to getting telegrams through the telephone, making frenzied hunts for a pencil to take them down, insisting firmly that she wanted a confirmatory copy sent to her, that she was quite startled to receive what she called to herself a 'real telegram' again.

> 'PLEASE BRING MRS BUTLER AND MIRANDA TO YOUR FLAT AT ONCE. NO TIME TO LOSE. IMPORTANT SEE DOCTOR FOR OPERATION.'

She went into the kitchen where Judith Butler was making quince jelly.

'Judy,' said Mrs Oliver, 'go and pack a few things, I'm going back to London and you're coming with me and Miranda, too.'

'It's very nice of you, Ariadne, but I've got a lot of things on here. Anyway, you needn't rush away today, need you?'

'Yes, I need to, I've been told to,' said Mrs Oliver.

'Who's told you – your housekeeper?'

'No,' said Mrs Oliver. 'Somebody else. One of the few people I obey. Come on. Hurry up.'

'I don't want to leave home just now. I can't.'

'You've got to come,' said Mrs Oliver. 'The car is ready. I brought it round to the front door. We can go at once.'

'I don't think I want to take Miranda. I could leave her here with someone, with the Reynolds or Rowena Drake.'

'Miranda's coming, too,' Mrs Oliver interrupted definitely. 'Don't make difficulties, Judy. This is serious. I don't see how you can even consider leaving her with the Reynolds. Two of the Reynolds children have been killed, haven't they?'

'Yes, yes, that's true enough. You think there's something wrong with that house. I mean there's someone there who – oh, what do I mean?'

'We're talking too much,' said Mrs Oliver. 'Anyway,' she added, 'if anyone is going to be killed, it seems to me that probably the most likely one would be Ann Reynolds.'

'What's the matter with the family? Why should they all get killed, one after another? Oh, Ariadne, it's *frightening*!'

'Yes,' said Mrs Oliver, 'but there are times when it's quite right to be frightened. I've just had a telegram and I'm acting upon it.'

'Oh, I didn't hear the telephone.'

'It didn't come through the telephone. It came to the door.'

She hesitated a moment, then she held it out to her friend.

'What's this mean? Operation?'

'Tonsils, probably,' said Mrs Oliver. 'Miranda had a bad throat last week, hadn't she? Well, what more likely than that she should be taken to consult a throat specialist in London?'

'Are you quite mad, Ariadne?'

'Probably,' said Mrs Oliver, 'raving mad. Come on. Miranda will enjoy being in London. You needn't worry. She's not going to have any operation. That's what's called "cover" in spy stories. We'll take her to a theatre, or an opera or the ballet, whichever way her tastes lie. On the whole I think it would be best to take her to the ballet.'

'I'm frightened,' said Judith.

Ariadne Oliver looked at her friend. She was trembling slightly. She looked more than ever, Mrs Oliver thought, like Undine. She looked divorced from reality.

'Come *on*,' said Mrs Oliver, 'I promised Hercule Poirot I'd bring you when he gave me the word. Well, he's given me the word.'

'What's going on in this place?' said Judith. 'I can't think why I ever came here.'

'I sometimes wondered why you did,' said Mrs Oliver, 'but there's no accounting for where people go to live. A friend of mine went to live in Moreton-in-the-Marsh the other day. I asked him why he wanted to go and live there. He said he'd always wanted to and thought about it. Whenever he retired he meant to go there. I said that I hadn't been to it myself but it sounded to me bound to be damp. What was it actually like? He said he didn't know what it was like because he'd never been there himself. But he had always wanted to live there. He was quite sane, too.'

'Did he go?'

'Yes.'

'Did he like it when he got there?'

'Well, I haven't heard that yet,' said Mrs Oliver. 'But people are very odd, aren't they? The things they want to do, the things they simply *have* to do . . .' She went to the garden and called, 'Miranda, we're going to London.'

Miranda came slowly towards them.

'Going to London?'

'Ariadne's going to drive us there,' said her mother. 'We'll go and see a theatre there. Mrs Oliver thinks perhaps she can get tickets for the ballet. Would you like to go to the ballet?'

'I'd love it,' said Miranda. Her eyes lighted up. 'I must go and say goodbye to one of my friends first.'

'We're going practically at once.'

'Oh, I shan't be as long as that, but I must explain. There are things I promised to do.'

She ran down the garden and disappeared through the gate.

'Who are Miranda's friends?' asked Mrs Oliver, with some curiosity.'

'I never really know,' said Judith. 'She never tells one things, you know. Sometimes I think that the only things that she really feels are her friends are the birds she looks at in the woods. Or squirrels or things like that. I think everybody likes her but I don't know that she has any particular friends. I mean, she doesn't bring back girls to tea and things like that. Not as much as other girls do. I think her best friend really was Joyce Reynolds.' She added vaguely: 'Joyce used to tell her fantastic things about elephants and tigers.' She roused herself. 'Well, I must go up and pack, I suppose, as you insist. But I don't want to leave here. There are lots of things I'm in the middle of doing, like this jelly and –'

'You've got to come,' said Mrs Oliver. She was quite firm about it.

Judith came downstairs again with a couple of suitcases just as Miranda ran in through the side door, somewhat out of breath.

'Aren't we going to have lunch first?' she demanded.

In spite of her elfin woodland appearance, she was a healthy child who liked her food.

'We'll stop for lunch on the way,' said Mrs Oliver. 'We'll stop at The Black Boy at Haversham. That would be about right. It's about three-quarters of an hour from here and they give you quite a good meal. Come on, Miranda, we're going to start now.'

'I shan't have time to tell Cathie I can't go to the pictures with her tomorrow. Oh, perhaps I could ring her up.'

'Well, hurry up,' said her mother.

Miranda ran into the sitting-room where the telephone was situated. Judith and Mrs Oliver put suitcases into the car. Miranda came out of the sitting-room.

'I left a message,' she said breathlessly. 'That's all right now.'

'I think you're mad, Ariadne,' said Judith, as they got into the car. 'Quite mad. What's it all *about*?'

'We shall know in due course, I suppose,' said Mrs Oliver. 'I don't know if I'm mad or he is.'

'He? Who?'

'Hercule Poirot,' said Mrs Oliver.

III

In London Hercule Poirot was sitting in a room with four other men. One was Inspector Timothy Raglan, looking respectful and poker-faced as was his invariable habit when in the presence of his superiors; the second was Superintendent Spence. The third was Alfred Richmond, Chief Constable of the County and the fourth was a man with a sharp, legal face from the Public Prosecutor's office. They looked at Hercule Poirot with varying expressions, or what one might describe as non-expressions.

'You seem quite sure, Monsieur Poirot.'

'I *am* quite sure,' said Hercule Poirot. 'When a thing arranges itself so, one realizes that it must be so, one only looks for reasons why it should not be so. If one does not find the reasons why it should not be so, then one is strengthened in one's opinion.'

'The motives seem somewhat complex, if I may say so.'

'No,' said Poirot, 'not complex really. But so simple that they are very difficult to see clearly.'

The legal gentleman looked sceptical.

'We shall have one piece of definite evidence very soon now,' said Inspector Raglan. 'Of course, if there has been a mistake on that point . . .'

'Ding dong dell, no pussy in the well?' said Hercule Poirot. 'That is what you mean?'

'Well, you must agree it is only a surmise on your part.'

'The evidence pointed to it all along. When a girl disappears, there are not many reasons. The first is that she has gone away with a man. The second is that she is dead. Anything else is very far-fetched and practically never happens.'

'There are no special points that you can bring to our attention, Monsieur Poirot?'

'Yes. I have been in touch with a well-known firm of estate agents. Friends of mine, who specialize in real estate in the West Indies, the Aegean, the Adriatic, the Mediterranean and other places. They specialize in sunshine and their clients are usually wealthy. Here is a recent purchase that might interest you.'

He handed over a folded paper.

'You think this ties up?'

'I'm sure it does.'

'I thought the sale of islands was prohibited by that particular government?'

'Money can usually find a way.'

'There is nothing else that you would care to dwell upon?'

'It is possible that within twenty-four hours I shall have for you something that will more or less clinch matters.'

'And what is that?'

'An eye-witness.'

'You mean –'

'An eye-witness to a crime.'

The legal man looked at Poirot with mounting disbelief.

'Where is this eye-witness now?'

'On the way to London, I hope and trust.'

'You sound – disturbed.'

'That is true. I have done what I can to take care of things, but I will admit to you that I am frightened. Yes, I am frightened in spite of the protective measure I have taken. Because, you see, we are – how shall I describe it? – we are up against ruthlessness, quick reactions, greed pushed beyond an expectable human limit and perhaps – I am not sure but I think it possible – a touch, shall we say, of madness? Not there originally, but cultivated. A seed that took root and grows fast. And now perhaps has taken charge, inspiring an inhuman rather than a human attitude to life.'

'We'll have to have a few extra opinions on this,' said the

legal man. 'We can't rush into things. Of course, a lot depends on the – er – forestry business. If that's positive, we'd have to think again.'

Hercule Poirot rose to his feet.

'I will take my leave. I have told you all that I know and all that I fear and envisage as possible. I shall remain in touch with you.'

He shook hands all round with foreign precision, and went out.

'The man's a bit of a mountebank,' said the legal man. 'You don't think he's a bit touched, do you? Touched in the head himself, I mean? Anyway, he's a pretty good age. I don't know that one can rely on the faculties of a man of that age.'

'I think you can rely upon him,' said the Chief Constable. 'At least, that is *my* impression. Spence, I've known you a good many years. You're a friend of his. Do you think he's become a little senile?'

'No, I don't,' said Superintendent Spence. 'What's your opinion, Raglan?'

'I've only met him recently, sir. At first I thought his – well, his way of talking, his ideas, might be fantastic. But on the whole I'm converted. I think he's going to be proved right.'

CHAPTER 24

I

Mrs Oliver had ensconced herself at a table in the window of The Black Boy. It was still fairly early, so the dining-room was not very full. Presently, Judith Butler returned from powdering her nose and sat down opposite her and examined the menu.

'What does Miranda like?' asked Mrs Oliver. 'We might as well order for her as well. I suppose she'll be back in a minute.'

'She likes roast chicken.'

'Well, that's easy then. What about you?'

'I'll have the same.'

'Three roast chickens,' Mrs Oliver ordered.

She leaned back, studying her friend.

'Why are you staring at me in that way?'

'I was thinking,' said Mrs Oliver.

'Thinking what?'

'Thinking really how very little I knew about you.'

'Well, that's the same with everybody, isn't it?'

'You mean, one never knows all about anyone.'

'I shouldn't think so.'

'Perhaps you're right,' said Mrs Oliver.

Both women were silent for some time.

'They're rather slow serving things here.'

'It's coming now, I think,' said Mrs Oliver.

A waitress arrived with a tray full of dishes.

'Miranda's a long time. Does she know where the dining-room is?'

'Yes, of course she does. We looked in on the way.' Judith got up impatiently. 'I'll have to go and fetch her.'

'I wonder if perhaps she gets car sick.'

'She used to when she was younger.'

She returned some four or five minutes later.

'She's not in the Ladies',' she said. 'There's a door outside it into the garden. Perhaps she went out that way to look at a bird or something. She's like that.'

'No time to look at birds today,' said Mrs Oliver. 'Go and call her or something. We want to get on.'

II

Elspeth McKay pricked some sausages with a fork, laid them on a baking dish, put it in the Frigidair and started to peel potatoes.

The telephone rang.

'Mrs McKay? Sergeant Goodwin here. Is your brother there?'

'No. He's in London today.'

'I've rung him there – he's left. When he gets back, tell him we've had a positive result.'

'You mean you've found a body in the well?'

'Not much use clamming up about it. The word's got around already.'

'Who is it? The *au pair* girl?'

'Seems like it.'

'Poor girl,' said Elspeth. 'Did she throw herself in – or what?'

'It wasn't suicide – she was knifed. It was murder all right.'

III

After her mother had left the Ladies' Room, Miranda waited for a minute or two. Then she opened the door, cautiously peered out, opened the side door to the garden which was close at hand and ran down the garden path that led round to the back yard of what had once been a coaching inn and was now a garage. She went out at a small door that enabled pedestrians to get into a lane outside. A little farther down the lane a car was parked. A man with beetling grey eyebrows and a grey beard was sitting in it reading a newspaper. Miranda opened the door and climbed in beside the driving-seat. She laughed.

'You do look funny.'

'Have a hearty laugh, there's nothing to stop you.'

The car started, went down the lane, turned right, turned left, turned right again and came out on a secondary road.

'We're all right for time,' said the grey-bearded man. 'At the right moment you'll see the double axe as it ought to be seen. And Kilterbury Down, too. Wonderful view.'

A car dashed past them so closely that they were almost forced into the hedge.

'Young idiots,' said the grey-bearded man.

One of the young men had long hair reaching over his shoulders and large, owlish spectacles. The other one affected a more Spanish appearance with side-burns.

'You don't think Mummy will worry about me?' asked Miranda.

'She won't have time to worry about you. By the time she worries about you, you'll have got where you want to be.'

IV

In London, Hercule Poirot picked up the telephone. Mrs Oliver's voice came over.

'We've lost Miranda.'

'What do you mean, lost her?'

'We had lunch at The Black Boy. She went to the loo. She didn't come back. Somebody said they saw her driving away with an elderly man. But it mightn't have been her. It might have been someone else. It –'

'Someone should have stayed with her. Neither of you ought

to have let her out of your sight. I told you there was danger. Is Mrs Butler very worried?'

'Of course she's worried. What do you think? She's frantic. She insists on ringing the police.'

'Yes, that would be the natural thing to do. I will ring them also.'

'But why should Miranda be in danger?'

'Don't you know? You ought to by now.' He added, 'The body's been found. I've just heard –'

'What body?'

'A body in a well.'

CHAPTER 25

'It's beautiful,' said Miranda, looking round her.

Kilterbury Ring was a local beauty spot though its remains were not particularly famous. They had been dismantled many hundreds of years ago. Yet here and there a tall megalithic stone still stood, upright, telling of a long past ritual worship. Miranda asked questions.

'Why did they have all these stones here?'

'For ritual. Ritual worship. Ritual sacrifice. You understand about sacrifice, don't you, Miranda?'

'I think so.'

'It has to be, you see. It's important.'

'You mean, it's *not* a sort of punishment? It's something else?'

'Yes, it's something else. You die so that others should live. You die so that beauty should live. Should come into being. That's the important thing.'

'I thought perhaps –'

'Yes, Miranda?'

'I thought perhaps you ought to die because what you've done has killed someone else.'

'What put that into your head?'

'I was thinking of Joyce. If I hadn't told her about something, she wouldn't have died, would she?'

'Perhaps not.'

'I've felt worried since Joyce died. I needn't have told her, need I? I told her because I wanted to have something worth while telling her. She'd been to India and she kept talking about it – about the tigers and about the elephants and their gold hangings and decorations and their trappings. And I think, too – suddenly I wanted somebody else to know, because you see I hadn't really thought about it before.' She added: 'Was – was *that* a sacrifice, too?'

'In a way.'

Miranda remained contemplative, then she said, 'Isn't it time yet?'

'The sun is not quite right yet. Another five minutes, perhaps, and then it will fall directly on the stone.'

Again they sat silent, beside the car.

'*Now*, I think,' said Miranda's companion, looking up at the sky where the sun was dipping towards the horizon. 'Now is a wonderful moment. No one here. Nobody comes up at this time of day and walks up to the top of Kilterbury Down to see Kilterbury Ring. Too cold in November and the blackberries are over. I'll show you the double axe first. The double axe on the stone. Carved there when they came from Mycenae or from Crete hundreds of years ago. It's wonderful, Miranda, isn't it?'

'Yes, it's very wonderful,' said Miranda. 'Show it me.'

They walked up to the topmost stone. Beside it lay a fallen one and a little farther down the slope a slightly inclined one leant as though bent with the weariness of years.

'Are you happy, Miranda?'

'Yes, I'm very happy.'

'There's the sign *here*.'

'Is that really the double axe?'

'Yes, it's worn with time but that's it. That's the symbol. Put your hand on it. And now – now we will drink to the past and the future and to beauty.'

'Oh, how lovely,' said Miranda.

A golden cup was put into her hand, and from a flask her companion poured a golden liquid into it.

'It tastes of fruit, of peaches. Drink it, Miranda, and you will be happier still.'

Miranda took the gilt cup. She sniffed at it.

'Yes. Yes, it does smell of peaches. Oh look, there's the sun. Really red gold – looking as though it was lying on the edge of the world.'

He turned her towards it.

'Hold the cup and *drink*.'

She turned obediently. One hand was still on the megalithic stone and its semi-erased sign. Her companion now was standing behind her. From below the inclined stone down the hill, two figures slipped out, bent half double. Those on the summit had their backs to them, and did not even notice them. Quickly but stealthily they ran up the hill.

'Drink to beauty, Miranda.'

'*Like hell she does!*' said a voice behind them.

A rose velvet coat shot over a head, a knife was knocked from the hand that was slowly rising. Nicholas Ransom caught hold of Miranda, clasping her tightly and dragging her away from the other two who were struggling.

'You bloody little idiot,' said Nicholas Ransom. 'Coming up here with a barmy murderer. You should have known what you were doing.'

'I did in a way,' said Miranda. 'I was going to be a sacrifice, I think, because you see it was all my fault. It was because of me that Joyce was killed. So it was right for me to be a sacrifice, wasn't it? It would be a kind of ritual killing.'

'Don't start talking nonsense about ritual killings. They've found that other girl. You know, the *au pair* girl who has been missing so long. A couple of years or something like that. They all thought she'd run away because she'd forged a Will. She hadn't run away. Her body was found in the well.'

'Oh!' Miranda gave a sudden cry of anguish. 'Not in the wishing well? Not in the wishing well that I wanted to find so badly? Oh, I don't want her to be in the wishing well. Who – who put her there?'

'The same person who brought you here.'

CHAPTER 26

Once again four men sat looking at Poirot. Timothy Raglan, Superintendent Spence and the Chief Constable had the pleased expectant look of a cat who is counting on a saucer of cream to materialize at any moment. The fourth man still had the expression of one who suspends belief.

'Well, Monsieur Poirot,' said the Chief Constable, taking charge of the proceedings and leaving the D.P.P. man to hold a watching brief. 'We're all here –'

Poirot made a motion with his hand. Inspector Raglan left the room and returned ushering in a woman of thirty odd, a girl, and two adolescent young men.

He introduced them to the Chief Constable. 'Mrs Butler, Miss Miranda Butler, Mr Nicholas Ransom and Mr Desmond Holland.'

Poirot got up and took Miranda's hand. 'Sit here by your mother, Miranda – Mr Richmond here who is what is called a Chief Constable, wants to ask you some questions. He wants you to answer them. It concerns something you saw – over a year ago now, nearer two years. You mentioned this to one person, and, so I understand, to one person only. Is that correct?'

'I told Joyce.'

'And what exactly did you tell Joyce?'

'That I'd seen a murder.'

'Did you tell anyone else?'

'No. But I think Leopold guessed. He listens, you know. At doors. That sort of thing. He likes knowing people's secrets.'

'You have heard that Joyce Reynolds, on the afternoon before the Hallowe'en party, claimed that she herself had seen a murder committed. Was that true?'

'No. She was just repeating what I'd told her – but pretending that it had happened to her.'

'Will you tell us now just what you did see.'

'I didn't know at first that it was a murder. I thought there had been an accident. I thought she'd fallen from up above somewhere.'

'Where was this?'

'In the Quarry Garden – in the hollow where the fountain used to be. I was up in the branches of a tree. I'd been looking at a squirrel and one has to keep very quiet, or they rush away. Squirrels are very quick.'

'Tell us what you saw.'

'A man and a woman lifted her up and were carrying her up the path. I thought they were taking her to a hospital or to the Quarry House. Then the woman stopped suddenly and said, "Someone is watching us," and stared at my tree. Somehow it made me feel frightened. I kept very still. The man said "Nonsense," and they went on. I saw there was blood on a scarf and there was a knife with blood on that – and I thought perhaps someone had tried to kill themselves – and I went on keeping very still.'

'Because you were frightened?'

'Yes, but I don't know why.'

'You didn't tell your mother?'

'No. I thought perhaps I oughtn't to have been there watching. And then the next day nobody said anything about an accident, so I forgot about it. I never thought about it again until –'

She stopped suddenly. The Chief Constable opened his mouth – then shut it. He looked at Poirot and made a very slight gesture.

'Yes, Miranda,' said Poirot, 'until what?'

'It was as though it was happening all over again. It was a green woodpecker this time, and I was being very still, watching it from behind some bushes. And those two were sitting there talking – about an island – a Greek island. She said something like, "It's all signed up. It's ours, we can go to it whenever we like. But we'd better go slow still – not rush things." And then the woodpecker flew away, and I moved. And she said – "Hush – be quiet – somebody's watching us." It was just the way she'd said it before, and she had just the same look on her face, and I was frightened again, and I remembered. And this time I *knew*. I knew it had been a murder I had seen and it had been a dead body they were carrying away to hide somewhere. You see, I wasn't a child any more. I *knew* – things and what they must mean – the blood and the knife and the dead body all limp –'

'When was this?' asked the Chief Constable. 'How long ago?'

Miranda thought for a moment.

'Last March – just after Easter.'

'Can you say definitely who these people were, Miranda?'

'Of course I can.' Miranda looked bewildered.

'You saw their faces?'

'Of course.'

'Who were they?'

'*Mrs Drake and Michael . . .*'

It was not a dramatic denunciation. Her voice was quiet, with something in it like wonder, but it carried conviction.

The Chief Constable said, 'You did not tell anyone. Why not?'

'I thought – I thought it might have been a sacrifice.'

'Who told you that?'

'Michael told me – he said sacrifices were necessary.'

Poirot said gently, 'You loved Michael?'

'Oh yes,' said Miranda, 'I loved him very much.'

CHAPTER 27

'Now I've got you here at last,' said Mrs Oliver, 'I want to know all about *everything*.'

She looked at Poirot with determination and asked severely:

'Why haven't you come sooner?'

'My excuses, Madame, I have been much occupied assisting the police with their inquiries.'

'It's criminals who do that. What on earth made you think of Rowena Drake being mixed up in a murder? Nobody else would have dreamed of it?'

'It was simple as soon as I got the vital clue.'

'What do you call the vital clue?'

'Water. I wanted someone who was at the party and who was *wet*, and who shouldn't have been wet. Whoever killed Joyce Reynolds would necessarily have got wet. You hold down a vigorous child with its head in a full bucket of water, and there will be struggling and splashing and you are bound to be wet. So something has got to happen to provide an innocent explanation of how you got wet. When everyone crowded into the dining-room for the Snapdragon, Mrs Drake took Joyce with her to the library. If your hostess asks you to come with her, naturally you go. And certainly Joyce had no suspicion of Mrs Drake. All Miranda had told her was that she had once seen a murder committed. And so Joyce was killed and her murderer was fairly well soaked with water. There must be a reason for that and she set about creating a reason. She had to get a witness as to *how* she got wet. She waited on the landing with an enormous vase of flowers filled with water. In due course Miss Whittaker came out from the Snapdragon room – it was hot in there. Mrs Drake pretended to start nervously, and let the vase go, taking care that it flooded her person as it crashed down to the hall below. She ran down the stairs and she and Miss Whittaker picked up the pieces and the flowers while Mrs Drake complained at the loss of her beautiful vase. She managed to give Miss Whittaker the impression that she had seen something or someone coming out of the room where a murder had been committed. Miss Whittaker took the statement at its face value, but when she mentioned it to Miss Emlyn, Miss Emlyn realized the really interesting thing about it. And so she urged Miss Whittaker to tell me the story.

'And *so*,' said Poirot, twirling his moustaches, 'I, too, knew who the murderer of Joyce was.'

'And all the time Joyce had never seen any murder committed at all!'

'Mrs Drake did not know that. But she had always suspected that someone had been there in the Quarry Wood when she and Michael Garfield had killed Olga Seminoff, and might have seen it happen.'

'When did *you* know it had been Miranda and not Joyce?'

'As soon as common sense forced me to accept the universal verdict that Joyce was a liar. Then Miranda was clearly indicated. She was frequently in the Quarry Wood, observing birds and squirrels. Joyce was, as Miranda told me, her best friend. She said: "We tell each other everything." Miranda was not at the party, so the compulsive liar Joyce could use the story her friend had told her of having once seen a murder committed – probably in order to impress *you*, Madame, the well-known crime writer.'

'That's right, blame it all on me.'

'No, no.'

'Rowena Drake,' mused Mrs Oliver. 'I still can't believe it of her.'

'She had all the qualities necessary. I have always wondered,' he added, 'exactly what sort of woman Lady Macbeth was. What would she be like if you met her in real life? Well, I think I *have* met her.'

'And Michael Garfield? They seem such an unlikely pair.'

'Interesting – Lady Macbeth and Narcissus, an unusual combination.'

'Lady Macbeth,' Mrs Oliver murmured thoughtfully.

'She was a handsome woman – efficient and competent – a born administrator – an unexpectedly good actress. You should have heard her lamenting over the death of the little boy Leopold and weeping large sobs into a dry handkerchief.'

'Disgusting.'

'You remember I asked you who, in your opinion, were or were not nice people.'

'Was Michael Garfield in love with her?'

'I doubt if Michael Garfield has ever loved anyone but himself. He wanted money – a lot of money. Perhaps he believed at first he could influence Mrs Llewellyn-Smythe to dote upon him to the extent of making a Will in his favour – but Mrs Llewellyn-Smythe was not that kind of woman.'

'What about the forgery? I still don't understand that. What was the point of it all?'

'It was confusing at first. Too much forgery, one might say. But if one considered it, the purpose of it was clear. You had only to consider what actually happened.

'Mrs Llewellyn-Smythe's fortune all went to Rowena Drake. The codicil produced was so obviously forged that any lawyer would spot it. It would be contested, and the evidence of experts would result in its being upset, and the original Will would stand. As Rowena Drake's husband had recently died she would inherit everything.'

'But what about the codicil that the cleaning woman witnessed?'

'My surmise is that Mrs Llewellyn-Smythe discovered that Michael Garfield and Rowena Drake were having an affair –

probably before her husband died. In her anger Mrs Llewellyn-Smythe made a codicil to her Will leaving everything to her *au pair* girl. Probably the girl told Michael about this – she was hoping to marry him.'

'I thought it was young Ferrier?'

'That was a plausible tale told me by Michael. There was no confirmation of it.'

'Then if he knew there was a real codicil why didn't he marry Olga and get hold of the money that way?'

'Because he doubted whether she really *would* get the money. There is such a thing as undue influence. Mrs Llewellyn-Smythe was an elderly woman and a sick woman also. All her preceding Wills had been in favour of her own kith and kin – good sensible Wills such as law courts approve of. This girl from foreign parts had been known to her only a year – and had no kind of claim upon her. That codicil even though genuine *could* have been upset. Besides, I doubt if Olga could have put through the purchase of a Greek island – or would even have been willing to do so. She had no influential friends, or contacts in business circles. She was attracted to Michael, but she looked upon him as a good prospect matrimonially, who would enable her to live in England – which is what she wanted to do.'

'And Rowena Drake?'

'She was infatuated. Her husband had been for many years a crippled invalid. She was middle-aged but she was a passionate woman, and into her orbit came a young man of unusual beauty. Women fell for him easily – but he wanted – not the beauty of women – but the exercise of his own creative urge to make beauty. For that he wanted money – a lot of money. As for love – he only loved himself. He was Narcissus. There is an old French song I heard many years ago –'

He hummed softly.

'Regarde, Narcisse
Regarde dans l'eau
Regarde, Narcisse, que tu es beau
Il n'y a au monde
Que la Beauté
Et la Jeunesse,

Hélas! Et la Jeunesse . . .
Regarde, Narcisse . . .
Regarde dans l'eau . . .'

'I can't believe – I simply can't believe that anyone would do murder just to make a garden on a Greek island,' said Mrs Oliver unbelievingly.

'Can't you? Can't you visualize how he held it in his mind? Bare rock, perhaps, but so shaped as to hold possibilities. Earth, cargoes of fertile earth to clothe the bare bones of the rocks – and then plants, seeds, shrubs, trees. Perhaps he read in the paper of a shipping millionaire who had created an island garden for the woman he loved. And so it came to him – *he* would make a garden, not for a woman, but – for himself.'

'It still seems to me quite mad.'

'Yes. That happens. I doubt if he even thought of his motive as sordid. He thought of it only as necessary for the creation of more beauty. He'd gone mad on creation. The beauty of the Quarry Wood, the beauty of other gardens he'd laid out and made – and now he envisaged even more – a whole island of beauty. And there was Rowena Drake, infatuated with him. What did she mean to him but the source of money with which he could create beauty. Yes – he had become mad, perhaps. Whom the gods destroy, they first drive mad.'

'He really wanted his island so much? Even with Rowena Drake tied round his neck as well? Bossing him the whole time?'

'Accidents can happen. I think one might possibly have happened to Mrs Drake in due course.'

'One more murder?'

'Yes. It started simply. Olga had to be removed because she knew about the codicil – and she was also to be the scapegoat, branded as a forger. Mrs Llewellyn-Smythe had hidden the original document, so I think that young Ferrier was given money to produce a similar forged document. So obviously forged that it would arouse suspicion at once. That sealed *his* death warrant. Lesley Ferrier, I soon decided, had had no arrangement or love affair with Olga. That was a suggestion made to me by Michael Garfield, but I think it was Michael who paid money to Lesley. It was Michael Garfield who was laying siege to the *au pair* girl's affections, warning her to keep quiet about this and not tell her employer, speaking of possible marriage in the future but at the same time marking her down cold-bloodedly as the victim whom he and Rowena Drake would need if the money was to come to them. It was not necessary for Olga Seminoff to be accused of forgery, or prosecuted. She needed only to be *suspected* of it. The forgery appeared to benefit her. It could have been done by her very easily, there was evidence to the effect that she did copy her employer's handwriting and if she was suddenly to disappear, it would be assumed that she had been not only a forger, but quite possibly might have assisted her employer to die suddenly. So on a suitable occasion Olga Seminoff died. Lesley Ferrier was killed in what is purported to have been a gang knifing or a knifing by a jealous woman. But the knife that was found in the well corresponds very closely with the knife wounds that he suffered. I knew that Olga's body must be hidden somewhere in this neighbourhood, but I had no idea where until I heard Miranda one day inquiring about a wishing well, urging Michael Garfield to take her there. And he was refusing. Shortly afterwards when I was talking to Mrs Goodbody, I said I wondered where that girl had disappeared to, and she said "Ding dong dell, pussy's in the well" and then I was quite sure the girl's body was in the wishing well. I discovered it was in the wood, in the Quarry Wood, on an incline not far from Michael Garfield's cottage and I thought that Miranda could have seen either the actual murder or the disposal of the body later. Mrs Drake and Michael feared that someone had been a witness – but they had no idea who it was – and as nothing happened they were lulled into security. They made their plans – they were in no hurry, but they set things in motion. She talked about buying land abroad – gave people the idea she wanted to get away from Woodleigh Common. Too many sad associations, referring always to her grief over her husband's death. Everything was nicely in train and then came the shock of Hallowe'en and Joyce's sudden assertion of having witnessed a murder. So now Rowena knew, or thought she knew, who it had been in the wood that day. So she acted quickly. But there was more to come. Young Leopold asked for money – there were things he wanted to buy, he said. What he guessed or knew is uncertain, but he was Joyce's brother, and so they probably thought he knew far more than he really did. And so – he, too, died.'

'You suspected her because of the water clue,' said Mrs Oliver. 'How did you come to suspect Michael Garfield?'

'He fitted,' said Poirot simply. 'And then – the last time I spoke to Michael Garfield, I was sure. He said to me, laughing – "Get thee beyond me, Satan. Go and join your police friends." And I knew then, quite certainly. *It was the other way round.* I said to myself: "*I* am leaving *you behind* me, Satan." A Satan so young and beautiful as Lucifer can appear to mortals . . .'

There was another woman in the room – until now she had not spoken, but now she stirred in her chair.

'Lucifer,' she said. 'Yes, I see now. He was always that.'

'He was very beautiful,' said Poirot, 'and he loved beauty. The beauty that he made with his brain and his imagination and his hands. To it he would sacrifice everything. In his own way, I think, he loved the child Miranda – but he was ready to sacrifice her – to save himself. He planned her death very carefully – he made of it a ritual and, as one might put it, indoctrinated her with the idea. She was to let him know if she were leaving Woodleigh Common – he instructed her to meet him at the Inn where you and Mrs Oliver lunched. She was to have been found on Kilterbury Ring – there by the sign of the double axe, with a golden goblet by her side – a ritual sacrifice.'

'Mad,' said Judith Butler. 'He must have been mad.'

'Madame, your daughter is safe – but there is something I would like to know very much.'

'I think you deserve to know anything I can tell you, Monsieur Poirot.'

'She is your daughter – *was she also Michael Garfield's daughter?*'

Judith was silent for a moment, and then she said, 'Yes.'

'But she doesn't know that?'

'No. She has no idea. Meeting him here was a pure coincidence. I knew him when I was a young girl. I fell wildly in love with him and then – and then I got afraid.'

'Afraid?'

'Yes. I don't know why. Not of anything he would do or that sort of thing, just afraid of his nature. His gentleness, but behind it, a coldness and a ruthlessness. I was even afraid of his passion for beauty and for creation in his work. I didn't tell him I was going to have a child. I left him – I went away and the baby was born. I invented the story of a pilot husband who had had a crash. I moved about rather restlessly. I came to Woodleigh Common more or less by chance. I had got contacts in Medchester where I could find secretarial work.

'And then one day Michael Garfield came here to work in the Quarry Wood. I don't think I minded. Nor did he. All that was over long ago, but later, although I didn't realize how often Miranda went there to the Wood, I *did* worry –'

'Yes,' said Poirot, 'there was a bond between them. A natural affinity. I saw the likeness between them – only Michael Garfield, the follower of Lucifer the beautiful, was evil, and your daughter has innocence and wisdom, and there is no evil in her.'

He went over to his desk and brought back an envelope. Out of it he drew a delicate pencil drawing.

'Your daughter,' he said.

Judith looked at it. It was signed 'Michael Garfield.'

'He was drawing her by the stream,' said Poirot, 'in the Quarry Wood. He drew it, he said, so that he should not forget. He was afraid of forgetting. It wouldn't have stopped him killing her, though.'

Then he pointed to a pencilled word across the top left hand corner.

'Can you read that?'

She spelt it out slowly.

'Iphigenia.'

'Yes,' said Poirot, 'Iphigenia. Agamemnon sacrificed his daughter, so that he should get a wind to take his ships to Troy. Michael would have sacrificed his daughter so that he should have a new Garden of Eden.'

'He knew what he was doing,' said Judith. 'I wonder – if he would ever have had regrets?'

Poirot did not answer. A picture was forming in his mind of a young man of singular beauty lying by the megalithic stone marked with a double axe, and still clasping in his dead fingers the golden goblet he had seized and drained when retribution had come suddenly to save his victim and to deliver him to justice.

It was so that Michael Garfield had died – a fitting death, Poirot thought – but, alas, there would be no garden blossoming on an island in the Grecian Seas . . .

Instead there would be Miranda – alive and young and beautiful.

He raised Judith's hand and kissed it.

'Goodbye, Madame, and remember me to your daughter.'

'She ought always to remember you and what she owes you.'

'Better not – some memories are better buried.'

He went on to Mrs Oliver.

'Good night, chère Madame. Lady Macbeth and Narcissus. It has been remarkably interesting. I have to thank you for bringing it to my notice –'

'That's right,' said Mrs Oliver in an exasperated voice, 'blame it all on me as usual!'

ELEPHANTS CAN REMEMBER

To Molly Myers
in return for many kindnesses

CHAPTER 1

A LITERARY LUNCHEON

Mrs Oliver looked at herself in the glass. She gave a brief, sideways look towards the clock on the mantelpiece, which she had some idea was twenty minutes slow. Then she resumed her study of her coiffure. The trouble with Mrs Oliver was – and she admitted it freely – that her styles of hairdressing were always being changed. She had tried almost everything in turn. A severe pompadour at one time, then a windswept style where you brushed back your locks to display an intellectual brow, at least she hoped the brow was intellectual. She had tried tightly arranged curls, she had tried a kind of artistic disarray. She had to admit that it did not matter very much today what her type of hairdressing was, because today she was going to do what she very seldom did, wear a hat.

On the top shelf of Mrs Oliver's wardrobe there reposed four hats. One was definitely allotted to weddings. When you went to a wedding, a hat was a 'must'. But even then Mrs Oliver kept two. One, in a round bandbox, was of feathers. It fitted closely to the head and stood up very well to sudden squalls of rain if they should overtake one unexpectedly as one passed from a car to the interior of the sacred edifice, or as so often nowadays, a registrar's office.

The other, and more elaborate, hat was definitely for attending a wedding held on a Saturday afternoon in summer. It had flowers and chiffon and a covering of yellow net attached with mimosa.

The other two hats on the shelf were of a more all-purpose character. One was what Mrs Oliver called her 'country house hat', made of tan felt suitable for wearing with tweeds of almost any pattern, with a becoming brim that you could turn up or turn down.

Mrs Oliver had a cashmere pullover for warmth and a thin pullover for hot days, either of which was suitable in colour to go with this. However, though the pullovers were frequently worn, the hat was practically never worn. Because, really, why put on a hat just to go to the country and have a meal with your friends?

The fourth hat was the most expensive of the lot and it had extraordinarily durable advantages about it. Possibly, Mrs Oliver sometimes thought, because it was so expensive. It consisted of a kind of turban of various layers of contrasting velvets, all of rather becoming pastel shades which would go with anything.

Mrs Oliver paused in doubt and then called for assistance.

'Maria,' she said, then louder, 'Maria. Come here a minute.'

Maria came. She was used to being asked to give advice on what Mrs Oliver was thinking of wearing.

'Going to wear your lovely smart hat, are you?' said Maria.

'Yes,' said Mrs Oliver. 'I wanted to know whether you think it looks best this way or the other way round.'

Maria stood back and took a look.

'Well, that's back to front you're wearing it now, isn't it?'

'Yes, I know,' said Mrs Oliver. 'I know that quite well. But I thought somehow it looked better that way.'

'Oh, why should it?' said Maria.

'Well, it's meant, I suppose. But it's got to be meant by me as well as the shop that sold it,' said Mrs Oliver.

'Why do you think it's better the wrong way round?'

'Because you get that lovely shade of blue and the dark brown, and I think that looks better than the other way which is green with the red and the chocolate colour.'

At this point Mrs Oliver removed the hat, put it on again and tried it wrong way round, right way round and sideways, which both she and Maria disapproved of.

'You can't have it the wide way. I mean, it's wrong for your face, isn't it? It'd be wrong for anyone's face.'

'No. That won't do. I think I'll have it the right way round, after all.'

'Well, I think it's safer always,' said Maria.

Mrs Oliver took off the hat. Maria assisted her to put on a well cut, thin woollen dress of a delicate puce colour, and helped her to adjust the hat.

'You look ever so smart,' said Maria.

That was what Mrs Oliver liked so much about Maria. If

given the least excuse for saying so, she always approved and gave praise.

'Going to make a speech at the luncheon, are you?' Maria asked.

'A speech!' Mrs Oliver sounded horrified. 'No, of course not. You know I never make speeches.'

'Well, I thought they always did at these here literary luncheons. That's what you're going to, isn't it? Famous writers of 1973 – or whichever year it is we've got to now.'

'I don't need to make a speech,' said Mrs Oliver. 'Several other people who *like* doing it will be making speeches, and they are much better at it than I would be.'

'I'm sure you'd make a lovely speech if you put your mind to it,' said Maria, adjusting herself to the rôle of a tempter.

'No, I shouldn't,' said Mrs Oliver. 'I know what I can do and I know what I can't. I can't make speeches. I get all worried and nervy and I should probably stammer or say the same thing twice. I should not only feel silly, I should probably look silly. Now it's all right with words. You can write words down or speak them into a machine or dictate them. I can do things with words so long as I know it's not a speech I'm making.'

'Oh well. I hope everything'll go all right. But I'm sure it will. Quite a grand luncheon, isn't it?'

'Yes,' said Mrs Oliver, in a deeply depressed voice. 'Quite a grand luncheon.'

And why, she thought, but did not say, why on earth am I going to it? She searched her mind for a bit because she always really liked knowing what she was going to do instead of doing it first and wondering why she had done it afterwards.

'I suppose,' she said, again to herself and not to Maria, who had had to return rather hurriedly to the kitchen, summoned by a smell of overflowing jam which she happened to have on the stove, 'I wanted to see what it felt like. I'm always being asked to literary lunches or something like that and I never go.'

Mrs Oliver arrived at the last course of the grand luncheon with a sigh of satisfaction as she toyed with the remains of the meringue on her plate. She was particularly fond of meringues and it was a delicious last course in a very delicious luncheon.

Nevertheless, when one reached middle age, one had to be careful with meringues. One's teeth? They looked all right, they had the great advantage that they could not ache, they were white and quite agreeable-looking – just like the real thing. But it was true enough that they were *not* real teeth. And teeth that were not real teeth – or so Mrs Oliver believed – were not really of high class material. Dogs, she had always understood, had teeth of real ivory, but human beings had teeth merely of bone. Or, she supposed, if they were false teeth, of plastic. Anyway, the point was that you mustn't get involved in some rather shame-making appearance, which false teeth might lead you into. Lettuce was a difficulty, and salted almonds, and such things as chocolates with hard centres, clinging caramels and the delicious stickiness and adherence of meringues. With a sigh of satisfaction, she dealt with the final mouthful. It had been a good lunch, a very good lunch.

Mrs Oliver was fond of her creature comforts. She had enjoyed the luncheon very much. She had enjoyed the company, too. The luncheon, which had been given to celebrated female writers, had fortunately not been confined to female writers only. There had been other writers, and critics, and those who read books as well as those who wrote them. Mrs Oliver had sat between two very charming members of the male sex. Edwin Aubyn, whose poetry she always enjoyed, an extremely entertaining person who had had various entertaining experiences in his tours abroad, and various literary and personal adventures. Also he was interested in restaurants and food and they had talked very happily about food, and left the subject of literature aside.

Sir Wesley Kent, on her other side, had also been an agreeable luncheon companion. He had said very nice things about her books, and had had the tact to say things that did not make her feel embarrassed, which many people could do almost without trying. He had mentioned one or two reasons why he had liked one or other of her books, and they had been the right reasons, and therefore Mrs Oliver had thought favourably of him for that reason. Praise from men, Mrs Oliver thought to herself, is always acceptable. It was women who gushed. Some of the things that women wrote to her! Really! Not always women, of course. Sometimes emotional young men from very far away countries. Only last week she had received a fan letter beginning 'Reading your book, I feel what a noble woman you must be.' After reading *The Second Goldfish* he had then gone off into an intense kind of literary ecstasy which was, Mrs Oliver felt, completely unfitting. She was not unduly modest. She thought the detective stories she wrote were quite good of their kind. Some were not so good and some were much better than others. But there was no reason, so far as she could see, to make anyone think that she was a noble woman. She was a lucky woman who had established a happy knack of writing what quite a lot of people wanted to read. Wonderful luck that was, Mrs Oliver thought to herself.

Well, all things considered, she had got through this ordeal very well. She had quite enjoyed herself, talked to some nice people. Now they were moving to where coffee was being handed round and where you could change partners and chat with other people. This was the moment of danger, as Mrs Oliver knew well. This was now where other women would come and attack her. Attack her with fulsome praise, and where she always felt lamentably inefficient at giving the right answers because there weren't really any right answers that you could give. It went really rather like a travel book for going abroad with the right phrases.

Question: 'I *must* tell you how very fond I am of reading your books and how wonderful I think they are.'

Answer from flustered author, 'Well, that's very kind. I am so glad.'

'You must understand that I've been waiting to meet you for months. It really is wonderful.'

'Oh, it's very nice of you. Very nice indeed.'

It went on very much like that. Neither of you seemed to be able to talk about anything of outside interest. It had to be all about your books, or the other woman's books if you knew what her books were. You were in the literary web and you weren't good at this sort of stuff. Some people could do it, but Mrs Oliver was bitterly aware of not having the proper capacity. A foreign friend of hers had once put her, when she was staying at an embassy abroad, through a kind of course.

'I listen to you,' Albertina had said in her charming, low, foreign voice, 'I have listened to what you say to that young man who came from the newspaper to interview you. You have not got – no! you have not got the pride you should have in your work.

You should say "Yes, I write well. I write better than anyone else who writes detective stories."'

'But I don't,' Mrs Oliver had said at that moment. 'I'm not bad, but –'

'Ah, do not say "I don't" like that. You must say you *do*; even if you do not think you do, you ought to *say* you do.'

'I wish, Albertina,' said Mrs Oliver, 'that you could interview these journalists who come. You would do it so well. Can't you pretend to be me one day, and I'll listen behind the door?'

'Yes, I suppose I could do it. It would be rather fun. But they would know I was not you. They know your face. But you must say "Yes, yes, I know that I am better than anyone else." You must say that to everybody. They should know it. They should announce it. Oh yes – it is terrible to hear you sitting there and say things as though you *apologize* for what you are. It must not be like that.'

It had been rather, Mrs Oliver thought, as though she had been a budding actress trying to learn a part, and the director had found her hopelessly bad at taking direction. Well, anyway, there'd be not much difficulty here. There'd be a few waiting females when they all got up from the table. In fact, she could see one or two hovering already. That wouldn't matter much. She would go and smile and be nice and say 'So kind of you. I'm so pleased. One is so glad to know people like one's books.' All the stale old things. Rather as you put a hand into a box and took out some useful words already strung together like a necklace of beads. And then, before very long now, she could leave.

Her eyes went round the table because she might perhaps see some friends there as well as would-be admirers. Yes, she did see in the distance Maurine Grant, who was great fun. The moment came, the literary women and the attendant cavaliers who had also attended the lunch, rose. They streamed towards chairs, towards coffee tables, towards sofas, and confidential corners. The moment of peril, Mrs Oliver often thought of it to herself, though usually at cocktail and not literary parties because she seldom went to the latter. At any moment the danger might arise, as someone whom you did not remember but who remembered you, or someone whom you definitely did not want to talk to but whom you found you could not avoid. In this case it was the first dilemma that came to her. A large woman. Ample proportions, large white champing teeth. What in French could have been called *une femme formidable*, but who definitely had not only the French variety of being formidable, but the English one of being supremely bossy. Obviously she either knew Mrs Oliver, or was intent on making her acquaintance there and then. The last was how it happened to go.

'Oh, Mrs Oliver,' she said in a high-pitched voice. 'What a pleasure to meet you today. I have wanted to for so long. I simply adore your books. So does my son. And my husband used to insist on never travelling without at least two of your books. But come, do sit down. There are so many things I want to ask you about.'

Oh well, thought Mrs Oliver, not my favourite type of woman, this. But as well her as any other.

She allowed herself to be conducted in a firm way rather as a police officer might have done. She was taken to a settee for two across a corner, and her new friend accepted coffee and placed coffee before her also.

'There. Now we are settled. I don't suppose you know my name. I am Mrs Burton-Cox.'

'Oh yes,' said Mrs Oliver, embarrassed, as usual. Mrs Burton-Cox? Did she write books also? No, she couldn't really remember anything about her. But she seemed to have heard the name. A faint thought came to her. A book on politics, something like that? Not fiction, not fun, not crime. Perhaps a high-brow intellectual with political bias? That ought to be easy, Mrs Oliver thought. with relief. I can just let her talk and say 'How interesting!' from time to time.

'You'll be very surprised, really, at what I'm going to say,' said Mrs Burton-Cox. 'But I have felt, from reading your books, how sympathetic you are, how much you understand of human nature. And I feel that if there is anyone who can give me an answer to the question I want to ask, you will be the one to do so.'

'I don't think, really . . .' said Mrs Oliver, trying to think of suitable words to say that she felt very uncertain of being able to rise to the heights demanded of her.

Mrs Burton-Cox dipped a lump of sugar in her coffee and crunched it in a rather carnivorous way, as though it was a bone.

Ivory teeth, perhaps, thought Mrs Oliver vaguely. Ivory? Dogs had ivory, walruses had ivory and elephants had ivory, of course. Great big tusks of ivory. Mrs Burton-Cox was saying:

'Now the first thing I must ask you – I'm pretty sure I am right, though – you have a goddaughter, haven't you? A goddaughter who's called Celia Ravenscroft?'

'Oh,' said Mrs Oliver, rather pleasurably surprised. She felt she could deal perhaps with a goddaughter. She had a good many goddaughters – and godsons, for that matter. There were times, she had to admit as the years were growing upon her, when she couldn't remember them all. She had done her duty in due course, one's duty being to send toys to your godchildren at Christmas in their early years, to visit them and their parents, or to have them visit you during the course of their upbringing, to take the boys out from school perhaps, and the girls also. And then, when the crowning days came, either the twenty-first birthday at which a godmother must do the right thing and let it be acknowledged to be done, and do it handsomely, or else marriage which entailed the same type of gift and a financial or other blessing. After that godchildren rather receded into the middle or far distance. They married or went abroad to foreign countries, foreign embassies, or taught in foreign schools or took up social projects. Anyway, they faded little by little out of your life. You were pleased to see them if they suddenly, as it were, floated up on the horizon again. But you had to remember to think when you had seen them last, whose daughters they were, what link had led to your being chosen as a godmother.

'Celia Ravenscroft,' said Mrs Oliver, doing her best. 'Yes, yes, of course. Yes, definitely.'

Not that any picture rose before her eyes of Celia Ravenscroft, not, that is, since a very early time. The christening. She'd gone to Celia's christening and had found a very nice Queen Anne silver strainer as a christening present. Very nice. Do nicely for straining milk and would also be the sort of thing a goddaughter could always sell for a nice little sum if she wanted ready money at any time. Yes, she remembered the strainer very well indeed. Queen Anne – Seventeen-eleven it had been. Britannia mark. How much easier it was to remember silver coffee-pots or strainers or christening mugs than it was the actual child.

'Yes,' she said, 'yes, of course. I'm afraid I haven't seen Celia for a very long time now.'

'Ah yes. She is, of course, a rather impulsive girl,' said Mrs Burton-Cox. 'I mean, she's changed her ideas very often. Of course, very intellectual, did very well at university, but – her political notions – I suppose all young people have political notions nowadays.'

'I'm afraid I don't deal much with politics,' said Mrs Oliver, to whom politics had always been anathema.

'You see, I'm going to confide in you. I'm going to tell you exactly what it is I want to know. I'm sure you won't mind. I've heard from so many people how kind you are, how willing always.'

I wonder if she's going to try and borrow money from me, thought Mrs Oliver, who had known many interviews that began with this kind of approach.

'You see, it is a matter of the greatest moment to me. Something that I really feel I *must* find out. Celia, you see, is going to marry – or thinks she is going to marry – my son, Desmond.'

'Oh, indeed!' said Mrs Oliver.

'At least, that is their idea at present. Of course, one has to know about people, and there's something I want very much to know. It's an extraordinary thing to ask anyone and I couldn't go – well, I mean, I couldn't very well go and ask a stranger, but I don't feel you are a stranger, dear Mrs Oliver.'

Mrs Oliver thought, I wish you did. She was getting nervous now. She wondered if Celia had had an illegitimate baby or was going to have an illegitimate baby, and whether she, Mrs Oliver, was supposed to know about it and give details. That would be very awkward. On the other hand, thought Mrs Oliver, I haven't seen her now for five or six years and she must be about twenty-five or -six, so it would be quite easy to say I don't know anything.

Mrs Burton-Cox leaned forward and breathed hard.

'I want you to tell me because I'm sure you must know or perhaps have a very good idea how it all came about. Did her mother kill her father or was it the father who killed the mother?'

Whatever Mrs Oliver had expected, it was certainly not that. She stared at Mrs Burton-Cox unbelievingly.

'But I don't –' She stopped. 'I – I can't understand. I mean – what reason –'

'Dear Mrs Oliver, you must *know* . . . I mean, such a famous case . . . Of course, I know it's a long time ago now, well, I suppose ten – twelve years at least, but it did cause a lot of attention at the time. I'm sure you'll remember, you *must* remember.'

Mrs Oliver's brain was working desperately. Celia was her goddaughter. That was quite true. Celia's mother – yes, of course. Celia's mother had been Molly Preston-Grey, who had been a friend of hers, though not a particularly intimate one, and of course she had married a man in the Army, yes – what was his name – Sir Something Ravenscroft. Or was he an ambassador? Extraordinary, one couldn't remember these things. She couldn't even remember whether she herself had been Molly's bridesmaid. She thought she had. Rather a smart wedding at the Guards Chapel or something like that. But one *did* forget so. And after that she hadn't met them for years – they'd been out somewhere – in the Middle East? In Persia? In Iraq? One time in Egypt? Malaya? Very occasionally, when they had been visiting England, she met them again. But they'd been like one of those photographs that one takes and looks at. One knows the people vaguely who are in it but it's so faded that you really can't recognize them or remember who they were. And she couldn't remember now whether Sir Something Ravenscroft and Lady Ravenscroft, born Molly Preston-Grey, had entered much into her life. She didn't think so. But then . . . Mrs Burton-Cox was still looking at her. Looking at her as though disappointed in her lack of *savoir-faire*, her inability to remember what had evidently been a *cause célèbre*.

'Killed? You mean – an accident?'

'Oh no. Not an accident. In one of those houses by the sea. Cornwall, I think. Somewhere where there were rocks. Anyway, they had a house down there. And they were both found on the cliff there and they'd been shot, you know. But there was nothing really by which the police could tell whether the wife shot the husband and then shot herself, or whether the husband shot the wife and then shot himself. They went into the evidence of the – you know – of the bullets and the various things, but it was very difficult. They thought it might be a suicide pact and – I forget what the verdict was. Something – it could have been misadventure or something like that. But of course everyone knew it must have been *meant*, and there were a lot of stories that went about, of course, at the time –'

'Probably all invented ones,' said Mrs Oliver hopefully, trying to remember even one of the stories if she could.

'Well, maybe. Maybe. It's very hard to say, I know. There were tales of a quarrel either that day or before, there was some talk of another man, and then of course there was the usual talk about some other woman. And one never knows which way it was about. I think things were hushed up a good deal because General Ravenscroft's position was rather a high one, and I think it was said that he'd been in a nursing home that year, and he'd been very run down or something, and that he really didn't know what he was doing.'

'I'm really afraid,' said Mrs Oliver, speaking firmly, 'that I must say that I don't know anything about it. I do remember, now you mention it, that there was such a case, and I remember the names and that I knew the people, but I never knew what happened or anything at all about it. And I really don't think I have the least idea . . .'

And really, thought Mrs Oliver, wishing she was brave enough to say it, how on earth *you* have the impertinence to ask me such a thing I don't know.

'It's very important that I should know,' Mrs Burton-Cox said.

Her eyes, which were rather like hard marbles, started to snap.

'It's important, you see, because of my boy, my dear boy wanting to marry Celia.'

'I'm afraid I can't help you,' said Mrs Oliver. 'I've never heard anything.'

'But you *must* know,' said Mrs Burton-Cox. 'I mean, you write these wonderful stories, you know all about crime. You know who commits crimes and why they do it, and I'm sure that all sorts of people will tell you the story behind the story, as one so much thinks of these things.'

'I don't know anything,' said Mrs Oliver, in a voice which no longer held very much politeness, and definitely now spoke in tones of distaste.

'But you do see that really one doesn't know who to go to ask about it? I mean, one couldn't go to the police after all these years, and I don't suppose they'd tell you anyway because obviously they were trying to hush it up. But I feel it's important to get the *truth*.'

'I only write books,' said Mrs Oliver coldly. 'They are entirely fictional. I know nothing personally about crime and have no opinions on criminology. So I'm afraid I can't help you in *any* way.'

'But you could ask your goddaughter. You could ask Celia.'

'Ask Celia!' Mrs Oliver stared again. 'I don't see how I could do *that*. She was – why, I think she must have been quite a child when this tragedy happened.'

'Oh, I expect she knew all about it, though,' said Mrs Burton-Cox. 'Children always know everything. And she'd tell you. I'm sure she'd tell *you*.'

'You'd better ask her yourself, I should think,' said Mrs Oliver.

'I don't think I could really do that,' said Mrs Burton-Cox. 'I don't think, you know, that Desmond would like it. You know he's rather – well, he's rather touchy where Celia is concerned and I really don't think that – no – I'm sure she'd tell you.'

'I really shouldn't dream of asking her,' said Mrs Oliver. She made a pretence of looking at her watch. 'Oh dear,' she said, 'what a long time we've been over this delightful lunch. I must run now, I have a very important appointment. Goodbye, Mrs – er – Bedley-Cox, so sorry I can't help you but these things are rather delicate and – does it really make any difference anyway, from your point of view?'

'Oh, I think it makes *all* the difference.'

At that moment, a literary figure whom Mrs Oliver knew well drifted past. Mrs Oliver jumped up to catch her by the arm.

'Louise, my dear, how lovely to see you. I hadn't noticed you were here.'

'Oh, Ariadne, it's a long time since I've seen *you*. You've grown a lot thinner, haven't you?'

'What nice things you always say to me,' said Mrs Oliver, engaging her friend by the arm and retreating from the settee. 'I'm rushing away because I've got an appointment.'

'I suppose you got tied up with that awful woman, didn't you?' said her friend, looking over her shoulder at Mrs Burton-Cox.

'She was asking me the most extraordinary questions,' said Mrs Oliver.

'Oh. Didn't you know how to answer them?'

'No. They weren't any of my business anyway. I didn't know anything about them. Anyway, I wouldn't have wanted to answer them.'

'Was it about anything interesting?'

'I suppose,' said Mrs Oliver, letting a new idea come into her head. 'I suppose it might be interesting, only –'

'She's getting up to chase you,' said her friend. 'Come along. I'll see you get out and give you a lift to anywhere you want to go if you haven't got your car here.'

'I never take my car about in London, it's so awful to park.'

'I know it is. Absolutely deadly.'

Mrs Oliver made the proper goodbyes. Thanks, words of greatly expressed pleasure, and presently was being driven round a London square.

'Eaton Terrace, isn't it?' said the kindly friend.

'Yes,' said Mrs Oliver, 'but where I've got to go now is – I think it's Whitefriars Mansions. I can't quite remember the name of it, but I know where it is.'

'Oh, flats. Rather modern ones. Very square and geometrical.'

'That's right,' said Mrs Oliver.

CHAPTER 2

FIRST MENTION OF ELEPHANTS

Having failed to find her friend Hercule Poirot at home, Mrs Oliver had to resort to a telephone enquiry.

'Are you by any chance going to be at home this evening?' asked Mrs Oliver.

She sat by her telephone, her fingers tapping rather nervously on the table.

'Would that be –?'

'Ariadne Oliver,' said Mrs Oliver, who was always surprised to find she had to give her name because she always expected all her friends to know her voice as soon as they heard it.

'Yes, I shall be at home all this evening. Does that mean that I may have the pleasure of a visit from you?'

'It's very nice of you to put it that way,' said Mrs Oliver. 'I don't know that it will be such a pleasure.'

'It is always a pleasure to see you, *chère Madame*.'

'I don't know,' said Mrs Oliver. 'I might be going to – well, bother you rather. Ask things. I want to know what you think about something.'

'That I am always ready to tell anyone,' said Poirot.

'Something's come up,' said Mrs Oliver. 'Something tiresome and I don't know what to do about it.'

'And so you will come and see me. I am flattered. Highly flattered.'

'What time would suit you?' said Mrs Oliver.

'Nine o'clock? We will drink coffee together, perhaps, unless you prefer a Grenadine or a *Sirop de Cassis*. But no, you do not like that. I remember.'

'George,' said Poirot, to his invaluable manservant, 'we are to receive tonight the pleasure of a visit from Mrs Oliver. Coffee, I think, and perhaps a liqueur of some kind. I am never sure what she likes.'

'I have seen her drink kirsch, sir.'

'And also, I think, *crème de menthe*. But kirsch, I think, is what she prefers. Very well then,' said Poirot. 'So be it.'

Mrs Oliver came punctual to time. Poirot had been wondering, while eating his dinner, what it was that was driving Mrs Oliver to visit him, and why she was so doubtful about what she was doing. Was she bringing him some difficult problem, or was she acquainting him with a crime? As Poirot knew well, it could be anything with Mrs Oliver. The most commonplace things or the most extraordinary things. They were, as you might say, all alike to her. She was worried, he thought. Ah well, Hercule Poirot thought to himself, he could deal with Mrs Oliver. He always had been able to deal with Mrs Oliver. On occasion she maddened him. At the same time he was really very much attached to her.

They had shared many experiences and experiments together. He had read something about her in the paper only that morning – or was it the evening paper? He must try and remember it before she came. He had just done so when she was announced.

She came into the room and Poirot deduced at once that his diagnosis of worry was true enough. Her hair-do, which was fairly elaborate, had been ruffled by the fact that she had been running her fingers through it in the frenzied and feverish way that she did sometimes. He received her with every sign of pleasure, established her in a chair, poured her some coffee and handed her a glass of kirsch.

'Ah!' said Mrs Oliver, with the sigh of someone who has relief. 'I expect you're going to think I'm awfully silly, but still . . .'

'I see, or rather, I saw in the paper that you were attending a literary luncheon today. Famous women writers. Something of that kind. I thought you never did that kind of thing.'

'I don't usually,' said Mrs Oliver, 'and I shan't ever do it again.'

'Ah. You suffered much?' Poirot was quite sympathetic.

He knew Mrs Oliver's embarrassing moments. Extravagant praise of her books always upset her highly because, as she had once told him, she never knew the proper answers.

'You did not enjoy it?'

'Up to a point I did,' said Mrs Oliver, 'and then something very tiresome happened.'

'Ah. And that is what you have come to see me about.'

'Yes, but I really don't know why. I mean, it's nothing to do with you and I don't think it's the sort of thing you'd even be interested in. And I'm not really interested in it. At least, I suppose I must be or I wouldn't have wanted to come to you to know what you thought. To know what – well, what you'd do if you were me.'

'That is a very difficult question, that last one,' said Poirot. 'I know how I, Hercule Poirot, would act in anything, but I do not know how you would act, well though I know you.'

'You must have some idea by this time,' said Mrs Oliver. 'You've known me long enough.'

'About what – twenty years now?'

'Oh, I don't know. I can never remember what years are, what dates are. You know, I get mixed up. I know 1939 because that's when the war started and I know other dates because of queer things, here and there.'

'Anyway, you went to your literary luncheon. And you did not enjoy it very much.'

'I enjoyed the lunch but it was afterwards . . .'

'People said things to you,' said Poirot, with the kindliness of a doctor demanding symptoms.

'Well, they were just getting ready to say things to me. Suddenly one of those large, bossy women who always manage to dominate everyone and who can make you feel more uncomfortable than anyone else, descended on me. You know, like somebody who catches a butterfly or something, only she'd have needed a butterfly-net. She sort of rounded me up and pushed me on to a settee and then she began to talk to me, starting about a goddaughter of mine.'

'Ah yes. A goddaughter you are fond of?'

'I haven't seen her for a good many years,' said Mrs Oliver, 'I can't keep up with all of them, I mean. And then she asked me a most worrying question. She wanted me – oh dear, how very difficult it is for me to tell this –'

'No, it isn't,' said Poirot kindly. 'It is quite easy. Everyone tells everything to me sooner or later. I'm only a foreigner, you see, so it does not matter. It is easy because I am a foreigner.'

'Well, it is rather easy to say things to you,' said Mrs Oliver. 'You see, she asked me about the girl's father and mother. She asked me whether her mother had killed her father or her father had killed her mother.'

'I beg your pardon,' said Poirot.

'Oh, I know it sounds mad. Well, I thought it was mad.'

'Whether your goddaughter's mother had killed her father, or whether her father had killed her mother.'

'That's right,' said Mrs Oliver.

'But – was that a matter of fact? Had her father killed her mother or her mother killed her father?'

'Well, they were both found shot,' said Mrs Oliver. 'On the top of a cliff. I can't remember if it was in Cornwall or in Corsica. Something like that.'

'Then it was true, then, what she said?'

'Oh yes, that part of it was true. It happened years ago. Well, but I mean – why come to me?'

'All because you were a crime writer,' said Poirot. 'She no doubt said you knew all about crime. This was a real thing that happened?'

'Oh yes. It wasn't something like what would A do – or what would be the proper procedure if your mother had killed your father or your father had killed your mother. No, it was something that really happened. I suppose really I'd better tell you all about it. I mean, I can't remember all about it but it was quite well known at the time. It was about – oh, I should think it was about twelve years ago at least. And, as I say, I can remember the names of the people because I did know them. The wife had been at school with me and I'd known her quite well. We'd been friends. It was a well-known case – you know, it was in all the papers and things like that. Sir Alistair Ravenscroft and Lady Ravenscroft. A very happy couple and he was a colonel or a general and she'd been with him and they'd been all over the world. Then they bought this house somewhere – I think it was abroad but I can't remember. And then there were suddenly accounts of this case in the papers. Whether somebody else had killed them or whether they'd been assassinated or something, or whether they killed each other. I think it was a revolver that had been in the house for ages and – well, I'd better tell you as much as I can remember.'

Pulling herself slightly together, Mrs Oliver managed to give Poirot a more or less clear *résumé* of what she had been told. Poirot from time to time checked on a point here or there.

'But why?' he said finally, 'why should this woman want to know this?'

'Well, that's what I want to find out,' said Mrs Oliver. 'I could get hold of Celia, I think. I mean, she still lives in London. Or perhaps it's Cambridge she lives in, or Oxford – I think she's got a degree and either lectures here or teaches somewhere, or does something like that. And – very modern, you know. Goes about with long-haired people in queer clothes. I don't think she takes drugs. She's quite all right and – just very occasionally I hear from her. I mean, she sends a card at Christmas and things like that. Well, one doesn't think of one's godchildren all the time, and she's quite twenty-five or -six.'

'Not married?'

'No. Apparently she is going to marry – or that is the idea – Mrs – What's the name of that woman again? – oh yes, Mrs Brittle – no – Burton-Cox's son.'

'And Mrs Burton-Cox does not want her son to marry this girl because her father killed her mother or her mother killed her father?'

'Well, I suppose so,' said Mrs Oliver. 'It's the only thing I can think. But what does it matter which? If one of your parents killed the other, would it really matter to the mother of the boy you were going to marry, which way round it was?'

'That is a thing one might have to think about,' said Poirot. 'It is – yes, you know it is quite interesting. I do not mean it is very interesting about Sir Alistair Ravenscroft or Lady Ravenscroft. I seem to remember vaguely – oh, some case like this one, or it might not have been the same one. But it is very strange about Mrs Burton-Cox. Perhaps she is a bit touched in the head. Is she very fond of her son?'

'Probably,' said Mrs Oliver. 'Probably she doesn't want him to marry this girl at all.'

'Because she may have inherited a predisposition to murder the man she marries – or something of that kind?'

'How do I know?' said Mrs Oliver. 'She seems to think that I can tell her, and she's really not told *me* enough, has she? But why, do you think? What's behind it all? What does it *mean*?'

'It would be almost interesting to find out,' said Poirot.

'Well, that's why I've come to you,' said Mrs Oliver. 'You like finding out things. Things that you can't see the reason for at first. I mean, that nobody can see the reason for.'

'Do you think Mrs Burton-Cox has any preference?' said Poirot.

'You mean that she'd rather the husband killed the wife, or the wife killed the husband? I don't think so.'

'Well,' said Poirot, 'I see your dilemma. It is very intriguing. You come home from a party. You've been asked to do something that is very difficult, almost impossible, and – you wonder what is the proper way to deal with such a thing.'

'Well, what would you think is the proper way?' said Mrs Oliver.

'It is not easy for me to say,' said Poirot. 'I'm not a woman. A woman whom you do not really know, whom you had met at a party, has put this problem to you, asked you to do it, giving no discernible reason.'

'Right,' said Mrs Oliver. 'Now what does Ariadne do? What does A do, in other words, if you were reading this as a problem in a newspaper?'

'Well, I suppose,' said Poirot, 'there are three things that A could do. A could write a note to Mrs Burton-Cox and say, "I'm very sorry but I really feel I cannot oblige you in this matter," or whatever words you like to put. B. You get into touch with your goddaughter and you tell her what has been asked of you by the mother of the boy, or the young man, or whatever he is, whom she is thinking of marrying. You will find out from her if she is really thinking of marrying this young man. If so, whether she has any idea or whether the young man has said anything to her about what his mother has got in her head. And there will be other interesting points, like finding out what this girl thinks of the mother of the young man she wants to marry. The third thing you could do,' said Poirot, 'and this really is what I firmly advise you to do, is . . .'

'I know,' said Mrs Oliver, 'one word.'

'Nothing,' said Poirot.

'Exactly,' said Mrs Oliver. 'I know that is the simple and proper thing to do. Nothing. It's darned cheek to go and tell a girl who's my goddaughter what her future mother-in-law is going about saying, and asking people. But –'

'I know,' said Poirot, 'it is human curiosity.'

'I want to know why that odious woman came and said what she did to me,' said Mrs Oliver. 'Once I know that I could relax and forget all about it. But until I know that . . .'

'Yes,' said Poirot, 'you won't sleep. You'll wake up in the night and, if I know you, you will have the most extraordinary and extravagant ideas which presently, probably, you will be able to make into a most attractive crime story. A whodunit – a thriller. All sorts of things.'

'Well, I suppose I could if I thought of it that way,' said Mrs Oliver. Her eyes flashed slightly.

'Leave it alone,' said Poirot. 'It will be a very difficult plot to undertake. It seems as though there could be no good reason for this.'

'But I'd like to make *sure* that there *is* no good reason.'

'Human curiosity,' said Poirot. 'Such a very interesting thing.' He sighed. 'To think what we owe to it throughout history. Curiosity. I don't know who invented curiosity. It is said to be usually associated with the cat. Curiosity killed the cat. But I should say really that the Greeks were the inventors of curiosity. They wanted to *know*. Before them, as far as I can see, nobody wanted to know *much*. They just wanted to know what the rules of the country they were living in were, and how they could avoid having their heads cut off or being impaled on spikes or something disagreeable happening to them. But they either obeyed or disobeyed. They didn't want to know *why*. But since then a lot of people have wanted to know *why* and all sorts of things have happened because of that. Boats, trains, flying machines and atom bombs and penicillin and cures for various illnesses. A little boy watches his mother's kettle raising its lid because of the steam. And the next thing we know is we have railway trains, leading on in due course to railway strikes and all that. And so on and so on.'

'Just tell me,' said Mrs Oliver, 'do you think I'm a terrible nosey-parker?'

'No, I don't,' said Poirot. 'On the whole I don't think you are a woman of great curiosity. But I can quite see you getting in a het-up state at a literary party, busy defending yourself against too much kindness, too much praise. You ran yourself instead into a very awkward dilemma, and took a very strong dislike to the person who ran you into it.'

'Yes. She's a very tiresome woman, a very disagreeable woman.'

'This murder in the past of this husband and wife who were supposed to get on well together and no apparent signs of a quarrel was known. One never really read about any cause for it, according to you?'

'They were shot. Yes, they were shot. It could have been a suicide pact. I think the police thought it was at first. Of course, one can't find out about things all those years afterwards.'

'Oh yes,' said Poirot, 'I think I could find out something about it.'

'You mean – through the exciting friends you've got?'

'Well, I wouldn't say the exciting friends, perhaps. Certainly there are knowledgeable friends, friends who could get certain records, look up the accounts that were given of the crime at the time, some access I could get to certain records.'

'You could find out things,' said Mrs Oliver hopefully, 'and then tell me.'

'Yes,' said Poirot, 'I think I could help you to know at any rate the full facts of the case. It'll take a little time, though.'

'I can see that if you do that, which is what I want you to do, *I've* got to do something myself. I'll have to see the girl. I've got to see whether she knows anything about all this, ask her if she'd like me to give her mother-in-law-to-be a raspberry or whether there is any other way in which I can help her. And I'd like to see the boy she's going to marry, too.'

'Quite right,' said Poirot. 'Excellent.'

'And I suppose,' said Mrs Oliver, 'there might be people –' She broke off, frowning.

'I don't suppose people will be very much good,' said Hercule Poirot. 'This is an affair of the past. A *cause célèbre* perhaps at the time. But what is a *cause célèbre* when you come to think of it? Unless it comes to an astonishing *dénouement*, which this one didn't. Nobody remembers it.'

'No,' said Mrs Oliver, 'that is quite true. There was a lot about it in the papers and mentions of it for some time, and then it just – faded out. Well, like things do now. Like that girl, the other day. You know, who left her home and they couldn't find her anywhere. Well, I mean, that was five or six years ago and then suddenly a little boy, playing about in a sand heap or a gravel pit or something, suddenly came across her dead body. Five or six years later.'

'That is true,' said Poirot. 'And it is true that knowing from that body how long it is since death and what happened on the particular day and going back over various events of which there is a written record, one may in the end turn up a murderer. But it will be more difficult in your problem since it seems the answer must be one of two things: that the husband disliked his wife and wanted to get rid of her, or that the wife hated her husband or else had a lover. Therefore, it might have been a passionate crime or something quite different. Anyway, there would be nothing, as it were, to find out about it. If the police could not find out at the time, then the motive must have been a difficult one, not easy to see. Therefore it has remained a nine days' wonder, that is all.'

'I suppose I can go to the daughter. Perhaps that is what that odious woman was getting me to do – wanted me to do. She thought the daughter knew – well, the daughter might have known,' said Mrs Oliver. 'Children do, you know. They know the most extraordinary things.'

'Have you any idea how old this goddaughter of yours would have been at the time?'

'Well, I have if I reckon it up, but I can't say off-hand. I think she might have been nine or ten, but perhaps older, I don't know. I think that she was away at school at the time. But that may be just my fancy, remembering back what I read.'

'But you think Mrs Burton-Cox's wish was to make you get information from the daughter? Perhaps the daughter knows something, perhaps she said something to the son, and the son said something to his mother. I expect Mrs Burton-Cox tried to question the girl herself and got rebuffed, but thought the famous Mrs Oliver, being both a godmother and also full of criminal knowledge, might obtain information. Though why it should matter to her, I still don't see,' said Poirot. 'And it does not seem to me that what you call vaguely "people" can help after all this time.' He added, 'Would anybody remember?'

'Well, that's where I think they might,' said Mrs Oliver.

'You surprise me,' said Poirot, looking at her with a somewhat puzzled face. '*Do* people remember?'

'Well,' said Mrs Oliver, 'I was really thinking of elephants.'

'Elephants?'

As he had thought often before, Poirot thought that really Mrs Oliver was the most unaccountable woman. Why suddenly elephants?

'I was thinking of elephants at the lunch yesterday,' said Mrs Oliver.

'Why were you thinking of elephants?' said Poirot, with some curiosity.

'Well, I was really thinking of teeth. You know, things one tries to eat, and if you've got some sort of false teeth – well, you can't do it very well. You know, you've got to know what you can eat and what you can't.'

'Ah!' said Poirot, with a deep sigh. 'Yes, yes. The dentists, they can do much for you, but not everything.'

'Quite so. And then I thought of – you know – our teeth being only bone and so not awfully good, and how nice it would be to be a dog, who has real ivory teeth. And then I thought of anyone else who has ivory teeth, and I thought about walruses and – oh, other things like that. And I thought about elephants. Of course when you think of ivory you do think of elephants, don't you? Great big elephant tusks.'

'That is very true,' said Poirot, still not seeing the point of what Mrs Oliver was saying.

'So I thought that what we've really got to do is to get at the people who are like elephants. Because elephants, so they say, don't forget.'

'I have heard the phrase, yes,' said Poirot.

'Elephants don't forget,' said Mrs Oliver. 'You know, a story children get brought up on? How someone, an Indian tailor, stuck a needle or something in an elephant's tusk. No. Not a tusk, his trunk, of course, an elephant's trunk. And the next time the elephant came past he had a great mouthful of water and he splashed it out all over the tailor though he hadn't seen him for several years. He hadn't forgotten. He remembered. That's the point, you see. Elephants remember. What I've got to do is – I've got to get in touch with some elephants.'

'I do not know yet if I quite see what you mean,' said Hercule Poirot. 'Who are you classifying as elephants? You sound as though you were going for information to the Zoo.'

'Well, it's not exactly like that,' said Mrs Oliver. 'Not elephants, as elephants, but the way people up to a point would resemble elephants. There are some people who *do* remember. In fact, one does remember queer things, I mean there are a lot of things that *I* remember very well. They happened – I remember a birthday party I had when I was five, and a pink cake – a lovely pink cake. It had a sugar bird on it. And I remember the day my canary flew away and I cried. And I remember another day when I went into a field and there was a bull there and somebody said it would gore me, and I was terrified and wanted to run out of the field.

Well, I remember that quite well. It was a Tuesday too. I don't know why I should remember it was a Tuesday, but it was a Tuesday. And I remember a wonderful picnic with blackberries. I remember getting pricked terribly, but getting more blackberries than anyone else. It was wonderful! By that time I was nine, I think. But one needn't go back as far as that. I mean, I've been to hundreds of weddings in my life, but when I look back on a wedding there are only two that I remember *particularly.* One where I was a bridesmaid. It took place in the New Forest, I remember, and I can't remember who was there actually. I think it was a cousin of mine getting married. I didn't know her very well but she wanted a good many bridesmaids and, well, I came in handy, I suppose. But I know another wedding. That was a friend of mine in the Navy. He was nearly drowned in a submarine, and then he was saved, and then the girl he was engaged to, her people didn't want her to marry him but then he did marry her after that and I was one of her bridesmaids at the marriage. Well, I mean, there's always things you *do* remember.'

'I see your point,' said Poirot. 'I find it interesting. So you will go *à la recherche des éléphants*?'

'That's right. I'd have to get the date right.'

'There,' said Poirot, 'I hope I may be able to help you.'

'And then I'll think of people I knew about at that time, people that I may have known who also knew the same friends that I did, who probably knew General What-not. People who may have known them abroad, but whom I also knew although I mayn't have seen them for a good many years. You can look up people, you know, that you haven't seen for a long time. Because people are always quite pleased to see someone coming up out of the past, even if they can't remember very much about you. And then you naturally will talk about the things that were happening at that date, that you remember about.'

'Very interesting,' said Poirot. 'I think you are very well equipped for what you propose to do. People who knew the Ravenscrofts either well or not very well; people who lived in the same part of the world where the things happened or who might have been staying there. More difficult, but I think one could get at it. And so, somehow or other one would try different things. Start a little talk going about what happened, what they think happened, what anyone else has ever told you about what might have happened. About any love-affairs the husband or wife had, about any money that somebody might have inherited. I think you could scratch up a lot of things.'

'Oh dear,' said Mrs Oliver. 'I'm afraid really I'm just a nosey-parker.'

'You've been given an assignment,' said Poirot, 'not by someone you like, not by someone you wish to oblige, but someone you entirely dislike. That does not matter. You are still on a quest, a quest of knowledge. You take your own path. It is the path of the elephants. The elephants *may* remember. *Bon voyage*,' said Poirot.

'I beg your pardon,' said Mrs Oliver.

'I'm sending you forth on your voyage of discovery,' said Poirot. '*À la recherche des éléphants*.'

'I expect I'm mad,' said Mrs Oliver sadly. She brushed her hands through her hair again so that she looked like the old picture books of Struwelpeter. 'I was just thinking of starting a story about a Golden Retriever. But it wasn't going well. I couldn't get started, if you know what I mean.'

'All right, abandon the Golden Retriever. Concern yourself only with elephants.'

BOOK I • ELEPHANTS

CHAPTER 3

GREAT AUNT ALICE'S GUIDE TO KNOWLEDGE

'Can you find my address book for me, Miss Livingstone?'

'It's on your desk, Mrs Oliver. In the left-hand corner.'

'I don't mean that one,' said Mrs Oliver. 'That's the one I'm using now. I mean my last one. The one I had last year, or perhaps the one before that again.'

'Has it been thrown away, perhaps?' suggested Miss Livingstone.

'No, I don't throw away address books and things like that because so often you want one. I mean some address that you haven't copied into the new one. I expect it may be in one of the drawers of the tallboys.'

Miss Livingstone was a fairly new arrival, replacing Miss Sedgwick. Ariadne Oliver missed Miss Sedgwick. Sedgwick knew so many things. She knew the places where Mrs Oliver sometimes put things, the kind of places Mrs Oliver kept things in. She remembered the names of people Mrs Oliver had written nice letters to, and the names of people that Mrs Oliver, goaded beyond endurance, had written rather rude things to. She was invaluable, or rather, had been invaluable. 'She was like – what was the book called?' Mrs Oliver said, casting her mind back. 'Oh yes, I know – a big brown book. All Victorians had it. *Enquire Within Upon Everything*. And you could too! How to take iron mark stains off linen, how to deal with curdled mayonnaise, how to start a chatty letter to a bishop. Many, many things. It was all there in *Enquire Within Upon Everything*.' Great Aunt Alice's great standby.

Miss Sedgwick had been just as good as Aunt Alice's book. Miss Livingstone was not at all the same thing. Miss Livingstone stood there always, very long-faced with a sallow skin, looking purposefully efficient. Every line of her face said 'I am very efficient.' But she wasn't really, Mrs Oliver thought. She only knew all the places where former literary employers of hers had kept things and where she clearly considered Mrs Oliver ought to keep them.

'What I want,' said Mrs Oliver, with firmness and the determination of a spoilt child, 'is my 1970 address book. And I think 1969 as well. Please look for it as quick as you can, will you?'

'Of course, of course,' said Miss Livingstone.

She looked round her with the rather vacant expression of someone who is looking for something she has never heard of before but which efficiency may be able to produce by some unexpected turn of luck.

If I don't get Sedgwick back, I shall go mad, thought Mrs Oliver to herself. I can't deal with this thing if I don't have Sedgwick.

Miss Livingstone started pulling open various drawers in the furniture in Mrs Oliver's so-called study and writing-room.

'Here is last year's,' said Miss Livingstone happily. 'That will be much more up-to-date, won't it? 1971.'

'I don't want 1971,' said Mrs Oliver.

Vague thoughts and memories came to her.

'Look in that tea-caddy table,' she said.

Miss Livingstone looked round, looking worried.

'That table,' said Mrs Oliver, pointing.

'A desk book wouldn't be likely to be in a tea-caddy,' said Miss Livingstone, pointing out to her employer the general facts of life.

'Yes, it could,' said Mrs Oliver. 'I seem to remember.'

Edging Miss Livingstone aside, she went to the tea-caddy table, raised the lid, looked at the attractive inlaid work inside. 'And it *is* here,' said Mrs Oliver, raising the lid of a papier-mâché round canister, devised to contain Lapsang Souchong as opposed to Indian tea, and taking out a curled-up small brown notebook.

'Here it is,' she said.

'That's only 1968, Mrs Oliver. Four years ago.'

'That's about right,' said Mrs Oliver, seizing it and taking it back to the desk. 'That's all for the present, Miss Livingstone, but you might see if you can find my birthday book somewhere.'

'I didn't know . . .'

'I don't use it now,' said Mrs Oliver, 'but I used to have one once. Quite a big one, you know. Started when I was a child. Goes on for years. I expect it'll be in the attic upstairs. You know, the one we use as a spare room sometimes when it's only boys coming for holidays, or people who don't mind. The sort of chest or bureau thing next to the bed.'

'Oh. Shall I look and see?'

'That's the idea,' said Mrs Oliver.

She cheered up a little as Miss Livingstone went out of the room. Mrs Oliver shut the door firmly behind her, went back to the desk and started looking down the addresses written in faded ink and smelling of tea.

'Ravenscroft. Celia Ravenscroft. Yes. 14 Fishacre Mews, S.W.3. That's the Chelsea address. She was living there then. But there was another one after that. Somewhere like Strand-on-the-Green near Kew Bridge.'

She turned a few more pages.

'Oh yes, this seems to be a later one. Mardyke Grove. That's off Fulham Road, I think. Somewhere like that. Has she got a telephone number? It's very rubbed out, but I think – yes, I think that's right – Flaxman . . . Anyway, I'll try it.'

She went across to the telephone. The door opened and Miss Livingstone looked in.

'Do you think that perhaps –'

'I found the address I want,' said Mrs Oliver. 'Go on looking for that birthday book. It's important.'

'Do you think you could have left it when you were in Sealy House?'

'No, I don't,' said Mrs Oliver. 'Go on looking.'

She murmured, as the door closed, 'Be as long as you like about it.'

She dialled the telephone and waited, opening the door to call up the stairs: 'You might try that Spanish chest. You know, the one that's bound with brass. I've forgotten where it is now. Under the table in the hall, I think.'

Mrs Oliver's first dialling was not successful. She appeared to have connected herself to a Mrs Smith Potter, who seemed both annoyed and unhelpful and had no idea what the present telephone number might be of anyone who had lived in that particular flat before.

Mrs Oliver applied herself to an examination of the address book once more. She discovered two more addresses which were hastily scrawled over other numbers and did not seem wildly helpful. However, at the third attempt a somewhat illegible Ravenscroft seemed to emerge from the crossings out and initials and addresses.

A voice admitted to knowing Celia.

'Oh dear, yes. But she hasn't lived here for *years*. I think she was in Newcastle when I last heard from her.'

'Oh dear,' said Mrs Oliver, 'I'm afraid I haven't got that address.'

'No, I haven't got it either,' said the kindly girl. 'I think she went to be secretary to a veterinary surgeon.'

It did not sound very hopeful. Mrs Oliver tried once or twice more. The addresses in the latest of her two address books were no use, so she went back a bit further. She struck oil, as you might put it, when she came to the last one, which was for the year 1967.

'Oh, you mean Celia,' said a voice. 'Celia Ravenscroft, wasn't it? Or was it Finchwell?'

Mrs Oliver just prevented herself in time from saying, 'No, and it wasn't redbreast either.'

'A very competent girl,' said the voice. 'She worked for me for over a year and a half. Oh yes, very competent. I would have been quite happy if she had stayed longer. I think she went from here to somewhere in Harley Street, but I think I've got her address somewhere. Now let me see.' There was a long pause while Mrs X – name unknown – was seeing. 'I've got one address here. It seems to be in Islington somewhere. Do you think that's possible?'

Mrs Oliver said that anything was possible and thanked Mrs X very much and wrote it down.

'So difficult, isn't it, trying to find people's addresses. They do send them to you usually. You know, a sort of postcard or something of that kind. Personally I always seem to lose it.'

Mrs Oliver said that she herself also suffered in this respect. She tried the Islington number. A heavy, foreign voice replied to her.

'You want, yes – you tell me what? Yes, who live here?'

'Miss Celia Ravenscroft?'

'Oh yes, that is very true. Yes, yes she lives here. She has a room on the second floor. She is out now and she not come home.'

'Will she be in later this evening?'

'Oh, she be home very soon now, I think, because she come home to dress for party and go out.'

Mrs Oliver thanked her for the information and rang off.

'Really,' said Mrs Oliver to herself, with some annoyance, 'girls!'

She tried to think how long it was since she had last seen her goddaughter, Celia. One lost touch. That was the whole point. Celia, she thought, was in London now. If her boyfriend was in London, or if the mother of her boyfriend was in London – all of it went together. Oh dear, thought Mrs Oliver, this really makes my head ache. 'Yes, Miss Livingstone?' she turned her head.

Miss Livingstone, looking rather unlike herself and decorated with a good many cobwebs and a general coating of dust, stood looking annoyed in the doorway holding a pile of dusty volumes.

'I don't know whether any of these things will be any use to you, Mrs Oliver. They seem to go back for a great many years.' She was disapproving.

'Bound to,' said Mrs Oliver.

'I don't know if there's anything particular you want me to search for.'

'I don't think so,' said Mrs Oliver, 'if you'll just put them on the corner of the sofa there I can look at them this evening.'

Miss Livingstone, looking more disapproving every moment, said, 'Very good, Mrs Oliver. I think I will just dust them first.'

'That will be very kind of you,' said Mrs Oliver, just stopping herself in time from saying – 'and for goodness' sake dust yourself as well. You've got six cobwebs in your left ear.'

She glanced at her watch and rang the Islington number again. The voice that answered this time was purely Anglo-Saxon and had a crisp sharpness about it that Mrs Oliver felt was rather satisfactory.

'Miss Ravenscroft? – Celia Ravenscroft?'

'Yes, this is Celia Ravenscroft.'

'Well, I don't expect you'll remember me very well. I'm Mrs Oliver. Ariadne Oliver. We haven't seen each other for a long time, but actually I'm your godmother.'

'Oh yes, of course. I know that. No, we haven't seen each other for a long time.'

'I wonder very much if I could see you, if you could come and see me, or whatever you like. Would you like to come to a meal or . . .'

'Well, it's rather difficult at present, where I'm working. I could come round this evening, if you like. About half past seven or eight. I've got a date later but . . .'

'If you do that I shall be very, very pleased,' said Mrs Oliver.

'Well, of course I will.'

'I'll give you the address.' Mrs Oliver gave it.

'Good. I'll be there. Yes, I know where that is, quite well.'

Mrs Oliver made a brief note on the telephone pad, and looked with some annoyance at Miss Livingstone, who had just come into the room struggling under the weight of a large album.

'I wondered if this could possibly be it, Mrs Oliver?'

'No, it couldn't,' said Mrs Oliver. 'That's got cookery recipes in it.'

'Oh dear,' said Miss Livingstone, 'so it has.'

'Well, I might as well look at some of them anyway,' said Mrs Oliver, removing the volume firmly. 'Go and have another look. You know, I've thought about the linen cupboard. Next door to the bathroom. You'd have to look on the top shelf above the bath towels. I do sometimes stick papers and books in there. Wait a minute. I'll come up and look myself.'

Ten minutes later Mrs Oliver was looking through the pages of a faded album. Miss Livingstone, having entered her final stage of martyrdom, was standing by the door. Unable to bear the sight of so much suffering, Mrs Oliver said,

'Well, that's all right. You might just take a look in the desk in the dining-room. The old desk. You know, the one that's broken a bit. See if you can find some more address books. Early ones. Anything up to about ten years old will be worth while having a look at. And after that,' said Mrs Oliver, 'I don't think I shall want anything more today.'

Miss Livingstone departed.

'I wonder,' said Mrs Oliver to herself, releasing a deep sigh as she sat down. She looked through the pages of the birthday book. 'Who's better pleased? She to go or I to see her go?

After Celia has come and gone, I shall have to have a busy evening.'

Taking a new exercise book from the pile she kept on a small table by her desk, she entered various dates, possible addresses and names, looked up one or two more things in the telephone book and then proceeded to ring up Monsieur Hercule Poirot.

'Ah, is that you, Monsieur Poirot?'

'Yes, madame, it is I myself.'

'Have you done anything?' said Mrs Oliver.

'I beg your pardon – have I done what?'

'Anything,' said Mrs Oliver. 'What I asked you about yesterday.'

'Yes, certainly. I have put things in motion. I have arranged to make certain enquiries.'

'But you haven't made them yet,' said Mrs Oliver, who had a poor view of what the male view was of doing something.

'And you, *chère madame*?'

'I have been very busy,' said Mrs Oliver.

'Ah! And what have you been doing, madame?'

'Assembling elephants,' said Mrs Oliver, 'if that means anything to you.'

'I think I can understand what you mean, yes.'

'It's not very easy, looking into the past,' said Mrs Oliver. 'It is astonishing, really, how many people one does remember when one comes to look up names. My word, the silly things they write in birthday books sometimes, too. I can't think why when I was about sixteen or seventeen or even thirty, I wanted people to write in my birthday book. There's a sort of quotation from a poet for every particular day in the year. Some of them are terribly silly.'

'You are encouraged in your search?'

'Not quite encouraged,' said Mrs Oliver. 'But I still think I'm on the right lines. I've rung up my goddaughter –'

'Ah. And you are going to see her?'

'Yes, she is coming to see me. Tonight between seven and eight, if she doesn't run out on me. One never knows. Young people are very unreliable.'

'She appeared pleased that you had rung her up?'

'I don't know,' said Mrs Oliver, 'not particularly pleased. She's got a very incisive voice and – I remember now, the last time I saw her, that must be about six years ago, I thought then that she was rather frightening.'

'Frightening? In what way?'

'What I mean is that she was more likely to bully me than I would be to bully her.'

'That may be a good thing and not a bad thing.'

'Oh, do you think so?'

'If people have made up their minds that they do not wish to like you, that they are quite sure they do not like you, they will get more pleasure out of making you aware of the fact and in that way will release more information to you than they would have done if they were trying to be amiable and agreeable.'

'Sucking up to me, you mean? Yes, you have something there. You mean then they tell you things that they thought would please you. And the other way they'd be annoyed with you and they'd say things that they'd hope would annoy you. I wonder if Celia's like that? I really remember her much better when she was five years old than at any other age. She had a nursery governess and she used to throw her boots at her.'

'The governess at the child, or the child at the governess?'

'The child at the governess, of course!' said Mrs Oliver.

She replaced the receiver and went over to the sofa to examine the various piled-up memories of the past. She murmured names under her breath.

'Mariana Josephine Pontarlier – of course, yes, I haven't thought of her for years – I thought she was dead. Anna Braceby – yes, yes, she lived in that part of the world – I wonder now –'

Continuing all this, time passed – she was quite surprised when the bell rang. She went out herself to open the door.

CHAPTER 4

CELIA

A tall girl was standing on the mat outside. Just for a moment Mrs Oliver was startled looking at her. So this was Celia. The impression of vitality and of life was really very strong. Mrs Oliver had the feeling which one does not often get.

Here, she thought, was someone who *meant* something. Aggressive, perhaps, could be difficult, could be almost dangerous perhaps. One of those girls who had a mission in life, who was dedicated to violence, perhaps, who went in for causes. But interesting. Definitely interesting.

'Come in, Celia,' she said. 'It's such a long time since I saw you. The last time, as far as I remember, was at a wedding. You were a bridesmaid. You wore apricot chiffon, I remember, and large bunches of – I can't remember what it was, something that looked like Golden Rod.'

'Probably *was* Golden Rod,' said Celia Ravenscroft. 'We sneezed a lot – with hay fever. It was a terrible wedding. I know. Martha Leghorn, wasn't it? Ugliest bridesmaids' dresses I've ever seen. Certainly the ugliest I've ever worn!'

'Yes. They weren't very becoming to anybody. You looked better than most, if I may say so.'

'Well, it's nice of you to say that,' said Celia. 'I didn't feel my best.'

Mrs Oliver indicated a chair and manipulated a couple of decanters.

'Like sherry or something else?'

'No. I'd like sherry.'

'There you are, then. I suppose it seems rather odd to you,' said Mrs Oliver. 'My ringing you up suddenly like this.'

'Oh no, I don't know that it does particularly.'

'I'm not a very conscientious godmother, I'm afraid.'

'Why should you be, at my age?'

'You're right there,' said Mrs Oliver. 'One's duties, one feels, end at a certain time. Not that I ever really fulfilled mine. I don't remember coming to your Confirmation.'

'I believe the duty of a godmother is to make you learn your catechism and a few things like that, isn't it? Renounce the devil and all his works in my name,' said Celia. A faint, humorous smile came to her lips.

She was being very amiable but all the same, thought Mrs Oliver, she's rather a dangerous girl in some ways.

'Well, I'll tell you why I've been trying to get hold of you,' said Mrs Oliver. 'The whole thing is rather peculiar. I don't often go out to literary parties, but as it happened I did go out to one the day before yesterday.'

'Yes, I know,' said Celia. 'I saw mention of it in the paper, and you had your name in it, too, Mrs Ariadne Oliver, and I rather wondered because I know you don't usually go to that sort of thing.'

'No,' said Mrs Oliver. 'I rather wish I hadn't gone to that one.'

'Didn't you enjoy it?'

'Yes, I did in a way because I hadn't been to one before. And so – well, the first time there's always something that amuses you. But,' she added, 'there's usually something that annoys you as well.'

'And something happened to annoy you?'

'Yes. And it's connected in an odd sort of way with you. And I thought – well, I thought I ought to tell you about it because I didn't like what happened. I didn't like it at all.'

'Sounds intriguing,' said Celia, and sipped her sherry.

'There was a woman there who came and spoke to me. I didn't know her and she didn't know me.'

'Still, I suppose that often happens to you,' said Celia.

'Yes, invariably,' said Mrs Oliver. 'It's one of the – hazards of literary life. People come up to you and say "I do love your books so much and I'm so pleased to be able to meet you." That sort of thing.'

'I was secretary to a writer once. I do know about that sort of thing and how difficult it is.'

'Yes, well, there was some of that too, but that I was prepared for. And then this woman came up to me and she said "I believe you have a goddaughter called Celia Ravenscroft."'

'Well, that was a bit odd,' said Celia. 'Just coming up to you and saying that. It seems to me she ought to have led into it more gradually. You know, talking about your books first and how much she'd enjoyed the last one, or something like that. And then sliding into me. What had she got against me?'

'As far as I know she hadn't got anything against you,' said Mrs Oliver.

'Was she a friend of mine?'

'I don't know,' said Mrs Oliver.

There was a silence. Celia sipped some more sherry and looked very searchingly at Mrs Oliver.

'You know,' she said, 'you're rather intriguing me. I can't see quite what you're leading into.'

'Well,' said Mrs Oliver, 'I hope you won't be angry with me.'

'Why should I be angry with you?'

'Well, because I'm going to tell you something, or repeat something, and you might say it's no business of mine or I ought to keep quiet about it and not mention it.'

'You've aroused my curiosity,' said Celia.

'Her name she mentioned to me. She was a Mrs Burton-Cox.'

'Oh!' Celia's 'Oh' was rather distinctive. 'Oh.'

'You know her?'

'Yes, I know her,' said Celia.

'Well, I thought you must because –'

'Because of what?'

'Because of something she said.'

'What – about me? That she knew me?'

'She said that she thought her son might be going to marry you.'

Celia's expression changed. Her eyebrows went up, came down again. She looked very hard at Mrs Oliver.

'You want to know if that's so or not?'

'No,' said Mrs Oliver, 'I don't particularly want to know. I merely mention that because it's one of the first things she said to me. She said because you were my goddaughter, I might be able to ask you to give me some information. I presume that she meant that if the information was given to me I was to pass it on to her.'

'What information?'

'Well, I don't suppose you'll like what I'm going to say now,' said Mrs Oliver. 'I didn't like it myself. In fact, it gives me a very nasty feeling all down my spine because I think it was – well, such awful cheek. Awful bad manners. Absolutely unpardonable. She said, "Can you find out if her father murdered her mother or if her mother murdered her father."'

'She said that to you? Asked you to do *that*?'

'Yes.'

'And she didn't know you? I mean, apart from being an authoress and being at the party?'

'She didn't know me at all. She'd never met me, I'd never met her.'

'Didn't you find that extraordinary?'

'I don't know that I'd find anything extraordinary that that woman said. She struck me,' said Mrs Oliver, 'if I may say so, as a particularly odious woman.'

'Oh yes. She is a particularly odious woman.'

'And are you going to marry her son?'

'Well, we've considered the question. I don't know. You knew what she was talking about?'

'Well, I know what I suppose anyone would know who was acquainted with your family.'

'That my father and mother, after he had retired from the Army, bought a house in the country, that they went out one day for a walk together, a walk along the cliff path. That they were found there, both of them shot. There was a revolver lying there. It belonged to my father. He had two revolvers in the house, it seems. There was nothing to say whether it was a suicide pact or whether my father killed my mother and then shot himself, or my mother shot my father and then killed herself. But perhaps you know all this already.'

'I know it after a fashion,' said Mrs Oliver. 'It happened I think about twelve years ago.'

'About that, yes.'

'And you were about twelve or fourteen at the time.'

'Yes . . .'

'I don't know much about it,' said Mrs Oliver. 'I wasn't even in England myself. At the time – I was on a lecture tour in America. I simply read it in the paper. It was given a lot of space in the press because it was difficult to know the real facts – there did not seem to be any motive. Your father and mother had always been happy together and lived on good terms. I remember that being mentioned. I was interested because I had known your father and mother when we were all much younger, especially your mother. I was at school with her. After that our ways led apart. I married and went somewhere and she married and went out, as far as I remember, to Malaya or some place like that, with her soldier husband. But she did ask me to be godmother to one of her children. You. Since your mother and father were living abroad, I saw very little of them for many years. I saw you occasionally.'

'Yes. You used to take me out from school. I remember that. Gave me some specially good feeds, too. Lovely food you gave me.'

'You were an unusual child. You liked caviar.'

'I still do,' said Celia, 'though I don't get it offered to me very often.'

'I was shocked to read this mention of things in the paper. Very little was said. I gathered it was a kind of open verdict. No particular motive. Nothing to show. No accounts of a quarrel, there was no suggestion of there having been an attack from outside. I was shocked by it,' said Mrs Oliver, 'and then I forgot it. I wondered once or twice what could have led to it, but as I was not in the country – I was doing a tour at the time, in America as I've said – the whole thing passed out of my mind. It was some years later when I next saw you and naturally I did not speak of it to you.'

'No,' said Celia, 'I appreciate that.'

'All through life,' Mrs Oliver said, 'one comes across very curious things that happen to friends or to acquaintances. With friends, of course, very often you have some idea of what led to – whatever the incident might be. But if it's a long time since you've heard them discussed or talked to them, you are quite in the dark and there is nobody that you can show too much curiosity to about the occasion.'

'You were always very nice to me,' said Celia. 'You sent me nice presents, a particularly nice present when I was twenty-one, I remember.'

'That's the time when girls need some extra cash in hand,' said Mrs Oliver, 'because there are so many things they want to do and have just then.'

'Yes, I always thought you were an understanding person and not – well, you know what some people are like. Always questioning, and asking things and wanting to know all about you. You never asked questions. You used to take me out to shows, or give me nice meals, and talk to me as though, well, as though everything was all right and you were just a distant relation of the family. I've appreciated that. I've known so many nosey-parkers in my life.'

'Yes. Everyone comes up against that sooner or later,' said Mrs Oliver. 'But you see now what upset me at this particular party. It seems an extraordinary thing to be asked to do by a complete stranger like Mrs Burton-Cox. I couldn't imagine why she should want to know. It was no business of hers, surely. Unless –'

'You thought it was, unless it was something to do with my marrying Desmond. Desmond is her son.'

'Yes, I suppose it could have been, but I couldn't see how, or what business it was of hers.'

'Everything's her business. She's nosey – in fact she's what you said she was, an odious woman.'

'But I gather Desmond isn't odious.'

'No. No, I'm very fond of Desmond and Desmond is fond of me. I don't like his mother.'

'Does he like his mother?'

'I don't really know,' said Celia. 'I suppose he might like her – anything's possible, isn't it? Anyway, I don't want to get married at present, I don't feel like it. And there are a lot of – oh, well, difficulties, you know, there are a lot of fors and againsts. It must have made you feel rather curious,' said Celia. 'I mean, why Mrs Nosey Cox should have asked you to try and worm things out of me and then run along and spill it all to her – Are you asking me that particular question by the way?'

'You mean, am I asking you whether you think or know that your mother killed your father or your father killed your mother, or whether it was a double suicide. Is that what you mean?'

'Well, I suppose it is, in a way. But I think I have to ask you also, *if* you were wanting to ask me that, whether you were doing so with the idea of giving Mrs Burton-Cox the information you obtained, in case you did receive any information from me.'

'No,' said Mrs Oliver. 'Quite decidedly no. I shouldn't dream of telling the odious woman anything of the sort. I shall tell her quite firmly that it is not any business of hers or of mine, and that I have no intention of obtaining information from you and retailing it to her.'

'Well, that's what I thought,' said Celia. 'I thought I could trust you to that extent. I don't mind telling you what I do know. Such as it is.'

'You needn't. I'm not asking you for it.'

'No. I can quite see that. But I'll give you the answer all the same. The answer is – nothing.'

'Nothing,' said Mrs Oliver thoughtfully.

'No. I wasn't there at the time. I mean, I wasn't in the house at the time. I can't remember now quite where I was. I think I was at school in Switzerland, or else I was staying with a school friend during the school holidays. You see, it's all rather mixed up in my mind by now.'

'I suppose,' said Mrs Oliver doubtfully, 'it wouldn't be likely that you *would* know. Considering your age at the time.'

'I'd be interested,' said Celia, 'to know just what you feel about that. Do you think it would be likely for me to know all about it? Or not to know?'

'Well, you said you weren't in the house. If you'd been in the house at the time, then yes, I think it would be quite likely that you might know something. Children do. Teenagers do. People of that age know a lot, they see a lot, they don't talk about it very often. But they do know things that the outside world wouldn't know, and they do know things that they wouldn't be willing, shall we say, to tell to police enquirers.'

'No. You're being quite sensible. I wouldn't've known. I don't think I did know. I don't think I had any idea. What did the police think? You don't mind my asking you that, I hope, because I should be interested. You see, I never read any account of the inquest or anything like that or the enquiry into it.'

'I think they thought it was a double suicide, but I don't think they ever had any inkling as to the reason for it.'

'Do you want to know what I think?'

'Not if you don't want me to know,' said Mrs Oliver.

'But I expect you are interested. After all, you write crime stories about people who kill themselves or kill each other, or who have reasons for things. I should think you would be interested.'

'Yes, I'll admit that,' said Mrs Oliver. 'But the last thing I want to do is to offend you by seeking for information which is no business of mine to know.'

'Well, I wondered,' said Celia. 'I've often wondered from time to time why, and how, but I knew very little about things. I mean, about how things were going on at home. The holidays before that I had been away on exchange on the Continent, so I hadn't seen my mother and father really very recently. I mean, they'd come out to Switzerland and taken me out from school once or twice, but that was all. They seemed much as usual, but they seemed older. My father, I think, was ailing. I mean, getting feebler. I don't know if it was heart or what it was. One doesn't really think about that. My mother, too, she was going rather nervy. Not hypochondriac but a little inclined to fuss over her health. They were on good terms, quite friendly. There wasn't anything that I noticed. Only sometimes one would, well, sometimes one gets ideas. One doesn't think they're true or necessarily right at all, but one just wonders if –'

'I don't think we'd better talk about it any more,' said Mrs Oliver. 'We don't need to know or find out. The whole thing's over and done with. The verdict was quite satisfactory. No means to show, or motive, or anything like that. But there was no question of your father having deliberately killed your mother, or of your mother having deliberately killed your father.'

'If I thought which was most likely,' said Celia, 'I would think my father killed my mother. Because, you see, it's more natural for a man to shoot anyone, I think. To shoot a woman for whatever reason it was. I don't think a woman, or a woman like my mother, would be so likely to shoot my father. If she wanted him dead, I should think she might have chosen some other method. But I don't think either of them wanted the other one dead.'

'So it could have been an outsider.'

'Yes, but what does one mean by an outsider?' said Celia.

'Who else was there living in the house?'

'A housekeeper, elderly, rather blind and rather deaf, a foreign girl, an au pair girl, she'd been my governess once – she was awfully nice – she came back to look after my mother who had been in hospital – And there was an aunt whom I never loved much. I don't think any of them could have been likely to have any grudge against my parents. There was nobody who profited by their deaths, except, I suppose, myself and my brother Edward, who was four years younger than I was. We inherited what money there was but it wasn't very much. My father had his pension, of course. My mother had a small income of her own. No. There was nothing there of any importance.'

'I'm sorry,' said Mrs Oliver. 'I'm sorry if I've distressed you by asking all this.'

'You haven't distressed me. You've brought it up in my mind a little and it has interested me. Because, you see, I am of an age now that I wish I did know. I knew and was fond of them, as one is fond of parents. Not passionately, just normally, but I realize I don't know what they were really *like*. What their life was like. What *mattered* to them. I don't know anything about it at all. I wish I did know. It's like a burr, something sticking into you, and you can't leave it alone. Yes. I would like to know. Because then, you see, I shouldn't have to think about it any more.'

'So you do? Think about it?'

Celia looked at her for a moment. She seemed to be trying to come to a decision.

'Yes,' she said, 'I think about it nearly all the time. I'm getting to have a thing about it, if you know what I mean. And Desmond feels the same.'

CHAPTER 5

OLD SINS HAVE LONG SHADOWS

Hercule Poirot let the revolving door wind him round. Arresting the swing of it with one hand, he stepped forward into the small restaurant. There were not many people there. It was an unfashionable time of day, but his eyes soon saw the man he had come to meet. The square, solid bulk of Superintendent Spence rose from the table in one corner.

'Good,' he said. 'You have arrived here. You had no difficulty in finding it?'

'None at all. Your instructions were most adequate.'

'Let me introduce you now. This is Chief Superintendent Garroway. Monsieur Hercule Poirot.'

Garroway was a tall, thin man with a lean, ascetic face, grey hair which left a small round spot like a tonsure, so that he had a faint resemblance to an ecclesiastic.

'This is wonderful,' said Poirot.

'I am retired now, of course,' said Garroway, 'but one remembers. Yes, certain things one remembers, although they are past and gone, and the general public probably remembers nothing about them. But yes.'

Hercule Poirot very nearly said 'Elephants do remember,' but checked himself in time. That phrase was so associated in his mind now with Mrs Ariadne Oliver that he found it difficult to restrain it from his tongue in many clearly unsuitable categories.

'I hope you have not been getting impatient,' said Superintendent Spence.

He pulled forward a chair, and the three men sat down. A menu was brought. Superintendent Spence, who was clearly addicted to this particular restaurant, offered tentative words of advice. Garroway and Poirot made their choice. Then, leaning back a little in their chairs and sipping glasses of sherry, they contemplated each other for some minutes in silence before speaking.

'I must apologize to you,' said Poirot, 'I really must apologize to you for coming to you with my demands about an affair which is over and done with.'

'What interests me,' said Spence, 'is what has interested you. I thought first that it was unlike you to have this wish to delve in the past. It is connected with something that has occurred nowadays, or is it sudden curiosity about a rather inexplicable, perhaps, case? Do you agree with that?'

He looked across the table.

'Inspector Garroway,' he said, 'as he was at that time, was the officer in charge of the investigations into the Ravenscroft shooting. He was an old friend of mine and so I had no difficulty in getting in touch with him.'

'And he was kind enough to come here today,' said Poirot, 'simply because I must admit to a curiosity which I am sure I have no right to feel about an affair that is past and done with.'

'Well, I wouldn't say that,' said Garroway. 'We all have interests in certain cases that are past. Did Lizzie Borden really kill her father and mother with an axe? There are people who still do not think so. Who killed Charles Bravo and why? There are several different ideas, mostly not very well founded. But still people try to find alternative explanations.'

His keen, shrewd eyes looked across at Poirot.

'And Monsieur Poirot, if I am not mistaken, has occasionally shown a leaning towards looking into cases, going back, shall we say, for murder, back into the past, twice, perhaps three times.'

'Three times, certainly,' said Superintendent Spence.

'Once, I think I am right, by request of a Canadian girl.'

'That is so,' said Poirot. 'A Canadian girl, very vehement, very passionate, very forceful, who had come here to investigate a murder for which her mother had been condemned to death, although she died before sentence was carried out. Her daughter was convinced that her mother had been innocent.'

'And you agreed?' said Garroway.

'I did not agree,' said Poirot, 'when she first told me of the matter. But she was very vehement and very sure.'

'It was natural for a daughter to wish her mother to have been innocent and to try and prove against all appearances that she was innocent,' said Spence.

'It was just a little more than that,' said Poirot. 'She convinced me of the type of woman her mother was.'

'A woman incapable of murder?'

'No,' said Poirot, 'it would be very difficult, and I am sure both of you agree with me, to think there is anyone quite incapable of murder if one knows what kind of person they are, what led up to it. But in that particular case, the mother never protested her innocence. She appeared to be quite content to be sentenced. That was curious to begin with. Was she a defeatist? It did not seem so. When I began to enquire, it became clear that she was not a defeatist. She was, one would say, almost the opposite of it.'

Garroway looked interested. He leaned across the table, twisting a bit of bread off the roll on his plate.

'And was she innocent?'

'Yes,' said Poirot. 'She was innocent.'

'And that surprised you?'

'Not by the time I realized it,' said Poirot. 'There were one or two things – one thing in particular – that showed she *could not* have been guilty. One fact that nobody had appreciated at the time. Knowing that one had only to look at what there was, shall we say, on the menu in the way of looking elsewhere.'[1]

Grilled trout was put in front of them at this point.

'There was another case, too, where you looked into the past, not quite in the same way,' continued Spence. 'A girl who said at a party that she had once seen a murder committed.'[2]

'There again one had to – how shall I put it? – step backwards instead of forward,' said Poirot. 'Yes, that is very true.'

'And had the girl seen the murder committed?'

'No,' said Poirot, 'because it was the wrong girl. This trout is delicious,' he added, with appreciation.

'They do all fish dishes very well here,' said Superintendent Spence.

He helped himself from the sauce boat proffered to him.

'A most delicious sauce,' he added.

Silent appreciation of food filled the next three minutes.

'When Spence came along to me,' said Superintendent Garroway, 'asking if I remembered anything about the Ravenscroft case, I was intrigued and delighted at once.'

'You haven't forgotten all about it?'

'Not the Ravenscroft case. It wasn't an easy case to forget about.'

'You agree,' said Poirot, 'that there were discrepancies about it? Lack of proof, alternative solutions?'

'No,' said Garroway, 'nothing of that kind. All the evidence recorded the visible facts. Deaths of which there were several former examples, yes, all plain sailing. And yet –'

'Well?' said Poirot.

'And yet it was all wrong,' said Garroway.

'Ah,' said Spence. He looked interested.

'That's what you felt once, isn't it?' said Poirot, turning to him.

1 *Five Little Pigs*
2 *Hallowe'en Party*

'In the case of Mrs McGinty. Yes.'[3]

'You weren't satisfied,' said Poirot, 'when that extremely difficult young man was arrested. He had every reason for doing it, he looked as though he had done it, everyone thought he had done it. But you knew he hadn't done it. You were so sure of it that you came to me and told me to go along to see what I could find out.'

'See if you could help – and you did help, didn't you?' said Spence.

Poirot sighed.

'Fortunately, yes. But what a tiresome young man he was. If ever a young man deserved to be hanged, not because he had done a murder but because he wouldn't help anyone to prove that he hadn't. Now we have the Ravenscroft case. You say, Superintendent Garroway, something was wrong?'

'Yes, I felt quite sure of it if you understand what I mean.'

'I do understand,' said Poirot. 'And so does Spence. One does come across these things sometimes. The proofs are there, the motive, the opportunity, the clues, the *mise-en-scène*, it's all there. A complete blueprint, as you might say. But all the same, those whose profession it is, *know*. They know that it's all wrong, just like a critic in the artistic world knows when a picture is all wrong. Knows when it's a fake and not the real thing.'

'There wasn't anything I could do about it, either,' said Superintendent Garroway. 'I looked into it, around it, up above it and down below it, as you might say. I talked to the people. There was nothing there. It looked like a suicide pact, it had all the marks of the suicide pact. Alternatively, of course, it could be a husband who shot a wife and then himself, or a wife who shot her husband and then herself. All those three things happen. When one comes across them, one knows they have happened. But in most cases one has some idea of *why*.'

'There wasn't any real idea of *why* in this case, was that it?' said Poirot.

'Yes. That's it. You see, the moment you begin to enquire into a case, to enquire about people and things, you get a very good picture as a rule of what their lives have been like. This

[3] *Mrs McGinty's Dead*

was a couple, ageing, the husband with a good record, a wife affectionate, pleasant, on good terms together. That's a thing one soon finds out about. They were happy living together. They went for walks, they played picquet, and poker patience with each other in the evenings, they had children who caused them no particular anxiety. A boy in school in England and a girl in a *pensionnat* in Switzerland. There was nothing wrong with their lives as far as one could tell. From such medical evidence as one could obtain, there was nothing definitely wrong with their health. The husband had suffered from high blood pressure at one time, but was in good condition by the taking of suitable medicaments which kept him on an even keel. His wife was slightly deaf and had had a little minor heart trouble, nothing to be worried about. Of course it could be, as does happen sometimes, that one or other of them had fears for their health. There are a lot of people who are in good health but are quite convinced they have cancer, are quite sure that they won't live another year. Sometimes that leads to their taking their own life. The Ravenscrofts didn't seem that kind of person. They seemed well balanced and placid.'

'So what did you really think?' said Poirot.

'The trouble is that I couldn't think. Looking back, I said to myself it was suicide. It could only have been suicide. For some reason or other they decided that life was unbearable to them. Not through financial trouble, not through health difficulties, not because of unhappiness. And there, you see, I came to a full stop. It had all the marks of suicide. I cannot see any other thing that could have happened except suicide. They went for a walk. In that walk they took a revolver with them. The revolver lay between the two bodies. There were blurred fingerprints of both of them. Both of them in fact had handled it, but there was nothing to show who had fired it last. One tends to think the husband perhaps shot his wife and then himself. That is only because it seems more likely. Well, why? A great many years have passed. When something reminds me now and again, something I read in the papers of bodies, a husband's and wife's bodies somewhere, lying dead, having taken their own lives apparently, I think back and then I wonder again what happened in the Ravenscroft case. Twelve years ago or fourteen and I still remember the Ravenscroft case and wonder – well, just the one word, I think. Why – why –

why? Did the wife really hate her husband and want to get rid of him? Did they go on hating each other until they could bear it no longer?'

Garroway broke off another piece of bread and chewed at it.

'You got some idea, Monsieur Poirot? Has somebody come to you and told you something that has awakened your interest particularly? Do you know something that might explain the "Why"?'

'No. All the same,' said Poirot, 'you must have had a theory. Come now, you had a theory?'

'You're quite right, of course. One does have theories. One expects them all, or one of them at least, to work out, but they don't usually. I think that my theory was in the end that you couldn't look for the cause, because one didn't know enough. What *did* I know about them? General Ravenscroft was close on sixty, his wife was thirty-five. All I knew of them, strictly speaking, was the last five or six years of their lives. The General had retired on a pension. They had come back to England from abroad and all the evidence that came to me, all the knowledge, was of a brief period during which they had first a house at Bournemouth and then moved to where they lived in the home where the tragedy took place. They had lived there peacefully, happily, their children came home there for school holidays. It was a peaceful period, I should say, at the end of what one presumed was a peaceful life. I knew of their life after retirement in England, of their family. There was no financial motive, no motive of hatred, no motive of sexual involvement, of intrusive love-affairs. No. But there *was* a period before that. What did I know about that? What I knew was a life spent mostly abroad with occasional visits home, a good record for the man, pleasant remembrances of her from friends of the wife's. There was no outstanding tragedy, dispute, nothing that one knew of. But then I mightn't have known. One doesn't know. There was a period of, say, twenty-thirty years, years from childhood to the time they married, the time they lived abroad in Malaya and other places. Perhaps the root of the tragedy was there. There is a proverb my grandmother used to repeat: *Old sins have long shadows*. Was the cause of death some long shadow, a shadow from the past? That's not an easy thing to find out about. You find out about a man's record, what friends or acquaintances say, but you don't know any inner details. Well, I think little by little the theory grew up in my mind that that would have been the place to look, if I could have looked. Something that had happened then, in another country, perhaps. Something that had been thought to be forgotten, to have passed out of existence, but which still perhaps existed. A grudge from the past, some happening that nobody knew about, that had happened elsewhere, not in their life in England, but which may have been there. If one had known where to look for it.'

'Not the sort of thing, you mean,' said Poirot, 'that anybody would remember. I mean, remember nowadays. Something that no friends of theirs in England, perhaps, would have known about.'

'Their friends in England seem to have been mostly made since retirement, though I suppose old friends did come and visit them or see them occasionally. But one doesn't hear about things that happened in the past. People forget.'

'Yes,' said Poirot, thoughtfully. 'People forget.'

'They're not like elephants,' said Superintendent Garroway, giving a faint smile. 'Elephants, they always say, remember everything.'

'It is odd that you should say that,' said Poirot.

'That I should say that about long sins?'

'Not so much that. It was your mention of elephants that interested me.'

Superintendent Garroway looked at Poirot with some surprise. He seemed to be waiting for more. Spence also cast a quick glance at his old friend.

'Something that happened out East, perhaps,' he suggested. 'I mean – well, that's where elephants come from, isn't it? Or from Africa. Anyway, who's been talking to you about elephants?' he added.

'A friend of mine happened to mention them,' said Poirot. 'Someone *you* know,' he said to Superintendent Spence. 'Mrs Oliver.'

'Oh, Mrs Ariadne Oliver. Well!' He paused.

'Well what?' said Poirot.

'Well, does she know something, then?' he asked.

'I do not think so as yet,' said Poirot, 'but she might know something before very long.' He added thoughtfully, 'She's that kind of person. She gets around, if you know what I mean.'

'Yes',' said Spence. 'Yes. Has she got any ideas?' he asked.

'Do you mean Mrs Ariadne Oliver, the writer?' asked Garroway with some interest.

'That's the one,' said Spence.

'Does she know a good deal about crime? I know she writes crime stories. I've never known where she got her ideas from or her facts.'

'Her ideas,' said Poirot, 'come out of her head. Her facts – well, that's more difficult.' He paused for a moment.

'What are you thinking of, Poirot, something in particular?'

'Yes,' said Poirot. 'I ruined one of her stories once, or so she tells me. She had just had a very good idea about a fact, something that had to do with a long-sleeved woollen vest. I asked her something over the telephone and it put the idea for the story out of her head. She reproaches me at intervals.'

'Dear, dear,' said Spence. 'Sounds rather like that parsley that sank into the butter on a hot day. You know. Sherlock Holmes and the dog who did nothing in the night time.'

'Did they have a dog?' asked Poirot.

'I beg your pardon?'

'I said did they have a dog? General and Lady Ravenscroft. Did they take a dog for that walk with them on the day they were shot? The Ravenscrofts.'

'They had a dog – yes,' said Garroway. 'I suppose, I suppose they did take him for a walk most days.'

'If it had been one of Mrs Oliver's stories,' said Spence, 'you ought to have found the dog howling over the two dead bodies. But that didn't happen.'

Garroway shook his head.

'I wonder where the dog is now?' said Poirot.

'Buried in somebody's garden, I expect,' said Garroway. 'It's fourteen years ago.'

'So we can't go and ask the dog, can we?' said Poirot. He added thoughtfully, 'A pity. It's astonishing, you know, what dogs can know. Who was there exactly in the house? I mean on the day when the crime happened?'

'I brought you a list,' said Superintendent Garroway, 'in case you like to consult it. Mrs Whittaker, the elderly cook-housekeeper. It was her day out so we couldn't get much from her that was helpful. A visitor was staying there who had been governess to the Ravenscroft children once, I believe. Mrs Whittaker was rather deaf and slightly blind. She couldn't tell us anything of interest, except that recently Lady Ravenscroft had been in hospital or in a nursing home – for nerves but not illness, apparently. There was a gardener, too.'

'But a stranger might have come from outside. A stranger from the past. That's your idea, Superintendent Garroway?'

'Not so much an idea as just a theory.'

Poirot was silent, he was thinking of a time when he had asked to go back into the past, had studied five people out of the past who had reminded him of the nursery rhyme 'Five little pigs.' Interesting it had been, and in the end rewarding, because he had found out the truth.

CHAPTER 6

AN OLD FRIEND REMEMBERS

When Mrs Oliver returned to the house the following morning, she found Miss Livingstone waiting for her.

'There have been two telephone calls, Mrs Oliver.'

'Yes?' said Mrs Oliver.

'The first one was from Crichton and Smith. They wanted to know whether you had chosen the lime-green brocade or the pale blue one.'

'I haven't made up my mind yet,' said Mrs Oliver. 'Just remind me tomorrow morning, will you? I'd like to see it by night light.'

'And the other was from a foreigner, a Mr Hercule Poirot, I believe.'

'Oh, yes,' said Mrs Oliver. 'What did he want?'

'He asked if you would be able to call and see him this afternoon.'

'That will be quite impossible,' said Mrs Oliver. 'Ring him up, will you? I've got to go out again at once, as a matter of fact. Did he leave a telephone number?'

'Yes, he did.'

'That's all right, then. We won't have to look it up again. All right. Just ring him. Tell him I'm sorry that I can't but that I'm out on the track of an elephant.'

'I beg your pardon?' said Miss Livingstone.

'Say that I'm on the track of an elephant.'

'Oh yes,' said Miss Livingstone, looking shrewdly at her employer to see if she was right in the feelings that she sometimes had that Mrs Ariadne Oliver, though a successful novelist, was at the same time not quite right in the head.

'I've never hunted elephants before,' said Mrs Oliver. 'It's quite an interesting thing to do, though.'

She went into the sitting-room, opened the top volume of the assorted books on the sofa, most of them looking rather the worse for wear, since she had toiled through them the evening before and written out a paper with various addresses.

'Well, one has got to make a start somewhere,' she said. 'On the whole I think that if Julia hasn't gone completely off her rocker by now, I might start with her. She always had ideas and after all, she knew that part of the country because she lived near there. Yes, I think we'll start with Julia.'

'There are four letters here for you to sign,' said Miss Livingstone.

'I can't be bothered now,' said Mrs Oliver. 'I really can't spare a moment. I've got to go down to Hampton Court, and it's quite a long ride.'

The Honourable Julia Carstairs, struggling with some slight difficulty out of her armchair, the difficulty that those over the age of seventy have when rising to their feet after prolonged rest, even a possible nap, stepped forward, peering a little to see who it was who had just been announced by the faithful retainer who shared the apartment which she occupied in her status of a member of 'Homes for the Privileged'. Being slightly deaf, the name had not come clearly to her. Mrs Gulliver. Was that it? But she didn't remember a Mrs Gulliver. She advanced on slightly shaky knees, still peering forward.

'I don't expect you'll remember me, it's so many years since we met.'

Like many elderly people, Mrs Carstairs could remember voices better than she did faces.

'Why,' she exclaimed, 'it's – dear me, it's Ariadne! My dear, how very nice to see you.'

Greetings passed.

'I just happened to be in this part of the world,' explained Mrs Oliver. 'I had to come down to see someone not far from here. And then I remembered that looking in my address book last night I had seen that this was quite near where you had your apartment. Delightful, isn't it?' she added, looking round.

'Not too bad,' said Mrs Carstairs. 'Not quite all it's written up to be, you know. But it has many advantages. One brings one's own furniture and things like that, and there is a central restaurant where you can have a meal, or you can have your own things, of course. Oh yes, it's very good, really. The grounds are charming and well kept up. But sit down, Ariadne, do sit down. You look very well. I saw you were at a literary lunch the other day, in the paper. How odd it is that one just sees something in the paper and almost the next day one meets the person. Quite extraordinary.'

'I know,' said Mrs Oliver, taking the chair that was offered her. 'Things do go like that, don't they.'

'You are still living in London?'

Mrs Oliver said yes, she was still living in London. She then entered into what she thought of in her own mind, with vague memories of going to dancing class as a child, as the first figure of the Lancers. Advance, retreat, hands out, turn round twice, whirl round, and so on.

She enquired after Mrs Carstairs's daughter and about the two grandchildren, and she asked about the other daughter, what she was doing. She appeared to be doing it in New Zealand. Mrs Carstairs did not seem to be quite sure what it was. Some kind of social research. Mrs Carstairs pressed an electric bell that rested on the arm of her chair, and ordered Emma to bring tea. Mrs Oliver begged her not to bother. Julia Carstairs said:

'Of course Ariadne has got to have tea.'

The two ladies leant back. The second and third figures of the Lancers. Old friends. Other people's children. The death of friends.

'It must be years since I saw you last,' said Mrs Carstairs.

'I think it was at the Llewellyns' wedding,' said Mrs Oliver. 'Yes, that must have been about it. How terrible Moira looked as a bridesmaid. That dreadfully unbecoming shade of apricot they wore.'

'I know. It didn't suit them.'

'I don't think weddings are nearly as pretty as they used to be in our day. Some of them seem to wear such very peculiar clothes. The other day one of my friends went to a wedding and she said the bridegroom was dressed in some sort of quilted white satin and ruffles at his neck. Made of Valenciennes lace, I believe. *Most* peculiar. And the girl was wearing a very peculiar trouser suit. Also white but it was stamped with green shamrocks all over.'

'Well, my dear Ariadne, can you imagine it. Really, extraordinary. In church too. If I'd been a clergyman I'd have refused to marry them.'

Tea came. Talk continued.

'I saw my goddaughter, Celia Ravenscroft, the other day,' said Mrs Oliver. 'Do you remember the Ravenscrofts? Of course, it's a great many years ago.'

'The Ravenscrofts? Now wait a minute. That was that very sad tragedy, wasn't it? A double suicide, didn't they think it was? Near their house at Overcliffe.'

'You've got such a wonderful memory, Julia,' said Mrs Oliver.

'Always had. Though I have difficulties with names sometimes. Yes, it was very tragic, wasn't it.'

'Very tragic indeed.'

'One of my cousins knew them very well in Malaya, Roddy Foster, you know. General Ravenscroft had had a most distinguished career. Of course he was a bit deaf by the time he retired. He didn't always hear what one said very well.'

'Do you remember them quite well?'

'Oh yes. One doesn't really forget people, does one? I mean, they lived at Overcliffe for quite five or six years.'

'I've forgotten her Christian name now,' said Mrs Oliver.

'Margaret, I think. But everyone called her Molly. Yes, Margaret. So many people were called Margaret, weren't they, at about that time? She used to wear a wig, do you remember?'

'Oh yes,' said Mrs Oliver. 'At least I can't quite remember, but I think I do.'

'I'm not sure she didn't try to persuade me to get one. She said it was so useful when you went abroad and travelled. She had four different wigs. One for evening and one for travelling and one – very strange, you know. You could put a hat on over it and not really disarrange it.'

'I didn't know them as well as you did,' said Mrs Oliver. 'And of course at the time of the shooting I was in America on a lecture tour. So I never really heard any details.'

'Well, of course, it was a great mystery,' said Julia Carstairs. 'I mean to say, one didn't know. There were so many different stories going about.'

'What did they say at the inquest – I suppose they had an inquest?'

'Oh yes, of course. The police had to investigate it. It was one of those indecisive things, you know, in that the death was due to revolver shots. They couldn't say definitely what had occurred. It seemed possible that General Ravenscroft had shot his wife and then himself, but apparently it was just as probable that Lady Ravenscroft had shot her husband and then herself. It seemed more likely, I think, that it *was* a suicide pact, but it couldn't be said definitely how it came about.'

'There seemed to be no question of its being a crime?'

'No, no. It was said quite clearly there was no suggestion of foul play. I mean there were no footprints or any signs of anyone coming near them. They left the house to go for a walk after tea, as they so often did. They didn't come back again for dinner and the manservant or somebody or the gardener – whoever it was – went out to look for them, and found them both dead. The revolver was lying by the bodies.'

'The revolver belonged to him, didn't it?'

'Oh yes. He had two revolvers in the house. These ex-military people so often do, don't they? I mean, they feel safer what with everything that goes on nowadays. A second revolver was still in the drawer in the house, so that he – well, *he* must have gone out deliberately with the revolver, presumably. I don't think it likely that she'd have gone out for a walk carrying a revolver.'

'No. No, it wouldn't have been so easy, would it?'

'But there was nothing apparently in the evidence to show that there was any unhappiness or that there'd been any quarrel between them or that there was any reason why they should commit suicide. Of course one never knows what sad things there are in people's lives.'

'No, no,' said Mrs Oliver. 'One never knows. How very true that is, Julia. Did you have any idea yourself?'

'Well, one always wonders, my dear.'

'Yes,' said Mrs Oliver, 'one always wonders.'

'It might be of course, you see, that he had some disease. I think he might have been told he was going to die of cancer, but that wasn't so, according to the medical evidence. He was quite healthy. I mean, he had – I think he had had a – what do they call those things? – coronary, is that what I mean? It sounds like a crown, doesn't it, but it's really a heart attack, isn't it? He'd had that but he'd recovered from it, and she was, well, she was very nervy. She was neurotic always.'

'Yes, I seem to remember that,' said Mrs Oliver. 'Of course I didn't know them well, but –' she asked suddenly – 'was she wearing a wig?'

'Oh. Well, you know, I can't really remember that. She always wore her wig. One of them, I mean.'

'I just wondered,' said Mrs Oliver. 'Somehow I feel if you were going to shoot yourself or even shoot your husband, I don't think you'd wear your wig, do you?'

The ladies discussed this point with some interest.

'What do you really think, Julia?'

'Well, as I said, dear, one wonders, you know. There were things said, but then there always are.'

'About him or her?'

'Well, they said that there was a young woman, you know. Yes, I think she did some secretarial work for him. He was writing his memoirs of his career abroad – I believe commissioned by a publisher at that – and she used to take dictation from him. But some people said – well, you know what they do say sometimes, that perhaps he had got – er – tied up with this girl in some way. She wasn't very young. She was over thirty, and not very good-looking and I don't think – there were no scandals about her or anything, but still, one doesn't know. People thought he might have shot his wife because he wanted to – well, he might have wanted to marry her, yes. But

I don't really think people said that sort of thing and *I* never believed it.'

'What did you think?'

'Well, of course I wondered a little about *her.*'

'You mean that a man was mentioned?'

'I believe there was something out in Malaya. Some kind of story I heard about her. That she got embroiled with some young man much younger than herself. And her husband hadn't liked it much and it had caused a bit of scandal. I forget where. But anyway, that was a long time ago and I don't think anything ever came of it.'

'You don't think there was any talk nearer home? No special relationship with anyone in the neighbourhood? There wasn't any evidence of quarrels between them, or anything of that kind?'

'No, I don't think so. Of course I read everything about it at the time. One did discuss it, of course, because one couldn't help feeling there might be some – well, some really very tragic love story connected with it.'

'But there wasn't, you think? They had children, didn't they. There was my goddaughter, of course.'

'Oh yes, and there was a son. I think he was quite young. At school somewhere. The girl was only twelve, no – older than that. She was with a family in Switzerland.'

'There was no – no mental trouble, I suppose, in the family?'

'Oh, you mean the boy – yes, *might* be of course. You do hear very strange things. There was that boy who shot his father – that was somewhere near Newcastle, I think. Some years before that. You know. He'd been very depressed and at first I think they said he tried to hang himself when he was at the university, and then he came and shot his father. But nobody quite knew why. Anyway, there wasn't anything of that sort with the Ravenscrofts. No, I don't think so, in fact I'm pretty sure of it. I can't help thinking, in some ways –'

'Yes, Julia?'

'I can't help thinking that there might have been a man, you know.'

'You mean that she –'

'Yes, well – well, one thinks it rather likely, you know. The wigs, for one thing.'

'I don't quite see how the wigs come into it.'

'Well, wanting to improve her appearance.'

'She was thirty-five, I think.'

'More. More. Thirty-six, I think. And, well, I know she showed me the wigs one day, and one or two of them really made her look quite attractive. And she used a good deal of make-up. And that had all started just after they had come to live there, I think. She was rather a good-looking woman.'

'You mean, she might have met someone, some man?'

'Well, that's what I've always thought,' said Mrs Carstairs. 'You see, if a man's getting off with a girl, people notice it usually because men aren't so good at hiding their tracks. But a woman, it might be – well, I mean like someone she'd met and nobody knew much about it.'

'Oh, do you really think so, Julia?'

'No I don't really think so,' said Julia, 'because I mean, people always do know, don't they? I mean, you know, servants know, or gardeners or bus drivers. Or somebody in the neighbourhood. And they know. And they talk. But still, there could have been something like that, and either he found out about it . . .'

'You mean it was a crime of jealousy?'

'I think so, yes.'

'So you think it's more likely that he shot her, then himself, than that she shot him and then herself.'

'Well, I should think so, because I think if she were trying to get rid of him – well, I don't think they'd have gone for a walk together and she'd have to have taken the revolver with her in a handbag and it would have been rather a bigger handbag if so. One has to think of the practical side of things.'

'I know,' said Mrs Oliver. 'One does. It's very interesting.'

'It must be interesting to you, dear, because you write these crime stories. So I expect really you would have better ideas. You'd know more what's likely to happen.'

'I don't know what's likely to happen,' said Mrs Oliver, 'because, you see, in all the crimes that I write, I've invented the crimes. I mean, what I want to happen, happens in my stories. It's not something that actually has happened or that could happen. So I'm really the worst person to talk about it. I'm interested to know what you think because you know people very well, Julia, and you knew them well. And I think she might have said something to you one day – or he might.'

'Yes. Yes, now wait a minute when you say that, that seems to bring something back to me.'

Mrs Carstairs leaned back in her chair, shook her head doubtfully, half closed her eyes and went into a kind of coma. Mrs Oliver remained silent with a look on her face which women are apt to wear when they are waiting for the first signs of a kettle coming to the boil.

'She did say something once, I remember, and I wonder what she meant by it,' said Mrs Carstairs. 'Something about starting a new life – in connection I think with St Teresa. St Teresa of Avila. . . .'

Mrs Oliver looked slightly startled.

'But how did St Teresa of Avila come into it?'

'Well, I don't know really. I think she must have been reading a Life of her. Anyway, she said that it was wonderful how women get a sort of second wind. That's not quite the term she used, but something like that. You know, when they are forty or fifty or that sort of age and they suddenly want to begin a new life. Teresa of Avila did. She hadn't done anything special up till then except being a nun, then she went out and reformed all the convents, didn't she, and flung her weight about and became a great Saint.'

'Yes, but that doesn't seem quite the same thing.'

'No, it doesn't,' said Mrs Carstairs. 'But women do talk in a very silly way, you know, when they are referring to love-affairs when they get on in life. About how it's never too late.'

CHAPTER 7

BACK TO THE NURSERY

Mrs Oliver looked rather doubtfully at the three steps and the front door of a small, rather dilapidated-looking cottage in the side street. Below the windows some bulbs were growing, mainly tulips.

Mrs Oliver paused, opened the little address book in her hand, verified that she was in the place she thought she was, and rapped gently with the knocker after having tried to press a bell-push of possible electrical significance but which did not seem to yield any satisfactory bell ringing inside, or anything of that kind. Presently, not getting any response, she knocked again. This time there were sounds from inside. A shuffling sound of feet, some asthmatic breathing and hands apparently trying to manage the opening of the door. With this noise there came a few vague echoes in the letter-box.

'Oh, drat it. Drat it. Stuck again, you brute, you.'

Finally, success met these inward industries, and the door, making a creaky and rather doubtful noise, was slowly pulled open. A very old woman with a wrinkled face, humped shoulders and a general arthritic appearance, looked at her visitor. Her face was unwelcoming. It held no sign of fear, merely of distaste for those who came and knocked at the home of an Englishwoman's castle. She might have been seventy or eighty, but she was still a valiant defender of her home.

'I dunno what you've come about and I –' she stopped. 'Why,' she said, 'it's Miss Ariadne. Well I never now! It's Miss Ariadne.'

'I think you're wonderful to know me,' said Mrs Oliver. 'How are you, Mrs Matcham?'

'Miss Ariadne! Just think of that now.'

It was, Mrs Ariadne Oliver thought, a long time ago since she had been addressed as Miss Ariadne, but the intonation of the voice, cracked with age though it was, rang a familiar note.

'Come in, m'dear,' said the old dame, 'come in now. You're lookin' well, you are. I dunno how many years it is since I've seen you. Fifteen at least.'

It was a good deal more than fifteen but Mrs Oliver made no corrections. She came in. Mrs Matcham was shaking hands, her hands were rather unwilling to obey their owner's orders. She managed to shut the door and, shuffling her feet and limping, entered a small room which was obviously one that was kept for the reception of any likely or unlikely visitors whom Mrs Matcham was prepared to admit to her home. There were large numbers of photographs, some of babies, some of adults. Some in nice leather frames which were slowly drooping but had not quite fallen to pieces yet. One in a silver frame by now rather tarnished, representing a young woman in presentation Court Dress with feathers rising up on her head. Two naval officers, two military gentlemen, some photographs of naked babies sprawling on rugs. There was a sofa and two chairs. As bidden, Mrs Oliver sat in a chair. Mrs Matcham pressed herself down on the sofa and pulled a cushion into the hollow of her back with some difficulty.

'Well, my dear, fancy seeing you. And you're still writing your pretty stories, are you?'

'Yes,' said Mrs Oliver, assenting to this though with a slight doubt as to how far detective stories and stories of crime and general criminal behaviour could be called 'pretty stories'. But that, she thought, was very much a habit of Mrs Matcham's.

'I'm all alone now,' said Mrs Matcham. 'You remember Gracie, my sister? She died last autumn, she did. Cancer it was. They operated but it was too late.'

'Oh dear, I'm so sorry,' said Mrs Oliver.

Conversation proceeded for the next ten minutes on the subject of the demise, one by one, of Mrs Matcham's last remaining relatives.

'And you're all right, are you? Doing all right? Got a husband now? Oh now, I remember, he's dead years ago, isn't he? And what brings you here, to Little Saltern Minor?'

'I just happened to be in the neighbourhood,' said Mrs Oliver, 'and as I've got your address in my little address book with me, I thought I'd just drop in and – well, see how you were and everything.'

'Ah! And talk about old times, perhaps. Always nice when you can do that, isn't it?'

'Yes, indeed,' said Mrs Oliver, feeling some relief that this particular line had been indicated to her since it was more or less what she had come for. 'What a lot of photographs you've got,' she said.

'Ah, I have, an' that. D'you know, when I was in that Home – silly name it had. Sunset House of Happiness for the Aged, something like that it was called, a year and a quarter I lived there till I couldn't stand it no more, a nasty lot they were, saying you couldn't have any of your own things with you. You know, everything had to belong to the Home. I don't say as it wasn't comfortable, but you know, I like me own things around me.

My photos and my furniture. And then there was ever so nice a lady, came from a Council she did, some society or other, and she told me there was another place where they had homes of their own or something and you could take what you liked with you. And there's ever such a nice helper as comes in every day to see if you're all right. Ah, very comfortable I am here. Very comfortable indeed. I've got all my own things.'

'Something from everywhere,' said Mrs Oliver, looking round.

'Yes, that table – the brass one – that's Captain Wilson, he sent me that from Singapore or something like that. And that Benares brass too. That's nice, isn't it? That's a funny thing on the ashtray. That's Egyptian, that is. It's a scarabee, or some name like that. You know. Sounds like some kind of scratching disease but it isn't. No, it's a sort of beetle and it's made out of some stone. They call it a precious stone. Bright blue. A lazy – a lavis – a lazy lapin or something like that.'

'Lapis lazuli,' said Mrs Oliver.

'That's right. That's what it is. Very nice, that is. That was my archaeological boy what went digging. He sent me that.'

'All your lovely past,' said Mrs Oliver.

'Yes, all my boys and girls. Some of them as babies, some of them I had from the month, and the older ones. Some of them when I went to India and that other time when I was in Siam. Yes. That's Miss Moya in her Court dress. Ah, she was a pretty thing. Divorced two husbands, she has. Yes. Trouble with his lordship, the first one, and then she married one of those pop singers and of course that couldn't take very well. And then she married someone in California. They had a yacht and went places, I think. Died two or three years ago and only sixty-two. Pity dying so young, you know.'

'You've been to a lot of different parts of the world yourself, haven't you?' said Mrs Oliver. 'India, Hong Kong, then Egypt, and South America, wasn't it?'

'Ah yes, I've been about a good deal.'

'I remember,' said Mrs Oliver, 'when I was in Malaya, you were with a service family then, weren't you? A General somebody. Was it – now wait a minute, I can't remember the name – it wasn't General and Lady Ravenscroft, was it?'

'No, no, you've got the name wrong. You're thinking of when I was with the Barnabys. That's right. You came to stay with them. Remember? You were doing a tour, you were, and you came and stayed with the Barnabys. You were an old friend of hers. He was a Judge.'

'Ah yes,' said Mrs Oliver. 'It's difficult a bit. One gets names mixed up.'

'Two nice children they had,' said Mrs Matcham. 'Of course they went to school in England. The boy went to Harrow and the girl went to Roedean, I think it was, and so I moved on to another family after that. Ah, things have changed nowadays. Not so many amahs, even, as there used to be. Mind you, the amahs used to be a bit of a trouble now and then. I got on with our one very well when I was with the Barnabys, I mean. Who was it you spoke of? The Ravenscrofts? Well, I remember them. Yes – I forget the name of the place where they lived now. Not far from us. The families were acquainted, you know. Oh yes, it's a long time ago, but I remember it all. I was still out there with the Barnabys, you know. I stayed on when the children went to school to look after Mrs Barnaby. Look after her things, you know, and mend them and all that. Oh yes, I was there when that awful thing happened. I don't mean the Barnabys, I mean to the Ravenscrofts. Yes, I shall never forget that. Hearing about it, I mean. Naturally I wasn't mixed up in it myself, but it was a terrible thing to happen, wasn't it?'

'I should think it must have been,' said Mrs Oliver.

'It was after you'd gone back to England, a good long time after that, I think. A nice couple they were. Very nice couple and it was a shock to them.'

'I don't really remember now,' said Mrs Oliver.

'I know. One forgets things. I don't myself. But they said she'd always been queer, you know. Ever since the time she was a child. Some early story there was. She took a baby out of the pram and threw it in the river. Jealousy, they said. Other people said she wanted the baby to go to heaven and not wait.'

'Is it – is it Lady Ravenscroft, you mean?'

'No, of course I don't. Ah, you don't remember as well as I do. It was the sister.'

'Her sister?'

'I'm not sure now whether it was her sister or his sister. They said she'd been in a kind of mental place for a long time, you know. Ever since she was about eleven or twelve years old. They kept her there and then they said she was all right again and she came out. And she married someone in the Army. And then there was trouble. And the next thing they heard, I believe, was that she'd been put back again in one of them loony-bin places. They treat you very well, you know. They have a suite, nice rooms and all that. And they used to go and see her, I believe. I mean the General did or his wife. The children were brought up by someone else, I think, because they were afraid-like. However, they said she was all right in the end. So she came back to live with her husband, and then he died or something. Blood pressure I think it was, or heart. Anyway, she was very upset and she came out to stay with her brother or her sister – whichever it was – she seemed quite happy there and everything, and ever so fond of children, she was. It wasn't the little boy, I think, he was at school. It was the little girl, and another little girl who'd come to play with her that afternoon. Ah well, I can't remember the details now. It's so long ago. There was a lot of talk about it. There was some as said, you know, as it wasn't her at all. They thought it was the amah that had done it, but the amah loved them and she was very, very upset. She wanted to take them away from the house. She said they weren't safe there, and all sorts of things like that. But of course the others didn't believe in it and then this came about and I gather they think it must have been whatever her name was – I can't remember it now. Anyway, there it was.'

'And what happened to this sister, either of General or Lady Ravenscroft?'

'Well, I think, you know, as she was taken away by a doctor and put in some place and went back to England, I believe, in the end. I dunno if she went to the same place as before, but she was well looked after somewhere. There was plenty of money, I think, you know. Plenty of money in the husband's family. Maybe she got all right again. But well, I haven't thought of it for years. Not till you came here asking me stories about General and Lady Ravenscroft. I wonder where they are now. They must have retired before now, long ago.'

'Well, it was rather sad,' said Mrs Oliver. 'Perhaps you read about it in the papers.'

'Read what?'

'Well, they bought a house in England and then –'

'Ah now, it's coming back to me. I remember reading something about that in the paper. Yes, and thinking then that I knew the name Ravenscroft, but I couldn't quite remember when and how. They fell over a cliff, didn't they? Something of that kind.'

'Yes,' said Mrs Oliver, 'something of that kind.'

'Now look here, dearie, it's so nice to see you, it is. You must let me give you a cup of tea.'

'Really,' said Mrs Oliver, 'I don't need any tea. Really, I don't want it.'

'Of course you want some tea. If you don't mind now, come into the kitchen, will you? I mean, I spend most of my time there now. It's easier to get about there. But I take visitors always into this room because I'm proud of my things, you know. Proud of my things and proud of all the children and the others.'

'I think,' said Mrs Oliver, 'that people like you must have had a wonderful life with all the children you've looked after.'

'Yes. I remember when you were a little girl, you liked to listen to the stories I told you. There was one about a tiger, I remember, and one about monkeys – monkeys in a tree.'

'Yes,' said Mrs Oliver, 'I remember those. It was a very long time ago.'

Her mind swept back to herself, a child of six or seven, walking in button boots that were rather too tight on a road in England, and listening to a story of India and Egypt from an attendant Nanny. And this was Nanny. Mrs Matcham was Nanny. She looked round the room as she followed her hostess out. At the pictures of girls, of schoolboys, of children and various middle-aged people, all mainly photographed in their best clothes and sent in nice frames or other things because they hadn't forgotten Nanny. Because of them, probably, Nanny was having a reasonably comfortable old age with money supplied. Mrs Oliver felt a sudden desire to burst out crying. This was so unlike her that she was able to stop herself by an effort of will. She followed Mrs Matcham to the kitchen. There she produced the offering she had brought.

'Well, I never! A tin of Tophole Thathams tea. Always my

favourite. Fancy you remembering. I can hardly ever get it nowadays. And that's my favourite tea biscuits. Well, you are a one for never forgetting. What was it they used to call you – those two little boys who came to play – one would call you Lady Elephant and the other one called you Lady Swan. The one who called you Lady Elephant used to sit on your back and you went about the floor on all fours and pretended to have a trunk you picked things up with.'

'You don't forget many things, do you, Nanny?' said Mrs Oliver.

'Ah,' said Mrs Matcham. 'Elephants don't forget. That's the old saying.'

CHAPTER 8

MRS OLIVER AT WORK

Mrs Oliver entered the premises of Williams & Barnet, a well-appointed chemist's shop also dealing with various cosmetics. She paused by a kind of dumb waiter containing various types of corn remedies, hesitated by a mountain of rubber sponges, wandered vaguely towards the prescription desk and then came down past the well-displayed aids to beauty as imagined by Elizabeth Arden, Helena Rubinstein, Max Factor and other benefit providers for women's lives.

She stopped finally near a rather plump girl and enquired for certain lipsticks, then uttered a short cry of surprise.

'Why, Marlene – it is Marlene, isn't it?'

'Well, I never. It's Mrs Oliver. I am pleased to see you. It's wonderful, isn't it? All the girls will be very excited when I tell them that you've been in to buy things here.'

'No need to tell them,' said Mrs Oliver.

'Oh, now I'm sure they'll be bringing out their autograph books!'

'I'd rather they didn't,' said Mrs Oliver. 'And how are you, Marlene?'

'Oh, getting along, getting along,' said Marlene.

'I didn't know whether you'd be working here still.'

'Well, it's as good as any other place, I think, and they treat you very well here, you know. I had a rise in salary last year and I'm more or less in charge of this cosmetic counter now.'

'And your mother? Is she well?'

'Oh yes. Mum will be pleased to hear I've met you.'

'Is she still living in her same house down the – the road past the hospital?'

'Oh yes, we're still there. Dad's not been so well. He's been in hospital for a while, but Mum keeps along very well indeed. Oh, she will be pleased to hear I've seen you. Are you staying here by any chance?'

'Not really,' said Mrs Oliver. 'I'm just passing through, as a matter of fact. I've been to see an old friend and I wonder now –' she looked at her wrist-watch. 'Would your mother be at home now, Marlene? I could just call in and see her. Have a few words before I have to get on.'

'Oh, do do that,' said Marlene. 'She'd be ever so pleased. I'm sorry I can't leave here and come with you, but I don't think – well, it wouldn't be viewed very well. You know I can't get off for another hour and a half.'

'Oh well, some other time,' said Mrs Oliver. 'Anyway, I can't quite remember – was it number 17 or has it got a name?'

'It's called Laurel Cottage.'

'Oh yes, of course. How stupid of me. Well, nice to have seen you.'

She hurried out plus one unwanted lipstick in her bag, and drove her car down the main street of Chipping Bartram and turned, after passing a garage and a hospital building, down a rather narrow road which had quite pleasant small houses on either side of it.

She left the car outside Laurel Cottage and went in. A thin, energetic woman with grey hair, of about fifty years of age, opened the door and displayed instant signs of recognition.

'Why, so it's you, Mrs Oliver. Ah well, now. Not seen you for years and years, I haven't.'

'Oh, it's a very long time.'

'Well, come in then, come in. Can I make you a nice cup of tea?'

'I'm afraid not,' said Mrs Oliver, 'because I've had tea already with a friend, and I've got to get back to London. As it happened,

I went into the chemist for something I wanted and I saw Marlene there.'

'Yes, she's got a very good job there. They think a lot of her in that place. They say she's got a lot of enterprise.'

'Well, that's very nice. And how are you, Mrs Buckle? You look very well. Hardly older than when I saw you last.'

'Oh, I wouldn't like to say that. Grey hairs, and I've lost a lot of weight.'

'This seems to be a day when I meet a lot of friends I knew formerly,' said Mrs Oliver, going into the house and being led into a small, rather over-cluttered sitting-room. 'I don't know if you remember Mrs Carstairs – Mrs Julia Carstairs.'

'Oh, of course I do. Yes, rather. She must be getting on.'

'Oh yes, she is, really. But we talked over a few old days, you know. In fact, we went as far as talking about that tragedy that occurred. I was in America at the time so I didn't know much about it. People called Ravenscroft.'

'Oh, I remember that well.'

'You worked for them, didn't you, at one time, Mrs Buckle?'

'Yes. I used to go in three mornings a week. Very nice people they were. You know, real military lady and gentleman, as you might say. The old school.'

'It was a very tragic thing to happen.'

'Yes, it was, indeed.'

'Were you still working for them at that time?'

'No. As a matter of fact, I'd given up going there. I had my old Aunt Emma come to live with me and she was rather blind and not very well, and I couldn't really spare the time any more to go out doing things for people. But I'd been with them up to about a month or two before that.'

'It seemed such a terrible thing to happen,' said Mrs Oliver. 'I understand that they thought it was a suicide pact.'

'I don't believe that,' said Mrs Buckle. 'I'm sure they'd never have committed suicide together. Not people like that. And living so pleasantly together as they did. Of course, they hadn't lived there very long.'

'No, I suppose they hadn't,' said Mrs Oliver. 'They lived somewhere near Bournemouth, didn't they, when they first came to England?'

'Yes, but they found it was a bit too far for getting to London from there, and so that's why they came to Chipping Bartram. Very nice house it was, and a nice garden.'

'Were they both in good health when you were working for them last?'

'Well, he felt his age a bit as most people do. The General, he'd had some kind of heart trouble or a slight stroke. Something of that kind, you know. They'd take pills, you know, and lie up a bit from time to time.'

'And Lady Ravenscroft?'

'Well, I think she missed the life she'd had abroad, you know. They didn't know so very many people there, although they got to know a good many families, of course, being the sort of class they were. But I suppose it wasn't like Malaya or those places. You know, where you have a lot of servants. I suppose gay parties and that sort of thing.'

'You think she missed her gay parties?'

'Well, I don't know that exactly.'

'Somebody told me she'd taken to wearing a wig.'

'Oh, she'd got several wigs,' said Mrs Buckle, smiling slightly. 'Very smart ones and very expensive. You know, from time to time she'd send one back to the place she'd got it from in London, and they'd re-dress it for her again and send it. There were all kinds. You know, there was one with auburn hair, and one with little grey curls all over her head. Really, she looked very nice in that one. And two – well, not so attractive really but useful for – you know – windy days when you wanted something to put on when it might be raining. Thought a lot about her appearance, you know and spent a lot of her money on clothes.'

'What do you think was the cause of the tragedy?' said Mrs Oliver. 'You see, not being anywhere near here and not seeing any of my friends at that time because I was in America, I missed hearing anything about it and, well, one doesn't like to ask questions or write letters about things of that kind. I suppose there must have been some cause. I mean, it was General Ravenscroft's own revolver that was used, I understand.'

'Oh yes, he had two of those in the house because he said that no house was safe without. Perhaps he was right there, you know. Not that they'd had any trouble beforehand as far as I know. One afternoon a rather nasty sort of fellow came along to the door. Didn't like the look of him, I didn't. Wanted to see the General. Said he'd been in the General's regiment when he was a young fellow. The General asked him a few questions and I think thought as how he didn't – well, thought he wasn't very reliable. So he sent him off.'

'You think then that it was someone outside that did it?'

'Well, I think it must have been because I can't see any other thing. Mind you, I didn't like the man who came and did the gardening for them very much. He hadn't got a very good reputation and I gather he'd had a few jail sentences earlier in his life. But of course the General took up his references and he wanted to give him a chance.'

'So you think the gardener might have killed them?'

'Well, I – I always thought that. But then I'm probably wrong. But it doesn't seem to me – I mean, the people who said there was some scandalous story or something about either her or him and that either he'd shot her or she'd shot him, that's all nonsense, I'd say. No, it was some outsider. One of these people that – well, it's not as bad as it is nowadays because that, you must remember, was before people began getting all this violence idea. But look at what you read in the papers every day now. Young men, practically only boys still, taking a lot of drugs and going wild and rushing about, shooting a lot of people for nothing at all, asking a girl in a pub to have a drink with them and then they see her home and next day her body's found in a ditch. Stealing children out of prams from their mothers, taking a girl to a dance and murdering her or strangling her on the way back. If anything, you feel as anyone can do anything. And anyway, there's that nice couple, the General and his wife, out for a nice walk in the evening, and there they were, both shot through the head.'

'Was it through the head?'

'Well, I don't remember exactly now and of course I never saw anything myself. But anyway, just went for a walk as they often did.'

'And they'd not been on bad terms with each other?'

'Well, they had words now and again, but who doesn't?'

'No boyfriend or girlfriend?'

'Well, if you can use that term of people of that age, oh, I mean there was a bit of talk here and there, but it was all nonsense. Nothing to it at all. People always want to say something of that kind.'

'Perhaps one of them was – ill.'

'Well, Lady Ravenscroft had been up to London once or twice consulting a doctor about something and I rather think she was going into hospital, or planning to go into hospital for an operation of some kind though she never told me exactly what it was. But I think they managed to put her right – she was in this hospital for a short time. No operation, I think. And when she came back she looked very much younger. Altogether, she'd had a lot of face treatment and you know, she looked so pretty in these wigs with curls on them. Rather as though she'd got a new lease of life.'

'And General Ravenscroft?'

'He was a very nice gentleman and I never heard or knew of any scandal about him and I don't think there was any. People say things, but then they want to say something when there's been a tragedy of any kind. It seems to me perhaps as he might have had a blow on the head in Malaya or something like that. I had an uncle or a great-uncle, you know, who fell off his horse there once. Hit it on a cannon or something and he was very queer afterwards. All right for about six months and then they had to put him into an asylum because he wanted to take his wife's life the whole time. He said she was persecuting him and following him and that she was a spy for another nation. Ah, there's no saying what things happen or can happen in families.'

'Anyway, you don't think there was any truth in some of the stories about them that I have happened to hear of, bad feeling between them so that one of them shot the other and then shot himself or herself.'

'Oh no, I don't.'

'Were her children at home at the time?'

'No. Miss – er – oh what was her name now, Rosie? No. Penelope?'

'Celia,' said Mrs Oliver. 'She's my goddaughter.'

'Oh, of course she is. Yes, I know that now. I remember you coming and taking her out once. She was a high-spirited girl, rather bad-tempered in some ways, but she was very fond of her father and mother, I think. No, she was away at a school in Switzerland when it happened, I'm glad to say, because it would have been a terrible shock to her if she'd been at home and the one who saw them.'

'And there was a boy, too, wasn't there?'

'Oh yes. Master Edward. His father was a bit worried about him, I think. He looked as though he disliked his father.'

'Oh, there's nothing in that. Boys go through that stage. Was he very devoted to his mother?'

'Well, she fussed over him a bit too much, I think, which he found tiresome. You know, they don't like a mother fussing over them, telling them to wear thicker vests or put an extra pullover on. His father, he didn't like the way he wore his hair. It was – well they weren't wearing hair like the way they are nowadays, but they were beginning to, if you know what I mean.'

'But the boy wasn't at home at the time of the tragedy?'

'No.'

'I suppose it was a shock to him?'

'Well, it must have been. Of course, I wasn't going to the house any more at that time so I didn't hear so much. If you ask me, I didn't like that gardener. What was his name now – Fred, I think. Fred Wizell. Some name like that. Seems to me if he'd done a bit of – well, a bit of cheating or something like that and the General had found him out and was going to sack him, I wouldn't put it past him.'

'To shoot the husband and wife?'

'Well, I'd have thought it more likely he'd just have shot the General. If he shot the General and the wife came along, then he'd have had to shoot her too. You read things like that in books.'

'Yes,' said Mrs Oliver thoughtfully, 'one does read all sorts of things in books.'

'There was the tutor. I didn't like him much.'

'What tutor?'

'Well, there was a tutor for the boy earlier. You know, he couldn't pass an exam and things at the earlier school he was at – prep school or something. So they had a tutor for him. He was there for about a year, I think. Lady Ravenscroft liked him very much. She was musical, you know, and so was this tutor. Mr Edmunds, I think his name was. Rather a namby-pamby sort of young man, I thought myself, and it's my opinion that General Ravenscroft didn't care for him much.'

'But Lady Ravenscroft did.'

'Oh, they had a lot in common, I think. And I think she was the one really that chose him rather more than the General. Mind you, he had very nice manners and spoke to everyone nicely and all that –'

'And did – what's-his-name?'

'Edward? Oh yes, he liked him all right, I think. Almost a bit of hero-worship. Anyway, don't you believe any stories you hear about scandals in the family or her having an affair with anyone or General Ravenscroft with that rather po-faced girl who did filing work for him and all that sort of thing. No. Whoever that wicked murderer was, it's one who came from outside. The police never got on to anyone, a car was seen near there but there was nothing to it and they never got any further. But all the same I think one ought to look about for somebody perhaps who'd known them in Malaya or abroad or somewhere else, or even when they were first living at Bournemouth. One never knows.'

'What did your husband think about it?' said Mrs Oliver. 'He wouldn't have known as much about them as you would, of course, but still he might have heard a lot.'

'Oh, he heard a lot of talk, of course. In the George and Flag, of an evening, you know. People saying all sorts of things. Said as she drank and that cases of empty bottles had been taken out of the house. Absolutely untrue, that was, I know for a fact. And there was a nephew as used to come and see them sometimes. Got into trouble with the police in some way, he did, but I don't think there was anything in that. The police didn't, either. Anyway, it wasn't at that time.'

'There was no one else really living in the house, was there, except the General and Lady Ravenscroft?'

'Well, she had a sister as used to come sometimes, Lady Ravenscroft did. She was a half-sister, I think. Something like that. Looked rather like Lady Ravenscroft. She made a bit of trouble between them, I always used to think, when she came for a visit. She was one of those who likes stirring things up, if you know what I mean. Just said things to annoy people.'

'Was Lady Ravenscroft fond of her?'

'Well, if you ask me, I don't think she was really. I think the sister more or less wished herself on to them sometimes and she didn't like not to have her, but I think she found it pretty trying to have her there. The General quite liked her because she played cards well. Played chess and things with him and he enjoyed that. And she was an amusing woman in a way. Mrs Jerryboy or something like that, her name was. She was a widow, I think. Used to borrow money from them, I think, too.'

'Did you like her?'

'Well, if you don't mind my saying so, ma'am, no, I didn't like her. I disliked her very much. I thought she was one of those trouble-makers, you know. But she hadn't been down for some time before the tragedy happened. I don't really remember very much what she was like. She had a son as came with her once or twice. Didn't like him very much. Shifty, I thought.'

'Well,' said Mrs Oliver. 'I suppose nobody will really ever know the truth. Not now. Not after all this time. I saw my goddaughter the other day.'

'Did you now, ma'am. I'd be interested to hear about Miss Celia. How is she? All right?'

'Yes. She seems quite all right. I think she's thinking perhaps of getting married. At any rate she's got a –'

'Got a steady boy-friend, has she?' said Mrs Buckle. 'Ah well, we've all got that. Not that we all marry the first one we settle on. Just as well if you don't, nine times out of ten.'

'You don't know a Mrs Burton-Cox, do you?' asked Mrs Oliver.

'Burton-Cox? I seem to know that name. No, I don't think so. Wasn't living down here or come to stay with them or anything? No, not that I remember. Yet I did hear something. Some old friend of General Ravenscroft, I think, which he'd known in Malaya. But I don't know.' She shook her head.

'Well,' said Mrs Oliver, 'I mustn't stay gossiping with you any longer. It's been so nice to see you and Marlene.'

CHAPTER 9

RESULTS OF ELEPHANTINE RESEARCH

'A telephone call for you,' said Hercule Poirot's manservant, George. 'From Mrs Oliver.'

'Ah yes, George. And what had she to say?'

'She wondered if she could come and see you this evening, sir, after dinner.'

'That would be admirable,' said Poirot. 'Admirable. I have had a tiring day. It will be a stimulating experience to see Mrs Oliver. She is always entertaining as well as being highly unexpected in the things she says. Did she mention elephants, by the way?'

'Elephants, sir? No, I do not think so.'

'Ah. Then it would seem perhaps that the elephants have been disappointing.'

George looked at his master rather doubtfully. There were times when he did not quite understand the relevance of Poirot's remarks.

'Ring her back,' said Hercule Poirot, 'tell her I shall be delighted to receive her.'

George went away to carry out this order, and returned to say that Mrs Oliver would be there about quarter to nine.

'Coffee,' said Poirot. 'Let coffee be prepared and some *petit-fours*. I rather think I ordered some in lately from Fortnum and Mason.'

'A liqueur of any kind, sir?'

'No, I think not. I myself will have some *Sirop de Cassis*.'

'Yes, sir.'

Mrs Oliver arrived exactly on time. Poirot greeted her with every sign of pleasure.

'And how are you, *chère madame*?'

'Exhausted,' said Mrs Oliver.

She sank down into the armchair that Poirot indicated.

'Completely exhausted.'

'Ah. *Qui va à la chasse* – oh, I cannot remember the saying.'

'I remember it,' said Mrs Oliver. 'I learnt it as a child. "*Qui va à la chasse perd sa place*."'

'That, I am sure, is not applicable to the chase you have been conducting. I am referring to the pursuit of elephants, unless that was merely a figure of speech.'

'Not at all,' said Mrs Oliver. 'I have been pursuing elephants madly. Here, there and everywhere. The amount of petrol I have used, the amount of trains I have taken, the amount of letters I've written, the amount of telegrams I've sent – you wouldn't believe how exhausting it all is.'

'Then repose yourself. Have some coffee.'

'Nice, strong, black coffee – yes, I will. Just what I want.'

'Did you, may I ask, get any results?'

'Plenty of results,' said Mrs Oliver. 'The trouble is, I don't know whether any of them are any use.'

'You learn facts, however?'

'No. Not really. I learnt things that people told me were facts, but I strongly doubt myself whether any of them *were* facts.'

'They were hearsay?'

'No. They were what I said they would be. They were memories. Lots of people who had memories. The trouble is, when you remember things you don't always remember them right, do you?'

'No. But they are still what you might describe perhaps as results. Is not that so?'

'And what have you done?' said Mrs Oliver.

'You are always so stern, madame,' said Poirot. 'You demand that I run about, that I also do things.'

'Well, have you run about?'

'I have not run about, but I have had a few consultations with others of my own profession.'

'It sounds far more peaceful than what I have been doing,' said Mrs Oliver. 'Oh, this coffee is nice. It's really strong. You wouldn't believe how tired I am. And how muddled.'

'Come, come. Let us have good expectancy. You have got things. You have got something, I think.'

'I've got a lot of different suggestions and stories. I don't know whether any of them are true.'

'They could be not true, but still be of use,' said Poirot.

'Well, I know what you mean,' said Mrs Oliver, 'and that's what I think, too. I mean, that's what I thought when I went about it. When people remember something and tell you about it – I mean, it's often not quite actually what occurred, but it's what they themselves thought occurred.'

'But they must have had something on which to base it,' said Poirot.

'I've brought you a list of a kind,' said Mrs Oliver. 'I don't need to go into details of where I went or what I said or why, I went out deliberately for – well, information one couldn't perhaps get from anybody in this country now. But it's all from people who knew something about the Ravenscrofts, even if they hadn't known them very well.'

'News from foreign places, do you mean?'

'Quite a lot of them were from foreign places. Other people who knew them here rather slightly or from people whose aunts or cousins or friends knew them long ago.'

'And each one that you've noted down had *some* story to tell – some reference to the tragedy or to people involved?'

'That's the idea,' said Mrs Oliver. 'I'll tell you roughly, shall I?'

'Yes. Have a *petit-four*.'

'Thank you,' said Mrs Oliver.

She took a particularly sweet and rather bilious-looking one and champed it with energy.

'Sweet things,' she said, 'really give you a lot of vitality, I always think. Well now, I've got the following suggestions. These things have usually been said to me starting by: – "Oh yes, of course!" "How sad it was, that whole story!" "Of course, I think everyone knows really what happened." That's the sort of thing.'

'Yes.'

'These people *thought* they knew what happened. But there weren't really any very good reasons. It was just something someone had told them, or they'd heard either from friends or servants or relations or things like that. The suggestions, of course, are all the kind that you might think they were. A. That General Ravenscroft was writing his memoirs of his Malayan days and that he had a young woman who acted as his secretary and took dictation and typed things for him and was helping him, that she was a nice-looking girl and no doubt there was something there. The result being – well, there seemed to be two schools of thought. One school of thought was that he shot his wife because he hoped to marry the girl, and then when he had shot her, immediately was horror-stricken at what he'd done and shot himself . . .'

'Exactly,' said Poirot. 'A romantic explanation.'

'The other idea was that there had been a tutor who came to give lessons to the son who had been ill and away from his prep school for six months or so – a good-looking young man.'

'Ah yes. And the wife had fallen in love with the young man. Perhaps had an affair with him?'

'That was the idea,' said Mrs Oliver. 'No kind of evidence. Just romantic suggestion again.'

'And therefore?'

'Therefore I think the idea was that the General probably shot his wife and then in a fit of remorse shot himself. There was another story that the General had had an affair, and his wife found out about it, that she shot him and then herself. It's always been slightly different every time. But nobody really knew anything. I mean, it's always just a likely story every time. I mean, the General may have had an affair with a girl or lots of girls or just another married woman, or it might have been the wife who had an affair with someone. It's been a different someone in each story I've been told. There was nothing definite about it or any evidence for it. It's just the gossip that went around about twelve or thirteen years ago, which people have rather forgotten about now. But they remember enough about it to tell one a few names and get things only moderately wrong about what happened. There was an angry gardener who happened to live on the place, there was a nice elderly cook-housekeeper, who was rather blind and rather deaf, but nobody seems to suspect that she had anything to do with it. And so on. I've got all the names and possibilities written down. The names of some of them wrong and some of them right. It's all very difficult. His wife had been ill, I gather, for some short time, I think it was some kind of fever that she had. A lot of her hair must have fallen out because she bought four wigs. There were at least four new wigs found among her things.'

'Yes. I, too, heard that,' said Poirot.

'Who did you hear it from?'

'A friend of mine in the police. He went back over the accounts of the inquest and the various things in the house. Four wigs! I would like to have your opinion on that, madame. Do you think that four wigs seems somewhat excessive?'

'Well, I do really,' said Mrs Oliver. 'I had an aunt who had a wig, and she had an extra wig, but she sent one back to be redressed and wore the second one. I never heard of anyone who had four wigs.'

Mrs Oliver extracted a small notebook from her bag, ruffled the pages of it, searching for extracts.

'Mrs Carstairs, she's seventy-seven and rather gaga. Quote from her: "I do remember the Ravenscrofts quite well. Yes, yes, a very nice couple. It's very sad, I think. Yes. Cancer it was!" I asked her which of them had cancer,' said Mrs Oliver, 'but Mrs Carstairs had rather forgotten about that. She said she thought the wife came to London and consulted a doctor and had an operation and then came home and was very miserable, and her husband was very upset about her. So of course he shot her and himself.'

'Was that her theory or did she have an exact knowledge?'

'I think it was entirely theory. As far as I can see and hear in the course of my investigations,' said Mrs Oliver, making rather a point of this last word, 'when anybody has heard that any of their friends whom they don't happen to know very well have sudden illness or consult doctors, they always think it's cancer. And so do the people themselves, I think. Somebody else – I can't read her name here, I've forgotten, I think it began with T – she said that it was the husband who had cancer. He was very unhappy, and so was his wife. And they talked it over together and they couldn't bear the thought of it all, so they decided to commit suicide.'

'Sad and romantic,' said Poirot.

'Yes, and I don't think really true,' said Mrs Oliver. 'It is worrying, isn't it? I mean, the people remembering so much and that they really mostly seem to have made it up themselves.'

'They have made up the solution of something they knew about,' said Poirot. 'That is to say, they know that somebody comes to London, say, to consult a doctor, or that somebody has been in hospital for two or three months. That is a *fact* that they know.'

'Yes,' said Mrs Oliver, 'and then when they come to talk about it a long time afterwards, they've got the solution for it which they've made up themselves. That isn't awfully helpful, is it?'

'It is helpful,' said Poirot. 'You are quite right, you know, in what you said to me.'

'About elephants?' said Mrs Oliver, rather doubtfully.

'About elephants,' said Poirot. 'It is important to know certain facts which have lingered in people's memories although they may not know exactly what the fact was, why it happened or what led to it. But they might easily know something that we do not know and that we have no means of learning. So there have been memories leading to theories – theories of infidelity, of illness, of suicide pacts, of jealousy, all these things have been suggested to you. Further search could be made as to points if they seem in any way probable.'

'People like talking about the past,' said Mrs Oliver. 'They like talking about the past really much more than they like talking about what's happening now, or what happened last year. It brings things back to them. They tell you, of course, first about a lot of other people that you don't want to hear about and then you hear what the other people that they've remembered knew about somebody else that they didn't know but they heard about. You know, so that the General and Lady Ravenscroft you hear about is at one remove, as it were. It's like family relationships,' she said. 'You know, first cousin once removed, second cousin twice removed, all the rest of it. I don't think I've been really very helpful, though.'

'You must not think that,' said Poirot. 'I am pretty sure that you will find that some of these things in your agreeable little purple-coloured notebook will have something to do with the past tragedy. I can tell you from my own enquiries into the official accounts of these two deaths, that they have remained a mystery. That is, from the police point of view. They were an affectionate couple, there was no gossip or hearsay much about them of any sex trouble, there was no illness discovered such as would have caused anyone to take their own lives. I talk now only of the time, you understand, immediately preceding the tragedy. But there was a time before that, further back.'

'I know what you mean,' said Mrs Oliver, 'and I've got something about that from an old Nanny. An old Nanny who is now – I don't know, she might be a hundred, but I think she's only about eighty. I remember her from my childhood days. She used to tell me stories about people in the Services abroad – India, Egypt, Siam and Hong Kong and the rest.'

'Anything that interested you?'

'Yes,' said Mrs Oliver, 'there was some tragedy that she talked about. She seemed a bit uncertain about what it was. I'm not sure that it had anything to do with the Ravenscrofts, it might have been to do with some other people out there because she doesn't remember surnames and things very well. It was a mental case in one family. Someone's sister-in-law. Either General Whoever-it-was's sister or Mrs Who-ever-it-was's sister. Somebody who'd been in a mental home for years. I gathered she'd killed her own children or tried to kill her own children long ago, and then she'd been supposed to be cured or paroled or something and came out to Egypt, or Malaya or wherever it was. She came out to stay with the people. And then it seems there was some other tragedy, connected again, I think, with children or something of that kind. Anyway, it was something that was hushed up. But I wondered. I mean, if there was something mental in the family, either Lady Ravenscroft's family or General Ravenscroft's family. I don't think it need have been as near as a sister. It could have been a cousin or something like that. But – well, it seemed to me a possible line of enquiry.'

'Yes,' said Poirot, 'there's always possibility and something that waits for many years and then comes home to roost from somewhere in the past. That is what someone said to me. *Old sins have long shadows*.'

'It seemed to me,' said Mrs Oliver, 'not that it was likely or even that old Nanny Matcham remembered it right or even really about it being the people she thought it was. But it *might* have fitted in with what that awful woman at the literary luncheon said to me.'

'You mean when she wanted to know . . .'

'Yes. When she wanted me to find out from the daughter, my

godchild, whether her mother had killed her father or whether her father had killed her mother.'

'And she thought the girl might know?'

'Well, it's likely enough that the girl would know. I mean, not at the time – it might have been shielded from her – but she might know things about it which would make her be aware what the circumstances were in their lives and who was likely to have killed whom, though she would probably never mention it or say anything about it or talk to anyone about it.'

'And you say that woman – this Mrs –'

'Yes. I've forgotten her name now. Mrs Burton something. A name like that. She said something about her son had this girlfriend and that they were thinking of getting married. And I can quite see you might want to know, if so, whether her mother or father had criminal relations in their family – or a loony strain. She probably thought that if it was the mother who killed the father it would be very unwise for the boy to marry her, whereas if the father had killed the mother, she probably wouldn't mind as much,' said Mrs Oliver.

'You mean that she would think that the inheritance would go in the female line?'

'Well, she wasn't a very clever type of woman. Bossy,' said Mrs Oliver. 'Thinks she knows a lot, but no. I think you might think that way if you were a woman.'

'An interesting point of view, but possible,' said Poirot. 'Yes, I realize that.' He sighed. 'We have a lot to do still.'

'I've got another side light on things, too. Same thing, but second hand, if you know what I mean. You know. Someone says "The Ravenscrofts? Weren't they that couple who adopted a child? Then it seems, after it was all arranged, and they were absolutely stuck on it – very, very keen on it, one of their children had died in Malaya, I think – but at any rate they had adopted this child and then its own mother wanted it back and they had a court case or something. But the court gave them the custody of the child and the mother came and tried to kidnap it back."'

'There are simpler points,' said Poirot, 'arising out of your report, points that I prefer.'

'Such as?'

'Wigs. Four wigs.'

'Well,' said Mrs Oliver, 'I thought that was interesting you but I don't know why. It doesn't seem to *mean* anything. The other story was just somebody mental. There are mental people who are in homes or loony-bins because they have killed their children or some other child, for some absolutely batty reason, no sense to it at all. I don't see why that would make General and Lady Ravenscroft want to kill themselves.'

'Unless one of them was implicated,' said Poirot.

'You mean that General Ravenscroft may have killed someone, a boy – an illigitimate child, perhaps, of his wife's or of his own? No, I think we're getting a bit too melodramatic there. Or she might have killed her husband's child or her own.'

'And yet,' said Poirot, 'what people seem to be, they usually are.'

'You mean –?'

'They seemed an affectionate couple, a couple who lived together happily without disputes. They seem to have had no case history of illness beyond a suggestion of an operation, of someone coming to London to consult some medical authority, a possibility of cancer, of leukaemia, something of that kind, some future that they could not face. And yet, somehow we do not seem to get at something beyond what is *possible*, but not yet what is *probable*. If there was anyone else in the house, anyone else at the time, the police, my friends that is to say, who have known the investigation at the time, say that nothing told was really compatible with anything else but with the facts. For some reason, those two didn't want to go on living. *Why*?'

'I knew a couple,' said Mrs Oliver, 'in the war – the second war, I mean – they thought that the Germans would land in England and they had decided if that happened they would kill themselves. I said it was very stupid. They said it would be impossible to go on living. It still seems to me stupid. You've got to have enough courage to live through something. I mean, it's not as though your death was going to do any good to anybody else. I wonder –'

'Yes, what do you wonder?'

'Well, when I said that I wondered suddenly if General and Lady Ravenscroft's deaths did any good to anyone else.'

'You mean somebody inherited money from them?'

'Yes. Not quite as blatant as that. Perhaps somebody would

have a better chance of doing well in life. Something there was in their life that they didn't want either of their two children ever to hear about or to know about.'

Poirot sighed.

'The trouble with you, is,' he said, 'you think so often of something that well *might* have occurred, that *might* have been. You give me ideas. Possible ideas. If only they were probable ideas also. *Why*? Why were the deaths of those two necessary? Why is it – they were not in pain, they were not in illness, they were not deeply unhappy from what one can see. Then why, in the evening of a beautiful day, did they go for a walk to a cliff and taking the dog with them . . .'

'What's the dog got to do with it?' said Mrs Oliver.

'Well, I wondered for a moment. Did they take the dog, or did the dog follow them? Where does the dog come in?'

'I suppose it comes in like the wigs,' said Mrs Oliver. 'Just one more thing that you can't explain and doesn't seem to make sense. One of my elephants said the dog was devoted to Lady Ravenscroft, but another one said the dog bit her.'

'One always comes back to the same thing,' said Poirot. 'One wants to know more.' He sighed. 'One wants to know more about the people, and how can you know people separated from you by a gulf of years.'

'Well, you've done it once or twice, haven't you?' said Mrs Oliver. 'You know – something about where a painter was shot or poisoned. That was near the sea on a sort of fortification or something. You found out who did that, although you didn't know any of the people.'

'No. I didn't know any of the people, but I learnt about them from the other people who were there.'[1]

'Well, that's what I'm trying to do,' said Mrs Oliver, 'only I can't get near enough. I can't get to anyone who really knew anything, who was really involved. Do you think really we ought to give it up?'

'I think it would be very wise to give it up,' said Poirot, 'but there is a moment when one no longer wants to be wise. One wants to find out more. I have an interest now in that couple

[1] *Five Little Pigs*

of kindly people, with two nice children. I presume they are nice children?'

'I don't know the boy,' said Mrs Oliver, 'I don't think I've ever met him. Do you want to see my goddaughter? I could send her to see you, if you like.'

'Yes, I think I would like to see her, meet her some way. Perhaps she would not wish to come and see me, but a meeting could be brought about. It might, I think, be interesting. And there is someone else I would like to see.'

'Oh! Who is that?'

'The woman at the party. The bossy woman. Your bossy friend.'

'She's no friend of mine,' said Mrs Oliver. 'She just came up and spoke to me, that's all.'

'You could resume acquaintance with her?'

'Oh yes, quite easily. I would think she'd probably jump at it.'

'I would like to see her. I would like to know why she wants to know these things.'

'Yes. I suppose that might be useful. Anyway –' Mrs Oliver sighed – 'I shall be glad to have a rest from elephants. Nanny – you know, the old Nanny I talked about – she mentioned elephants and that elephants didn't forget. That sort of silly sentence is beginning to haunt me. Ah well, *you* must look for more elephants. It's your turn.'

'And what about you?'

'Perhaps I could look for swans.'

'*Mon dieu*, where do swans come in?'

'It is only what I remember, which Nanny reminded me of. That there were little boys I used to play with and one used to call me Lady Elephant and the other one used to call me Lady Swan. When I was Lady Swan I pretended to be swimming about on the floor. When I was Lady Elephant they rode on my back. There are no swans in this.'

'That is a good thing,' said Poirot. 'Elephants are quite enough.'

CHAPTER 10

DESMOND

Two days later, as Hercule Poirot drank his morning chocolate, he read at the same time a letter that had been among his correspondence that morning. He was reading it now for the second time. The handwriting was a moderately good one, though it hardly bore the stamp of maturity.

Dear Monsieur Poirot,

I am afraid you will find this letter of mine somewhat peculiar, but I believe it would help if I mentioned a friend of yours. I tried to get in touch with her to ask her if she would arrange for me to come and see you, but apparently she had left home. Her secretary – I am referring to Mrs Ariadne Oliver, the novelist – her secretary seemed to say something about her having gone on a safari in East Africa. If so, I can see she may not return for some time. But I'm sure she would help me. I would indeed like to see you so much. I am badly in need of advice of some kind.

Mrs Oliver, I understand, is acquainted with my mother, who met her at a literary luncheon party. If you could give me an appointment to visit you one day I should be very grateful. I can suit my time to anything you suggested. I don't know if it is helpful at all but Mrs Oliver's secretary did mention the word 'elephants'. I presume this has something to do with Mrs Oliver's travels in East Africa. The secretary spoke as though it was some kind of password. I don't really understand this but perhaps you will. I am in a great state of worry and anxiety and I would be very grateful if you could see me.

Yours truly,
Desmond Burton-Cox.

'*Nom d'un petit bonhomme!*' said Hercule Poirot.

'I beg your pardon, sir?' said George.

'A mere ejaculation,' said Hercule Poirot. 'There are some things, once they have invaded your life, which you find very difficult to get rid of again. With me it seems to be a question of elephants.'

He left the breakfast table, summoned his faithful secretary,

Miss Lemon, handed her the letter from Desmond Cox and gave her directions to arrange an appointment with the writer of the letter.

'I am not too occupied at the present time,' he said. 'Tomorrow will be quite suitable.'

Miss Lemon reminded him of two appointments which he already had, but agreed that that left plenty of hours vacant and she would arrange something as he wished.

'Something to do with the Zoological Gardens?' she enquired.

'Hardly,' said Poirot. 'No, do not mention elephants in your letter. There can be too much of anything. Elephants are large animals. They occupy a great deal of the horizon. Yes. We can leave elephants. They will no doubt arise in the course of the conversation I propose to hold with Desmond Burton-Cox.'

'Mr Desmond Burton-Cox,' announced George, ushering in the expected guest.

Poirot had risen to his feet and was standing beside the mantelpiece. He remained for a moment or two without speaking, then he advanced, having summed up his own impression. A somewhat nervous and energetic personality. Quite naturally so, Poirot thought. A little ill at ease but managing to mask it very successfully. He said, extending a hand,

'Mr Hercule Poirot?'

'That is right,' said Poirot. 'And your name is Desmond Burton-Cox. Pray sit down and tell me what I can do for you, the reasons why you have come to see me.'

'It's all going to be rather difficult to explain,' said Desmond Burton-Cox.

'So many things are difficult to explain,' said Hercule Poirot, 'but we have plenty of time. Sit down.'

Desmond looked rather doubtfully at the figure confronting him. Really, a very comic personality, he thought. The egg-shaped head, the big moustaches. Not somehow very imposing. Not quite, in fact, what he had expected to encounter.

'You – you are a detective, aren't you?' he said. 'I mean you – you find out things. People come to you to find out, or to ask you to find out things for them.'

'Yes,' said Poirot, 'that is one of my tasks in life.'

'I don't suppose that you know what I've come about or that you know anything much about me.'

'I know something,' said Poirot.

'You mean Mrs Oliver, your friend Mrs Oliver. She's told you something?'

'She told me that she had had an interview with a goddaughter of hers, a Miss Celia Ravenscroft. That is right, is it not?'

'Yes. Yes, Celia told me. This Mrs Oliver, is she – does she also know my mother – know her well, I mean?'

'No. I do not think that they know each other well. According to Mrs Oliver, she met her at a literary luncheon recently and had a few words with her. Your mother, I understand, made a certain request to Mrs Oliver.'

'She'd no business to do so,' said the boy.

His eyebrows came down over his nose. He looked angry now, angry – almost revengeful.

'Really,' he said. 'Mothers – I mean –'

'I understand,' said Poirot. 'There is much feeling these days, indeed perhaps there always has been. Mothers are continually doing things which their children would much rather they did not. Am I right?'

'Oh you're right enough. But my mother – I mean, she interferes in things in which really she has no concern.'

'You and Celia Ravenscroft, I understand, are close friends. Mrs Oliver understood from your mother that there was some question of marriage. Perhaps in the near future?'

'Yes, but my mother really doesn't need to ask questions and worry about things which are – well, no concern of hers.'

'But mothers are like that,' said Poirot. He smiled faintly. He added, 'You are, perhaps, very much attached to your mother?'

'I wouldn't say that,' said Desmond. 'No, I certainly wouldn't say that. You see – well, I'd better tell you straight away, she's not really my mother.'

'Oh, indeed. I had not understood that.'

'I'm adopted,' said Desmond. 'She had a son. A little boy who died. And then she wanted to adopt a child so I was adopted, and she brought me up as her son. She always speaks of me as her son, and thinks of me as her son, but I'm not really. We're not a bit alike. We don't look at things the same way.'

'Very understandable,' said Poirot.

'I don't seem to be getting on,' said Desmond, 'with what I want to ask you.'

'You want me to do something to find out something, to cover a certain line of interrogation?'

'I suppose that does cover it. I don't know how much you know about – about well, what the trouble is all about.'

'I know a little,' said Poirot. 'Not details. I do not know very much about you or about Miss Ravenscroft, whom I have not yet met. I'd like to meet her.'

'Yes, well, I was thinking of bringing her to talk to you but I thought I'd better talk to you myself first.'

'Well, that seems quite sensible,' said Poirot. 'You are unhappy about something? Worried? You have difficulties?'

'Not really. No. No, there shouldn't be any difficulties. There aren't any. What happened is a thing that happened years ago when Celia was only a child, or a schoolgirl at least. And there was a tragedy, the sort of thing that happens – well, it happens every day, any time. Two people you know whom something has upset very much and they commit suicide. A sort of suicide pact, this was. Nobody knew very much about it or why, or anything like that. But, after all, it happens and it's no business really of people's children to worry about it. I mean, if they know the facts that's quite enough, I should think. And it's no business of my mother's *at all.*'

'As one journeys through life,' said Poirot, 'one finds more and more that people are often interested in things that are none of their own business. Even more so than they are in things that *could* be considered as their own business.'

'But this is all over. Nobody knew much about it or anything. But, you see, my mother keeps asking questions. Wants to know things, and she's got at Celia. She's got Celia into a state where she doesn't really know whether she wants to marry me or not.'

'And you? You know if you want to marry her still?'

'Yes, of course I know. I mean to marry her. I'm quite determined to marry her. But she's got upset. She wants to know things. She wants to know why all this happened and she thinks – I'm sure she's wrong – she thinks that my mother knows something about it. That she's heard something about it.'

'Well, I have much sympathy for you,' said Poirot, 'but it seems to me that if you are sensible young people and if you want to marry, there is no reason why you should not. I may say that I have been given some information at my request about this sad tragedy. As you say, it is a matter that happened years ago. There was no full explanation of it. There never has been. But in life one cannot have explanations of all the sad things that happen.'

'It was a suicide pact,' said the boy. 'It couldn't have been anything else. But – well . . .'

'You want to know the cause of it. Is that it?'

'Well, yes, that's it. That's what Celia's been worried about, and she's almost made me worried. Certainly my mother is worried, though, as I've said, it's absolutely no business of hers. I don't think any fault is attached to anyone. I mean, there wasn't a row or anything. The trouble is, of course, that we don't know. Well, I mean, I shouldn't know anyway because I wasn't there.'

'You didn't know General and Lady Ravenscroft or Celia?'

'I've known Celia more or less all my life. You see, the people I went to for holidays and her people lived next door to each other when we were very young. You know – just children. And we always liked each other, and got on together and all that. And then of course, for a long time all that passed over. I didn't meet Celia for a great many years after that. Her parents, you see, were in Malaya, and so were mine. I think they met each other again there – I mean my father and mother. My father's dead, by the way. But I think when my mother was in Malaya she heard things and she's remembered now what she heard and she's worked herself up about them and she sort of – sort of thinks things that can't possibly be true. I'm sure they aren't true. But she's determined to worry Celia about them. I want to know what really happened. Celia wants to know what really happened. What it was all about. And why? And how? Not just people's silly stories.'

'Yes,' said Poirot, 'it is not unnatural perhaps that you should both feel that. Celia, I should imagine, more than you. She is more disturbed by it than you are. But, if I may say so, does it really matter? What matters is the *now*, the *present*. The girl you want to marry, the girl who wants to marry you – what has the past to do with you? Does it matter whether her parents had a suicide pact or whether they died in an aeroplane accident or one of them was killed in an accident and the other one later committed suicide? Whether there were love-affairs which came into their lives and made for unhappiness.'

'Yes,' said Desmond Burton-Cox, 'yes, I think what you say is sensible and quite right but – well, things have been built up in such a way that I've got to make sure that Celia is satisfied. She's – she's a person who *minds* about things although she doesn't talk about them much.'

'Has it not occurred to you,' said Hercule Poirot, 'that it may be very difficult, if not impossible, to find out what really happened.'

'You mean which of them killed the other or why, or that one shot the other and then himself. Not unless – not unless there had been *something*.'

'Yes, but that something would have been in the past, so why does it matter now?'

'It oughtn't to matter – it wouldn't matter but for my mother interfering, poking about in things. It wouldn't have mattered. I don't suppose that, well, Celia's ever thought much about it. I think probably that she was away at school in Switzerland at the time the tragedy happened and nobody told her much and, well, when you're a teenager or younger still you just accept things as something that happened, but that's not anything to do with you really.'

'Then don't you think that perhaps you're wanting the impossible?'

'I want you to find out,' said Desmond. 'Perhaps it's not the kind of thing that you can find out, or that you like finding out –'

'I have no objection to finding out,' said Poirot. 'In fact one has even a certain – curiosity, shall I say. Tragedies, things that arise as a matter of grief, surprise, shock, illness, they are human tragedies, human things, and it is only natural that if one's attention is drawn to them one should want to know. What I say is, is it wise or necessary to rake up things?'

'Perhaps it isn't,' said Desmond, 'but you see . . .'

'And also,' said Poirot, interrupting him, 'don't you agree with me that it is rather an impossible thing to do after all this time?'

'No,' said Desmond, 'that's where I *don't* agree with you. I think it would be quite possible.'

'Very interesting,' said Poirot. 'Why do you think it would be quite possible?'

'Because –'

'Of what? You have a reason.'

'I think there are people who would know. I think there are people who *could* tell you if they were willing to tell you. People, perhaps, who would not wish to tell me, who would not wish to tell Celia, but *you* might find out from them.'

'That is interesting,' said Poirot.

'Things happened,' said Desmond. 'Things happened in the past. I – I've sort of heard about them in a vague way. There was some mental trouble. There was someone – I don't know who exactly, I think it might have been Lady Ravenscroft – I think she was in a mental home for years. Quite a long time. Some tragedy had happened when she was quite young. Some child who died or an accident. Something that – well, she was concerned in it in some way.'

'It is not what you know of your own knowledge, I presume?'

'No. It's something my mother said. Something she heard. She heard it in Malaya, I think. Gossip there from other people. You know how they get together in the Services, people like that, and the women all gossip together – all the memsahibs. Saying things that mightn't be true at all.'

'And you want to know whether they were true or were not true?'

'Yes, and I don't know how to find out myself. Not now, because it was a long time ago and I don't know who to ask. I don't know who to go to, but until we really find out what did happen and why –'

'What you mean is,' said Poirot, 'at least I think I am right only this is pure surmise on my part, Celia Ravenscroft does not want to marry you unless she is quite sure that there is no mental flaw passed to her presumably by her mother. Is that it?'

'I think that is what she has got into her head somehow. And I think my mother put it there. I think it's what my mother wants to believe. I don't think she's any reason really for believing it except ill-mannered spite and gossip and all the rest of it.'

'It will not be a very easy thing to investigate,' said Poirot.

'No, but I've heard things about you. They say that you're very clever at finding out what did happen. Asking people questions and getting them to tell you things.'

'Whom do you suggest I should question or ask? When you say Malaya, I presume you are not referring to people of Malayan nationality. You are speaking of what you might call the mem-sahib days, the days when there were Service communities in Malaya. You are speaking of English people and the gossip in some English station there.'

'I don't really mean that that would be any good now. I think whoever it was who gossiped, who talked – I mean, it's so long ago now that they'd have forgotten all about it, that they are probably dead themselves. I think that my mother's got a lot of things wrong, that she's heard things and made up more things about them in her mind.'

'And you still think that I would be capable –'

'Well, I don't mean that I want you to go out to Malaya and ask people things. I mean, none of the people would be there now.'

'So you think you could not give me names?'

'Not those sort of names,' said Desmond.

'But some names?'

'Well, I'll come out with what I mean. I think there are two people who might know what happened and why. Because, you see, they'd have been *there*. They'd have *known*, really known, of their own knowledge.'

'You do not want to go to them yourself?'

'Well, I could. I have in a way, but I don't think, you see, that they – I don't know. I wouldn't like to ask some of the things I want to ask. I don't think Celia would. They're very nice, and that's *why* they'd know. Not because they're nasty, not because they gossip, but because they might have helped. They might have done something to make things better, or have tried to do so, only they couldn't. Oh, I'm putting it all so badly.'

'No,' said Poirot, 'you are doing it very well, and I am interested and I think you have something definite in your mind. Tell me, does Celia Ravenscroft agree with you?'

'I haven't said too much to her. You see, she was very fond of Maddy and of Zélie.'

'Maddy and Zélie?'

'Oh well, that's their names. Oh, I must explain. I haven't done it very well. You see, when Celia was quite a child – at the time when I first knew her, as I say, when we were living next door in the country – she had a French sort of – well, I suppose nowadays we call it an *au pair* girl but it was called a governess then. You know, a French governess. A mademoiselle. And you see, she was very nice. She played with all of us children and Celia always called her "Maddy" for short – and all the family called her Maddy.'

'Ah yes. The mademoiselle.'

'Yes, you see being French I thought – I thought perhaps she would tell you things that she knew and wouldn't wish to speak about to other people.'

'Ah. And the other name you mentioned?'

'Zélie. The same sort of thing, you see. A mademoiselle. Maddy was there, I think, for about two or three years and then, later, she went back to France, or Switzerland I think it was, and this other one came. Younger than Maddy was and we didn't call her Maddy. Celia called her Zélie. She was very young, pretty and great fun. We were all frightfully fond of her. She played games with us and we all loved her. The family did. And General Ravenscroft was very taken with her. They used to play games together, picquet, you know and lots of things.'

'And Lady Ravenscroft?'

'Oh she was devoted to Zélie too, and Zélie was devoted to her. That's why she came back again after she'd left.'

'Came back?'

'Yes, when Lady Ravenscroft was ill, and had been in hospital, Zélie came back and was sort of companion to her and looked after her. I don't know, but I believe, I think, I'm almost sure that she was there when it – the tragedy – happened. And so, you see she'd *know* – what really happened.'

'And you know her address? You know where she is now?'

'Yes. I know where she is. I've got her address. I've got both their addresses. I thought perhaps you could go and see her, or both of them. I know it's a lot to ask –' He broke off.

Poirot looked at him for some minutes. Then he said: 'Yes, it is a possibility – certainly – a possibility.'

BOOK 2 • LONG SHADOWS

CHAPTER 11

SUPERINTENDENT GARROWAY AND POIROT COMPARE NOTES

Superintendent Garroway looked across the table at Poirot. His eyes twinkled. At his side George delivered a whisky and soda. Passing on to Poirot, he put down a glass filled with a dark purple liquid.

'What's your tipple?' said Superintendent Garroway, with some interest.

'A syrup of black currant,' said Poirot.

'Well, well,' said Superintendent Garroway, 'everyone to their own taste. What was it Spence told me? He told me you used to drink something called a tisane, wasn't it? What's that, a variant of French piano or something?'

'No,' said Poirot, 'it's useful for reducing fevers.'

'Ah. Invalid dope of some kind.' He drank from his glass. 'Well,' he said, 'here's to suicide!'

'It *was* suicide?' Poirot asked.

'What else can it be?' said Superintendent Garroway. 'The things you wanted to know!' He shook his head. His smile grew more pronounced.

'I am sorry,' said Poirot, 'to have troubled you so much. I am like the animal or the child in one of your stories by Mr Kipling. I Suffer from Insatiable Curiosity.'

'Insatiable curiosity,' said Superintendent Garroway. 'Nice stories he wrote, Kipling. Knew his stuff, too. They told me once that that man could go for one short tour round a destroyer and know more about it than one of the top engineers in the Royal Navy.'

'Alas,' said Hercule Poirot. 'I do not know everything. Therefore, you see, I have to ask questions. I am afraid that I sent you rather a long list of questions.'

'What intrigued me,' said Superintendent Garroway, 'is the

way you jumped from one thing to another. Psychiatrists, doctors' reports, how money was left, who had money, who got money. Who expected money and didn't get money, particulars of ladies' hairdressing, wigs, name of the supplier of wigs, charming rose-coloured cardboard boxes they came in by the way.'

'You knew all these things,' said Poirot. 'That has amazed me, I can assure you.'

'Ah well, it was a puzzling case and of course we made full notes on the subject. None of this was any good to us but we kept the files and it was all there if one wanted to look for it.'

He pushed a piece of paper across the table.

'Here you are. Hairdressers. Bond Street. Expensive firm. Eugene and Rosentelle was the name of it. They moved later. Same firm but went into business in Sloane Street. Here's the address, but it's a Pet Shop now. Two of their assistants retired some years ago now, but they were the top assistants serving people then, and Lady Ravenscroft was on their list. Rosentelle lives in Cheltenham now. Still in the same line of business – Calls herself a Hair Stylist – That's the up-to-date term – and you add Beautician. Same man, different hat, as one used to say in my young days.'

'Ah-ha?' said Poirot.

'Why ah-ha?' asked Garroway.

'I am immensely obliged to you,' said Hercule Poirot. 'You have presented me with an idea. How strange it is the way ideas arrive into one's head.'

'You've too many ideas in your head already,' said the Superintendent, 'that's one of your troubles – you don't need any more. Now then, I've checked up as well as I could on the family history – nothing much there. Alistair Ravenscroft was of Scottish extraction. Father was a clergyman – two uncles in the Army – both quite distinguished. Married Margaret Preston-Grey – well-born girl – presented at Court and all the rest of it. No family scandals. You were quite right about her being one of twin sisters. Don't know where you picked that up – Dorothea and Margaret Preston-Grey – known colloquially as Dolly and Molly. The Preston-Greys lived at Hatters Green in Sussex. Identical twins – usual kind of history of that kind of twin. Cut their first tooth the same day – both got scarlet fever the same month – wore the same kind of clothes – fell in love with the same kind of man – got married about the same time – both husbands in the Army. Family doctor who attended the family when they were young died some years ago, so there's nothing of interest to be got out of him. There was an early tragedy, though, connected with one of them.'

'Lady Ravenscroft?'

'No, the other one – she married a Captain Jarrow – had two children; the younger one, a boy of four, was knocked down by a wheelbarrow or some kind of child's garden toy – or a spade or a child's hoe. Hit him on his head and he fell into an artificial pond or something and drowned. Apparently it was the older child, a girl of nine who did it. They were playing together and quarrelled, as children do. Doesn't seem much doubt, but there *was* another story. Someone said the mother did it – got angry and hit him – and someone else said it was a woman who lived next door who hit him. Don't suppose it's of any interest to you – no bearing on a suicide pact entered into by the mother's sister and her husband years after.'

'No,' said Poirot, 'it does not seem to. But one likes to know background.'

'Yes,' said Garroway, 'as I told you, one has to look into the past. I can't say we'd thought of looking into the past as long ago as this. I mean, as I've said, all this was some years before the suicide.'

'Were there any proceedings at the time?'

'Yes. I managed to look up the case. Accounts of it. Newspaper accounts. Various things. There were some doubts about it, you know. The mother was badly affected. She broke down completely and had to go into hospital. They do say she was never the same woman again afterwards.'

'But they thought she had done it?'

'Well, that's what the doctor thought. There was no direct evidence, you understand. She said that she had seen this happen from a window, that she'd seen the older child, the girl, hit the boy and push him in. But her account – well, I don't think they believed it at the time. She talked so wildly.'

'There was, I suppose, some psychiatric evidence?'

'Yes. She went to a nursing home or hospital of some kind, she was definitely a mental case. She was a good long time in one or two different establishments having treatment, I believe under the care of one of the specialists from St Andrew's Hospital in London. In the end she was pronounced cured, and released after about three years, and sent home to lead a normal life with her family.'

'And she was then quite normal?'

'She was always neurotic, I believe –'

'Where was she at the time of the suicide? Was she staying with the Ravenscrofts?'

'No – she had died nearly three weeks before that. She was staying with them at Overcliffe when it happened. It seemed again to be an illustration of the identical twin destiny. She walked in her sleep – had suffered from that over a period of years, it seems. She had had one or two minor accidents that way. Sometimes she took too many tranquillizers and that resulted in her walking round the house and sometimes out of it during the night. She was following a path along the cliff edge, lost her footing and fell over the cliff. Killed immediately – they didn't find her until the next day. Her sister, Lady Ravenscroft, was terribly upset. They were very devoted to each other and she had to be taken to hospital suffering from shock.'

'Could this tragic accident have led to the Ravenscrofts' suicide some weeks later?'

'There was never a suggestion of such a thing.'

'Odd things happen with twins as you say – Lady Ravenscroft might have killed herself because of the link between her and her twin sister. Then the husband may have shot himself because possibly he felt guilty in some way –'

Superintendent Garroway said: 'You have too many ideas, Poirot. Alistair Ravenscroft couldn't have had an affair with his sister-in-law without everyone knowing about it. There was nothing of that kind – if that's what you've been imagining.'

The telephone rang – Poirot rose and answered it. It was Mrs Oliver.

'Monsieur Poirot, can you come to tea or sherry tomorrow? I have got Celia coming – and later on the bossy woman. That's what you wanted, isn't it?'

Poirot said it was just what he wanted.

'I've got to dash now,' said Mrs Oliver. 'Going to meet an old War Horse – provided by my elephant No. 1, Julia Carstairs. I think she's got his name wrong – she always does – but I hope she's got his address right.'

CHAPTER 12

CELIA MEETS HERCULE POIROT

'Well, madame,' said Poirot, 'and how did you fare with Sir Hugo Foster?'

'To begin with his name wasn't Foster – it was Fothergill. Trust Julia to get a name wrong. She's always doing it.'

'So elephants are not always reliable in the names they remember?'

'Don't talk of elephants – I've finished with elephants.'

'And your War Horse?'

'Quite an old pet – but useless as a source of information. Obsessed by some people called Barnet who did have a child killed in an accident in Malaya. But nothing to do with the Ravenscrofts. I tell you I've finished with elephants –'

'Madame, you have been most persevering, most noble.'

'Celia is coming along in about half an hour's time. You wanted to meet her, didn't you? I've told her that you are – well, helping me in this matter. Or would you rather she came to see you?'

'No,' said Poirot, 'I think I should like her to come in the way you have arranged.'

'I don't suppose she'll stay very long. If we get rid of her in about an hour, that would be all right, just to think over things a bit, and then Mrs Burton-Cox is coming.'

'Ah yes. That will be interesting. Yes, that will be very interesting.'

Mrs Oliver sighed. 'Oh dear, it's a pity, though, isn't it?' She said again, 'We do have too much material, don't we?'

'Yes,' said Poirot. 'We do not know what we are looking for. All we know of still is, in all probability, the double suicide of a married couple who lived quiet and happy lives together. And what have we got to show for cause, for reason? We've gone forward and back to the right, to the left, to the west, to the east.'

'Quite right,' said Mrs Oliver. 'Everywhere. We haven't been to the North Pole yet,' she added.

'Nor to the South Pole,' said Poirot.

'So what is there, when it all comes to it?'

'Various things,' said Poirot. 'I have made here a list. Do you want to read it?'

Mrs Oliver came over and sat beside him and looked over his shoulder.

'Wigs,' she said, pointing to the first item. 'Why wigs first?'

'Four wigs,' said Poirot, 'seem to be interesting. Interesting and rather difficult to solve.'

'I believe the shop she got her wigs from has gone out of the trade now. People go to quite different places for wigs and they're not wearing so many as they did just then. People used to wear wigs to go abroad. You know, because it saves bother in travelling.'

'Yes, yes,' said Poirot, 'we will do what we can with wigs. Anyway, that is one thing that interests me. And then there are other stories. Stories of mental disturbance in the family. Stories of a twin sister who was mentally disturbed and spent a good many years of her life in a mental home.'

'It doesn't seem to lead anywhere,' said Mrs Oliver. 'I mean to say, I suppose she could have come and shot the two of them, but I don't really see why.'

'No,' said Poirot, 'the fingerprints on the revolver were definitely only the fingerprints of General Ravenscroft and his wife, I understand. Then there are stories of a child, a child in Malaya was murdered or attacked, possibly by this twin sister of Lady Ravenscroft. Possibly by some quite different woman – possibly by an amah or a servant. Point two. You know a little more about money.'

'Where does money come into it?' said Mrs Oliver, in some surprise.

'It does not come into it,' said Poirot. 'That is what is so interesting. Money usually comes in. Money someone got as a result of that suicide. Money lost as a result of it. Money somewhere causing difficulties, causing trouble, causing covetousness and desire. It is difficult, that. Difficult to see. There does not seem to have been any large amount of money anywhere. There are various stories of love-affairs, women who were attractive to the husband, men who were attractive to the wife. An affair on one side or the other could have led to suicide or to murder. It very often does. Then we come to what at the moment inclines me to the most interest. That is why I am so anxious to meet Mrs Burton-Cox.'

'Oh. That awful woman. I don't see why you think she's important. All she did was to be a noseyparker and want me to find out things.'

'Yes, but why did she want you to find out things? It seems to me very odd, that. It seems to me that that is something that one has to find out about. She is the link, you see.'

'The link?'

'Yes. We do not know what the link was, where it was, how it was. All we know is that she wants desperately to learn more about this suicide. Being a link, she connects both with your godchild, Celia Ravenscroft, and with the son who is not her son.'

'What do you mean – not her son?'

'He is an adopted son,' said Poirot. 'A son she adopted because her own son died.'

'How did her own child die? Why? When?'

'All these things I asked myself. She could be a link, a link of emotion, a wish for revenge through hatred, through some love-affair. At any rate I must see her. I must make up my mind about her. Yes, I cannot help but think that is very important.'

There was a ring at the bell and Mrs Oliver went out of the room to answer it.

'This, I think, could be Celia,' she said. 'You're sure it's all right?'

'By me, yes,' said Poirot. 'By her also, I hope.'

Mrs Oliver came back a few minutes later. Celia Ravenscroft was with her. She had a doubtful, suspicious look.

'I don't know,' she said, 'if I –' She stopped, staring at Hercule Poirot.

'I want to introduce you,' said Mrs Oliver, 'to someone who is helping me, and I hope is helping you also. That is, helping you in what you want to know and to find out. This is

Monsieur Hercule Poirot. He has special genius in finding out things.'

'Oh,' said Celia.

She looked very doubtfully at the egg-shaped head, the monstrous moustaches and the small stature.

'I think,' she said, rather doubtfully, 'that I have heard of him.'

Hercule Poirot stopped himself with a slight effort from saying firmly 'Most people have heard of me.' It was not quite as true as it used to be because many people who had heard of Hercule Poirot and known him, were now reposing with suitable memorial stones over them, in churchyards. He said,

'Sit down, mademoiselle. I will tell you this much about myself. That when I start an investigation I pursue it to the end. I will bring to light the truth and if it is, shall we say, truly the truth that you want, then I will deliver that knowledge to you. But it may be that you want reassuring. That is not the same thing as the truth. I can find various aspects that might reassure you. Will that be enough? If so, do not ask for more.'

Celia sat down in the chair he had pushed towards her, and looked at him rather earnestly. Then she said,

'You don't think I'd care for the truth, is that it?'

'I think,' said Poirot, 'that the truth might be – a shock, a sorrow, and it might be that you would have said "Why did I not leave all this behind? Why did I ask for knowledge? It is painful knowledge about which I can do nothing helpful or hopeful." It is a double suicide by a father and a mother that I – well, we'll admit it – that I loved. It is not a disadvantage to love a mother and father.'

'It seems to be considered so nowadays occasionally,' said Mrs Oliver. 'New article of belief, shall we say.'

'That's the way I've been living,' said Celia. 'Beginning to wonder, you know. Catching on to odd things that people said sometimes. People who looked at me rather pityingly. But more than that. With curiosity as well. One begins to find out, you know, things about people, I mean. People you meet, people you know, people who used to know your family. I don't want this life. I want . . . you think I don't really want it but I do – I want truth. I'm able to deal with truth. Just tell me something.'

It was not a continuation of the conversation. Celia had turned on Poirot with a separate question. Something which had replaced what had been in her mind just previously.

'You saw Desmond, didn't you?' she said. 'He went to see you. He told me he had.'

'Yes. He came to see me. Did you not want him to do so?'

'He didn't ask me.'

'If he had asked you?'

'I don't know. I don't know whether I should have forbidden him to do so, told him on no account to do such a thing, or whether I should have encouraged it.'

'I would like to ask you one question, mademoiselle. I want to know if there is one clear thing in your mind that matters to you, that could matter to you more than anything else.'

'Well, what is that?'

'As you say, Desmond Burton-Cox came to see me. A very attractive and likeable young man, and very much in earnest over what he came to say. Now that – that is the really important thing. The important thing is if you and he really wish to marry – because that *is* serious. That is – though young people do not always think so nowadays – that is a link together for life. Do you want to enter into that state? It matters. What difference can it make to you or to Desmond whether the death of two people was a double suicide or something quite different?'

'You think it *is* something quite different – or, it was?'

'I do not as yet know,' said Poirot. 'I have reason to believe that it might be. There are certain things that do not accord with a double suicide, but as far as I can go on the opinion of the police – and the police are very reliable, Mademoiselle Celia, very reliable – they put together all the evidence and they thought very definitely that it could be nothing else but a double suicide.'

'But they never knew the cause of it? That's what you mean.'

'Yes,' said Poirot, 'that's what I mean.'

'And don't you know the cause of it, either? I mean, from looking into things or thinking about them, or whatever you do?'

'No, I am not sure about it,' said Poirot. 'I think there might be something very painful to learn and I am asking you whether you will be wise enough to say: "The past is the past. Here is a young man whom I care for and who cares for me. This is the future we are spending together, not the past."'

'Did he tell you he was an adopted child?' asked Celia.

'Yes, he did.'

'You see, what business is it really, of hers? Why should she come worrying Mrs Oliver here, trying to make Mrs Oliver ask me questions, find out things? She's not his own mother.'

'Does he care for her?'

'No,' said Celia. 'I'd say on the whole he dislikes her. I think he always has.'

'She's spent money on him, schooling and on clothes and on all sorts of different things. And you think *she* cares for *him*?'

'I don't know. I don't think so. She wanted, I suppose, a child to replace her own child. She'd had a child who died in an accident, that was why she wanted to adopt someone, and her husband had died quite recently. All these dates are so difficult.'

'I know, I know. I would like perhaps to know one thing.'

'About her or about him?'

'Is he provided for financially?'

'I don't know quite what you mean by that. He'll be able to support me – to support a wife. I gather some money was settled on him when he was adopted. A sufficient sum, that is. I don't mean a fortune or anything like that.'

'There is nothing that she could – withhold?'

'What, you mean that she'd cut off the money supplies if he married me? I don't think she's ever threatened to do that, or indeed that she could do it. I think it was all fixed up by lawyers or whoever arranges adoptions. I mean, they make a lot of fuss, these adoption societies, from all I hear.'

'I would ask you something else which you might know but nobody else does. Presumably Mrs Burton-Cox knows it. Do you know who his actual mother was?'

'You think that might have been one of the reasons for her being so nosey and all that? Something to do with, as you say, what he was really. I don't know. I suppose he might have been an illegitimate child. They're the usual ones that go for adoption, aren't they? She might have known something about his real mother or his real father, or something like that. If so, she didn't tell him. I gather she just told him the silly things they suggest you should say. That it is just as nice to be adopted because it shows you really were wanted. There's a lot of silly slop like that.'

'I think some societies suggest that that's the way you should break the news. Does he or you know of any blood relations?'

'I don't know. I don't think he knows, but I don't think it worries him at all. He's not that kind of a worrier.'

'Do you know if Mrs Burton-Cox was a friend of your family, of your mother and father? Did you ever meet her as far as you can remember, when you were living in your own home in the early days?'

'I don't think so. I think Desmond's mother – I mean, I think Mrs Burton-Cox went to Malaya. I think perhaps her husband died out in Malaya, and that Desmond was sent to school in England while they were out there and that he was boarded with some cousins or people who take in children for holidays. And that's how we came to be friends in those days. I always remembered him, you know. I was a great hero-worshipper. He was wonderful at climbing trees and he taught me things about birds' nests and birds' eggs. So it seemed quite natural, when I met him again I mean, met him at the university, and we both talked about where we'd lived and then he asked me my name. He said "Only your Christian name I know," and then we remembered quite a lot of things together. It's what made us, you might say, get acquainted. I don't know everything about him. I don't know *anything*. I want to know. How can you arrange your life and know what you're going to do with your life if you don't know all about the things that affect you, that really happened?'

'So you tell me to carry on with my investigation?'

'Yes, if it's going to produce any results, though I don't think it will be because in a way, well, Desmond and I have tried our hand at finding out a few things. We haven't been very successful. It seems to come back to this plain fact which isn't really the story of a life. It's the story of a death, isn't it? Of two deaths, that's to say. When it's a double suicide, one thinks of it as one death. Is it in Shakespeare or where does the quotation come from – "And in death they were not divided."' She turned to Poirot again. 'Yes, go on. Go on finding out. Go on telling Mrs Oliver or telling me direct. I'd rather you told me direct.' She turned towards Mrs Oliver. 'I don't mean to be horrid to you, Godmother. You've been a very nice godmother to me always, but – but I'd like it straight from the horse's mouth. I'm afraid that's rather rude, Monsieur Poirot, but I didn't mean it that way.'

'No,' said Poirot, 'I am content to be the horse's mouth.'

'And you think you will be?'

'I always believe that I can.'

'And it's always true, is it?'

'It is usually true,' said Poirot. 'I do not say more than that.'

CHAPTER 13

MRS BURTON-COX

'Well,' said Mrs Oliver as she returned into the room after seeing Celia to the door. 'What do you think of her?'

'She is a personality,' said Poirot, 'an interesting girl. Definitely, if I may put it so, she is somebody, not anybody.'

'Yes, that's true enough,' said Mrs Oliver.

'I would like you to tell me something.'

'About her? I don't really know her very well. One doesn't really, with godchildren. I mean, you only see them, as it were, at stated intervals rather far apart.'

'I didn't mean her. Tell me about her mother.'

'Oh. I see.'

'You knew her mother?'

'Yes. We were in a sort of *pensionnat* in Paris together. People used to send girls to Paris then to be finished,' said Mrs Oliver. 'That sounds more like an introduction to a cemetery than an introduction into Society. What do you want to know about her?'

'You remember her? You remember what she was like?'

'Yes. As I tell you, one doesn't entirely forget things or people because they're in the past.'

'What impression did she make on you?'

'She was beautiful,' said Mrs Oliver. 'I do remember that. Not when she was about thirteen or fourteen. She had a lot of puppy fat then. I think we all did,' she added, thoughtfully.

'Was she a personality?'

'It's difficult to remember because, you see, she wasn't my

only friend or my greatest friend. I mean, there were several of us together – a little pack, as you might say. People with tastes more or less the same. We were keen on tennis and we were keen on being taken to the opera and we were bored to death being taken to the picture galleries. I really can only give you a general idea.

'Molly Preston-Grey. That was her name.'

'You both had boyfriends?'

'We had one or two passions, I think. Not for pop singers, of course. They hadn't happened yet. Actors usually. There was one rather famous variety actor. A girl – one of the girls – had him pinned up over her bed and Mademoiselle Girand, the French mistress, on no account allowed that actor to be pinned up there. "*Ce n'est pas convenable*," she said. The girl didn't tell her that he was her father! We laughed,' added Mrs Oliver. 'Yes, we laughed a good deal.'

'Well, tell me more about Molly or Margaret Preston-Grey. Does this girl remind you of her?'

'No, I don't think she does. No. They are not alike. I think Molly was more – was more emotional than this girl.'

'There was a twin sister, I understand. Was she at the same *pensionnat*?'

'No, she wasn't. She might have been since they were the same age, but no, I think she was in some entirely different place in England. I'm not sure. I have a feeling that the twin sister Dolly, whom I had met once or twice very occasionally and who of course at that time looked exactly like Molly – I mean they hadn't started trying to look different, have different hair-dos and all that, as twins do usually when they grow up. I think Molly was devoted to her sister Dolly, but she didn't talk about her very much. I have a feeling – nowadays, I mean, I didn't have it then – that there might have been something a bit wrong perhaps with the sister even then. Once or twice, I remember, there were mentions of her having been ill or gone away for a course of treatment somewhere. Something like that. I remember once wondering whether she was a cripple. She was taken once by an aunt on a sea voyage to do her health good.' She shook her head. 'I can't really remember, though. I just had a feeling that Molly was devoted to her and would have liked to have protected her in some way. Does that seem nonsense to you?'

'Not at all,' said Hercule Poirot.

'There were other times, I think, when she didn't want to talk about her. She talked about her mother and her father. She was fond of them, I think, in the ordinary sort of way. Her mother came once to Paris and took her out, I remember. Nice woman. Not very exciting or good-looking or anything. Nice, quiet, kindly.'

'I see. So you have nothing to help us there? No boyfriends?'

'We didn't have so many boyfriends then,' said Mrs Oliver. 'It's not like nowadays when it's a matter of course. Later, when we were both back again at home we more or less drifted apart. I think Molly went abroad somewhere with her parents. I don't think it was India – I don't think so. Somewhere else I think it was. Egypt perhaps. I think now they were in the Diplomatic Service. They were in Sweden at one time, and after that somewhere like Bermuda or the West Indies. I think he was a Governor or something there. But those sort of things one doesn't really remember. Molly was very keen on the music master, which was very satisfying to us both and I should think much less troublesome than boyfriends seem to be nowadays. I mean, you adored – longed for the day when they came again to teach you. They were, I have no doubt, quite indifferent to you. But one dreamt about them at night and I remember having a splendid kind of daydream in which I nursed my beloved Monsieur Adolphe when he had cholera and I gave him, I think, blood transfusions to save his life. How very silly one is. And think of all the other things you think of doing! There was one time when I was quite determined to be a nun and later on I thought I'd be a hospital nurse. Well, I suppose we shall have Mrs Burton-Cox in a moment. I wonder how she will react to you?'

Poirot gazed at his watch.

'We shall be able to see that fairly soon.'

'Have we anything else we ought to talk about first?'

'I think there are a few things we might compare notes on. As I say, there are one or two things that I think could do with investigation. An elephant investigation for you, shall we say? And an understudy for an elephant for me.'

'What an extraordinary thing to say,' said Mrs Oliver. 'I told you I was done with elephants.'

'Ah,' said Poirot, 'but elephants perhaps have not done with you.'

The front doorbell sounded once again. Poirot and Mrs Oliver looked at each other.

'Well,' said Mrs Oliver, 'here we go.'

She left the room once more. Poirot heard sounds of greeting going on outside and in a moment or two Mrs Oliver returned, ushering the somewhat massive figure of Mrs Burton-Cox.

'What a delightful flat you have,' said Mrs Burton-Cox. 'So charming of you to have spared time – your very valuable time, I'm sure – you asked me to come and see you.' Her eyes shot sideways to Hercule Poirot. A faint expression of surprise passed over her face. For a moment her eyes went from him to the baby grand piano that stood in one window. It occurred to Mrs Oliver that Mrs Burton-Cox was thinking that Hercule Poirot was a piano-tuner. She hastened to dispel this illusion.

'I want to introduce you,' she said, 'to M. Hercule Poirot.'

Poirot came forward and bent over her hand.

'I think he is the only person who might be able to help you in some way. You know. What you were asking me about the other day concerning my godchild, Celia Ravenscroft.'

'Oh yes, how kind of you to remember. I do so hope you can give me a little more knowledge of what really happened.'

'I'm afraid I haven't been very successful,' said Mrs Oliver, 'and that is really why I asked M. Poirot to meet you. He is a wonderful person, you know, for information on things generally. Really on top of his profession. I cannot tell you how many friends of mine he has assisted and how many, well, I can really call them mysteries, he has elucidated. And this was such a tragic thing to have happened.'

'Yes, indeed,' said Mrs Burton-Cox. Her eyes were still somewhat doubtful. Mrs Oliver indicated chairs and remarked,

'Now what will you have? A glass of sherry? It's too late for tea, of course. Or would you prefer a cocktail of some kind?'

'Oh, a glass of sherry. You are very kind.'

'Monsieur Poirot?'

'I, too,' said Poirot.

Mrs Oliver could not help being thankful that he had not asked for *Sirop de Cassis* or one of his favourite fruit drinks. She got out glasses and a decanter.

'I have already indicated to Monsieur Poirot the outlines of the enquiry you want to make.'

'Oh yes,' said Mrs Burton-Cox.

She seemed rather doubtful and not so sure of herself as it would seem she was in the natural habit of being.

'These young people,' she said to Poirot, 'so difficult nowadays. These young people. My son, such a dear boy, we have great hopes of his doing well in the future. And then there is this girl, a very charming girl, who, as probably Mrs Oliver told you, is her goddaughter, and – well, of course one never knows. I mean these friendships spring up and very often they don't last. They are what we used to call calf love, you know, years ago, and it is very important to know a little at least about the – antecedents of people. You know, what their families are like. Oh, of course I know Celia's a very well-born girl and all that, but there *was* this tragedy. Mutual suicide, I believe, but nobody has been really able to enlighten me at all on what led to it or what led up to it, shall we say. I have no actual friends who were friends in common with the Ravenscrofts and so it is very difficult for me to have ideas. I know Celia is a charming girl and all that, but one would like to know, to know more.'

'I understand from my friend, Mrs Oliver, that you wanted to know something specifically. You wanted to know, in fact –'

'What you said you wanted to know,' said Mrs Oliver, chipping in with some firmness, 'was whether Celia's father shot her mother and then himself or whether Celia's mother shot her father and then herself.'

'I feel it makes a difference,' said Mrs Burton-Cox. 'Yes, definitely I feel it makes a difference.'

'A very interesting point of view,' said Poirot.

His tone was not very encouraging.

'Oh, the emotional background, shall I say, the emotional events that led up to all this. In a marriage, you must admit, one has to think of the children. The children, I mean, that are to come. I mean heredity. I think now we realize that heredity does more than environment. It leads to certain formation of character and certain very grave risks that one might not want to take.'

'True,' said Poirot. 'The people who undertake the risks are the ones that have to make the decision. Your son and this young lady, it will be their choice.'

'Oh, I know, I know. Not mine. Parents are never allowed to choose, are they, or even to give any advice. But I would like to know something about it, yes, I would like to know very much. If you feel that you could undertake any – investigation I suppose is the word you would use. But perhaps – perhaps I am being a very foolish mother. You know. Over-anxious about my dear son. Mothers are like that.'

She gave a little whinney of laughter, putting her head slightly on one side.

'Perhaps,' she said, as she tipped up the sherry glass, 'perhaps you will think about it and I also will let you know. Perhaps the exact points and things that I am worried about.'

She looked at her watch.

'Oh dear. Oh dear, I'm late for another appointment. I shall have to go. I am so sorry, dear Mrs Oliver, to have to run away so soon, but you know what it is. I had great difficulties finding a taxi this afternoon. One after another just turned his head aside and drove straight past me. All very, very difficult, isn't it? I think Mrs Oliver has your address, has she not?'

'I will give you my address,' said Poirot. He removed a card from his pocket and handed it to her.

'Oh yes, yes. I see. Monsieur Hercule Poirot. You are French, is that right?'

'I am Belgian,' said Poirot.

'Oh yes, yes. Belgique. Yes, yes, I quite understand. I am so pleased to have met you and I feel so hopeful. Oh dear, I must go very, very fast.'

Shaking Mrs Oliver warmly by the hand, then extending the same hand to Poirot, she left the room and the door sounded in the hall.

'Well, what do you think of that?' said Mrs Oliver.

'What do you?' said Poirot.

'She ran away,' said Mrs Oliver. 'She ran away. You frightened her in some way.'

'Yes,' said Poirot, 'I think you've judged quite right.'

'She wanted me to get things out of Celia, she wanted me to get some knowledge out of Celia, some expression, some sort of secret she suspected was there, but she doesn't want a real proper investigation, does she?'

'I think not,' said Poirot. 'That is interesting. Very interesting. She is well-to-do, you think?'

'I should say so. Her clothes are expensive, she lives at an expensive address, she is – it's difficult to make out. She's a pushing woman and a bossy woman. She sits on a lot of committees. There's nothing, I mean, suspicious about her. I've asked a few people. Nobody likes her very much. But she's a sort of public-spirited woman who takes part in politics, all those sort of things.'

'Then what is wrong with her?' said Poirot.

'You think there is something wrong with her? Or do you just not like her, like I do?'

'I think there is something there that she does not want to come to light,' said Poirot.

'Oh. And are you going to find out what it is?'

'Naturally, if I can,' said Poirot. 'It may not be easy. She is in retreat. She was in retreat when she left us here. She was afraid of what questions I was going to ask her. Yes. It is interesting.' He sighed. 'One will have to go back, you know, even farther than one thought.'

'What, back into the past again?'

'Yes. Somewhere in the past, in more cases than one, there is something that one will have to know before we can come back again to what happened – what is it now? – fifteen years ago, twenty years ago, at a house called Overcliffe. Yes. One will have to go back again.'

'Well, that's that,' said Mrs Oliver. 'And now, what is there to do? What is this list of yours?'

'I have heard a certain amount of information through police records on what was found in the house. You will remember that among the things there were four wigs.'

'Yes,' said Mrs Oliver, 'you said that four wigs were too many.'

'It seemed to be a little excessive,' said Poirot. 'I have also got certain useful addresses. The address of a doctor that might be helpful.'

'The doctor? You mean, the family doctor?'

'No, not the family doctor. The doctor who gave evidence at an inquest on a child who met with an accident. Either pushed by an older child or possibly by someone else.'

'You mean by the mother?'

'Possibly the mother, possibly by someone else who was in the house at the time. I know the part of England where that happened, and Superintendent Garroway has been able to trace him, through sources known to him and also through journalistic friends of mine, who were interested in this particular case.'

'And you're going to see – he must be a very old man by now.'

'It is not him I shall go to see, it is his son. His son is also qualified as a specialist in various forms of mental disorders. I have an introduction to him and he might be able to tell me something interesting. There have also been enquiries into a case of money.'

'What do you mean by money?'

'Well, there are certain things we have to find out. That is one of the things in anything which might be a crime. Money. Who has money to lose by some happening, who has money to gain by something happening. That, one has to find out.'

'Well, they must have found out in the case of the Ravenscrofts.'

'Yes, that was all quite natural, it seems. They had both made normal wills, leaving in each case, the money to the other partner. The wife left her money to the husband and the husband left his money to his wife. Neither of them benefited by what happened because they both died. So that the people who did profit, were the daughter, Celia, and a younger child, Edward, who I gather is now at a university abroad.'

'Well, that won't help. Neither of the children were there or could have had anything to do with it.'

'Oh no, that is quite true. One must go further – further back, further forward, further sideways to find out if there is some financial motive somewhere that is – well, shall we say, significant.'

'Well, don't ask me to do that sort of thing,' said Mrs Oliver,

'I've no real qualifications for that. I mean, that's come up, I suppose, fairly reasonable in the – well, in the elephants that I've talked to.'

'No. I think the best thing for you to do would be to, shall we say, take on the subject of the wigs.'

'Wigs?'

'There had been a note made in the careful police report at the time of the suppliers of the wigs, who were a very expensive firm of hairdressers and wig-makers in London, in Bond Street. Later, that particular shop closed and the business was transferred somewhere else. Two of the original partners continued to run it and I understand it has now been given up, but I have here an address of one of the principal fitters and hairdressers, and I thought perhaps that it would come more easily if enquiries were made by a woman.'

'Ah,' said Mrs Oliver, 'me?'

'Yes, you.'

'All right. What do you want me to do?'

'Pay a visit to Cheltenham to an address I shall give you and there you will find a Madame Rosentelle. A woman no longer young but who was a very fashionable maker of ladies' hair adornments of all kinds, and who was married, I understand, to another in the same profession, a hairdresser who specialized in surmounting the problems of gentlemen's baldness. Toupees and other things.'

'Oh dear,' said Mrs Oliver, 'the jobs you do give me to do. Do you think they'll remember anything about it?'

'Elephants remember,' said Hercule Poirot.

'Oh, and who are you going to ask questions of? This doctor you talked about?'

'For one, yes.'

'And what do you think he'll remember?'

'Not very much,' said Poirot, 'but it seems to me possible that he might have heard about a certain accident. It must have been an interesting case, you know. There must be records of the case history.'

'You mean of the twin sister?'

'Yes. There were two accidents as far as I can hear connected with her. One when she was a young mother living in the country, at Hatters Green I think the address was, and again later when she was in Malaya. Each time an accident which resulted in the death of a child. I might learn something about –'

'You mean that as they were twin sisters, that Molly – my Molly I mean – might also have had mental disability of some kind? I don't believe it for a minute. She wasn't like that. She was affectionate, loving, very good-looking, emotional and – oh, she was a terribly nice person.'

'Yes. Yes, so it would seem. And a very happy person on the whole, would you say?'

'Yes. She was a happy person. A *very* happy person. Oh, I know I never saw anything of her later in life, of course; she was living abroad. But it always seemed to me on the very rare occasions when I got a letter or went to see her that she was a happy person.'

'And the twin sister you did not really know?'

'No. Well, I think she was . . . well, quite frankly she was in an institution of some kind, I think, on the rare occasions that I saw Molly. She wasn't at Molly's wedding, not as a bridesmaid even.'

'That is odd in itself.'

'I still don't see what you're going to find out from that.'

'Just information,' said Poirot.

CHAPTER 14

DR WILLOUGHBY

Hercule Poirot got out of the taxi, paid the fare and a tip, verified the fact that the address he had come to was the address corresponding to that written down in his little notebook, took carefully a letter from his pocket addressed to Dr Willoughby, mounted the steps to the house and pressed the bell. The door was opened by a manservant. On reception of Poirot's name he was told that Dr Willoughby was expecting him.

He was shown into a small, comfortable room with bookshelves up the side of it, there were two armchairs drawn to the fire and a tray with glasses on it and two decanters. Dr Willoughby rose to greet him. He was a man between fifty and sixty with a lean, thin body, a high forehead, dark-haired and with very piercing grey eyes. He shook hands and motioned him to a seat. Poirot produced the letter from his pocket.

'Ah, yes.'

The doctor took it from him, opened it, read it and then, placing it beside him, looked at Poirot with some interest.

'I had already heard,' he said, 'from Superintendent Garroway and also, I may say, from a friend of mine in the Home Office, who also begged me to do what I can for you in the matter that interests you.'

'It is a rather serious favour to ask, I know,' said Poirot, 'but there are reasons which make it important for me.'

'Important for you after this number of years?'

'Yes. Of course I shall quite understand if those particular events have passed out of your mind altogether.'

'I can't say they've done that. I am interested, as you may have heard, in special branches of my profession, and have been for many years.'

'Your father, I know, was a very celebrated authority on them.'

'Yes, he was. It was a great interest in his life. He had a lot of theories, some of them triumphantly proved right and some of them which proved disappointing. It is, I gather, a mental case you are interested in?'

'A woman. Her name was Dorothea Preston-Grey.'

'Yes. I was quite a young man at the time. I was already interested in my father's line of thought although my theories and his did not always agree. The work he did was interesting and the work I did in collaboration interested me very much. I don't know what your particular interest was in Dorothea Preston-Grey, as she was at the time, Mrs Jarrow later.'

'She was one of twins, I gather,' said Poirot.

'Yes. That was at that moment, I may say, my father's particular field of study. There was a project on hand at that time, to follow up the general lives of selected pairs of identical twins. Those who were brought up in the same environment, those who through various chances of life were brought up in entirely different environments. To see how alike they remained, how similar the things were that happened to them. Two sisters, perhaps, or two brothers who had hardly spent any of their life together and yet in an extraordinary way the same things seemed to happen to them at the same time. It was all – indeed it has been all – extremely interesting. However, that is not your interest in the matter, I gather.'

'No,' said Poirot, 'it is a case, I think – the part of it that is to say that I'm interested in – of an accident to a child.'

'That is so. It was in Surrey, I think. Yes, a very pleasant area, that, in which people lived. Not very far from Camberley, I think. Mrs Jarrow was a young widow at that time and she had two small children. Her husband had recently died in an accident. She was, as a result –'

'Mentally disturbed?' asked Poirot.

'No, she was not thought to be so. She was deeply shocked by her husband's death and had a great sense of loss, but she was not recovering very satisfactorily in the impression of her own doctor. He did not quite like the way her convalescence was tending, and she did not seem to be getting over her bereavement in the way that he would have liked. It seemed to be causing her rather peculiar reactions. Anyway, he wanted a consultation and my father was asked by him to come and see what he could make of it. He found her condition interesting, and at the same time he thought it held very decided dangers, and he seemed to think that it would be as well if she was put under observation in some nursing home where particular care could be taken. Things like that. Even more so after the case when this accident to the child happened. There were two children, and according to Mrs Jarrow's account of what happened, it was the older child, a girl who attacked the little boy who was four or five years younger than she was, hitting him with a garden spade or hoe, so that he fell into an ornamental pond they had in the garden and was drowned. Well, these things, as you know, happen quite often among children. Children are pushed in a perambulator into a pond sometimes because an older child, being jealous, thinks that "Mummy will have so much less trouble if only Edward or Donald, or whatever his name is, wasn't here," or, "It would be much nicer for her." It all results from jealousy. There did not seem to be any particular cause or evidence of jealousy in this case, though. The child had not resented the birth of her brother. On the other hand, Mrs Jarrow had not wanted this second child. Although her husband had been pleased to have this second child coming, Mrs Jarrow did not want it. She had tried two doctors with the idea of having an abortion but did not succeed in finding one who would perform what was then an illegal operation. It was said by one of the servants, and also by a boy who was bringing a telegram, I believe, to the house, that it was a woman who attacked the boy, not the other child. And one of the servants said very definitely she had been looking out of the window and that it was her mistress. She said, "I don't think the poor thing knows what she is doing nowadays. You know, just since the master died she's been in, oh, such a state as never was." Well, as I say, I don't know exactly what you want to know about the case. A verdict was brought in of accident, it was considered to be an accident, and the children had been said to be playing together, pushing each other, etcetera, and that therefore it was undoubtedly a very unfortunate accident. It was left at that, but my father when consulted, and after a conversation with Mrs Jarrow and certain tests, questionnaires, sympathetic remarks to her and questions, he was quite sure she had been responsible for what happened. According to his advice it would be advisable for her to have mental treatment.'

'But your father *was* quite sure that *she* had been responsible?'

'Yes. There was a school of treatment at the time which was very popular and which my father believed in. That school's belief was that after sufficient treatment, lasting sometimes quite a long time, a year or longer, people could resume a normal everyday life, and it was to their advantage to do so. They could be returned to live at home and with a suitable amount of attention, both medical and from those, usually near relatives, who were with them and could observe them living a normal life, everything would go well. This, I may say, did meet with success at first in many cases, but later there was a difference. Several cases had most unfortunate results. Patients who appeared to be cured came home to their natural surroundings, to a family, a husband, their mothers and fathers, and slowly relapsed, so that very often tragedies or near tragedies occurred. One case my father was bitterly disappointed in – also a very important case in his knowledge – was a woman who came back to live with the same friend she lived with before.

All seemed to be going happily but after about five or six months she sent urgently for a doctor and when he came said, "I must take you upstairs because you will be angry at what I have done, and you will have to send for the police, I am afraid. I know that must happen. But you see, I was commanded to do this. I saw the Devil looking out of Hilda's eyes. I saw the Devil there so I knew what I had to do. I knew I had to kill her." The woman was lying dead in a chair, strangled, and after her death her eyes had been attacked. The killer died in a mental home with never any feeling about her crime except that it had been a necessary command laid upon her because it was her duty to destroy the Devil.'

Poirot shook his head sadly –

The doctor went on: 'Yes. Well, I consider that in a mild way Dorothea Preston-Grey suffered from a form of mental disorder that was dangerous and that she could only be considered safe if she lived under supervision. This was not generally accepted, I may say, at the time, and my father did consider it most inadvisable. Once she had been committed to a very pleasant nursing home a very good treatment was given. And again, after a period of years she appeared to be completely sane, left the establishment, lived in an ordinary life with a very pleasant nurse more or less in charge of her, though considered in the household as a lady's maid. She went about, made friends and sooner or later went abroad.'

'To Malaya,' said Poirot.

'Yes. I see you've been correctly informed. She went to Malaya to stay with her twin sister.'

'And there another tragedy happened?'

'Yes. A child of a neighbour was attacked. It was thought at first by an amah, and afterwards I believe one of the native servants, a bearer, was suspected. But there again there seemed no doubt that Mrs Jarrow had, for one of those mental reasons known only to her, been guilty of the attack. There was no definite evidence, I understand, which could be brought against her. I think General – I forget his name now –'

'Ravenscroft?' said Poirot.

'Yes, yes, General Ravenscroft agreed to arrange for her to go back to England and again undergo medical treatment. Is that what you wanted to know?'

'Yes,' said Poirot, 'that is what I have partly heard already, but mainly I may say, by hearsay, which is not dependable. What I want to ask you was, this was a case concerned with identical twins. What about the other twin? Margaret Preston-Grey. Afterwards the wife of General Ravenscroft. Was she likely to be affected by the same malady?'

'There was never any medical case about her. She was perfectly sane. My father was interested, visited her once or twice and talked to her because he had so often seen cases of almost identical illnesses or mental disturbances happen between identical twins who had started life very devoted to each other.'

'Only started life, you said?'

'Yes. On certain occasions a state of animosity can arise between identical twins. It follows on a first keen protective love one for the other, but it can degenerate into something which is nearer hatred, if there is some emotional strain that could trigger it off or could arouse it, or any emotional crisis to account for animosity arising between two sisters.

'I think there might have been that here. General Ravenscroft as a young subaltern or captain or whatever he was, fell deeply in love, I think, with Dorothea Preston-Grey, who was a very beautiful girl. Actually the more beautiful of the two – she also fell in love with him. They were not officially engaged, but General Ravenscroft transferred his affections fairly soon to the other sister, Margaret. Or Molly as she was called. He fell in love with her, and asked her to marry him. She returned his affection and they were married as soon as it became feasible in his career. My father had no doubt that the other twin, Dolly, was bitterly jealous of her sister's marriage and that she continued to be in love with Alistair Ravenscroft and to resent his marriage. However, she got over it all, married another man in due course – a thoroughly happy marriage, it seemed, and later she used frequently to go to visit the Ravenscrofts, not only on that one occasion in Malaya, but later when they were in another station abroad and after they returned home. She was by that time apparently cured again, was no longer in any kind of mental dejection and lived with a very reliable nurse companion and staff of servants. I believe, or so my father had always told me, that Lady Ravenscroft, Molly, remained very devoted to her sister. She felt very protective towards her and loved her dearly. She wanted often, I think, to see more of her than she did, but General Ravenscroft was not so keen on her doing so. I think it possible that the slightly unbalanced Dolly – Mrs Jarrow – continued to feel a very strong attachment to General Ravenscroft, which I think may have been embarrassing and difficult for him, though I believe that his wife was quite convinced that her sister had got over any feelings of jealousy or anger.'

'I understand Mrs Jarrow was staying with the Ravenscrofts about three weeks or so before the tragedy of their suicide happened.'

'Yes, that was quite true. Her own tragic death happened then. She was quite frequently a sleep-walker. She went out one night walking in her sleep and had an accident, falling down a portion of the cliff to which a pathway which had been discarded appeared to lead. She was found the next day and I believe died in hospital without recovering consciousness. Her sister Molly was extremely upset and bitterly unhappy about this, but I would like to say, which you probably want to know, I do not think that this can in any way be held responsible for the subsequent suicide of the married couple who were living so happily together. Grief for a sister's or a sister-in-law's death would hardly lead you to commit suicide. Certainly not to a double suicide.'

'Unless, perhaps,' said Hercule Poirot, 'Margaret Ravenscroft had been responsible for her sister's death.'

'Good heavens!' said Dr Willoughby – 'surely you are not suggesting –'

'That it was Margaret who followed her sleep-walking sister, and that it was Margaret's hand that was stretched out to push Dorothea over the cliff edge?'

'I refuse absolutely,' said Dr Willoughby, 'to accept any such idea.'

'With people,' said Hercule Poirot, 'one never knows.'

CHAPTER 15

EUGENE AND ROSENTELLE, HAIR STYLISTS AND BEAUTICIANS

Mrs Oliver looked at Cheltenham with approval. As it happened, she had never been to Cheltenham before. How nice, said Mrs Oliver to herself, to see some houses that are really like houses, proper houses.

Casting her mind back to youthful days, she remembered that she had known people, or at least her relations, her aunts, had known people who lived at Cheltenham. Retired people usually. Army or Navy. It was the sort of place, she thought, where one would like to come and live if one had spent a good deal of time abroad. It had a feeling of English security, good taste and pleasant chat and conversation.

After looking in one or two agreeable antique shops, she found her way to where she wanted – or rather Hercule Poirot wanted her – to go. It was called The Rose Green Hairdressing Saloons. She walked inside it and looked round. Four or five people were in process of having things done to their hair. A plump young lady left her client and came forward with an enquiring air.

'Mrs Rosentelle?' said Mrs Oliver, glancing down at a card. 'I understand she said she could see me if I came here this morning. I don't mean,' she added, 'having anything done to my hair, but I wanted to consult her about something and I believe a telephone call was made and she said if I came at half past eleven she could spare me a short time.'

'Oh yes,' said the girl. 'I think Madam is expecting someone.'

She led the way through a passage down a short flight of steps and pushed a swing door at the bottom of it. From the hairdressing saloon they had passed into what was obviously Mrs Rosentelle's house. The plump girl knocked at the door and said, 'The lady to see you,' as she put her nose in, and then asked rather nervously, 'What name did you say?'

'Mrs Oliver,' said Mrs Oliver.

She walked in. It had a faint effect of what might have been yet another showroom. There were curtains of rose gauze and roses on the wallpaper and Mrs Rosentelle, a woman Mrs Oliver thought of as roughly her own age or possibly a good many years older, was just finishing what was obviously a cup of morning coffee.

'Mrs Rosentelle?' said Mrs Oliver.

'Yes?'

'You did expect me?'

'Oh yes. I didn't quite understand what it was all about. The lines are so bad on the telephone. That is quite all right, I have about half an hour to spare. Would you like some coffee?'

'No, thank you,' said Mrs Oliver. 'I won't keep you any longer than I need. It is just something that I want to ask you about, that you may happen to remember. You have had quite a long career, I understand, in the hairdressing business.'

'Oh yes. I'm quite thankful to give over to the girls now. I don't do anything myself these days.'

'Perhaps you still advise people?'

'Yes, I do that.' Mrs Rosentelle smiled.

She had a nice, intelligent face with well arranged, brown hair, with somewhat interesting grey streaks in it here and there.

'I'm not sure what it's all about.'

'Well, really I wanted to ask you a question about, well, I suppose in a way about wigs generally.'

'We don't do as much in wigs now as we used to do.'

'You had a business in London, didn't you?'

'Yes. First in Bond Street and then we moved to Sloane Street but it's very nice to live in the country after all that, you know. Oh yes, my husband and I are very satisfied here. We run a small business but we don't do much in the wig line nowadays,' she said, 'though my husband does advise and get wigs designed for men who are bald. It really makes a big difference, you know, to many people in their business if they don't look too old and it often helps in getting a job.'

'I can quite imagine that,' said Mrs Oliver.

From sheer nervousness she said a few more things in the way of ordinary chat and wondered how she would start on her subject. She was startled when Mrs Rosentelle leant forward and said suddenly, 'You are Ariadne Oliver, aren't you? The novel writer?'

'Yes,' said Mrs Oliver, 'as a matter of fact –' she had her usual somewhat shame-faced expression when she said this, that was habitual to her – 'yes, I do write novels.'

'I'm so fond of your books. I've read a lot of them. Oh, this is very nice indeed. Now tell me in what way can I help you?'

'Well, I wanted to talk about wigs and about something that happened a great many years ago and probably you mayn't remember anything about it.'

'Well, I rather wonder – do you mean fashions of years ago?'

'Not exactly. It's a woman, a friend of mine – actually I was at school with her – and then she married and went out to Malaya and came back to England, and there was a tragedy later and one of the things I think that people found surprising after it was that she had so many wigs. I think they had been all supplied by you, by your firm, I mean.'

'Oh, a tragedy. What was her name?'

'Well, her name when I knew her was Preston-Grey, but afterwards her name was Ravenscroft.'

'Oh. Oh yes, that one. Yes, I do remember Lady Ravenscroft. I remember her quite well. She was so nice and really very, very good-looking still. Yes, her husband was a Colonel or a General or something and they'd retired and they lived in – I forget the county now –'

'– And there was what was supposed to be a double suicide,' said Mrs Oliver.

'Yes. Yes, I remember reading about it and saying, "Why that's our Lady Ravenscroft," and then there was a picture of them both in the paper, and I saw that it was so. Of course, I'd never seen him but it was her all right. It seemed so sad, so much grief. I heard that they discovered that she had cancer and they couldn't do anything about it so this happened. But I never heard any details or anything.'

'No,' said Mrs Oliver.

'But what is it you think I can tell you?'

'You supplied her with wigs and I understand the people investigating, I suppose the police, thought four wigs was quite a lot to have, but perhaps people did have four wigs at a time?'

'Well, I think that most people had two wigs at least,' said Mrs Rosentelle. 'You know, one to send back to be serviced, as you might say, and the other one that they wore while it was away.'

'Do you remember Lady Ravenscroft ordering an extra two wigs?'

'She didn't come herself. I think she'd been or was ill in hospital, or something, and it was a French young lady who came. I think a French lady who was companion to her or something like that. Very nice. Spoke perfect English. And she explained all about the extra wigs she wanted, sizes and colours and styles and ordered them. Yes. Fancy my remembering it. I suppose I wouldn't have except that about – oh it must have been a month later – a month, perhaps more, six weeks – I read about the suicide, you know. I'm afraid they gave her bad news at the hospital or wherever she was, and so she just couldn't face living any more, and her husband felt he couldn't face life without her –'

Mrs Oliver shook her head sadly – and continued her enquiries.

'They were different kinds of wigs, I suppose.'

'Yes, one had a very pretty grey streak in it, and then there was a party one and one for evening wear, and one close-cropped with curls. Very nice, that you could wear under a hat and it didn't get messed up. I was sorry not to have seen Lady Ravenscroft again. Even apart from her illness, she had been very unhappy about a sister who had recently died. A twin sister.'

'Yes, twins are very devoted, aren't they,' said Mrs Oliver.

'She'd always seemed such a happy woman before,' said Mrs Rosentelle.

Both women sighed. Mrs Oliver changed the subject.

'Do you think that I'd find a wig useful?' she asked.

The expert stretched out a hand and laid it speculatively on Mrs Oliver's head.

'I wouldn't advise it – you've got a splendid crop of hair – very thick still – I imagine –' a faint smile came to her lips – 'you enjoy doing things with it?'

'How clever of you to know that. It's quite true – I enjoy experimenting – it's such fun.'

'You enjoy life altogether, don't you?'

'Yes, I do. I suppose it's the feeling that one never knows what might be going to happen next.'

'Yet that feeling,' said Mrs Rosentelle, 'is just what makes so many people never stop worrying!'

CHAPTER 16

MR GOBY REPORTS

Mr Goby came into the room and sat, as indicated by Poirot, in his usual chair. He glanced around him before choosing what particular piece of furniture or part of the room he was about to address. He settled, as often before, for the electric fire, not turned on at this time of year. Mr Goby had never been known to address the human being he was working for directly. He selected always the cornice, a radiator, a television set, a clock, sometimes a carpet or a mat. Out of a briefcase he took a few papers.

'Well,' said Hercule Poirot, 'you have something for me?'

'I have collected various details,' said Mr Goby.

Mr Goby was celebrated all over London, indeed possibly all over England and even further, as a great purvēyor of information. How he performed these miracles nobody ever really quite knew. He employed a not excessive staff. Sometimes he complained that his legs, as he sometimes called them, were not as good as they used to be. But his results were still able to astonish people who had commissioned them.

'Mrs Burton-Cox,' he said, announcing the name much as though he had been the local churchwarden having his turn at reading the lessons. He might equally have been saying 'Third verse, fourth chapter, the book of Isaiah.'

'Mrs Burton-Cox,' he said again. 'Married Mr Cecil Aldbury, manufacturer of buttons on a large scale. Rich man. Entered politics, was MP for Little Stansmere. Mr Cecil Aldbury was killed in a car accident four years after their marriage. The only child of the marriage died in an accident shortly afterwards. Mr Aldbury's estate was inherited by his wife, but was not as much as had been expected since the firm had not been doing well of late years. Mr Aldbury also left quite a considerable sum of money to a Miss Kathleen Fenn, with whom it seemed he had been having intimate relations quite unknown to his wife. Mrs Burton-Cox continued her political career. Some three years after that she adopted a child which had been born to Miss Kathleen Fenn. Miss Kathleen Fenn insisted that the child was the son of the late Mr Aldbury. This, from what I have been able to learn in my enquiries, is somewhat difficult to accept,' continued Mr Goby. 'Miss Fenn had had many relationships, usually with gentlemen of ample means and generous dispositions, but after all, so many people have their price, have they not? I'm afraid this is quite a serious bill I may have to send you in.'

'Continue,' said Hercule Poirot.

'Mrs Aldbury, as she then was, agreed to adopt the child. A short while later she married Major Burton-Cox. Miss Kathleen Fenn became, I may say, a most successful actress and pop singer and made a very large amount of money. She then wrote to Mrs Burton-Cox saying she would be willing to take back the adopted child. Mrs Burton-Cox refused. Mrs Burton-Cox has been living quite comfortably since, I understand, Major Burton-Cox was killed in Malaya. He left her moderately well off. A further piece of information I have obtained is that Miss Kathleen Fenn, who died a very short while ago – eighteen months, I think – left a Will by which her entire fortune, which amounted by then to a considerable sum of money, was left to her natural son Desmond, at present known under the name of Desmond Burton-Cox.'

'Very generous,' said Poirot. 'Of what did Miss Fenn die?'

'My informant tells me that she contracted leukaemia.'

'And the boy has inherited his mother's money?'

'It was left in trust for him to acquire at the age of twenty-five.'

'So he will be independent, will have a substantial fortune? And Mrs Burton-Cox?'

'Has not been happy in her investments, it is understood. She has sufficient to live on but not much more.'

'Has the boy Desmond made a Will?' asked Poirot.

'That,' said Mr Goby, 'I fear I do not know as yet. But I have certain means of finding out. If I do, I will acquaint you with the fact without loss of time.'

Mr Goby took his leave, absent-mindedly bowing a farewell to the electric fire.

About an hour and a half later the telephone rang.

Hercule Poirot, with a sheet of paper in front of him, was making notes. Now and then he frowned, twirled his moustaches, crossed something out and re-wrote it and then proceeded onward. When the telephone rang he picked up the receiver and listened.

'Thank you,' he said, 'that was quick work. Yes . . . yes, I'm grateful. I really do not know sometimes how you manage these things . . . Yes, that sets out the position clearly. It makes sense of something that did not make sense before . . . Yes . . . I gather . . . yes, I'm listening . . . you are pretty sure that that *is* the case. He knows he is adopted . . . but he never has been told who his real mother was . . . yes. Yes, I see . . . Very well. You will clear up the other point too? Thank you.'

He replaced the receiver and started once more writing down words. In half an hour the telephone rang once more. Once again he picked up the phone.

'I'm back from Cheltenham,' said a voice which Poirot had no difficulty in recognizing.

'Ah, *chère madame*, you have returned? You have seen Mrs Rosentelle?'

'Yes. She is nice. Very nice. And you were quite right, you know, she *is* another elephant.'

'Meaning, *chère madame*?'

'I mean that she remembered Molly Ravenscroft.'

'And she remembered her wigs?'

'Yes.'

Briefly she outlined what the retired hairdresser had told her about the wigs.

'Yes,' said Poirot, 'that agrees. That is exactly what Superintendent Garroway mentioned to me. The four wigs that the police found. Curls, an evening type of head-dress, and two other plainer ones. Four.'

'So I really only told you what you knew already?'

'No, you told me something more than that. She said – that is what you told me just now, is it not? – that Lady Ravenscroft wanted two extra wigs to add to the two that she already had and that this was about three weeks to six weeks before the suicide tragedy occurred. Yes, that is interesting, is it not?'

'It's very natural,' said Mrs Oliver. 'I mean, you know that people, women, I mean, may do awful damage to things. To false hair and things of that kind. If it can't be re-dressed and cleaned, if it's got burnt or got stuff spilt on it you can't get out, or it's been dyed and dyed all wrong – something like that – well then, of course you have to get two new wigs or switches or whatever they are. I don't see what makes you excited about that.'

'Not exactly excited,' said Poirot, 'no. It is a point, but the more interesting point is what you have just added. It was a French lady, was it not, who brought the wigs to be copied or matched?'

'Yes. I gathered some kind of companion or something. Lady Ravenscroft had been or was in hospital or in a nursing home somewhere and she was not in good health and she could not come herself to make a choice or anything of that kind.'

'I see.'

'And so her French companion came.'

'Do you know the name of that companion by any chance?'

'No. I don't think Mrs Rosentelle mentioned it. In fact I don't think she knew. The appointment was made by Lady Ravenscroft and the French girl or woman just brought the wigs along for size and matching and all the rest of it, I suppose.'

'Well,' said Poirot, 'that helps me towards the further step that I am about to take.'

'What have *you* learnt?' said Mrs Oliver. 'Have you done *anything*?'

'You are always so sceptical,' said Poirot. 'You always consider that I do nothing, that I sit in a chair and repose myself.'

'Well I think you sit in a chair and think,' admitted Mrs Oliver, 'but I quite agree that you don't often go out and do things.'

'In the near future I think I may possibly go out and do things,' said Hercule Poirot, 'and that will please you. I may even cross the Channel though certainly not in a boat. A plane, I think is indicated.'

'Oh,' said Mrs Oliver., 'Do you want me to come too?'

'No,' said Poirot, 'I think it would be better if I went alone on this occasion.'

'You really *will* go?'

'Oh yes, oh yes. I will run about with all activity and so you should be pleased with me, madame.'

When he had rung off, he dialled another number which he looked up from a note he had made in his pocket-book. Presently he was connected to the person whom he wished to speak to.

'My dear Superintendent Garroway, it is Hercule Poirot who

addresses you. I do not derange you too much? You are not very busy at this moment?'

'No, I am not busy,' said Superintendent Garroway. 'I am pruning my roses, that's all.'

'There is something that I want to ask you. Quite a small thing.'

'About our problem of the double suicide?'

'Yes, about our problem. You said there was a dog in the house. You said that the dog went for walks with the family, or so you understood.'

'Yes, there was some mention made of a dog. I think it may have been either the housekeeper or someone who said that they went for a walk with the dog as usual that day.'

'In examination of the body was there any sign that Lady Ravenscroft had been bitten by a dog? Not necessarily very recently or on that particular day?'

'Well, it's odd you should say that. I can't say I'd have remembered about it if you hadn't mentioned such a thing. But yes, there were a couple of scars. Not bad ones. But again the housekeeper mentioned that the dog had attacked its mistress more than once and bitten her, though not very severely. Look here, Poirot, there was no rabies about, if that's what you are thinking. There couldn't have been anything of that kind. After all she was shot – they were both shot. There was no question of any septic poisoning or danger of tetanus.'

'I do not blame the dog,' said Poirot, 'it was only something I wanted to know.'

'One dog bite was fairly recent, about a week before, I think, or two weeks somebody said. There was no case of necessary injections or anything of that kind. It had healed quite well. What's that quotation?' went on Superintendent Garroway. '"*The dog it was that died.*" I can't remember where it comes from but –'

'Anyway, it wasn't the dog that died,' said Poirot. 'That wasn't the point of my question. I would like to have known that dog. He was perhaps a very intelligent dog.'

After he had replaced the receiver with thanks to the Superintendent, Poirot murmured: 'An intelligent dog. More intelligent perhaps than the police were.'

CHAPTER 17

POIROT ANNOUNCES DEPARTURE

Miss Livingstone showed in a guest. 'Mr Hercules Porrett.'

As soon as Miss Livingstone had left the room, Poirot shut the door after her and sat down by his friend, Mrs Ariadne Oliver.

He said, lowering his voice slightly, 'I depart.'

'You do what?' said Mrs Oliver, who was always slightly startled by Poirot's methods of passing on information.

'I depart. I make the departure. I take a plane to Geneva.'

'You sound as though you were UNO or UNESCO or something.'

'No. It is just a private visit that I make.'

'Have you got an elephant in Geneva?'

'Well, I suppose you might look at it that way. Perhaps two of them.'

'I haven't found out anything more,' said Mrs Oliver. 'In fact I don't know who I can go to, to find out any more.'

'I believe you mentioned, or somebody did, that your goddaughter, Celia Ravenscroft, had a young brother.'

'Yes. He's called Edward, I think. I've hardly ever seen him. I took him out once or twice from school, I remember. But that was years ago.'

'Where is he now?'

'He's at university, in Canada I think. Or he's taking some engineering course there. Do you want to go and ask him things?'

'No, not at the moment. I should just like to know where he is now. But I gather he was not in the house when this suicide happened?'

'You're not thinking – you're not thinking for a moment that *he* did it, are you? I mean, shot his father and his mother, both of them. I know boys do sometimes. Very queer they are sometimes when they're at a funny age.'

'He was not in the house,' said Poirot. 'That I know already from my police reports.'

'Have you found out anything else interesting? You look quite excited.'

'I am excited in a way. I have found out certain things that may throw light upon what we already know.'

'Well, what throws light on what?'

'It seems to me possible now that I can understand why Mrs Burton-Cox approached you as she did and tried to get you to obtain information for her about the facts of the suicide of the Ravenscrofts.'

'You mean she wasn't just being a nosey-parker?'

'No. I think there was some motive behind it. This is where, perhaps, money comes in.'

'Money? What's money got to do with that? She's quite well off, isn't she?'

'She has enough to live upon, yes. But it seems that her adopted son whom she regards apparently as her true son – he knows that he was adopted although he knows nothing about the family from which he really came. It seems that when he came of age he made a Will, possibly urged by his adopted mother to do so. Perhaps it was merely hinted to him by some friends of hers or possibly by some lawyer that she had consulted. Anyway, on coming of age he may have felt that he might as well leave everything to her, to his adopted mother. Presumably at that time he had nobody else to leave it to.'

'I don't see how that leads to wanting news about a suicide.'

'Don't you? She wanted to discourage the marriage. If young Desmond had a girl-friend, if he proposed to marry her in the near future, which is what a lot of young people do nowadays – they won't wait or think it over. In that case, Mrs Burton-Cox would not inherit the money he left, since the marriage would invalidate any earlier Will, and presumably if he did marry his girl he would make a new Will leaving everything to her and not to his adopted mother.'

'And you mean Mrs Burton-Cox didn't want that?'

'She wanted to find something that would discourage him from marrying the girl. I think she hoped, and probably really believed as far as that goes, that Celia's mother killed her husband, afterwards shooting herself. That is the sort of thing that might discourage a boy. Even if her father killed her mother, it is still a discouraging thought. It might quite easily prejudice and influence a boy at that age.'

'You mean he'd think that if her father or mother was a murderer, the girl might have murderous tendencies?'

'Not quite as crude as that but that might be the main idea, I should think.'

'But he wasn't rich, was he? An adopted child.'

'He didn't know his real mother's name or who she was, but it seems that his mother, who was an actress and a singer and who managed to make a great deal of money before she became ill and died, wanted at one time to get her child returned to her and when Mrs Burton-Cox would not agree to that, I should imagine she thought about this boy a great deal and decided that she would leave her money to him. He will inherit this money at the age of twenty-five, but it is held in trust for him until then. So of course Mrs Burton-Cox doesn't want him to marry, or only to marry someone that she really approves of or over whom she might have influence.'

'Yes, that seems to me fairly reasonable. She's not a nice woman though, is she?'

'No,' said Poirot, 'I did not think her a very nice woman.'

'And that's why she didn't want you coming to see her and messing about with things and finding out what she was up to.'

'Possibly,' said Poirot.

'Anything else you have learnt?'

'Yes, I have learnt – that is only a few hours ago really – when Superintendent Garroway happened to ring me up about some other small matters, but I did ask him and he told me that the housekeeper, who was elderly, had very bad eyesight.'

'Does that come into it anywhere?'

'It might,' said Poirot. He looked at his watch. 'I think,' he said, 'it is time that I left.'

'You are on your way to catch your plane at the airport?'

'No. My plane does not leave until tomorrow morning. But there is a place I have to visit today – a place that I wish to see with my own eyes. I have a car waiting outside now to take me there –'

'What is it you want to see?' Mrs Oliver asked with some curiosity.

'Not so much to *see* – to *feel*. Yes – that is the right word – to feel and to recognize what it will be that I feel . . .'

CHAPTER 18

INTERLUDE

Hercule Poirot passed through the gate of the churchyard. He walked up one of the paths, and presently, against a moss-grown wall he stopped, looking down on a grave. He stood there for some minutes looking first at the grave, then at the view of the Downs and sea beyond. Then his eyes came back again. Flowers had been put recently on the grave. A small bunch of assorted wild flowers, the kind of bunch that might have been left by a child, but Poirot did not think that it was a child who had left them. He read the lettering on the grave.

To the memory of
DOROTHEA JARROW
Died Sept 15th 1960

Also of
MARGARET RAVENSCROFT
Died Oct 3rd 1960
Sister of above

Also of
ALISTAIR RAVENSCROFT
Died Oct 3rd 1960
Her husband

In their Death they were not divided

Forgive us our trespasses
As we forgive those that trespass against us
Lord, have Mercy upon us
Christ, have Mercy upon us
Lord, have Mercy upon us

Poirot stood there a moment or two. He nodded his head once or twice. Then he left the churchyard and walked by a footpath that led out on to the cliff and along the cliff. Presently he stood still again looking out to the sea. He spoke to himself.

'I am sure now that I know what happened and why. I understand the pity of it and the tragedy. One has to go back such a long way. *In my end is my beginning*, or should one put it differently? "In my beginning was my tragic end"? The Swiss girl must have known – but will she tell me? The boy believes she will. For their sakes – the girl and the boy. They cannot accept life unless they know.'

CHAPTER 19

MADDY AND ZÉLIE

'Mademoiselle Rouselle?' said Hercule Poirot. He bowed.

Mademoiselle Rouselle extended her hand. About fifty, Poirot thought. A fairly imperious woman. Would have her way. Intelligent, intellectual, satisfied, he thought, with life as she had lived it, enjoying the pleasures and suffering the sorrows life brings.

'I have heard your name,' she said. 'You have friends, you know, both in this country and in France. I do not know exactly what I can do for you. Oh, I know that you explained, in the letter that you sent me. It is an affair of the past, is it not? Things that happened. Not exactly things that happened, but the clue to things that happened many, many years ago. But sit down. Yes. Yes, that chair is quite comfortable, I hope. There are some *petit-fours* and the decanter is on the table.'

She was quietly hospitable without any urgency. She was unworried but amiable.

'You were at one time a governess in a certain family,' said Poirot. 'The Preston-Greys. Perhaps now you hardly remember them.'

'Oh yes, one does not forget, you know, things that happen when you were young. There was a girl, and a boy about four or five years younger in the family I went to. They were nice children. Their father became a General in the Army.'

'There was also another sister.'

'Ah yes, I remember. She was not there when I first came. I

think she was delicate. Her health was not good. She was having treatment somewhere.'

'You remember their Christian names?'

'Margaret, I think was one. The other one I am not sure of by now.'

'Dorothea.'

'Ah yes. A name I have not often come across. But they called each other by shorter names. Molly and Dolly. They were identical twins, you know, remarkably alike. They were both very handsome young women.'

'And they were fond of each other?'

'Yes, they were devoted. But we are, are we not, becoming slightly confused? Preston-Grey is not the name of the children I went to teach. Dorothea Preston-Grey married a Major – ah, I cannot remember the name now. Arrow? No, Jarrow. Margaret's married name was –'

'Ravenscroft,' said Poirot.

'Ah, that. Yes. Curious how one cannot remember names. The Preston-Greys are a generation older. Margaret Preston-Grey had been in a *pensionnat* in this part of the world, and when she wrote after her marriage asking Madame Benoît, who ran that *pensionnat*, if she knew of someone who would come to her as nursery-governess to her children, I was recommended. That is how I came to go there. I spoke only of the other sister because she happened to be staying there during part of my time of service with the children. The children were a girl, I think then of six or seven. She had a name out of Shakespeare. I remember, Rosalind or Celia.'

'Celia,' said Poirot.

'And the boy was only about three or four. His name was Edward. A mischievous but lovable child. I was happy with them.'

'And they were happy, I hear, with you. They enjoyed playing with you and you were very kind in your playing with them.'

'*Moi, j'aime les enfants*,' said Mademoiselle Rouselle.

'They called you "Maddy", I believe.'

She laughed.

'Ah, I like hearing that word. It brings back past memories.'

'Did you know a boy called Desmond? Desmond Burton-Cox?'

'Ah yes. He lived I think in a house next door or nearly next door. We had several neighbours and the children very often came to play together. His name was Desmond. Yes, I remember.'

'You were there long, mademoiselle?'

'No. I was only there for three or four years at most. Then I was recalled to this country. My mother was very ill. It was a question of coming back and nursing her, although I knew it would not be perhaps for very long. That was true. She died a year and a half or two years at the most after I returned here. After that I started a small *pensionnat* out here, taking in rather older girls who wanted to study languages and other things. I did not visit England again, although for a year or two I kept up communication with the country. The two children used to send me a card at Christmas time.'

'Did General Ravenscroft and his wife strike you as a happy couple?'

'Very happy. They were fond of their children.'

'They were very well suited to each other?'

'Yes, they seemed to me to have all the necessary qualities to make their marriage a success.'

'You said Lady Ravenscroft was devoted to her twin sister. Was the twin sister also devoted to her?'

'Well, I had not very much occasion of judging. Frankly, I thought that the sister – Dolly, as they called her – was very definitely a mental case. Once or twice she acted in a very peculiar manner. She was a jealous woman, I think, and I understood that she had at one time thought she was engaged, or was going to be engaged, to General Ravenscroft. As far as I could see he'd fallen in love with her first, then later, however, his affections turned towards her sister, which was fortunate, I thought, because Molly Ravenscroft was a well-balanced and very sweet woman. As for Dolly – sometimes I thought she adored her sister, sometimes that she hated her. She was a very jealous woman and she decided too much affection was being shown to the children. There is one who could tell you about all this better than I. Mademoiselle Meauhourat. She lives in Lausanne and she went to the Ravenscrofts about a year and a half or two years after I had to leave. She was with them for some years. Later I believe she went back as companion to Lady Ravenscroft when Celia was abroad at school.'

'I am going to see her. I have her address,' said Poirot.

'She knows a great deal that I do not, and she is a charming and reliable person. It was a terrible tragedy that happened later. She knows if anyone does what led to it. She is very discreet. She has never told me anything. Whether she will tell you I do not know. She may do, she may not.'

Poirot stood for a moment or two looking at Mademoiselle Meauhourat. He had been impressed by Mademoiselle Rouselle, he was impressed also by the woman who stood waiting to receive him. She was not so formidable, she was much younger, at least ten years younger, he thought, and she had a different kind of impressiveness. She was alive, still attractive, eyes that watched you and made their own judgment on you, willing to welcome you, looking with kindliness on those who came her way but without undue softness. Here is someone, thought Hercule Poirot, very remarkable.

'I am Hercule Poirot, mademoiselle.'

'I know. I was expecting you either today or tomorrow.'

'Ah. You received a letter from me?'

'No. It is no doubt still in the post. Our posts are a little uncertain. No. I had a letter from someone else.'

'From Celia Ravenscroft?'

'No. It was a letter written by someone in close touch with Celia. A boy or a young man, whichever we like to regard him as, called Desmond Burton-Cox. He prepared me for your arrival.'

'Ah. I see. He is intelligent and he wastes no time, I think. He was very urgent that I should come and see you.'

'So I gathered. There's trouble, I understand. Trouble that he wants to resolve, and so does Celia. They think you can help them?'

'Yes, and they think that *you* can help *me*.'

'They are in love with each other and wish to marry.'

'Yes, but there are difficulties being put in their way.'

'Ah, by Desmond's mother, I presume. So he lets me understand.'

'There are circumstances, or have been circumstances, in

Celia's life that have prejudiced his mother against his early marriage to this particular girl.'

'Ah. Because of the tragedy, for it was a tragedy.'

'Yes, because of the tragedy. Celia has a godmother who was asked by Desmond's mother to try and find out from Celia the exact circumstances under which that suicide occurred.'

'There's no sense in that,' said Mademoiselle Meauhourat. She motioned with her hand. 'Sit down. Please sit down. I expect we shall have to talk for some little time. Yes, Celia could not tell her godmother – Mrs Ariadne Oliver, the novelist is it not? Yes, I remember. Celia could not give her the information because she has not got the information herself.'

'She was not there when the tragedy occurred, and no one told her anything about it. Is that right?'

'Yes, that is right. It was thought inadvisable.'

'Ah. And do you approve of that decision or disapprove of it?'

'It is difficult to be sure. Very difficult. I've not been sure of it in the years that have passed since then, and there are quite a lot. Celia, as far as I know, has never been worried. Worried, I mean, as to the why and wherefore. She's accepted it as she would have accepted an aeroplane accident or a car accident. Something that resulted in the death of her parents. She spent many years in a *pensionnat* abroad.'

'Actually I think the *pensionnat* was run by you, Mademoiselle Meauhourat.'

'That is quite true. I have retired recently. A colleague of mine is now taking it on. But Celia was sent out to me and I was asked to find for her a good place for her to continue her education, as many girls do come to Switzerland for that purpose. I could have recommended several places. At the moment I took her into my own.'

'And Celia asked you nothing, did not demand information?'

'No. It was, you see, before the tragedy happened.'

'Oh. I did not quite understand that.'

'Celia came out here some weeks before the tragic occurrence. I was at that time not here myself. I was still with General and Lady Ravenscroft. I looked after Lady Ravenscroft, acting as a companion to her rather than as a governess to Celia, who was still at that moment in boarding-school. But it was suddenly arranged that Celia should come to Switzerland and finish her education there.'

'Lady Ravenscroft had been in poor health, had she not?'

'Yes. Nothing very serious. Nothing as serious as she had herself feared at one time. But she had suffered a lot of nervous strain and shock and general worry.'

'You remained with her?'

'A sister whom I had living in Lausanne received Celia on her arrival and settled her into the institution which was only for about fifteen or sixteen girls, but there she would start her studies and await my return. I returned some three or four weeks later.'

'But you were at Overcliffe at the time it happened.'

'I was at Overcliffe. General and Lady Ravenscroft went for a walk, as was their habit. They went out and did not return. They were found dead, shot. The weapon was found lying by them. It was one that belonged to General Ravenscroft and had been always kept in a drawer in his study. The finger marks of both of them were found on that weapon. There was no definite indication of who had held it last. Impressions of both people, slightly smeared, were on it. The obvious solution was a double suicide.'

'You found no reason to doubt that?'

'The police found no reason, so I believe.'

'Ah,' said Poirot.

'I beg your pardon?' said Mademoiselle Meauhourat.

'Nothing. Nothing. Just something upon which I reflect.'

Poirot looked at her. Brown hair as yet hardly touched with grey, lips closed firmly together, grey eyes, a face which showed no emotion. She was in control of herself completely.

'So you cannot tell me anything more?'

'I fear not. It was a long time ago.'

'You remember that time well enough.'

'Yes. One cannot entirely forget such a sad thing.'

'And you agreed that Celia should not be told anything more of what had led up to this?'

'Have I not just told you that I had no extra information?'

'You were there, living at Overcliffe, for a period of time before the tragedy, were you not? Four or five weeks – six weeks perhaps.'

'Longer than that, really. Although I had been governess to Celia earlier, I came back this time, after she went to school, in order to help Lady Ravenscroft.'

'Lady Ravenscroft's sister was living with her also about that time, was she not?'

'Yes. She had been in hospital having special treatment for some time. She had shown much improvement and the authorities had felt – the medical authorities I speak of – that she would do better to lead a normal life with her own relations and the atmosphere of a home. As Celia had gone to school, it seemed a good time for Lady Ravenscroft to invite her sister to be with her.'

'Were they fond of each other, those two sisters?'

'It was difficult to know,' said Mademoiselle Meauhourat. Her brows drew together. It was as though what Poirot had just said aroused her interest. 'I have wondered, you know. I have wondered so much since, and at the time really. They were identical twins, you know. They had a bond between them, a bond of mutual dependence and love and in many ways they were very alike. But there were ways also in which they were not alike.'

'You mean? I should be glad to know just what you mean by that.'

'Oh, this has nothing to do with the tragedy. Nothing of that kind. But there was a definite, as I shall put it, a definite physical or mental flaw – whichever way you like to put it – some people nowadays hold the theory that there is some physical cause for any kind of mental disorder. I believe that it is fairly well recognized by the medical profession that identical twins are born either with a great bond between them, a great likeness in their characters which means that although they may be divided in their environment, where they are brought up, the same things will happen to them at the same time of life. They will take the same trend. Some of the cases quoted as medical example seem quite extraordinary. Two sisters, one living in Europe, one say in France, the other in England, they have a dog of the same kind which they choose at about the same date. They marry men singularly alike. They give birth perhaps to a child almost within a month of each other. It is as though they have to follow the pattern wherever they are and without knowing what the other one is doing. Then there is the opposite to that. A kind of revulsion, a hatred almost, that makes one sister draw apart, or one brother reject the other as though they seek to get away from the sameness, the likeness, the knowledge, the things they have in common. And that can lead to very strange results.'

'I know,' said Poirot. 'I have heard of it. I have seen it once or twice. Love can turn to hate very easily. It is easier to hate where you have loved than it is to be indifferent where you have loved.'

'Ah, you know that,' said Mademoiselle Meauhourat.

'Yes, I have seen it not once but several times. Lady Ravenscroft's sister was very like her?'

'I think she was still very like her in appearance, though, if I may say so, the expression on her face was very different. She was in a condition of strain as Lady Ravenscroft was not. She had a great aversion to children. I don't know why. Perhaps she had had a miscarriage in early life. Perhaps she had longed for a child and never had one, but she had a kind of resentment against children. A dislike of them.'

'That had led to one or two rather serious happenings, had it not?' said Poirot.

'Someone has told you that?'

'I have heard things from people who knew both sisters when they were in Malaya. Lady Ravenscroft was there with her husband and her sister, Dolly, came out to stay with them there. There was an accident to a child there, and it was thought that Dolly might have been partially responsible for it. Nothing was proved definitely, but I gather that Molly's husband took his sister-in-law home to England and she had once more to go into a mental home.'

'Yes, I believe that is a very good account of what happened. I do not of course know it of my own knowledge.'

'No, but there are things you do know, I think, from your own knowledge.'

'If so, I see no reason for bringing them back to mind now. Is it not better to leave things when at least they have been accepted?'

'There are other things that could have happened that day at

Overcliffe. It may have been a double suicide, it could have been a murder, it could have been several other things. You were told what had happened, but I think from one little sentence you just said, that you know what happened that day and I think you know what happened perhaps – or began to happen, shall we say? – some time before that. The time when Celia had gone to Switzerland and you were still at Overcliffe. I will ask you one question. I would like to know what your answer would be to it. It is not a thing of direct information, it is a question of what you believe. What were the feelings of General Ravenscroft towards those two sisters, the twin sisters?'

'I know what you mean.'

For the first time her manner changed slightly. She was no longer on her guard, she leaned forward now and spoke to Poirot almost as though she definitely found a relief in doing so.

'They were both beautiful,' she said, 'as girls. I heard that from many people. General Ravenscroft fell in love with Dolly, the mentally afflicted sister. Although she had a disturbed personality she was exceedingly attractive – sexually attractive. He loved her very dearly, and then I don't know whether he discovered in her some characteristic, something perhaps that alarmed him or in which he found a repulsion of some kind. He saw perhaps the beginnings of insanity in her, the dangers connected with her. His affections went to her sister. He fell in love with the sister and married her.'

'He loved them both, you mean. Not at the same time but in each case there was a genuine fact of love.'

'Oh, yes, he was devoted to Molly, relied on her and she on him. He was a very lovable man.'

'Forgive me,' said Poirot, 'you too were in love with him, I think.'

'You – you dare say that to me?'

'Yes. I dare say it to you. I am not suggesting that you and he had a love-affair, nothing of that kind. I'm only saying that you loved him.'

'Yes,' said Zélie Meauhourat. 'I loved him. In a sense, I still love him. There's nothing to be ashamed of. He trusted me and relied on me, but he was never in love with me. You can love and serve and still be happy. I wanted no more than I had. Trust, sympathy, belief in me –'

'And you did,' said Poirot, 'what you could to help him in a terrible crisis in his life. There are things you do not wish to tell me. There are things that I will say to you, things that I have gathered from various information that has come to me, that I know something about. Before I have come to see you I have heard from others, from people who have known not only Lady Ravenscroft, not only Molly, but who have known Dolly. And I know something of Dolly, the tragedy of her life, the sorrow, the unhappiness and also the hatred, the streak perhaps of evil, the love of destruction that can be handed down in families. If she loved the man she was engaged to she must have, when he married her sister, felt hatred perhaps towards that sister. Perhaps she never quite forgave her. But what of Molly Ravenscroft? Did she dislike her sister? Did she hate her?'

'Oh no,' said Zélie Meauhourat, 'she loved her sister. She loved her with a very deep and protective love. That I do know. It was she who always asked that her sister should come and make her home with her. She wanted to save her sister from unhappiness, from danger too, because her sister would often relapse into fits of rather dangerous rages. She was frightened sometimes. Well, you know enough. You have already said that there was a strange dislike of children from which Dolly suffered.'

'You mean that she disliked Celia?'

'No, no, not Celia. The other one, Edward. The younger one. Twice Edward had dangers of an accident. Once, some kind of tinkering with a car and once some outburst of violent annoyance. I know Molly was glad when Edward went back to school. He was very young, remember, much younger than Celia. He was only eight or nine, at preparatory school. He was vulnerable. Molly was frightened about him.'

'Yes,' said Poirot, 'I can understand that. Now, if I may I will talk of wigs. Wigs. The wearing of wigs. Four wigs. That is a lot for one woman to possess at one time. I know what they were like, what they looked like. I know that when more were needed, a French lady went to the shop in London and spoke about them and ordered them. There was a dog, too. A dog who went for a walk on the day of the tragedy with General Ravenscroft and his wife. Earlier that dog, some little time earlier, had bitten his mistress, Molly Ravenscroft.'

'Dogs are like that,' said Zélie Meauhourat. 'They are never quite to be trusted. Yes, I know that.'

'And I will tell you what I think happened on that day, and what happened before that. Some little time before that.'

'And if I will not listen to you?'

'You will listen to me. You may say that what I have imagined is false. Yes, you might even do that, but I do not think you will. I am telling you, and I believe it with all my heart, that what is needed here is the truth. It is not just imagining, it is not just wondering. There is a girl and a boy who care for each other and who are frightened of the future because of what may have happened and what there might be handed down from the father or the mother to the child. I am thinking of the girl, Celia. A rebellious girl, spirited, difficult perhaps to manage but with brains, a good mind, capable of happiness, capable of courage but needing – there are people who need – truth. Because they can face truth without dismay. They can face it with that brave acceptance you have to have in life if life is to be any good to you. And the boy that she loves, he wants that for her too. Will you listen to me?'

'Yes,' said Zélie Meauhourat, 'I am listening. You understand a great deal, I think, and I think you know more than I could have imagined you would know. Speak and I will listen.'

CHAPTER 20

COURT OF ENQUIRY

Once more Hercule Poirot stood on the cliff overlooking the rocks below and the sea breaking against them. Here where he stood the bodies of a husband and wife had been found. Here, three weeks before that a woman had walked in her sleep and fallen to her death.

'Why had these things happened?' That had been Superintendent Garroway's question.

Why? What had led to it?

An accident first – and three weeks later a double suicide. Old sins that had left long shadows. A beginning that had led years later to a tragic end.

Today there would be people meeting here. A boy and a girl who sought the Truth. Two people who knew the truth.

Hercule Poirot turned away from the sea and back along the narrow path that led to a house once called Overcliffe.

It was not very far. He saw cars parked against a wall. He saw the outline of a house against the sky. A house that was clearly empty – that needed repainting. A house agent's board hung there – announcing that 'this desirable property' was for sale. On the gate the word Overcliffe had a line drawn over it and the name Down House replaced it. He went to meet two people who were walking towards him. One was Desmond Burton-Cox and the other was Celia Ravenscroft.

'I got an order from the house agent,' said Desmond, 'saying we wanted to view it or however they put it. I've got the key in case we want to go inside. It's changed hands twice in the last five years. But there wouldn't be anything to see there now, would there?'

'I shouldn't think so,' said Celia. 'After all, it's belonged to lots of people already. Some people called Archer who first bought it, and then somebody called Fallowfield, I think. They said it was too lonely. And now these last people are selling it too. Perhaps they were haunted.'

'Do you really believe in haunted houses?' said Desmond.

'Well now, of course I don't think so really,' said Celia, 'but this might be, mightn't it? I mean, the sort of things that happened, the sort of place it is and everything . . .'

'I do not think so,' said Poirot. 'There was sorrow here and Death, but there was also Love.'

A taxi came along the road.

'I expect that's Mrs Oliver,' said Celia. 'She said she'd come by train and take a taxi from the station.'

Two women got out of the taxi. One was Mrs Oliver and with her was a tall, elegantly dressed woman. Since Poirot knew she was coming he was not taken by surprise. He watched Celia to see if she had any reactions.

'Oh!' Celia sprang forward.

She went towards the woman and her face had lit up.

'Zélie!' she said, 'it *is* Zélie? It is really Zélie! Oh, I am so pleased. I didn't know you were coming.'

'Monsieur Hercule Poirot asked me to come.'

'I see,' said Celia. 'Yes, yes, I suppose I see. But I – I didn't –' she stopped. She turned her head and looked at the handsome boy standing beside her. 'Desmond, was it – was it you?'

'Yes. I wrote to Mademoiselle Meauhourat – to Zélie, if I may still call her that.'

'You can always call me that, both of you,' said Zélie. 'I was not sure I wanted to come, I did not know if I was wise to come. That I still do not know, but I hope so.'

'I want to *know*,' said Celia. 'We both want to know. Desmond thought you could tell us something.'

'Monsieur Poirot came to see me,' said Zélie. 'He persuaded me to come today.'

Celia linked her arm in Mrs Oliver's.

'I wanted you to come too because you put this in hand, didn't you? You got Monsieur Poirot and you found out some things yourself, didn't you?'

'People told me things,' said Mrs Oliver, 'people whom I thought might remember things. Some of them did remember things. Some of them remembered them right and some of them remembered them wrong. That was confusing. Monsieur Poirot says that that does not really matter.'

'No,' said Poirot, 'it is just as important to know what is hearsay and what is certain knowledge. Because from one you can learn facts even if they are not quite the right facts or had not got the explanation that you think they had. With the knowledge that you got from me, madame, from the people whom you designated elephants –' he smiled a little.

'Elephants?!' said Mademoiselle Zélie.

'It is what she called them,' said Poirot.

'Elephants can remember,' explained Mrs Oliver. 'That was the idea I started on. And people can remember things that happened a long time ago just like elephants can. Not all people, of course, but they can usually remember *something*. There were a lot of people who did. I turned a lot of the things I heard over to Monsieur Poirot and he – he has made a sort of – oh, if he was a doctor I should call it a sort of diagnosis, I suppose.'

'I made a list,' said Poirot. 'A list of things that seemed to be pointers to the truth of what happened all those years ago. I shall read the various items to you to see perhaps if you who were concerned in all this, feel that they have any significance. You may not see their significance or you may see it plainly.'

'One wants to know,' said Celia. 'Was it suicide, or was it murder? Did somebody – some outside person – kill both my father and my mother, shoot them for some reason we don't know about, some motive? I shall always think there was something of that kind or something else. It's difficult, but –'

'We will stay here, I think,' said Poirot. 'We will not go into the house as yet. Other people have lived in it and it has a different atmosphere. We will perhaps go in if we wish when we have finished our court of enquiry here.'

'It's a court of enquiry, is it?' said Desmond.

'Yes. A court of enquiry into what happened.'

He moved towards some iron seats which stood near the shelter of a large magnolia near the house. Poirot took from the case he carried a sheet of paper with writing on it. He said to Celia:

'To you, it has got to be that way? A definite choice. Suicide or murder.'

'One of them must be true,' said Celia.

'I shall say to you that both are true, and more than those two. According to my ideas, we have here not only a murder and also a suicide, but we have as well what I shall call an execution, and we have a tragedy also. A tragedy of two people who loved each other and who died for love. A tragedy of love may not always belong to Romeo and Juliet, it is not necessarily only the young who suffer the pains of love and are ready to die for love. No. There is more to it than that.'

'I don't understand,' said Celia.

'Not yet.'

'Shall I understand?' said Celia.

'I think so,' said Poirot. 'I will tell you what I think happened and I will tell you how I came to think so. The first thing that struck me was the things that were not explained by the evidence that the police examined. Some things were very commonplace, were not evidence at all, you'd think. Among the possessions of the dead Margaret Ravenscroft, were four wigs.' He repeated with emphasis. '*Four* wigs.' He looked at Zélie.

'She did not use a wig all the time,' said Zélie. 'Only occasionally. If she travelled or if she'd been out and got very dishevelled and wanted to tidy herself in a hurry, or sometimes she'd use one that was suitable for evening wear.'

'Yes,' said Poirot, 'it was quite the fashion at that particular date. People certainly when they travelled abroad usually had a wig or two wigs. But in her possession were *four* wigs. Four wigs seemed to me rather a lot. I wondered *why* she needed four. According to the police whom I asked, it was not that she had any tendency to baldness, she had the ordinary hair a woman of her age would have and in good condition. All the same, I wondered about those. One of the wigs had a grey streak in it, I learnt later. It was her hairdresser who told me that. And one of the wigs had little curls. It was the latter wig she was wearing the day she died.'

'Is that significant in any way?' asked Celia. 'She might have been wearing any of them.'

'She might. I also learnt the housekeeper told the police that she had been wearing that particular wig almost all the time for the last few weeks before she died. It appeared to be her favourite one.'

'I can't see –'

'There was also a saying that Superintendent Garroway quoted to me – "Same man, different hat". It gave me furiously to think.'

Celia repeated, 'I don't see –'

Poirot said, 'There was also the evidence of the dog –'

'The dog – what did the dog do?'

'The dog bit her. The dog was said to be devoted to its mistress – but in the last few weeks of her life, the dog turned on her more than once and bit her quite severely.'

'Do you mean it knew she was going to commit suicide?' Desmond stared.

'No, something much simpler than that –'

'I don't –'

Poirot went on – 'No, it knew what no one else seemed to know. It knew she was not its mistress. She looked like its mistress – the housekeeper who was slightly blind and also deaf saw a woman who wore Molly Ravenscroft's clothes and the most recognizable of Molly Ravenscroft's wigs – the one with little curls all over the head. The housekeeper said only that her mistress had been rather different in her manner the last few weeks of her life – "Same man, different hat," had been Garroway's phrase. And the thought – the conviction – came to me then. Same *wig* – different *woman*. The dog knew – he knew by what his nose told him. A different woman, not the woman he loved – a woman whom he disliked and feared. And I thought, suppose that woman was not Molly Ravenscroft – but who could she be? Could she be Dolly – the twin sister?'

'But that's impossible,' said Celia.

'No – it was not impossible. After all, remember, they were twins. I must come now to the things that were brought to my notice by Mrs Oliver. The things people told her or suggested to her. The knowledge that Lady Ravenscroft had suggested to her. The knowledge that Lady Ravenscroft had recently been in hospital or in a nursing home and that she perhaps had known that she suffered from cancer, or thought that she did. Medical evidence was against that, however. She still might have thought she did, but it was not the case. Then I learnt little by little the early history of her and her twin sister, who loved each other very devotedly as twins do, did everything alike, wore clothes alike, the same things seemed to happen to them, they had illnesses at the same time, they married about the same time or not very far removed in time. And eventually, as many twins do, instead of wanting to do everything in the same fashion and the same way, they wanted to do the opposite. To be as unlike each other as they could. And even between them grew a certain amount of dislike. More than that. There was a reason in the past for that. Alistair Ravenscroft as a young man fell in love with Dorothea Preston-Grey, the elder twin of the two. But his affection shifted to the other sister, Margaret, whom he married. There was jealousy then, no doubt, which led to an estrangement between the sisters. Margaret continued to be deeply attached to her twin, but Dorothea no longer was devoted in any way to Margaret. That seemed to me to be the explanation of a great many things. Dorothea was a tragic figure. By no fault of her own but by some accident of genes, of birth, of hereditary characteristics, she was always mentally unstable. At quite an early age she had, for some reason which has never been made clear, a dislike of children. There is every reason to believe that a child came to its death through her action. The evidence was not definite, but it was definite enough for a doctor to advise that she should have mental treatment, and she was for some years treated in a mental home. When reported cured by doctors, she resumed normal life, came often to stay with her sister and went out to Malaya at a time when they were stationed out there, to join them there. And there, again, an accident happened. A child of a neighbour. And again, although perhaps there was no very definite proof, it seems again Dorothea might have been responsible for it. General Ravenscroft took her home to England and she was placed once more in medical care. Once again she appeared to be cured, and after psychiatric care it was again said that she could go once more and resume a normal life. Margaret believed this time that all would be well, and thought that she ought to live with them so that they could watch closely for any signs of any further mental disability. I don't think that General Ravenscroft approved. I think he had a very strong belief that just as someone can be born deformed, spastic or crippled in some way, she had a deformity of the brain which would recur from time to time and that she would have to be constantly watched and saved from herself in case some other tragedy happened.'

'Are you saying,' asked Desmond, 'that it was *she* who shot both the Ravenscrofts?'

'No,' said Poirot, 'that is not my solution. I think what happened was that Dorothea killed her sister, Margaret. They walked together on the cliff one day and Dorothea pushed Margaret over. The dormant obsession of hatred and resentment of the sister who, though so like herself, was sane and healthy, was too much for her. Hate, jealousy, the desire to kill all rose to the surface and dominated her. I think that there was one outsider who knew, who was here at the time that this happened. I think *you* knew, Mademoiselle Zélie.'

'Yes,' said Zélie Meauhourat, 'I knew. I was here at the time. The Ravenscrofts had been worried about her. That is when they saw her attempt to injure their small son, Edward. Edward was sent back to school and I and Celia went to my *pensionnat*. I came back here – after seeing Celia settled in. Once the house was empty except for myself, General Ravenscroft and Dorothea and Margaret, nobody had any anxiety. And then one day *it happened.* The two sisters went out together. Dolly returned alone. She seemed in a very queer and nervous state. She came in and sat down at the tea-table. It was then General Ravenscroft noticed that her right hand was covered with blood. He asked her if she had had a fall. She said, "Oh no, it was nothing. Nothing at all. I got scratched by a rose-bush." But there were no rose-bushes on the downs. It was a purely foolish remark and we were worried. If she had said a gorse bush, we might have accepted the remark. General Ravenscroft went out and I went after him. He kept saying as he walked, "Something has happened to Margaret. I'm sure something has happened to Molly." We found her on a ledge a little way down the cliff. She had been battered with a rock and stones. She was not dead but she had bled heavily. For a moment we hardly knew what we could do. We dared not move her. We must get a doctor, we felt, at once, but before we could do that she clung to her husband. She said, gasping for breath, "Yes, it was Dolly. She didn't know what she was doing. She didn't *know*, Alistair. You mustn't let her suffer for it. She's never known the things she does or why. She can't help it. She's never been able to help it. You must promise me, Alistair. I think I'm dying now. No – no, we won't have time to get a doctor and a doctor couldn't do anything. I've been lying here bleeding to death – and I'm very close to death. I know that, but promise me. *Promise* me you'll save her. Promise me you won't let the police arrest her. Promise me that she'll not be tried for killing me, not shut up for life as a criminal. Hide me somewhere so that my body won't be found. Please, please, it's the last thing I ask you. You whom I love more than anything in the world. If I could live for you I would, but I'm not going to live. I can feel that. I crawled a little way but that was all I could do. Promise me. And you, Zélie, you love me too. I know. You've loved me and been good to me and looked after me always. And you loved the children, so you *must* save Dolly. You must save poor Dolly. Please, please. For all the love we have for each other, Dolly must be saved."'

'And then,' said Poirot. 'What did you do? It seems to me that you must in some way between you –'

'Yes. She died, you know. She died within about ten minutes of those last words, and I helped him. I helped him to hide her body. It was a place a little further along the cliff. We carried her there and there were rocks and boulders and stones, and we covered her body as best we could. There was no path to it really, or no way. You had to scramble. We put her there. All Alistair said again and again was – "I promised her. I must keep my word. I don't know how to do it, I don't know how anyone can save her. I don't know. But –" Well, we did do it. Dolly was in the house. She was frightened, desperate with fright – but at the same time she showed a horrible kind of satisfaction. She said, "I always knew, I've known for years that Molly was really evil. She took you away from me, Alistair. You belonged to me – but she took you away from me and made you marry her and I always knew. Now I'm frightened. What'll they do to me – what'll they say? I can't be shut up again. I can't, I can't. I shall go mad. You won't let me be shut up. They'll take me away and they'll say I'm guilty of murder. It wasn't murder. I just had to do it. Sometimes I do have to do things. I wanted to see the blood, you know. I couldn't wait to see Molly die, though. I ran away. But I knew she would die. I just hoped you wouldn't find her. She just fell over the cliff. People would say it was an accident."'

'It's a horrible story,' said Desmond.

'Yes,' said Celia, 'it's a horrible story, but it's better to know. It's better to know, isn't it? I can't even feel sorry for her. I mean for my mother. I know she was sweet. I know there was never any trace of evil in her – she was good all through – and I know, I can understand, why my father didn't want to marry Dolly. He wanted to marry my mother because he loved her and he had found out by then that there was something wrong with Dolly. Something bad and twisted. But how – how did you do it all?'

'We told a good many lies,' said Zélie. 'We hoped the body would not be found so that later perhaps it might be removed in the night or something like that to somewhere where it could look as though she'd fallen down into the sea. But then we thought of the sleep-walking story. What we had to do was really quite simple. Alistair said, "It's frightening, you know. But I promised – I swore to Molly when she was dying. I swore I'd do as she asked – there's a way, a possible way to save Dolly, if only Dolly can do her part. I don't know if she's capable of it." I said, "Do what?" And Alistair said, "Pretend she's Molly and that it's Dorothea who walked in her sleep and fell to her death."

'We managed it. Took Dolly to an empty cottage we knew of and I stayed with her there for some days. Alistair said Molly had been taken to hospital suffering from shock after the discovery that her sister had fallen over the cliff whilst walking in her sleep at night. Then we brought Dolly back – brought her back as Molly – wearing Molly's clothes and Molly's wig. I got extra wigs – the kind with the curls which really did disguise her. The dear old housekeeper, Janet, couldn't see very well. Dolly and Molly were really very much alike, you know, and their voices were alike. Everyone accepted quite easily that it was Molly, behaving rather peculiarly now and then because of still suffering from shock. It all seemed quite natural. That was the horrible part of it –'

'But how could she keep it up?' asked Celia. 'It must have been dreadfully difficult.'

'No – she did not find it difficult – she had got, you see, what she wanted – what she had always wanted. She had got Alistair –'

'But Alistair – how could he bear it?'

'He told me why and how – on the day he had arranged for me to go back to Switzerland. He told me what I had to do and then he told me what *he* was going to do.

'He said: "There is only one thing for me to do. I promised Margaret that I wouldn't hand Dolly over to the police, that it should never be known that she was a murderess, that the children were never to know that they had a murderess for an aunt. No one need ever know that Dolly committed murder. She walked in her sleep and fell over the cliff – a sad accident and she will be buried here in the church, and under her own name."

'"How can you let that be done?" I asked – I couldn't bear it.

'He said: "Because of what I am going to do – you have got to know about it."

'"You see," he said, "Dolly has to be stopped from living. If she's near children she'll take more lives – poor soul; she's not fit to live. But you must understand, Zélie, that because of what I am going to do, I must pay with my own life, too – I shall live here quietly for a few weeks with Dolly playing the part of my wife – and then there will be another tragedy –"

'I didn't understand what he meant – I said, "Another accident? Sleep-walking again?" And he said, "No – what will be known to the world is that I and Molly have both committed suicide – I don't suppose the reason will ever be known. They may think it's because she was convinced she had cancer – or that I thought so – all sorts of things may be suggested. But you see – you must help me, Zélie. You are the only person who really loves me and loves Molly and loves the children. If Dolly has got to die, I am the only person who must do it. She won't be unhappy or frightened. I shall shoot her and then myself. Her fingerprints will show on the revolver because she handled it not long ago, and mine will be there too. Justice has to be done and I have to be the executioner. The thing I want you to know is that I did – that I still do – love them both. Molly more than my life. Dolly because I pity her so much for what she was born to be." He said, "Always remember that –"'

Zélie rose and came towards Celia. 'Now you know the truth,' she said. 'I promised your father that you should never know – I have broken my word. I never meant to reveal it to you or to anyone else. Monsieur Poirot made me feel differently. But – it's such a horrible story –'

'I understand how you felt,' said Celia. 'Perhaps you were right from your point of view, but I – I am glad to know because now a great burden seems to have been lifted off me –'

'Because now,' said Desmond, 'we both know. And it's something we'll never mind about knowing. It *was* a tragedy. As Monsieur Poirot here has said, it was a real tragedy of two people who loved each other. But they didn't kill each other, because they loved each other. One was murdered and the other executed a murderer for the sake of humanity so that more children shouldn't suffer. One can forgive him if he was wrong, but I don't think it *was* wrong really.'

'She was a frightening woman always,' said Celia. 'Even when I was a child I was frightened of her but I didn't know why. But I do know why now. I think my father was a brave man to do what he did. He did what my mother asked him to do, begged him to do with her dying breath. He saved her twin sister whom I think she'd always loved very dearly. I like to think – oh, it seems a silly thing for me to say –' she looked doubtfully at Hercule Poirot. 'Perhaps you won't think so. I expect you're a Catholic, but it's what's written on their tombstone. "In death they were not divided." It doesn't mean that they died together, but I think they *are* together. I think they came together afterwards. Two people who loved each other very much, and my poor aunt whom I'll try to feel more kindly about than I ever did – my poor aunt didn't have to suffer for what she couldn't perhaps help herself doing. Mind you,' said Celia, suddenly breaking into her ordinary everyday voice, 'she wasn't a nice person. You can't help not liking people if they're not nice people. Perhaps she *could* have been different if she tried, but perhaps she couldn't. And if so, one has to think of her as someone who was very ill – like somebody, for instance, who had plague in a village and they wouldn't let her go out or feed her and she couldn't go amongst other people because the whole village would have died. Something like that. But I'll try and be sorry for her. And my mother and father – I don't worry about them any more. They loved each other so much, and loved poor, unhappy, hating Dolly.'

'I think, Celia,' said Desmond, 'we'd better get married now as soon as possible. I can tell you one thing. My mother is never going to hear anything about this. She's not my own mother and she's not a person I can trust with this sort of secret.'

'Your adopted mother, Desmond,' said Poirot, 'I have good reason to believe was anxious to come between you and Celia and tried to influence you in the idea that from her mother and father she might have inherited some terrible characteristic. But you know, or you may not know and I see no reason why I should not tell you, you will inherit from the woman who was your real mother and who died not very long ago leaving all her money to you – you will inherit a very large sum when you reach the age of twenty-five.'

'If I marry Celia, of course we shall need the money to live on,' said Desmond. 'I quite understand. I know my present adopted mother is very keen on money and I often lend her money even now. She suggested my seeing a lawyer the other day because she said it was very dangerous now that I was over twenty-one, not leaving a Will behind me. I suppose she thought she'd get the money. I had thought of probably leaving nearly all the money to her. But of course now Celia and I are getting married I shall leave it to Celia – and I didn't like the way my mother tried to put me against Celia.'

'I think your suspicions are entirely correct,' said Poirot. 'I dare say she could tell herself that she meant it all for the best, that Celia's origin is something that you ought to know if there is a risk for you to take, but –'

'All right,' said Desmond, 'but – I know I'm being unkind. After all, she adopted me and brought me up and all the rest of it and I dare say if there's enough money I can settle some of it on her. Celia and I will have the rest and we're going to be happy together. After all, there are things that'll make us feel sad from time to time but we shan't worry any more, shall we, Celia?'

'No,' said Celia, 'we'll never worry again. I think they were rather splendid people, my mother and father. Mother tried to look after her sister all her life, but I suppose it was a bit too hopeless. You can't stop people from being like they are.'

'Ah, dear children,' said Zélie. 'Forgive me for calling you children because you are not. You are a grown man and woman. I know that. I am so pleased to have seen you again and to know I have not done any harm in what I did.'

'You haven't done any harm at all and it's lovely seeing you, dear Zélie.' Celia went to her and hugged her. 'I've always been terribly fond of you,' she said.

'And I was very fond of you too when I knew you,' said Desmond. 'When I lived next door. You had lovely games you played with us.'

The two young people turned.

'Thank you, Mrs Oliver,' said Desmond. 'You've been very kind and you've put in a lot of work. I can see that. Thank you, Monsieur Poirot.'

'Yes, thank you,' said Celia. 'I'm very grateful.'

They walked away and the others looked after them.

'Well,' said Zélie, 'I must leave now.' She said to Poirot, 'What about you? Will you have to tell anyone about this?'

'There is one person I might tell in confidence. A retired police force officer. He is no longer actively in the Service now. He is completely retired. I think he would not feel it is his duty to interfere with what time has now wiped out. If he was still in active service it might be different.'

'It's a terrible story,' said Mrs Oliver, 'terrible. And all those people I talked to – yes, I can see now, they all remembered *something*. Something that was useful in showing us what the truth was, although it was difficult to put together. Except for Monsieur Poirot, who can always put things together out of the most extraordinary things. Like wigs and twins.'

Poirot walked across to where Zélie was standing looking out over the view.

'You do not blame me,' he said, 'for coming to you, persuading you to do what you have done?'

'No. I am glad. You have been right. They are very charming, those two, and they are well suited, I think. They will be happy. We are standing here where two lovers once lived. Where two lovers died and I don't blame him for what he did. It may have been wrong, I suppose it was wrong, but I can't blame him. I think it was a brave act even if it was a wrong one.'

'You loved him too, did you not?' said Hercule Poirot.

'Yes. Always. As soon as I came to the house. I loved him dearly. I don't think he knew it. There was never anything, what you call, between us. He trusted me and was fond of me. I loved them both. Both him and Margaret.'

'There is something I would like to ask you. He loved Dolly as well as Molly, didn't he?'

'Right up to the end. He loved them both. And that's why he was willing to save Dolly. Why Molly wanted him to. Which did he love the best of those sisters? I wonder. That is a thing I shall perhaps never know,' said Zélie. 'I never did – perhaps I never shall.'

Poirot looked at her for a moment, then turned away. He rejoined Mrs Oliver.

'We will drive back to London. We must return to everyday life, forget tragedies and love-affairs.'

'Elephants can remember,' said Mrs Oliver, 'but we are human beings and mercifully human beings can forget.'

THE PALE HORSE

To John and Helen Mildmay White
with many thanks for the opportunity
given me to see justice done

FOREWORD

BY MARK EASTERBROOK

There are two methods, it seems to me, of approaching this strange business of the Pale Horse. In spite of the dictum of the White King, it is difficult to achieve simplicity. One cannot, that is to say, 'Begin at the beginning, go on to the end, and then stop.' For where is the beginning?

To a historian, that always is the difficulty. At what point in history does one particular portion of history begin.

In this case, you can begin at the moment when Father Gorman set forth from his presbytery to visit a dying woman. Or you can start before that, on a certain evening in Chelsea.

Perhaps, since I am writing the greater part of this narrative myself, it is there that I should begin.

CHAPTER I

MARK EASTERBROOK'S NARRATIVE

I

The Espresso machine behind my shoulder hissed like an angry snake. The noise it made had a sinister, not to say devilish, suggestion about it. Perhaps, I reflected, most of our contemporary noises carry that implication. The intimidating angry scream of jet planes as they flash across the sky; the slow menacing rumble of a tube train approaching through its tunnel; the heavy road transport that shakes the very foundations of your house . . . Even the minor domestic noises of today, beneficial in action though they may be, yet carry a kind of alert. The dish-washers, the refrigerators, the pressure cookers, the whining vacuum cleaners – 'Be careful,' they all seem to say. 'I am a genie harnessed to your service, but if your control of me fails . . .'

A dangerous world – that was it, a dangerous world.

I stirred the foaming cup placed in front of me. It smelt pleasant.

'What else will you have? Nice banana and bacon sandwich?'

It seemed an odd juxtaposition to me. Bananas I connected with my childhood – or occasionally *flambé* with sugar and rum. Bacon, in my mind, was firmly associated with eggs. However, when in Chelsea, eat as Chelsea does. I agreed to a nice banana and bacon sandwich.

Although I lived in Chelsea – that is to say, I had had a furnished flat there for the last three months – I was in every other way a stranger in these parts. I was writing a book on certain aspects of Mogul architecture, but for that purpose I could have lived in Hampstead or Bloomsbury or Streatham or Chelsea and it would have been all the same to me. I was oblivious of my surroundings except for the tools of my trade, and the neighbourhood in which I lived was completely indifferent to me, I existed in a world of my own.

On this particular evening, however, I had suffered from one of those sudden revulsions that all writers know.

Mogul architecture, Mogul Emperors, the Mogul way of life – and all the fascinating problems it raised, became suddenly as dust and ashes. What did they matter? Why did I want to write about them?

I flicked back various pages, rereading what I had written. It all seemed to me uniformly bad – poorly written and singularly devoid of interest. Whoever had said 'History is bunk' (Henry Ford?) had been absolutely right.

I pushed back my manuscript with loathing, got up and looked at my watch. The time was close on eleven p.m. I tried to remember if I had had dinner . . . From my inner sensations I thought not. Lunch, yes, at the Athenaeum. That was a long time ago.

I went and looked into the refrigerator. There was a small remnant of desiccated tongue. I looked at it without favour. So it was that I wandered out into the King's Road, and eventually turned into an Espresso Coffee Bar with the name Luigi written in red neon light across its window, and was now contemplating a bacon and banana sandwich whilst I reflected on the sinister implications of present-day noises and their atmospheric effects.

All of them, I thought, had something in common with my early memories of pantomime. Davy Jones arriving from his locker in clouds of smoke! Trap doors and windows that exuded the infernal powers of evil, challenging and defying a Good Fairy Diamond, or some such name, who in turn waved an inadequate-looking wand and recited hopeful platitudes as to the ultimate triumph of good in a flat voice, thus prefacing the inevitable 'song of the moment' which never had anything to do with the story of that particular pantomime.

It came to me suddenly that evil was, perhaps, necessarily always more impressive than good. It *had* to make a show! It had to startle and challenge! It was instability attacking stability. And in the end, I thought, stability will always win. Stability can survive the triteness of Good Fairy Diamond; the flat voice, the rhymed couplet, even the irrelevant vocal statement of 'There's a Winding Road runs down the Hill, To the Olde World Town I love.' All very poor weapons it would seem, and yet those weapons would inevitably prevail. The pantomime would end in the way it always ended. The staircase, and the descending cast in order of seniority, with Good Fairy Diamond, practising the Christian virtue of humility and not seeking to be first (or, in this case, last) but arriving about half-way through the procession, side by side with her late opponent, now seen to be no longer the snarling Demon King breathing fire and brimstone, but just a man dressed up in red tights.

The Espresso hissed again in my ear. I signalled for another cup of coffee and looked around me. A sister of mine was always accusing me of not being observant, not noticing what was going on. 'You live in a world of your own,' she would say accusingly. Now, with a feeling of conscious virtue, I took note of what was going on. It was almost impossible not to read about the coffee bars of Chelsea and their patrons every day in the newspapers; this was my chance to make my own appraisal of contemporary life.

It was rather dark in the Espresso, so you could not see very clearly. The clientele were almost all young people. They were, I supposed vaguely, what was called the off-beat generation. The girls looked, as girls always did look to me nowadays, dirty. They also seemed to be much too warmly dressed. I had noticed that when I had gone out a few weeks ago to dine with some friends. The girl who had sat next to me had been about twenty. The restaurant was hot, but she had worn a yellow wool pullover, a black skirt and black woollen stockings, and the perspiration poured down her face all through the meal. She smelt of perspiration-soaked wool and also, strongly, of unwashed hair. She was said, according to my friends, to be very attractive. Not to me! My only reaction was a yearning to throw her into a hot bath, give her a cake of soap and urge her to get on with it! Which just showed, I suppose, how out of touch with the times I was. Perhaps it came of having lived abroad so much. I recalled with pleasure Indian women with their beautifully-coiled black hair, and their saris of pure bright colours hanging in graceful folds, and the rhythmic sway of their bodies as they walked . . .

I was recalled from these pleasant thoughts by a sudden accentuation of noise. Two young women at the table next to me had started a quarrel. The young men who were with them tried to adjust things, but without avail.

Suddenly they were screaming at each other. One girl slapped the other's face, the second dragged the first from her chair. They fought each other like fishwives, screaming abuse hysterically. One was a tousled red-head, the other a lank-haired blonde.

What the quarrel was about, apart from terms of abuse, I did not gather. Cries and catcalls arose from other tables.

'Attagirl! Sock her, Lou!'

The proprietor behind the bar, a slim Italian-looking fellow with sideburns, whom I had taken to be Luigi, came to intervene in a voice that was pure cockney London.

'Nah then – break it up – break it up – You'll 'ave the whole street in in a minute. You'll 'ave the coppers here. Stop it, I say.'

But the lank blonde had the red-head by the hair and was tugging furiously as she screamed:

'You're nothing but a man-stealing bitch!'

'Bitch yourself.'

Luigi and the two embarrassed escorts forced the girls apart. In the blonde's fingers were large tufts of red hair. She held them aloft gleefully, then dropped them on the floor.

The door from the street was pushed open and Authority,

dressed in blue, stood on the threshold and uttered the regulation words majestically.

'What's going on here?'

Immediately a common front was presented to the enemy.

'Just a bit of fun,' said one of the young men.

'That's all,' said Luigi. 'Just a bit of fun among friends.'

With his foot he kicked the tufts of hair adroitly under the nearest table. The contestants smiled at each other in false amnesty.

The policeman looked at everybody suspiciously.

'We're just going now,' said the blonde sweetly. 'Come on, Doug.'

By a coincidence several other people were just going. Authority watched them go grimly. His eye said that he was overlooking it *this* time, but he'd got his eye on them. He withdrew slowly.

The red-head's escort paid the check.

'You all right?' said Luigi to the girl who was adjusting a headscarf. 'Lou served you pretty bad, tearing out your hair by the roots like that.'

'It didn't hurt,' said the girl nonchalantly. She smiled at him. 'Sorry for the row, Luigi.'

The party went out. The bar was now practically empty. I felt in my pocket for change.

'She's a sport all right,' said Luigi approvingly, watching the door close. He seized a floor brush and swept the tufts of red hair behind the counter.

'It must have been agony,' I said.

'*I'd* have hollered if it had been me,' admitted Luigi. 'But she's a real sport, Tommy is.'

'You know her well?'

'Oh, she's in here most evenings. Tuckerton, that's her name, Thomasina Tuckerton, if you want the whole set out. But Tommy Tucker's what she's called round here. Stinking rich, too. Her old man left her a fortune, and what does she go and do? Comes to Chelsea, lives in a slummy room half-way to Wandsworth Bridge, and mooches around with a gang all doing the same thing. Beats me, half of that crowd's got money. Could have any mortal thing they want; stay at the Ritz if they liked. But they seem to get a kick out of living the way they do. Yes – it beats me.'

'It wouldn't be your choice?'

'Ar, I've got sense!' said Luigi. 'As it is, I just cash in.'

I rose to go and asked what the quarrel was about.

'Oh, Tommy's got hold of the other girl's boy friend. He's not worth fighting about, believe me!'

'The other girl seemed to think he was,' I observed.

'Oh, Lou's very romantic,' said Luigi tolerantly.

It was not my idea of romance, but I did not say so.

II

It must have been about a week later that my eye was caught by a name in the Deaths column of *The Times*.

> *TUCKERTON. On October 2nd at Fallowfield Nursing Home, Amberley, Thomasina Ann, aged twenty, only daughter of the late Thomas Tuckerton, Esq., of Carrington Park, Amberley, Surrey. Funeral private. No flowers.*

III

No flowers for poor Tommy Tucker; and no more 'kicks' out of life in Chelsea. I felt a sudden fleeting compassion for the Tommy Tuckers of today. Yet after all, I reminded myself, how did I know that my view was the right one? Who was I to pronounce it a wasted life? Perhaps it was *my* life, my quiet scholarly life, immersed in books, shut off from the world, that was the wasted one. Life at second hand. Be honest now, was *I* getting kicks out of life? A very unfamiliar idea! The truth was, of course, that I didn't want kicks. But there again, perhaps I ought to? An unfamiliar and not very welcome thought.

I dismissed Tommy Tucker from my thoughts, and turned to my correspondence.

The principal item was a letter from my cousin Rhoda Despard, asking me to do her a favour. I grasped at this, since I was not feeling in the mood for work this morning, and it made a splendid excuse for postponing it.

I went out into King's Road, hailed a taxi, and was driven to the residence of a friend of mine, a Mrs Ariadne Oliver.

Mrs Oliver was a well-known writer of detective stories. Her maid, Milly, was an efficient dragon who guarded her mistress from the onslaughts of the outside world.

I raised my eyebrows inquiringly, in an unspoken question. Milly nodded a vehement head.

'You'd better go right up, Mr Mark,' she said. 'She's in a mood this morning. You may be able to help her snap out of it.'

I mounted two flights of stairs, tapped lightly on a door, and walked in without waiting for encouragement. Mrs Oliver's workroom was a good-sized room, the walls papered with exotic birds nesting in tropical foliage. Mrs Oliver herself, in a state apparently bordering on insanity, was prowling round the room, muttering to herself. She threw me a brief uninterested glance and continued to prowl. Her eyes, unfocused, swept round the walls, glanced out of the window, and occasionally closed in what appeared to be a spasm of agony.

'But why,' demanded Mrs Oliver of the universe, 'why doesn't the idiot say at once that he *saw* the cockatoo? Why shouldn't he? He couldn't have helped seeing it! But if he *does* mention it, it ruins everything. There must be a way . . . there must be . . .'

She groaned, ran her fingers through her short grey hair and clutched it in a frenzied hand. Then, looking at me with suddenly focused eyes, she said, 'Hallo, Mark. I'm going mad,' and resumed her complaint.

'And then there's Monica. The nicer I try to make her, the more irritating she gets . . . Such a stupid girl . . . Smug, too! Monica . . . Monica? I believe the name's wrong. Nancy? Would that be better? Joan? Everybody is always Joan. Anne is the same. Susan? I've had a Susan. Lucia? *Lucia?* Lucia? I believe I can *see* a Lucia. Red-haired. Polo-necked jumper . . . Black tights? Black stockings, anyway.'

This momentary gleam of good cheer was eclipsed by the memory of the cockatoo problem, and Mrs Oliver resumed her unhappy prowling, picking up things off tables unseeingly and putting them down again somewhere else. She fitted with some care her spectacle case into a lacquered box which already contained a Chinese fan and then gave a deep sigh and said:

'I'm glad it's you.'

'That's very nice of you.'

'It might have been anybody. Some silly woman who wanted me to open a bazaar, or the man about Milly's insurance card which Milly absolutely refuses to have – or the plumber (but that would be too much good fortune, wouldn't it?). Or, it might be someone wanting an interview – asking me all those embarrassing questions which are always the same every time. What made you first think of taking up writing? How many books have you written? How much money do you make? Etc. etc. I never know the answers to any of them and it makes me look such a fool. Not that any of that matters because I think I am going mad, over this cockatoo business.'

'Something that won't jell?' I said sympathetically. 'Perhaps I'd better go away.'

'No, don't. At any rate you're a distraction.'

I accepted this doubtful compliment.

'Do you want a cigarette?' Mrs Oliver asked with vague hospitality. 'There are some somewhere. Look in the typewriter lid.'

'I've got my own, thanks. Have one. Oh no, you don't smoke.'

'Or drink,' said Mrs Oliver. 'I wish I did. Like those American detectives that always have pints of rye conveniently in their collar drawers. It seems to solve all their problems. You know, Mark, I really can't think how anyone ever gets away with a murder in real life. It seems to me that the moment you've done a murder the whole thing is so terribly obvious.'

'Nonsense. You've done lots of them.'

'Fifty-five at least,' said Mrs Oliver. 'The murder part is quite easy and simple. It's the covering up that's so difficult. I mean, why *should* it be anyone else but you? You stick out a mile.'

'Not in the finished article,' I said.

'Ah, but what it costs me,' said Mrs Oliver darkly. 'Say what you like, it's not *natural* for five or six people to be on the spot when B is murdered and all have a motive for killing B – unless, that is, B is absolutely madly unpleasant and in that case nobody will mind whether he's been killed or not, and doesn't care in the least who's done it.'

'I see your problem,' I said. 'But if you've dealt with it successfully fifty-five times, you will manage to deal with it once again.'

'That's what I tell myself,' said Mrs Oliver, 'over and over again, but every single time I can't believe it, and so I'm in agony.'

She seized her hair again and tugged it violently.

'Don't,' I cried. 'You'll have it out by the roots.'

'Nonsense,' said Mrs Oliver. 'Hair's tough. Though when I had measles at fourteen with a very high temperature, it did come out – all round the front. Most shaming. And it was six whole months before it grew properly again. Awful for a girl – girls mind so. I thought of it yesterday when I was visiting Mary Delafontaine in that nursing home. Her hair was coming out just like mine did. She said she'd have to get a false front when she was better. If you're sixty it doesn't always grow again, I believe.'

'I saw a girl pull out another girl's hair by the roots the other night,' I said. I was conscious of a slight note of pride in my voice as one who has seen life.

'What extraordinary places have you been going to?' asked Mrs Oliver.

'This was in a coffee bar in Chelsea.'

'Oh *Chelsea!*' said Mrs Oliver. 'Everything happens there, I believe. Beatniks and sputniks and squares and the beat generation. I don't write about them much because I'm so afraid of getting the terms wrong. It's safer, I think, to stick to what you know.'

'Such as?'

'People on cruises, and in hotels, and what goes on in hospitals, and on parish councils – and sales of work – and music festivals, and girls in shops, and committees and daily women, and young men and girls who hike round the world in the interests of science, and shop assistants –'

She paused, out of breath.

'That seems fairly comprehensive to be getting on with,' I said.

'All the same, you might take me out to a coffee bar in Chelsea some time – just to widen my experience,' said Mrs Oliver wistfully.

'Any time you say. Tonight?'

'Not tonight. I'm too busy writing or rather worrying because I can't write. That's really the most tiresome thing about writing – though everything is tiresome really, except the one moment when you get what you think is going to be a wonderful idea, and can hardly wait to begin. Tell me, Mark, do you think it is possible to kill someone by remote control?'

'What do you mean by remote control? Press a button and set off a radioactive death ray?'

'No, no, not science fiction. I suppose,' she paused doubtfully, 'I really mean black magic.'

'Wax figures and pins in them?'

'Oh, wax figures are right out,' said Mrs Oliver scornfully. 'But queer things do happen – in Africa or the West Indies. People are always telling you so. How natives just curl up and die. Voodoo – or ju-ju . . . Anyway, you know what I mean.'

I said that much of that was attributed nowadays to the power of suggestion. Word is always conveyed to the victim that his death has been decreed by the medicine-man – and his subconscious does the rest.

Mrs Oliver snorted.

'If anyone hinted to me that I had been doomed to lie down and die, I'd take a pleasure in thwarting their expectations!'

I laughed.

'You've got centuries of good Occidental sceptical blood in your veins. No predispositions.'

'Then you think it *can* happen?'

'I don't know enough about the subject to judge. What put it into your head? Is your new masterpiece to be Murder by Suggestion?'

'No, indeed. Good old-fashioned rat poison or arsenic is good enough for me. Or the reliable blunt instrument. *Not* firearms if possible. Firearms are so tricky. But you didn't come here to talk to me about my books.'

'Frankly no – The fact is that my cousin Rhoda Despard has got a church fête and –'

'Never again!' said Mrs Oliver. 'You know what happened last time? I arranged a Murder Hunt, and the first thing that happened was a *real corpse*. I've never quite got over it!'

'It's not a Murder Hunt. All you'd have to do would be to sit in a tent and sign your own books – at five bob a time.'

'We-e-l-l-l,' said Mrs Oliver doubtfully. 'That might be all right. I shouldn't have to open the fête? Or say silly things? Or have to wear a hat?'

None of these things, I assured her, would be required of her.

'And it would only be for an hour or two,' I said coaxingly. 'After that, there'll be a cricket match – no, I suppose not this time of year. Children dancing, perhaps. Or a fancy dress competition –'

Mrs Oliver interrupted me with a wild scream.

'That's it,' she cried. '*A cricket ball!* Of course! He sees it from the window . . . rising up in the air . . . and it distracts him – and so he never mentions the cockatoo! What a good thing you came, Mark. You've been wonderful.'

'I don't quite see –'

'Perhaps not, but I do,' said Mrs Oliver. 'It's all rather complicated, and I don't want to waste time explaining. Nice as it's been to see you, what I'd really like you to do now is to go away. At once.'

'Certainly. About the fête –'

'I'll think about it. Don't worry me now. Now where on earth did I put my spectacles? Really, the way things just disappear . . .'

CHAPTER 2

I

Mrs Gerahty opened the door of the presbytery in her usual sharp pouncing style. It was less like answering a bell, than a triumphant manoeuvre expressing the sentiment 'I've caught you this time!'

'Well now, and what would you be wanting?' she demanded belligerently.

There was a boy on the doorstep, a very negligible looking boy – a boy not easily noticeable nor easily remembered – a boy like a lot of other boys. He sniffed because he had a cold in his head.

'Is this the priest's place?'

'Is it Father Gorman you're wanting?'

'He's wanted,' said the boy.

'Who wants him and where and what for?'

'Benthall Street. Twenty-three. Woman as says she's dying.

Mrs Coppins sent me. This is a Carthlick place all right, isn't it? Woman says the vicar won't do.'

Mrs Gerahty reassured him on this essential point, told him to stop where he was and retired into the presbytery. Some three minutes later a tall elderly priest came out carrying a small leather case in his hand.

'I'm Father Gorman,' he said. 'Benthall Street? That's round by the railway yards, isn't it?'

''Sright. Not more than a step, it isn't.'

They set out together, the priest walking with a free striding step.

'Mrs – Coppins, did you say? Is that the name?'

'She's the one what owns the house. Lets rooms, she does. It's one of the lodgers wants you. Name of Davis, I think.'

'Davis. I wonder now. I don't remember –'

'She's one of you all right. Carthlick, I mean. Said as no vicar would do.'

The priest nodded. They came to Benthall Street in a very short time. The boy indicated a tall dingy house in a row of other tall dingy houses.

'That's it.'

'Aren't you coming in?'

'I don't belong. Mrs C. gave me a bob to take the message.'

'I see. What's your name?'

'Mike Potter.'

'Thank you, Mike.'

'You're welcome,' said Mike, and went off whistling. The imminence of death for someone else did not affect him.

The door of No. 23 opened and Mrs Coppins, a large red-faced woman, stood on the threshold and welcomed the visitor with enthusiasm.

'Come in, come in. She's bad, I'd say. Ought to be in hospital, not here. I've rung up, but goodness knows when anybody will come nowadays. Six hours my sister's husband had to wait when he broke his leg. Disgraceful, I call it. Health Service, indeed! Take your money and when you want them where are they?'

She was preceding the priest up the narrow stairs as she talked.

'What's the matter with her?'

''Flu's what she's had. Seemed better. Went out too soon I'd say. Anyway she comes in last night looking like death. Took to her bed. Wouldn't eat anything. Didn't want a doctor. This morning I could see she was in a raging fever. Gone to her lungs.'

'Pneumonia?'

Mrs Coppins, out of breath by now, made a noise like a steam engine, which seemed to signify assent. She flung open a door, stood aside to let Father Gorman go in, said over his shoulder: 'Here's the Reverend for you. *Now* you'll be all right!' in a spuriously cheerful way, and retired.

Father Gorman advanced. The room, furnished with old-fashioned Victorian furniture, was clean and neat. In the bed near the window a woman turned her head feebly. That she was very ill, the priest saw at once.

'You've come . . . There isn't much time –' she spoke between panting breaths. '. . . Wickedness . . . such wickedness . . . I must . . . I must . . . I can't die like this . . . Confess – confess – my sin – grievous – grievous . . .' the eyes wandered . . . half closed . . .

A rambling monotone of words came from her lips.

Father Gorman came to the bed. He spoke as he had spoken so often – so very often. Words of authority – of reassurance . . . the words of his calling and of his belief. Peace came into the room . . . The agony went out of the tortured eyes . . .

Then, as the priest ended his ministry, the dying woman spoke again.

'Stopped . . . It must be stopped . . . You will . . .'

The priest spoke with reassuring authority.

'I will do what is necessary. You can trust me . . .'

A doctor and an ambulance arrived simultaneously a little later. Mrs Coppins received them with gloomy triumph.

'Too late as usual!' she said. 'She's gone . . .'

II

Father Gorman walked back through the gathering twilight. There would be fog to-night, it was growing denser rapidly. He paused for a moment, frowning. Such a fantastic extraordinary story . . . How much of it was born of delirium and high fever?

Some of it was true, of course – but how much? Anyway it was important to make a note of certain names whilst they were fresh in his memory. The St Francis Guild would be assembled when he got back. He turned abruptly into a small café, ordered a cup of coffee and sat down. He felt in the pocket of his cassock. Ah, Mrs Gerahty – he'd asked her to mend the lining. As usual, she hadn't! His notebook and a loose pencil and the few coins he carried about him, had gone through to the lining. He prised up a coin or two and the pencil, but the notebook was too difficult. The coffee came, and he asked if he could have a piece of paper.

'This do you?'

It was a torn paper bag. Father Gorman nodded and took it. He began to write – the *names* – it was important not to forget the names. Names were the sort of thing he did forget . . .

The café door opened and three young lads in Edwardian dress came in and sat down noisily.

Father Gorman finished his memorandum. He folded up the scrap of paper and was about to shove it into his pocket when he remembered the hole. He did what he had often done before, pressed the folded scrap down into his shoe.

A man came in quietly and sat down in a far corner. Father Gorman took a sip or two of the weak coffee for politeness' sake, called for his bill, and paid. Then he got up and went out.

The man who had just come in seemed to change his mind. He looked at his watch as though he had mistaken the time, got up, and hurried out.

The fog was coming on fast. Father Gorman quickened his steps. He knew his district very well. He took a shortcut by turning down the small street which ran close by the railway. He may have been conscious of steps behind him but he thought nothing of them. Why should he?

The blow from the cosh caught him completely unaware. He heeled forward and fell . . .

III

Dr Corrigan, whistling 'Father O'Flynn', walked into the D.D.I.'s room and addressed Divisional Detective-Inspector Lejeune in a chatty manner.

'I've done your padre for you,' he said.

'And the result?'

'We'll save the technical terms for the coroner. Well and truly coshed. First blow probably killed him, but whoever it was made sure. Quite a nasty business.'

'Yes,' said Lejeune.

He was a sturdy man, dark haired and grey eyed. He had a misleadingly quiet manner, but his gestures were sometimes surprisingly graphic and betrayed his French Huguenot ancestry.

He said thoughtfully:

'Nastier than would be necessary for robbery?'

'Was it robbery?' asked the doctor.

'One supposes so. His pockets were turned out and the lining of his cassock ripped.'

'They couldn't have hoped for much,' said Corrigan. 'Poor as a rat, most of these parish priests.'

'They battered his head in – to make sure,' mused Lejeune. 'One would like to know *why*.'

'Two possible answers,' said Corrigan. 'One, it was done by a vicious-minded young thug, who likes violence for violence's sake – there are plenty of them about these days, more's the pity.'

'And the other answer?'

The doctor shrugged his shoulders.

'Somebody had it in for your Father Gorman. Was that likely?'

Lejeune shook his head.

'Most unlikely. He was a popular man, well loved in the district. No enemies, as far as one can hear. And robbery's unlikely. Unless –'

'Unless what?' asked Corrigan. 'The police have a clue! Am I right?'

'He did have something on him that wasn't taken away. It was in his shoe, as a matter of fact.'

Corrigan whistled.

'Sounds like a spy story.'

Lejeune smiled.

'It's much simpler than that. He had a hole in his pocket. Sergeant Pine talked to his housekeeper. She's a bit of a slattern, it seems. Didn't keep his clothes mended in the way she might have done. She admitted that, now and again, Father Gorman would thrust a paper or a letter down the inside of his shoe – to prevent it from going down into the lining of his cassock.'

'And the killer didn't know that?'

'The killer never thought of that! Assuming, that is, that this piece of paper is what he may have been wanting – rather than a miserly amount of small change.'

'What was on the paper?'

Lejeune reached into a drawer and took out a flimsy piece of creased paper.

'Just a list of names,' he said.

Corrigan looked at it curiously.

Ormerod
Sandford
Parkinson
Hesketh-Dubois
Shaw
Harmondsworth
Tuckerton
Corrigan?
Delafontaine?

His eyebrows rose.

'I see *I'm* on the list!'

'Do any of the names mean anything to you?' asked the inspector.

'None of them.'

'And you've never met Father Gorman?'

'Never.'

'Then you won't be able to help us much.'

'Any ideas as to what this list means – if anything?'

Lejeune did not reply directly.

'A boy called at Father Gorman's about seven o'clock in the evening. Said a woman was dying and wanted the priest. Father Gorman went with him.'

'Where to? If you know.'

'We know. It didn't take long to check up. Twenty-three Benthall Street. House owned by a woman named Coppins. The sick woman was a Mrs Davis. The priest got there at a quarter past seven and was with her for about half an hour. Mrs Davis died just before the ambulance arrived to take her to hospital.'

'I see.'

'The next we hear of Father Gorman is at Tony's Place, a small down-at-heel café. Quite decent, nothing criminal about it, serves refreshment of poor quality and isn't much patronised. Father Gorman asked for a cup of coffee. Then apparently he felt in his pocket, couldn't find what he wanted and asked the proprietor, Tony, for a piece of paper. This –' he gestured with his finger, 'is the piece of paper.'

'And then?'

'When Tony brought the coffee, the priest was writing on the paper. Shortly afterwards he left, leaving his coffee practically untasted (for which I don't blame him), having completed this list and shoved it into his shoe.'

'Anybody else in the place?'

'Three boys of the Teddy boy type came in and sat at one table and an elderly man came in and sat at another. The latter went away without ordering.'

'He followed the priest?'

'Could be. Tony didn't notice when he went. Didn't notice what he looked like, either. Described him as an inconspicuous type of man. Respectable. The kind of man that looks like everybody else. Medium height, he thinks, dark blue overcoat – or could be brown. Not very dark and not very fair. No reason he should have had anything to do with it. One just doesn't know. He hasn't come forward to say he saw the priest in Tony's place – but it's early days yet. We're asking for anyone who saw Father Gorman between a quarter to eight and eight-fifteen to communicate with us. Only two people so far have responded: a woman and a chemist who had a shop nearby. I'll be going to see them presently. His body was found at eight-fifteen by two small boys in West Street – you know it? Practically an alleyway, bounded by the railway on one side. The rest – you know.'

Corrigan nodded. He tapped the paper.

'What's your feeling about this?'

'I think it's important,' said Lejeune.

'The dying woman told him something and he got these names

down on paper as soon as he could before he forgot them? The only thing is – would he have done that if he'd been told under seal of the confessional?'

'It needn't have been under a seal of secrecy,' said Lejeune. 'Suppose, for instance, these names have a connection of – say, blackmail –'

'That's your idea, is it?'

'I haven't any ideas yet. This is just a working hypothesis. These people were being blackmailed. The dying woman was either the blackmailer, or she knew about the blackmail. I'd say that the general idea was, repentance, confession, and a wish to make reparation as far as possible. Father Gorman assumed the responsibility.'

'And then?'

'Everything else is conjectural,' said Lejeune. 'Say it was a paying racket, and someone didn't want it to stop paying. Someone knew Mrs Davis was dying and that she'd sent for the priest. The rest follows.'

'I wonder now,' said Corrigan, studying the paper again. 'Why do you think there's an interrogation mark after the last two names?'

'It could be that Father Gorman wasn't sure he'd remembered those two names correctly.'

'It might have been Mulligan instead of Corrigan,' agreed the doctor with a grin. 'That's likely enough. But I'd say that with a name like Delafontaine, either you'd remember it or you wouldn't – if you know what I mean. It's odd that there isn't a single address–' He read down the list again.

'Parkinson – lots of Parkinsons. Sandford, not uncommon – Hesketh-Dubois – that's a bit of a mouthful. Can't be many of them.'

On a sudden impulse he leaned forward and took the telephone directory from the desk.

'E to L. Let's see. Hesketh, Mrs A . . . John and Co., Plumbers . . . Sir Isidore. Ah! here we are! Hesketh-Dubois, Lady, Forty-nine, Ellesmere Square, S.W.1. What say we just ring her up?'

'Saying what?'

'Inspiration will come,' said Doctor Corrigan airily.

'Go ahead,' said Lejeune.

'What?' Corrigan stared at him.

'I said go ahead,' Lejeune spoke airily. 'Don't look so taken aback.' He himself picked up the receiver. 'Give me an outside line.' He looked at Corrigan. 'Number?'

'Grosvenor 64578.'

Lejeune repeated it, then handed the receiver over to Corrigan.

'Enjoy yourself,' he said.

Faintly puzzled, Corrigan looked at him as he waited. The ringing tone continued for some time before anyone answered. Then, interspersed with heavy breathing, a woman's voice said:

'Grosvenor 64578.'

'Is that Lady Hesketh-Dubois's house?'

'Well – well, yes – I mean –'

Doctor Corrigan ignored these uncertainties.

'Can I speak to her, please?'

'No, that you can't do! Lady Hesketh-Dubois died last April.'

'Oh!' Startled, Dr Corrigan ignored the 'Who is it speaking, please?' and gently replaced the receiver.

He looked coldly at Inspector Lejeune.

'So that's why you were so ready to let me ring up.'

Lejeune smiled maliciously.

'We don't really neglect the obvious,' he pointed out.

'Last April,' said Corrigan thoughtfully. 'Five months ago. Five months since blackmail or whatever it was has failed to worry her. She didn't commit suicide, or anything like that?'

'No. She died of a tumour on the brain.'

'So now we start again,' said Corrigan, looking down at the list.

Lejeune sighed.

'We don't really know that list had anything to do with it,' he pointed out. 'It may have been just an ordinary coshing on a foggy night – and precious little hope of finding who did it unless we have a piece of luck . . .'

Dr Corrigan said:

'Do you mind if I continue to concentrate on this list?'

'Go ahead. I wish you all the luck in the world.'

'Meaning *I'm* not likely to get anywhere if *you* haven't! Don't be too sure. I shall concentrate on Corrigan. Mr or Mrs or Miss Corrigan – with a big interrogation mark.'

CHAPTER 3

I

'Well, really, Mr Lejeune, I don't see what more I can tell you! I told it all before to your sergeant. *I* don't know who Mrs Davis was, or where she came from. She'd been with me about six months. She paid her rent regular, and she seemed a nice quiet respectable person, and what more you expect me to say I'm sure I don't know.'

Mrs Coppins paused for breath and looked at Lejeune with some displeasure. He gave her the gentle melancholy smile which he knew by experience was not without its effect.

'Not that I wouldn't be willing to help if I could,' she amended.

'Thank you. That's what we need – help. Women know – they feel instinctively – so much more than a man can know.'

It was a good gambit, and it worked.

'Ah,' said Mrs Coppins. 'I wish Coppins could hear you. So hoity-toity and off-hand he always was. "Saying you know things when you haven't got anything to go on!" he'd say and snort. And nine times out of ten I was right.'

'That's why I'd like to hear what ideas you have about Mrs Davis. Was she – an unhappy woman, do you think?'

'Now as to that – no, I wouldn't say so. Businesslike. That's what she always seemed. Methodical. As though she'd got her life planned and was acting accordingly. She had a job, I understand, with one of these consumer research associations. Going around and asking people what soap powder they used, or flour, and what they spend on their weekly budget and how it's divided up. Of course I've always felt that sort of thing is snooping really – and why the Government or anyone else wants to know beats me! All you hear at the end of it is only what everybody has known perfectly well all along – but there, there's a craze for that sort of thing nowadays. And if you've got to have it, I should say that poor Mrs Davis would do the job very nicely. A pleasant manner, not nosy, just businesslike and matter-of-fact.'

'You don't know the actual name of the firm or association that employed her?'

'No, I don't, I'm afraid.'

'Did she ever mention relatives –?'

'No. I gathered she was a widow and had lost her husband many years ago. A bit of an invalid he'd been, but she never talked much about him.'

'She didn't mention where she came from – what part of the country?'

'I don't think she was a Londoner. Came from somewhere up north, I should say.'

'You didn't feel there was anything – well, mysterious about her?'

Lejeune felt a doubt as he spoke. If she was a suggestible woman – But Mrs Coppins did not take advantage of the opportunity offered to her.

'Well, I can't say really that I did. Certainly not from anything she ever *said*. The only thing that perhaps might have made me wonder was her suitcase. Good quality it was, but not new. And the initials on it had been painted over. J.D. – Jessie Davis. But originally it had been J. something else. H., I think. But it might have been an A. Still, I didn't think anything of that at the time. You can often pick up a good piece of luggage second-hand ever so cheap, and then it's natural to get the initials altered. She hadn't a lot of stuff – only the one case.'

Lejeune knew that. The dead woman had had curiously few personal possessions. No letters had been kept, no photographs. She had had apparently no insurance card, no bank book, no cheque book. Her clothes were of good everyday serviceable quality, nearly new.

'She seemed quite happy?' he asked.

'I suppose so.'

He pounced on the faint doubtful tone in her voice.

'You only *suppose* so?'

'Well, it's not the kind of thing you think about, is it? I should say she was nicely off, with a good job, and quite satisfied with her life. She wasn't the bubbling over sort. But of course, when she got ill –'

'Yes, when she got ill?' he prompted her.

'Vexed, she was at first. When she went down with 'flu, I mean. It would put all her schedule out, she said. Missing appointments and all that. But 'flu's 'flu, and you can't ignore it when it's there.

So she stopped in bed, and made herself tea on the gas ring, and took aspirin. I said why not have the doctor and she said no point in it. Nothing to do for 'flu but stay in bed and keep warm and I'd better not come near her to catch it. I did a bit of cooking for her when she got better. Hot soup and toast. And a rice pudding now and again. It got her down, of course, 'flu does – but not more than what's usual, I'd say. It's after the fever goes down that you get the depression – and she got that like everyone does. She sat there, by the gas fire, I remember, and said to me, "I wish one didn't have so much time to *think*. I don't like having time to think. It gets me down."'

Lejeune continued to look deeply attentive and Mrs Coppins warmed to her theme.

'Lent her some magazines, I did. But she didn't seem able to keep her mind on reading. Said once, I remember, "If things aren't all they should be, it's better not to know about it, don't you agree?" and I said, "That's right, dearie." And she said, "I don't know – I've never really been *sure*." And I said that was all right, then. And she said, 'Everything I've done has always been perfectly straightforward and above board. I've nothing to reproach *myself* with." And I said, "Of course you haven't, dear." But I did just wonder in my own mind whether in the firm that employed her there mightn't have been some funny business with the accounts maybe, and she'd got wind of it – but had felt it wasn't really her business.'

'Possible,' agreed Lejeune.

'Anyway, she got well again – or nearly so, and went back to work. I told her it was too soon. Give yourself another day or two, I said. And there, how right I was! Come back the second evening, she did, and I could see at once she'd got a high fever. Couldn't hardly climb the stairs. You must have the doctor, I says, but no, she wouldn't. Worse and worse she got, all that day, her eyes glassy, and her cheeks like fire, and her breathing terrible. And the next day in the evening she said to me, hardly able to get the words out: "A priest. I must have a priest. And quickly . . . or it will be too late." But it wasn't our vicar she wanted. It had to be a Roman Catholic priest. I never knew she was a Roman, never any crucifix about or anything like that.'

But there had been a crucifix, tucked away at the bottom of the suitcase. Lejeune did not mention it. He sat listening.

'I saw young Mike in the street and I sent him for that Father Gorman at St Dominic's. And I rang for the doctor, and the hospital on my own account, not saying nothing to her.'

'You took the priest up to her when he came?'

'Yes, I did. And left them together.'

'Did either of them say anything?'

'Well now, I can't exactly remember. I was talking myself, saying here was the priest and now she'd be all right, trying to cheer her up, but I do call to mind now as I closed the door I heard her say something about wickedness. Yes – and something, too, about a horse – horse-racing, maybe. I like a half-crown on myself occasionally – but there's a lot of crookedness goes on in racing, so they say.'

'Wickedness,' said Lejeune. He was struck by the word.

'Have to confess their sins, don't they, Romans, before they die? So I suppose that was it.'

Lejeune did not doubt that that was it, but his imagination was stirred by the word used. Wickedness . . .

Something rather special in wickedness, he thought, if the priest who knew about it was followed and clubbed to death . . .

II

There was nothing to be learnt from the other three lodgers in the house. Two of them, a bank clerk and an elderly man who worked in a shoe shop, had been there for some years. The third was a girl of twenty-two who had come there recently and had a job in a nearby department store. All three of them barely knew Mrs Davis by sight.

The woman who had reported having seen Father Gorman in the street that evening had no useful information to give. She was a Catholic who attended St Dominic's and she knew Father Gorman by sight. She had seen him turn out of Benthall Street and go into Tony's Place about ten minutes to eight. That was all.

Mr Osborne, the proprietor of the chemist's shop on the corner of Barton Street, had a better contribution to make.

He was a small, middle-aged man, with a bald domed head, a round ingenuous face, and glasses.

'Good evening, Chief Inspector. Come behind, will you?' He held up the flap of an old-fashioned counter. Lejeune passed behind and through a dispensing alcove where a young man in a white overall was making up bottles of medicine with the swiftness of a professional conjurer, and so through an archway into a tiny room with a couple of easy-chairs, a table and a desk. Mr Osborne pulled the curtain of the archway behind him in a secretive manner and sat down in one chair, motioning to Lejeune to take the other. He leaned forward, his eyes glinting in pleasurable excitement.

'It just happens that I *may* be able to assist you. It wasn't a busy evening – nothing much to do, the weather being unfavourable. My young lady was behind the counter. We keep open until eight on Thursdays always. The fog was coming on and there weren't many people about. I'd gone to the door to look at the weather, thinking to myself that the fog was coming up fast. The weather forecast had said it would. I stood there for a bit – nothing going on inside that my young lady couldn't deal with – face creams and bath salts and all that. Then I saw Father Gorman coming along on the other side of the street. I know him quite well by sight, of course. A shocking thing, this murder, attacking a man so well thought of as he is. "There's Father Gorman," I said to myself. He was going in the direction of West Street, it's the next turn on the left before the railway, as you know. A little way behind him there was another man. It wouldn't have entered my head to notice or think anything of that, but quite suddenly this second man came to a stop – quite abruptly, just when he was level with my door. I wondered why he'd stopped – and then I noticed that Father Gorman, a little way ahead, was slowing down. He didn't quite stop. It was as though he was thinking of something so hard that he almost forgot he was walking. Then he started on again, and this other man started to walk, too – rather fast. I thought – inasmuch as I thought at all, that perhaps it was someone who knew Father Gorman and wanted to catch him up and speak to him.'

'But in actual fact he could simply have been following him?'

'That's what I'm sure he was doing now – not that I thought anything of it at the time. What with the fog coming up, I lost sight of them both almost at once.'

'Can you describe this man at all?'

Lejeune's voice was not confident. He was prepared for the usual nondescript characteristics. But Mr Osborne was made of different mettle to Tony of Tony's Place.

'Well, yes, I think so,' he said with complacency. 'He was a tall man –'

'Tall? How tall?'

'Well – five eleven to six feet, at least, I'd say. Though he might have seemed taller than he was because he was very thin. Sloping shoulders he had, and a definite Adam's apple. Grew his hair rather long under his Homburg. A great beak of a nose. *Very* noticeable. Naturally I couldn't say as to the colour of his eyes. I saw him in profile as you'll appreciate. Perhaps fifty as to age. I'm going by the walk. A youngish man moves quite differently.'

Lejeune made a mental survey of the distance across the street, then back again to Mr Osborne, and wondered. He wondered very much . . .

A description such as that given by the chemist could mean one of two things. It could spring from an unusually vivid imagination – he had known many examples of that kind, mostly from women. They built up a fancy portrait of what they thought a murderer ought to look like. Such fancy portraits, however, usually contained some decidedly spurious details – such as rolling eyes, beetle brows, ape-like jaws, snarling ferocity. The description given by Mr Osborne sounded like the description of a real person. In that case it was possible that here was the witness in a million – a man who observed accurately and in detail – and who would be quite unshakable as to what he had seen.

Again Lejeune considered the distance across the street. His eyes rested thoughtfully on the chemist.

He asked: 'Do you think you would recognise this man if you saw him again?'

'Oh, yes.' Mr Osborne was supremely confident. 'I never forget a face. It's one of my hobbies. I've always said that if one of these wife murderers came into my place and bought a nice little package of arsenic, I'd be able to swear to him at the trial. I've always had my hopes that something like that would happen one day.'

'But it hasn't happened yet?'

Mr Osborne admitted sadly that it hadn't.

'And not likely to now,' he added wistfully. 'I'm selling this business. Getting a very nice price for it, and retiring to Bournemouth.'

'It looks a nice place you've got here.'

'It's got class,' said Mr Osborne, a note of pride in his voice. 'Nearly a hundred years we've been established here. My grandfather and my father before me. A good old-fashioned family business. Not that I saw it that way as a boy. Stuffy, I thought it. Like many a lad, I was bitten by the stage. Felt sure I could act. My father didn't try to stop me. "See what you can make of it, my boy," he said. "You'll find you're no Sir Henry Irving." And how right he was! Very wise man, my father. Eighteen months or so in repertory and back I came into the business. Took a pride in it, I did. We've always kept good solid stuff. Old-fashioned. But quality. But nowadays' – he shook his head sadly – 'disappointing for a pharmaceutist. All this toilet stuff. You've got to keep it. Half the profits come from all that muck. Powder and lipstick and face creams; and hair shampoos and fancy sponge bags. I don't touch the stuff myself. I have a young lady behind the counter who attends to all that. No, it's not what it used to be, having a chemist's establishment. However, I've a good sum put by, and I'm getting a very good price, and I've made a down payment on a very nice little bungalow near Bournemouth.'

He added:

'Retire whilst you can still enjoy life. That's my motto. I've got plenty of hobbies. Butterflies, for instance. And a bit of bird watching now and then. And gardening – plenty of good books on how to start a garden. And there's travel. I might go on one of these cruises – see foreign parts before it's too late.'

Lejeune rose.

'Well, I wish you the best of luck,' he said. 'And if, before you actually leave these parts, you *should* catch sight of that man –'

'I'll let you know at once, Mr Lejeune. Naturally. You can count on me. It will be a pleasure. As I've told you, I've a very good eye for a face. I shall be on the lookout. On the *qui vive*, as they say. Oh yes. You can rely on me. It will be a pleasure.'

CHAPTER 4

MARK EASTERBROOK'S NARRATIVE

I

I came out of the Old Vic, my friend Hermia Redcliffe beside me. We had been to see a performance of *Macbeth.* It was raining hard. As we ran across the street to the spot where I had parked the car, Hermia remarked unjustly that whenever one went to the Old Vic it always rained.

'It's just one of those things.'

I dissented from this view. I said that, unlike sundials, she remembered only the rainy hours.

'Now at Glyndebourne,' went on Hermia as I let in the clutch, 'I've always been lucky. I can't imagine it other than perfection: the music – the glorious flower borders – the white flower border in particular.'

We discussed Glyndebourne and its music for a while, and then Hermia remarked:

'We're not going to Dover for breakfast, are we?'

'Dover? What an extraordinary idea. I thought we'd go to the Fantasie. One needs some really good food and drink after all the magnificent blood and gloom of *Macbeth*, Shakespeare always makes me ravenous.'

'Yes. So does Wagner. Smoked salmon sandwiches at Covent Garden in the intervals are never enough to stay the pangs. As to why Dover, it's because you're driving in that direction.'

'One has to go round,' I explained.

'But you've overdone going round. You're well away on the Old (or is it the New?) Kent Road.'

I took stock of my surroundings and had to admit that Hermia, as usual, was quite right.

'I always get muddled here,' I said in apology.

'It is confusing,' Hermia agreed. 'Round and round Waterloo Station.'

Having at last successfully negotiated Westminster Bridge we resumed our conversation, discussing the production of *Macbeth* that we had just been viewing. My friend Hermia Redcliffe was a handsome young woman of twenty-eight. Cast in the heroic mould, she had an almost flawless Greek profile, and a mass of dark chestnut hair, coiled on the nape of her neck. My sister always referred to her as 'Mark's girl friend' with an intonation of inverted commas about the term that never failed to annoy me.

The Fantasie gave us a pleasant welcome and showed us to a small table against the crimson velvet wall. The Fantasie is deservedly popular, and the tables are close together. As we sat down, our neighbours at the next table greeted us cheerfully. David Ardingly was a lecturer in History at Oxford. He introduced his companion, a very pretty girl, with a fashionable hairdo, all ends, bits and pieces, sticking out at improbable angles on the crown of her head. Strange to say, it suited her. She had enormous blue eyes and a mouth that was usually half-open. She was, as all David's girls were known to be, extremely silly. David, who was a remarkably clever young man, could only find relaxation with girls who were practically half-witted.

'This is my particular pet, Poppy,' he explained. 'Meet Mark and Hermia. They're very serious and highbrow and you must try and live up to them. We've just come from *Do it for Kicks*. Lovely show! I bet you two are straight from Shakespeare or a revival of Ibsen.'

'*Macbeth* at the Old Vic,' said Hermia.

'Ah, what do you think of Batterson's production?'

'I liked it,' said Hermia. 'The lighting was very interesting. And I've never seen the banquet scene so well managed.'

'Ah, but what about the witches?'

'Awful!' said Hermia. 'They always are,' she added.

David agreed.

'A pantomime element seems bound to creep in,' he said. 'All of them capering about and behaving like a three-fold Demon King. You can't help expecting a Good Fairy to appear in white with spangles to say in a flat voice:

Your evil shall not triumph. In the end,
It is Macbeth who will be round the bend.'

We all laughed, but David, who was quick on the uptake, gave me a sharp glance.

'What gives with you?' he asked.

'Nothing. It was just that I was reflecting only the other day about Evil and Demon Kings in pantomime. Yes – and Good Fairies, too.'

'*A propos de* what?'

'Oh, in Chelsea at a coffee bar.'

'How smart and up to date you are, aren't you, Mark? All among the Chelsea set. Where heiresses in tights marry corner boys on the make. That's where Poppy ought to be, isn't it, duckie?'

Poppy opened her enormous eyes still wider.

'I hate Chelsea,' she protested. 'I like the Fantasie *much* better! Such lovely, lovely food.'

'Good for you, Poppy. Anyway, you're not really rich enough for Chelsea. Tell us more about *Macbeth*, Mark, and the awful witches. I know how I'd produce the witches if I were doing a production.'

David had been a prominent member of the O.U.D.S. in the past.

'Well, how?'

'I'd make them very ordinary. Just sly quiet old women. Like the witches in a country village.'

'But there aren't any witches nowadays?' said Poppy, staring at him.

'You say that because you're a London girl. There's still a witch in every village in rural England. Old Mrs Black, in the third cottage up the hill. Little boys are told not to annoy her, and she's given presents of eggs and a home-baked cake now and again. Because,' he wagged a finger impressively, 'if you get across her, your cows will stop giving milk, your potato crop will fail, or little Johnnie will twist his ankle. You must keep on the right side of old Mrs Black. Nobody says so outright – but they all *know*!'

'You're joking,' said Poppy, pouting.

'No, I'm not. I'm right, aren't I, Mark?'

'Surely all that kind of superstition has died out completely with education,' said Hermia sceptically.

'Not in the rural pockets of the land. What do you say, Mark?'

'I think perhaps you're right,' I said slowly. 'Though I wouldn't really know. I've never lived in the country much.'

'I don't see *how* you could produce the witches as ordinary old women,' said Hermia, reverting to David's earlier remark. 'They must have a supernatural atmosphere about them, surely.'

'Oh, but just think,' said David. 'It's rather like madness. If you have someone who raves and staggers about with straws in their hair and *looks* mad, it's not frightening at all! But I remember being sent once with a message to a doctor at a mental home and I was shown into a room to wait, and there was a nice elderly lady there, sipping a glass of milk. She made some conventional remark about the weather and then suddenly she leant forward and asked in a low voice:

'"*Is it your poor child who's buried there behind the fireplace?*" And then she nodded her head and said "*12.10 exactly. It's always at the same time every day. Pretend you don't notice the blood.*"

'It was the matter-of-fact way she said it that was so spine-chilling.'

'Was there *really* someone buried behind the fireplace?' Poppy wanted to know.

David ignored her and went on:

'Then take mediums. At one moment trances, darkened rooms, knocks and raps. Afterwards the medium sits up, pats her hair and goes home to a meal of fish and chips, just an ordinary quite jolly woman.'

'So your idea of the witches,' I said, 'is three old Scottish crones with second sight – who practise their arts in secret, muttering their spells round a cauldron, conjuring up spirits, but remaining themselves just an ordinary trio of old women. Yes – it could be impressive.'

'If you could ever get any actors to play it that way,' said Hermia drily.

'You have something there,' admitted David. 'Any hint of madness in the script and an actor is immediately determined to go to town on it! The same with sudden deaths. No actor can just quietly collapse and fall down dead. He has to groan, stagger, roll his eyes, gasp, clutch his heart, clutch his head, and make a terrific performance of it. Talking of performances, what did you think of Fielding's Macbeth? Great division of opinion among the critics.'

'I thought it was terrific,' said Hermia. 'That scene with the doctor, after the sleep-walking scene. "*Canst thou not minister to a mind diseas'd.*" He made clear what I'd never thought of before – that he was really ordering the doctor to kill her. And yet he loved his wife. He brought out the struggle between his fear and his love. That "*Thou shouldst have died hereafter*" was the most poignant thing I've ever known.'

'Shakespeare might get a few surprises if he saw his plays acted nowadays,' I said drily.

'Burbage and Co. had already quenched a good deal of his spirit, I suspect,' said David.

Hermia murmured:

'The eternal surprise of the author at what the producer has done to him.'

'Didn't somebody called Bacon really write Shakespeare?' asked Poppy.

'That theory is quite out of date nowadays,' said David kindly. 'And what do *you* know of Bacon?'

'He invented gunpowder,' said Poppy triumphantly.

'You see why I love this girl?' he said. 'The things she knows are always so unexpected. Francis, not Roger, my love.'

'I thought it interesting,' said Hermia, 'that Fielding played the part of Third Murderer. Is there a precedent for that?'

'I believe so,' said David. 'How convenient it must have been in those times,' he went on, 'to be able to call up a handy murderer whenever you wanted a little job done. Fun if one could do it nowadays.'

'But it is done,' protested Hermia. 'Gangsters. Hoods – or whatever you call them. Chicago and all that.'

'Ah,' said David. 'But what I meant was not gangsterdom, not racketeers or Crime Barons. Just ordinary everyday folk who want to get rid of someone. That business rival; Aunt Emily, so rich and so unfortunately long-lived; that awkward husband always in the way. How convenient if you could ring up Harrods and say "Please send along two good murderers, will you?"'

We all laughed.

'But one *can* do that in a way, can't one?' said Poppy.

We turned towards her.

'What way, poppet?' asked David.

'Well, I mean, people can do that if they want to . . . People like us, as you said. Only I believe it's very expensive.'

Poppy's eyes were wide and ingenuous, her lips were slightly parted.

'What *do* you mean?' asked David curiously.

Poppy looked confused.

'Oh – I expect – I've got it mixed. I meant the Pale Horse. All that sort of thing.'

'A pale *horse?* What kind of a pale horse?'

Poppy flushed and her eyes dropped.

'I'm being stupid. It's just something someone mentioned – but I must have got it all wrong.'

'Have some lovely Coupe Nesselrode,' said David kindly.

II

One of the oddest things in life, as we all know, is the way that when you have heard a thing mentioned, within twenty-four hours you nearly always come across it again. I had an instance of that the next morning.

My telephone rang and I answered it –

'Flaxman 73841.'

A kind of gasp came through the phone. Then a voice said breathlessly but defiantly:

'I've thought about it, and I'll come!'

I cast round wildly in my mind.

'Splendid,' I said, stalling for time. 'Er – is that –?'

'After all,' said the voice, 'lightning never strikes twice.'

'Are you sure you've got the right number?'

'Of course I have. You're Mark Easterbrook, aren't you?'

'Got it!' I said. 'Mrs Oliver.'

'Oh,' said the voice, surprised. 'Didn't you know who it was? I never thought of that. It's about that fête of Rhoda's. I'll come and sign books if she wants me to.'

'That's frightfully nice of you. They'll put you up, of course.'

'There won't be parties, will there?' asked Mrs Oliver apprehensively.

'You know the kind of thing,' she went on. 'People coming up to me and saying am I writing something just now – when you'd think they could see I'm drinking ginger ale or tomato juice and not writing at all. And saying they like my books – which of course is pleasing, but I've never found the right answer. If you say "I'm so glad" it sounds like "Pleased to meet you." A kind of stock phrase. Well, it is, of course. And you don't think they'll want me to go out to the Pink Horse and have drinks?'

'The Pink *Horse*?'

'Well, the Pale Horse. Pubs, I mean. I'm so bad in pubs. I can *just* drink beer at a pinch, but it makes me terribly gurgly.'

'Just what do you mean by the Pale Horse?'

'There's a pub called that down there, isn't there? Or perhaps I do mean the Pink Horse? Or perhaps that's somewhere else. I may have just imagined it. I do imagine quite a lot of things.'

'How's the Cockatoo getting on?' I asked.

'The Cockatoo?' Mrs Oliver sounded at sea.

'And the cricket ball?'

'Really,' said Mrs Oliver with dignity. 'I think you must be mad or have a hangover or something. Pink Horses and cockatoos and cricket balls.'

She rang off.

I was still considering this second mention of the Pale Horse when my telephone rang again.

This time, it was Mr Soames White, a distinguished solicitor who rang up to remind me that under the will of my godmother, Lady Hesketh-Dubois, I was entitled to choose three of her pictures.

'There is nothing outstandingly valuable, of course,' said Mr Soames White in his defeatist melancholy tones. 'But I understand that at some time you expressed admiration of some of the pictures to the deceased.'

'She had some very charming water colours of Indian scenes,' I said. 'I believe you already have written to me about this matter, but I'm afraid it slipped my memory.'

'Quite so,' said Mr Soames White. 'But probate has now been granted, and the executors, of whom I am one, are arranging for the sale of the effects of her London house. If you *could* go round to Ellesmere Square in the near future . . .'

'I'll go now,' I said.

It seemed an unfavourable morning for work.

III

Carrying the three water colours of my choice under my arm, I emerged from Forty-nine Ellesmere Square and immediately cannoned into someone coming up the steps to the front door. I apologised, received apologies in return, and was just about to hail a passing taxi when something clicked in my mind and I turned sharply to ask:

'Hallo – isn't it Corrigan?'

'It is – and – yes – you're Mark Easterbrook!'

Jim Corrigan and I had been friends in our Oxford days – but it must have been fifteen years or more since we had last met.

'Thought I knew you – but couldn't place you for the moment,' said Corrigan. 'I read your articles now and again – and enjoy them, I must say.'

'What about you? Have you gone in for research as you meant to do?'

Corrigan sighed.

'Hardly. It's an expensive job – if you want to strike out on your own. Unless you can find a tame millionaire, or a suggestible Trust.'

'Liver flukes, wasn't it?'

'What a memory! No, I went off liver flukes. The properties of the secretions of the Mandarian glands; that's my present-day interest. You wouldn't have heard of them! Connected with the spleen. Apparently serving no purpose whatever!'

He spoke with a scientist's enthusiasm.

'What's the big idea, then?'

'Well,' Corrigan sounded apologetic. 'I have a theory that they may influence behaviour. To put it very crudely, they may act rather as the fluid in your car brakes does. No fluid – the brakes don't act. In human beings, a deficiency in these secretions might – I only say *might* – make you a criminal.'

I whistled.

'And what happens to Original Sin?'

'What indeed?' said Dr Corrigan. 'The parsons wouldn't like it, would they? I haven't been able to interest anyone in my theory, unfortunately. So I'm a police surgeon, in N.W. division. Quite interesting. One sees a lot of criminal types. But I won't bore you with shop – unless you'll come and have some lunch with me?'

'I'd like to. But you were going in there,' I nodded towards the house behind Corrigan.

'Not really,' said Corrigan. 'I was just going to gatecrash.'

'There's nobody there but a caretaker.'

'So I imagined. But I wanted to find out something about the late Lady Hesketh-Dubois if I could.'

'I dare say I can tell you more than a caretaker could. She was my godmother.'

'Was she indeed? That's a bit of luck. Where shall we go to feed? There's a little place off Lowndes Square – not grand, but they do a special kind of sea food soup.'

We settled ourselves in the little restaurant – a cauldron of steaming soup was brought to us by a pale-faced lad in French sailor trousers.

'Delicious,' I said, sampling the soup. 'Now then, Corrigan, what do you want to know about the old lady? And incidentally, why?'

'Why's rather a long story,' said my friend. 'First tell me what kind of an old lady she was?'

I considered.

'She was an old-fashioned type,' I said. 'Victorian. Widow of an ex-Governor of some obscure island. She was rich and liked her comfort. Went abroad in the winters to Estoril and places like that. Her house is hideous, full of Victorian furniture and the worst and most ornate kind of Victorian silver. She had no children, but kept a couple of fairly well-behaved poodles whom she loved dearly. She was opinionated and a staunch Conservative. Kindly, but autocratic. Very set in her ways. What more do you want to know?'

'I'm not quite sure,' said Corrigan. 'Was she ever likely to have been blackmailed, would you say?'

'*Blackmailed?*' I asked in lively astonishment. 'I can imagine nothing more unlikely. What *is* this all about?'

It was then I heard for the first time of the circumstances of Father Gorman's murder.

I laid down my spoon and asked,

'This list of names? Have you got it?'

'Not the original. But I copied them out. Here you are.'

I took the paper he produced from his pocket and proceeded to study it.

'Parkinson? I know two Parkinsons. Arthur who went into the Navy. Then there's a Henry Parkinson in one of the Ministries. Ormerod – there's a Major Ormerod in the Blues – Sandford – our old Rector when I was a boy was Sandford. Harmondsworth? No – Tuckerton –' I paused. 'Tuckerton . . . Not Thomasina Tuckerton, I suppose?'

Corrigan looked at me curiously.

'Could be, for all I know. Who's she and what does she do?'

'Nothing now. Her death was in the paper about a week ago.'

'That's not much help, then.'

I continued with my reading. 'Shaw. I know a dentist called Shaw, and there's Jerome Shaw, Q.C. . . . Delafontaine – I've heard that name lately, but I can't remember where. Corrigan. Does that refer to you, by any chance?'

'I devoutly hope not. I've a feeling that it's unlucky to have your name on that list.'

'Maybe. What made you think of blackmail in connection with it?'

'It was Detective-Inspector Lejeune's suggestion if I remember rightly. It seemed the most likely possibility – But there are plenty of others. This may be a list of dope smugglers or drug addicts or secret agents – it may be anything in fact. There's only one thing sure, it was important enough for murder to be committed in order to get hold of it.'

I asked curiously: 'Do you always take such an interest in the police side of your work?'

He shook his head.

'Can't say I do. My interest is in criminal *character*. Background, upbringing, and particularly glandular health – all that!'

'Then why the interest in this list of names?'

'Blessed if I know,' said Corrigan slowly. 'Seeing my own name on the list, perhaps. Up the Corrigans! One Corrigan to the rescue of another Corrigan.'

'Rescue? Then you definitely see this as a list of victims – *not* a list of malefactors. But surely it *could* be either?'

'You're entirely right. And it's certainly odd that I should be so positive. Perhaps it's just a feeling. Or perhaps it's something to do with Father Gorman. I didn't come across him very often, but he was a fine man, respected by everyone and loved by his own flock. He was the good tough militant kind. I can't get it out of my head that he considered this list a matter of life or death . . .'

'Aren't the police getting anywhere?'

'Oh yes, but it's a long business. Checking here, checking there. Checking the antecedents of the woman who called him out that night.'

'Who was she?'

'No mystery about her, apparently. Widow. We had an idea that her husband might have been connected with horse-racing, but that doesn't seem to be so. She worked for a small commercial firm that does consumer research. Nothing wrong there. They are a reputable firm in a small way. They don't know much about her. She came from the north of England – Lancashire. The only odd thing about her is that she had so few personal possessions.'

I shrugged my shoulders.

'I expect that's true for a lot more people than we ever imagine. It's a lonely world.'

'Yes, as you say.'

'Anyway, you decided to take a hand?'

'Just nosing around. Hesketh-Dubois is an uncommon name. I thought if I could find out a little about the lady –' He left the sentence unfinished. 'But from what you tell me, there doesn't seem to be any possible lead there.'

'Neither a dope addict nor a dope smuggler,' I assured him. 'Certainly not a secret agent. Has led far too blameless a life to have been blackmailed. I can't imagine what kind of a list she could possibly be on. Her jewellery she keeps at the bank so she wouldn't be a hopeful prospect for robbery.'

'Any other Hesketh-Duboises that you know about? Sons?'

'No children. She's got a nephew and a niece, I think, but not of that name. Her husband was an only child.'

Corrigan told me sourly that I'd been a lot of help. He looked at his watch, remarked cheerfully that he was due to cut somebody up, and we parted.

I went home thoughtful, found it impossible to concentrate on my work, and finally, on an impulse, rang up David Ardingly.

'David? Mark here. That girl I met with you the other evening. Poppy. What's her other name?'

'Going to pinch my girl, is that it?'

David sounded highly amused.

'You've got so many of them,' I retorted. 'You could surely spare one.'

'You've got a heavyweight of your own, old boy. I thought you were going steady with her.'

'Going steady.' A repulsive term. And yet, I thought, struck suddenly with its aptitude, how well it described my relationship with Hermia. And why should it make me feel depressed? I had always felt in the back of my mind that some day Hermia and I would marry . . . I liked her better than anyone I knew. We had so much in common . . .

For no conceivable reason, I felt a terrible desire to yawn . . . Our future stretched out before me. Hermia and I going to plays of significance – that mattered. Discussions of art – of music. No doubt about it, Hermia was the perfect companion.

But not much fun, said some derisive imp, popping up from my subconscious. I was shocked.

'Gone to sleep?' asked David.

'Of course not. To tell the truth, I found your friend Poppy very refreshing.'

'Good word. She is – taken in small doses. Her actual name is Pamela Stirling, and she works in one of those arty flower places in Mayfair. You know, three dead twigs, a tulip with its petals pinned back and a speckled laurel leaf. Price three guineas.'

He gave me the address.

'Take her out and enjoy yourself,' he said in a kindly avuncular fashion. 'You'll find it a great relaxation. That girl knows nothing – she's absolutely empty headed. She'll believe anything you tell her. She's virtuous by the way, so don't indulge in any false hopes.'

He rang off.

IV

I invaded the portals of Flower Studies Ltd. with some trepidation. An overpowering smell of gardenia nearly knocked me backwards. A number of girls, dressed in pale green sheaths and all looking exactly like Poppy, confused me. Finally I identified her. She was writing down an address with some difficulty, pausing doubtfully over the spelling of Fortescue Crescent. As soon as she was at liberty, after having further difficulties connected with producing the right change for a five-pound note, I claimed her attention.

'We met the other night – with David Ardingly,' I reminded her.

'Oh *yes!*' agreed Poppy warmly, her eyes passing vaguely over my head.

'I wanted to ask you something.' I felt sudden qualms. 'Perhaps I'd better buy some flowers?'

Like an automaton who has had the right button pressed, Poppy said:

'We've some lovely roses, fresh in today.'

'These yellow ones, perhaps?' There were roses everywhere. 'How much are they?'

'Vewy vewy cheap,' said Poppy in a honeyed persuasive voice. 'Only five shillings each.'

I swallowed and said I would have six of them.

'And some of these vewy special leaves with them?'

I looked dubiously at the special leaves which appeared to be in an advanced state of decay. Instead I chose some bright green asparagus fern, which choice obviously lowered me in Poppy's estimation.

'There was something I wanted to ask you,' I reiterated as Poppy was rather clumsily draping the asparagus fern round the roses. 'The other evening you mentioned something called the Pale Horse.'

With a violent start, Poppy dropped the roses and the asparagus fern on the floor.

'Can you tell me more about it?'

Poppy straightened herself after stooping.

'What did you say?' she asked.

'I was asking you about the Pale Horse.'

'A pale horse? What do you mean?'

'You mentioned it the other evening.'

'I'm sure I never did anything of the kind! I've never heard of any such thing.'

'Somebody told you about it. Who was it?'

Poppy drew a deep breath and spoke very fast.

'I don't in the least know what you mean! And we're not supposed to talk to customers.' . . . She slapped paper round my choice. 'That will be thirty-five shillings, please.'

I gave her two pound notes. She thrust six shillings into my hand and turned quickly to another customer.

Her hands, I noticed, were shaking slightly.

I went out slowly. When I had gone a little way, I realised she had quoted the wrong price (asparagus fern was seven and six) and had also given me too much change. Her mistakes in arithmetic had previously been in the other direction.

I saw again the rather lovely vacant face and the wide blue eyes. There had been something showing in those eyes . . .

'Scared,' I said to myself. 'Scared stiff . . . Now why? *Why?*'

CHAPTER 5

MARK EASTERBROOK'S NARRATIVE

'What a relief,' sighed Mrs Oliver. 'To think it's over and nothing has happened!'

It was a moment of relaxation. Rhoda's fête had passed off in the manner of fêtes. Violent anxiety about the weather which in the early morning appeared capricious in the extreme. Considerable argument as to whether any stalls should be set up in the open, or whether everything should take place in the long barn and the marquee. Various passionate local disputes regarding tea arrangements, produce stalls, et cetera. Tactful settlement of same by Rhoda. Periodical escapes of Rhoda's delightful but undisciplined dogs who were supposed to be incarcerated in the house, owing to doubts as to their behaviour on this great occasion. Doubts fully justified! Arrival of pleasant but vague starlet in a profusion of pale fur, to open the fête, which she did very charmingly, adding a few moving words about the plight of refugees which puzzled everybody, since the object of the fête was the restoration of the church tower. Enormous success of the bottle stall. The usual difficulties about change. Pandemonium at tea-time when every patron wanted to invade the marquee and partake of it simultaneously.

Finally, blessed arrival of evening. Displays of local dancing in the long barn were still going on. Fireworks and a bonfire were scheduled, but the weary household had now retired to the house, and were partaking of a sketchy cold meal in the dining-room, indulging meanwhile in one of those desultory conversations where everyone utters their own thoughts, and pays little attention to those of other people. It was all disjointed and comfortable. The released dogs crunched bones happily under the table.

'We shall take more than we did for the Save the Children last year,' said Rhoda gleefully.

'It seems very extraordinary to me,' said Miss Macalister, the children's Scottish nursery governess, 'that Michael Brent should find the buried treasure three years in succession. I'm wondering if he gets some advance information?'

'Lady Brookbank won the pig,' said Rhoda. 'I don't think she wanted it. She looked terribly embarrassed.'

The party consisted of my cousin Rhoda, and her husband Colonel Despard, Miss Macalister, a young woman with red hair suitably called Ginger, Mrs Oliver, and the vicar, the Rev. Caleb Dane Calthrop and his wife. The vicar was a charming elderly scholar whose principal pleasure was finding some apposite comment from the classics. This, though often an embarrassment, and a cause of bringing the conversation to a close, was perfectly in order now. The vicar never required acknowledgement of his sonorous Latin, his pleasure in having found an apt quotation was its own reward.

'As Horace says . . .' he observed, beaming round the table.

The usual pause happened and then:

'I think Mrs Horsefall cheated over the bottle of champagne,' said Ginger thoughtfully. 'Her nephew got it.'

Mrs Dane Calthrop, a disconcerting woman with fine eyes, was studying Mrs Oliver thoughtfully. She asked abruptly:

'What did you expect to happen at this fête?'

'Well, really, a murder or something like that?'

Mrs Dane Calthrop looked interested.

'But why should it?'

'No reason at all. Most unlikely, really. But there was one at the last fête I went to.'

'I see. And it upset you?'

'Very much.'

The vicar changed from Latin to Greek.

After the pause, Miss Macalister cast doubts on the honesty of the raffle for the live duck.

'Very sporting of old Lugg at the King's Arms to send us twelve dozen beer for the bottle stall,' said Despard.

'King's Arms?' I asked sharply.

'Our local, darling,' said Rhoda.

'Isn't there another pub round here? The – Pale Horse, didn't you say,' I asked, turning to Mrs Oliver.

There was no such reaction here as I had half expected. The faces turned towards me were vague and uninterested.

'The Pale Horse isn't a pub,' said Rhoda. 'I mean, not *now*.'

'It *was* an old inn,' said Despard. 'Mostly sixteenth-century I'd say. But it's just an ordinary house now. I always think they should have changed the name.'

'Oh, *no*,' exclaimed Ginger. 'It would have been awfully silly to call it Wayside, or Fairview. I think the Pale Horse is *much* nicer, and there's a lovely old inn sign. They've got it framed in the hall.'

'Who's they?' I asked.

'It belongs to Thyrza Grey,' said Rhoda. 'I don't know if you saw her today? Tall woman with short grey hair.'

'She's very occult,' said Despard. 'Goes in for spiritualism and trances, and magic. Not quite black masses, but that sort of thing.'

Ginger gave a sudden peal of laughter.

'I'm sorry,' she said apologetically. 'I was just thinking of Miss Grey as Madame de Montespan on a black velvet altar.'

'Ginger!' said Rhoda. 'Not in front of the vicar.'

'Sorry, Mr Dane Calthrop.'

'Not at all,' said the vicar, beaming. 'As the ancients put it–' he continued for some time in Greek.

After a respectful silence of appreciation, I returned to the attack.

'I still want to know who are "they" – Miss Grey and who else?'

'Oh, there's a friend who lives with her. Sybil Stamfordis. She acts as medium, I believe. You must have seen her about – Lots of scarabs and beads – and sometimes she puts on a sari – I can't think why – she's never been in India –'

'And then there's Bella,' said Mrs Dane Calthrop. 'She's their cook,' she explained. 'And she's also a witch. She comes from the village of Little Dunning. She had quite a reputation for witchcraft there. It runs in the family. Her mother was a witch, too.'

She spoke in a matter-of-fact way.

'You sound as though you believe in witchcraft, Mrs Dane Calthrop,' I said.

'But of course! There's nothing mysterious or secretive about it. It's all quite matter-of-fact. It's a family asset that you inherit. Children are told not to tease your cat, and people give you a cottage cheese or a pot of home-made jam from time to time.'

I looked at her doubtfully. She appeared to be quite serious.

'Sybil helped us today by telling fortunes,' said Rhoda. 'She was in the green tent. She's quite good at it, I believe.'

'She gave me a lovely fortune,' said Ginger. 'Money in my hand. A handsome dark stranger from overseas, two husbands and six children. Really very generous.'

'I saw the Curtis girl come out giggling,' said Rhoda. 'And she was very coy with her young man afterwards. Told him not to think he was the only pebble on the beach.'

'Poor Tom,' said her husband. 'Did he make any comeback?'

'Oh, yes. "I'm not telling you what she promised *me*," he said. "Mebbe you wouldn't like it too well, my girl!"'

'Good for Tom.'

'Old Mrs Parker was quite sour,' said Ginger, laughing. '"'Tis all foolishness," that's what she said. "Don't you believe none of it, you two." But then Mrs Cripps piped up and said, "You know, Lizzie, as well as I do, that Miss Stamfordis sees things as others can't see, and Miss Grey knows to a day when there's going to be a death. Never wrong, she is! Fairly gives me the creeps sometimes." And Mrs Parker said: "Death – that's different. It's a gift." And Mrs Cripps said: "Anyway I wouldn't like to offend none of those three, that I wouldn't!"'

'It does all sound exciting. I'd love to meet them,' said Mrs Oliver wistfully.

'We'll take you over there tomorrow,' Colonel Despard promised. 'The old inn is really worth seeing. They've been very clever in making it comfortable without spoiling its character.'

'I'll ring up Thyrza tomorrow morning,' said Rhoda.

I must admit that I went to bed with a slight feeling of deflation.

The Pale Horse which had loomed in my mind as a symbol of something unknown and sinister had turned out to be nothing of the sort.

Unless, of course, there was another Pale Horse somewhere else?

I considered that idea until I fell asleep.

II

There was a feeling of relaxation next day, which was a Sunday. An after-the-party feeling. On the lawn the marquee and tents flapped limply in a damp breeze, awaiting removal by the caterer's men at early dawn on the morrow. On Monday we would all set to work to take stock of what damage had been done, and clear things up. Today, Rhoda had wisely decided, it would be better to go out as much as possible.

We all went to church, and listened respectfully to Mr Dane Calthrop's scholarly sermon on a text taken from Isaiah which seemed to deal less with religion than with Persian history.

'We're going to lunch with Mr Venables,' explained Rhoda afterwards. 'You'll like him, Mark. He's really a most interesting man. Been everywhere and done everything. Knows all sorts of out-of-the-way things. He bought Priors Court about three years ago. And the things he's done to it must have cost him a fortune. He had polio and is semi-crippled, so he has to go about in a wheeled chair. It's very sad for him because up to then he was a great traveller, I believe. Of course he's rolling in money, and, as I say, he's done up the house in a wonderful way – it was an absolute ruin, falling to pieces. It's full of the most gorgeous stuff. The sale rooms are his principal interest nowadays, I believe.'

Priors Court was only a few miles away. We drove there and our host came wheeling himself along the hall to meet us.

'Nice of you all to come,' he said heartily. 'You must be exhausted after yesterday. The whole thing was a great success, Rhoda.'

Mr Venables was a man of about fifty, with a thin hawk-like face and a beaked nose that stood out from it arrogantly. He wore an open-wing collar which gave him a faintly old-fashioned air.

Rhoda made introductions.

Venables smiled at Mrs Oliver.

'I met this lady yesterday in her professional capacity,' he said. 'Six of her books with signatures. Takes care of six presents for Christmas. Great stuff you write, Mrs Oliver. Give us more of it. Can't have too much of it.' He grinned at Ginger. '*You* nearly landed me with a live duck, young woman.' Then he turned to me. 'I enjoyed your article in the Review last month,' he said.

'It was awfully good of you to come to our fête, Mr Venables,' said Rhoda. 'After that generous cheque you sent us, I didn't really hope that you'd turn up in person.'

'Oh, I enjoy that kind of thing. Part of English rural life, isn't it? I came home clasping a most terrible Kewpie doll from the hoop-la, and had a splendid but unrealistic future prophesied me by Our Sybil, all dressed up in a tinsel turban with about a ton of fake Egyptian beads slung over her torso.'

'Good old Sybil,' said Colonel Despard. 'We're going there to tea with Thyrza this afternoon. It's an interesting old place.'

'The Pale Horse? Yes. I rather wish it had been left as an inn. I always feel that that place has had a mysterious and unusually wicked past history. It can't have been smuggling; we're not near enough to the sea for that. A resort for highwaymen, perhaps? Or rich travellers spent the night there and were never seen again. It seems, somehow, rather tame to have turned it into a desirable residence for three old maids.'

'Oh – I *never* think of them like that!' cried Rhoda. 'Sybil Stamfordis, perhaps – with her saris and her scarabs, and always seeing auras round people's heads – she *is* rather ridiculous. But there's something really awe-inspiring about Thyrza, don't you agree? You feel she knows just what you're thinking. She doesn't *talk* about having second sight – but everyone says that she has got it.'

'And Bella, far from being an old maid, has buried two husbands,' added Colonel Despard.

'I sincerely beg her pardon,' said Venables, laughing.

'With sinister interpretations of the deaths from the neighbours,' added Despard. 'It's said they displeased her, so she turned her eyes on them, and they slowly sickened and pined away!'

'Of course, I forgot, she is the local witch?'

'So Mrs Dane Calthrop says.'

'Interesting thing, witchcraft,' said Venables thoughtfully. 'All over the world you get variations of it – I remember when I was in East Africa –'

He talked easily, and entertainingly, on the subject. He spoke of medicine-men in Africa; of little-known cults in Borneo. He promised that, after lunch, he would show us some West African sorcerers' masks.

'There's everything in this house,' declared Rhoda with a laugh.

'Oh well –' he shrugged his shoulders – 'if you can't go out to everything – then everything must be made to come to you.'

Just for a moment there was a sudden bitterness in his voice. He gave a swift glance downwards towards his paralysed legs.

'"*The world is so full of a number of things*,"' he quoted. 'I think that's always been my undoing. There's so much I want to know about – to see! Oh well I haven't done too badly in my time. And even now – life has its consolations.'

'Why *here?*' asked Mrs Oliver suddenly.

The others had been slightly ill at ease, as people become when a hint of tragedy looms in the air. Mrs Oliver alone had been unaffected. She asked because she wanted to know. And her frank curiosity restored the light-hearted atmosphere.

Venables looked towards her inquiringly.

'I mean,' said Mrs Oliver, 'why did you come to live here, in this neighbourhood? So far away from things that are going on. Was it because you had friends here?'

'No. I chose this part of the world, since you are interested, because I had *no* friends here.'

A faint ironical smile touched his lips.

How deeply, I wondered, had his disability affected him? Had the loss of unfettered movement, of liberty to explore the world, bitten deep into his soul? Or had he managed to adapt himself to altered circumstances with comparative equanimity – with a real greatness of spirit?

As though Venables had read my thoughts, he said: 'In your article you questioned the meaning of the term "greatness" – you compared the different meanings attached to it – in the East and the West. But what do we all mean nowadays, here in England, when we use the term "a great man"? –'

'Greatness of intellect, certainly,' I said, 'and surely moral strength as well?'

He looked at me, his eyes bright and shining.

'Is there no such thing as an evil man, then, who can be described as great?' he asked.

'Of course there is,' cried Rhoda. 'Napoleon and Hitler and oh, lots of people. They were all great men.'

'Because of the effect they produced?' said Despard. 'But if one had known them personally – I wonder if one would have been impressed.'

Ginger leaned forward and ran her fingers through her carroty mop of hair.

'That's an interesting thought,' she said. 'Mightn't they, perhaps, have seemed pathetic, undersized little figures. Strutting, posturing, feeling inadequate, determined to *be* someone, even if they pulled the world down round them?'

'Oh, *no*,' said Rhoda vehemently. 'They couldn't have produced the results they did if they had been like that.'

'I don't know,' said Mrs Oliver. 'After all, the stupidest child can set a house on fire quite easily.'

'Come, come,' said Venables. 'I really can't go along with this modern playing down of evil as something that doesn't really exist. There *is* evil. And evil is powerful. Sometimes more powerful than good. It's there. It has to be recognised – and fought. Otherwise –' he spread out his hands. 'We go down to darkness.'

'Of course I was brought up on the devil,' said Mrs Oliver, apologetically. 'Believing in him, I mean. But you know he always did seem to me so *silly*. With hoofs and a tail and all that. Capering about like a ham actor. Of course I often have a master criminal in my stories – people like it – but really he gets harder and harder to do. So long as one doesn't know who he is, I can keep him impressive – but when it all comes out – he seems, somehow, so *inadequate*. A kind of anti-climax. It's much easier if you just have a bank manager who's embezzled the funds, or a husband who wants to get rid of his wife and marry the children's governess. So much more *natural* – if you know what I mean.'

Everyone laughed and Mrs Oliver said apologetically:

'I know I haven't put it very well – but you do see what I mean?'

We all said that we knew exactly what she meant.

CHAPTER 6

MARK EASTERBROOK'S NARRATIVE

It was after four o'clock when we left Priors Court. After a particularly delicious lunch, Venables had taken us on a tour of the house. He had taken a real pleasure in showing us his various possessions – a veritable treasure house the place was.

'He must be rolling in money,' I said when we had finally departed. 'Those jades – and the African sculpture – to say nothing of all his Meissen and Bow. You're lucky to have such a neighbour.'

'Don't we know it?' said Rhoda. 'Most of the people down here are nice enough – but definitely on the dull side. Mr Venables is positively exotic by comparison.'

'How did he make his money?' asked Mrs Oliver. 'Or has he always had it?'

Despard remarked wryly that nobody nowadays could boast of such a thing as a large inherited income. Death duties and taxation had seen to that.

'Someone told me,' he added, 'that he started life as a stevedore but it seems most unlikely. He never talks about his boyhood or his family –' He turned towards Mrs Oliver. 'A Mystery Man for you –'

Mrs Oliver said that people were always offering her things she didn't want –

The Pale Horse was a half-timbered building (genuine half-timbering not faked). It was set back a little way from the village street. A walled garden could be glimpsed behind it which gave it a pleasant old-world look.

I was disappointed in it, and said so.

'Not nearly sinister enough,' I complained. 'No atmosphere.'

'Wait till you get inside,' said Ginger.

We got out of the car and went up to the door, which opened as we approached.

Miss Thyrza Grey stood on the threshold, a tall, slightly masculine figure in a tweed coat and skirt. She had rough grey hair springing up from a high forehead, a large beak of a nose, and very penetrating light blue eyes.

'Here you are at last,' she said in a hearty bass voice. 'Thought you'd all got lost.'

Behind her tweed-clad shoulders I became aware of a face peering out from the shadows of the dark hall. A queer, rather formless face, like something made in putty by a child who had strayed in to play in a sculptor's studio. It was the kind of face, I thought, that you sometimes see amongst a crowd in an Italian or Flemish primitive painting.

Rhoda introduced us and explained that we had been lunching with Mr Venables at Priors Court.

'Ah!' said Miss Grey. 'That explains it! Fleshpots. That Italian cook of his! And all the treasures of the treasure house as well. Oh well, poor fellow – got to have something to cheer him up. But come in – come in. We're rather proud of our own little place. Fifteenth-century – and some of it fourteenth.'

The hall was low and dark with a twisting staircase leading up from it. There was a wide fireplace and over it a framed picture.

'The old inn sign,' said Miss Grey, noting my glance. 'Can't see much of it in this light. The Pale Horse.'

'I'm going to clean it for you,' said Ginger. 'I said I would. You let me have it and you'll be surprised.'

'I'm a bit doubtful,' said Thyrza Grey, and added bluntly, 'Suppose you ruin it?'

'Of course I shan't ruin it,' said Ginger indignantly. 'It's my job.'

'I work for the London Galleries,' she explained to me. 'Great fun.'

'Modern picture restoring takes a bit of getting used to,' said Thyrza. 'I gasp every time I go into the National Gallery nowadays. All the pictures look as though they'd had a bath in the latest detergent.'

'You can't really prefer them all dark and mustard coloured,' protested Ginger. She peered at the inn sign. 'A lot more would come up. The horse *may* even have a rider.'

I joined her to stare into the picture. It was a crude painting with little merit except the doubtful one of old age and dirt. The pale figure of a stallion gleamed against a dark indeterminate background.

'Hi, Sybil,' cried Thyrza. 'The visitors are crabbing our Horse, damn their impertinence!'

Miss Sybil Stamfordis came through a door to join us.

She was a tall willowy woman with dark, rather greasy hair, a simpering expression, and a fish-like mouth.

She was wearing a bright emerald green sari which did nothing to enhance her appearance. Her voice was faint and fluttery.

'Our dear, dear Horse,' she said. 'We fell in love with that old inn sign the moment we saw it. I really think it influenced us to buy the house. Don't you, Thyrza? But come in – come in.'

The room into which she led us was small and square and had probably been the bar in its time. It was furnished now with chintz and Chippendale and was definitely a lady's sitting-room, country style. There were bowls of chrysanthemums.

Then we were taken out to see the garden which I could see would be charming in summer, and then came back into the house to find tea had been laid. There were sandwiches and home-made cakes and as we sat down, the old woman whose face I had glimpsed for a moment in the hall came in bearing a silver teapot. She wore a plain dark green overall. The impression of a head made crudely from Plasticine by a child was borne out on closer inspection. It had a witless primitive face but I could not imagine why I had thought it sinister.

Suddenly I felt angry with myself. All this nonsense about a converted inn and three middle-aged women!

'Thank you, Bella,' said Thyrza.

'Got all you want?'

It came out almost as a mumble.

'Yes, thanks.'

Bella withdrew to the door. She had looked at nobody, but just before she went out, she raised her eyes and took a speedy glance at me. There was something in that look that startled me – though it was difficult to describe why. There was malice in it, and a curious intimate knowledge. I felt that without effort, and almost without curiosity, she had known exactly what thoughts were in my mind.

Thyrza Grey had noticed my reaction.

'Bella is disconcerting, isn't she, Mr Easterbrook?' she said softly. 'I noticed her look at you.'

'She's a local woman, isn't she?' I strove to appear merely politely interested.

'Yes. I dare say someone will have told you she's the local witch.'

Sybil Stamfordis clanked her beads.

'Now do confess, Mr – Mr –'

'Easterbrook.'

'Easterbrook. I'm sure you've heard that we all practise witchcraft. Confess now. We've got quite a reputation, you know –'

'Not undeserved, perhaps,' said Thyrza. She seemed amused. 'Sybil here has great gifts.'

Sybil sighed pleasurably.

'I was always attracted by the occult,' she murmured. 'Even as a child I realised that I had unusual powers. Automatic writing came to me quite naturally. I didn't even know what it *was*! I'd just sit there with a pencil in my hand – and not know a thing about what was happening. And of course I was always ultra-sensitive. I fainted once when taken to tea in a friend's house. Something awful had happened in that very room . . . I knew it! We got the explanation later. There had been a murder there – twenty-five years ago. In that very room!'

She nodded her head and looked round at us with great satisfaction.

'Very remarkable,' said Colonel Despard with polite distaste.

'Sinister things have happened in *this* house,' said Sybil darkly. 'But we have taken the necessary steps. The earth-bound spirits have been freed.'

'A kind of spiritual spring cleaning?' I suggested.

Sybil looked at me rather doubtfully.

'What a lovely coloured sari you are wearing,' said Rhoda.

Sybil brightened.

'Yes, I got it when I was in India. I had an interesting time there. I explored yoga, you know, and all that. But I could not help feeling that it was all too sophisticated – not near enough to the natural and the primitive. One must go back, I feel, to the beginnings, to the early primitive powers. I am one of the few women who have visited Haiti. Now there you really *do* touch the original springs of the occult. Overlaid, of course, by a certain amount of corruption and distortion. But the root of the matter is there.

'I was shown a great deal, especially when they learnt that I had twin sisters a little older than myself. The child who is born next after twins has special powers, so they told me. Interesting, wasn't it? Their death dances are wonderful. All the panoply of death, skulls and cross bones, and the tools of a gravedigger, spade, pick and hoe. They dress up as undertakers' mutes, top hats, black clothes –

'The Grand Master is Baron Samedi, and the Legba is the god he invokes, the god who "removes the barrier". You send the dead forth – to cause death. Weird idea, isn't it?

'Now this,' Sybil rose and fetched an object from the window sill. 'This is my Asson. It's a dried gourd with a network of beads and – you see these bits? – dried snake vertebrae.'

We looked politely, though without enthusiasm.

Sybil rattled her horrid toy affectionately.

'Very interesting,' said Despard courteously.

'I could tell you lots more –'

At this point my attention wandered. Words came to me hazily as Sybil continued to air her knowledge of sorcery and voodoo – Maître Carrefour, the *Coa*, the Guidé family –

I turned my head to find Thyrza looking at me quizzically.

'You don't believe any of it, do you?' she murmured. 'But

you're wrong, you know. You can't explain away *everything* as superstition, or fear, or religious bigotry. There *are* elemental truths and elemental powers. There always have been. There always will be.'

'I don't think I would dispute that,' I said.

'Wise man. Come and see my library.'

I followed her out through the french windows into the garden and along the side of the house.

'We made it out of the old stables,' she explained.

The stables and outbuildings had been reconstituted as one large room. The whole of one long wall was lined with books. I went across to them and was presently exclaiming.

'You've got some very rare works here, Miss Grey. Is this an original *Malleus Maleficorum?* My word, you have some treasures.'

'I have, haven't I?'

'That Grimoire – very rare indeed.' I took down volume after volume from the shelves. Thyrza watched me – there was an air of quiet satisfaction about her which I did not understand.

I put back *Sadducismus Triumphatus* as Thyrza said:

'It's nice to meet someone who can appreciate one's treasures. Most people just yawn or gape.'

'There can't be much about the practice of witchcraft, sorcery, and all the rest of it that you don't know,' I said. 'What gave you an interest in it in the first place?'

'Hard to say now . . . It's been so long . . . One looks into a thing idly – and then – one gets gripped! It's a fascinating study. The things people believed – and the damn' fool things they did!'

I laughed.

'That's refreshing. I'm glad you don't believe all you read.'

'You mustn't judge me by poor Sybil. Oh yes, I saw you looking superior! But you were wrong. She's a silly woman in a lot of ways. She takes voodoo, and demonology, and black magic and mixes everything up into a glorious occult pie – but she has the power.'

'The power?'

'I don't know what else you can call it . . . There *are* people who can become a living bridge between this world and a world of strange uncanny powers. Sybil is one of them. She is a first-class medium. She has never done it for money. But her gift is quite exceptional. When she and I and Bella –'

'Bella?'

'Oh yes. Bella has her own powers. We all have, in our different degrees. As a team –'

She broke off.

'Sorcerers Ltd?' I suggested with a smile.

'One could put it that way.'

I glanced down at the volume I was holding in my hand.

'Nostradamus and all that?'

'Nostradamus and all that.'

I said quietly: 'You *do* believe it, don't you?'

'I don't *believe*. I *know*.'

She spoke triumphantly – I looked at her.

'But how? In what way? For what reason?'

She swept her hand out towards the bookshelves –

'All that! So much of it nonsense! Such grand ridiculous phraseology! But sweep away the superstitions and the prejudices of the times – and the *core* is truth! You only dress it up – it's always been dressed up – to impress people.'

'I'm not sure I follow you.'

'My dear man, *why* have people come throughout the ages to the necromancer – to the sorcerer – to the witch-doctor? Only two reasons really. There are only two things that are wanted badly enough to risk damnation. The love potion or the cup of poison.'

'Ah.'

'So simple, isn't it? Love – and death. The love potion – to win the man you want – the black mass – to keep your lover. A draught to be taken at the full of the moon. Recite the names of devils or of spirits. Draw patterns on the floor or on the wall. All that's window dressing. The truth is the aphrodisiac in the draught!'

'And death?' I asked.

'Death?' She laughed, a queer little laugh that made me uncomfortable. 'Are *you* so interested in death?'

'Who isn't?' I said lightly.

'I wonder.' She shot me a glance, keen, searching. It took me aback.

'Death. There's always been a greater trade in that than there ever has been in love potions. And yet – how childish it all was in the past! The Borgias and their famous secret poisons. Do you know what they *really* used? Ordinary white arsenic! Just the same as any little wife poisoner in the back streets. But we've progressed a long way beyond that nowadays. Science has enlarged our frontiers.'

'With untraceable poisons?' My voice was sceptical.

'Poisons! That's *vieux jeu*. Childish stuff. There are new horizons.'

'Such as?'

'The *mind*. Knowledge of what the mind *is* – what it can *do* – what it can be *made* to do.'

'Please go on. This is most interesting.'

'The principle is well known. Medicine-men have used it in primitive communities for centuries. You don't need to kill your victim. All you need do is – *tell him to die*.'

'Suggestion? But it won't work unless the victim believes in it.'

'It doesn't work on Europeans, you mean,' she corrected me. 'It does sometimes. But that's not the point. We've gone further ahead than the witch-doctor has ever gone. The psychologists have shown the way. The desire for death! It's there – in everyone. Work on that! Work on the death wish.'

'It's an interesting idea.' I spoke with a muted scientific interest. 'Influence your subject to commit suicide? Is that it?'

'You're still lagging behind. You've heard of traumatic illnesses?'

'Of course.'

'People who, because of an unconscious wish to avoid returning to work, develop real ailments. Not malingering – real illnesses with symptoms, with actual pain. It's been a puzzle to doctors for a long time.'

'I'm beginning to get the hang of what you mean,' I said slowly.

'To destroy your subject, power must be exerted on his secret unconscious self. The death wish that exists in all of us must be stimulated, heightened.' Her excitement was growing. 'Don't you see? A *real* illness will be induced, caused by that death-seeking self. You wish to be ill, you wish to die – and so – you do get ill, and die.'

She had flung her head up now, triumphantly. I felt suddenly very cold. All nonsense, of course. This woman was slightly mad . . . And yet –

Thyrza Grey laughed suddenly.

'You don't believe me, do you?'

'It's a fascinating theory, Miss Grey – quite in line with modern thought, I'll admit. But how do you propose to stimulate this death wish that we all possess?'

'That's my secret. The way! The means! There are communications without contact. You've only to think of wireless, radar, television. Experiments in Extra-Sensory Perception haven't gone ahead as people hoped, but that's because they haven't grasped the first simple principle. You *can* accomplish it sometimes by accident – but once you know *how* it works, you could do it every time . . .'

'Can *you* do it?'

She didn't answer at once – then she said, moving away:

'You mustn't ask me, Mr Easterbrook, to give all my secrets away.'

I followed her towards the garden door –

'Why have you told me all this?' I asked.

'You understand my books. One needs sometimes to – to – well – talk to someone. And besides –'

'Yes?'

'I had the idea – Bella has it, too – that you – *may need us*.'

'*Need you*?'

'Bella thinks you came here – to find us. She is seldom at fault.'

'Why should I want to – "find you", as you put it?'

'That,' said Thyrza Grey softly, 'I do not know – yet.'

CHAPTER 7

MARK EASTERBROOK'S NARRATIVE

I

'So there you are! We wondered where you were.' Rhoda came through the open door, the others behind her. She looked round her. 'This is where you hold your *séances*, isn't it?'

'You're well informed,' Thyrza Grey laughed breezily. 'In a village everyone knows your business better than you do. We've a splendid sinister reputation, so I've heard. A hundred years ago it would have been sink or swim or the funeral pyre. My great-great-aunt – or one or two more greats – was burned as a witch, I believe, in Ireland. Those were the days!'

'I always thought you were Scottish?'

'On my father's side – hence the second sight. Irish on my mother's. Sybil is our pythoness, originally of Greek extraction. Bella represents Old English.'

'A *macabre* human cocktail,' remarked Colonel Despard.

'As you say.'

'Fun!' said Ginger.

Thyrza shot her a quick glance.

'Yes, it is in a way.' She turned to Mrs Oliver. 'You should write one of your books about a murder by black magic. I can give you a lot of dope about it.'

Mrs Oliver blinked and looked embarrassed.

'I only write very plain murders,' she said apologetically.

Her tone was of one who says 'I only do plain cooking.'

'Just about people who want other people out of the way and try to be clever about it,' she added.

'They're usually too clever for me,' said Colonel Despard. He glanced at his watch. 'Rhoda, I think –'

'Oh yes, we must go. It's much later than I thought.'

Thanks and good-byes were said. We did not go back through the house but round to a side gate.

'You keep a lot of poultry,' remarked Colonel Despard, looking into a wired enclosure.

'I hate hens,' said Ginger. 'They cluck in such an irritating way.'

'Mostly cockerels they be.' It was Bella who spoke. She had come out from a back door.

'White cockerels,' I said.

'Table birds?' asked Despard.

Bella said, 'They'm useful to us.'

Her mouth widened in a long curving line across the pudgy shapelessness of her face. Her eyes had a sly knowing look.

'They're Bella's province,' said Thyrza Grey lightly.

We said good-bye and Sybil Stamfordis appeared from the open front door to join in speeding the parting guests.

'I don't like that woman,' said Mrs Oliver, as we drove off. 'I don't like her *at all.*'

'You mustn't take old Thyrza too seriously,' said Despard indulgently. 'She enjoys spouting all that stuff and seeing what effect it has on you.'

'I didn't mean her. She's an unscrupulous woman, with a keen eye on the main chance. But she's not dangerous like the other one.'

'Bella? She *is* a bit uncanny, I'll admit.'

'I didn't mean her either. I meant the Sybil one. She *seems* just silly. All those beads and draperies and all the stuff about voodoo, and all those fantastic reincarnations she was telling us about. (Why is it that anybody who was a kitchenmaid or an ugly old peasant never seems to get reincarnated? It's always Egyptian Princesses or beautiful Babylonian slaves. Very fishy.) But all the same, though she's stupid, I have a feeling that she could really *do* things – make queer things happen. I always put things badly – but I mean she could be *used* – by something – in a way just because she *is* so silly. I don't suppose anyone understands what I mean,' she finished pathetically.

'I do,' said Ginger. 'And I shouldn't wonder if you weren't right.'

'We really ought to go to one of their *séances*,' said Rhoda wistfully. 'It might be rather fun.'

'No, you don't,' said Despard firmly. 'I'm not having you getting mixed up in anything of that sort.'

They fell into a laughing argument. I roused myself only when I heard Mrs Oliver asking about trains the next morning.

'You can drive back with me,' I said.

Mrs Oliver looked doubtful.

'I think I'd better go by train –'

'Oh, come now. You've driven with me before. I'm a most reliable driver.'

'It's not that, Mark. But I've got to go to a funeral tomorrow. So I mustn't be late in getting back to town.' She sighed. 'I do *hate* going to funerals.'

'Must you?'

'I think I must in this case. Mary Delafontaine was a very old friend – and I think she'd *want* me to go. She was that sort of person.'

'Of course,' I exclaimed. 'Delafontaine – of course.'

The others stared at me, surprised.

'Sorry,' I said. 'It's only – that – well, I was wondering where I'd heard the name Delafontaine lately. It was you, wasn't it?' I looked at Mrs Oliver. 'You said something about visiting her – in a nursing home.'

'Did I? Quite likely.'

'What did she die of?'

Mrs Oliver wrinkled her forehead.

'Toxic polyneuritis – something like that.'

Ginger was looking at me curiously. She had a sharp penetrating glance.

As we got out of the car, I said abruptly:

'I think I'll go for a bit of a walk. Such a lot of food. That wonderful lunch and tea on top of it. It's got to be worked off somehow.'

I went off briskly before anyone could offer to accompany me. I wanted badly to get by myself and sort out my ideas.

What was all this business? Let me at least get it clear to myself. It had started, had it not, with that casual but startling remark by Poppy, that if you wanted to 'get rid of someone' the Pale Horse was the place to go.

Following on that, there had been my meeting with Jim Corrigan, and his list of 'names' – as connected with the death of Father Gorman. On that list had been the name of Hesketh-Dubois, and the name of Tuckerton, causing me to hark back to that evening at Luigi's coffee bar. There had been the name of Delafontaine, too, vaguely familiar. It was Mrs Oliver who had mentioned it, in connection with a sick friend. The sick friend was now dead.

After that, I had, for some reason which I couldn't quite identify, gone to beard Poppy in her floral bower. And Poppy had denied vehemently any knowledge of such an institution as the Pale Horse. More significant still, Poppy had been afraid.

Today – there had been Thyrza Grey.

But surely the Pale Horse and its occupants was one thing and that list of names something separate, quite unconnected. Why on earth was I coupling them together in my mind?

Why should I imagine for one moment that there was any connection between them?

Mrs Delafontaine had presumably lived in London. Thomasina Tuckerton's home had been somewhere in Surrey. No one on the list had any connection with the little village of Much Deeping. Unless –

I was just coming abreast of the King's Arms. The King's Arms was a genuine pub with a superior look about it and a freshly-painted announcement of Lunches, Dinners and Teas.

I pushed its door open and went inside. The bar, not yet open, was on my left, on my right was a minute lounge smelling of stale smoke. By the stairs was a notice: *Office*. The office consisted of a glass window, firmly closed and a printed card. PRESS BELL. The whole place had the deserted air of a pub at this particular time of day. On a shelf by the office window was a battered registration book for visitors. I opened it and flicked through the pages. It was not much patronised. There were five or six entries, perhaps, in a week, mostly for one night only. I flicked back the pages, noting the names.

It was not long before I shut the book. There was still no one about. There were really no questions I wanted to ask at this stage. I went out again into the soft damp afternoon.

Was it only coincidence that someone called Sandford and someone else called Parkinson had stayed at the King's Arms during the last year? Both names were on Corrigan's list. Yes, but they were not particularly uncommon names. But I had noted one other name – the name of Martin Digby. If it was the Martin Digby I knew, he was the great-nephew of the woman I had always called Aunt Min – Lady Hesketh-Dubois.

I strode along, not seeing where I was going. I wanted very badly to talk to someone. To Jim Corrigan. Or to David Ardingly. Or to Hermia with her calm good sense. I was alone with my chaotic thoughts and I didn't want to be alone. What I wanted, frankly, was someone who would argue me out of the things that I was thinking.

It was after about half an hour of tramping muddy lanes that I finally turned in at the gates of the vicarage, and made my way up a singularly ill-kept drive, to pull a rusty-looking bell at the side of the front door.

II

'It doesn't ring,' said Mrs Dane Calthrop, appearing at the door with the unexpectedness of a genie.

I had already suspected that fact.

'They've mended it twice,' said Mrs Dane Calthrop. 'But it never lasts. So I have to keep alert. In case it's something important. It's important with you, isn't it?'

'It – well – yes, it is important – to me, I mean.'

'That's what I meant, too . . .' She looked at me thoughtfully. 'Yes, it's quite bad, I can see – Who do you want? The vicar?'

'I – I'm not sure –'

It had been the vicar I came to see – but now, unexpectedly, I was doubtful. I didn't quite know why. But immediately Mrs Dane Calthrop told me.

'My husband's a very good man,' she said. 'Besides being the vicar, I mean. And that makes things difficult sometimes. Good people, you see, don't really understand evil.' She paused and then said with a kind of brisk efficiency, 'I think it had better be *me*.'

A faint smile came to my lips. 'Is evil your department?' I asked.

'Yes, it is. It's important in a parish to know all about the various – well – sins that are going on.'

'Isn't sin your husband's province? His official business, so to speak.'

'The forgiveness of sins,' she corrected me. 'He can give absolution. I can't. But I,' said Mrs Dane Calthrop with the utmost cheerfulness, 'can get sin arranged and classified for him.

And if one knows about it one can help to prevent its harming other people. One can't help the people themselves. *I* can't, I mean. Only God can call to repentance, you know – or perhaps you don't know. A lot of people don't nowadays.'

'I can't compete with your expert knowledge,' I said, 'but I would like to prevent people being – harmed.'

She shot me a quick glance.

'It's like that, is it? You'd better come in and we'll be comfortable.'

The vicarage sitting-room was big and shabby. It was much shaded by a gargantuan Victorian shrubbery that no one seemed to have had the energy to curb. But the dimness was not gloomy for some peculiar reason. It was, on the contrary, restful. All the large shabby chairs bore the impress of resting bodies in them over the years. A fat clock on the chimney-piece ticked with a heavy comfortable regularity. Here there would always be time to talk, to say what you wanted to say, to relax from the cares brought about by the bright day outside.

Here, I felt, round-eyed girls who had tearfully discovered themselves to be prospective mothers, had confided their troubles to Mrs Dane Calthrop and received sound, if not always orthodox, advice; here angry relatives had unburdened themselves of their resentment over their in-laws; here mothers had explained that their Bob was *not* a bad boy; just high-spirited, and that to send him away to an approved school was absurd. Husbands and wives had disclosed marital difficulties.

And here was I, Mark Easterbrook, scholar, author, man of the world, confronting a grey-haired weather-beaten woman with fine eyes, prepared to lay my troubles in her lap. Why? I didn't know. I only had that odd surety that she was the right person.

'We've just had tea with Thyrza Grey,' I began.

Explaining things to Mrs Dane Calthrop was never difficult. She leaped to meet you.

'Oh I see. It's upset you? These three are a bit much to take, I agree. I've wondered myself . . . So much boasting. As a rule, in my experience, the really wicked don't boast. They can keep quiet about their wickedness. It's if your sins aren't really bad that you want so much to talk about them. Sin's such a wretched, mean, ignoble little thing. It's terribly necessary to make it seem grand and important. Village witches are usually silly ill-natured old women who like frightening people and getting something for nothing that way. Terribly easy to do, of course. When Mrs Brown's hens die all you have to do is nod your head and say darkly: "Ah, her Billy teased my Pussy last Tuesday week." Bella Webb *might*, be only a witch of that kind. But she might, she just *might*, be something more . . . Something that's lasted on from a very early age and which crops up now and then in country places. It's frightening when it does, because there's real malevolence – not just a desire to impress. Sybil Stamfordis is one of the silliest women I've ever met – but she really is a medium – whatever a medium may be. Thyrza – I don't know . . . What did she say to you? It was something that she said that's upset you, I suppose?'

'You have great experience, Mrs Dane Calthrop. Would you say, from all you know and have heard, that a human being could be destroyed from a distance, without visible connection, by another human being?'

Mrs Dane Calthrop's eyes opened a little wider.

'When you say destroyed, you mean, I take it, *killed?* A plain physical fact?'

'Yes.'

'I should say it was nonsense,' said Mrs Dane Calthrop robustly.

'Ah!' I said, relieved.

'But of course I might be wrong,' said Mrs Dane Calthrop. 'My father said that airships were nonsense, and my great-grandfather probably said that railway trains were nonsense. They were both quite right. At that time they both were impossible. But they're not impossible now. What does Thyrza do, activate a death ray or something? Or do they all three draw pentagrams and wish?'

I smiled.

'You're making things come into focus,' I said. 'I must have let that woman hypnotise me.'

'Oh no,' said Mrs Dane Calthrop. 'You wouldn't do that. You're not really the suggestible type. There must have been something else. Something that happened *first*. Before all this.'

'You're quite right.' I told her, then, as simply as I could with an economy of words, of the murder of Father Gorman, and of the casual mention in the night-club of the Pale Horse. Then I took from my pocket the list of names I had copied from the paper Dr Corrigan had shown me.

Mrs Dane Calthrop looked down at it, frowning.

'I see,' she said. 'And these people? What have they all in common?'

'We're not sure. It might be blackmail – or dope –'

'Nonsense,' said Mrs Dane Calthrop. 'That's not what's worrying you. What you really believe is – *that they're all dead?*'

I gave a deep sigh.

'Yes,' I said. 'That's what I believe. But I don't really *know* that that is so. Three of them are dead. Minnie Hesketh-Dubois, Thomasina Tuckerton, Mary Delafontaine. All three died in their beds from natural causes. Which is what Thyrza Grey claims would happen.'

'You mean she claims she *made* it happen?'

'No, no. She wasn't speaking of any actual people. She was expounding what she believes to be a scientific possibility.'

'Which appears on the face of it to be nonsense,' said Mrs Dane Calthrop thoughtfully.

'I know. I would just have been polite about it and laughed to myself, if it hadn't been for that curious mention of the Pale Horse.'

'Yes,' said Mrs Dane Calthrop musingly. 'The Pale Horse. That's suggestive.'

She was silent a moment. Then she raised her head.

'It's bad,' she said. 'It's very bad. Whatever is behind it, it's got to be *stopped.* But you know that.'

'Well yes . . . But what can one do?'

'That you'll have to find out. But there's no time to be lost.' Mrs Dane Calthrop rose to her feet, a whirlwind of activity. 'You must get down to it – *at once.*' She considered. 'Haven't you got some friend who could help you?'

I thought. Jim Corrigan? A busy man with little time, and already probably doing all he could. David Ardingly – but would David believe a word? Hermia? Yes, there was Hermia. A clear brain, admirable logic. A tower of strength if she could be persuaded to become an ally. After all, she and I – I did not finish the sentence. Hermia was my steady – Hermia was the person.

'You've thought of someone? Good.'

Mrs Dane Calthrop was brisk and businesslike.

'I'll keep an eye on the Three Witches. I still feel that they are – somehow – not *really* the answer. It's like when the Stamfordis woman dishes out a lot of idiocy about Egyptian mysteries and prophecies from the Pyramid texts. All she says is plain balderdash, but there *are* Pyramids and texts and temple mysteries. I can't help feeling that Thyrza Grey has got hold of something, found out about it, or heard it talked about, and is using it in a kind of wild hotchpotch to boost her own importance and control of occult powers. People are so proud of wickedness. Odd, isn't it, that people who are good are never proud of it? That's where Christian humility comes in, I suppose. They don't even know they are good.'

She was silent for a moment and then said:

'What we really need is a *link* of some kind. A link between one of these names and the Pale Horse. Something tangible.'

CHAPTER 8

Detective-Inspector Lejeune heard the well-known tune 'Father O'Flynn' being whistled outside in the passage and raised his head as Dr Corrigan came in.

'Sorry to disoblige everybody,' said Corrigan, 'but the driver of that Jaguar hadn't any alcohol in him at all . . . What P.C. Ellis smelt on his breath must have been Ellis's imagination or halitosis.'

But Lejeune at the moment was uninterested in the daily run of motorists' offences.

'Come and take a look at this,' he said.

Corrigan took the letter handed to him. It was written in a small neat script. The heading was Everest, Glendower Close, Bournemouth.

Dear Inspector Lejeune,

You may remember that you asked me to get in touch with you if I should happen to see the man who was following Father Gorman on the night that he was killed. I kept a good look-out in the neighbourhood of my establishment, but never caught a glimpse of him again.

Yesterday, however, I attended a church fête in a village about twenty miles from here. I was attracted by the fact that Mrs Oliver, the well-known detective writer, was going to be there autographing her own books. I am a great reader of detective stories and I was quite curious to see the lady.

What I did see, to my great surprise, was the man I described to you as having passed my shop the night Father Gorman was killed. Since then, it would seem, he must have met with an accident, as on this occasion he was propelling himself in a wheeled chair. I made some discreet inquiries as to who he might be, and it seems he is a local resident of the name of Venables. His place of residence is Priors Court, Much Deeping. He is said to be a man of considerable means.

Hoping these details may be of some service to you,
Yours truly,
Zachariah Osborne

'Well?' said Lejeune.

'Sounds most unlikely,' said Corrigan dampingly.

'On the face of it, perhaps. But I'm not so sure –'

'This Osborne fellow – he couldn't really have seen *anyone's* face very clearly on a foggy night like that. I expect this is just a chance resemblance. You know what people are. Ring up all over the country to say they've seen a missing person – and nine times out of ten there's no resemblance even to the printed description!'

'Osborne's not like that,' said Lejeune.

'What is he like?'

'He's a respectable dapper little chemist, old-fashioned, quite a character, and a great observer of persons. One of the dreams of his life is to be able to come forward and identify a wife poisoner who has purchased arsenic at his shop.'

Corrigan laughed.

'In that case, this is clearly an example of wishful thinking.'

'Perhaps.'

Corrigan looked at him curiously.

'So you think there may be something in it? What are you going to do about it?'

'There will be no harm, in any case, in making a few discreet inquiries about this Mr Venables of –' he referred to the letter – 'of Priors Court, Much Deeping.'

CHAPTER 9

MARK EASTERBROOK'S NARRATIVE

I

'What exciting things happen in the country!' said Hermia lightly.

We had just finished dinner. A pot of black coffee was in front of us –

I looked at her. The words were not quite what I had expected. I had spent the last quarter of an hour telling her my story. She had listened intelligently and with interest. But her response was not at all what I had expected. The tone of her voice was indulgent – she seemed neither shocked nor stirred.

'People who say that the country is dull and the towns full of excitement don't know what they are talking about,' she went on. 'The last of the witches have gone to cover in the tumble-down cottage, black masses are celebrated in remote manor houses by decadent young men. Superstition runs rife in isolated hamlets. Middle-aged spinsters clank their false scarabs and hold *séances* and planchettes run luridly over sheets of blank paper. One could really write a very amusing series of articles on it all. Why don't you try your hand?'

'I don't think you really understand what I've been telling you, Hermia.'

'But I *do*, Mark! I think it's all *tremendously* interesting. It's a page out of history, all the lingering forgotten lore of the Middle Ages.'

'I'm not interested historically,' I said irritably. 'I'm interested in the facts. In a list of names on a sheet of paper. I know what has happened to some of those people. What's going to happen or has happened to the rest?'

'Aren't you letting yourself get rather carried away?'

'No,' I said obstinately. 'I don't think so. I think the menace is real. And I'm not alone in thinking so. The vicar's wife agrees with me.'

'Oh, the vicar's wife!' Hermia's voice was scornful.

'No, not "*the vicar's wife*" like that! She's a very unusual woman. This whole thing is *real*, Hermia.'

Hermia shrugged her shoulders.

'Perhaps.'

'But *you* don't think so?'

'I think your imagination is running away with you a little, Mark. I dare say your middle-aged pussies are quite genuine in believing it all *themselves*. I'm sure they're very nasty old pussies!'

'But not really sinister?'

'Really, Mark, how *can* they be?'

I was silent for a moment. My mind wavered – turning from light to darkness and back again. The darkness of the Pale Horse, the light that Hermia represented. Good everyday sensible light – the electric light bulb firmly fixed in its socket, illuminating all the dark corners. Nothing there – nothing at all – just the everyday objects you always find in a room. But yet – but yet – Hermia's light, clear as it might make things seem, was after all an *artificial* light . . .

My mind swung back, resolutely, obstinately . . .

'I want to look into it all, Hermia. Get to the bottom of what's going on.'

'I agree. I think you should. It might be quite interesting. In fact, really rather fun.'

'Not fun!' I said sharply.

I went on:

'I wanted to ask if you'd help me, Hermia.'

'Help you? How?'

'Help me to investigate. Get right down to what this is all about.'

'But Mark dear, just at present I'm most terribly busy. There's my article for the Journal. And the Byzantium thing. And I've promised two of my students –'

Her voice went on reasonably – sensibly – I hardly listened.

'I see,' I said. 'You've too much on your plate already.'

'That's it.' Hermia was clearly relieved at my acquiescence. She smiled at me. Once again I was struck by her expression of indulgence. Such indulgence as a mother might show over her little son's absorption in his new toy.

Damn it all, I wasn't a little boy. I wasn't looking for a mother – certainly not that kind of a mother. My own mother had been charming and feckless; and everyone in sight, including her son, had adored looking after *her*.

I considered Hermia dispassionately across the table.

So handsome, so mature, so intellectual, so well read! And so – how could one put it? So – yes, so damnably *dull*!

II

The next morning I tried to get hold of Jim Corrigan – without success. I left a message, however, that I'd be in between six and seven, if he could come for a drink. He was a busy man, I knew, and I doubted if he would be able to come at such short notice, but he turned up all right at about ten minutes to seven. While I was getting him a whisky he wandered round looking at my pictures and books. He remarked finally that he wouldn't have minded being a Mogul Emperor himself instead of a hard-pressed over-worked police surgeon.

'Though, I dare say,' he remarked as he settled down in a chair, 'that they suffered a good deal from woman trouble. At least I escape that.'

'You're not married, then?'

'No fear. And no more are you, I should say, from the comfortable mess in which you live. A wife would tidy all that up in next to no time.'

I told him that I didn't think women were as bad as he made out.

I took my drink to the chair opposite him and began:

'You must wonder why I wanted to get hold of you so urgently, but as a matter of fact something has come up that may have a bearing on what we were discussing the last time we met.'

'What was that? – oh, of course. The Father Gorman business.'

'Yes – But first, does the phrase The Pale Horse mean anything to you?'

'The Pale *Horse* . . . The *Pale* Horse – No, I don't think so – why?'

'Because I think it's possible that it might have a connection with that list of names you showed me – I've been down in the country with friends – at a place called Much Deeping, and they took me to an old pub, or what was once a pub, called the Pale Horse.'

'Wait a bit! Much Deeping? Much Deeping . . . Is it anywhere near Bournemouth?'

'It's about fifteen miles or so from Bournemouth.'

'I suppose you didn't come across anyone called Venables down there?'

'Certainly I did.'

'You did?' Corrigan sat up in some excitement. 'You certainly have a knack of going places! What is he like?'

'He's a most remarkable man.'

'He is, is he? Remarkable in what way?'

'Principally in the force of his personality. Although he's completely crippled by polio –'

'Corrigan interrupted me sharply –

'*What?*'

'He had polio some years ago. He's paralysed from the waist down.'

Corrigan threw himself back in his chair with a look of disgust.

'That tears it! I thought it was too good to be true.'

'I don't understand what you mean.'

Corrigan said, 'You'll have to meet the D.D.I. Divisional Detective-Inspector Lejeune. He'll be interested in what you have to say. When Gorman was killed, Lejeune asked for information from anyone who had seen him in the street that night. Most of the answers were useless, as is usual. But there was a pharmacist, name of Osborne, who has a shop in those parts. He reported having seen Gorman pass his place that night, and he also saw a man who followed close after him – naturally he didn't think anything of it at that time. But he managed to describe this chap pretty closely – seemed quite sure he'd know him again. Well, a couple of days ago Lejeune got a letter from Osborne. He's retired, and living in Bournemouth. He'd been over to some local fête and he said he'd seen the man in question there. He was at the fête in a wheeled chair. Osborne asked who he was and was told his name was Venables.'

He looked at me questioningly. I nodded.

'Quite right,' I said. 'It was Venables. He was at the fête. But he couldn't have been the man who was walking along a street in Paddington following Father Gorman. It's physically impossible. Osborne made a mistake.'

'He described him very meticulously. Height about six feet, a prominent beaked nose, and a noticeable Adam's apple. Correct?'

'Yes. It fits Venables. But all the same –'

'I know. Mr Osborne isn't necessarily as good as he thinks he is at recognising people. Clearly he was misled by the coincidence of a chance resemblance. But it's disturbing to have you come along shooting your mouth off about that very district – talking about some pale horse or other. What is this pale horse? Let's have your story.'

'You won't believe it,' I warned him. 'I don't really believe it myself.'

'Come on. Let's have it.'

I told him of my conversation with Thyrza Grey. His reaction was immediate.

'What unutterable balderdash!'

'It is, isn't it?'

'Of course it is! What's the matter with you, Mark? White cockerels. Sacrifices, I suppose! A medium, the local witch, and a middle-aged country spinster who can send out a death ray guaranteed lethal. It's mad, man – absolutely mad!'

'Yes, it's mad,' I said heavily.

'Oh! stop agreeing with me, Mark. You make me feel there's something in it when you do that. *You* believe there's something in it, don't you?'

'Let me ask you a question first. This stuff about everybody having a secret urge or wish for death. Is there any scientific truth in that?'

Corrigan hesitated for a moment. Then he said:

'I'm not a psychiatrist. Strictly between you and me I think half these fellows are slightly barmy themselves. They're punch drunk on theories. And they go much too far. I can tell you that the police aren't at all fond of the expert medical witness who's always being called in for the defence to explain away a man's having killed some helpless old woman for the money in the till.'

'You prefer your glandular theory?'

He grinned.

'All right. All right. I'm a theorist, too. Admitted. But there's a good physical reason behind my theory – if I can ever get at it. But all this subconcious stuff! Pah!'

'You don't believe in it?'

'Of course I *believe* in it. But these chaps take it much too far. The unconscious "death wish" and all that, there's *something* in it, of course, but not nearly so much as they make out.'

'But there *is* such a thing,' I persisted.

'You'd better go and buy yourself a book on psychology and read all about it.'

'Thyrza Grey claims that she knows all there is to know.'

'Thyrza Grey!' he snorted. 'What does a half-baked spinster in a country village know about mental psychology?'

'She says she knows a lot.'

'As I said before, balderdash!'

'That,' I remarked, 'is what people have always said about any discovery that doesn't accord with recognised ideas. Frogs twitching their legs on railings –'

He interrupted me.

'So you've swallowed all this, hook, line and sinker?'

'Not at all,' I said. 'I just wanted to know if there is any scientific basis for it.'

Corrigan snorted.

'Scientific basis my foot!'

'All right. I just wanted to know.'

'You'll be saying next she's the Woman with the Box.'

'What Woman with a box?'

'Just one of the wild stories that turns up from time to time – by Nostradamus out of Mother Shipton. Some people will swallow anything.'

'You might at least tell me how you are getting on with that list of names.'

'The boys have been hard at work, but these things take time and a lot of routine work. Names without addresses or Christian names aren't easy to trace or identify.'

'Let's take it from a different angle. I'd be willing to bet you one thing. Within a fairly recent period – say a year to a year and a half – *every one of those names has appeared on a death certificate.* Am I right?'

He gave me a queer look.

'You're right – for what it's worth.'

'That's the thing they all have in common – death.'

'Yes, but that mayn't mean as much as it sounds, Mark. Have you any idea how many people die every day in the British Isles? And some of those names are quite common – which doesn't help.'

'Delafontaine,' I said. 'Mary Delafontaine. That's not a very common name, is it? The funeral was last Tuesday, I understand.'

He shot me a quick glance.

'How do you know that? Saw it in the paper. I suppose.'

'I heard it from a friend of hers.'

'There was nothing fishy about her death. I can tell you that. In fact, there's been nothing questionable about any of the deaths the police have been investigating. If they were "accidents" it *might* be suspicious. But the deaths are all perfectly normal deaths. Pneumonia, cerebral haemorrhage, tumour on the brain, gall stones, one case of polio – nothing in the least suspicious.'

I nodded.

'Not accident,' I said. 'Not poisoning. Just plain illnesses leading to death. Just as Thyrza Grey claims.'

'Are you really suggesting that that woman can cause someone she's never seen, miles away, to catch pneumonia and die of it?'

'*I'm* not suggesting such a thing. *She* did. *I* think it's fantastic and I'd *like* to think it's impossible. But there *are* certain curious factors. There's the casual mention of a Pale Horse – in connection with the removal of unwanted persons. There *is* a place called the Pale Horse – and the woman who lives there practically boasts that such an operation is possible. Living in that neighbourhood is a man who is recognised very positively as the man who was seen following Father Gorman on the night that he was killed – the night when he had been called to a dying woman who was heard to speak of "great wickedness". Rather a lot of coincidences, don't you think?'

'The man couldn't have been Venables, since according to you, he's been paralysed for years.'

'It isn't possible, from the medical point of view, that that paralysis could be faked?'

'Of course not. The limbs would be atrophied.'

'That certainly seems to settle the question,' I admitted. I sighed. 'A pity. If there is a – I don't know quite what to call it – an organisation that specialises in "Removals – Human" Venables is the kind of brain I can see running it. The things he has in that house of his represent a fantastic amount of money. Where does that money come from?'

I paused – and then said:

'All these people who have died – tidily – in their beds, of this, that and the other – were there people who profited by their deaths?'

'Someone always profits by a death – in greater or lesser degree. There were no notably suspicious circumstances, if that is what you mean.'

'It isn't quite.'

'Lady Hesketh-Dubois, as you probably know, left about fifty thousand net. A niece and a nephew inherit. Nephew lives in Canada. Niece is married and lives in North of England. Both could do with the money. Thomasina Tuckerton was left a very large fortune by her father. If she died unmarried before the age of twenty-one, it reverts to her stepmother. Stepmother seems quite a blameless creature. Then there's your Mrs Delafontaine – money left to a cousin –'

'Ah yes. And the cousin?'

'In Kenya with her husband.'

'All splendidly absent,' I commented.

Corrigan threw me an annoyed glance.

'Of the three Sandfords who've kicked the bucket, one left a wife much younger than himself who has married again – rather quickly. Deceased Sandford was an R.C., and wouldn't have given her a divorce. A fellow called Sidney Harmondsworth who died of cerebral haemorrhage was suspected at the Yard of augmenting his income by discreet blackmail. Several people in high places must be greatly relieved that he is no more.'

'What you're saying in effect is that all these deaths were *convenient* deaths. What about Corrigan?'

Corrigan grinned.

'Corrigan is a common name. Quite a lot of Corrigans have died – but not to the particular advantage of anyone in particular so far as we can learn.'

'That settles it. *You're* the next prospective victim. Take good care of yourself.'

'I will. And don't think that your Witch of Endor is going to strike me down with a duodenal ulcer, or Spanish 'flu. Not a case-hardened doctor!'

'Listen, Jim. I want to investigate this claim of Thyrza Grey's. Will you help me?'

'No, I won't! I can't understand a clever educated fellow like you being taken in by such balderdash.'

I sighed.

'Can't you use another word? I'm tired of that one.'

'Poppycock, if you like it better.'

'I don't much.'

'Obstinate fellow, aren't you, Mark?'

'As I see it,' I said, 'somebody has to be!'

CHAPTER 10

Glendower Close was very very new. It swept round in an uneven semi-circle and at its lower end the builders were still at work. About half-way along its length was a gate inscribed with the name of Everest.

Visible, bent over the garden border, planting bulbs, was a rounded back which Inspector Lejeune recognised without difficulty as that of Mr Zachariah Osborne. He opened the gate and passed inside. Mr Osborne rose from his stooping position and turned to see who had entered his domain. On recognising his visitor, an additional flush of pleasure rose to his already flushed face. Mr Osborne in the country was looking very much the same as Mr Osborne in his shop in London. He wore stout country shoes and was in his shirt sleeves, but even this déshabillé detracted little from the dapper neatness of his appearance. A fine dew of perspiration showed on the shining baldness of his domed head. This he carefully wiped with a pocket handkerchief before advancing to meet his visitor.

'Inspector Lejeune!' he exclaimed pleasurably. 'I take this as an honour. I do indeed, sir. I received your acknowledgement of my letter, but I never hoped to see you in person. Welcome to my little abode. Welcome to Everest. The name surprises you perhaps? I have always been deeply interested in the Himalayas. I followed every detail of the Everest expedition. What a triumph for our country. Sir Edmund Hillary! What a man! What endurance! As one who has never had to suffer any personal discomfort, I do appreciate the courage of those who go forth to scale unconquered mountains or sail through ice-bound seas to discover the secrets of the Pole. But come inside and partake, I beg of you, of some simple refreshment.'

Leading the way, Mr Osborne ushered Lejeune into the small bungalow which was the acme of neatness, though rather sparsely furnished.

'Not quite settled yet,' explained Mr Osborne. 'I attend local sales whenever possible. There is good stuff to be picked up that way, at a quarter of the cost one would have to pay in a shop. Now what can I offer you? A glass of sherry? Beer? A cup of tea? I could have the kettle on in a jiffy.'

Lejeune expressed a preference for beer.

'Here we are, then,' said Mr Osborne, returning a moment later with two brimming pewter tankards. 'We will sit and take our rest. Everest. Ha ha! The name of my house has a double meaning. I am always fond of a little joke.'

Those social amenities satisfied, Mr Osborne leaned forward hopefully.

'My information was of service to you?'

Lejeune softened the blow as much as possible.

'Not as much as we hoped, I am afraid.'

'Ah, I confess I am disappointed. Though, really, there is, I realise, no reason to suppose that a gentleman proceeding in the same direction as Father Gorman should necessarily be his murderer. That was really too much to hope for. And this Mr Venables is well-to-do and much respected locally, I understand, moving in the best social circles.'

'The point is,' said Lejeune, 'that it could not have been Mr Venables that you saw on that particular evening.'

'Oh, but it was. I have absolutely no doubt in my own mind. I am *never* mistaken about a face.'

'I'm afraid you must have been this time,' said Lejeune gently. 'You see, Mr Venables is a victim of polio. For over three years he has been paralysed from the waist down, and is unable to use his legs.'

'Polio!' ejaculated Mr Osborne. 'Oh dear, dear . . . That does seem to settle the matter. And yet – You'll excuse me, Inspector Lejeune. I hope you won't take offence. But that really is so? I mean you have definite medical evidence as to that?'

'Yes, Mr Osborne. We have. Mr Venables is a patient of Sir William Dugdale of Harley Street, a most eminent member of the medical profession.'

'Of course, of course. F.R.C.P. A very well known name! Oh dear, I seem to have fallen down badly. I was so very sure. And to trouble you for nothing.'

'You mustn't take it like that,' said Lejeune quickly. 'Your information is still very valuable. It is clear that the man you saw must bear a very close resemblance to Mr Venables – and since Mr Venables is a man of distinctly unusual appearance, that is extremely valuable knowledge to have. There cannot be many persons answering to that description.'

'True, true.' Mr Osborne cheered up a little. 'A man of the criminal classes resembling Mr Venables in appearance. There certainly cannot be many such. In the files at Scotland Yard –'

He looked hopefully at the inspector.

'It may not be quite so simple as that,' said Lejeune slowly. 'The man may not have a record. And in any case, as you said just now there is as yet no reason to assume that this particular man had anything to do with the attack on Father Gorman.'

Mr Osborne looked depressed again.

'You must forgive me. Wishful thinking, I am afraid, on my part . . . I should so like to have been able to give evidence at a murder trial . . . And they would not have been able to shake me, I assure you of that. Oh no, I should have stuck to my guns!'

Lejeune was silent, considering his host thoughtfully. Mr Osborne responded to the silent scrutiny.

'Yes?'

'Mr Osborne, *why* would you have stuck to your guns, as you put it?'

Mr Osborne looked astonished.

'Because I am so certain – oh – oh yes, I see what you mean. The man was *not* the man. So I have no business to feel certain. And yet I do –'

Lejeune leaned forward. 'You may have wondered why I have come to see you today. Having received medical evidence that the man seen by you could not have been Mr Venables, why am I here?'

'Quite. Quite. Well, then, Inspector Lejeune, why did you come?'

'I came,' said Lejeune, 'because the very positiveness of your identification impressed me. I wanted to know on what grounds your certainty was based. It was a foggy night, remember. I have been to your shop. I have stood where you stood in your doorway and looked across the street. On a foggy night it seemed to me that a figure at that distance would be very insubstantial, that it would be almost impossible to distinguish features clearly.'

'Up to a point, of course, you are quite right. Fog *was* setting in. But it came, if you understand me, in patches. It cleared for a short space every now and then. It did so at the moment that I saw Father Gorman walking fast along the opposite pavement. That is why I saw him and the man who followed shortly after him so clearly. Moreover, just when the second man was abreast of me, he flicked on a lighter to relight his cigarette. His profile at that moment was very clear – the nose, the chin, the pronounced Adam's apple. That's a striking-looking man, I thought. I've never seen *him* about before. If he'd ever been into my shop I'd have remembered him, I thought. So, you see –'

Mr Osborne broke off.

'Yes, I see,' said Lejeune thoughtfully.

'A brother,' suggested Mr Osborne hopefully. 'A twin brother, perhaps? Now that *would* be a solution.'

'The identical twin solution?' Lejeune smiled and shook his head. 'So very convenient in fiction. But in real life –' he shook his head. 'It doesn't happen, you know. It really doesn't happen.'

'No . . . No, I suppose not. But possibly an ordinary brother. A close family resemblance –' Mr Osborne looked wistful.

'As far as we can ascertain,' Lejeune spoke carefully, 'Mr Venables has not got a brother.'

'As far as you can ascertain?' Mr Osborne repeated the words.

'Though of British nationality, he was born abroad, his parents only brought him to England when he was eleven years old.'

'You don't know very much about him really, then? About his family, I mean?'

'No,' said Lejeune, thoughtfully. 'It isn't easy to find out very much about Mr Venables – without, that is to say, going and asking him – and we've no grounds for doing that.'

He spoke deliberately. There were ways of finding out things without going and asking, but he had no intention of telling Mr Osborne so.

'So if it wasn't for the medical evidence,' he said, getting to his feet, 'you'd be sure about the identification?'

'Oh yes,' said Mr Osborne, following suit. 'It's quite a hobby of mine, you know, memorising faces.' He chuckled. 'Many a customer I've surprised that way. "How's the asthma?" I'd say to someone – and she'd look quite surprised. "You came in last March," I'd say, "with a prescription. One of Dr Hargreaves's." And wouldn't she look surprised! Did me a lot of good in business. It pleases people to be remembered, though I wasn't as good with names as with faces. I started making a hobby of the thing quite young. If Royalty can do it, I used to say to myself, you can do it, Zachariah Osborne! After a while it becomes automatic. You hardly have to make an effort.'

Lejeune sighed.

'I'd like to have a witness like you in the box,' he said. 'Identification is always a tricky business. Most people can't tell you anything at all. They'll say things like: "Oh, tallish, I think. Fair-haired – well, not very fair, sort of middling. Ordinary sort of face. Eyes blue – or grey – or perhaps brown. Grey mackintosh – or it may have been dark blue."'

Mr Osborne laughed.

'Not much good to you, that sort of thing.'

'Frankly, a witness like you would be a godsend!'

Mr Osborne looked pleased.

'It's a gift,' he said modestly. 'But mind you, I've cultivated my gift. You know the game they play at children's parties – a lot of objects brought in on a tray and a few minutes given to memorise them. I can score a hundred per cent every time. Quite surprises people. How wonderful, they say. It's not wonderful. It's a knack. Comes with practice.' He chuckled. 'I'm not a bad conjurer either. I do a bit to amuse the kiddies at Christmas-time. Excuse me, Mr Lejeune, what *have* you got in your breast pocket?'

He leaned forward and extracted a small ash-tray.

'Tut, tut, sir, and you in the police force!'

He laughed heartily and Lejeune laughed with him. Then Mr Osborne sighed.

'It's a nice little place I've got here, sir. The neighbours seem pleasant and friendly. It's the life I've been looking forward to for years, but I'll admit to you, Mr Lejeune, that I miss the interest of my own business. Always someone coming in and out. Types, you know, lots of types to study. I've looked forward to having my little bit of garden, and I've got quite a lot of interests. Butterflies, as I told you, and a bit of bird watching now and again. I didn't realise that I'd miss what I might call the human element so much.

'I'd looked forward to going abroad in a small way. Well, I've taken one week-end trip to France. Quite nice, I must say – but I felt, very strongly, that England's really good enough for me. I didn't care for the foreign cooking, for one thing. They haven't the least idea, as far as I can see, how to do eggs and bacon.'

He sighed again.

'Just shows you what human nature is. Looked forward no end to retiring, I did. And now – do you know I've actually played with the idea of buying a small share in a pharmaceutical business here in Bournemouth – just enough to give me an interest, no need to be tied to the shop all the time. But I'd feel in the middle of things again. It will be the same with you, I expect. You'll make plans ahead, but when the time comes, you'll miss the excitement of your present life.'

Lejeune smiled.

'A policeman's life is not such a romantically exciting one as you think, Mr Osborne. You've got the amateur's view of crime. Most of it is dull routine. We're not always chasing down criminals, and following up mysterious clues. It can be quite a dull business, really.'

Mr Osborne looked unconvinced.

'You know best,' he said. 'Good-bye, Mr Lejeune, and I'm sorry indeed that I haven't been able to help you. If there was anything – anytime –'

'I'll let you know,' Lejeune promised him.

'That day at the fête, it seemed such a chance,' Osborne murmured sadly.

'I know. A pity the medical evidence is so definite, but one can't get over that sort of thing, can one?'

'Well –' Mr Osborne let the word linger, but Lejeune did not notice it. He strode away briskly. Mr Osborne stood by the gate looking after him.

'Medical evidence,' he said. 'Doctors indeed! If he knew half what I know about doctors – innocents, that's what *they* are! Doctors indeed!'

CHAPTER 11

MARK EASTERBROOK'S NARRATIVE

I

First Hermia. Now Corrigan.

All right, then, I was making a fool of myself!

I was accepting balderdash as solid truth. I had been hypnotised by that phony woman Thyrza Grey into accepting a farrago of nonsense. I was a credulous, superstitious ass.

I decided to forget the whole damned business. What was it to do with me anyway?

Through the mist of disillusionment, I heard the echoes of Mrs Dane Calthrop's urgent tones.

'*You've got to DO something!*'

All very well – to say things like that.

'*You need someone to help you . . .*'

I had needed Hermia. I had needed Corrigan. But neither of them would play. There was no one else.

Unless –

I sat – considering the idea.

On an impulse I went to the telephone and rang Mrs Oliver.

'Hallo. Mark Easterbrook here.'

'Yes?'

'Can you tell me the name of that girl who was staying in the house for the fête?'

'I expect so. Let me see . . . Yes, of course, Ginger. That was her name.'

'I know that. But her other name.'

'What other name?'

'I doubt if she was christened Ginger. And she must have a surname.'

'Well, of course. But I've no idea what it is. One never seems to hear any surnames nowadays. It's the first time I'd ever met her.' There was a slight pause and then Mrs Oliver said, 'You'll have to ring up Rhoda and ask her.'

I didn't like that idea. Somehow I felt shy about it.

'Oh, I can't do that,' I said.

'It's perfectly simple,' said Mrs Oliver encouragingly. 'Just say you've lost her address and can't remember her name and you'd promised to send her one of your books, or the name of a shop that sells cheap caviare, or to return a handkerchief which she lent you when your nose bled one day, or the address of a rich friend who wants a picture restored. Any of those do? I can think of lots more if you'd like.'

'One of those will do beautifully,' I assured her.

I rang off, dialled 100 and presently was speaking to Rhoda.

'Ginger?' said Rhoda. 'Oh, she lives in a Mews. Calgary Place. Forty-five. Wait a minute. I'll give you her telephone number.' She went away and returned a minute later. 'It's Capricorn 35987. Got it?'

'Yes, thanks. But I haven't got her name. I never heard it.'

'Her name? Oh, her *surname*, you mean. Corrigan. Katherine Corrigan. What did you say?'

'Nothing. Thanks, Rhoda.'

It seemed to me an odd coincidence. Corrigan. Two Corrigans. Perhaps it was an omen.

I dialled Capricorn 35987.

II

Ginger sat opposite me at a table in the White Cockatoo where we had met for a drink. She looked refreshingly the same as she had looked at Much Deeping – a tousled mop of red hair, an engaging freckled face and alert green eyes. She was wearing her London artistic livery of skin-tight pants, a Sloppy Joe jersey and black woollen stockings – but otherwise she was the same Ginger. I liked her very much.

'I've had to do a lot of work to track you down,' I said. 'Your surname and your address and your telephone number – all unknown. I've got a problem.'

'That's what my daily always says. It usually means that I have to buy her a new saucepan scourer or a carpet brush, or something dull.'

'You don't have to buy anything,' I assured her.

Then I told her. It didn't take quite so long as the story I had told to Hermia, because she was already familiar with the Pale Horse and its occupants. I averted my eyes from her as I finished the tale. I didn't want to see her reaction. I didn't want to see indulgent amusement, or stark incredulity. The whole thing sounded more idiotic than ever. No one (except Mrs Dane Calthrop) could possibly feel about it as I felt. I drew patterns on the plastic table top with a stray fork.

Ginger's voice came briskly.

'That's all, is it?'

'That's all,' I admitted.

'What are you going to do about it?'

'You think – I *should* do something about it?'

'Well, of course! *Someone's* got to do something! You can't have an organisation going about bumping people off and not do *anything*.'

'But what *can* I do?'

I could have fallen on her neck and hugged her.

She was sipping *Pernod* and frowning. Warmth spread over me. I was no longer alone.

Presently she said musingly:

'You'll have to find out what it all means.'

'I agree. But how?'

'There seem to be one or two leads. Perhaps I can help.'

'Would you? But there's your job.'

'Plenty could be done out of office hours.' She frowned again as she thought.

'That girl,' she said at last. 'The one at supper after the Old Vic. Poppy or something. She knows about it – she must do – to say what she did.'

'Yes, but she got frightened, and sheered off when I tried to ask her questions. She was scared. She definitely wouldn't talk.'

'That's where I can help,' said Ginger confidently. 'She'd tell me things she wouldn't tell you. Can you arrange for us to meet? Your friend and her and you and me? A show, or dinner or something?' Then she looked doubtful. 'Or is that too expensive?'

I assured her that I could support the expense.

'As for you –' Ginger thought a minute. 'I believe,' she said slowly, 'that your best bet would be the Thomasina Tuckerton angle.'

'But how? She's dead.'

'And somebody wanted her dead, if your ideas are correct! And arranged it with the Pale Horse. There seem two possibilities. The stepmother, or else the girl she had the fight with at Luigi's and whose young man she had pinched. She was going to marry him, perhaps. That wouldn't suit the stepmother's book – or the girl's – if she was crazy enough about the young man. Either of them might have gone to the Pale Horse. We might get a lead there. What was the girl's name, or don't you know?'

'I think it was Lou.'

'Ash blonde lank hair, medium height, rather bosomy?'

I agreed with the description.

'I think I've met her about. Lou Ellis. She's got a bit of money herself –'

'She didn't look like it.'

'They don't – but she has, all right. Anyway, she could afford to pay the Pale Horse's fees. They don't do it for nothing, I suppose.'

'One would hardly imagine so.'

'You'll have to tackle the stepmother. It's more up your street than mine. Go and see her –'

'I don't know where she lives or anything.'

'Luigi knows something about Tommy's home. He'll know what county she lives in, I should imagine. A few books of reference ought to do the rest. But what idiots we are! You saw the notice in *The Times* of her death. You've only got to go and look in their files.'

'I'll have to have a pretext for tackling the stepmother,' I said thoughtfully.

Ginger said that that would be easy.

'You're *someone*, you see,' she pointed out. 'A historian, and you lecture and you've got letters after your name. Mrs Tuckerton will be impressed, and probably tickled to death to see you.'

'And the pretext?'

'Some feature of interest about her house?' suggested Ginger vaguely. 'Sure to have something if it's an old one.'

'Nothing to do with my period,' I objected.

'She won't know that,' said Ginger. 'People always think that anything over a hundred years old must interest a historian or an archaeologist. Or how about a picture? There must be some old pictures of some kind. Anyway, you make an appointment and you arrive and you butter her up and be charming, and then you say you once met her daughter – her stepdaughter – and say how sad etc. . . . And then, bring in, quite suddenly, a reference to the Pale Horse. Be a little sinister if you like.'

'And then?'

'And then you observe the reaction. If you mention the Pale Horse out of the blue, and she has a guilty conscience, I defy anyone not to show *some* sign.'

'And if she does – what next?'

'The important thing is, that we'll know we're on the right track. Once we're *sure*, we can go full steam ahead.'

She nodded thoughtfully.

'There's something else. Why do you think the Grey woman told you all she did tell you? Why was she so forthcoming?'

'The common-sense answer is because she's potty.'

'I don't mean that. I mean – why *you?* You in particular? I just wondered if there might be some kind of tie up?'

'Tie up with what?'

'Wait just a minute – while I get my ideas in order.'

I waited. Ginger nodded twice emphatically and then spoke.

'Supposing – just supposing – it went like this. The Poppy girl knows all about the Pale Horse in a vague kind of way – not through personal knowledge, but by hearing it talked about. She sounds the sort of girl that wouldn't be noticed much by anyone when they were talking – but she'd quite likely take in a lot more than they thought she did. Rather silly people are often like that. Say she was overheard talking to you about it that night, and someone ticks her off. Next day you come and ask her questions, and she's been scared, so she won't talk. But the fact that you've come and asked her also gets around. Now what would be the reason for your asking questions? You're not the police. The *likely* reason would be that you're a possible *client*.'

'But surely –'

'It's logical, I tell you. You've heard rumours of this thing – you want to find out about it – for your own purposes. Presently you appear at the fête in Much Deeping. You are brought to the Pale Horse – presumably because you've asked to be taken there – and what happens? Thyrza Grey goes straight into her sales talk.'

'I suppose it's a possibility.' I considered . . . 'Do you think she can do what she claims to do, Ginger?'

'Personally I'd be inclined to say of course she can't! But odd things *can* happen. Especially with things like hypnotism. Telling someone to go and take a bite out of a candle the next afternoon at four o'clock, and they do it without having any idea *why*. That *sort* of thing. And electric boxes where you put in a drop of blood and it tells you if you're going to have cancer in two years' time. It all sounds rather bogus – but perhaps not entirely bogus. About Thyrza – I don't *think* it's true – but I'm terribly afraid it *might* be!'

'Yes,' I said sombrely, 'that explains it very well.'

'I might put in a bit of work on Lou,' said Ginger thoughtfully. 'I know lots of places where I can run across her. Luigi might know a few things too.

'But the first thing,' she added, 'is to get in touch with Poppy.'

The latter was arranged fairly easily. David was free three nights ahead, we settled on a musical show, and he arrived, with Poppy in tow. We went to the Fantasie for supper and I noticed that Ginger and Poppy after a prolonged retirement to powder their noses, reappeared on excellent terms with each other. No controversial subjects were raised during the party on Ginger's instructions. We finally parted and I drove Ginger home.

'Not much to report,' she said cheerfully. 'I've been on to Lou. The man they quarrelled about was Gene Pleydon, by the way. A nasty bit of goods, if you ask me. Very much on the make. The girls all adore him. He was making quite a play for Lou and then Tommy came along. Lou says he didn't care for her a bit, he was after her money – but she'd probably want to think that. Anyway, he dropped Lou like a hot coal and she was naturally sore about it. According to her, it wasn't much of a row – just a few girlish high spirits.'

'Girlish high spirits! She tugged Tommy's hair out by the roots.'

'I'm just telling you what Lou told me.'

'She seems to have been very forthcoming.'

'Oh, they all like talking about their affairs. They'll talk to anyone who will listen. Anyway, Lou has got another boy friend now – another dud, I'd say, but she's already crazy about him. So it doesn't look to me as though she'd been a client of the Pale Horse. I brought the term up, but it didn't register. I think we can wash her out. Luigi doesn't think there was much in it, either. On the other hand, he thinks Tommy *was* serious about Gene. And Gene was going for her in a big way. What have you done about the stepmother?'

'She was abroad. She comes back tomorrow. I've written her a letter – or rather I got my secretary to write it, asking for an appointment.'

'Good. We're getting things moving. I hope everything doesn't peter out.'

'If it gets us anywhere!'

'Something will,' said Ginger enthusiastically. 'That reminds me. To go back to the beginning of all this, the theory is that Father Gorman was killed after being called out to a dying woman, and that he was murdered because of something she told him or confessed to him. What happened to that woman? Did she die? And who was she? There ought to be some lead there.'

'She died. I don't really know much about her. I think her name was Davis.'

'Well, couldn't you find out more?'

'I'll see what I can do.'

'If we could get at her background, we might find out how she knew what she did know.'

'I see your point.'

I got Jim Corrigan on the telephone early the next morning and put my query to him.

'Let me see now. We did get a bit further, but not much. Davis wasn't her real name, that's why it took a little time to check up on her. Half a moment, I jotted down a few things . . . Oh yes, here we are. Her real name was Archer, and her husband had been a small-time crook. She left him and went back to her maiden name.'

'What sort of a crook was Archer? And where is he now?'

'Oh, very small stuff. Pinched things from department stores. Unconsidered trifles here and there. He had a few convictions. As to where he is now, he's dead.'

'Not much there.'

'No, there isn't. The firm Mrs Davis was working for at the time of her death, the C.R.C. (Customers' Reactions Classified), apparently didn't know anything about her, or her background.'

I thanked him and rang off.

CHAPTER 12

MARK EASTERBROOK'S NARRATIVE

Three days later Ginger rang me up.

'I've got something for you,' she said. 'A name and address. Write it down.'

I took out my notebook.

'Go ahead.'

'Bradley is the name and the address is Seventy-eight Municipal Square Buildings, Birmingham.'

'Well, I'm damned, what is all this?'

'Goodness knows! I don't. I doubt if Poppy does really!'

'Poppy? Is this –'

'Yes. I've been working on Poppy in a big way. I told you I

could get something out of her if I tried. Once I got her softened up, it was easy.'

'How did you set about it?' I asked curiously.

Ginger laughed.

'Girls-together stuff. You wouldn't understand. The point is that if a girl tells things to another girl it doesn't really count. She doesn't think it matters.'

'All in the trade union so to speak?'

'You could put it like that. Anyway, we lunched together, and I yapped a bit about my love life – and various obstacles – married man with impossible wife – Catholic – wouldn't divorce him – made his life hell. And how she was an invalid, always in pain, but not likely to die for years. Really much better for her if she *could* die. Said I'd a good mind to try the Pale Horse, but I didn't really know how to set about it – and would it be terribly expensive? And Poppy said yes, she thought it would. She'd heard they charged the earth. And I said "Well, I *have* expectations." Which I have, you know – a great-uncle – a poppet and I'd hate him to die, but the fact came in useful. Perhaps, I said, they'd take something on account? But how did one set about it? And then Poppy came across with that name and address. You had to go to him first, she said, to settle the business side.'

'It's fantastic!' I said.

'It is, rather.'

We were both silent for a moment.

I said incredulously: 'She told you quite openly? She didn't seem – scared?'

Ginger said impatiently: 'You don't understand. Telling me didn't count. And after all, Mark, if what we think is true the business has to be more or less advertised, hasn't it? I mean they must want new "clients" all the time.'

'We're mad to believe anything of the kind.'

'All right. We're mad. Are you going to Birmingham to see Mr Bradley?'

'Yes,' I said. 'I'm going to see Mr Bradley. If he exists.'

I hardly believed that he did. But I was wrong. Mr Bradley did exist.

Municipal Square Buildings was an enormous honeycomb of

offices. Seventy-eight was on the third floor. On the ground-glass door was neatly printed in black: *C. R. Bradley, COMMISSION AGENT*. And below, in smaller letters: *Please enter*.

I entered.

There was a small outer office, empty, and a door marked *PRIVATE*, half ajar. A voice from behind it said:

'Come in, please.'

The inner office was larger. It had a desk, one or two comfortable chairs, a telephone, a stack of box files, and Mr Bradley sitting behind the desk.

He was a small dark man, with shrewd dark eyes. He wore a dark business suit and looked the acme of respectability.

'Just shut the door, will you?' he said pleasantly. 'And sit down. That chair's quite comfortable. Cigarette? No? Well now, what can I do for you?'

I looked at him. I didn't know how to begin. I hadn't the least idea what to say. It was, I think, sheer desperation that led me to attack with the phrase I did. Or it may have been the small beady eyes.

'How much?' I said.

It startled him a little, I was glad to note, but not in the way that he ought to have been startled. He did not assume, as I would have assumed in his place, that someone not quite right in the head had come into his office.

His eyebrows rose.

'Well, well, well,' he said. 'You don't waste much time, do you?'

I held to my line.

'What's the answer?'

He shook his head gently in a slightly reproving manner.

'That's not the way to go about things. We must proceed in the proper manner.'

I shrugged my shoulders.

'As you like. What's the proper manner?'

'We haven't introduced ourselves yet, have we? I don't know your name.'

'At the moment,' I said, 'I don't really think I feel inclined to tell it to you.'

'Cautious.'

'Cautious.'

'An admirable quality – though not always practicable. Now who sent you to me? Who's our mutual friend?'

'Again I can't tell you. A friend of mine has a friend who knows a friend of yours.'

Mr Bradley nodded his head.

'That's the way a lot of my clients come,' he said. 'Some of the problems are rather – delicate. You know my profession, I presume?'

He had no intention of waiting for my reply. He hastened to give me the answer.

'Turf Commission Agent,' he said. 'You're interested, perhaps, in – horses?'

There was just the faintest pause before the last word.

'I'm not a racing man,' I said non-committally.

'There are many aspects of the horse. Racing, hunting, hacking. It's the sporting aspect that interests me. Betting.' He paused for a moment and then asked casually – almost too casually:

'Any particular horse you had in mind?'

I shrugged my shoulders and burnt my boats.

'A pale horse . . .'

'Ah, very good, excellent. You yourself, if I may say so, seem to be rather a *dark* horse. Ha ha! You mustn't be nervous. There really is no need to be nervous.'

'That's what *you* say,' I said rather rudely.

Mr Bradley's manner became more bland and soothing.

'I can quite understand your feelings. But I can assure you that you needn't have any anxiety. I'm a lawyer myself – disbarred, of course,' he added parenthetically, in what was really almost an engaging way. 'Otherwise I shouldn't be here. But I can assure you that I know my law. Everything I recommend is perfectly legal and above board. It's just a question of a bet. A man can bet on anything he pleases, whether it will rain tomorrow, whether the Russians can send a man to the moon, or whether your wife's going to have twins. You can bet whether Mrs B. will die before Christmas, or whether Mrs C. will live to be a hundred. You back your judgement or your intuition or whatever you like to call it. It's as simple as that.'

I felt exactly as though I were being reasssured by a surgeon before an operation. Mr Bradley's consulting-room manner was perfect.

I said slowly:

'I don't really understand this business of the Pale Horse.'

'And that worries you? Yes, it worries a lot of people. More things in heaven and earth, Horatio, and so on and so on. Frankly, I don't understand it myself. But it gets results. It gets results in the most marvellous way.'

'If you could tell me more about it –'

I had settled on my role now – cautious, eager – but scared. It was obviously an attitude with which Mr Bradley had frequently had to cope.

'Do you know the place at all?'

I made a quick decision. It would be unwise to lie.

'I – well – yes – I was with some friends. They took me there –'

'Charming old pub. Full of historical interest. And they've done wonders in restoring it. You met her, then. My friend, Miss Grey, I mean?'

'Yes – yes, of course. An extraordinary woman.'

'Isn't she? Yes, isn't she? You've hit it exactly. An extraordinary woman. And with extraordinary powers.'

'The things she claims! Surely – quite – well – impossible?'

'Exactly. That's the whole point. The things she claims to be able to know and *do* are impossible! Everybody would say so. In a court of law, for instance –'

The black beady eyes were boring into mine. Mr Bradley repeated the words with designed emphasis.

'In a court of law, for instance – the whole thing would be ridiculed! If that woman stood up and confessed to murder, murder by remote control or "will power" or whatever nonsensical name she likes to use, that confession couldn't be acted upon! Even if her statement was true (which of course sensible men like you and I don't believe for one moment!) it couldn't be admitted legally. Murder by remote control isn't murder in the eyes of the law. It's just nonsense. That's the whole beauty of the thing – as you'll appreciate if you think for a moment.'

I understood that I was being reassured. Murder committed by occult powers was not murder in an English court of law. If I were to hire a gangster to commit murder with a cosh or a knife, I was committed with him – an accomplice before the fact – I had conspired with him. But if I commissioned Thyrza Grey to use her black arts – those black arts were not admissible. That was what, according to Mr Bradley, was the beauty of the thing.

All my natural scepticism rose up in protest. I burst out heatedly:

'But damn it all, it's fantastic,' I shouted. 'I don't believe it. It's impossible.'

'I agree with you. I really do. Thyrza Grey is an extraordinary woman, and she certainly has some extraordinary powers, but one *can't* believe all the things she claims for herself. As you say, it's too fantastic. In this age, one really can't credit that someone can send out thought-waves or whatever it is, either oneself or through a medium, sitting in a cottage in England and cause someone to sicken and die of a convenient disease out in Capri or somewhere like that.'

'But that *is* what she claims?'

'Oh yes. Oh course she *has* powers – she is Scottish and what is called second sight is a peculiarity of that race. It really does exist. What I do believe, and believe without a doubt, is this': he leaned forward, wagging a forefinger impressively, 'Thyrza Grey does know – beforehand – when someone is going to die. It's a gift. And she has it.'

He leaned back, studying me. I waited.

'Let's assume a hypothetical case. Someone, yourself or another, would like very much to know when – let's say Great-Aunt Eliza – is going to die. It's useful, you must admit, to know something like that. Nothing unkind in it, nothing wrong – just a matter of business convenience. What plans to make? Will there be, shall we say, a useful sum of money coming in by next November? If you knew that, definitely, you might take up some valuable option. Death is such a chancy matter. Dear old Eliza might live, pepped up by doctors, for another ten years. You'd be delighted, of course, you're fond of the dear old girl, but how useful it would be to *know*.'

He paused and then leaned a little farther forward.

'Now that's where *I* come in. I'm a betting man. I'll bet on anything – naturally on my own terms. You come to see me.

Naturally you wouldn't want to bet on the old girl's passing out. That would be repulsive to your finer feelings. So we put it this way. You bet me a certain sum that Aunt Eliza will be hale and hearty still next Christmas, I bet you that she won't.'

The beady eyes were on me, watching . . .

'Nothing against that, is there? Simple. We have an argument on the subject. I say Aunt E. is lined up for death, you say she isn't. We draw up a contract and sign it. I give you a date. I say that a fortnight either way from that date Auntie E.'s funeral service will be read. You say it won't. If you're right – *I* pay *you*. If you're wrong, you – pay *me!*'

I looked at him. I tried to summon up the feelings of a man who wants a rich old lady out of the way. I shifted it to a blackmailer. Easier to throw oneself into that part. Some man had been bleeding me for years. I couldn't bear it any longer. I wanted him dead. I hadn't the nerve to kill him myself, but I'd give anything – yes, anything –'

I spoke – my voice was hoarse. I was acting the part with some confidence.

'What terms?'

Mr Bradley's manner underwent a rapid change. It was gay, almost facetious.

'That's where we came in, isn't it? Or rather where you came in, ha ha. "How much?" you said. Really quite startled me. Never heard anyone come to the point so soon.'

'What terms?'

'That depends. It depends on several different factors. Roughly it depends on the amount there is at stake. In some cases it depends on the funds available to the client. An inconvenient husband – or a blackmailer or something of that kind – would depend on how much my client could afford to pay. I don't – let me make that clear – bet with poor clients – except in the kind of case I have just been outlining. In that case it would depend on the amount of Aunt Eliza's estate. Terms are by mutual agreement. We both want something out of it, don't we? The odds, however, work out usually at five hundred to one.'

'Five hundred to one? That's pretty steep.'

'My wager is pretty steep. If Aunt Eliza were pretty well booked for the tomb, you'd know it already, and you wouldn't come to me. To prophesy somebody's death to within two weeks means pretty long odds. Five thousand pounds to one hundred isn't at all out of the way.'

'Supposing you lose?'

Mr Bradley shrugged his shoulders.

'That's just too bad. I pay up.'

'And if I lose, I pay up. Supposing I don't?'

Mr Bradley leaned back in his chair. He half closed his eyes.

'I shouldn't advise that,' he said softly. 'I really shouldn't.'

Despite the soft tone, I felt a faint shiver pass over me. He had uttered no direct menace. But the menace was there.

I got up. I said:

'I – I must think it over.'

Mr Bradley was once more his pleasant and urbane self.

'Certainly think it over. Never rush into anything. If you decide to do business, come back, and we will go into the matter fully. Take your time. No hurry in the world. Take your time.'

I went out with those words echoing in my ears.

'Take your time . . .'

CHAPTER 13

MARK EASTERBROOK'S NARRATIVE

I approached my task of interviewing Mrs Tuckerton with the utmost reluctance. Goaded to it by Ginger, I was still far from convinced of its wisdom. To begin with I felt myself unfitted for the task I had set myself. I was doubtful of my ability to produce the needed reaction, and I was acutely conscious of masquerading under false colours.

Ginger, with the almost terrifying efficiency which she was able to display when it suited her, had briefed me by telephone.

'It will be quite simple. It's a Nash house. Not the usual style one associates with him. One of his near-Gothic flights of fancy.'

'And why should I want to see it?'

'You're considering writing an article or a book on the influences that cause fluctuation of an architect's style. That sort of thing.'

'Sounds very bogus to me,' I said.

'Nonsense,' said Ginger robustly. 'When you get on to learned subjects, or arty ones, the most incredible theories are propounded and written about, in the utmost seriousness, by the most unlikely people. I could quote you chapters of tosh.'

'That's why you would really be a much better person to do this than I am.'

'That's where you are wrong,' Ginger told me. 'Mrs T. can look you up in *Who's Who* and be properly impressed. She can't look me up there.'

I remained unconvinced, though temporarily defeated.

On my return from my incredible interview with Mr Bradley, Ginger and I had put our heads together. It was less incredible to her than it was to me. It afforded her, indeed, a distinct satisfaction.

'It puts an end to whether we're imagining things or not,' she pointed out. 'Now we know that an organisation *does* exist for getting unwanted people out of the way.'

'By supernatural means!'

'You're so hidebound in your thinking. It's all that wispiness and the false scarabs that Sybil wears. It puts you off. And if Mr Bradley had turned out to be a quack practitioner, or a pseudo-astrologer, you'd still be unconvinced. But since he turns out to be a nasty down-to-earth little legal crook – or that's the impression you give me –'

'Near enough,' I said.

'Then that makes the whole thing come into line. However phony it may sound, those three women at the Pale Horse have got hold of something that *works*.'

'If you're so convinced, then why Mrs Tuckerton?'

'Extra check,' said Ginger. 'We know what Thyrza Grey *says* she can do. We know how the financial side is worked. We know a little about three of the victims. We want to know more about the client angle.'

'And suppose Mrs Tuckerton shows no signs of having been a client?'

'Then we'll have to investigate elsewhere.'

'Of course, I may boob it,' I said gloomily.

Ginger said that I must think better of myself than that.

So here I was, arriving at the front door of Carraway Park.

It certainly did not look like my preconceived idea of a Nash house. In many ways it was a near castle of modest proportions. Ginger had promised to supply me with a recent book on Nash architecture, but it had not arrived in time, so I was here somewhat inadequately briefed.

I rang the bell, and a rather seedy-looking man in an alpaca coat opened the door.

'Mr Easterbrook?' he said. 'Mrs Tuckerton's expecting you.'

He showed me into an elaborately furnished drawing-room. The room made a disagreeable impression upon me. Everything in it was expensive, but chosen without taste. Left to itself, it could have been a room of pleasant proportions. There were one or two good pictures, and a great many bad ones. There was a great deal of yellow brocade. Further cogitations were interrupted by the arrival of Mrs Tuckerton herself. I arose with difficulty from the depths of a bright yellow brocade sofa.

I don't know what I had expected, but I suffered a complete reversal of feeling. There was nothing sinister here; merely a completely ordinary young to middle-aged woman. Not a very interesting woman, and not, I thought, a particularly nice woman. The lips, in spite of a generous application of lipstick, were thin and bad-tempered. The chin receded a little. The eyes were pale blue and gave the impression that she was appraising the price of everything. She was the sort of woman who undertipped porters and cloakroom attendants. There are a lot of women of her type to be met in the world, though mainly less expensively dressed, and not so well made-up.

'Mr Easterbrook?' She was clearly delighted by my visit. She even gushed a little. 'I'm *so* pleased to meet you. Fancy your being interested in this house. Of course I knew it was built by John Nash, my husband told me so, but I never realised that it would be interesting to a person like *you*!'

'Well, you see, Mrs Tuckerton, it's not quite his usual style, and that makes it interesting to – er –'

She saved me the trouble of continuing.

'I'm afraid I'm terribly stupid about that sort of thing – architecture, I mean, and archaeology and all that. But you mustn't mind my ignorance –'

I didn't mind at all. I preferred it.

'Of course all that sort of thing is terribly interesting,' said Mrs Tuckerton.

I said that we specialists, on the contrary, were usually terribly dull and very boring on our own particular subject.

Mrs Tuckerton said she was sure that *that* wasn't true, and would I like to have tea first and see the house afterwards, or see round the house and then have tea.

I hadn't bargained for tea – my appointment had been for three-thirty, but I said that perhaps the house first.

She showed me round, chatting vivaciously most of the time, and thus relieving me of uttering any architectural judgements.

It was lucky, she said, that I'd come now. The house was up for sale – 'It's too big for me – since my husband's death' – and she believed there was a purchaser already, though the agents had only had it on their books for just over a week.

'I wouldn't have liked you to see it when it was empty. I think a house needs to be lived in, if one is really to appreciate it, don't you, Mr Easterbrook?'

I would have preferred this house unlived in, and unfurnished, but naturally I could not say so. I asked her if she was going to remain in the neighbourhood.

'Really, I'm not quite sure. I shall travel a little first. Get into the sunshine. I hate this miserable climate. Actually I think I shall winter in Egypt. I was there two years ago. Such a wonderful country, but I expect *you* know all about it.'

I knew nothing about Egypt and said so.

'I expect you're just being modest,' she said gaily and vaguely. 'This is the dining-room. It's octagonal. That's right, isn't it? No corners.'

I said she was quite right and praised the proportions.

Presently, the tour was completed, we returned to the drawing-room and Mrs Tuckerton rang for tea. It was brought in by the seedy-looking manservant. There was a vast Victorian silver teapot which could have done with a clean.

Mrs Tuckerton sighed as he left the room.

'After my husband died, the married couple he had had for nearly twenty years insisted on leaving. They said they were retiring, but I heard afterwards that they took another post. A very highly-paid one. I think it's absurd, myself, to pay these high wages. When you think what servants' board and lodging costs – to say nothing of their laundry.'

Yes, I thought, mean. The pale eyes, the tight mouth – avarice was there.

There was no difficulty in getting Mrs Tuckerton to talk. She liked talking. She liked, in particular, talking about herself. Presently, by listening with close attention, and uttering an encouraging word now and then, I knew a good deal about Mrs Tuckerton. I knew, too, more than she was conscious of telling me.

I knew that she had married Thomas Tuckerton, a widower, five years ago. She had been 'much, much younger than he was.' She had met him at a big seaside hotel where she had been a bridge hostess. She was not aware that that last fact had slipped out. He had had a daughter at school near there – 'so difficult for a man to know what to do with a girl when he takes her out.

'Poor Thomas, he was so lonely . . . His first wife had died some years back and he missed her very much.'

Mrs Tuckerton's picture of herself continued. A gracious kindly woman taking pity on this ageing lonely man. His deteriorating health and her devotion.

'Though, of course, in the last stages of his illness I couldn't really have *any* friends of my own.'

Had there been, I wondered, some men friends whom Thomas Tuckerton had thought undesirable? It might explain the terms of his will.

Ginger had looked up the terms of his will for me at Somerset House.

Bequests to old servants, to a couple of godchildren, and then provision for his wife – sufficient, but not unduly generous. A sum in trust, the income to be enjoyed during her lifetime. The residue of his estate, which ran into a sum of six figures, to his daughter Thomasina Ann, to be hers absolutely at the age of twenty-one, or on her marriage. If she died before twenty-one unmarried, the money was to go to her stepmother. There had been, it seemed, no other members of the family.

The prize, I thought, had been a big one. And Mrs Tuckerton liked money . . . It stuck out all over her. She had never had any money of her own, I was sure, till she married her elderly widower. And then, perhaps, it had gone to her head. Hampered, in her life with an invalid husband, she had looked forward to the time when she would be free, still young, and rich beyond her wildest dreams.

The will, perhaps, had been a disappointment. She had dreamed of something better than a moderate income. She had looked forward to expensive travel, to luxury cruises, to clothes, jewels – or possibly to the sheer pleasure of money itself – mounting up in the bank.

Instead the girl was to have all that money! The girl was to be a wealthy heiress. The girl who, very likely, had disliked her stepmother and shown it with the careless ruthlessness of youth. The girl was to be the rich one – unless . . .

Unless . . . ? Was that enough? Could I really believe that the blonde-haired meretricious creature talking platitudes so glibly was capable of seeking out the Pale Horse, and arranging for a young girl to die?

No, I couldn't believe it . . .

Nevertheless, I must do my stuff. I said, rather abruptly:

'I believe, you know, I met your daughter – stepdaughter – once.'

She looked at me in mild surprise, though without much interest.

'Thomasina? Did you?'

'Yes, in Chelsea.'

'Oh, Chelsea! Yes, it would be . . .' She sighed. 'These girls nowadays. So difficult. One doesn't seem to have *any* control over them. It upset her father very much. *I* couldn't do anything about it, of course. She never listened to anything *I* said.' She sighed again. 'She was nearly grown-up, you know, when we married. A stepmother –' she shook her head.

'Always a difficult position,' I said sympathetically.

'I made allowances – did my best in every way.'

'I'm sure you did.'

'But it was absolutely no use. Of course Tom wouldn't allow her to be actually rude to me, but she sailed as near to the wind as she could. She really made life quite impossible. In a way it was a relief to me when she insisted on leaving home, but I could quite understand how Tom felt about it. She got in with a most undesirable set.'

'I – rather gathered that,' I said.

'Poor Thomasina,' said Mrs Tuckerton. She adjusted a stray lock of blonde hair. Then she looked at me. 'Oh, but perhaps you don't know. She died about a month ago. Encephalitis – very sudden. It's a disease that attacks young people, I believe – so sad.'

'I did know she was dead,' I said.

I got up.

'Thank you, Mrs Tuckerton, very much indeed for showing me your house.' I shook hands.

Then as I moved away, I turned back.

'By the way,' I said, 'I think you know the Pale Horse, don't you?'

There wasn't any doubt of the reaction. Panic, sheer panic, showed in those pale eyes. Beneath the make-up, her face was suddenly white and afraid.

Her voice came shrill and high:

'Pale Horse? What do you mean by the Pale Horse? I don't know anything about the Pale Horse.'

I let mild surprise show in my eyes.

'Oh – my mistake. There's a very interesting old pub – in Much Deeping. I was down there the other day and was taken to see it. It's been charmingly converted, keeping all the atmosphere. I certainly *thought* your name was mentioned – but perhaps it was your stepdaughter who had been down there – or someone else of the same name.' I paused. 'The place has got – quite a reputation.'

I enjoyed my exit line. In one of the mirrors on the wall I saw Mrs Tuckerton's face reflected. She was staring after me. She was very, very frightened and I saw just how she would look in years to come . . . It was not a pleasant sight.

CHAPTER 14

MARK EASTERBROOK'S NARRATIVE

I

'So now we're quite sure,' said Ginger.

'We were sure before.'

'Yes – reasonably so. But this does clinch it.'

I was silent for a moment or two. I was visualising Mrs

Tuckerton journeying to Birmingham. Entering the Municipal Square Buildings – meeting Mr Bradley. Her nervous apprehension . . . his reassuring bonhomie. His skilful underlining of the lack of risk. (He would have had to underline that very hard with Mrs Tuckerton.) I could see her going away, not committing herself. Letting the idea take root in her mind. Perhaps she went to see her stepdaughter, or her stepdaughter came home for a weekend. There could have been talk, hints of marriage. And all the time the thought of the MONEY – not just a little money, not a miserly pittance – but lots of money, big money, money that enabled you to do everything you had ever wanted! And all going to this degenerate, ill-mannered girl, slouching about in the coffee bars of Chelsea in her jeans and her sloppy jumpers, with her undesirable degenerate friends. Why should a girl like that, a girl who was no good and would never be any good, have all that beautiful money?

And so – another visit to Birmingham. More caution, more reassurance. Finally, a discussion on terms. I smiled involuntarily. Mr Bradley would not have had it all his own way. She would have been a hard bargainer. But in the end, the terms had been agreed, some document duly signed, and then what?

That was where imagination stopped. That was what we didn't know.

I came out of my meditation to see Ginger watching me.

She asked: 'Got it all worked out?'

'How did you know what I was doing?'

'I'm beginning to know the way your mind works. You were working it out, weren't you, following her – to Birmingham and all the rest of it?'

'Yes. But I was brought up short. At the moment when she had settled things in Birmingham – *What happens next?*'

We looked at each other.

'Sooner or later,' said Ginger, '*someone* has got to find out exactly what happens at the Pale Horse.'

'How?'

'I don't know . . . It won't be easy. Nobody who's actually been there, who's actually *done* it, will ever tell. At the same time, they're the only people who *can* tell. It's difficult . . . I wonder . . .'

'We could go to the police?' I suggested.

'Yes. After all, we've got something fairly definite now. Enough to act upon, do you think?'

I shook my head doubtfully.

'Evidence of intent. But is that enough? It's this death wish nonsense. Oh,' I forestalled her interruption, 'it mayn't be nonsense – but it would *sound* like it in court. We've no idea, even, of what the actual procedure is.'

'Well, then, we've got to know. But how?'

'One would have to see – or hear – with one's own eyes and ears. But there's absolutely no place one could hide oneself in that great barn of a room – and I suppose that's where it – whatever "it" is – must take place.'

Ginger sat up very straight, gave her head a kind of toss, rather like an energetic terrier, and said:

'There's only one way to find out what does really happen. You've got to be a genuine *client*.'

I stared at her.

'A genuine client?'

'Yes. You or I, it doesn't matter which, has got to want somebody put out of the way. One of us has got to go to Bradley and fix it up.'

'I don't like it,' I said sharply.

'Why?'

'Well – it opens up dangerous possibilities.'

'For us?'

'Perhaps. But I was really thinking about the – victim. We've got to have a victim – we've got to give him a name. It can't be just invention. They might check up – in fact, they'd almost certainly check up, don't you agree?'

Ginger thought a minute and then nodded.

'Yes. The victim's got to be a real person with a real address.'

'That's what I don't like,' I said.

'And we've got to have a real reason for getting rid of him.'

We were silent for a moment, considering this aspect of the situation.

'The person, whoever it was, would have to agree,' I said slowly. 'It's a lot to ask.'

'The whole set-up has got to be good,' said Ginger, thinking it out. 'But there's one thing, you were absolutely right in what you were saying the other day. The weakness of the whole thing is that they're in a cleft stick. The business has got to be secret – but not too secret. Possible clients have got to be able to hear about it.'

'What puzzles me,' I said, 'is that the police don't seem to have heard about it. After all, they're usually aware of what kind of criminal activities are going on.'

'Yes, but I think that the reason for that is, that this is in every sense of the word, an *amateur* show. It's not professional. No professional criminals are employed or involved. It's not like hiring gangsters to bump people off. It's all – *private*.'

I said that I thought she had something there.

Ginger went on:

'Suppose now that you, or I (we'll examine both possibilities), are desperate to get rid of someone. Now who is there that you and I could want to do away with? There's my dear old Uncle Mervyn – I'll come into a very nice packet when he pops off. I and some cousin in Australia are the only ones left of the family. So there's a motive there. But he's over seventy and more or less ga-ga, so it would really seem more sensible for me to wait for natural causes – unless I was in some terrible hole for money – and that really would be quite difficult to fake. Besides, he's a pet, and I'm very fond of him, and ga-ga or not ga-ga, he quite enjoys life, and I wouldn't want to deprive him of a minute of it – or even risk such a thing! What about you? Have you got any relatives who are going to leave you money?'

I shook my head.

'No one at all.'

'Bother. It could be blackmail, perhaps? That would take a lot of fixing, though. You're not really vulnerable enough. If you were an M.P., or in the Foreign Office, or an up and coming Minister it would be different. The same with me. Fifty years ago it would have been easy. Compromising letters, or photographs in the altogether, but really nowadays, who *cares?* One can be like the Duke of Wellington and say "Publish and be damned!" Well, now, what else is there? Bigamy?' She fixed me with a reproachful stare. 'What a pity it is you've never been married. We could have cooked something up if you had.'

Some expression on my face must have given me away. Ginger was quick.

'I'm sorry,' she said. 'Have I raked up something that hurts?'

'No,' I said. 'It doesn't hurt. It was a long time ago, I rather doubt if there's anyone now who knows about it.'

'You married someone?'

'Yes. Whilst I was at the University. We kept it dark. She wasn't – well, my people would have cut up rough. I wasn't even of age. We lied about our ages.'

I was silent a moment or two, reliving the past.

'It wouldn't have lasted,' I said slowly. 'I know that now. She was pretty and she could be very sweet . . . but . . .'

'What happened?'

'We went to Italy in the long vacation. There was an accident – a car accident. She was killed outright.'

'And you?'

'I wasn't in the car. She was – with a friend.'

Ginger gave me a quick glance. I think she understood the way it had been. The shock of my discovery that the girl I had married was not the kind that makes a faithful wife.

Ginger reverted to practical matters.

'You were married in England?'

'Yes. Registry office in Peterborough.'

'But she died in Italy?'

'Yes.'

'So there will be no record of her death in England?'

'No.'

'Then what more do you want? It's an answer to prayer! Nothing could be simpler! You're desperately in love with someone and you want to marry her – *but* you don't know whether your wife is still alive. You've parted years ago and never heard from her since. Dare you risk it? While you're thinking it out, sudden reappearance of the wife! She turns up out of the blue, refuses to give you a divorce, and threatens to go to your young woman and spill the beans.'

'Who's my young woman?' I asked, slightly confused. 'You?'

Ginger looked shocked.

'Certainly not. I'm quite the wrong type – I'd probably go and live in sin with you. No, you know quite well who I mean – and she'll be exactly right, I should say. The statuesque brunette you go around with. Very highbrow and serious.'

'Hermia Redcliffe?'

'That's right. Your steady.'

'Who told you about her?'

'Poppy, of course. She's rich, too, isn't she?'

'She's extremely well off. But really –'

'All right, all right. *I'm* not saying you're marrying her for her money. You're not the kind. But nasty minds like Bradley's could easily think so . . . Very well then. Here's the position. You are about to pop the question to Hermia when up turns the unwanted wife from the past. She arrives in London and the fat's in the fire. You urge a divorce – she won't play. She's vindictive. And then – you hear of the Pale Horse. I'll bet anything you like that Thyrza, and that half-witted peasant Bella, thought that that was why you came that day. They took it as a tentative approach, and that's why Thyrza was so forthcoming. It *was* a sales talk they were giving you.'

'It could have been, I suppose.' I went over that day in my mind.

'And your going to Bradley soon after fits in perfectly. You're hooked! You're a prospect –'

She paused triumphantly. There was something in what she said – but I didn't quite see . . .

'I still think,' I said, 'that they'll investigate very carefully.'

'Sure to,' Ginger agreed.

'It's all very well to invent a fictitious wife, resurrected from the past – but they'll want *details* – where she lives – all that. And when I try to hedge –'

'You won't need to hedge. To do the thing properly the wife has got to be there – and she will be there! –

'Brace yourself,' said Ginger. '*I'm your wife!*'

II

I stared at her. Goggled, I suppose, would be a better term. I wonder, really, that she didn't burst out laughing.

I was just recovering myself when she spoke again.

'There's no need to be so taken aback,' she said. 'It's not a proposal.'

I found my tongue.

'You don't know what you're saying.'

'Of course I do. What I'm suggesting is perfectly feasible – and it has the advantage of not dragging some innocent person into possible danger.'

'It's putting yourself in danger.'

'That's my lookout.'

'No, it isn't. And anyway, it wouldn't hold water for a moment.'

'Oh yes, it would. I've been thinking it out. I arrive at a furnished flat, with a suitcase or two with foreign labels. I take the flat in the name of Mrs Easterbrook – and who on earth is to say I'm not Mrs Easterbrook?'

'Anyone who knows you.'

'Anyone who knows me won't see me. I'm away from my job, ill. A spot of hair dye – what was your wife, by the way, dark or blonde? – not that it really matters.'

'Dark,' I said mechanically.

'Good, I'd hate a bleach. Different clothes and lots of make-up, and my best friend wouldn't look at me twice! And since you haven't had a wife in evidence for the last fifteen years or so – no one's likely to spot that I'm *not* her. Why should anyone in the Pale Horse doubt that I'm who I say I am? If you're prepared to sign papers wagering large sums of money that I'll stay alive, there's not likely to be any doubt as to my being the bona fide article. You're not connected with the police in any way – you're a genuine client. They can verify the marriage by looking up old records in Somerset House. They can check up on your friendship with Hermia and all that – so why should there by any doubts?'

'You don't realise the difficulties – the risk.'

'Risk – Hell!' said Ginger. 'I'd love to help you win a miserly hundred pounds or whatever it is from that shark Bradley.'

I looked at her. I liked her very much . . . Her red hair, her freckles, her gallant spirit. But I couldn't let her take the risks she wanted to take.

'I can't stand for it, Ginger,' I said. 'Suppose – something happened.'

'To me?'

'Yes.'

'Isn't that my affair?'

'No. I got you in on all this.'

She nodded thoughtfully.

'Yes, perhaps you did. But who got there first doesn't matter much. We're both *in* it now – and we've got to do *something*. I'm being serious now, Mark. I'm not pretending this is all just fun. If what we believe to be true is true, it's a sickening beastly thing. And it's got to be *stopped*! You see, it's not hot-blooded murder, from hate or jealousy; it's not even murder from cupidity, the human frailty of murder for gain but taking the risk yourself. It's murder as a *business* – murder that takes no account of who or what the victim may be.

'That is,' she added, 'if the whole thing is true?'

She looked at me in momentary doubt.

'It *is* true,' I said. 'That's why I'm afraid for you.'

Ginger put both elbows on the table, and began to argue.

We thrashed it out, to and fro, ding dong, repeating ourselves whilst the hands of the clock on my mantelpiece moved slowly round.

Finally Ginger summed up.

'It's like this. I'm forewarned and forearmed. I *know* what someone is trying to do to me. And I don't believe for one moment she can do it! If everyone's got a "desire for death" mine isn't well developed! I've good health. And I simply cannot believe that I'll develop gallstones, or meningitis just because – old Thyrza draws pentagrams on the floor, or Sybil throws a trance – or whatever it is those women do do.'

'Bella sacrifices a white cock, I should imagine,' I said thoughtfully.

'You must admit it's all terribly bogus!'

'We don't know what actually *does* happen,' I pointed out.

'No. That's why it's important to find out. But do you believe, really believe, that because of what three women can do in the barn of the Pale Horse, I, in a flat in London, will develop some fatal disease? You *can't!*'

'No,' I said. 'I can't believe it.

'But,' I added. 'I do . . .'

We looked at each other.

'Yes,' said Ginger. 'That's our weakness.'

'Look here,' I said. 'Let's make it the other way round. Let me be the one in London. You be the client. We can cook up something –'

But Ginger was vigorously shaking her head.

'No, Mark,' she said. 'It won't work that way. For several reasons. The most important is that I'm known at the Pale Horse already – as my carefree self. They could get all the dope about my life from Rhoda – and there's nothing there. But you are in the ideal position already – you're a nervous client, sniffing around, not able yet to commit yourself. No, it's got to be this way.'

'I don't like it. I don't like to think of you – alone in some place under a false name – with nobody to keep an eye on you. I think, before we embark on this, we ought to go to the police – now – before we try anything else.'

'I'm agreeable to that,' said Ginger slowly. 'In fact I think it's what you ought to do. You've got something to go on. What police? Scotland Yard?'

'No,' I said. 'I think Divisional Detective-Inspector Lejeune is the best bet.'

CHAPTER 15

MARK EASTERBROOK'S NARRATIVE

I liked Divisional Detective-Inspector Lejeune at first sight. He had an air of quiet ability. I thought, too, that he was an imaginative man – the kind of man who would be willing to consider possibilities that were not orthodox.

He said:

'Dr Corrigan has told me of his meeting with you. He's taken a great interest in this business from the first. Father Gorman, of course, was very well known and respected in the district. Now you say you have some special information for us?'

'It concerns,' I said, 'a place called the Pale Horse.'

'In, I understand, a village called Much Deeping?'

'Yes.'

'Tell me about it.'

I told him of the first mention of the Pale Horse at the Fantasie. Then I described my visit to Rhoda, and my introduction to the 'three weird sisters'. I related, as accurately as I could, Thyrza

Grey's conversation on that particular afternoon.

'And you were impressed by what she said?'

I felt embarrassed.

'Well, not really. I mean, I didn't seriously believe –'

'Didn't you, Mr Easterbrook? I rather think you did.'

'I suppose you're right. One just doesn't like admitting how credulous one is.'

Lejeune smiled.

'But you've left something out, haven't you? You were already interested when you came to Much Deeping – why?'

'I think it was the girl looking so scared.'

'The young lady in the flower shop?'

'Yes. She'd thrown out her remark about the Pale Horse so casually. Her being so scared seemed to underline the fact that there was – well, something to be scared about. And then I met Dr Corrigan and he told me about the list of names. Two of them I already knew. Both were dead. A third name seemed familiar. Afterwards I found that she, too, had died.'

'That would be Mrs Delafontaine?'

'Yes.'

'Go on.'

'I made up my mind that I'd got to find out more about this business.'

'And you set about it. How?'

I told him of my call on Mrs Tuckerton. Finally I came to Mr Bradley and the Municipal Square Buildings in Birmingham.

I had his full interest now. He repeated the name.

'Bradley,' he said. 'So Bradley's in this?'

'You know him?'

'Oh yes, we know all about Mr Bradley. He's given us a lot of trouble. He's a smooth dealer, an adept at never doing anything that we can pin on him. He knows every trick and dodge of the legal game. He's always just on the right side of the line. He's the kind of man who could write a book like those old cookery books, "A hundred ways of evading the law." But murder, such a thing as organised murder – I should have said that that was right off his beat. Yes – right off his beat –'

'Now that I've told you about our conversation, could you act upon it?'

Lejeune slowly shook his head.

'No, we couldn't act on it. To begin with, there were no witnesses to your conversation. It was just between the two of you and he could deny the whole thing if he wanted to! Apart from that, he was quite right when he told you that a man can bet on anything. He bets somebody won't die – and he loses. What is there criminal about that? Unless we can connect Bradley in some way with the actual crime in question – and that, I imagine, will not be easy.'

He left it with a shrug of his shoulders. He paused a minute and then said,

'Did you, by any chance, come across a man called Venables when you were down in Much Deeping?'

'Yes,' I said, 'I did. I was taken over to lunch with him one day.'

'Ah! What impression, if I may ask, did he make upon you?'

'A very powerful impression. He's a man of great personality. An invalid.'

'Yes. Crippled by polio.'

'He can only move about in a wheeled chair. But his disability seems to have heightened his determination to live and enjoy living.'

'Tell me all you can about him.'

I described Venables's house, his art treasures, the range and sweep of his interests.

Lejeune said:

'It's a pity.'

'What is a pity?'

He said drily: 'That Venables is a cripple.'

'Excuse me, but you are quite certain he really is a cripple? He couldn't be – well – faking the whole thing?'

'We're as sure of his being a cripple as one can be sure of anything. His doctor is Sir William Dugdale of Harley Street, a man absolutely above suspicion. We have Sir William's assurance that the limbs are atrophied. Our little Mr Osborne may be certain that Venables was the man he saw walking along Barton Street that night. But he's wrong.'

'I see.'

'As I say, it's a pity, because if there is such a thing as an organisation for private murder, Venables is the kind of man who would be capable of planning it.'

'Yes; that's what I thought.'

With his forefinger Lejeune traced interlacing circles on the table in front of him. Then he looked up sharply.

'Let's assemble what we've got; adding to our own knowledge the knowledge you've brought us. It seems reasonably certain that there *is* some agency or organisation that specialises in what one might call the removal of unwanted persons. There's nothing crude about the organisation. It doesn't employ ordinary thugs or gunmen . . . There's nothing to show that the victims haven't died a perfectly natural death. I may say that in addition to the three deaths you've mentioned, we've got a certain amount of rather indefinite information about some of the others – deaths were from natural causes in each instance, but there were those who profited by these deaths. No evidence, mind you.

'It's clever, damnably clever, Mr Easterbrook. Whoever thought it out – and it's been thought out in great detail – has brains. We've only got hold of a few scattered names. Heaven knows how many more of them there are – how widespread the whole thing may be. And we've only got the few names we have got, by the accident of a woman knowing herself to be dying, and wanting to make her peace with heaven.'

He shook his head angrily, and then went on:

'This woman, Thyrza Grey; you say she boasted to you about her powers! Well, she can do so with impunity. Charge her with murder, put her in the dock, let her trumpet to heaven and a jury that she has released people from the toils of this world by will power or weaving spells – or what have you. She wouldn't be guilty according to the law. She's never been near the people who died, we've checked on that, she hasn't sent them poisoned chocolates through the post or anything of that kind. According to her own account, she just sits in a room and employs telepathy! Why, the whole thing would be laughed out of Court!'

I murmured:

'But Lu and Aengus laugh not. Nor any in the high celestial House.'

'What's that?'

'Sorry. A quotation from the "Immortal Hour".'

'Well, it's true enough. The devils in Hell are laughing but not the Host of Heaven. It's an – an *evil* business, Mr Easterbrook.'

'Yes,' I said. 'It's a word that we don't use very much nowadays. But it's the only word applicable here. That's why –'

'Yes?'

Lejeune looked at me inquiringly.

I spoke in a rush. 'I think there's a chance – a possible chance – of getting to know a bit more about all this. I and a friend of mine have worked out a plan. You may think it very silly –'

'I'll be the judge of that.'

'First of all, I take it from what you've said, that you are sure in your mind that there *is* such an organisation as the one we've been discussing, and that it works?'

'It certainly works.'

'But you don't know *how* it works? The first steps are already formulated. The individual I call the client hears vaguely about this organisation, gets to know more about it, is sent to Mr Bradley in Birmingham, and decides that he will go ahead. He enters into some agreement with Bradley, and then is, or so I presume, sent to the Pale Horse. But what happens after *that*, we don't know! What, exactly, *happens* at the Pale Horse? Somebody's got to go and find out.'

'Go on.'

'Because until we *do* know, exactly, what Thyrza Grey actually *does*, we can't get any further – Your police doctor, Jim Corrigan, says the whole idea is poppycock – but is it? Inspector Lejeune, is it?'

Lejeune sighed.

'You know what I'd answer – what any sane person would answer – the answer would be "Yes, of course it is!" – but I'm speaking now unofficially. Very odd things have happened during the last hundred years. Would anyone have believed seventy years ago that a person could hear Big Ben strike twelve on a little box and, after it had finished striking, hear it again with his own ears through the window, from the actual clock itself – and no jiggery pokery. But Big Ben struck *once* – not twice – the sound was brought to the ears of the person by two different kinds of waves! Would you believe you could hear a man speaking in New York in your own drawing-room, without so much as a connecting wire?

Would you have believed –? Oh! a dozen other things – things that are now everyday knowledge that a child gabbles off!'

'In other words, anything's possible?'

'That's what I mean. If you ask me if Thyrza Grey can kill someone by rolling her eyes or going into a trance, or projecting her will, I still say "No." But – I'm not sure – How can I be? If she's stumbled on something –'

'Yes,' I said. 'The supernatural seems supernatural. But the science of tomorrow is the supernatural of today.'

'I'm not talking officially, mind,' Lejeune warned me.

'Man, you're talking sense. And the answer is, someone has got to go and see what actually *happens*. That's what I propose to do – go and see.'

Lejeune stared at me.

'The way's already paved,' I said.

I settled down then, and told him about it. I told him exactly what I and a friend of mine planned to do.

He listened, frowning and pulling at his lower lip.

'Mr Easterbrook, I see your point. Circumstances have, so to speak, given you the entrée. But I don't know whether you fully realise that what you are proposing to do may be dangerous – these are dangerous people. It may be dangerous for you – but it will certainly be dangerous for your friend.'

'I know,' I said, 'I know . . . We've been over it a hundred times. I don't like her playing the part she's going to play. But she's determined – absolutely determined. Damn it all, she wants to!'

Lejeune said unexpectedly:

'She's a red-head, didn't you say?'

'Yes,' I said, startled.

'You can never argue with a red-head,' said Lejeune. 'Don't I know it!'

I wondered if his wife was one.

CHAPTER 16

MARK EASTERBROOK'S NARRATIVE

I felt absolutely no nervousness on my second visit to Bradley. In fact, I enjoyed it.

'Think yourself into the part,' Ginger urged me, before I set off, and that was exactly what I tried to do.

Mr Bradley greeted me with a welcoming smile.

'Very pleased to see you,' he said, advancing a podgy hand. 'So you've been thinking your little problem over, have you? Well, as I said, no hurry. Take your time.'

I said, 'That's just what I can't do. It's – well – it's rather urgent . . .'

Bradley looked me over. He noted my nervous manner, the way I avoided his eyes, the clumsiness of my hands as I dropped my hat.

'Well, well,' he said. 'Let's see what we can do about things. You want to have a little bet on something, is that it? Nothing like a sporting flutter to take one's mind off one's – er – troubles.'

'It's like this –' I said, and came to a dead stop.

I left it to Bradley to do his stuff. He did it.

'I see you're a bit nervous,' he said. 'Cautious. I approve of caution. Never say anything your mother shouldn't hear about! Now, perhaps you have some idea that this office of mine might have a bug in it?'

I didn't understand and my face showed it.

'Slang term for a microphone,' he explained. 'Tape recorders. All that sort of thing. No, I give you my personal word of honour that there's nothing of that sort here. Our conversation will not be recorded in any way. And if you don't believe me,' his candour was quite engaging – 'and why should you? – you've a perfect right to name a place of your own, a restaurant, the waiting-room in one of our dear English railway stations; and we'll discuss the matter there instead.'

I said that I was sure it was quite all right here.

'Sensible! That sort of thing wouldn't pay us, I assure you. Neither you nor I is going to say a word that, in legal parlance, could be "used against us". Now let's start this way. There's something worrying you. You find me sympathetic and you feel you'd like to tell me about it. I'm a man of experience and I might be able to advise you. A trouble shared is a trouble halved, as they say. Suppose we put it like that?'

We put it like that, and I stumbled into my story.

Mr Bradley was very adroit. He prompted; eased over difficult words and phrases. So good was he, that I felt no difficulty at all in telling him about my youthful infatuation for Doreen and our secretive marriage.

'Happens so often,' he said, shaking his head. 'So often. Understandable! Young man with ideals. Genuinely pretty girl. And there you are. Man and wife before you can say Jack Robinson. And what comes of it?'

I went on to tell him what came of it.

Here I was purposefully vague over details. The man I was trying to present would not have gone into sordid details. I presented only a picture of disillusionment – a young fool realising that he had been a young fool.

I let it be assumed that there had been a final quarrel. If Bradley took it that my young wife had gone off with another man, or that there had been another man in the offing all along – that was good enough.

'But you know,' I said anxiously, 'although she wasn't – well, wasn't quite what I thought her, she was really a very sweet girl. I'd never have thought that she'd be like this – that she'd behave like this, I mean.'

'What exactly has she been doing to you?'

What my 'wife' had done to me, I explained, was to come back.

'What did you think happened to her?'

'I suppose it seems extraordinary – but I really *didn't* think. Actually, I suppose, I assumed she must be dead.'

Bradley shook his head at me.

'Wishful thinking. Wishful thinking. Why *should* she be dead?'

'She never wrote or anything. I never heard from her.'

'The truth is you wanted to forget all about her.'

He was a psychologist in his way, this beady-eyed little lawyer.

'Yes,' I said gratefully. 'You see, it wasn't as though I wanted to marry someone else.'

'But you do now, eh, is that it?'

'Well –' I showed reluctance.

'Come now, tell Papa,' said the odious Bradley.

I admitted, shamefacedly, that, yes, lately, I *had* considered marrying . . .

But I stuck my toes in and refused firmly to give him any details about the girl in question. I wasn't going to have her brought into this. I wasn't going to tell him a thing about her.

Again, I think my reaction here was the correct one. He did not insist. Instead he said:

'Quite natural, my dear sir. You've got over your nasty experience in the past. You've found someone, no doubt, thoroughly suited to you. Able to share your literary tastes and your way of life. A true companion.'

I saw then that he knew about Hermia. It would have been easy. Any inquiries made about me would have revealed the fact that I had only one close woman friend. Bradley, since receiving my letter making the appointment, must have found out all about me, all about Hermia. He was fully briefed.

'What about divorce?' he asked. 'Isn't that the natural solution?'

I said: 'There's no question of divorce. She – my wife – won't hear of it!'

'Dear, dear. What is her attitude towards you, if I may ask?'

'She – er – she wants to come back to me. She – she's utterly unreasonable. She knows there's someone, and – and –'

'Acting nasty . . . I see . . . Doesn't look as though there's any way out, unless of course . . . But she's quite young . . .'

'She'll live for years,' I said bitterly.

'Oh, but you never know, Mr Easterbrook. She's been living abroad, you say?'

'So she tells me. I don't know where she's been.'

'May have been out East. Sometimes, you know, you pick up a germ out in those parts – dormant for years! And then you came back home, and suddenly it blows up. I've known two or three cases like that. Might happen in this case. If it will cheer you up,' he paused, 'I'd bet a small amount on it.'

I shook my head.

'She'll live for years.'

'Well, the odds are on your side, I admit . . . But let's have a wager on it. Fifteen hundred to one the lady dies between now and Christmas: how's that?'

'Sooner! It will have to be sooner. I can't wait. There are things –'

I was purposely incoherent. I don't know whether he thought that matters between Hermia and myself had gone so far that I couldn't stall for time – or that my 'wife' threatened to go to Hermia and make trouble. He may have thought that there was another man making a play for Hermia. I didn't mind what he thought. I wanted to stress urgency.

'Alter the odds a bit,' he said. 'We'll say eighteen hundred to one your wife's a goner in under a month. I've got a sort of feeling about it.'

I thought it was time to bargain – and I bargained. Protested that I hadn't got that amount of money. Bradley was skilful. He knew, by some means or other, just what sum I could raise in an emergency. He knew that Hermia had money. His delicate hint that later, when I was married, I wouldn't feel the loss of my bet, was proof of that. Moreover, my urgency put him in a fine position. He wouldn't come down.

When I left him the fantastic wager was laid and accepted.

I signed some form of I.O.U. The phraseology was too full of legal phrases for me to understand. Actually I very much doubted that it had any legal significance whatever.

'Is this legally binding?' I asked him.

'I don't think,' said Mr Bradley, showing his excellent dentures, 'that it will ever be put to the test.' His smile was not a very nice one. 'A bet's a bet. If a man doesn't pay up –'

I looked at him.

'I shouldn't advise it,' he said softly. 'No, I shouldn't advise it. We don't like welshers.'

'I shan't welsh,' I said.

'I'm sure you won't, Mr Easterbrook. Now for the er – arrangements. Mrs Easterbrook, you say, is in London. Where, exactly?'

'Do you have to know?'

'I have to have full details – the next thing to do is to arrange an appointment with Miss Grey – you remember Miss Grey?'

I said of course I remembered Miss Grey.

'An amazing woman. Really an amazing woman. Most gifted. She'll want something your wife has worn – a glove – handkerchief – anything like that –'

'But why? In the name of –'

'I know, I know. Don't ask *me* why. I've not the least idea. Miss Grey keeps her secrets to herself.'

'But what happens? What does she *do*?'

'You really must believe me, Mr Easterbrook, when I tell you that honestly I haven't the least idea! I don't know – and what is more, *I don't want to know* – let's leave it at that.'

He paused, and then went on in an almost fatherly tone.

'My advice is as follows, Mr Easterbrook. Pay a visit to your wife. Soothe her down, let her think that you're coming round to the idea of a reconciliation. I should suggest that you have to go abroad for a few weeks, but that on your return etc., etc. . . .'

'And then?'

'Having purloined a trifle of daily wear in an unobtrusive manner, you will go down to Much Deeping.' He paused thoughtfully. 'Let me see. I think you mentioned on your previous visit that you had friends – relations – in the neighbourhood?'

'A cousin.'

'That makes it very simple. This cousin will doubtless put you up for a day or so.'

'What do most people do? Stay at the local inn?'

'Sometimes, I believe – or they motor over from Bournemouth. Something of that kind – but I know very little about the matter.'

'What – er – is my cousin likely to think?'

'You express yourself as intrigued by the inhabitants of the Pale Horse. You want to participate in a *séance* there. Nothing can sound simpler. Miss Grey and her medium friend often indulge in *séances*. You know what spiritualists are. You go protesting that of course it's nonsense, but that it will interest you. That is all, Mr Easterbrook. As you see, nothing can be simpler –'

'And – and, after that?'

He shook his head smiling.

'That's all I can tell you. All, in fact, that I know. Miss Thyrza Grey will then be in charge. Don't forget to take the glove, or handkerchief, or whatever it is with you. Afterwards, I would suggest that you take a little trip abroad. The Italian Riviera is very pleasant at this time of year. Just for a week or two, say.'

I said that I didn't want to go abroad. I said I wanted to stay in England.

'Very well, then, but definitely *not* London. No, I must strongly advise, not London.'

'Why not?'

Mr Bradley looked at me reprovingly.

'Clients are guaranteed complete – er – safety,' he said. '*If* they obey orders.'

'What about Bournemouth? Would Bournemouth do?'

'Yes, Bournemouth would be adequate. Stay at a hotel, make a few acquaintances, be seen in their company. The blameless life – that is what we aim at. You can always go on to Torquay if you get tired of Bournemouth.'

He spoke with the affability of a travel agent.

Once again I had to shake his podgy hand.

CHAPTER 17

MARK EASTERBROOK'S NARRATIVE

I

'Are you really going to a *séance* at Thyrza's?' Rhoda demanded.

'Why not?'

'I never knew you were interested in that sort of thing, Mark.'

'I'm not really,' I said truthfully. 'But it's such a queer set-up, those three. I'm curious to see what sort of a show they put on.'

I did not find it really easy to put on a light manner. Out of the tail of my eye, I saw Hugh Despard looking at me thoughtfully. He was a shrewd man, with an adventurous life behind him. One of those men who have a kind of sixth sense where danger is concerned. I think he scented its presence now – realised that something more important than idle curiosity was at stake.

'Then I shall come with you,' said Rhoda gleefully. 'I've always wanted to go.'

'You'll do nothing of the sort, Rhoda,' growled Despard.

'But I don't really believe in spirits and all that, Hugh. You know I don't. I just want to go for the fun of it!'

'That sort of business isn't fun,' said Despard. 'There may be something genuine to it, there probably is. But it doesn't have a good effect on people who go out of "idle curiosity".'

'Then you ought to dissuade Mark, too.'

'Mark's not my responsibility,' said Despard.

But again he gave me that quick sidelong look. He knew, I was quite sure, that I had a purpose.

Rhoda was annoyed, but she got over it, and when we chanced to meet Thyrza Grey in the village a little later that morning, Thyrza herself was blunt upon the matter.

'Hallo, Mr Easterbrook, we're expecting you this evening. Hope we can put on a good show for you. Sybil's a wonderful medium, but one never knows beforehand what results one will get. So you mustn't be disappointed. One thing I do ask you. Keep an open mind. An honest inquirer is always welcome – but a frivolous, scoffing approach is bad.'

'I wanted to come too,' said Rhoda. 'But Hugh is so frightfully prejudiced. You know what he's like.'

'I wouldn't have had you, anyway,' said Thyrza. 'One outsider is quite enough.'

She turned to me.

'Suppose you come and have a light meal with us first,' she said. 'We never eat much before a *séance*. About seven o'clock? Good, we'll be expecting you.'

She nodded, smiled, and strode briskly away. I stared after her, so engrossed in my surmises, that I entirely missed what Rhoda was saying to me.

'What did you say? I'm sorry.'

'You've been very odd lately, Mark. Ever since you arrived. Is anything the matter?'

'No, of course not. What should be the matter?'

'Have you got stuck with the book? Something like that?'

'The book?' Just for a moment I couldn't remember anything about the book. Then I said hastily, 'Oh yes, the book. It's getting on more or less all right.'

'I believe you're in love,' said Rhoda accusingly. 'Yes, that's it. Being in love has a very bad effect on men – it seems to addle their wits. Now women are just the opposite – on top of the world, looking radiant and twice as good-looking as usual. Funny, isn't it, that it should suit women, and only make a man look like a sick sheep?'

'Thank you!' I said.

'Oh, don't be cross with me, Mark. I think it's a very good thing really – and I'm delighted. She's really very nice.'

'Who's nice?'

'Hermia Redcliffe, of course. You seem to think I know nothing about *anything*. I've seen it coming on for ages. And she really is just the person for you – good-looking and clever; absolutely suitable.'

'That,' I said, 'is one of the cattiest things you could say about anyone.'

Rhoda looked at me.

'It is rather,' she said.

She turned away and said she had to go and give a pep talk to the butcher. I said that I would go and pay a call at the vicarage.

'But not' – I forestalled any comment – 'in order to ask the vicar to put the banns up!'

II

Coming to the vicarage was like coming home.

The front door was hospitably open, and as I stepped inside I was conscious of a burden slipping from my shoulders.

Mrs Dane Calthrop came through a door at the back of the hall, carrying for some reason unfathomable to me an enormous plastic pail of bright green.

'Hallo, it's you,' she said. 'I thought it would be.'

She handed me the pail. I had no idea what to do with it and stood looking awkward.

'Outside the door, on the step,' said Mrs Calthrop impatiently, as though I ought to have known.

I obeyed. Then I followed her into the same dark shabby room we had sat in before. There was a rather moribund fire there, but Mrs Dane Calthrop poked it into flame and dumped a log on it. Then she motioned me to sit down, plumped down herself, and fixed me with a bright impatient eye.

'Well?' she demanded. 'What have you done?'

From the vigour of her manner we might have had a train to catch.

'You told me to do something. I am doing something.'

'Good. What?'

I told her. I told her everything. In some unspoken way I told her things I did not quite know myself.

'Tonight?' said Mrs Dane Calthrop thoughtfully.

'Yes.'

She was silent for a minute, obviously thinking. Unable to help myself I blurted out,

'I don't like it. My God, I don't like it.'

'Why should you?'

That, of course, was unanswerable.

'I'm so horribly afraid for her.'

She looked at me kindly.

'You don't know,' I said, 'how – how brave she is. If, in some way, they manage to harm her . . .'

Mrs Dane Calthrop said slowly:

'I don't see – I really don't see – *how* they can harm her in the way you mean.'

'But they have harmed – other people.'

'It would seem so, yes . . .' She sounded dissatisfied.

'In any other way, she will be all right. We've taken every imaginable precaution. No *material* harm *can* happen to her.'

'But it's material harm that these people claim to be able to produce,' Mrs Dane Calthrop pointed out. 'They claim to be able to work through the mind on the body. Illness – disease. Very interesting if they *can*. But quite horrible! And it's got to be *stopped*, as we've already agreed.'

'But she's the one who's taking the risk,' I muttered.

'Someone has to,' said Mrs Dane Calthrop calmly. 'It upsets your pride, that it shouldn't be you. You've got to swallow that. Ginger's ideally suited for the part she's playing. She can control her nerves and she's intelligent. She won't let you down.'

'I'm not worrying about *that*!'

'Well, stop worrying at all. It won't do *her* any good. Don't let's shirk the issue. If she dies as a result of this experiment, then she dies in a good cause.'

'My God, you're brutal!'

'Somebody has to be,' said Mrs Dane Calthrop. 'Always envisage the worst. You've no idea how that steadies the nerves.

You begin at once to be sure that it can't be as bad as what you imagine.'

She nodded at me reassuringly.

'You may be right,' I said doubtfully.

Mrs Dane Calthrop said with complete certainty that of course she was right.

I proceeded to details.

'You're on the telephone here?'

'Naturally.'

I explained what I wanted to do.

'After this – this business tonight is over, I may want to keep in close touch with Ginger. Ring her up every day. If I could telephone from here?'

'Of course. Too much coming and going at Rhoda's. You want to be sure of not being overheard.'

'I shall stay on at Rhoda's for a bit. Then perhaps go to Bournemouth. I'm not supposed to – go back to London.'

'No use looking ahead,' Mrs Dane Calthrop said. 'Not beyond tonight.'

'Tonight . . .' I got up. I said a thing that was out of character. 'Pray for me – for us,' I said.

'Naturally,' said Mrs Dane Calthrop, surprised that I should need to ask.

As I went out of the front door a sudden curiosity made me say,

'Why the pail? What's it *for*?'

'The pail? Oh, it's for the schoolchildren, to pick berries and leaves from the hedges – for the church. Hideous, isn't it, but so handy.'

I looked out over the richness of the autumn world. Such soft still beauty . . .

'Angels and Ministers of grace defend us,' I said.

'Amen,' said Mrs Dane Calthrop.

III

My reception at the Pale Horse was conventional in the extreme. I don't know what particular atmospheric effect I had expected – but it was not this.

Thyrza Grey, wearing a plain dark wool dress, opened the door, said in a businesslike tone: 'Ah, here you are. Good. We'll have supper straight away –'

Nothing could have been more matter-of-fact, more completely ordinary . . .

The table was laid for a simple meal at the end of the panelled hall. We had soup, an omelette, and cheese. Bella waited on us. She wore a black stuff dress and looked more than ever like one of the crowd in an Italian primitive. Sybil struck a more exotic note. She had on a long dress of some woven peacock-coloured fabric, shot with gold. Her beads were absent on this occasion, but she had two heavy gold bracelets clasping her wrists. She ate a minute portion of omelette but nothing else. She spoke little, treating us to a far-away wrapped-up-in-higher-things mood. It ought to have been impressive. Actually it was not. The effect was theatrical and unreal.

Thyrza Grey provided what conversation there was – a brisk chatty commentary on local happenings. She was this evening the British country spinster to the life, pleasant, efficient, uninterested in anything beyond her immediate surroundings.

I thought to myself, I'm mad, completely mad. What is there to fear here? Even Bella seemed to-night only a half-witted old peasant woman – like hundreds of other women of her kind – inbred, untouched by education or a broader outlook.

My conversation with Mrs Dane Calthrop seemed fantastic in retrospect. We had worked ourselves up to imagine goodness knows what. The idea of Ginger – Ginger with her dyed hair and assumed name – being in danger from anything these three very ordinary women could do, was positively ludicrous!

The meal came to an end.

'No coffee,' said Thyrza apologetically. 'One doesn't want to be overstimulated.' She rose. 'Sybil?'

'Yes,' said Sybil, her face taking on what she clearly thought was an ecstatic and other-world expression. 'I must go and PREPARE . . .'

Bella began to clear the table. I wandered over to where the old inn sign hung. Thyrza followed me.

'You can't really see it at all by this light,' she said.

That was quite true. The faint pale image against the dark encrusted grime of the panel could hardly be distinguished as that of a horse. The hall was lit by feeble electric bulbs shielded by thick vellum shades.

'That red-haired girl – what's her name? – Ginger something – who was staying down here – said she'd do a spot of cleaning and restoring on it,' said Thyrza. 'Don't suppose she'll ever remember about it, though.' She added casually, 'She works for some gallery or other in London.'

It gave me a strange feeling to hear Ginger referred to lightly and casually.

I said, staring at the picture:

'It might be interesting.'

'It's not a good painting, of course,' said Thyrza. 'Just a daub. But it goes with the place – and it's certainly well over three hundred years old.'

'Ready.'

We wheeled abruptly.

Bella, emerging out of the gloom, was beckoning.

'Time to get on with things,' said Thyrza, still brisk and matter-of-fact.

I followed her as she led the way out to the converted barn.

As I have said, there was no entrance to it from the house. It was a dark overcast night, no stars. We came out of the dense outer blackness into the long lighted room.

The barn, by night, was transformed. By day it had seemed a pleasant library. Now it had become something more. There were lamps, but these were not turned on. The lighting was indirect and flooded the room with a soft but cold light. In the centre of the floor was a kind of raised bed or divan. It was spread with a purple cloth, embroidered with various cabbalistic signs.

On the far side of the room was what appeared to be a small brazier, and next to it a big copper basin – an old one by the look of it.

On the other side, set back almost touching the wall, was a heavy oak-backed chair. Thyrza motioned me towards it.

'Sit there,' she said.

I sat obediently. Thyrza's manner had changed. The odd thing was that I could not define exactly in what the change consisted. There was none of Sybil's spurious occultism about it. It was more as though an everyday curtain of normal trivial life had been lifted. Behind it was the real woman, displaying something of the manner of a surgeon approaching the operating table for a difficult and dangerous operation. This impression was heightened when she went to a cupboard in the wall and took from it what appeared to be a kind of long overall. It seemed to be made, when the light caught it, of some metallic woven tissue. She drew on long gauntlets of what looked like a kind of fine mesh rather resembling a 'bullet-proof vest' I had once been shown.

'One has to take precautions,' she said.

The phrase struck me as slightly sinister.

Then she addressed me in an emphatic deep voice.

'I must impress upon you, Mr Easterbrook, the necessity of remaining absolutely still where you are. On no account must you move from that chair. It might not be safe to do so. This is no child's game. I am dealing with forces that are dangerous to those who do not know how to handle them!' She paused and then asked, 'You have brought what you were instructed to bring?'

Without a word, I drew from my pocket a brown suède glove and handed it to her.

She took it and moved over to a metal lamp with a gooseneck shade. She switched on the lamp and held the glove under its rays which were of a peculiar sickly colour, turning the glove from its rich brown to a characterless grey.

She switched off the lamp, nodding in approval.

'Most suitable,' she said. 'The physical emanations from its wearer are quite strong.'

She put it down on top of what appeared to be a large radio cabinet at the end of the room. Then she raised her voice a little. 'Bella. Sybil. We are ready.'

Sybil came in first. She wore a long black cloak over her peacock dress. This she flung aside with a dramatic gesture. It slid down, looking like an inky pool on the floor. She came forward.

'I do hope it will be all right,' she said. 'One never knows. Please don't adopt a sceptical frame of mind, Mr Easterbrook. It does so hinder things.'

'Mr Easterbrook has not come here to mock,' said Thyrza.

There was a certain grimness in her tone.

Sybil lay down on the purple divan. Thyrza bent over her, arranging her draperies.

'Quite comfortable?' she asked solicitously.

'Yes, thank you, dear.'

Thyrza switched off some lights. Then she wheeled up what was, in effect, a kind of canopy on wheels. This she placed so that it overshadowed the divan and left Sybil in a deep shadow in the middle of outlying dim twilight.

'Too much light is harmful to a complete trance,' she said.

'Now, I think, we are ready. Bella?'

Bella came out of the shadows. The two women approached me. With her right hand Thyrza took my left. Her left hand took Bella's right. Bella's left hand found my right hand. Thyrza's hand was dry and hard, Bella's was cold and boneless – it felt like a slug in mine and I shivered in revulsion.

Thyrza must have touched a switch somewhere, for music sounded faintly from the ceiling. I recognised it as Mendelssohn's funeral march.

'*Mise en scène*,' I said to myself rather scornfully. 'Meretricious trappings!' I was cool and critical – but nevertheless aware of an undercurrent of some unwanted emotional apprehension.

The music stopped. There was a long wait. There was only the sound of breathing. Bella's slightly wheezy, Sybil's deep and regular.

And then, suddenly, Sybil spoke. Not, however, in her own voice. It was a man's voice, as unlike her own mincing accents as could be. It had a guttural foreign accent.

'I am here,' the voice said.

My hands were released. Bella flitted away into the shadows. Thyrza said: 'Good evening. Is that Macandal?'

'I am Macandal.'

Thyrza went to the divan and drew away the protecting canopy. The soft light flowed down on to Sybil's face. She appeared to be deeply asleep. In this repose her face looked quite different.

The lines were smoothed away. She looked years younger. One could almost say that she looked beautiful.

Thyrza said:

'Are you prepared, Macandal, to submit to my desire and my will?'

The new deep voice said:

'I am.'

'Will you undertake to protect the body of the Dossu that lies here and which you now inhabit, from all physical injury and harm? Will you dedicate its vital force to my purpose, that that purpose may be accomplished through it?'

'I will.'

'Will you so dedicate this body that death may pass through it, obeying such natural laws as may be available in the body of the recipient?'

'The dead must be sent to cause death. It shall be so.'

Thyrza drew back a step. Bella came up and held out what I saw was a crucifix. Thyrza placed it on Sybil's breast in a reversed position. Then Bella brought a small green phial. From this Thyrza poured out a drop or two on to Sybil's forehead, and traced something with her finger. Again I fancied that it was the sign of the cross upside down.

She said to me, briefly, 'Holy water from the Catholic church at Garsington.'

Her voice was quite ordinary, and this, which ought to have broken the spell, did not do so. It made the whole business, somehow, more alarming.

Finally she brought that rather horrible rattle we had seen before. She shook it three times and then clasped Sybil's hand round it.

She stepped back and said:

'All is ready –'

Bella repeated the words:

'All is ready –'

Thyrza addressed me in a low tone:

'I don't suppose you're much impressed, are you, by all the ritual? Some of our visitors are. To you, I dare say, it's all so much mumbo jumbo . . . But don't be too sure. Ritual – a pattern of words and phrases sanctified by time and usage, has an effect on the human spirit. What causes the mass hysteria of crowds? We don't know exactly. But it's a phenomenon that exists. These old-time usages, they have their part – a necessary part, I think.'

Bella had left the room. She came back now, carrying a white cock. It was alive and struggling to be free.

Now with white chalk she knelt down and began to draw signs on the floor round the brazier and the copper bowl. She set down the cock with its back on the white curving line round the bowl and it stayed there motionless.

She drew more signs, chanting as she did so, in a low guttural voice. The words were incomprehensible to me, but as she knelt and swayed, she was clearly working herself up to some pitch of obscene ecstasy.

Watching me, Thyrza said: 'You don't like it much? It's old, you know, very old. The death spell according to old recipes handed from mother to daughter.'

I couldn't fathom Thyrza. She did nothing to further the effect on my senses which Bella's rather horrible performances might well have had. She seemed deliberately to take the part of a commentator.

Bella stretched out her hands to the brazier and a flickering flame sprang up. She sprinkled something on the flames and a thick cloying perfume filled the air.

'We are ready,' said Thyrza.

The surgeon, I thought, picks up his scalpel . . .

She went over to what I had taken to be a radio cabinet. It opened up and I saw that it was a large electrical contrivance of some complicated kind.

It moved like a trolley and she wheeled it slowly and carefully to a position near the divan.

She bent over it, adjusted the controls, murmuring to herself:

'Compass, north-north-east . . . degrees . . . that's about right.' She took the glove and adjusted it in a particular position, switching on a small violet light beside it.

Then she spoke to the inert figure on the divan.

'Sybil Diana Helen, you are set free from your mortal sheath which the spirit Macandal guards safely for you. You are free to be at one with the owner of this glove. Like all human beings, her goal in life is towards death. There is no final satisfaction but death. Only death solves all problems. Only death gives true peace. All great ones have known it. Remember Macbeth. "After life's fitful fever he sleeps well." Remember the ecstasy of Tristan and Isolde. Love and death. Love and death. But the greatest of these is death . . .'

The words rang out, echoing, repeating – the big box-like machine had started to emit a low hum, the bulbs in it glowed – I felt dazed, carried away. This, I felt, was no longer something at which I could mock. Thyrza, her power unleashed, was holding that prone figure on the divan completely enslaved. She was using her. Using her for a definite end. I realised vaguely why Mrs Oliver had been frightened, not of Thyrza but of the seemingly silly Sybil. Sybil had a power, a natural gift, nothing to do with mind or intellect; it was a physical power, the power to separate herself from her body. And, so separated, her mind was not hers, but Thyrza's. And Thyrza was using her temporary possession.

Yes, but the box? Where did the box come in?

And suddenly all my fear was transferred to the box! What devilish secret was being practised through its agency? Could there be physically-produced rays of some kind that acted on the cells of the mind? Of a particular mind?

Thyrza's voice went on:

'The weak spot . . . there is always a weak spot . . . deep in the tissues of the flesh . . . Through weakness comes strength – the strength and peace of death . . . Towards death – slowly, naturally, towards death – the true way, the natural way. The tissues of the body obey the mind . . . Command them – command them . . . Towards death . . . Death, the Conqueror . . . Death . . . soon . . . very soon . . . Death . . . Death . . . DEATH!'

Her voice rose in a great swelling cry . . . And another horrible animal cry came from Bella. She rose up, a knife flashed . . . there was a horrible strangled squawk from the cockerel . . . Blood dripped into the copper bowl. Bella came running, the bowl held out . . .

She screamed out:

'Blood . . . the *blood* . . . BLOOD!'

Thyrza whipped out the glove from the machine. Bella took it, dipped it in the blood, returned it to Thyrza who replaced it.

Bella's voice rose again in that high ecstatic call . . .

'The blood . . . the blood . . . the blood . . .'

She ran round and round the brazier, then dropped twitching to the floor. The brazier flickered and went out.

I felt horribly sick. Unseeing, clutching the arm of my chair, my head seemed to be whirling in space . . .

I heard a click, the hum of the machine ceased.

Then Thyrza's voice rose, clear and composed:

'The old magic and the new. The old knowledge of belief, the new knowledge of science. Together, they will prevail . . .'

CHAPTER 18

MARK EASTERBROOK'S NARRATIVE

'Well, what was it like?' demanded Rhoda eagerly at the breakfast table.

'Oh, the usual stuff,' I said nonchalantly.

I was uneasily conscious of Despard's eye on me. A perceptive man.

'Pentagrams drawn on the floor?'

'Lots of them.'

'Any white cocks?'

'Naturally. That was Bella's part of the fun and games.'

'And trances and things?'

'As you say, trances and things.'

Rhoda looked disappointed.

'You seem to have found it rather dull,' she said in an aggrieved voice.

I said that these things were all much of a muchness. At any rate, I'd satisfied my curiosity.

Later, when Rhoda had departed to the kitchen, Despard said to me:

'Shook you up a bit, didn't it?'

'Well –'

I was anxious to make light of the whole thing, but Despard was not an easy man to deceive.

I said slowly, 'It was – in a way – rather beastly.'

He nodded.

'One doesn't really believe in it,' said Despard. 'Not with one's reasoning mind – but these things have their effect. I've seen a good deal of it in East Africa. The witch-doctors there have a terrific hold on the people, and one has to admit that odd things happen which can't be explained in any rational manner.'

'Deaths?'

'Oh yes. If a man knows he's been marked down to die, he dies.'

'The power of suggestion, I suppose.'

'Presumably.'

'But that doesn't quite satisfy you?'

'No – not quite. There are cases difficult of explanation by any of our glib Western scientific theories. The stuff doesn't usually work on Europeans – (though I have known cases). But if the belief is there in your blood – you've had it!' He left it there.

I said thoughtfully: 'I agree with you that one can't be too didactic. Odd things happen even in this country. I was at a hospital one day in London. A girl had come in – neurotic subject, complaining of terrible pain in bones, arm, etc. Nothing to account for it. They suspected she was a victim of hysteria. Doctor told her cure could be effected by a red-hot rod being drawn down the arm. Would she agree to try it? She did.

'The girl turned her head away and screwed up her eyes. The doctor dipped a glass rod in cold water and drew it down the inside of her arm. The girl screamed with agony. He said, "You'll be all right now." She said, "I expect so, but it was awful. It burnt." The queer thing to me was – not that she believed that she had been burnt, but that her arm actually was burnt. The flesh was actually blistered everywhere the rod had touched it.'

'Was she cured?' Despard asked curiously.

'Oh yes. The neuritis, or whatever it was, never reappeared. She had to be treated for the burnt arm, though.'

'Extraordinary,' said Despard. 'It goes to show, doesn't it?'

'The doctor was startled himself.'

'I bet he was . . .' He looked at me curiously.

'Why were you really so keen to go to that *séance* last night?'

I shrugged my shoulders.

'Those three women intrigue me. I wanted to see what sort of show they would put up.'

Despard said no more. I don't think he believed me. As I have said, he was a perceptive man.

Presently I went along to the vicarage. The door was open but there seemed to be no one in the house.

I went to the little room where the telephone was, and rang up Ginger.

It seemed an eternity before I heard her voice.

'Hallo!'

'Ginger!'

'Oh, it's *you*. What happened?'

'You're all right?'

'Of course I'm all right. Why shouldn't I be?'

Waves of relief swept over me.

There was nothing wrong with Ginger; the familiar challenge of her manner did me a world of good. How could I ever have believed that a lot of mumbo jumbo could hurt so normal a creature as Ginger?

'I just thought you might have had bad dreams or something,' I said rather lamely.

'Well, I didn't. I expected to have, but all that happened was that I kept waking up and wondering if I felt anything peculiar happening to me. I really felt almost indignant because nothing did happen to me –'

I laughed.

'But go on – tell me,' said Ginger. 'What's it all about?'

'Nothing much out of the ordinary. Sybil lay on a purple couch and went into a trance.'

Ginger gave a spurt of laughter.

'Did she? How wonderful! Was it a velvet one and did she have nothing on?'

'Sybil is no Madame de Montespan. And it wasn't a black mass. Actually Sybil wore quite a lot of clothes, peacock blue, and lots of embroidered symbols.'

'Sounds most appropriate and Sybil-like. What did Bella do?'

'That really was rather beastly. She killed a white cock and then dipped your glove in the blood.'

'Oo – nasty . . . What else?'

'Lots of things,' I said.

I thought that I was doing quite well. I went on:

'Thyrza gave me the whole bag of tricks. Summoned up a spirit – Macandal was, I think, the name. And there were coloured lights and chanting. The whole thing would have been quite impressive to some people – scared 'em out of their wits.'

'But it didn't scare you?'

'Bella did scare me a bit,' I said. 'She had a very nasty-looking knife, and I thought she might lose her head and add me to the cock as a second victim.'

Ginger persisted:

'Nothing else frightened you?'

'I'm not influenced by that sort of thing.'

'Then why did you sound so thankful to hear I was all right?'

'Well, because –' I stopped.

'All right,' said Ginger obligingly. 'You needn't answer that one. And you needn't go out of your way to play down the whole thing. *Something* about it impressed you.'

'Only, I think, because they – Thyrza, I mean – seemed so calmly confident of the result.'

'Confident that what you've been telling me about could actually *kill* a person?'

Ginger's voice was incredulous.

'It's daft,' I agreed.

'Wasn't Bella confident, too?'

I considered. I said:

'I think Bella was just enjoying herself killing cocks and working herself up into a kind of orgy of ill wishing. To hear her moaning out "The Blood . . . the blood" was really something.'

'I wish I'd heard it,' said Ginger regretfully.

'I wish you had,' I said. 'Frankly, the whole thing was quite a performance.'

'You're all right now, aren't you?' said Ginger.

'What do you mean – all right?'

'You weren't when you rang me up, but you are now.'

She was quite correct in her assumption. The sound of her cheerful normal voice had done wonders for me. Secretly, though, I took off my hat to Thyrza Grey. Bogus though the whole business might have been, it had infected my mind with doubt and apprehension. But nothing mattered now. Ginger was all right – she hadn't had so much as a bad dream.

'And what do we do next?' demanded Ginger. 'Have I got to stay put for another week or so?'

'If I want to collect a hundred pounds from Mr Bradley, yes.'

'You'll do that if it's the last thing you ever do . . . Are you staying on with Rhoda?'

'For a bit. Then I'll move on to Bournemouth. You're to ring me every day, mind, or I'll ring you – that's better. I'm ringing from the vicarage now.'

'How's Mrs Dane Calthrop?'

'In great form. I told her all about it, by the way.'

'I thought you would. Well, good-bye for now. Life is going to be very boring for the next week or two. I've brought some work with me to do – and a good many of the books that one always means to read but never has the time to.'

'What does your gallery think?'

'That I'm on a cruise.'

'Don't you wish you were?'

'Not really,' said Ginger . . . Her voice was a little odd.

'No suspicious characters approached you?'

'Only what you might expect. The milkman, the man to read the gas meter, a woman asking me what patent medicines and cosmetics I used, someone asking me to sign a petition to abolish nuclear bombs and a woman who wanted a subscription for the blind. Oh, and the various flat porters, of course. Very helpful. One of them mended a fuse for me.'

'Seems harmless enough,' I commented.

'What were you expecting?'

'I don't really know.'

I had wished, I suppose, for something overt that I could tackle.

But the victims of the Pale Horse died of their own free will . . . No, the word free was *not* the one to use. Seeds of physical weakness in them developed by a process that I did not understand.

Ginger rebuffed a weak suggestion of mine about a false gas meter man.

'He had genuine credentials,' she said. 'I asked for them! He was only the man who gets up on a ladder inside the bathroom and reads off the figures and writes them down. He's far too grand to touch pipes or gas jets. And I can assure you he hasn't arranged an escape of gas in my bedroom.'

No, the Pale Horse did not deal with accidental gas escapes – nothing so concrete!

'Oh! I had one other visitor,' said Ginger. 'Your friend, Dr Corrigan. He's nice.'

'I suppose Lejeune sent him.'

'He seemed to think he ought to rally to a namesake. Up the Corrigans!'

I rang off, much relieved in mind.

I got back to find Rhoda busy on the lawn with one of her dogs. She was anointing it with some unguent.

'The vet's just gone,' she said. 'He says it's ringworm. It's frightfully catching, I believe. I don't want the children getting it – or the other dogs.'

'Or even adult human beings,' I suggested.

'Oh, it's usually children who get it. Thank goodness they're away at school all day – keep quiet, Sheila. Don't wriggle.

'This stuff makes the hair fall out,' she went on. 'It leaves bald spots for a bit but it grows again.'

I nodded, offered to help, was refused, for which I was thankful, and wandered off again.

The curse of the country, I have always thought, is that there are seldom more than three directions in which you can go for a walk. In Much Deeping, you could either take the Garsington road, or the road to Long Cottenham, or you could go up Shadhanger Lane to the main London-Bournemouth road two miles away.

By the following day at lunch-time, I had sampled both the Garsington and the Long Cottenham roads. Shadhanger Lane was the next prospect.

I started off, and on my way was struck by an idea. The entrance to Priors Court opened off Shadhanger Lane. Why should I not go and call on Mr Venables?

The more I considered the idea, the more I liked it. There would be nothing suspicious about my doing so. When I had been staying down here before, Rhoda had taken me over there. It would be easy and natural to call and ask if I might be shown again some particular object that I had not had time really to look at and enjoy on that occasion.

The recognition of Venables by this chemist – what was his name – Ogden? – Osborne? – was interesting, to say the least of it. Granted that, according to Lejeune, it would have been quite impossible for the man in question to have been Venables owing to the latter's disability, yet it was intriguing that a mistake should have been made about a man living in this particular neighbourhood – and a man, one had to admit, who fitted in so well in character.

There was something mysterious about Venables. I had felt it from the first. He had, I was sure, first-class brains. And there was something about him – what word could I use? – the word vulpine came to me. Predatory – destructive. A man, perhaps, too clever to be a killer himself – but a man who could organise killing very well if he wanted to.

As far as all that went, I could fit Venables into the part perfectly. The master mind behind the scenes. But this chemist, Osborne, had claimed that he had *seen Venables walking along a London street.* Since that was impossible, then the identification was worthless, and the fact that Venables lived in the vicinity of the Pale Horse meant nothing.

All the same, I thought, I would like to have another look at Mr Venables. So in due course I turned in at the gates of Priors Court and walked up the quarter mile of winding drive.

The same manservant answered the door, and said that Mr Venables was at home. Excusing himself for leaving me in the hall, 'Mr Venables is not always well enough to see visitors,' he went away, returning a few moments later with the information that Mr Venables would be delighted to see me.

Venables gave me a most cordial welcome, wheeling his chair forward and greeting me quite as an old friend.

'Very nice of you to look me up, my dear fellow. I heard you were down here again, and was going to ring up our dear Rhoda this evening and suggest you all come over for lunch or dinner.'

I apologised for dropping in as I had, but said that it was a sudden impulse. I had gone for a walk, found that I was passing his gate, and decided to gate-crash.

'As a matter of fact,' I said, 'I'd love to have another look at your Mogul miniatures. I hadn't nearly enough time to see them properly the other day.'

'Of course you hadn't. I'm glad you appreciate them. Such exquisite detail.'

Our talk was entirely technical after this. I must admit that I enjoyed enormously having a closer look at some of the really wonderful things he had in his possession.

Tea was brought in and he insisted that I partake of it.

Tea is not one of my favourite meals but I appreciated the smoky China tea, and the delicate cups in which it was served. There was hot buttered anchovy toast, and a plum cake of the luscious old-fashioned kind that took me back to tea-time at my grandmother's house when I was a little boy.

'Home-made,' I said approvingly.

'Naturally! A bought cake never comes into *this* house.'

'You have a wonderful cook, I know. Don't you find it difficult to keep a staff in the country, as far away from things as you are here?'

Venables shrugged his shoulders. 'I must have the best. I insist upon it. Naturally – one has to pay! I pay.'

All the natural arrogance of the man showed here. I said dryly: 'If one is fortunate enough to be able to do that, it certainly solves many problems.'

'It all depends, you know, on what one wants out of life. If one's desires are strong enough – that is what matters. So many people make money without a notion of what they want it to do for them! As a result they get entangled in what one might call the money-making machine. They are slaves. They go to their offices early and leave late; they never stop to *enjoy*. And what do they get for it? Larger cars, bigger houses, more expensive mistresses or wives – and, let me say, bigger headaches.'

He leaned forward.

'Just the *getting* of money – that is really the be all and end all for most rich men. Plough it back into bigger enterprises, make more money still. But *why?* Do they ever stop to ask themselves why? They don't know.'

'And you?' I asked.

'I –' he smiled. 'I knew what I wanted. Infinite leisure in which to contemplate the beautiful things of this world, natural and artificial. Since to go and see them in their natural surroundings has of late years been denied me, I have them brought from all over the world to me.'

'But money still has to be got before that can happen.'

'Yes, one must plan one's coups – and that involves quite a lot of planning – but there is no need, really no need nowadays, to serve any sordid apprenticeship.'

'I don't know if I quite understand you.'

'It's a changing world, Easterbrook. It always has been – but now the changes come more rapidly. The tempo has quickened – one must take advantage of that.'

'A changing world,' I said thoughtfully.

'It opens up new vistas.'

I said apologetically:

'I'm afraid, you know, that you're talking to a man whose face is set in the opposite direction – towards the past – not towards the future.'

Venables shrugged his shoulders.

'The future? Who can foresee that? I speak of today – now – the immediate moment! I take no account of anything else. The new techniques are here to use. Already we have machines that can supply us with the answer to questions in seconds – compared to hours or days of human labour.'

'Computers? The electronic brain?'

'Things of that kind.'

'Will machines take the place of men eventually?'

'Of *men*, yes. Men who are only units of manpower – that is. But Man, no. There has to be Man the Controller, Man the Thinker, who works out the questions to ask the machines.'

I shook my head doubtfully.

'Man, the Superman?' I put a faint inflection of ridicule into my voice.

'Why not, Easterbrook? Why not? Remember, we know – or are beginning to know – something about Man the human animal. The practice of what is sometimes, incorrectly, called brain-washing has opened up enormously interesting possibilities in that direction. Not only the body, but the *mind* of man, responds to certain stimuli.'

'A dangerous doctrine,' I said.

'Dangerous?'

'Dangerous to the doctored man.'

Venables shrugged his shoulders.

'All life is dangerous. We forget that, we who have been reared in one of the small pockets of civilisation. For that is all that civilisation really is, Easterbrook. Small pockets of men here and there who have gathered together for mutual protection and who thereby are able to outwit and control Nature. They have beaten the jungle – but that victory is only temporary. At any moment, the jungle will once more take command. Proud cities that were, are now mere mounds of earth, overgrown with rank vegetation, and the poor hovels of men who just manage to keep alive, no more. Life is always dangerous – never forget that. In the end, perhaps, not only great natural forces, but the work of our own hands may destroy it. We are very near to that happening at this moment . . .'

'No one can deny that, certainly. But I'm interested in your theory of power – power over mind.'

'Oh that –' Venables looked suddenly embarrassed. 'Probably I exaggerated.'

I found his embarrassment and partial withdrawal of his former claim interesting. Venables was a man who lived much alone. A man who is alone develops the need to talk – to someone – anyone. Venables had talked to me – and perhaps not wisely.

'Man the Superman,' I said. 'You've rather sold me on some modern version of the idea, you know.'

'There's nothing new about it, certainly. The formula of the Superman goes back a long way. Whole philosophies have been built on it.'

'Of course. But it seems to me that your Superman is – a Superman with a difference . . . A man who could wield power – and never be *known* to wield power. A man who sits in his chair and pulls the strings.'

I looked at him as I spoke. He smiled.

'Are you casting me for the part, Easterbrook? I wish it were indeed so. One needs something to compensate for – *this!*'

His hand struck down on the rug across his knees, and I heard the sudden sharp bitterness in his voice.

'I won't offer you my sympathy,' I said. 'Sympathy is very little good to a man in your position. But let me say that if we *are* imagining such a character – a man who can turn unforeseen disaster into triumph – you would be, in my opinion, exactly that type of man.'

He laughed easily.

'You're flattering me.'

But he was pleased, I saw that.

'No,' I said. 'I have met enough people in my life to recognise the unusual, the extra gifted man, when I meet him.'

I was afraid of going too far; but can one ever, really, go too far with flattery? A depressing thought! One must take it to heart and avoid the pitfall oneself.

'I wondered,' he said thoughtfully, 'what actually makes you say that? All this?' He swept a careless hand round the room.

'That is a proof,' I said, 'that you are a rich man who knows how to buy wisely, who has appreciation and taste. But I feel that there is more to it than mere possession. You set out to acquire beautiful and interesting things – and you have practically hinted that they were not acquired through the medium of laborious toil.'

'Quite right, Easterbrook, quite right. As I said, only the fool toils. One must think, plan the campaign in every detail. The secret of all success is something quite simple – but it has to be thought of! Something simple. One thinks of it, one puts it into execution – and there you are!'

I stared at him. Something simple – something as simple as the removal of unwanted persons? Fulfilling a need. An action performed without danger to anybody except the victim. Planned by Mr Venables sitting in his wheeled chair, with his great hooked nose like the beak of a bird of prey, and his prominent Adam's apple moving up and down. Executed by – whom? Thyrza Grey?

I watched him as I said:

'All this talk of remote control reminds me of something that odd Miss Grey said.'

'Ah, our dear Thyrza!' His tone was smooth, indulgent (but had there been a faint flicker of the eyelids?). 'Such nonsense as those two dear ladies talk! And they believe it, you know, they really believe it. Have you been yet – (I'm sure they'll insist on your going) – to one of these ridiculous *séances* of theirs?'

I had a momentary hesitation whilst I decided rapidly what my attitude here ought to be.

'Yes,' I said, 'I – I did go to a *séance*.'

'And you found it great nonsense? Or were you impressed?'

I avoided his eyes and presented to my best ability a man who is ill at ease.

'I – oh well – of course I didn't really believe in any of it. They seem very sincere but –' I looked at my watch. 'I'd no idea it was so late. I must hurry back. My cousin will wonder what I am doing.'

'You have been cheering up an invalid on a dull afternoon. My regards to Rhoda. We must arrange another luncheon party soon. Tomorrow I am going to London. There is an interesting sale at Sotheby's. Medieval French ivories. Exquisite! You will appreciate them, I am sure, if I succeed in acquiring them.'

We parted on this amicable note. Was there an amused and malicious twinkle in his eye as he registered my awkwardness over the *séance?* I thought so, but I could not be sure. I felt it quite likely that I was now imagining things.

CHAPTER 19

MARK EASTERBROOK'S NARRATIVE

I went out into the late afternoon. Darkness had already fallen, and since the sky was overcast, I moved rather uncertainly down the winding drive. I looked back once at the lighted windows of the house. In doing so, I stepped off the gravel on to the grass and collided with someone moving in the opposite direction.

It was a small man, solidly made. We exchanged apologies. His voice was a rich deep bass with a rather fruity and pedantic tone.

'I'm so sorry . . .'

'Not at all. Entirely my fault, I assure you . . .'

'I have never been here before,' I explained, 'so I don't quite know where I'm going. I ought to have brought a torch.'

'Allow me.'

The stranger produced a torch from his pocket, switched it on and handed it to me. By its light I saw that he was a man of middle age, with a round cherubic face, a black moustache and spectacles. He wore a good quality dark raincoat and can only be described as the acme of respectability. All the same, it did just cross my mind to wonder why he was not using his torch himself since he had it with him.

'Ah,' I said rather idiotically. 'I see. I have stepped off the drive.'

I stepped back on it, then offered him back the torch.

'I can find my way now.'

'No, no, pray keep it until you get to the gate.'

'But you – you are going to the house?'

'No, no. I am going the same way that you are. Er – down the drive. And then up to the bus stop. I am catching a bus back to Bournemouth.'

I said, 'I see,' and we fell into step side by side. My companion seemed a little ill at ease. He inquired if I also were going to the bus stop. I replied that I was staying in the neighbourhood.

There was again a pause and I could feel my companion's embarrassment growing. He was the kind of man who does not like feeling in any way in a false position.

'You have been to visit Mr Venables?' he asked, clearing his throat.

I said that that was so, adding, 'I took it that you also were on your way to the house?'

'No,' he said. 'No . . . As a matter of fact –' he paused. 'I live in Bournemouth – or at least near Bournemouth. I have just moved into a small bungalow there.'

I felt a faint stirring in my mind. What had I recently heard about a bungalow at Bournemouth? Whilst I was trying to remember, my companion, becoming even more ill at ease, was finally impelled to speak.

'You must think it very odd – I admit, of course, it *is* odd – to find someone wandering in the grounds of a house when the – er – person in question is not acquainted with the owner of the house. My reasons are a little difficult to explain, though I assure you that I have reasons. But I can only say that although I have only recently settled in Bournemouth, I am quite well known there, and I could bring forward several esteemed residents to vouch for me personally. Actually, I am a pharmacist who has recently sold an old-established business in London, and I have retired to this part of the world which I have always found very pleasant – very pleasant indeed.'

Enlightenment came to me. I thought I knew who the little man was. Meanwhile he was continuing in full spate.

'My name is Osborne, Zachariah Osborne, and as I say I have – had rather – a very nice business in London – Barton Street –

Paddington Green. Quite a good neighbourhood in my father's time, but sadly changed now – oh yes, very much changed. Gone down in the world.'

He sighed, and shook his head.

Then he resumed:

'This *is* Mr Venables's house, is it not? I suppose – er – he is a friend of yours?'

I said with deliberation:

'Hardly a friend. I have only met him once before to-day, when I was taken to lunch with him by some friends of mine.'

'Ah yes – I see . . . Yes, precisely.'

We had come now to the entrance gates. We passed through them. Mr Osborne paused irresolutely. I handed him back his torch.

'Thank you,' I said.

'Not at all. You're welcome. I–' He paused, then words came from him in a rush.

'I shouldn't like you to think . . . I mean, technically, of course, I *was* trespassing. But not, I assure you, from any motive of vulgar curiosity. It must have seemed to you most peculiar – my position – and open to misconstruction. I really would like to explain – to – er – clarify my position.'

I waited. It seemed the best thing to do. My curiosity, vulgar or not, was certainly aroused. I wanted it satisfied.

Mr Osborne was silent for about a minute, then he made up his mind.

'I really would like to explain to you, Mr – er –'

'Easterbrook. Mark Easterbrook.'

'Mr Easterbrook. As I say, I would welcome the chance of explaining my rather odd behaviour. If you have the time–? It is only five minutes' walk up the lane to the main road. There is quite a respectable little café at the petrol station close to the bus stop. My bus is not due for over twenty minutes. If you would allow me to offer you a cup of coffee?'

I accepted. We walked up the lane together. Mr Osborne, his anguished respectability appeased, chatted cosily of the amenities of Bournemouth, its excellent climate, its concerts and the nice class of people who lived there.

We reached the main road. The petrol station was on the corner with the bus stop just beyond it. There was a small clean café, empty except for a young couple in a corner. We entered and Mr Osborne ordered coffee and biscuits for two.

Then he leaned forward across the table and unburdened himself.

'This all stems from a case you may have seen reported in the newspapers some time ago. It was not a very sensational case, so it did not make the headlines – if that is the correct expression. It concerned the Roman Catholic parish priest of the district in London where I have – had – my shop. He was set upon one night and killed. Very distressing. Such happenings are far too frequent nowadays. He was, I believe, a good man – though I myself do not hold with the Roman doctrine. However that may be, I must explain my particular interest. There was a police announcement that they were anxious to interview anyone who had seen Father Gorman on the night in question. By chance I had happened to be standing outside the door of my establishment that evening about eight o'clock and had seen Father Gorman go by. Following him at a short distance was a man whose appearance was unusual enough to attract my attention. At the time, of course, I thought nothing of the matter, but I am an observant man, Mr Easterbrook, and I have the habit of mentally registering what people look like. It is quite a hobby of mine, and several people who have come to my shop have been surprised when I say to them, "Ah yes, I think you came in for this same preparation last March?" It pleases them, you know, to be remembered. Good business, I have found it. Anyway, I described the man I had seen to the police. They thanked me and that was that.

'Now I come to the rather surprising part of my story. About ten days ago I came over to a church fête in the little village at the bottom of the lane we have just walked up – and what was my surprise to see this same man I have mentioned. He must have had, or so I thought, an accident, since he was propelling himself in a wheeled chair. I inquired about him and was told he was a rich local resident of the name of Venables. After a day or two to debate the matter, I wrote to the police officer to whom I had made my original statement. He came down to Bournemouth – Inspector Lejeune was his name. He seemed sceptical, however, as to whether this was indeed the man I had seen on the night of the murder. He informed me that Mr Venables had been crippled for some years, as a result of polio. I must, he said, have been misled by a chance resemblance.'

Mr Osborne came to an abrupt halt. I stirred the pale fluid in front of me and took a cautious sip. Mr Osborne added three lumps of sugar to his own cup.

'Well, that seems to settle that,' I said.

'Yes,' said Mr Osborne. 'Yes . . .' His voice was markedly dissatisfied. Then he leaned forward again, his round bald head shining under the electric bulb, his eyes quite fanatical behind his spectacles . . .

'I must explain a little more. As a boy, Mr Easterbrook, a friend of my father's, another pharmacist, was called to give evidence in the case of Jean Paul Marigot. You may remember – he poisoned his English wife – an arsenical preparation. My father's friend identified him in court as the man who signed a false name in his poison register. Marigot was convicted and hanged. It made a great impression on me – I was nine years old at the time – an impressionable age. It was my great hope that some day, I, too, might figure in a *cause célèbre* and be the instrument of bringing a murderer to justice! Perhaps it was then that I began to make a study of memorising faces. I will confess to you, Mr Easterbrook, though it may seem to you quite ridiculous, that for many, many years now I have contemplated the possibility that some man, determined to do away with his wife, might enter my shop to purchase what he needed.'

'Or, I suppose, a second Madeleine Smith,' I suggested.

'Exactly. Alas,' Mr Osborne sighed, 'that has never happened. Or, if so, the person in question has never been brought to justice. That occurs, I would say, more frequently than it is quite comfortable to believe. So this identification, though not what I had hoped, opened up at least a *possibility* that I might be a witness in a murder case!'

His face beamed with childish pleasure.

'Very disappointing for you,' I said sympathetically.

'Ye-es.' Again Mr Osborne's voice held that odd note of dissatisfaction.

'I'm an obstinate man, Mr Easterbrook. As the days have passed by I have felt more and more sure that I *was right*. That the man I saw *was* Venables and no other. Oh!' he raised a hand in protest as I was about to speak. 'I know. It was inclined to be foggy. I was some distance away – but what the police have not taken into consideration is that I have made a study of recognition. It was not just the features, the pronounced nose, the Adam's apple; there is the carriage of the head, the angle of the neck on the shoulders. I said to myself "Come, come, admit you were mistaken." But I continued to feel that I had *not* been mistaken. The police said it was impossible. But *was* it impossible? That's what I asked myself.'

'Surely, with a disability of that kind –'

He stopped me by waving an agitated forefinger.

'Yes, yes, but my experiences, under the National Health – Well, really it would surprise you what people are prepared to do – and what they get away with! I wouldn't like to say that the medical profession are credulous – a plain case of malingering they will spot soon enough. But there are ways – ways that a chemist is more likely to appreciate than a doctor. Certain drugs, for instance, other quite harmless-seeming preparations. Fever can be induced – various rashes and skin irritations – dryness of throat, or increase of secretions –'

'But hardly atrophied limbs,' I pointed out.

'Quite, quite. But who says that Mr Venables's limbs *are* atrophied?'

'Well – his doctor, I suppose?'

'Quite. But I have tried to get a little information on that point. Mr Venables's doctor is in London, a Harley Street man – true, he *was* seen by the local doctor here when he first arrived. But that doctor has now retired and gone to live abroad. The present man *has never attended Mr Venables*. Mr Venables goes up once a month to Harley Street.'

I looked at him curiously.

'That still seems to me to present no loophole for er – er –'

'You don't know the things I know,' said Mr Osborne. 'A humble example will suffice. Mrs H. – drawing insurance benefits for over a year. Drew them in three separate places – only in one place she was Mrs C. and in another place Mrs T. . . . Mrs C. and Mrs T. lent her their cards for a consideration, and so she collected the money three times over.'

'I don't see –'

'Suppose – just suppose –' The forefinger was now wiggling excitedly, 'our Mr V. makes contact with a genuine polio case in poor circumstances. He makes a proposition. The man resembles him, let us say, in a general kind of way, no more. Genuine sufferer calling himself Mr V. calls in specialist, and is examined, so that the case history is all correct. Then Mr V. takes house in country. Local G.P. wants to retire soon. Again genuine sufferer calls in doctor, is examined. And there you are! Mr Venables well documented as a polio sufferer with atrophied limbs. He is seen locally (when he is seen) in a wheeled chair, etc.'

'His servants would know, surely,' I objected. 'His valet.'

'But supposing it is a gang – the valet is one of the gang. What could be simpler? Some of the other servants, too, perhaps.'

'But *why*?'

'Ah,' said Mr Osborne. 'That's another question, isn't it? I won't tell you *my* theory – I expect you'd laugh at it. But there you are – a very nice *alibi* set up for a man who might want an alibi. He could be here, there and everywhere, and nobody would know. Seen walking about in Paddington? Impossible! He's a helpless cripple living in the country, etc.' Mr Osborne paused and glanced at his watch. 'My bus is due. I must be quick. I get to brooding about this you see. Wondered if I could do anything to prove it, as you might say. So I thought I'd come out here (I've time on my hands, these days. I almost miss my business sometimes), go into the grounds and – well, not to put too fine a point upon it, do a bit of spying. Not very nice, you'll say – and I agree. But if it's a case of getting at the truth – of bringing a criminal to book . . . If, for instance, I spotted our Mr Venables having a quiet walk around in the grounds, well, there you are! And then I thought, if they don't pull the curtains too soon – (and you may have noticed people don't when daylight saving first ends – they've got in the habit of expecting it to be dark an hour later) – I might creep up and take a peep. Walking about his library, maybe, never dreaming that anyone would be spying on him? Why should he? No one suspects him as far as he knows!'

'Why are you so sure the man you saw that night was Venables?'

'I *know* it was Venables!'

He shot to his feet.

'My bus is coming. Pleased to have met you, Mr Easterbrook, and it's a weight off my mind to have explained what I was doing there at Priors Court. I dare say it seems a lot of nonsense to *you.*'

'It doesn't altogether,' I said. 'But you haven't told me what you think Mr Venables is up to.'

Mr Osborne looked embarrassed and a little sheepish.

'You'll laugh, I dare say. Everybody says he's rich but nobody seems to know *how he made his money*. I'll tell you what *I* think. I think he's one of those master criminals you read about. You know – plans things, and has a gang that carries them out. It may sound silly to you but I –'

The bus had stopped. Mr Osborne ran for it –

I walked home down the lane very thoughtful . . . It was a fantastic theory that Mr Osborne had outlined, but I had to admit that there might just possibly be something in it.

CHAPTER 20

MARK EASTERBROOK'S NARRATIVE

1

Ringing up Ginger on the following morning, I told her that I was moving to Bournemouth the next day.

'I've found a nice quiet little hotel called (heaven knows why) the Deer Park. It's got a couple of nice unobtrusive side exits. I *might* sneak up to London and see you.'

'You oughtn't to really, I suppose. But I must say it *would* be rather heaven if you did. The boredom! You've no idea! If you couldn't come here, I could sneak out and meet you somewhere.'

Something suddenly struck me.

'Ginger! Your voice . . . It's different somehow . . .'

'Oh that! It's all right. Don't worry.'

'But your *voice?*'

'I've just got a bit of a sore throat or something, that's all.'

'Ginger!'

'Now look, Mark, anyone can have a sore throat. I'm starting a cold, I expect. Or a touch of 'flu.'

''Flu? Look here, don't evade the point. Are you all right, or aren't you?'

'Don't fuss. I'm all right.'

'Tell me exactly how you're feeling. Do you feel as though you might be starting 'flu?'

'Well – perhaps . . . Aching a bit all over, you know the kind of thing –'

'Temperature?'

'Well, perhaps a bit of a temperature . . .'

I sat there, a horrible cold sort of feeling stealing over me. I was frightened. I knew, too, that however much Ginger might refuse to admit it, Ginger was frightened also.

Her voice spoke again.

'Mark – don't panic. You *are* panicking – and really there's nothing to panic about.'

'Perhaps not. But we've got to take every precaution. Ring up your doctor and get him to come and see you. At once.'

'All right . . . But – he'll think I'm a terrible fuss-pot.'

'Never mind. *Do* it! Then, when he's been, ring me back.'

After I had rung off, I sat for a long time staring at the black inhuman outline of the telephone. Panic – I mustn't give way to panic . . . There was always 'flu about at this time of year . . . The doctor would be reassuring . . . perhaps it would be only a slight chill . . .

I saw in my mind's eye Sybil in her peacock dress with its scrawled symbols of evil. I heard Thyrza's voice, willing, commanding . . . On the chalked floor, Bella, chanting her evil spells, held up a struggling white cock . . .

Nonsense, all nonsense . . . Of course it was all superstitious nonsense . . .

The box – not so easy, somehow, to dismiss the box. The box represented, not human superstition, but a development of scientific possibility . . . But it wasn't possible – it couldn't be possible that –

Mrs Dane Calthrop found me there, sitting staring at the telephone. She said at once:

'What's happened?'

'Ginger,' I said, 'isn't feeling well . . .'

I wanted her to say that it was all nonsense. I wanted her to reassure me. But she didn't reassure me.

'That's bad,' she said. 'Yes, I think that's bad.'

'It's not possible,' I urged. 'It's not possible for a moment that they can do what they say!'

'Isn't it?'

'You don't believe – you can't believe –'

'My dear Mark,' said Mrs Dane Calthrop, 'both you and Ginger have already admitted the possibility of such a thing, or you wouldn't be doing what you are doing.'

'And our believing makes it worse – makes it more likely!'

'You don't go so far as *believing* – you just admit that, with evidence, you might believe.'

'Evidence? What evidence?'

'Ginger's becoming ill is evidence,' said Mrs Dane Calthrop.

I hated her. My voice rose angrily.

'Why must you be so pessimistic? It's just a simple cold – something of that kind. Why must you persist in believing the worst?'

'Because if it's the worst, we've got to face it – not bury our heads in the sand until it's too late.'

'You think that this ridiculous mumbo jumbo *works?* These trances and spells and cock sacrifices and all the bag of tricks?'

'*Something* works,' said Mrs Dane Calthrop. 'That's what we've got to face. A lot of it, most of it, I think, is *trappings*. It's just to create atmosphere – atmosphere is important. But concealed amongst the trappings, there must be the real thing – the thing that *does* work.'

'Something like radio activity at a distance?'

'Something of that kind. You see, people are discovering things all the time – frightening things. Some variation of this new knowledge might be adapted by some unscrupulous person for their own purposes – Thyrza's father was a physicist, you know –'

'But *what? What?* That damned box! If we could get it examined? If the police –'

'Police aren't very keen on getting a search warrant and removing property without a good deal more to go on than we've got.'

'If I went round there and smashed up the damned thing?'

Mrs Dane Calthrop shook her head.

'From what you told me, the damage, if there *has* been damage, was done that night.'

I dropped my head in my hands and groaned.

'I wish we'd never started this damned business.'

Mrs Dane Calthrop said firmly: 'Your motives were excellent. And what's done is done. You'll know more when Ginger rings back after the doctor has been. She'll ring Rhoda's, I suppose –'

I took the hint.

'I'd better get back.'

'I'm being stupid,' said Mrs Dane Calthrop suddenly as I left. 'I know I'm being stupid. *Trappings!* We're letting ourselves be obsessed by trappings. I can't help feeling that we're thinking the way they *want* us to think.'

Perhaps she was right. But I couldn't see any other way of thinking.

Ginger rang me two hours later.

'He's been,' she said. 'He seemed a bit puzzled, but he says it's probably 'flu. There's quite a lot about. He's sent me to bed and is sending along some medicine. My temperature is quite high. But it would be with 'flu, wouldn't it?'

There was a forlorn appeal in her hoarse voice, under its surface bravery.

'You'll be all right,' I said miserably. 'Do you hear? You'll be all right. Do you feel very awful?'

'Well – fever – and aching, and everything hurts, my feet and my skin. I hate anything touching me . . . And I'm so hot.'

'That's the fever, darling. Listen, I'm coming up to you! I'm leaving now – at once. No, don't protest.'

'All right. I'm glad you're coming, Mark. I dare say – I'm not so brave as I thought . . .'

II

I rang up Lejeune.

'Miss Corrigan's ill,' I said.

'What?'

'You heard me. She's ill. She's called her own doctor. He says perhaps 'flu. It may be. But it may not. I don't know what *you* can do. The only idea that occurs to me is to get some kind of specialist on to it.'

'What kind of specialist?'

'A psychiatrist – or psychoanalyst, or psychologist. A psycho something. A man who knows about suggestion and hypnotism and brainwashing and all that kind of thing. There *are* people who deal with that kind of thing?'

'Of course there are. Yes. There are one or two Home Office men who specialise in it. I think you're dead right. It may be just 'flu – but it may be some kind of psycho-business about which nothing much is known. Lord, Easterbrook, this may be just what we've been hoping for!'

I slammed down the receiver. We might be learning something about psychological weapons – but all that I cared about was Ginger, gallant and frightened. We hadn't really believed, either of us – or had we? No, of course we hadn't. It had been a game – a cops and robbers game. But it wasn't a game.

The Pale Horse was proving itself a reality.

I dropped my head into my hands and groaned.

CHAPTER 21

MARK EASTERBROOK'S NARRATIVE

I

I doubt if I shall ever forget the next few days. It appears to me now as a kind of bewildered kaleidoscope without sequence or form. Ginger was removed from the flat to a private nursing home. I was allowed to see her only at visiting hours.

Her own doctor, I gather, was inclined to stand on his high horse about the whole business. He could not understand what the fuss was all about. His own diagnosis was quite clear – broncho pneumonia following on influenza, though complicated by certain slightly unusual symptoms, but that, as he pointed out, 'happens all the time. No case is ever "typical". And some people don't respond to antibiotics.'

And, of course, all that he said was true. Ginger had broncho pneumonia. There was nothing mysterious about the disease from which she was suffering. She just had it – and had it badly.

I had one interview with the Home Office psychologist. He was a quaint little cock robin of a man, rising up and down on his toes, with eyes twinkling through very thick lenses.

He asked me innumerable questions, half of which I could see no point in whatever, but there must have been a point, for he nodded sapiently at my answers. He entirely refused to commit himself, wherein he was probably wise. He made occasional pronouncements in what I took to be the jargon of his trade. He tried, I think, various forms of hypnotism on Ginger, but by what seemed to be universal consent, no one would tell me very much. Possibly because there was nothing to tell.

I avoided my own friends and acquaintances, yet the loneliness of my existence was insupportable.

Finally, in an excess of desperation, I rang up Poppy at her flower shop. Would she come out and dine with me. Poppy would love to do so.

I took her to the Fantasie. Poppy prattled happily and I found her company very soothing. But I had not asked her out only for her soothing qualities. Having lulled her into a happy stupor with delicious food and drink, I began a little cautious probing. It seemed to be possible that Poppy might know something without being wholly conscious of what it was she knew. I asked her if she remembered my friend Ginger. Poppy said, 'Of course,' opening her big blue eyes, and asked what Ginger was doing nowadays.

'She's very ill,' I said.

'Poor pet.' Poppy looked as concerned as it was possible for her to look, which was not very much.

'She got herself mixed up with something,' I said. 'I believe she asked your advice about it. Pale Horse stuff. Cost her a terrible lot of money.'

'Oh,' exclaimed Poppy, eyes wider still. 'So it was *you*!'

For a moment or two I didn't understand. Then it dawned upon me that Poppy was identifying me with the 'man' whose invalid wife was the bar to Ginger's happiness. So excited was she by this revelation of our love life that she quite failed to be alarmed by the mention of the Pale Horse.

She breathed excitedly:

'Did it work?'

'It went a bit wrong somehow.' I added, '*The dog it was that died.*'

'What dog?' asked Poppy, at sea.

I saw that words of one syllable would always be needed where Poppy was concerned.

'The – er – business seems to have recoiled upon Ginger. Did you ever hear of that happening before?'

Poppy never had.

'Of course,' I said, 'this stuff they do at the Pale Horse down in Much Deeping – you know about that, don't you?'

'I didn't know where it was. Down in the country somewhere.'

'I couldn't quite make out from Ginger what it is they do . . .'

I waited carefully.

'Rays, isn't it?' said Poppy vaguely. 'Something like that. From outer space,' she added helpfully. 'Like the Russians!'

I decided that Poppy was now relying on her limited imagination.

'Something of that kind,' I agreed. 'But it must be quite dangerous. I mean, for Ginger to get ill like this.'

'But it was your wife who was to be ill and die, wasn't it?'

'Yes,' I said, accepting the role Ginger and Poppy had planted on me. 'But it seems to have gone wrong – backfired.'

'You mean –?' Poppy made a terrific mental effort. 'Like when you plug an electric iron in wrong and you get a shock?'

'Exactly,' I said. 'Just like that. Did you ever know that sort of thing happen before?'

'Well, not that way –'

'What way, then?'

'Well, I mean if one didn't pay up – afterwards. A man I knew wouldn't.' Her voice dropped in an awe-stricken fashion. 'He was killed in the tube – fell off the platform in front of a train.'

'It might have been an accident.'

'Oh no,' said Poppy, shocked at the thought. 'It was THEM.'

I poured some more champagne into Poppy's glass. Here, I felt, in front of me was someone who might be helpful if only you could tear out of her the disassociated facts that were flitting about in what she called her brain. She had heard things said, and assimilated about half of them, and got them jumbled up and nobody had been very careful what they said because it was 'only Poppy'.

The maddening thing was that I didn't know what to ask her. If I said the wrong thing she would shut up in alarm like a clam and go dumb on me.

'My wife,' I said, 'is still an invalid, but she doesn't seem any worse.'

'That's too bad,' said Poppy sympathetically, sipping champagne.

'So what do I do next?'

Poppy didn't seem to know.

'You see it was Ginger who – *I* didn't make any of the arrangements. Is there anyone I could get at?'

'There's a place in Birmingham,' said Poppy doubtfully.

'That's closed down,' I said. 'Don't you know anyone else who'd know anything about it?'

'Eileen Brandon *might* know something – but I don't think so.'

The introduction of a totally unexpected Eileen Brandon startled me. I asked who Eileen Brandon was.

'She's terrible really,' said Poppy. 'Very dim. Has her hair very tightly permed, and *never* wears stiletto heels. She's the end.' She added by way of explanation, 'I was at school with her – but she was pretty dim then. She was frightfully good at geography.'

'What's she got to do with the Pale Horse?'

'Nothing really. It was only an idea she got. And so she chucked it up.'

'Chucked what up?' I asked, bewildered.

'Her job with C.R.C.'

'What's C.R.C.?'

'Well, I don't really know exactly. They just say C.R.C. Something about Customers' Reactions or Research. It's quite a small show.'

'And Eileen Brandon worked for them? What did she have to do?'

'Just go round and ask questions – about toothpaste or gas stoves, and what kind of sponges you used. Too too depressing and dull. I mean, who *cares*?'

'Presumably C.R.C.' I felt a slight prickling of excitement.

It was a woman employed by an association of this kind who had been visited by Father Gorman on the fatal night. And – yes – of course, someone of that kind had called on Ginger at the flat . . .

Here was a link of some kind.

'Why did she chuck up her job? Because she got bored?'

'I don't think so. They paid quite well. But she got a sort of idea about it – that it wasn't what it seemed.'

'She thought that it might be connected, in some way, with the Pale Horse? Is that it?'

'Well, I don't know. Something of that kind . . . Anyway, she's working in an Espresso coffee bar off Tottenham Court Road now.'

'Give me her address.'

'She's not a bit your type.'

'I don't want to make sexual advances to her,' I said brutally. 'I want some hints on Customers Research. I'm thinking of buying some shares in one of those things.'

'Oh, I see,' said Poppy, quite satisfied with this explanation.

There was nothing more to be got out of her, so we finished up the champagne, and I took her home and thanked her for a lovely evening.

II

I tried to ring Lejeune next morning – but failed. However, after some difficulty I managed to get through to Jim Corrigan.

'What about that psychological pipsqueak you brought along to see me, Corrigan? What does he say about Ginger?'

'A lot of long words. But I rather think, Mark, that he's yours truly baffled. And you know, people do *get* pneumonia. There's nothing mysterious or out of the way about that.'

'Yes,' I said. 'And several people we know of, whose names were on a certain list, have died of broncho pneumonia, gastro-enteritis, bulbar paralysis, tumour on the brain, epilepsy, para-typhoid and other well-authenticated diseases.'

'I know how you feel . . . But what can we do?'

'She's worse, isn't she?' I asked.

'Well – yes . . .'

'Then something's *got* to be done.'

'Such as?'

'I've got one or two ideas. Going down to Much Deeping, getting hold of Thyrza Grey and forcing her, by scaring the living daylights out of her, to reverse the spell or whatever it is –'

'Well – that might work.'

'Or – I might go to Venables –'

Corrigan said sharply:

'Venables? But he's out. How can he possibly have any connection with it? He's a cripple.'

'I wonder. I might go there and snatch off that rug affair and see if this atrophied limbs business is true or false!'

'We've looked into all that –'

'Wait. I ran into that little chemist chap, Osborne, down in Much Deeping. I want to repeat to you what he suggested to me.'

I outlined to him Osborne's theory of impersonation.

'That man's got a bee in his bonnet,' said Corrigan. 'He's the kind of man who has always got to be right.'

'But Corrigan, tell me, *couldn't* it be as he said? It's *possible*, isn't it?'

After a moment or two Corrigan said slowly,

'Yes. I have to admit it's *possible* . . . But several people would have to be in the know – and would have to be paid very heavily for holding their tongues.'

'What of that? He's rolling in money, isn't he? Has Lejeune found out yet how he's made all that money?'

'No. Not exactly . . . I'll admit this to you. There's something wrong about the fellow. He's got a past of some kind. The money's all very cleverly accounted for, in a lot of ways. It isn't possible to check up on it all without an investigation which might take years. The police have had to do that before – when they've been up against a financial crook who has covered his traces by a web of infinite complexity. I believe the Inland Revenue has been smelling around Venables for some time. But he's clever. What do you see him as – the head of the show?'

'Yes. I do. I think he's the man who plans it all.'

'Perhaps. He sounds as though he'd have the kind of brains for that, I agree. But surely he wouldn't have done anything so crude as killing Father Gorman himself!'

'He might have if there was sufficient urgency. Father Gorman might have had to be silenced before he could pass on what he had learnt from that woman about the activities of the Pale Horse. Besides –'

I stopped short.

'Hallo – you still there?'

'Yes, I was thinking . . . Just an idea that occurred to me . . .'

'What was it?'

'I've not got it clear yet . . . Just that real safety could only be achieved one way. I haven't worked it out yet . . . Anyway, I must go now. I've got a rendezvous at a coffee bar.'

'Didn't know you were in the Chelsea coffee bar set!'

'I'm not. My coffee bar is in Tottenham Court Road, as a matter of fact.'

I rang off and glanced at the clock.

I started for the door when the telephone rang.

I hesitated. Ten to one, it was Jim Corrigan again, ringing back to know more about my idea.

I didn't want to talk to Jim Corrigan just now.

I moved towards the door whilst the telephone rang on persistently, naggingly.

Of course, it might be the hospital – Ginger –

I couldn't risk that. I strode across impatiently and jerked the receiver off its hook.

'Hallo?'

'Is that you, Mark?'

'Yes, who is it?'

'It's me, of course,' said the voice reproachfully. 'Listen, I want to tell you something.'

'Oh, it's you.' I recognised the voice of Mrs Oliver. 'Look here, I'm in a great hurry, got to go out. I'll ring you back later.'

'That won't do at all,' said Mrs Oliver, firmly. 'You've got to listen to me now. It's important.'

'Well, you'll have to be quick. I've got an appointment.'

'Pooh,' said Mrs Oliver. 'You can always be late for an appointment. Everybody is. They'll think all the more of you.'

'No, really, I've got to –'

'Listen, Mark. This is important. I'm sure it is. It *must* be!'

I curbed my impatience as best I could, glancing at the clock.

'Well?'

'My Milly had tonsilitis. She was quite bad and she's gone to the country – to her sister –'

I gritted my teeth.

'I'm frightfully sorry about that, but really –'

'Listen. I've not begun yet. Where was I? Oh yes. Milly had to go to the country and so I rang up the agency I always go to – the Regency – such a silly name I always think – like a cinema –'

'I really must –'

'And said what could they send? And they said it was very difficult just now – which they always say as a matter of fact – but they'd do what they could –'

Never had I found my friend Ariadne Oliver so maddening.

'– and so, this morning a woman came along, and who do you think she turned out to be?'

'I can't imagine. Look –'

'A woman called Edith Binns – comic name, isn't it? – and *you* actually know her.'

'No, I don't. I never heard of a woman called Edith Binns.'

'But you do know her and you saw her not very long ago. She had been with that godmother of yours for years. Lady Hesketh-Dubois.'

'Oh, with her!'

'Yes. She saw you the day you came to collect some pictures.'

'Well, that's all very nice and I expect you're very lucky to find her. I believe she's most trustworthy and reliable and all that. Aunt Min said so. But really – now –'

'*Wait*, can't you? I haven't got to the point. She sat and talked a great deal about Lady Hesketh-Dubois and her last illness, and all that sort of thing, because they do love illnesses and death and then she said it.'

'Said what?'

'The thing that caught my attention. She said something like: "Poor dear lady, suffering like she did. That nasty thing on her brain, a growth, they say, and she in quite good health up to just before. And pitiful it was to see her in the nursing home and all her hair, nice thick white hair it was, and always blued regularly once a fortnight, to see it coming out all over the pillow. Coming out in handfuls. And then, Mark, I thought of Mary Delafontaine, that friend of mine. *Her hair came out.* And I remembered what you told me about some girl you'd seen in a Chelsea coffee place fighting with another girl, and getting her hair all pulled out in handfuls. Hair doesn't come out as easily as that, Mark. You try – just try to pull your own hair, just a little bit of it, out by the roots!

Just *try* it! You'll see. It's not natural, Mark, for all those people to have hair that comes out by the roots. It's not natural. It must be some special kind of new illness – it must *mean* something.'

I clutched the receiver and my head swam. Things, half-remembered scraps of knowledge, drew together. Rhoda and her dogs on the lawn – an article I had read in a medical journal in New York – Of course . . . Of course!

I was suddenly aware that Mrs Oliver was still quacking happily.

'Bless you,' I said. 'You're wonderful!'

I slammed back the receiver, then took it off again. I dialled a number and was lucky enough this time to get Lejeune straight away.

'Listen,' I said, 'is Ginger's hair coming out by the roots in handfuls?'

'Well – as a matter of fact I believe it is. High fever, I suppose.'

'Fever my foot,' I said. 'What Ginger's suffering from, what they've all suffered from, is thallium poisoning. Please God, we may be in time . . .'

CHAPTER 22

MARK EASTERBROOK'S NARRATIVE

I

'Are we in time? Will she live?'

I wandered up and down. I couldn't sit still.

Lejeune sat watching me. He was patient and kind.

'You can be sure that everything possible is being done.'

It was the same old answer. It did nothing to comfort me.

'Do they know how to treat thallium poisoning?'

'You don't often get a case of it. But everything possible will be tried. If you ask me, I think she'll pull through.'

I looked at him. How could I tell if he really believed what he was saying? Was he just trying to soothe me?

'At any rate, they've verified that it *was* thallium.'

'Yes, they've verified that.'

'So that's the simple truth behind the Pale Horse. Poison.

No witchcraft, no hypnotism, no scientific death rays. Plain poisoning! And she flung that at me, damn her. Flung it in my face. Laughing in her cheek all the while, I expect.'

'Who are you talking about?'

'Thyrza Grey. That first afternoon when I went to tea there. Talked about the Borgias and all the build up of "rare and untraceable poisons"; the poisoned gloves and all the rest of it. "Common white arsenic," she said, "and nothing else." This was just as simple. All that hooey! The trance and the white cocks and the brazier and the pentagrams and the voodoo and the reversed crucifix – all that was for the crudely superstitious. And the famous "box" was another bit of hooey for the contemporary-minded. We don't believe in spirits and witches and spells nowadays, but we're a gullible lot when it comes to "rays" and "waves" and psychological phenomena. That box, I bet, is nothing but a nice little assembly of electrical show-off, coloured bulbs and humming valves. Because we live in daily fear of radio fall out and strontium 90 and all the rest of it, we're amenable to suggestion along the line of scientific talk. The whole set-up at the Pale Horse was bogus! The Pale Horse was a stalking horse, neither more nor less. Attention was to be focused on that, so that we'd never suspect what might be going on in another direction. The beauty of it was that it was quite safe for them. Thyrza Grey could boast out loud about what occult powers she had or could command. She could never be brought into court and tried for murder on that issue. Her box could have been examined and proved to be harmless. Any court would have ruled that the whole thing was nonsense and impossible! And, of course, that's exactly what it *was*.'

'Do you think they're all three in it?' asked Lejeune.

'I shouldn't think so. Bella's belief in witchcraft is genuine, I should say. She believes in her own powers and rejoices in them. The same with Sybil. She's got a genuine gift of mediumship. She goes into a trance and she doesn't know what happens. She believes everything that Thyrza tells her.'

'So Thyrza is the ruling spirit?'

I said slowly:

'As far as the Pale Horse is concerned, yes. But she's not the real *brains* of the show. The real brain works behind the scenes.

He plans and organises. It's all beautifully dove-tailed, you know. Everyone has his or her job, and no one has anything on anyone else. Bradley runs the financial and legal side. Apart from that, he doesn't know what happens elsewhere. He's handsomely paid, of course; so is Thyrza Grey.'

'You seem to have got it all taped to your satisfaction,' said Lejeune drily.

'I haven't. Not yet. But we know the basic necessary fact. It's the same as it has been through the ages. Crude and simple. Just plain poison. The dear old death potion.'

'What put thallium into your head?'

'Several things suddenly came together. The beginning of the whole business was the thing I saw that night in Chelsea. A girl whose hair was being pulled out by the roots by another girl. And she said: "*It didn't really hurt.*" It wasn't bravery, as I thought; it was simple fact. It didn't hurt.

'I read an article on thallium poisoning when I was in America. A lot of workers in a factory died one after the other. Their deaths were put down to astonishingly varied causes. Amongst them, if I remember rightly, were paratyphoid, apoplexy, alcoholic neuritis, bulbar paralysis, epilepsy, gastro-enteritis, and so on. Then there was a woman who poisoned seven people. Diagnosis included brain tumour, encephalitis, and lobar pneumonia. The symptoms vary a good deal, I understand. They may start with diarrhoea and vomiting, or there may be a stage of intoxication, again it may begin with pain in the limbs, and be put down as polyneuritis or rheumatic fever or polio – one patient was put in an iron lung. Sometimes there's pigmentation of the skin.'

'You talk like a medical dictionary!'

'Naturally. I've been looking it up. But one thing always happens sooner or later. *The hair falls out.* Thallium used to be used for depilation at one time – particularly for children with ringworm. Then it was found to be dangerous. But it's occasionally given internally, but with very careful dosage going by the weight of the patient. It's mainly used nowadays for rats, I believe. It's tasteless, soluble, and easy to buy. There's only one thing, poisoning mustn't be suspected.'

Lejeune nodded.

'Exactly,' he said. 'Hence the insistence by the Pale Horse

that the murderer must stay away from his intended victim. No suspicion of foul play ever arises. Why should it? There's no interested party who *could* have had access to food or drink. No purchase of thallium or any other poison is ever made by him or her. That's the beauty of it. The real work is done by someone who has no connection whatever with the victim. Someone, I think, who appears once and once only.'

He paused.

'Any ideas on that?'

'Only one. A common factor appears to be that on every occasion some pleasant harmless-seeming woman calls with a questionnaire on behalf of a domestic research unit.'

'You think that that woman is the one who plants the poison? As a sample? Something like that?'

'I don't think it's quite as simple as that,' I said slowly. 'I have an idea that the women are quite genuine. But they come into it somehow. I think we may be able to find out something if we talk to a woman called Eileen Brandon, who works in an Espresso off Tottenham Court Road.'

II

Eileen Brandon had been fairly accurately described by Poppy – allowing, that is to say, for Poppy's own particular point of view. Her hair was neither like a chrysanthemum, nor an unruly birds' nest. It was waved back close to her head, she wore the minimum of make-up and her feet were encased in what is called, I believe, sensible shoes. Her husband had been killed in a motor accident, she told us, and left her with two small children. Before her present employment, she had been employed by a firm called Customers' Reactions Classified for over a year. She had left of her own accord as she had not cared for the type of work.

'Why didn't you care for it, Mrs Brandon?'

Lejeune asked the question. She looked at him.

'You're a detective-inspector of police? Is that right?'

'Quite right, Mrs Brandon.'

'You think there's something wrong about that firm?'

'It's a matter I'm inquiring into. Did you suspect something of that kind? Is that why you left?'

'I've nothing definite to go upon. Nothing definite that I could tell you.'

'Naturally. We understand that. This is a confidential inquiry.'

'I see. But there is really very little I could say.'

'You can say why you wanted to leave.'

'I had a feeling that there were things going on that I didn't know about.'

'You mean you didn't think it was a genuine concern?'

'Something of the kind. It didn't seem to me to be run in a business-like way. I suspected that there must be some ulterior object behind it. But what that object was I still don't know.'

Lejeune asked more questions as to exactly what work she had been asked to do. Lists of names in a certain neighbourhood had been handed out. Her job was to visit those people, ask certain questions, and note down the answers.

'And what struck you as wrong about that?'

'The questions did not seem to me to follow up any particular line of research. They seemed desultory, almost haphazard. As though – how can I put it? – they were a cloak for something else.'

'Have you any idea what the something else might have been?'

'No. That's what puzzled me.'

She paused a moment and then said doubtfully:

'I did wonder, at one time, whether the whole thing could have been organised with a view perhaps to burglaries, a spying out of the land, so to speak. But that couldn't be it, because I was never asked for any description of the rooms, fastenings, etc, or when the occupants of the flat or house were likely to be out or away.'

'What articles did you deal with in the questions?'

'It varied. Sometimes it was foodstuffs. Cereals, cake mixes, or it might be soap flakes and detergents. Sometimes cosmetics, face powders, lipsticks, creams, etc. Sometimes patent medicines or remedies, brands of aspirin, cough pastilles, sleeping pills, pep pills, gargles, mouth-washes, indigestion remedies and so on.'

'You were not asked,' Lejeune spoke casually, 'to supply samples of any particular goods?'

'No. Nothing of that kind.'

'You merely asked questions and noted down the answers?'

'Yes.'

'What was supposed to be the object of these inquiries?'

'That was what seemed so odd. We were never told exactly. It was supposed to be done in order to supply information to certain manufacturing firms – but it was an extraordinarily amateurish way of going about it. Not systematic at all.'

'Would it be possible, do you think, that amongst the questions you were told to ask, there was just one question or one group of questions, that was the object of the enterprise, and that the others might have been camouflage?'

She considered the point, frowning a little, then she nodded.

'Yes,' she said. 'That would account for the haphazard choice – but I haven't the least idea *what* question or questions were the important ones.'

Lejeune looked at her keenly.

'There must be more to it than what you've told us,' he said gently.

'That's the point, there isn't really. I just felt there was something wrong about the whole set-up. And then I talked to another woman, a Mrs Davis –'

'You talked to a Mrs Davis – yes?'

Lejeune's voice remained quite unchanged.

'She wasn't happy about things, either.'

'And why wasn't she happy?'

'She'd overheard something.'

'What had she overheard?'

'I told you I couldn't be definite. She didn't tell me in so many words. Only that from what she had overheard, the whole set-up was a racket of some kind. "It's not what it seems to be." That is what she said. Then she said: "Oh well, it doesn't affect us. The money's very good and we're not asked to do anything that's against the law – so I don't see that we need bother our heads about it".'

'That was all?'

'There was one other thing she said. I don't know what she meant by it. She said: "Sometimes I feel like Typhoid Mary." At the time I didn't know what she meant.'

Lejeune took a paper from his pocket and handed it to her.

'Do any of the names on that list mean anything to you? Did you call upon any of them that you can remember?'

'I wouldn't remember.' She took the paper. 'I saw so many . . .' She paused as her eye went down the list. She said:

'Ormerod.'

'You remember an Ormerod?'

'No. But Mrs Davis mentioned him once. He died very suddenly, didn't he? Cerebral haemorrhage. It upset her. She said, "He was on my list a fortnight ago. Looked like a man in the pink of condition." It was after that that she made the remark about Typhoid Mary. She said, "Some of the people I call on seem to curl up their toes and pass out just from having one look at me." She laughed about it and said it was a coincidence. But I don't think she liked it much. However, she said she wasn't going to worry.'

'And that was all?'

'Well –'

'Tell me.'

'It was some time later. I hadn't seen her for a while. But we met one day in a restaurant in Soho. I told her that I'd left the C.R.C. and got another job. She asked me why, and I told her I'd felt uneasy, not knowing what was going on. She said: "Perhaps you've been wise. But it's good money and short hours. And after all, we've all got to take our chance in this life! I've not had much luck in *my* life and why should I care what happens to other people?" I said: "I don't understand what you're talking about. What exactly *is* wrong with that show?" She said: "I can't be sure, but I'll tell you I recognised someone the other day. Coming out of a house where he'd no business to be and carrying a bag of tools. What was he doing with those I'd like to know?" She asked me, too, if I'd ever come across a woman who ran a pub called the Pale Horse somewhere. I asked her what the Pale Horse had to do with it.'

'And what did she say?'

'She laughed and said "Read your Bible".'

Mrs Brandon added: 'I don't know what she meant. That was the last time I saw her. I don't know where she is now, whether she's still with C.R.C. or whether she's left.'

'Mrs Davis is dead,' said Lejeune.

Eileen Brandon looked startled.

'Dead! But – how?'

'Pneumonia, two months ago.'

'Oh, I see. I'm sorry.'

'Is there anything else you can tell us, Mrs Brandon?'

'I'm afraid not. I have heard other people mention that phrase – the Pale Horse, but if you ask them about it, they shut up at once. They look afraid, too.'

She looked uneasy.

'I – I don't want to be mixed up in anything dangerous, Inspector Lejeune. I've got two small children. Honestly, I don't know anything more than I've told you.'

He looked at her keenly – then he nodded his head and let her go.

'That takes us a little further,' said Lejeune when Eileen Brandon had gone. 'Mrs Davis got to know too much. She tried to shut her eyes to the meaning of what was going on, but she must have had a very shrewd suspicion of what it was. Then she was suddenly taken ill, and when she was dying, she sent for a priest and told him what she knew and suspected. The question is, how much *did* she know? That list of people, I should say, is a list of people she had called on in the course of her job, and who had subsequently died. Hence the remark about Typhoid Mary. The real question is, who was it she "recognised" coming out of a house where he had no business to be, and pretending to be a workman of some kind? That must have been the knowledge that made her dangerous. If she recognised him, he may have recognised her – and he may have realised that she *had* recognised him. If she'd passed on that particular item to Father Gorman, then it was vital that Father Gorman should be silenced at once before he could pass it on.'

He looked at me.

'You agree, don't you? That must have been the way of it.'

'Oh yes,' I said. 'I agree.'

'And you've an idea, perhaps, who the man is?'

'I've an idea, but –'

'I know. We haven't a particle of evidence.'

He was silent a moment. Then he got up.

'But we'll get him,' he said. 'Make no mistake. Once we know definitely who it is, there are always ways. We'll try every damned one of them!'

CHAPTER 23

MARK EASTERBROOK'S NARRATIVE

It was some three weeks later that a car drove up to the front door of Priors Court.

Four men got out. I was one of them. There was also Detective-Inspector Lejeune and Detective-Sergeant Lee. The fourth man was Mr Osborne, who could hardly contain his delight and excitement at being allowed to be one of the party.

'You must hold your tongue, you know,' Lejeune admonished him.

'Yes, indeed, Inspector. You can count on me absolutely. I won't utter a word.'

'Mind you don't.'

'I feel it's a privilege. A great privilege, though I don't quite understand –'

But nobody was entering into explanations at this moment.

Lejeune rang the bell and asked for Mr Venables.

Looking rather like a deputation, the four of us were ushered in.

If Venables was surprised at our visit, he did not show it. His manner was courteous in the extreme. I thought again, as he wheeled his chair a little back so as to widen the circle round him, what a very distinctive appearance the man had. The Adam's apple moving up and down between the wings of his old-fashioned collar, the haggard profile with its curved nose like a bird of prey.

'Nice to see you again, Easterbrook. You seem to spend a lot of time down in this part of the world nowadays.'

There was a faint malice in his tone, I thought. He resumed:

'And – Detective-Inspector Lejeune, is it? That rouses my curiosity, I must admit. So peaceful in these parts, so free from crime. And yet, a detective-inspector calls! What can I do for you, Detective-Inspector?'

Lejeune was very quiet, very suave.

'There is a matter on which we think you might be able to assist us, Mr Venables.'

'That has a rather familiar ring, does it not? In what way do you think I can assist you?'

'On October seventh – a parish priest of the name of Father Gorman was murdered in West Street, Paddington. I have been given to understand that you were in the neighbourhood at that time – between 7.45 and 8.15 in the evening, and you may have seen something that may have a bearing on the matter?'

'Was I really in the neighbourhood at that time? Do you know, I doubt it, I very much doubt it. As far as I can recall I have never been in that particular district of London. Speaking from memory, I do not even think I was in London at all just then. I go to London occasionally for an interesting day in the sale room, and now and then for a medical check up.'

'With Sir William Dugdale of Harley Street, I believe.'

Mr Venables stared at him coldly.

'You are very well informed, Inspector.'

'Not quite so well as I should like to be. However, I'm disappointed that you can't assist me in the way that I hoped. I think I owe it to you to explain the facts connected with the death of Father Gorman.'

'Certainly, if you like. It is a name I have never heard until now.'

'Father Gorman had been called out on that particular foggy evening to the death-bed of a woman nearby. She had become entangled with a criminal organisation, at first almost unwittingly, but later certain things made her suspect the seriousness of the matter. It was an organisation which specialised in the removal of unwanted persons – for a substantial fee, naturally.'

'Hardly a new idea,' murmured Venables. 'In America –'

'Ah, but there were some novel features about this particular organisation. To begin with, the removals were ostensibly brought about by what might perhaps be called psychological means. What is referred to as a "death wish", said to be present in everyone, is stimulated –'

'So that the person in question obligingly commits suicide? It sounds, if I may say so, Inspector, too good to be true.'

'Not suicide, Mr Venables. The person in question dies a perfectly natural death.'

'Come now. Come now. Do you really believe that? How very unlike our hard-headed police force!'

'The headquarters of this organisation are said to be a place called the Pale Horse.'

'Ah, *now* I begin to understand. So that is what brings you to our pleasant rural neighbourhood; my friend Thyrza Grey, and her nonsense! Whether she believes it herself or not, I've never been able to make out. But nonsense it is! She has a silly mediumistic friend, and the local witch cooks her dinners (quite brave to eat them – hemlock in the soup any moment!). And the three old dears have worked up quite a local reputation. Very naughty, of course, but don't tell me Scotland Yard, or wherever you come from, take it all seriously?'

'We take it very seriously indeed, Mr Venables.'

'You really believe that Thyrza spouts some high-falutin' nonsense, Sybil throws a trance, and Bella does black magic, and as a result somebody dies?'

'Oh no, Mr Venables – the cause of death is simpler than that –' He paused a moment.

'The cause is thallium poisoning.'

There was a momentary pause –

'*What* did you say?'

'Poisoning – by thallium salts. Quite plain and straightforward. Only it had to be covered up – and what better method of covering up than a pseudo-scientific, psychological set-up – full of modern jargon and reinforced by old superstitions. Calculated to distract attention from the plain fact of administration of poison.'

'Thallium,' Mr Venables frowned. 'I don't think I've ever heard of it.'

'No? Used extensively as rat poison, occasionally as a depilatory for children with ringworm. Can be obtained quite easily. Incidentally there's a packet of it tucked away in a corner of your potting shed.'

'In *my* potting shed? It sounds most unlikely.'

'It's there all right. We've examined some of it for testing purposes –'

Venables became slightly excited.

'Someone must have put it there. I know nothing about it! Nothing at all.'

'Is that so? You're a man of some wealth, aren't you, Mr Venables?'

'What has that got to do with what we are talking about?'

'The Inland Revenue have been asking some awkward questions lately, I believe? As to source of income, that is.'

'The curse of living in England is undoubtedly our system of taxation. I have thought very seriously of late of going to live in Bermuda.'

'I don't think you'll be going to Bermuda just yet awhile, Mr Venables.'

'Is that a threat, Inspector? Because if so –'

'No, no, Mr Venables. Just an expression of opinion. Would you like to hear just how this little racket was worked?'

'You are certainly determined to tell me.'

'It's very well organised. Financial details are arranged by a debarred solicitor called Mr Bradley. Mr Bradley has an office in Birmingham. Prospective clients visit him there, and do business. This is to say, there is a bet on whether someone will die within a stated period . . . Mr Bradley, who is fond of a wager, is usually pessimistic in his prognostications. The client is usually more hopeful. When Mr Bradley wins his bet, the money has to be paid over promptly – or else something unpleasant is liable to happen. That is all Mr Bradley has to do – make a bet. Simple, isn't it?

'The client next visits the Pale Horse. A show is put on by Miss Thyrza Grey and her friends, which usually impresses him in the way it is meant to do.

'Now for the simple facts behind the scenes.

'Certain women, *bona-fide* employees of one of the many consumer research concerns, are detailed to canvass a particular neighbourhood with a questionnaire. "What bread do you prefer? What toilet articles and cosmetics? What laxative, tonics, sedatives, indigestion mixtures, etc.?" People nowadays are conditioned to answering quizzes. They seldom object.

'And so to – the last step. Simple, bold, successful! The only action performed by the originator of the scheme in person. He may be wearing a mansion flat porter's uniform, he may be a man calling to read the gas or the electric meter. He may be a plumber, or an electrician, or a workman of some kind. Whatever he is, he will have what appear to be the proper credentials with him if anyone asks to see them. Most people don't. Whatever role he is playing, his real object is simple – the substitution of a preparation he brings with him for a similar article which he knows (by reason of the C.R.C. questionnaires) that his victim uses. He may tap pipes, or examine meters, or test water pressure – but that is his real object. Having accomplished it, he leaves, and is not seen in that neighbourhood again.

'And for a few days perhaps nothing happens. But sooner or later, the victim displays symptoms of illness. A doctor is called in, but has no reason to suspect anything out of the ordinary. He may question what food and drink, etc., the patient has taken, but he is unlikely to suspect the ordinary proprietary article that the patient has taken for years.

'And you see the beauty of the scheme, Mr Venables? The only person who knows *what the head of the organisation actually does* – is the head of the organisation himself. *There is no one to give him away.*'

'So how do *you* know so much?' demanded Mr Venables pleasantly.

'When we have suspicions of a certain person, there are ways of making sure.'

'Indeed? Such as?'

'We needn't go into all of them. But there's the camera, for instance. All kinds of ingenious devices are possible nowadays. A man can be snapped without his suspecting the fact. We've got some excellent pictures, for instance, of a uniformed flat porter, and a gas man and so on. There are such things as false moustaches, different dentures, etc., but our man has been recognised, quite easily – first by Mrs Mark Easterbrook, alias Miss Katherine Corrigan, and also by a woman called Edith Binns. Recognition is an interesting thing, Mr Venables. For instance, this gentleman here, Mr Osborne, is willing to swear he saw you following Father Gorman in Barton Street on the night of the seventh of October about eight o'clock.'

'And I *did* see you!' Mr Osborne leaned forward, twitching with excitement. 'I described you exactly!'

'Rather too exactly, perhaps,' said Lejeune. 'Because you *didn't* see Mr Venables that night when you were standing outside the doorway of your shop. *You weren't standing there at all.* You were across the street *yourself* – following Father Gorman until he turned into West Street, and you came up with him *and killed him* . . .'

Mr Zachariah Osborne said:

'What?'

It might have been ludicrous. It *was* ludicrous! The dropped jaw, the staring eyes . . .

'Let me introduce you, Mr Venables, to Mr Zachariah Osborne, pharmacist, late of Barton Street, Paddington. You'll feel a personal interest in him when I tell you that Mr Osborne, who has been under observation for some time, was unwise enough to plant a packet of thallium salts in your potting shed. Not knowing of your disability, he'd amused himself by casting you as the villain of the piece; and being a very obstinate, as well as a very stupid man, he refused to admit he'd made a bloomer.'

'Stupid? You dare to call *me* stupid? If you knew – if you'd any idea what I've done – what I can do – I –'

Osborne shook and spluttered with rage.

Lejeune summed him up carefully. I was reminded of a man playing a fish.

'You shouldn't have tried to be so clever, you know,' he said reprovingly. 'Why, if you'd just sat back in that shop of yours, and let well alone, I shouldn't be here now, warning you, as it's my duty to do, that anything you say will be taken down and –'

It was then that Mr Osborne began to scream.

CHAPTER 24

MARK EASTERBROOK'S NARRATIVE

'Look here, Lejeune, there are lots of things I want to know.'

The formalities over, I had got Lejeune to myself. We were sitting together with two large tankards of beer opposite us.

'Yes, Mr Easterbrook? I gather it was a surprise to you.'

'It certainly was. My mind was set on Venables. You never gave me the least hint.'

'I couldn't afford to give hints, Mr Easterbrook. You have to play these things close to your chest. They're tricky. The truth is we hadn't a lot to go on. That's why we had to stage the show in the way we did with Venables's co-operation. We had to lead Osborne right up the garden path and then turn on him suddenly and hope to break him down. And it worked.'

'Is he mad?' I asked.

'I'd say he's gone over the edge now. He wasn't to begin with, of course, but it does something to you, you know. Killing people. It makes you feel powerful and larger than life. It makes you feel you're God Almighty. But you're not. You're only a nasty bit of goods that's been found out. And when that fact's presented to you suddenly your ego just can't stand it. You scream and you rant and you boast of what you've done and how clever you are. Well, you saw him.'

I nodded. 'So Venables was in on the performance you put up,' I said. 'Did he like the idea of co-operating?'

'It amused him, I think,' said Lejeune. 'Besides, he was impertinent enough to say that one good turn deserves another.'

'And what did he mean by that cryptic remark?'

'Well, I shouldn't be telling you this,' said Lejeune, 'this is off the record. There was a big outbreak of bank robberies about eight years ago. The same technique every time. *And* they got away with it! The raids were cleverly planned by someone who took no part in the actual operation. That man got away with a lot of money. We may have had our suspicions who it was, but we couldn't prove it. He was too clever for us. Especially on the financial angle. And he's had the sense never to try and repeat his success. I'm not saying more. He was a clever crook but he wasn't a murderer. No lives were lost.'

My mind went back to Zachariah Osborne. 'Did you always suspect Osborne?' I asked. 'Right from the beginning?'

'Well, he would draw attention to himself,' said Lejeune. 'As I told him, if he'd only sat back and done nothing, we'd never have dreamed that the respectable pharmacist, Mr Zachariah Osborne, had anything to do with the business. But it's a funny thing, that's just what murderers can't do. There they are, sitting pretty, safe as houses. But they can't let well alone. I'm sure I don't know why.'

'The desire for death,' I suggested. 'A variant of Thyrza Grey's theme.'

'The sooner you forget all about Miss Thyrza Grey and the things she told you, the better,' said Lejeune severely. 'No,' he said thoughtfully, 'I think really it's loneliness. The knowledge that you're such a clever chap, but that there's nobody you can talk to about it.'

'You haven't told me when you started to suspect him,' I said.

'Well, straight away he started telling lies. We asked for anyone who'd seen Father Gorman that night to communicate with us. Mr Osborne communicated and the statement he made was a palpable lie. He'd seen a man following Father Gorman and he described the features of that man, but he couldn't possibly have seen him across the street on a foggy night. An aquiline nose in profile he might have seen, but not an Adam's apple. That was going too far. Of course, that lie might have been innocent enough. Mr Osborne might just want to make himself important. Lots of people *are* like that. But it made me focus my attention on Mr Osborne and he was really rather a curious person. At once he started to tell me a lot about himself. Very unwise of him. He gave me a picture of someone who had always wanted to be more important than he was. He'd not been content to go into his father's old-fashioned business. He'd gone off and tried his fortunes on the stage, but he obviously hadn't been a success. Probably, I should say, because he couldn't take production. Nobody was going to dictate to *him* the way he should play a part! He was probably genuine enough when he told of his ambition to be a witness in a murder trial, successfully identifying a man who had come in to buy poison. His mind ran on those lines a good deal, I should think. Of course we don't know at what point, and when, the idea occurred to him that he might become a really big criminal, a man so clever that he could never be brought to justice.

'But that's all surmise. To go back. Osborne's description of the man he had seen that night was interesting. It was so obviously a description of a real person whom he had at one time seen. It's extraordinarily difficult, you know, to make up a description of anybody. Eyes, nose, chin, ears, bearing, all the rest of it. If you try it you'll find yourself unconsciously describing somebody that you've noticed somewhere – in a tram or a train or an omnibus. Osborne was obviously describing a man with somewhat unusual characteristics. I'd say that he noticed Venables sitting in his car one day in Bournemouth and was struck by his appearance – if he'd seen him that way, he wouldn't realise the man was a cripple.

'Another reason that kept me interested in Osborne was that he was a pharmacist. I thought it just possible that that list we had might tie up with the narcotic trade somewhere. Actually that wasn't so, and I might, therefore, have forgotten all about Mr Osborne if Mr Osborne himself hadn't been determined to keep in the picture. He wanted, you see, to know just what we were doing, and so he writes to say that he's seen the man in question at a church fête in Much Deeping. He still didn't know that Mr Venables was a paralysis case. When he did find that out he hadn't the sense to shut up. That was his vanity. Typical criminal's vanity. He wasn't going to admit for one moment that he'd been wrong. Like a fool, he stuck to his guns and put forward all sorts of preposterous theories. I had a very interesting visit to him at his bungalow in Bournemouth. The name of it ought to have given the show away. Everest. That's what he called it. And he'd hung up a picture of Mount Everest in the hall. Told me how interested he was in Himalayan exploration. But that was the kind of cheap joke that he enjoyed. Ever rest. That was his trade – his profession. He did give people eternal rest on payment of a suitable fee. It was a wonderful idea, one's got to hand him that. The whole set-up was clever. Bradley in Birmingham, Thyrza Grey holding her *séances* in Much Deeping. And who was to suspect Mr Osborne who had no connection with Thyrza Grey, no connection with Bradley and Birmingham, no connection with the victim. The actual mechanics of the thing was child's play to a pharmacist. As I say, if only Mr Osborne had had the sense to keep quiet.'

'But what did he do with the money?' I asked. 'After all, he did it for money presumably?'

'Oh, yes, he did it for the money. Had grand visions, no doubt, of himself travelling, entertaining, being a rich and important person. But of course he wasn't the person he imagined himself to be. I think his sense of power was exhilarated by the actual performance of murder. To get away with murder again and again intoxicated him, and what's more, he'll enjoy himself in the dock. You see if he doesn't. The central figure with all eyes upon him.'

'But what did he *do* with the money?' I demanded.

'Oh, that's very simple,' said Lejeune, 'though I don't know that I should have thought of it unless I'd noticed the way he'd furnished the bungalow. He was a miser, of course. He loved money and he wanted money, but not for spending. That bungalow was sparsely furnished and all with stuff that he'd bought cheap at sales. He didn't like spending money, he just wanted to *have* it.'

'Do you mean he banked it all?'

'Oh no,' said Lejeune. 'I'd say we'll find it somewhere under the floor in that bungalow of his.'

Both Lejeune and I were silent for some minutes while I contemplated the strange creature that was Zachariah Osborne.

'Corrigan,' said Lejeune dreamily, 'would say it was all due to some gland in his spleen or his sweetbread or something either over-functioning or under-producing – I never can remember which. I'm a simple man – I think he's just a wrong 'un – What beats me – it always does – is how a man can be so clever and yet be such a perfect fool.'

'One imagines a master mind,' I said, 'as some grand and sinister figure of evil.'

Lejeune shook his head. 'It's not like that at all,' he said. 'Evil is not something superhuman, it's something *less* than human. Your criminal is someone who wants to be important, but who never will be important, because he'll always be less than a man.'

CHAPTER 25

MARK EASTERBROOK'S NARRATIVE

I

At Much Deeping everything was refreshingly normal.

Rhoda was busy doctoring dogs. This time, I think, it was deworming. She looked up as I came in and asked me if I would like to assist. I refused and asked where Ginger was.

'She's gone over to the Pale Horse.'

'What?'

'She said she had something to do there.'

'But the house is empty.'

'I know.'

'She'll overtire herself. She's not fit yet –'

'How you fuss, Mark. Ginger's all right. Have you seen Mrs Oliver's new book? It's called *The White Cockatoo*. It's over on the table there.'

'God bless Mrs Oliver. And Edith Binns, too.'

'Who on earth is Edith Binns?'

'A woman who has identified a photograph. Also faithful retainer to my late godmother.'

'Nothing you say seems to make sense. What's the matter with you?'

I did not reply, but set out for the Pale Horse.

Just before I got there, I met Mrs Dane Calthrop.

She greeted me enthusiastically.

'All along I knew I was being stupid,' she said. 'But I didn't see how. Taken in by trappings.'

She waved an arm towards the inn, empty and peaceful in the late autumn sunshine.

'The wickedness was never there – not in the sense it was supposed to be. No fantastic trafficking with the Devil, no black and evil splendour. Just parlour tricks done for money – and human life of no account. That's real wickedness. Nothing grand or big – just petty and contemptible.'

'You and Inspector Lejeune would seem to agree about things.'

'I like that man,' said Mrs Dane Calthrop. 'Let's go into the Pale Horse and find Ginger.'

'What's she doing there?'

'Cleaning up something.'

We went in through the low doorway. There was a strong smell of turpentine. Ginger was busy with rags and bottles. She looked up as we entered. She was still very pale and thin, a scarf wound round her head where the hair had not yet grown, a ghost of her former self.

'*She's* all right,' said Mrs Dane Calthrop, reading my thoughts as usual.

'Look!' said Ginger triumphantly.

She indicated the old inn sign on which she was working.

The grime of years removed, the figure of the rider on the horse was plainly discernible; a grinning skeleton with gleaming bones.

Mrs Dane Calthrop's voice, deep and sonorous, spoke behind me:

'Revelation, Chapter Six, Verse Eight. *And I looked and behold a pale horse: and his name that sat on him was Death, and Hell followed with him . . .*'

We were silent for a moment or two, and then Mrs Dane Calthrop, who was not one to be afraid of anti-climax, said,

'So that's that,' in the tone of one who puts something in the wastepaper basket.

'I must go now,' she added. 'Mothers' Meeting.'

She paused in the doorway, nodded at Ginger, and said unexpectedly:

'You'll make a good mother.'

For some reason Ginger blushed crimson . . .

'Ginger,' I said, 'will you?'

'Will I what? Make a good mother?'

'You know what I mean.'

'Perhaps . . . But I'd prefer a firm offer.'

I made her a firm offer . . .

II

After an interlude, Ginger demanded:

'Are you quite sure you don't want to marry that Hermia creature?'

'Good lord!' I said. 'I quite forgot.'

I took a letter from my pocket.

'This came three days ago, asking me if I'd come to the Old Vic with her to see *Love's Labour's Lost.*'

Ginger took the letter out of my hand and tore it up.

'If you want to go to the Old Vic in future,' she said firmly, 'you'll go with me.'